D0841504

IN THE FALL

IN THE FALL

Jeffrey Lent

PICADOR

First published 2000 by Grove/Atlantic, N.Y.

First published in Great Britain in 2000 by Picador
an imprint of Macmillan Publishers Ltd
25 Eccleston Place, London SW1W 9NF
Basingstoke and Oxford
Associated companies throughout the world
www.macmillan.co.uk

ISBN 0 330 39175 5 (Hardback)
ISBN 0 330 39275 1 (Trade paperback)

All characters, locations, and situations are products of
imagination or are used fictitiously. While effort has been made
to adhere to historical record, events and geography may have been
altered for narrative texture.

The 'Mother-in-Law' song comes from *Songs of Old Vermont*,
by the late Harold Harrington of North Pomfret, Vermont, and was
released on Droll Yankees records.

3 5 7 9 8 6 4 2

A CIP catalogue record for this book is available from
the British Library.

Printed and bound in Great Britain by
Mackays of Chatham plc, Chatham, Kent

for Marion

the sweet long road

And for their unstinting support and enthusiasm,

Michael Hill and Holley Bishop

Prologue

The boy woke in the dark house and knew he was alone. It was knowing this that woke him. The house was not empty, he just was alone in it. He stood and dressed and went down through the house in the dark. From the kitchen, he could see the lantern light past the overgrown pasture beyond the barn. He took his jacket from the peg and held the door to settle it back into the frame without noise. Under the big hemlocks and tamaracks surrounding the house, he crossed the soft dirt track of the drive and stepped into the tangle of sumac and blackberries and young popples, keeping a clump of sumac between him and the light. He was not afraid of the dark. He was afraid of being in the house. The lantern sat on an upturned stone. His father was digging with a spade in the woods floor, piling the soil he lifted onto a canvas tarp laid next to the hole he was making. The boy heard the soft noise of dirt slipping off the spade. The hole was round, not wide but deep. His father worked carefully, prying free stones, small rocks, with the tip of the blade. When the handle disappeared halfway into the ground his father stopped, set down the spade and from the edge of the tarp took up one of three coffee cans and got down on his knees to position it in the bottom of the hole. Still on his knees, he packed handfuls of dirt around the can and only when it was covered did he rise to finish the job. He worked slowly, transferring the soil from the tarp back to the hole. When he was done, he tamped the soil with the flat of the blade, the sound gentle blows in the night. He set aside the spade and shook the tarp for the last traces of dirt and then took up a metal-tined rake and pulled the leaves and understory trash

1

back over the hole, raking back and forth until he was satisfied with his job. Then he moved a short distance in the woods, the boy moving with him, a soft unwatched dance within the thicket. He watched as his father dug another hole, the same careful job as the first, another small grave for a coffee can. And when this was done, they both moved again and one more hole was dug and filled and finished, covered over, hidden. When his father was done, he sat on a stone, lighted a cigarette and smoked it. The boy watched, knowing he had to get back to the house before his father but only wanting enough time and no more. The cigarette tip made an orange flare in the dark as his father inhaled and the release of smoke from his lungs would come float through the brush where the boy stood and he'd breathe in all he could—as if it were his father's presence. The night after his little sister died and his mother still lay sick his father had sent him to bed but it had been his mother that woke him, standing at the foot of his bed with the girl held by the hand, his mother saying nothing but watching him while Claire waved to him. It was not long after this that his father came up the stairs to send the boy out with a lantern to shovel snow from the drive out through the hemlocks to the road, shoveling uselessly against the four-foot snowfall, crying as he worked, raging in an effort he already knew was for nothing. When his father came into the brittle orange and purple dawn to stop him, to still his shovel, to tell him his mother was dead, even then he would not stop, but dug at the snow as if into his own bursting heart. Seeing the two of them together, side by side in his room. A silent farewell. His mother and sister had come to him on their way out of the house to view him once more. This was enough then to be scared of being alone in the house. It was not the dark. He had no fear of the dark outside.

His father ground the cigarette against the sides of his trousers, broke the butt apart and scattered it, and still the boy waited. Then his father took up the tarp and passed it through his hands along one edge until he held the corners and draped it down before him, his arms spread wide. For a moment the tarp hid both father and lantern—a screen over the scene, the tarp backlit from the lantern—and then his father brought the corners together and folded the tarp against the length of his body, placed it under one arm and reached down with the other to gather up the rake and shovel. It was time to go. His father took up the lantern as the boy turned back to the house, moving swiftly through the dark, the house a blank silhouette against the night sky. He heard his father behind him, his wind a ragged suck as if he pulled himself forward by drawing in the air—his lungs still weak with the winter's influenza which he'd carried into the house but risen from, just when Claire had sickened with it and then their mother. They did not have it near as long as his father but both drowned in it. The boy had not been sick at all. With the noise his father was making he guessed he could have run, and not been seen or heard, but he wanted nothing more than just to beat his father back to the house. To lie in bed and hear him come in.

Whatever was in the coffee cans, whatever was buried in the woods behind him, he did not know. Something secret laid away, something hidden deep now in the earth, out of sight, gone. Without ever having once been told, he knew it was his father's business buried out there, not his. Curious as any boy, he still knew to leave it be.

Part I

Randolph

One

The boy's grandfather came down off the hill farm above the Bethel road south of Randolph early in the summer of 1862, leaving behind his mother and the youngest girl still at home along with a dwindling flock of Merino sheep and a slowly building herd of milk cows. Norman Pelham was barely seventeen, but he was well built in his homemade fine-stitched suit of clothes. His silent manner and extra height deflected any question of his age. His father drove him in the wagon and neither spoke during the hour trip to the depot in Randolph. The summer dust rose up through the trace chains and settled on the braided bobs of the team's tails. Norman was a serious youth who doubted that the secession of near half the states in the union would be quickly resolved. Still, his death seemed remote and unlikely. He planned to do his part as well as he could, but no hero's blood pumped through his veins. He had no desire for glory beyond traveling back up that same road one day. But he did not speak with his father of these things and his father offered nothing of his own fears that morning. Instead they tracked the course of crows over the valley and watched as men they knew worked at the first cutting of hay in the broad flat fields along the river. Some of those men rested their scythes to lift a hat or arm in greeting, some had sons already at the depot or in Brattleboro and some would soon follow. Father and son would incline their heads to the greetings with no need for words, for all knew their destination. They rode on to the strained creak of harness leather above the heavy wheels crumbling the road dust, the father's heart clattering as if loosed from a pivot in his chest and the heart of the boy also in fearsome ratchet. There had been no argument between them, no discussions of fitness or age. The father would have gone himself but could not. The boy was not going in his place. The boy was going on his own.

In Randolph, they drew the team up away from the depot and backed the wagon around so it was headed home. The team stood with dropped heads, sweat lather foaming around their backpads. The father wrapped the lines once in a loose loop around the brake lever and stepped down out of the wagon. Norman climbed down the other side and reached behind to lift out a valise with twin straps that held a winter coat, canvas pants, a boiled white shirt, a small inscribed Bible, extra socks and a razor. All but the razor had been brought at his mother's urging. Norman had planned to carry the razor in his pocket, confident he could always find a strop and soap of some kind. He thought the army might even provide these things. He didn't know; there was no one to ask.

There was a crowd around the depot, which was strung with homemade bunting. His father reached out, took his hand, and they both grasped hard, then dropped the other's hand at the same moment, as if from long practice.

"Well," his father said, his eyes drifting over the wagonbed toward the team.

"Keep an eye on my sheep," Norman said.

"Yuht," his father said. And then added, "Dodge them bullets."

"I'll do her."

His father nodded. "I'll get on to home then."

Norman raised the valise and held it against his back, with his elbow in the air. He echoed his father. "Yuht." As he turned away and walked toward the crowd, he realized for the first time that he would be around far more people than he was used to, yet knew all he needed to do was keep quiet and he could be as alone as he liked.

He rode the train south to Brattleboro for the rest of the day. Around him, men were eating food out of sacks or bound-up in cloth. Norman opened the valise, intent upon retrieving the razor and leaving the rest behind him, and found there on top a piece of cold mutton, tied up in paper and string, and a loaf of new bread along with a half dozen hardboiled eggs. As he peeled the shells off the eggs, he thought of her egg money going with him. After he ate all the mutton and bread, he closed the valise and kept it held tight between his feet, razor and all.

In Brattleboro the next morning he signed the muster rolls and was issued a uniform and gun as well as a dozen or more other related items. He lived in a tent with five other men from rare and unknown parts of Vermont and went through a couple of weeks of drills and simple training that struck him as having little to do with anything at all. He learned over time that he was fortunate in having officers who were neither ambitious nor career men, but who had age and experience. In early July, they rode trains south and joined the thronged mass of the Army of the Potomac. Norman now carried only his razor in one pocket and his small Bible in another. He'd saved also his extra socks.

It was late September of 1865 before he passed through Bethel on his way back to the hill farm, months after his fellow members of the 2nd Vermont had returned in pairs or small groups. Although word of him had spread beyond that group of veterans, they would not speak of him; any of them who were approached by his mother would only assure her he'd be along any day and last they'd seen him he was fine. There were still those few whose eyes rose over whatever length of road they could see from time to time to see if the figure in the distance was him. Some among them even doubted he'd come at all, but even those doubts were less of a judgment than a curiosity. They were not the sort of men to place themselves in another's shoes and would not voice an opinion unless the matter bore directly upon them. And this with Norman did not. Still, they watched the road.

So they saw him pass along the road that Indian-summer morning with the sugarbush maples flaring on the hillsides and the hilltop sheep pastures overgrown with young cherry and maple. Word ran along the road ahead of him so near all his neighbors and townspeople saw him walking in the long easy stride of one who counted walking in months and years not miles, a rucksack cut from an issue blanket strapped to his back and by his side a girl near his own height in a sunfaded blue dress and carrying her own cardboard suitcase bound with rough twine. Norman wore his army brogans while the girl walked barefoot in the dust, her own pair of wornout boots tied together by the laces and slung over one shoulder. Norman raised his hand to greet those he saw and most nodded or waved back. And those that hung back in barn doorways or stood behind curtains he paid no attention to, satisfied to pass them by and telling himself he held no malice to those who ignored him. At one point the girl said to him, "They watching us."

"They been watching us all along the way."

"They has been. But these your folks."

"All they got is the right to look."

"Maybe."

"No maybe about it," he said. "They can look all they want and think what they like, it don't matter to me and it don't matter to you." And he meant what he said; he'd walked through any fear he might be wrong back in southern Virginia. There was nothing cocksure or militant in how he felt, just his own certainty at having settled his fears and doubts. If there was any hesitation left in him it came from his great tenderness for her, his knowledge of the cruelty a person may inflict upon another and his determination to shield her from any damage that his own people might cast upon her. He was not simple in love but ferocious with it.

They turned off the road less than a mile from Randolph village to climb the half mile of gravel track to the hill farm where only his mother and youngest sister now waited, his father kicked in the head by the old mare as he bent to pick up a dropped dime two years before. The letter with this news had reached him just days before the battle of Fredericksburg in which men died before, beside and twice behind him as his body recalled his father's advice and he dropped in a long swivel from his knees to rise again with the breech-loading Springfield coming up before him. His older sisters married and gone, Miriam on a farm in Iowa, Ethel to a paper-goods man out of St. Louis. As he and the girl passed the final house along the way, the farmwife was in the side yard stringing laundry, with her arms full and her mouth agape with pins, and so was unable to wave or call greeting but just watched them pass by, the neighbor boy grown war-hardened and the green-eyed girl with her African body so lovely in the fall sunshine, her skin the color and luster of hand-rubbed heartpine. Norman called out and the girl raised a hand in a gesture the woman read as saying You're over there and I'm over here and I'm going to stay right here unless you invite me otherwise. As they continued on up the hill, Norman thought he heard the soft spatter of clothespins falling into the grass behind them.

He was wounded twice. The first time was at Gettysburg when the 2nd Vermont found the breach in the flank of Pickett's fated charge and waded in to turn the battle, charging across the field through the offal of dead and dying men and horses, the siren of battle at full crescendo. Norman was wounded as a red-eyed cavalryman swept through them with his sabre flaring in the dying summer light and sliced Norman's right arm deep to the bone and the sabre flew up from the blow and was coming down again. Norman had dropped his Springfield but raised his left arm as he threw his body against the man's horse behind the long blade and drew the man down on top of him, knocking the wind from himself and leaving it to others to drag the rebel man from Norman and run bayonets through him. They saved the sabre and presented it to him when he returned to the company from the hospital at Lee's old home outside Washington but he did not want it, still able to feel the sweat coming from the cavalryman's mustache and chin as he came down on him, still able to smell his glaze of fear and death as they struck the earth and the sky darkened with the bodies of his comrades closing over them.

The second wound came almost two years later outside Richmond after that city fell and Lee's army was crumbling before them. It was late in the day when the company crossed a small stream with the dogwoods blooming and the few spring leaves on the trees fine and pale, the size of mouse ears. The men they were pursuing had gained enough ground to turn their one fieldpiece upon the 2nd and fire off a final canister of grapeshot that blew apart a dozen feet from where he crouched with the others in poison ivy and trout lilies, hearing the whistle of the grape coming in. While the shell fell short, it sent something hard through the air, a piece of tree perhaps, which struck Norman in the head, tore apart his left ear and left him unconscious and alone while the company camped around him. Sometime during the night he woke and, still senseless, crawled off in the manner of a sick animal seeking better shelter in which to die. He awoke in mighty pain at dawn next to a hedgerow somewhere in Virginia, his ear a throbbing thing attached to him and his brain ill and scattered, shivering with the dew already burning off before the rising sun and his tongue thick with wanting water. He'd rolled onto his good side to keep his ear in the air and away from the ground. He slept some like that and waking again saw a girl squatting there beside him, her face serious as death itself and her hands cupping a dipper gourd of water as she asked him, "Is you dead?"

He lay there etching her against the pan of his brain: the fine raised cheekbones that brought all focus of her face to her wide eyes already bright before the sun added light to them. The fine cleft chin he wanted to hold as an apple and the lips cracked with her own fearsome journey and still lovely as if chiseled from a piece of veined rose marble. Still he could barely speak from pain but felt he must or she would flee, thinking him dead or somehow dangerous, and so he said, "I just need to lay here a bit." Then, his head and ear booming, he asked, "Is that water you got there?"

She nodded and held the back of his head as he drank and then settled him slow back onto the ground and he slept again. When he woke later she was still there and the gourd was full again and she helped raise him up and gave him water. The sun was up but they sat in the thin shade from the hedge. She had biscuits and a hunk of ham with the mold scraped off and she fed some of that to him and he slept more. At full dusk he was awake again and heard whippoorwills calling each other off in the darkening woods. The girl stood over him this time. She said, "You got to get up and walk. It ain't far but you got to go. Another night here fever gonna carry you off. I spent too much time to have that happen." He saw that she had blankets looped long and narrow over one shoulder. She said, "You ain't that bad hurt. You ain't dead. Rise on up now." And when he was standing, his body pressed to hers and one arm around her and one of hers around him, he asked her name and she paused, her face turned away from him down into the folds of the blankets she carried. She said, "Leah."

"Why that's a pretty name," he said. "From the Bible."

And again slowly as if gauging him she said, "I guess so. Anyway its my name."

He wanted to tell her she was prettier than her name, any name, but the words were wrong; that, and he was still seeing her blackness, still thinking of her as the most beautiful colored girl he'd ever seen. As the land fell away with the dark, the pain in his head was made a lesser thing against the girl beside him.

They moved that way into the night, the girl leading him through fields as he struggled to find his own balance and when that would not happen finally let himself move along with her as with a current. She led him down through a woods of old oaks and into a narrow ravine with a small stream and he guessed this was where she had carried his water from. In the dark she brought him to a hidden dugout shored with logs and shielded with a thicket of rhododendron, the open front of the dugout half covered by a hand-laid drywall of stone, old enough so the surfaces of the stones were soft with moss. Inside she made a fire with flint and steel, and in the light they ate the rest of her ham and she brought more water up from the stream. She kept the fire small but with the food it warmed them. She asked where he was from and he told her and she asked where that was and he said up by Canada and she knew where that was. He asked where she was from and she thought about it and then said, "Round here." He didn't know if she was lying or telling the truth and knew it wasn't his business to probe. She had every reason not to trust him and he realized how exceptional her care of him was, how great her risk had been and in her eyes still likely was. He sat with her in the cave, built he guessed by her own kind. Word of this place and others like it passed along a vein of trust, a line of knowledge outside the reach of his own race, and he looked at her, feeling he was beginning to know her. The idea of sex bloomed in his mind and he moved a little away from her and took up one of the two blankets, leaving the most room he could for her by the fire and told her, "You've been awful helpful. I just want to tell you that. Dawn tomorrow I'll get out of your hair and get on and find my regiment. They'll prob-ably go ahead and shoot me for deserting anyway." And seeing her eyes flare at this he said, "That's a joke. I bet they think I'm dead. Probably think I'm a ghost when they see me."

She made a face at him that was not quite a smile. "You're not any ghost."

He grinned at her. "Not yet anyhow."

"Some strange kind of man, that's what you are."

"What're you talking about?"

She shook her head and said, "Scuse me." Her tone sudden with spleen she stepped around him, ducking low until she was outside, and he lay and watched her disappear in the darkness. When she came back she was silent and so was he. Something had been extended from both of them, some straw bridge from one to the other, but then it had fallen apart and not either of them knowing what made it fall but both know-ing it was gone. As children both feeling the fault and afraid to admit it. So they said nothing.

During the night she moved him close to the scant coals and wrapped in her own blanket had spooned against his back and so he woke at bare dawn with her against him and he lay without moving until there was light in the treetops and she stirred behind him. Through both their blankets, he felt the long muscles of her thighs against the backs of his and her torso and breasts pressed tight to his back and one arm flat against his chest inside his own blanket. Only when he felt her wake fully and leave the dugout did he move at all, so that when she returned he was up with his blanket folded, moving his arms and legs to wake. She led him to the stream and there ordered him onto his hands and knees and held his head in her hands and lowered the wound into the shock of water, letting her fingers run over his scalp to clear the matted blood and woods-trash, her touch warm even in the cold water. When he stood he found his balance and she stepped back from him and as if accusing said, "Should have done that yesterday."

Still breathless he said, "It would've killed me then."

She gripped his forearm and he felt the bite of her nails and she said, "Don't you tell nobody about this place, you hear me?" There was no protest before this fury and so he only nodded, once and short but looking straight into her eyes. He wanted again to touch her or say some words to her but she'd already turned and was walking away into the woods, looking back once with impatience or scorn, so he followed her because it was all he could do.

She led him in a straight line up the side of the ravine and through the woods again and he had no way of knowing if it was the same route they'd taken the night before or a different direction altogether. Then she led him across a field to a small height of wooded land until they looked down on a field beyond a road with the camp of the 2nd Vermont. He started forward, the smell of food rising from cookfires, and then turned back but she stayed in the underbrush and he said, "Come on down with me. There's food."

She shook her head.

"Come on. I guess I ate up all your food. Least you could let me do, it seems to me."

She shook her head again and then said, "You go on, Mister Norman Pelham." When he stepped toward her she held out a hand, palm raised out and flat to stop him. She stepped back, her hand still out, one step at a time until she placed a briar thicket overgrown with honeysuckle between them. He stood listening to her slipping away until no sound came from the woods and she was gone. He thought of following her back to the field on the other side but suddenly knew she would not be in sight. And so he stood there a long while and then turned and went down to the encampment.

When his wounds were dressed and he was fed, he told his story leaving out the part about the girl and it was listened to but only just; a rumor had come down late the night before from Appomattox Court House and there was talk of going home or going on into North Carolina where an army under Johnston was still in full fight. Others said that army was nothing but a fragment and Sherman would mop it as a barkeep would the overflow suds from a bucket of beer. Others reminded them they'd considered Lee done for before this and been proved wrong. It was all talk to Norman; even the idea of a surrender left him idly numbed and he was quiet among the men. He sat that night by the bright circle of the rail-fence fire, unable to see beyond the wall of dark but imagining her in the dugout with the small fire even as he knew she would've moved on from there, was likely miles away along her own route of hidden road. Norman wondered if she'd heard the rumor and what it might mean to her and once felt clearly that she was out there looking right back at him. He stood then, making a show of stretching his body, his face turned toward the wooded height, and then felt a fool, knowing she was not there. He moved out to the rim of light to pee and then back for a tin cup of the overboiled coffee they all sat drinking. An hour after midnight a horse clattered hard down the road and the war was done for them.

The next day they passed through two towns as they made their way back toward Washington and both times the townspeople stood silent watching them with empty faces and the troops were quiet also, as if they were all at the same funeral, the viewers and the procession all indispensable. In both towns Norman's eyes searched through the colored people but did not see her. He was already unsure if he'd recognize her until his eyes found one and then another tall woman and knew immediately each was not the one he sought. He wondered how long that surety would last and did not let himself consider why this was important.

Twice during the afternoon he saw movement off the roadside, once behind a hedgerow and once again farther off along a wooded edge, and both times he looked to the men around him to see if they too had seen anything and wondered if he'd imagined it or even why he might think it was her at all. The countryside was filled with people: men deserted and foraging from both armies, colored people some still bound as slaves and others runaway, white children competing with the deserters for what game or roots the land might offer up. There were women also, both white and black who'd come out to the encampments to offer what they had to offer for whatever they could get for it. Still he watched hard through the afternoon for another flicker of movement and saw nothing at all.

They camped that night in a well-built barn with overhanging sheds on both sides. The men tore out planking from empty mule stalls for fires, the rail fences already stripped away, and the woman of the house brought down a kettle of potato soup made with milk and butter although they saw no cow. The surrender meant something to someone somewhere but nothing yet to these men on the road and nothing yet to the people they imposed upon, except the chance to acknowledge the imposition, and so they filled their tin cups and thanked her one by one and she nodded to each and stood silent until the soup was gone and then carried the kettle back to the house.

After midnight he was walking sentry, the Springfield loose alongside him held in just one hand, his tunic unbuckled, open to more than just the spring night. In the darkness he paused and as he stood looking at those men the idea of leaving them frightened him a little. He wondered if the men there he knew from Bethel or Randolph or Royalton or Chelsea would come upon him in years ahead and nod their greeting and pass along by as if this were all nothing more but a great and forever silent part of their lives. Norman knew how glad he'd be back up on the farm with his arms bloody on February mornings from birthing lambs or his back burned and sore from lifting forkfuls of hay from the hot fields. The war was already breaking apart into fragments for his memory to hold, the odd things: the squirrel racing back along the road through the advancing troops that first day at Second Bull Run; the summer mist burning off the Potomac as they marched north into Pennsylvania two summers before; the man out on the field

well before him who landed on his back and for a long moment seemed
to hold the cannonball with both arms to his belly before he flew apart
under it; the boy face up and his mouth open to the air, flies already
pooled around his eyes as he called a woman's name, his tone plaintive
as if she were nearby and ignoring him. These sights and others, each
forever etched in its own small box of his mind. Life after this was not
so simple a thing as going home and carrying on from where he'd left
off, and he remembered his father's death, a news that at the time
seemed just one more in a long chain of life poured out upon the ground.
Now he could begin to feel it as the hole he'd forever carry forward with
himself: not having the chance to not talk about the war with his father, not even having that silent presence there beside him as he birthed
those lambs or dug that potato ground. He was watching his fellows and
himself all at once when from behind him she said, "Norman don't you
shoot me with that gun of yours."

He turned slow and saw her face split in half with shadow and light,
her eyes wide, her nostrils flared as if to breathe him in and her lips
parted like the mouth of a bell. He took a step closer and said, "I thought
that was maybe you follering us." Smiling.

"You never seen me."

"Seen something."

"Sho." She snorted this at him and he almost laughed. "Something
in your head I guess."

"Well," he said. "You were there and now you're here."

"I didn't follow nothing. Been here waiting."

"That right?"

She nodded. He could see she wore a different dress, once a deep
green now faded to old moss.

"Waiting for what?" And he immediately wanted to bite back the
words from the night.

But she only said, "Waiting for that woman to get done with her
charity while you all tore up her barn. Waiting to see you walk out here
sometime tonight. Waiting to see if you jump up in the air already running when you see me like you see a spook. You still got time for that I
guess."

"I'm sentry tonight. If I tore off running who knows what would
happen. So I'm standing right here I guess."

"Sentry sposed to walk around I thought."

He shrugged. "War's over. I guess you heard that."

Now she shrugged. "You think that's gonna change a thing, Mister Norman Pelham?" Before he could respond she reached out one hand and ran her fingers down his forearm, and he felt the flesh of his arm rise up to meet her. She was speaking not of her life or the lives of her people or even the people all around them but of the sudden and irrevocable breach each had made in the other. And nothing said out yet in the air between them, nothing said to make it real, as if words could do such a thing. So he only asked, "You get anything to eat today?"

"Some folks shared what they had." She watching him now as if seeing he'd finally figured things out. Or maybe afraid he knew the words to break it apart. So he touched her upper arm and felt the chill of her skin, smooth and tight with cold. And said, "I need to find you a coat."

"I got a coat. Out there." Pointing out into the dark with her chin. "With my blankets and mess." Norman shuddered with the complicated ripple of knowledge that the next minutes hours days would circuit his life; he'd learned early in the war to avoid reading signs or portents into any one small thing because the larger ones pay no attention to those small events. Hope and desire or dread are puny human attributes beside the work of a dreadful god or a careless universe but at this moment he knew his life was some way shapable. He was breathless that long moment and then Leah moved forward so her face was in full light now and he told her, "You wait right here. You wait just one minute. Please. Here, hold this." He thrust the Springfield into her hands and turned to lope back up to the fire, where he poured out a can of coffee and took biscuits and bacon from the racks by the fire, stuffing his tunic pockets to a bulge. He was turning to leave when he saw Goundry watching him, the fervently quiet small blacksmith from Poultney now captain of the company, whose voice just carried the five feet between them.

"What're you doing, Pelham?"

"Something to eat sir?"

"Hungry?" Goundry eyeing the tunic.

"Yessir."

Goundry nodded. "Where the hell's your rifle, Pelham?"

Norman inclined his head. "Back there. Right by the barn sir. I just wanted to get this food."

Goundry nodded again. "Is your head feeling all right, son?"

"It's fine sir."

Goundry held him with his eyes. Then he said, "By Jesus I'm glad this thing's done with. Get out of here, Pelham."

He found her crouched in the shadow beside one of the mule-stall partitions, his rifle held upright between her legs, the barrel hugged against her chest. He took her hand and helped her stand and she said, "Some man came out the back of the barn and peed there so I hid down here."

He traded her the can of coffee for his rifle and told her, "I've got some bread and bacon too. You know some place we could set down?"

She took him by the hand and led him over what had been vegetable gardens and then past a chicken yard, down a dirt track with a pair of empty cabins on each side, and behind these was a smaller structure made of heavy logs with no windows but with a door busted apart, pieces of timber still splinted upright by strap hinges. Inside she hung a blanket from nails over the doorway and lit a candle stub and he saw her suitcase and bedroll on the floor and a small rude bench made of a split log with unpeeled limbs splayed as legs. A short length of stout chain was bolted into the log wall, the chain ending in a manacle roughly cut open with the marks of the slipped chisel. They sat on the bench and shared the coffee and she ate some of the biscuit and the bacon he sliced off for her, ate with a vast controlled manner that made clear how hungry she was, and while she declined more than a small amount of the food he cleared his pockets and set the rest on the edge of the bench in a natural sort of way. They sat silent on the bench in the guttering candlelight, the boy younger than he thought he was and the girl older than she thought she was. He saw slight spasms running over her upper body and he unbuttoned his tunic and saw her watching him, her mouth tight and her eyes flat, and he took the tunic off and put it around her shoulders and sat there beside her with his suspenders up over his woolen undershirt. She crossed her arms to take the tunic edges in opposite hands and drew it close around her and in so doing leaned a little so her shoulder touched his and she said, "Norman, what do you want with me?"

He thought about this and only would say, "I guess I could ask the same thing."

Without pause she said, "Ask then."

So he did and she said, "I want to go to Up-by-Canada."

"Vermont," he said.

"Ver-mont," she said, breaking the word in two parts and he thought Yes that's right, that verde monte, that old green hill of Champlain—his Randolph Academy brought back clear by the girl's usage—but he only said, "It's a long ways from here."

"Already walked one of those. I can walk another." Then, "Less you don't want me to."

Norman looked away from her now, looked down at his hands joined together between his knees, his elbows and forearms flat on his thighs, and was quiet until his voice came and then he said, "I don't know." He could hear her breathing beside him, could feel slight movement in her shoulder against his and felt a patience from her as she waited for him and he knew what for and didn't know how to say it and so only said, "I don't barely know you."

"Course you don't," she said. "What it takes to know a person you tell me soon's you know. I don't know, not me. You got brothers, sisters?"

"Sisters," he said, "three of em."

But she kept right on talking as if he'd said nothing. "Your mama and daddy. You known those people all your life but you don't know what they really all about inside. And you think they all gonna sit around waiting for you to know, Norman? You think even they themselves know? Not like they like to, I tell you that. You and me sitting here strange as can be to one another but here we are, ain't that right? And what you call that? You call that a accident? I walked maybe three hundred miles to meet up with you Norman and didn't even know it was you till I seen you laying there under that briar clump and how'd I know then that you'd wake up to be you? I didn't. You know what I'm telling you Norman?"

All he could do was nod his head, just once.

She said, "I look at you, you know what I see? Norman?"

"I got no idea."

"I see a man gentle right down in his soul. All the way down."

Then she was quiet and when she spoke again her voice had lost a little edge and he heard it right away, a little less certainty and he felt this loss in his chest like hot water. She said, "So me. You look at me what do you see? Norman?"

His face furrowed like a spring field, wanting to get this just right. He had no idea what to say and kept looking at her hoping she'd wait for him, hoping she'd be patient. Hoping he'd find his way not out but through this.

She didn't wait. She said, "You see a little nigger girl wanting to eat up your biscuit, your bacon, whatever you got? You see me thinking my taking care of you once overnight is something I can trade for lots more than that? Or maybe even just nigger pussy ready for you to say the right words, do the right thing? That what you see, Norman?" And she was reared back away from him now, sitting still on the bench, upright as if at a great distance, her back arched like a drawn bow, eyes burning wide open as her soul welled up but not at all ready to pour out without something back from him. He watched his hands turning one over the other, the fingers lacing and relacing until he realized she was watching him do this. He slid around and lifted his right leg over the bench so he sat spraddle-legged facing her front on. With his face collapsed in sheer terror, he said to her, "Leah. All I see is the most lovely girl I've ever seen."

She stood off the bench away from him and said, "I told you the truth, Norman. I told you the truth. But you lying to me if that's all you see."

And without even thinking about it he said, "What I see is the most lovely girl and one fat wide world of trouble. Trouble for both of us. That's what I see."

And now she stepped back over the bench to face him and said, "You got that right. You got that just exactly right." He reached and took one of her hands and sat looking down at their hands lying one into the other, the small slip of warmth between his fingers, her life lying up against his, and still not looking at her he said, "Don't you ever talk that way to me again Leah."

"What way?" Her voice low, already knowing, needing to ask, needing him to tell her.

So he said, "That nigger-this nigger-that business."

"White men talk any way they want to a colored girl."

"Am I white men to you then?"

She reached her free hand and took his other hand and put it against her breastbone just below her throat and told him, "My daddy's a white man, Norman."

"I figured something like that," he said; in truth he hadn't thought that far. So again without thinking he said, "He doesn't talk that way does he?" His hand warming to the heat of her, his brain on the buttons down her dress-front.

She tilted her chin to look at him. "My daddy has never even said my name to me." Her voice tight with disgust, venom, a loathing that was distinct and almost covered all what sadness she had but that he knew was there, knew it the same way she believed his soul to be gentle. He scooted toward her on the bench and she brought her knees in tight to the bench to let him come close and he put his arms around her and she laid her head against him and he sat there, holding her like that.

From the bench to her blankets on the floorboards of the little stockade was not a long way to go but they took a long time moving there, seeming to travel down inch by inch in a locked body motion that neither led nor followed but went with them trembling. Once down, they wrestled with limbs made slow and heavy, his fingers thick with the buttons of her dress and her breasts out then, nipples like summer blackcaps against thick honey, and she shuddered under his tongue. She astride him and with one hand he swept the dress up over her hips and opened his flies with the other, but she arched away from him even as he strained toward her, his thumb once traveling down the length of her as she opened under, the wet there breathtaking. Still she held off from him, their mouths smothering each other, tongues each hot and sharp to the other, almost struggling until she broke away, rolling over to lie beside him, her legs still spread and her dress open to the waist, and she said, "If you'd got it in I would've let you." He rolled over on top of her and as he entered she said, her voice now a wet thing in his ear, "I could just melt all over you," and with that he was done, thrusting from the small of his back and her soft cries falling into his ears like thin slices of bird-flight entering his brain. She reached down and held him to her after he was finished and told him, "Don't leave, don't go."

So he stayed until he slipped from her and still he lay there, the wet between them sealing one to the other. Neither one now wanting or able
to leave.

Walking up that final half mile of rough track above Randolph with
the farmhouse not yet in sight, the crown of the elms over the house
stretched ahead where the road cut an opening through the trees, the
girl already thought she knew something of the place to which she'd
come, having walked through half the state just to get here, as well as
all the rest of the north that lay behind them now. The boy paced slow
with so much home after so long finally in sight, both with those long
days and too-short nights behind them; those and the weeks they spent
outside Washington where after Lincoln's assassination Norman waited
with his company through a mourning for the president. They stayed
through most of May to walk together one final time as a military force
down Pennsylvania Avenue in the Grand Review of the Army of the
Potomac, Norman waiting with great agitation while Leah disappeared
into the swamped springtime of the capital, a place at odds with itself,
wildly festive with the war's end and murderously foul from the dead
president. After four long days, she reappeared with lye-burned mottled
hands and a pure gleefulness nothing could diminish; she was working
in the basement of a hotel scrubbing linens and ironing them to a slick
starched stiffness but earning cash money, in fact a sum that gave
Norman pause; during the years of the war he'd come to think of money
in the abstract and at those random intervals when his pay arrived he
wired it through to his sheep account at the bank in Randolph. Those
first six weeks passed and they went their own way, disregarding the
packed trains leaving for Philadelphia or New York or Boston and
walking up the country through the lush and easy summer, sleeping in
woods or fields with hedgerow cover and buying food when they needed
it. At times they had to fend off dogs and small boys with their name-
calling and meanness strident and forgivable for their age and ignorance.
Only once, outside Port Royal, New York, did a man on horseback block
their passage, inquiring the price of the nigger whore. And Norman
brought the man down from his horse, an easy job after that long-dead

cavalryman, and thrashed him there in the dust of the road, three other men off in the distance watching and not involving themselves. It was not the watchers but Leah who stopped him, who began kicking him in the muscles on the backs of his calves and screaming at him until he gave way. They continued up the road, leaving the man lying and his horse standing off some distance in a field, blowing its nostrils clear, and Norman and Leah walked by the watching men and Norman met their gaze and wished them a good day. So they walked to Vermont, to home for both, and told each other stories along the way. Outside a river town in northern Massachusetts they married each other standing naked in the moonlight in the Connecticut River, the water end-of-summer low and syrup-colored even in the night, the rings thin gold bands he'd bought three days previous and carried as they watched and waited for the right place and time. Late the following day they crossed into Vermont and Leah grew quiet, her animation screwed now to a tight focus, watching around her as if careful observation would offer keys or clues to the place she would assume among this landscape. As if her silence before this spectrum offered her protection against any hostilities or animosity.

They came up that first sharp knee of the home-place hill and the land opened out not so much in a bowl as a series of wide ledges that held the farmstead: the haymeadows and sheep pastures and the high field where potatoes were grown, the orchard just above the house and barns, to where the sugar house stood flanked by the bush of great maples rising in crown over it all, the final pitch of the hillside steep again at the top amongst granite outcroppings and ranks of spruce. Norman's gait gained with the sudden leveling of the track and the place there before him, his feet for the first time in years striking ground as if each separate egg of gravel and patch of dusty hardpan were known through the soles of his boots, Leah still apace beside him, her head high and her gaze steady before her, her eyes sweeping at first to draw it all in but settling on the house under the elms. Without looking at him she said, "Reckon they seen us yet?"

As she spoke a figure broke out from the apple trees heavy with ripe fruit. Norman saw the baskets under the trees and the narrow picking ladder and thought Cider—could not smell it yet but could taste it— and then the girl hurtling down the road toward them, short-legged and strong, twice the little girl he'd left behind, still small but grown, her schoolgirl breasts rising against her shirtwaist like young apples as she ran toward him, her voice calling out his name.

Beside him Leah softly echoed her. "Nawmin."

The girl spied Leah and gathered herself down to a walk and Norman saw the moment when she misstepped, saw her head cock like a puppy's at something strange, and yet she came on, her eyes on Leah even as Norman stepped the last three feet and pulled her against him. Before he could speak she said, "Seems to me, a man or stout boy would've been more useful around, you had to bring one of them home." And she stepped back from Norman then, her eyes already wiser as she looked Leah up and down.

"Maybe you'll find out, Miss Quickmouth," Leah said, "that I'm a good bit stouter than you like."

Connie shrugged this away. "There's work enough to share," she said. "I guess you already learned how to work."

"Worked all my life. I learned how to let my mind work for me too. Sometimes before I opened my mouth. I know my manners."

"Well, la."

"Ain't no la about it. There was, you'd be behaving different."

"That's enough," Norman said.

Connie said, "You're a feisty one."

"I wasn't, you think I'd be here? Since your brother forgot himself, my name's Leah." She held out a hand. Connie looked at Norman and then back at the hand.

Norman said, "My little sister. Constance. Connie, we call her."

Connie let Leah take her hand and then both women let go. Norman said, "Where's Mother?"

Connie said, "Up to the house." And looked at Norman as if just thinking of something. She half turned and looked back at him. "You don't look like I remember."

He nodded. "You've grown some too."

"That's not what I meant."

He nodded again, both brother and sister using this time to take measure of the other, recognizing each as familiar stranger to be learned anew, some parts of each never to be glimpsed. Norman strove for the ordinary, some tentative linkage to all that lost. "You making cider?"

"Getting ready. Pressed some last week a little too rough. Sheep liked the pomace though."

"Jug of cider's about the only thing I can think of that might clear all this road out of my throat."

She grinned. "You'll have to help then." And glanced again at Leah.

Norman said, "I believe I recall how to crank a press."

"You'll want some dinner first."

"About anything."

"I could run help get things started."

"Sure," he said. "You do that. Carry your news along with you."

"You home is news enough." Her eyes cut once more to Leah; then she turned and flew up the road.

"So tell me Norman. That the easy part?"

"I guess," he said. "She didn't intend meanness. You're a shock. You have to allow that for folks. Otherwise you'll just be disappointed every time."

They went a little ways and Leah said, "Tell me you love me," and he did and she reached to take his hand. Norman took stock of the sheep in one high meadow, of the milk cows in higher grass of better pasture close to the barn and also of the broken axle off the wagon that sat upright against it like no one knew what to do next. There were other things, simple benign neglect adding up in his mind, an accounting freed of blame, more in the nature of inventory. Halfway to the house he felt her fingers begin to slip from his and he took a firm grip to hold her there beside him. He thought her only nervous and when she wrapped his hand tight with hers he thought she was fine again. He did not look at her. And so could not see the fear pass over her face or the swift knowing that ran through her, that the woman in the house ahead of her would take one look and read the weakness there that trembled constant as water running, the pith of despair and turmoil of her soul. She said nothing. Together they skirted the front of the house around to the side entry through the long woodshed and small toolshop into the kitchen, where he knew his mother and sister both waited. Leah walked alongside him.

His mother was an old woman. She was stooped over the oven of the range and she turned to place a beanpot on the table where Connie sat silent. His mother placed her hands flat on the table and looked at

Norman as she said his name. Her face was fierce and worn like tree-bark, her hair pulled back tight as always but dappled gray like a Percheron. Her hands on the table thick with raised veins and spots the color of new rust. She'd grown old in three years.

So he only said, "Beans."

She demurred. "It's Saturday you know. They was for supper. But it happened I started them early yesterday. Before milking. So they're ready. I haven't steamed the brown bread yet, you'll have to make do with loaf-bread. There's pickle."

"Leah, my mother. Mother, this is Leah."

Leah said, "Missus Pelham." And her body swayed beside him as if almost to dip a curtsy. "Pleased to meet you." Erect now, not moving.

Mrs. Pelham remained behind the table, a guarded patience upon her face as if she'd seen wondrous and terrible things before and was waiting for this one to reveal which it was. She had never seen a black woman. And meeting her for the first time not in the village but here in her own kitchen. Brought by her warrior son. The woman was with him. That much was all she knew. So she inclined her head and responded. "I'm sure. You two set. I've got buttermilk and spring water and that's it. No cider, fresh or hard. I've not put any barrels up these past two years. Too much work for just the girl and me, without anyone to drink it. So you'll make do. But set; you must be famished walking all the way back up here." Her eyes on Norman as she added, "Other men rode trains at least part of the way."

Stretching for the beanpot, he said, "I should've got back here to help you. I wanted to see the country. Thought I might not get the chance again. And I figured you and sprout here was capable." And then added, "So we took our time."

"You took your time."

"Yes ma'am." Grinning at her, not yet realizing he couldn't be both the boy-child miscreant and the unassailable man. He dug the spoon to the bottom of the pot and lifted the seasoning onion up through the beans and divided it half onto his plate and half onto Leah's, then scooped beans onto his own plate and handed her the spoon.

Connie said, "Could be others might like some of that bean-onion."

"Could be," said Norman. "Could be some been eating bean-onions while others ate stale biscuit and bacon in the mud and rain. Sprout, you've grown up." To see if he could make her blush. She did not, but her eyes clouded with hostility.

She said, "I started to the Academy this fall."

Mrs. Pelham said, "Connie, go bring up some buttermilk."

"Not for me," Norman said. "Spring water's all I want." Eyeing it where the iron pipe ran in through the wall, ending over the soapstone sink, the line laid the summer before the war by Norman and his father from the spring high on the hill above the house, the water fed by gravity, running in a steady thin stream year round, draining through clean cheesecloth clamped in a small pouch over the end of the pipe. He said, "I've drank more mud than water, enough so that spring ran in my dreams."

"Perhaps Lee would—"

"Leah," she said.

"Yes, that's right." Mrs. Pelham said, agreeing to nothing. "Perhaps Leah would care for buttermilk."

"Thank you, no. Water would be fine. But I could get it." She started to rise.

"Set. There's no servants here but we can take care of a guest." Inflecting slightly on the last word and moving to the sink, filling a pitcher and placing it on the table, this time coming around to stand behind them and reach the pitcher through, placing it between them. She stayed there, her hand on the pitcher until Norman looked up at her, her eyes stark with brightness, a faint flutter around her mouth as she gazed on the bright slender band on his left hand. Her voice a husk, stripped of fluid as she said, "Oh Lord, Norman. What have you done?"

Leah swung her head sideways to look up but Mrs. Pelham was gone, her skirts swept by her movement. She opened the door of the small parlor and closed it after her. The sound a small clap in the stillness. Leah released a held breath. She said to him, "Go after her. Go talk to your mother, Norman."

"No." Connie stood up fast, her chair a rough scrape backwards. "No. I'll go. You two just set there. Set there and eat your damned beans." When he spoke her full name, she turned back as if his speaking had not lessened her angry confusion but charged it further, her small face pinched upon itself, her curls tossed adrift by the speed of her movement. "You waltz on in here in your own sweet time without a word about Father or how we made out alone here and set down to eat up the supper in the middle of the day and that's not enough, no sir, not for you, but you drag along home with you this . . . this . . . colored woman and set her down at the table to feed her while your own mother stands waiting a kind word or embrace from you, feeding her up our supper—"

"That's enough," Norman said. "Leah's my wife. We're married."

"Married?"

"That's right." His tone meant to settle the matter.

"Norman Pelham," his sister said all in one breath, "you've lost your mind," as she walked a mannered step through to the closed parlor and shut the door behind her soft as nothing at all.

"They not delighted with me," Leah said.

"That's all right," Norman said, wondering not only why he'd failed to write his mother some warning or caution but why he'd not even thought to. And stranger still, he felt a tingling of excitement at this failure, excitement real as his balls tightening. He looked at the woman next to him and said, "I am."

Sunday morning Mrs. Pelham and Connie hitched the mare that killed his father to the high-seated two-wheeled cart and took it to town: to church and, Norman was sure, much more than a usual simple worship and social. It would be late afternoon before they returned. He spent the morning at his father's old desk, reviewing what passed for accounts and then writing a letter to the horse trader in Chelsea. He would not keep the team with the killer mare. This done he began a close count of the sheep, walking over the high pasture and tallying with a pencil stub on a sheet of brown wrapping paper, always watching Leah as she went back and forth outside, working at the tub, scouring their clothes with lye soap and hand-wringing them before draping them onto the lilac and hydrangea that bordered the back of the house. The clothes from the height of land small bright flags that served to bring the careless summer over him so that he did not fret over the number of ram lambs or the three ewes he absolutely could not find but allowed himself a fine moment at the edge of a stone ledge looking down over it all; this was his and he was needed here and he'd returned to it. He came down off the hill before the middle of the day to find Leah and led her back into the house, up the stairs to the attic where the night before he had taken her, instead of to his old room down just from his sister's and close to where his mother lay not sleeping. They'd climbed up the small cramped stairs to pull out and shake loose an old feather ticking where they made their bed, and now he was on his back in the empty house with her above him, Norman deep with solace as her face pitched and roamed over him, he watching the steady come and go of mud daubers along the rafters. In the afternoon he stripped down the broken axle, readying it for the smith and then went through the barns, taking stock of the small lay-in of hay and the dairy tie-up, having already run his eye over the five cows in the pasture, small brown and dun Jerseys that all looked poor to him. He'd never cared for cows but accepted the five were there to stay and likely more of them. Then he walked through the empty pig shed and scattered shellcorn to bring out the ranging hens, the flock greater and older than it should have been. They'd be eating a lot of stewed hen this winter. He killed a young roasting rooster and took it to Leah, who sat on the ground in a clean skirt and shirtwaist under the appletrees, her legs bared to above her knee and her chin wet with apple juice. He held up the rooster and said, "It won't hurt to have supper ready when they come back."

"Un-uh," she said. "I'm not messing with her kitchen."

He said, "There's potatoes and carrots and parsnips on the hill. There's winter squash on the old manure pile by the barn. You could bake a pie from these apples. There's fresh cream in the pans down basement. It's your kitchen." He dropped the rooster on the ground next to where she sat. He said, "It's my farm."

He climbed the track up the hillside, passing the sugarhouse, not willing to look inside at the buckets with rusted hoops and rotted staves, continuing on through the sugar bush, the ancient maple trunks thick-barked and dense, some capable of holding five or six buckets, from there following the track around the shoulder of the mountain into other mixed hardwood of beech and birch, ash, ironwood and hickory. The woods a carnage of color, the early autumn-smell sweet as if death could be that way. A partridge blew out of the litter beside the track, and Norman flinched without hesitation. He wondered if everything would somehow always remind him of the war. If a partridge could ever be just that again.

He came around the mountain above the wildland of a small gore and walked another quarter of a mile before coming upon Ballous'. A shake-sided one-story dwelling more cabin than house but for the length of it. Backed up against a granite outcropping the builder had used as backside for the fireplace and chimney. The front door open to the afternoon and Ballou himself seated there, as if waiting for Norman. Dressed in green woolen pants, leather braces up over red underwear, the clothing not so much dirty as having gained a texture from the forest loam, sawdust, deer and fish entrails. His long hair greased behind his ears and his face sharp-shaven, features like a fisher-cat. Smoking a long-stemmed clay pipe, the only one Norman had ever seen, the stem and bowl the color of antler from handling and tobacco stain.

"Heard you was back."

"Yuht." Not surprised the news had leapfrogged up the mountain.

"One a them boys hellcattin down to Randol' last night, chasing some little skirt come weaseling back at dawn with word a you. Boys no good for nothin but they got to do her, young like that. Not me, no. Not no more. One old woman is much for me, right? You be learned that soon, eh?"

"You been keeping my mother in wood?"

"Yuht, sure. No complain?"

"Nope. Not at all. Just there's only two–three cords back behind the house."

"She been buying as she needed. Pretty much."

"Uh-huh." Angry but not sure at whom. "You got any yarded up?"

"Got plenty down. Not sawed and split."

"Not too hard to get to?" Norman watching him.

Ballou grinned, feral amber teeth. "All I cutting here on the backside a you. What I want your wood for, I got all this?" Spreading his arms.

Norman ignored this, certain come winter or spring he'd find stumps in the far reach of his own land, knowing Ballou enjoyed selling her own wood to his mother. He said, "I need ten cords for the winter."

"Them nigger women don't know no snow. Got to keep em warm and it take more than what you got, eh, Norman?"

"Henri, you got that much wood or not?"

Ballou sucked his pipestem. "How soon you want this ten cord?"

"Two weeks."

"No."

"Two weeks."

"Can't be done."

"Your boys around?"

Ballou looked around the yard as if to spy them there. He shrugged. "Out the woods somewhere."

"You got plenty of help then."

Ballou fired the dead pipe. The smoke smelling like the day itself. When it was well lighted he said, "October fifteen. Ten cord."

"Split and stacked."

Ballou spit. Agreeing.

"I pay when it's done."

"Half and half. I got to have something keep the boys out the woods."

"Five cords, half. The other five, the rest."

Ballou shrugged. "You want some tea?"

"Thanks, Henri, but I got to get on. I got lots to do. Give my best to your Missus."

"That war, she bad, eh?"

Norman nodded. "Yuht."

Ballou gazed off, done with it. He looked back at Norman and said, "Well get on with you then. The boys and me we start this week. Come a load and meet your own Missus, eh?"

Norman went back around the mountain, the afternoon failing, the light rich as butter. The two-wheeled cart was out in the yard before the open barn doors, resting its horseless shafts on the ground. Connie came from the barn and picked up the shafts and backed the cart around into the barn, Norman guessing she'd arrived home and left the mare to stand in the yard while she went to change from her good clothes before coming back out to stable the horse and wheel the cart away. Wondering if his mother was milking. He decided to leave them alone, all three of them, for a little while, feeling some things might be worked out better with him absent. The kitchen showed a clear smoke rising with heat vapors at the chimney top. He settled at the base of a maple, his back against the rough soothing ridges of the trunk and his knees up. He could still see the farm.

Intending to sort his plans and purposes for the coming days, not only what must be said and done but also what must be established, for whatever lapses might be made then would be lapses with them forever; he knew this, and knew also that payments would be extruded, the least of them in cash or kind. Telling himself he'd known these things, these costs, all the summer long, right down to the first day that he woke to her looming beside him. Telling himself no event lies or falls unconnected to others and that will is only the backbone needed to face these things head on. Determined then to pay attention. As if his father spoke, calling for him to look sharp.

Gazing out over the bowl of his small fortress, watching a wedge of geese tracking over the far ridge following the branch of the river south, Norman found himself thinking of Ballou: the man as wild goose pursuing his own course without concern of what others cared or thought of him. Norman's father ever bastardizing his name even to his face, as if his unwillingness to commit body and soul to a patch of rock-studded ground was crime enough without the taint of otherness about him already; the French Canadian unreliable but content to live on the unclaimed wildland above the small gore. Ballou was out on snowshoes all winter long running traplines and felling trees if a market appeared on the horizon, the rest of the year happy to fish, hunt and attend horse races or run hounds. Ballou was among the first of only a few who paid out hard money in gold coin for substitutes for his three boys, not waiting for the draft. Offering no explanation, his smile tight and scornful as if he saw the others fools not to appreciate that life was short and bittersweet enough without being blown apart to serve some other men's ideas of how things should be. Norman felt that he and Ballou had just executed a short and easy turn of dance with one another: firewood bought; money paid. And Norman now deflated with the effort as if it had stripped some layer from his soul. Knowing the worst men could do to one another wasn't the clear gore of Marye's Heights or the wreckage of Petersburg but the relentless small decades of generations of Sweetboro, North Carolina. Which all the efforts of battle might change but not erase from the thinking walking talking breath of the woman

down the valley before him. What was he to say, Rest easy now? With
both of them knowing however far the distance and unlikely the location she would never, and so neither would he, assume that some peace
or ease was theirs to hold the way others assume that peace could be held.
Live quiet, was what she'd said. But without knowing exactly what they
were headed to, he knew while it might be possible it could never be
certain. He wondered if that was why Ballou paid that gold money, as
much to save his sons as to announce his intention to live quiet. Would
make it so with all the fiber and gut he could string out of himself to
ward off everything else. Whatever good it might do.

What she told him about Sweetboro she'd told him only after they'd
left Washington and were traveling north through the war-blown
countryside of northern Virginia and through the western arm of Maryland and into Pennsylvania. Camped in the barn of a man they'd met
along the road, the man with a yoke of young balking oxen that Norman
stepped forward and helped goad. The man who did not offer his home
but his barn-loft with good bright barley straw, the man with a woman
a head taller than he who stood at the half-door of her kitchen and
watched Norman and Leah cross the yard to the barn, the door holding back three round-faced boys no more than six to ten. The man crossing from the house in the summer evening with a crock of sauerkraut
baked with spare ribs, a fresh wheat loaf on top that steamed when they
broke it open. Leah watching his back until he closed the kitchen door
behind him again and only then reaching to eat.

Norman said, "You don't care for that feller much."

Her mouth brilliant with grease she said without pause, "It's not him.
I don't trust his woman."

Norman almost asked what to trust and then stopped himself, letting his quiet run along under him as he ate his supper. It was the first
hot food he'd had not prepared by the army or purchased out the back
door of a rooming house or hotel. Since Washington there'd been
a wariness, a caution near skittish of strangers about her that she'd
not so much hidden as simply acted upon without direct reference,
making clear she'd prefer camping in hedge or thicket than asking
at a house. She wouldn't linger in towns or around groups of people,
especially groups of men; she would startle at the sound of galloping
horses approaching on the road. Recalling the town in Maryland where

a police officer had hurried toward them, cutting it seemed across the street to meet them and how Leah had folded herself against Norman's side even as the man passed them with no more than a glance. In the pale green twilight he carried the crock back to the kitchen door and thanked the woman, returning to the barn to lie in the straw opposite Leah atop a spread blanket. He said, "Why's that woman bother you?"

As though she was not sure she was going to tell him she said, "The way she look at us. Everybody look. But some people, like this woman, seem like she trying to line my face up with something else, something she heard or been told or maybe even some picture she seen somewhere. Or like she memorizing me, like she want to get every little line down right. It's more than not liking me cause I'm me or even that I'm me with you."

Norman was quiet awhile, thinking everything she said was true and sure also it was not. When he spoke again it was dark with the summer stars out the open loft door of the barn showing bats slipping out from under the ridgeline, cutting slim arcs against the night sky. He said, "You going to tell me the rest of it now or you want to wait some while longer?"

"Tell what?"

"Whatever it is that gets you so spooked around strangers. Whatever it is you done wherever it is you come from. Something makes you think somebody's watching for you. Or might be."

"You got that all figured out."

He shrugged even though he guessed she couldn't see it. "I guess you'll tell me when you're ready. Although it might not hurt if I knew what it was we're looking out for. Or not."

"I'm not keeping nothing from you Norman."

"Didn't say you were."

"I just ain't told you everything yet is all."

"I guess there's plenty about me you don't know too."

"You hush up Norman. Trying to talk to you." He could not see this but knew she was frowning in the dark. Then she began speaking and her voice gained a flatness he hadn't heard before, without passion or tone, the voice older than she, as if the voice of the place she spoke of, the voices held there and rising from that place through her.

She told him of Sweetboro: the late February afternoon alone in the kitchen of the house, with her mother Helen and the old woman Rey not three dozen steps out the back door in their cabin, Leah alone heating flatirons on the stove and pressing the clothing of the white people, all now gone to Raleigh but for the younger son somewhere in the house behind the kitchen door. The white people were clutched near to panic with disarray: firstborn Spencer dead almost a year defending Petersburg and the younger Alex just fourteen run off two months before and returned almost immediately with his right arm gone to the elbow, the pus-stained wrappings among what Leah ironed because everything the white people wore in any way when washed was also ironed. Alex would not leave the house, as if his arm lost was somehow not enough, that it was disgrace to have come back at all. Mebane took his wife and two daughters to the capital where life was only less grim because there were more white people to share it with. Leah was not so much happy with the white people gone as no longer caring; the rumors of the past four years she'd learned to ignore, but what was clear was the state of the white people and she knew things had in some fundamental way already changed, even if she still stood with rising steam burning her nostrils as she pressed their underclothes.

Mebane the youngest son of a youngest son who went from the coastal plain rice fields below Wilmington to Chapel Hill and then for no reason clear to anyone, brought his bride to Sweetboro where he practiced law and spent much of his time traveling the thirty miles southwest to Raleigh while she kept house with Rey and another slave, Peter, a man brought to tend the stable and the flower gardens that fell in steps between the house and the redclay street. His wife became pregnant almost immediately with Spencer, but four years passed before Alex was born and it was during this time that Helen was bought from Mebane's brother. Seventeen years ago: Helen at the time two years younger than Leah now was. Mebane would still from time to time pass through the kitchen to nod at Helen before passing out the back steps to wait for her in the cabin, his eyes never more than glancing off Leah like fingers flicking a fly, his eyes the same wetglass green as hers. Other times he'd come to her mother at night, less cautious, taking no notice of the girl or the old woman behind their curtains, his rut then loud and jubilant. Where Leah first heard the words that other white men and boys would direct at her. Where she would lie awake without moving, her face stiff as if held together by will, the breath under her ribs a small sharp thing, waiting for him to finish and leave, waiting for the smell of him to drain out of the night before falling back to sleep. As the February afternoon folded without notice to dusk, the rain still steady down and the kitchen steaming with warmth, her right hand slid the iron back and forth and her left moved fanlike both before and behind the iron. Something pleasant in the sway of her torso over the board, pleasant in the slight clutch of leg muscles anchoring her over it all. Happy to be left alone, to feel left alone. And so only a little less happy when Alex came through the connecting door from the dining room across from where she stood, thinking he would come and go and she would still be alone in the short evening.

He sat at the table across from where she worked, his good arm up on the table, palm flat, the stump of the other flat against his side, the cauterized tip still swaddled with bandage that seeped a clear pus that yellowed in the cloth. He was a pretty boy, with a pouched lower lip and his father's ginger hair swept back in ordered waves from his forehead. His skin was smooth, made more so by faint feathers of beard. His crumpled clothes gave the idea he no longer cared how he looked. She continued ironing, not looking up at him, pressing the same shirt slowly over with a cool iron. She couldn't help but wonder about the missing arm, where it was, what had happened to it. She only knew it had been removed, what fragments and pieces of it were left. She still thought of it as a whole thing. Sure a part of his soul had been lost with that arm. Wondered where that hand was and what it grasped for. His other hand on the table, fingers drumming now. She knew he was waiting for her to look at him. It was too hot in the kitchen and she broke sweat.

"What's to eat?"

She didn't look up, her arm still moving. "Same as always. Field peas, turnips, collards, some cornbread. All of it cold though."

"Colored food."

She shrugged, still not looking at him. "It's what they is. You want better you should've gone off with the rest of them."

"Yes," he said. "I spect they're eating oysters and champagne. Beefsteak maybe."

"I don't know," she said. "All I know is what's here."

His fingers drummed hard and fast on the tabletop, then stopped. "Get me something to eat."

"I'm working."

"You already ironed that thing three times."

She stayed quiet.

He said, "Get me some dinner."

"I'm busy. You feed yourself."

"Look at me."

"I done looked at you. You still able to feed yourself, I can see."

He slapped his hand on the table hard. "Goddammit, I said look at me."

She stepped away to the stove and placed the cold iron on it and brought a hot one back and set it on the end of the board. She took up the shirt and folded it and placed it on the pile and dipped to lift another from the basket and laid it over the board. Then she looked at him and said, "What you want, Mister Lex?"

A shroud of darkness ran over his boy's face, not strong enough to break the softness of his skin but something laced through the muscles beneath the surface, a tautness there; and for the first time she feared him. This fear angered her and so angry at the manchild before her she only said again, "What you want, Mister Lex?" This time the title over her tongue the juice of a bitter weed.

"You know what Mama told me before they all lit out for Raleigh?"

She said nothing. His eyes dark, wet.

"She told me there was nobody but myself to blame. I said I was just trying to do my part. She told me I was a fool, my part wasn't anything I thought it was, nobody's part was what they thought it was anymore. She said we all had new parts coming and not one of us could know what they was. But we could be smart enough to figure out to wait until they was revealed. And me sitting there like this and her telling me that. Like she was angry at me. Like she somehow blamed me. Like she blamed me for the future somehow."

Leah said, "She a tough woman," and didn't know she knew this until she said it.

His eyes shot from her face as if she'd said nothing. He said, "It was mostly old men and boys like me. What men there was was worn out.

Cold like you never known. Grown men barefoot in the wintertime. When the fight come each one lit up with a rage. Men furious wild with right. One minute you're red as bears' eyes and the next you're flat on the ground with the world all gone to pain and men climbing over you running and you thinking about your daddy sitting on his fat ass down there and knowing it's men like him that keep this thing going at the same time you know somehow it's men like him keep it from working. My arm wasn't nothing next to that. It made me sit up and puke. It still makes me want to puke."

She was ironing again. She didn't want to talk about his father. She said, "Seems to me your mama was maybe right."

"What's that mean?"

Picking her way. "It don't mean nothing. Just, things change. Folks get used to most anything."

He was quiet a little while, watching her. She was wet under her arms and could smell herself and guessed he could too. After a bit he said, "Know what I saw coming back down home?"

She folded the shirt and turned to the stove with the iron and set it there and turned back, standing now before the stove, a pace away from the table. "What'd you see?"

"Come across a pair of wagons. Hooped over with canvas covers, a skinny old team of oxen hitched up to each wagon. The wagons filled up with house stuff, feather ticks and furniture, nothing too big but all of it looked nice what I could see. Old men and little children and women in the wagons. Six men bareback on mules carrying pitchforks and hog-butchering knives, one with a scythe. What do you think of that?"

"I don't think nothing. Lots people moving round now."

"They was all niggers. A whole troop of niggers. Heading north in broad daylight. In ox wagons with pilfered belongings. Going what? Six–eight miles a day? Some great old escape. A dash to freedom. Two of the ones on muleback rode up with their rusted weapons with edges whetted to shine like water and sat there and asked me what I was doing. 'What you wanting here white boy,' they said to me. 'Jus keep moving on,' they said. 'Jus keep one foot front of the other and you'll get your little white ass on home.' And I didn't say nothing to em, just kept walking right on by those spavined mules and them old wagons

and them oxen near dead anyhow and didn't look back at em, the whole
time feeling those pitchfork tines running right on through my lungs,
knowing they was looking at me like they'd like to do that. I went on
all day until it was dark and never met anybody looking for em at all.
Them out there in broad daylight, brazen as that. Like they was riding
angels not oxen to the skinny bosom of Lincoln himself. Like there
wasn't near the whole state of Virginia to get through and it filled up
with thousands of men all too happy to shoot runaway niggers. They
going along serious but easy too, like it was just what they was doing. I
bet them women and old men setting up there on those ticks even went
along singing. What do you think about that?"

She stepped away from the stove and went and stood before the door
where it was cooler. Now just down the side of the table from him. She
felt her breathing, a tremble along her ribcage. His eyes wide, focused
on her, each an even distribution of mockery and anger. Back in the
house a clock struck six, the tones each separate and round with brass
clarity. She could picture the clock, the cherubs twining to reach from
the pedestal to hold up the sphere of time. She said, "Ain't no business
of mine what those folks up to."

"I wasn't asking what you thought they was up to."

"What you asking then?"

"What do you think?"

She pushed off the door and took a step toward the table, toward him,
and stopped. She folded her arms over her chest and said, "Why you
messing with me? Why you can't just leave me be?"

He ran his fingertips over the boards of the tabletop like stroking the
strings of an instrument. Then he put his elbow on the table and held
his chin with his hand. "Free," he said. "That old freedom song. That
old road north. That what you want, Leah?"

She shrugged her shoulders, still holding herself. The sweat chill
against her now, the smell rising now fear sharp as chopped onion.

He went on. "How do you think that would be? I bet you ain't even
thought that far. I bet you think you get up north and those folks sweep
you up like long-lost cousins and set you up pretty in a little house and
bring you food and clothes and pretty little things to set around the
house, little knickknacks. And take you on into their church and let their
god sweep down onto you and raise you up to providence? And let their

sons walk out afternoons with you and bring you home and feed you dinner and then let them marry you. You think it's going to be like that? Or maybe you think you'll just set right here and we can swap places. You all would move on in here and wear my mother's clothes and maybe even set up on the back gallery and look down at her on her hands and knees weeding out the vegetable patch, and Daddy would drive you all whenever you took a whim to go downtown and pass some new law what white folks could or could not do. Maybe you think it's going to be like that. Maybe you think that old stick rail reading off a piece of paper in another country going to change things here and maybe you think this sweet country that's home to you and me both is falling apart and you're going to get whatever you want. I bet that's it. I bet that's what you think it will be. I'm right, ain't I? Stand there like a free woman and speak the truth to me for once in your life, like a proud free woman would do. Come on now."

"I don't think nothing about it." And then bold and scared by his words she said, her voice low to a mumble, "I reckon I'd work. Work like I do now, maybe here, maybe some other place. I don't know. But for myself. So my work all my own. But I don't know a thing about it. You and me both, Alex, we don't know what's coming, what it mean."

His face blackened over, and she knew he'd wanted to hear something else from her, some fear of clinging to what she knew. And thought how young he was and clear and bright with danger. Thinking of those glistening pitchfork tines he'd spoken of.

He still held his chin but his legs were spread long out beside the table, crossed at the ankles. His stump lying flat against his side. He said, "You're a stupid bitch. Ain't anything going to change. Not one goddamn thing. It might get all rearranged but it ain't going to change. You'll still be a nigger girl and the rest of the world'll still be white. Nothing going to change."

She nodded as if agreeing, all the while sure he was wrong in some way she couldn't explain to him. So all she said was, "We'll see, I guess. Comes to that."

He nodded back and she saw he was not agreeing either. He looked at her, a long pause until her feet became sore with wanting to move under his look. Then he grinned at her and said, "So tell me: When old Spence was home last two Novembers ago did he screw you? I'm just curious. He talked about it. Said you was ripe and ready for it. But he never said he had. So did he?"

And she was rigid again upright between table and door, sweating again and thinking of Spencer. Slender tall and well made with his mother's frame but their daddy's ginger hair and hawked nose. His eyes also. It was Spencer the one the summer she was twelve who found her crouched in tangled honeysuckle and briar canes in the grown-over lot off a lane three streets away, found her in the high green summer dusk with her arms locked around her knees rocking and leaning against the red oak growing in the side of the lot, away from the cellar hole of the house burned out before either of them were born, found her with her dress torn and blooded and streaked with the red clay, the clay matted also in her hair and grimed on her face, caked there like mud with her crying, rocking back and forth and shaking and crying in the hot summer-still dusk, everything around them very quiet but for a dog barking some streets away. She heard him coming, heard him calling her name just above a whisper so she knew he knew where to find her and why and so she sat still and did not run, her head still down on her arms but waiting for him as he stepped through the tall grass and briars straight on to the tree not to the cellar hole as if he'd thought it through since hearing whatever he'd heard. Knowing she'd be there, as if he'd asked himself how far he'd go and where that would be if something like that happened to him. And came to her and knelt down with a boy's clumsy tenderness and held her head against his thin chest until her fresh crying stopped, Spencer not speaking but crooning soft like to a child and after her crying stopped he lifted her to her feet and led her through the lanes and backyards, cutting through as straight a line as he could to home and still avoid anyone out in the evening. His colt's legs slowed to a cautious easy pace for her until they came through the back garden gate off the lane and her mother came off the stepstone before the cabin door and ran to her. Spencer then followed to the cabin door and reached to touch Helen's shoulder and say, "I just want you to know I didn't have nothing to do with this. I went and got her soon's I heard word of it." And her mother turning swift and saying, "Leave us be! Don't you talk to nobody about this, not your daddy, not nobody!" And her mother talking nonstop after the door closed in her hushed whisper of white boys, white men, as she lifted the dress from Leah and bathed her standing naked no longer bleeding in the center of the cabin, her hands gentle against the harsh bitten-off flow of her words, each word dropping like a small fleck of the dried blood from Leah's thighs. Leah not listening but crying silent and remembering only that he'd come as soon as he'd heard.

And Spencer home that last time two Novembers ago, silent and restless around the house and yard as if he no longer knew how to relax around people. The day Leah found him sitting one knee crossed over the other on a stump of firewood behind the garden shed, when she came from the garden to hang the fork she'd been using to dig the Irish potatoes for dinner the next day, Spencer wearing only the trousers from his uniform and an open-necked white shirt of his father's, the pants already worn and patched but nothing like the wornout home-dyed stuff she'd see on men in the years to come. He was smoking a short thin cigar wrapped in black leaf, leaning back so the stump tilted under him and blowing the smoke out into the quiescent golden air of late fall, and she saw he was waiting for her and he said, "Hey girl, how you been?" and took the fork from her and hung it on the nail. She told him she'd been fine and asked about him, but he only stepped to her and took her by the upper arms and held her with her back against the shed wall and leaned and kissed her, his mouth soft, pliable against hers, lips easy against her and she held her mouth still against his kiss not stiff or remote but as if just waiting until he figured out he was doing the wrong thing. He lifted his lips from hers and grazed against her cheek, the soft ends of his mustache slipping along the folds of her nose as if they belonged there and the moment his mouth was gone from hers she wanted it back and she reached her mouth up to find his, her mouth open once she covered his and he groaned against her as his body slipped forward and pressed over the length of her and she moved a little against him. He drank at her mouth as his hands came off her shoulders across where her throat spread to her breastbone and down to hold her breasts through the cotton shirtwaist, the weak sun coming into her eyes spangling over his shoulder and the air sweet as lying down and she closed her eyes as a sound came rising up from deep below her lungs and sliding from her mouth into his and he stopped, his hands falling from her as he reared back his head and looked at her, his eyes wide with pride and sadness, longing gone hollow as if he stood outside himself watching not just

himself but the both of them and he placed his hands on the shed and
pushed away from her, pushed his body back to stand over his own feet
and not against her anymore and he said, "I'm sorry. I'm sorry Leah.
I'm so sorry." Stood like that looking at her and her looking back at him
for a long moment and she not saying anything and when he saw she
would not and seemed to know all that was running through her he
turned away, his eyes at the last terrible and sad, and he went to bend
by the stump and pick up the gone-out cigar and walked down along
the garden to the back gate and out into the lane. She stood where she
was, her legs trembling and her mind hot with not being able to think,
watching after where he'd gone and after a moment she could smell faint
the smoke floating back, a sieve of scent from him already gone and she
looked at her hands, still smeared with clay from picking out the potatoes and rubbed them against the front of the apron over her skirt and
then wound her fingers tight together and wrung them, watching the
edges of the joints turn a pale whiteblue against the pressure, and out
loud she said "Stupid" and walked back out to the garden to lift up the
basket of potatoes and go to the kitchen.

And stood now in that same kitchen facing his younger brother and
thinking what he'd said of Spencer was likely true, knowing enough to
know people held many versions and forms revolving like trials around
their own true self; but saw now that there was something wrong with
that brother's eyes, too wet, too dark, too wide, as if his brain worked at
unusual speed and his eyes raced to keep pace with the workings behind them, and with great and true calm she said, "Spencer always was
good to me. Was a gentleman. Treated me right. Treated me like a sister." Her own eyes steady on him as she said this, feeling undistorted
and stalwart to something she couldn't put name to but emotion, one
of love and memory combined, sentiment from her as pitch to amber
from a loblolly pine. Knowing the manchild before her would not
understand this or would not be able to allow understanding and was
patient with serenity before his reaction.

Which was simple and nothing more than what she expected. Some
part of her as he stood even thinking it was what she wanted. As if unknown but inevitable. As if that door finally glimpsed. He crossed swift
to her and she saw and heard and felt each footfall in her chest as if syn-
chronized to her heartbeat. When he stood before her she saw a waver

once in his eyes and she thought Go on and the waver was gone. The wounded soldier a head shorter than she before him.

He struck her with his one balled fist hard just below her ribcage and she fell forward toward him and the fist came off her and raised to clip her chin, snapping her teeth together and a sound came from her, a drawn half-cry, half-sob, and he caught her as she sagged, grasping her wrist and turning it under itself as she was spun with her back to him. He pressed her wrist up deep below her shoulder blades and she felt the joint of her shoulder strain. He held it there and pressed up behind her and moved her forward toward the table, she still bent forward with no wind. Then her torso was flat against the table and he dropped her wrist to reach down and lift her skirts over her hips, her cheek harsh against the oiled planks, smelling the taint of old food, her nose burned raw by the shove down. All the time Alex not speaking, his breath ragged and raw like a rusted crosscut blade moving through punked timber, his hand swimming over her bared rear and then down between her legs, opening her. His fingers were soft from his weeks in bed or sitting upright in a chair, and she was wet under them and ashamed and shocked by the betrayal of her body, as if her body was somehow to blame. She knew it was not but still felt it open to him. Then his hand was gone and he used it to open the flies of his trousers, Leah hearing the buttons pop open with the soft snick of fabric. She got both hands flat against the table and didn't just come upright but backwards also, her right elbow leading to drive into his open crotch, to strike hard into his scrotum. He sagged away from her, mewling sounds from his lips and it was only then she realized he'd been chanting the whole time, words not to her but to himself, words meant to carry him forward: 'little nigger bitch, little nigger bitch.' She was upright now and stepped to the stove and turned back, raising the hot iron over where he was still crouched, both his arms over his crotch as if that was what was wrong with him, as if that was what she meant to hurt and she brought the iron down against the side of his head, not even as hard as she meant to. His head seemed to bounce from his shoulder and raise up again to face her, a cry just starting from his lips when she brought it down again, the edge of it catching hard and deep just above his ear. This time she saw it split his scalp, saw the fine auburn hair part and render up torn whiteness like marrow that then ran quick with blood, not gushing but filling his hair and draining down onto his face. He tried to raise both arms to stop her, and then tried to cover the bloodflow from his head but only the one hand reached there, a small ineffectual cap over the flush of blood. Then that hand fell away, lank against him and his head tilted back as his eyes rolled up awful whites toward her. His head was a mat of blood and his pants were tangled down around his thighs. Her breath was hot with great infrequent blasts, and she stepped back and set the iron back on the stove. The smell of burned hair and blood rose from it. She looked at him. He lay not moving. She stepped forward and words came more hiss than sound, "Fuck that white fuck," and she raised her foot and kicked him hard in his open slack genitals. It was full dark outside and the light was dim from the one lamp on the table. She bent and cupped the chimney and blew out the wick. She went out the door into the sleeting rain. She pulled the door shut hard and silent behind her.

She moved fast, not running, not yet, past the cabin with her mother and Rey and around the garden, the rain wetting her quickly. She went around the stable, empty of horses all gone to war, to rap hard the door of the small attached shed, the one paned windowglass lit low from within and a voice called for her to enter, the voice so low as to be missed in the rain but she was straining for it and pushed the door and stepped inside. The old man sitting at what had once been a cobbler's bench in the center of the room, his bed off to one side and a small table and single chair the only other furniture. A small fire in the grate. One wall hung with harness, this the fancy set he and Mebane had hid from the requisition officers, the brass buckles and ornamental rivets like gold in the low light. He had a bridle on the pommel of the bench, polishing the brass with an ash slurry and fine cloth. He kept working as she came in but with his eyes on her, not speaking, waiting for her.

"I got to go Peter." Only now aware not only of her heart hammering but a feeling over her as if she would break into a thousand parts if she paused. As if her skin was thin frost over an upsurging hot liquid.

"That so." His hand still worrying a small circle with the rag. Studying her, his face blank.

She wanted to swallow before she spoke and could not; she crossed to the bucket and raised the dipper and drank and faced him again. "I got to go now, Peter."

He nodded and said, "Bad night to travel."

"Mister Lex lying over there in the kitchen dead. Knocked me round and tried to stick his thing in me and I busted his head open with a iron. So you pardon me but it seem like a fine night to travel." Saying it put it behind her. She grew calmer, rapturous with motion, as if her nerve cells were already out before her in the wet night. Watching Peter fold his polish rag slow and evenly and place it on the bench before him. Then he stood. His eyes on her hard and fierce, not angry but clenched wide open. He did not speak. He stepped to the connecting door into the stable and from the back of the door took down a heavy greatcoat, ragged at the collar and cuffs and torn once low in the back. She'd never seen the coat before; it was the navy wool of the Union army. He laid it over the small table and from under his bed came out with a pair of boots and two pairs of socks and said, "Set down and get this on your feet." While she put the boots on he found a sack and put three cold sweet potatoes still black with fireplace ash in the sack and folded it over and lifted the coat as she stood and put it around her shoulders. He put the sack in one of the coat pockets and told her, "Carry your shoes out and drop em in the lane back the garden. Don' carry em far. Leave em right by the gate. Your mama find em in the mornin'. Cut crossways and don' let nobody see you, white or colored. Get down in the bottom under the train trestle, opposite end of the bottom from that. Couple big oak trees there, you know?"

She nodded.

"Wait there. Anybody there, cut back up through and get to the colored burying ground. But they ain't gon' be anybody down in that bottom. Wait there or the burying ground until a man come find you. Won't be long, maybe a hour but it seem like a long time. Just wait there."

And then she paused, arrested now, alone. And said, "You ain't goin take me?"

"Gon' to go clean your mess child. You don' need me hold your hand."

"Peter—" she started but he cut her off.

"Get on out of here," he said. "You ain't got no time at all to spare right now. Just git. Watch your step. Watch out around you. Git."

And so like that she left there, left her mother without farewell but to pause with a wet face in the rain a moment outside the gate, looking back at the pale windowlight of the cabin, left the white man both father and owner of her who behaved toward her as if she were nothing more than a dream of herself; but mostly she left Peter. That last fall before the war, following the summer she was raped, Peter took her one evening to his shed where he boiled water and made her peppermint tea. He sat on the edge of his bed facing her, she in the only chair holding the hot tin cup of tea just letting the smell rise up through her nose and flood through her as he talked to her, talked as no person ever had, explaining to her with words simple and precise what was happening in the world beyond her that was her world also and never telling her what she could or might think of these things but only how he felt and saw and believed. She sat listening as to a madman or someone speaking a tongue unknown to her and he finished as she drained the last of the tea. That might have been the end of it but for what he did next: rising and sliding the bolt in the door, he brought out a thin broken-spined primer and made her come sit on the bed beside him as he opened the book and read the first simple page to her. He then used his finger to trace out the words and the sounds and made her repeat them after him, over and over until it was memorized, just that first page with its poor printing of two children hand in hand at the top of the page. Then he closed the book and took her to the fireplace and knelt at the hearth and scraped back a layer of ash onto the bricks. He spread it thin and even and began to trace letters for her there, making her say them, making the sounds, having her say cape and cart over and over until he could ask her and she could make the sound without the word and know how it fit. That night ended with her promise solemn to die before telling anyone of what they did there. Daytimes he still ignored her although she watched him now, watched the dip and twist of his grayed head as he moved with the horses or in the flower gardens, knowing he knew she watched him and those odd evenings he'd sign to her and she'd slip away from the cabin and go to him and drink that sweet tea and learn to read. She used up the first book and after that another, several years more advanced, and after that pieces and fragments of newspapers, some only weeks old and others several years out of date that he'd burn after she mastered them. In the second year, he made her begin to trace the letters herself and make sentences of her own. And some evenings, when the reading and writing was done with, he told her also what he knew of the world beyond them, telling her news of the war and what he heard from the north or heard about the north, his authority never questioned, never given as absolute but as knowledge greater than any she might have otherwise.

But it was not until the wet February night when she left through the freezing rain without looking back once she dropped her shoes outside the lane gate that she understood it had only been for her. She'd always assumed that he shared something both could dream of or hold to, but she'd been wrong to think that. It was only for her that he held out what slender things were his to give and that night knew he would take no thanks for it. So she went through that night knowing it was love he sent her away with, sent her toward what would be the first of many meetings in the dark with strangers who might lead her a ways until they could point to a landmark or a sleeping place for the daylight hours. Other times only someone who passed on directions and landmarks and if she was lucky a bundle with some food in it. She passed the first of two months of living by darkness and lying by day in some shelter: brambles, brush, woods, twice a hayloft and once a thin pallet of blankets under a bed in a slave cabin. All as if with Peter standing far back at the beginning watching her move ahead, moving north and all as if she was racing down a long twisted channel of night straight into Norman lying bleeding and stuporous in the noontime heat and light. At first she was afraid of him because the wound to his head seemed a duplicate of how she'd killed Alex. Then, as she crouched watching him, she felt as if he'd been sent to her as restitution, as if the world were offering her atonement and rescue all at once. Knowing she could not walk away from this, feeling as if all her life had folded over itself to bring her to this moment, to this man, this lying near-dead Union man. And so she went to the creek in the woods three fields away and brought back the gourd of water to drip into his mouth and smear onto his lips until his tongue began to work and his throat to swallow.

She told him all this plain and simple and true as she could. Everything as it happened. But what she did not tell, what she did not trust yet enough to tell, was some part of her responsible for it all. Something in her she could not name or touch but which ran through her deep and solid as a vein in rock—that something in her had drawn all this upon her. That something in her cried out into the nameless dark for punishment of some sort. That she deserved all misfortune that came her way. She did not think it was her race or even the cir-cumstances of her life thus far. It was, she thought, something wrong in herself.

He came down from the sugar bush into the blue-dusk bowl of the farm and entered the barn basement tie-up where his mother was up in the loft, forking down hay to the stalled horses. He let the five milk cows free of their stanchions and followed their shit-caked hindquar-ters as they filed out into the night pasture and slid the door shut after them. He took up the yoke over his shoulders and carried the double buckets of milk out of the barn, wordless meeting his mother as she came down the ladder from the loft and saw what he was doing. He crossed the yard into the cellar of the house, the stone-vaulted chambers cool and moist. In the cooling room, he poured the milk out into the long pans and laid them out by the well square-sided with even slabs of granite, the water in the well from the same source-spring as what flowed into the kitchen overhead. Here he could smell food and heard girl-voices warbling with laughter over his head. He skimmed the cream from the morning pans and dropped the clots into jars and fastened the bails and lowered the jars into the water to sit overnight. His mother came in behind him and spoke his name. He turned to her and said, "I was remiss not letting you know. I failed you not get-ting home sooner. Whatever spree I was on I still ought to have let you know. Truth is I never thought to."

She nodded, meaning she knew that much. She said, "Father passed, I'd thought they'd send you home."

"Would've I'd asked."

She nodded again. She studied him, as to fathom, to reconcile the man before her. Then she said, "You surely brought a surprise."

"Surprise to me too."

She cleared her throat. Pronouncement, he thought. She said, "Fa-ther left things clear. We need to set down together."

He nodded. "I've money in the bank."

"I know it." She paused and then went on. "I always expected you'd find some girl soon's you were home. I always supported the abolition. Little it was but I did my part, knitting things that went forward to those folks journeying on toward Canada. You didn't know that. It was quiet, you know. But Norman, this."

He looked down, studied the earth-packed floor. The smell of the room sweet and sour at once with the new milk and cream and the dank wet coming through the stone foundations and the faint cleanth rising from the water. His eyes off his mother he looked up to the low rafters and said, "I brought her."

His mother looked now up. She said, "She's taken over my kitchen. Just like that."

"That was me. I told her to fix a supper for us. Whatever it is is all my doing. And by Jesus I could eat that chicken all myself. You can't imagine how it smells to me."

His mother nodded. And was crying now, silent, the tears running over her face. Her hands wrung before her, tugged and clenched and twisted in her apron. He stepped the two feet and reached and laid his hand flat on her forearm. The first time he'd touched her since arriving home. Then laid his other hand on her other arm. She looked up at him, her eyes great and wide and wet. She said, her voice husked, "You recall that old song, Norman? I used to sing it when you were a baby, me jolly and disbelieving."

He looked down at her and shook his head. "I don't recall you singing."

And she held his eyes and her hands curled up over his arms and her voice low and pliant with her whisper sang,

> "We're gettin ready for the mother-in-law,
> gettin ready for the fray.
> When she puts her face inside this place
> we'll make the old girl feel quite gay.
> There's a little ell room on the third floor up
> where the beetles up the wall do climb.
> Mother, mother, mother,
> Mother, mother, mother.
> We'll have a lively time."

He wrapped his arms around her back and drew her against him, feeling her now as an old woman the same way he'd seen her the afternoon before. She came against him and laid her head sideways against his chest and he stood high craned over her, holding her and feeling as awkward and rough as if he'd been new split from some great tree, some man made from some material and propped up for all to see. He held his mother close against him, his breath warm against her shoulder coming back onto his face. He thought again of the woman waiting upstairs for him and of all she'd left behind and also brought with her to this place. It was her courage somehow that allowed him to hold his mother so close and long against him.

Two

She could not keep a baby. She mis-
carried four times in five years, each event a tragedy of silence endured
at a scream-pitch within as Norman spoke in quiet tones that made her
hate him a little, his assurances that they would try again, his certainty
each would be the one to swell forth and thrive. Beyond the terror of
her failure lay the restlessness of the small souls, lacking even the infants' headstone awarded to earlier generations of Pelham child-death.
The fourth was the worst in a way: a trauma of blood late in her fourth
month, the blood thick and rich and darkening fast against the linen,
the day outside brilliant against deep snowbanks of February, the window beside her bed hung with sparkling dripping icicles, the pain as if
all of her body was clenched tight to hold the creature within her, a fish
not to be grasped in swollen viscous liquids. They had kept this one secret
until she began to show visibly and it seemed settled within her. Alone,
Norman laid the creature too small for him to comprehend truly as a
child in a cut-down egg crate and buried it in a place he would not tell
her: under the lilacs beside the kitchen where the south sun had softened the soil at the foundation and where she could not see him working from the bed above on the other side of the house. He then carried
the bundled linens high up to the woodlot and burned them with a brush
pile on a day of soft wet falling snow while she was still in bed, and yet
clearly she smelled the smoke of the blood-soaked cloth, the stench of
her own failure passing downhill through the snowscreen. She rose silent that day from her bed and resumed her work, unable to not think
of what small remains burned also there above her. The doctor was a

portly man who wore pince-nez and heavy wool vested suits, abrupt and hesitant with Leah, ineffectual beyond assuring her this happened to many women, not helped by her silence over her own history and not improving upon her impression when she overheard him telling Norman that after all half the fun was in the trying. The doctor's hands were delicate and timid, trembling slightly as they came upon her and she knew he drank but could not help but think it was her skin that caused their tremor.

Throughout that spring and summer she worked alongside or separate from Norman, caring daily for the long pens of laying hens they'd built into what had once been the basement dairy of the barn, the pens stretching outside in wired runs on the south-facing open slope, dividing the several hundred hens by breed: Rhode Island and New Hampshire Reds, Barred Rocks, Plymouth Rocks and Silver-laced Wyandottes. Daily gathering the eggs in baskets and carrying them to the house basement to candle them and pack them in straw in wooden crates which twice a week were driven to the depot in Randolph where they were shipped to Boston; daily also working in the brooder house newly built according to plans from the agricultural school at the university in Burlington, raking the litter and spreading pine tar on young fowl wounded by others, clipping beaks when she found the warrior bird, culling the sick. She talked to the hens as she went among them, a low fluttering tone of speech half-directed at them and half to herself. She knew them all and would wring a neck when egg production dropped off. Six times a year the brooder house was emptied: young hens joining the laying flock, the young cocks packed two dozen to a crate and shipped south for the live market.

Most of the chicken they ate themselves was stewed, old hens eating more than they laid. Tough meat cooked slow and wet and well seasoned until it fell from the bone, made sweet with patience. Eaten in spring with dandelion greens or fiddleheads or asparagus and sometimes the small dense morels Norman would carry back from the woods, cradling them in his cap held in his hands; in summer with garden vegetables and sometimes great fried slices of the puffballs that would spring up in the pastures like brilliant white boulders; in fall and winter with the great Hubbards or Irish potatoes stored down basement along with carrots and parsnips packed in crates of sand. Always something good to eat and work enough to keep them both long-muscled and hard, both young and fresh enough with strength so that even the long stretching summer days, light by four and still light at half past nine at night, were not long enough. And they could not make a baby. After the fourth miscarriage they stopped speaking of the problem or what might be the cause and went through that spring and summer with the first true remove about them, a slight skim of distance walked with both through everyday, neither willing or able or even conscious to admit to themselves or the other that this was happening to them. Still coming together in the night, both still endless with appetite and it was not then, at the end of the day as dark and sleep came over them, but during the day that both carried the small discontent of attendant fear.

He woke one August midnight to the bed alone, the room cool with pewtered moonlight. He lay waiting even as he knew she was not in the house. Finally he rose and went to the window to stand and was there more than an hour before he saw her coming down from the granite ledges of the high sheep pasture, wearing the old shirt of his that she slept summers in. Still stood as she came into the house and he saw the faint flare of light from a kitchen lamp spread from the window below onto the dark of the yard, stood listening long enough to know that she was cooking something, baking something, and would not be back to bed, not soon.

When he rose again at four-thirty and went downstairs the kitchen was seasoned with steaming loaves and a pair of blackberry pies and he thought She was up there picking berries in the dark. She was still wearing only her nightshirt and was turning eggs in the pan, coffee already hot on the stove. He went to her and held her from behind, his elbows against her sides and his hands over her breasts and so felt the familiar new weight to them even as she spoke, her voice steady as her body was tight. "Trying again, Norman."

"That's right," he said. "That's good."

She slid the egg pan to the cold end of the stove. She didn't turn around to face him. She said, "You got to tell me it's going to be all right."

"Sure," he said. "Sure it is."

She still wasn't moving. Letting his hands hold her, letting his body come up against her backside, but not giving anything into this embrace. She said, "No. You got to promise me."

He didn't understand. "We just have to see I guess."

She turned then, still inside his arms and took his shirtfront in her fists, the hands small hard-curled knobs, tugging him toward her and pushing him back, a wild rocking, her eyes sprung wide and flaring. "You got to promise me Norman. You got to promise me."

He stood there while she pummeled him, making no effort to stop her as if he deserved this, as if it were all his doing, his fault, as if he deserved not this simple sharp beating but something far worse; pressed between grinding stones. He held her until her breath was gone to sobs and her hands lay flat and still on his chest, all the while keeping his hands at rest against her back and when she was done and cried against him he still said nothing. Just held her standing there in the kitchen ripe with yeast. Then soft to a near silent whisper he said, hating himself for not being sure of it, not able to believe himself but sure it must be said, "I promise."

Bringing her home, what he had not foreseen was not so much the drift away of his own family but the estrangement, the voluntary withdrawal, the displacement he felt toward the neighbors and villagers themselves. Times he felt he'd lost something and times he felt if he'd returned alone it would be the same: as if not the dark-skinned woman but the war he found her in was where he'd lost any sense of common-hold with other men. As if the affairs of humans had been revealed to him as puny maunderings, rife with self-interest and greed, little more than spinning of blood and brood to enthrall all inward toward a latch onto the world that was not so much a turning away from the dark as blunt refusal to acknowledge how frail the light was. Norman did not hold himself separate through any belief he was beyond or above all this but a lack of interest so sincere as to frighten him a little when he paused too long upon it. All he wanted was his daily round of work, the blood pleasure of sweat and muscle fatigue and the satisfaction of mild accomplishment and to follow this then with the woman who seemed such a part of him as if she'd stepped whole out from some corner of his soul; as if he'd lacked a part of himself never known missing until confronted with it: this he wanted and—as the years brought the miscarriages—children with her, at first children for her and then clear as grief after the third miscarriage, children for himself as well. He was to wonder silent if that failure of wanting on his part had played some role in those lost children. And he was to learn as well that she was not only that missing part of himself but a self full-blown in contradiction and turmoil far too great to have ever only been held silent in himself. Her temper roiled from her as easily as her passion; often he thought of them as each the backside of the other. He did not know rage in himself except in that one unending sweep of war years and that was not a rage to inform his life once left behind; as if that raised spectre of the human was now too great for him to confront, let him go mend harness or cultivate potatoes. He did not know if this began with the war's end or his finding Leah; there was no way of distinction. He wondered if he'd been this way perhaps even as a child but there was no one to ask and no way to formulate the question even if there had been. That child was a stranger to him, as much lost as his father. As much lost as the world of his neighbors and townsfolk.

That first year he'd learned much. He learned more than Leah. Because what he learned constricted the world he'd thought he'd known. Leah reported village children following her through the streets and one bold boy who stepped forward and without asking took her arm in his hands and rubbed at her skin as if to loosen the pigment. Also the gawking and murmurs as she passed. Even the women standing side by side with hands flapped loose against their mouths as if to conceal the words they meant for her to hear as she passed. Even the merchants who ignored her until other latecomers had come and gone. It was all more or less what she had expected. Not the place she had come from. And so was puzzled first and then reluctant and then adamant with refusal when Norman offered to do what shopping must be done. This not a possibility she'd consider. So it was left to Norman to set limits of whom they would and would not trade with, she smart enough perhaps even before him to not demand reasons. It was the place he knew, not she. So they carried trade in sundries and dry goods to Allen Bros. because Ira Allen offered the same clipped milk-eyed service to anyone, Leah or Norman or a grimed child wanting a penny's worth of horehound or lemon drops. To Gould the harness maker for that work as well as boots and shoes and to Mose Chase for smithing parts for the machinery and implements. It was Chase who built the stoves and shaded lights for the brooder houses. Contracted with Flannagan the Irish farrier from Bethel to come twice a year with his ox-drawn wagon to the farm, spring and fall to shoe the horses, adding heavy caulks in the fall against the ice. Because it was the Randolph farrier Harringdon who caught Norman by the sleeve to ask if it was true those dusk women's slit went sideways, Norman saying as if passing on fresh news that No it was just like the mares the smith tupped, up and down like all the rest of creation. The woman Norman did not know who came upon him on the street and beat his face with her open hands, him standing silent before her rant over her lost husband and both boys, as if their deaths were for nothing than for him to bring home love. Worse than all this were the handful of veterans missing a limb or more who would not speak but ran eyes hot over him as if he were their loss, him walking with both arms and the woman up the hill. There was nothing to be said. Not to them, not to the rest. He did his business and went home.

There was little they needed of the village. One time weekly or twice as the season called for, one or the other would drive the load of eggs and perhaps crates of young roasters to the station and then pick up what passed for mail and penciled list in pocket make the short rounds. They had all they wanted otherwise and so cared less for the town than it for them. First Tuesday of March, Norman went to Town Meeting and sat throughout, feeling his presence huge with silent condemnation before his neighbors. Business was conducted. He would speak his aye or nay and had done enough. Every other November he'd go down to vote. Beyond this he felt no civic drive; let them make their choices, it all came to the same thing. He left these obligations eager for the farm and whatever chore was postponed. Eager for the sight of her. He was twenty-six and she twenty-two after her fourth miscarriage the summer she was pregnant again. He did not understand his age; it made no sense to him. He did not know himself in the mirror or reflected in the other young men of the village he saw time to time. The middle-aged tradesmen seemed worn out from nothing. It was the silent old men he felt kinship toward. The ones he guessed who understood that life was partial at best. Everything else was grandiose imagination. He wanted nothing more than his feet on the ground. It was a tremendous thing to ask for. When Leah made him promise their child would come, it was the first time since the grapeshot concussed beside him that he felt he could not carry on all alone. His fear was so great that he could not ponder it, could not let it tag his days. He sat down at the pigeon-holed desk that same night and wrote a letter.

His mother had moved herself and Connie to the village three weeks after Norman first brought Leah home almost six years before. Cora Pelham then telling her son the move was for the girl, that she'd been overheard telling girlfriends of the noise coming through the attic floorboards nightly; Norman with heat in his face accepting this, knowing it was the one way his mother could silence him to acquiescence even as she went on in a burst of apparent candor explaining that it was only natural for a young married man to satisfy himself upon his wife, he watching her through this for the certain deception in her face, unwilling to accept that she might have lain with his father as burden. Realizing she censored with her actions even as she draped words over them. He listened with an odd slow pity, not sure if it was for her or his dead father.

"What I think, you're spoiling her." Holding her ribboned hat in her lap, her loosed hair flaying her face, the curls grown out to a thick bundle.

"Could be." The reins tight against the backs of the bays, the geldings he'd traded for just after the war, getting rid of the team that included the mare that killed their father. "Could be just what she needs. Some peace of mind. Might do the trick. And, long's you're willing, won't hurt, is how I see it."

"It's why I came," Connie said. "But I won't wait on her." And then added, "I wouldn't wait on anybody."

Norman watched a bobolink bending a roadside stalk. Careless, he said, "Wasn't thinking of anybody waiting on anyone. Just a set of hands to lighten the load."

"I'm a set of hands then."

"I was thinking more the company of a woman."

"Mother wouldn't do for that."

It was not a question but he answered anyway. "She's well settled at Breedlove's. I believe she's happy off the farm and wouldn't want to come back except I asked."

"I was happy off the farm too."

"My asking was no commandment."

"If you don't know it was, you know less than I thought, Norman. It is fine to be back though. I doubt my lungs'll ever clear all that crud."

"I couldn't ever tell if you were happy or not, down to Manchester."

"It wasn't happy or no. Not much in the way of opportunity for a single woman in these hills."

"Thought you might catch a husband down there." As they came upon it the bobolink lifted and coasted over the road before the trotting team, planing down into the river elms on the other side. The horses' backs sweat shining.

"Oh," she said, "I guess I could, that was what I wanted." Her tone defiant with failure. He glanced at her, his compact pretty sister, and wondered what that story might be and if he'd hear it. Not from her. Leah perhaps. She went on. "Mostly, it was the awful monotony of the work. Five days ten and a half hours a day and a half of Saturday cooped up inside with the dust and noise from the looms and spinning machines. It wasn't the work itself, just there seemed nothing human about it. Funny to say that, working with thousands of other people around you and comparing it to chasing cows across a pasture and thinking the cows more human than the woman at the next stitcher over. I liked the work all right and I liked making the money but I was ready enough to come home time your letter came asking. I worked next to people came into that mill when they were twelve or thirteen and will be there till they die or close to it. I couldn't imagine that for myself, never once. Truth is I thought it would lead to something else and I guess maybe it has. Although there's no telling what I'll do when you're done with me."

He thought of Leah creating a minor poultry industry with no model and said, "When we chuck you out the door like a broken chair. Can't say for sure but it seems to me there's maybe more opportunity in the old burg than you're thinking. And you've got plenty of time to find out. Might even be some single young fellers around town; you never know."

She snorted. "Any still around Randolph are ones still wet behind the ears or lacking the gumption to go west."

"Like your brother," he said.

She looked at him. They'd turned off onto the road leading up to the farm. That spring Norman had leveled it, drawing a loaded stone boat up and down to flatten and smooth the gravel down into the dirt, working with a pick and shovel at the worst washes and clearing the ditches by hand. The road now in the end of August hardpacked and almost black, cool in the shade. The team kept their gait easily up the grade. Connie said, "No. You don't lack gumption. Imagination either. I just don't know what your problem is, Norman."

"Could be there's not one."

"You still holding on to that flock of sheep?" Imp's grin.

He smiled back at her. "Devil me about my sheep. That poultry puts a nice dollar in the wallet but it wouldn't feel like a farm without the sheep. The wool price makes it a loss to shear and ship but the market's good down to Boston for the spring lamb."

She turned her hat in her hands, nervous now as they came over the rise into the bowl of the farm. "A man's a strange creature, Norman. Each and every one is capable of great surprise, maybe even to themselves."

"Likely so. I like to think I've used up my share of surprise."

"You should hope so, Norman."

Norman and Leah in the pantry off the kitchen, the shelves lined with hot-packed summer vegetables in glass jars with glass lids and rubber seals and metal bails, tins of flour and meal, crocks of pickle and sacks of dried beans; they stood talking in tones urgent, hushed, as if the speaking suffered threat of interruption. Leah held his hands and stood close to him, her breath sweetly cooling in the close warmth of the summer afternoon.

"I'm not going to lie in the bed for six months. I couldn't do it. I couldn't even if somebody was to tell me, the doctor, somebody. I couldn't stand it. Who says that's what I should do, anyway? Who says it's even me? Could be something with you. You thought about that, Norman?"

"Nobody's saying lie in bed. Not me. Not Connie."

"Course not. Some white woman tending me."

"All it is, is to help out. And she's not some white woman."

"You think I can't do it, don't you? You think I can't make us a baby, don't you? Think there's something wrong with me inside, something messed up or maybe just missing. Maybe you think it's from when those boys done me I was a little girl. Just not right. Not a whole woman. Maybe you beginning to regret me even."

"Doctor said you're fine. I don't think none of all the rest of that."

"What that doctor know? Old drunk man."

"Knows enough to tell you and me both you're a fine healthy young woman and nothing wrong but bad luck. You made me promise you a promise I'm doing my by Jesus best to keep. And the first thing I thought of was to get somebody in here so it wasn't all on you. And I did that."

"I don't want no help."

"She's not help. She's my sister."

"I don't want anybody Norman. I want it just you and me." Her hands clenched tight around his. As if her hands would convey all that her soul might not send otherwise. "I don't want no one tiptoeing round the house thinking I can't maybe do it. I don't want no one feeling sorry for me." Her eyes brilliant with panic and hatred. Of just what Norman was not sure. Something much greater than his sister in the house. He felt himself stretched out as a thin hot wire. He remembered his mother telling him the younger Potter girl throughout the war each time they met would ask after him. He wondered if it might have been different with her. He suspected it would've been. And not. Like remorse for he knew not what he longed for the fields, the woods, the barn. Some task to take to hand. Work, tinker, trial, work some more. There. His head ached with not knowing what to do. And so was tender, not because he felt tender but with a desperate calm he prayed to convey.

"Right now, seems to me, there's nothing to regret. Nothing to feel sorry about, you or anyone else. Far as I'm concerned you're going to have a baby. Way I understand it, plenty of women have a hard time the first time around. There's nothing to know. It's something greater than what we can understand. It's providential." He took a breath. His hands had moved out of hers and rested loose around her breasts, knowing she liked this soft touch, knowing the swelling of her breasts was magnified to her by his touch. He went on, suddenly deeply sad. "It's all we can do. It's all we have."

Her voice a whisper he felt more than heard. "It is providential. I can feel that. It's a punishment on me."

"Leah."

"It's true."

"Leah."

Her voice up now she said, "Don't you try and pacify me Norman Pelham."

He stood silent, his hands ridiculous on her body: great lumpen scabbed things. He took his hands from her and didn't know what to do with them. He reached and traced an invisible line on a shelf edge. Then pushed both hands in his trouser pockets and felt this action someway defiant and so pulled them out and hooked his thumbs low in his suspenders, the fingers curled in loose fists. As if guarding his own belly. He gave up. He said, "You start into that business and it never stops. Trying to pin one event to another. Look at me. I killed men. I killed as many as I could, without trying to be a hero or some such. Now maybe, according to your notion, the Lord was angry with me for doing that and so it was Him caused my father to fumble that dime right smack behind that old mare what was always ready to kick. Maybe the Lord made her born that way so she could wait all those years just to be in the right place in time to kick Father in the head. Or maybe it wasn't me at all. Maybe Father did some wrong none of us knows about. And so it was all lined up because of that. Or maybe not. Maybe he just dropped the dime. Maybe that's all it was."

Her face was turned a quarter sideways. As a murmur she said, "An eye for an eye."

"I always took that to mean to fear the Lord's retribution. The wrath of Him. If He was to spend all His time meting judgment and punishment and reward during this short lifetime what would be the point of face-to-face judgment? Seems to me it'd all be a jumbled-up thing nobody could sort out."

Her smile broke small and crooked across her cheeks. Unable to stop it, she said, "You oughtn't make jokes about that."

"Goodness," he said. Now was able to shove his hands in his pockets. "I'm serious as forty below."

"You know I always liked Connie. She always been kind to me." She paused and Norman was also thinking of others less kind. Leah went on. "I just have to get used to the idea. I always just wanted it to be you and me."

"I know it."

"Might could help," she relented.

"Couldn't hurt."

"Here she come now." Both listened to the double-step fast slap of bare feet down the stairs and his sister came into the kitchen. Both turned from the pantry to her. Out of her traveling clothes, wearing a simple white summer dress with her hair loose and grown out to her shoulders, she said, "Here it is almost September and my feet tender as June. Some things, you go without and you forget all about until you get it back again and wonder how you ever managed. Little things like going barefoot in summertime." And she gently hitched her dress and skipped a quick toe-and-heel about the table, coming to a stop before them, laughing. Norman felt Leah's hand flat against his back, stroking. Connie said, "Now you tell me what to do. I'm not going to raise a hand unless I'm told to. Otherwise I'm just going to go out and shuffle my feet in the dooryard dust like one of those old hens."

"I guess there's plenty to do," said Norman.

"Go on," said Leah. "Go shuffle your feet. We'll let you know, we can use help."

It turned into a brutish wet fall of cold streaming rains that mired the farmyard like April and made pools in the poultry runs. The old cow paths up the meadows ran as brooks through the last lush uncropped growth of grass. The leaf change was brilliant in the wet: watercolors through the streaked windowglass. They picked apples in the rain and pressed four barrels of cider on the hayloft floor, the sheep crying from the sheepshed at the smell of the pomace. They wrapped the best of the apples in newsprint and packed them loosely in crates in the cellar. Norman dug the last of the potatoes in the rain and spread them on the barn floor to dry. The giant Hubbards were left in a storage room in the barn. At the end of the month there was a single placid day of feeble Indian summer and that night the cold returned. Three days later it snowed to cover the ground and by mid-November there were two feet of snow over everything and the winter pattern set. Paths to the barn and sheds were dug and redug. Norman used the stone boat to pack a track down to the road, which the ox teams were already packing with the giant rollers. The sleigh trip to the village was in brutish cold, the heated soapstones under the horsehide robes little more than a pale offering. He rose twice each night to fill the stoves in the brooder house and henhouse, the long snakes of stovepipe suspended by wires two thirds of the way to the ceiling before venting outside; this the most central feature of the modern plan. On dark storm days he lit great kerosene lamps in the laying pens, the lamps with wide skirts of metal about their tops to reflect the light down. The hens continued laying. It was a miracle of sorts; as a boy he'd not eaten a fresh egg from November until the spring.

The sleigh went out odd weekdays when there were enough eggs to ship and always on Sunday, with Connie alone behind the bays, hard upright and driving the team with taut reins and tight-curled hands as her father'd taught her. Bundled against the cold, she wore the one black velvet-ribboned hat she'd brought back from Manchester, going to the congregational church service and most Sundays afterward returning to Breedlove's with her mother to take Sunday dinner there from the old widowed Breedlove woman. Mrs. Pelham continued to board there, renting an extra room as well for the mending and hemming and occasional fancywork she took in. Mrs. Pelham did not visit the farm; Norman and Leah did not attend church.

When Connie quizzed her mother she replied that she held no ill will to the Negro girl but could not forgive her son. Asked what there was to forgive she chalked with anger and said nothing. Connie told her, "You'll change your tune soon's there's a grandbaby." Her mother turned to Mrs. Breedlove and asked for another cup of the tea the old woman brewed from white pine needles against the winter's agues. She took up a molasses cookie and nibbled it, putting her daughter in mind of a mouse before a cheese wheel. Mrs. Breedlove spoke.

"I found the Reverend Potwin pallid this morning. Perhaps I was distracted."

"It was cold to the church," Mrs. Pelham responded.

"Some might've used the chance to bestir us."

"He is no fancy speaker."

"Plain speech is best. If it has a destination."

"Perhaps you *were* distracted. I enjoyed the homily."

"I believe he was extemporizing. I'm seventy-four years old and sound as a post. He was at sixes and sevens if you ask me."

Connie said, "We all have our off days."

Both women looked at her, blinking, as if to learn who she was and why she was at their table. Connie took up her cup of awful tea and imitated sipping. The old women continued their vague dissection of the morning. Connie yearned for the warm farmhouse kitchen. The mantel clock read one fifteen. She might leave by two. The old women would only note her departure if it was early. Life with Norman and Leah might be temporary, might not be her own life—the one coming she was sure—but it was pleasant, oddly soothing. Even the winter day-to-day was vivid, each action etched. Visiting her mother was like being submerged in a neutral heavy liquid, the old women like salamanders resting in warm pond water.

From behind she did not look pregnant but her belly grew high and round and she seemed to walk around it, as if moving her belly through the space before her. Nights she would wake to find Norman's hand over it and she would cover his with her own. She felt a true calm, not from certainty that she would bear this child to life but as if her body had someway stilled her mind and all else was simply passage, the small collapse of time that each nightfall and daybreak brought. Her unease over Connie's arrival had less to do with any intrusion than her own nervousness in the company of women; she had never known another woman as confidant, companion or friend. She did not realize this about herself until Connie had been there some weeks and proved clever about taking over no one's work, simply waiting until there was a job to be done and no one but herself to do it.

By the time of that first beginning snow cover the three had settled into easy routines. The women were alone much in the house; Norman save in the worst weather spent free time up in the woodlot felling and skidding trees out to the sawpit for the next winter's sixteen cords. Connie and Leah worked together, candling and packing the day's eggs, cooking and baking, cleaning house, three times daily touring the laying pens and brooder house for problems, once a week boiling the big kettle on the stove for laundry, often just sitting in the parlor mending or making clothes, and it was weeks after it began that Leah realized she no longer lifted anything or carried anything, that without obvious effort or awkward excuse her sister-in-law was there before she thought to move and the work was done. They spoke only of the present, as if both had no desire to unwrap their pasts before the other. It was so easy as to seem natural. Leah was secure within this and believed herself happy. Then one afternoon they sat sewing in the parlor, Leah mending a tear from the sawteeth in Norman's woolen pants before cutting a patch to sew over it, when she looked over at Connie on the horsehide sofa, a great ball of homespun wool from the unsold attic fleece lying beside her as her hands flew in crisscross with needles flashing, a small thing in her lap taking form as she lifted and turned it. Leah stopped her work and watched and then her voice betraying her said, "What's that you're working on?"

"A set of little suits for your baby. The cap's finished. It's small and so I'll make another larger." She turned the piece over in her lap, the needles never stopping. "I think this'll be more useful than a blanket wrap since I've put arms on it. Easier for you I should guess. And I'll make a larger one to go with the other cap. Should get you through that first year, cold days like this."

Leah continued sewing up the tear, watching the speed of the woman across from her, watching the soft thing in her lap take a shape and form, her own fingers working the needle and thread in and out of the pantleg at a pace not meant to try and match her sister-in-law but faster than she ever worked and she not watching. The needle ran deep into her left forefinger. The tears came from her in torn sobs that bent her double, her face down now close upon her stalled work. Bent over her swollen belly as if to hide or cover or save it from anything outside of her. As if it was all of her and she betrayed it with her tears. Then felt Connie's hands on her knees. Not pressing, just there upon her. Leah slowly recovered, felt her breath coming back. Lifted her head slowly just enough to face Connie, her face hushed and serious, waiting. Kind. Leah said, "Look at me. Must be the baby makes me act like this."

Connie didn't take her hands away. She said, "Norman treats you good, doesn't he?"

"Yes. Oh yes."

"And others?"

Leah paused, letting what was asked settle. "Nobody's mean. I don't believe no one intends any meanness."

"Well, shit on a stick," Connie said. Leah choked: laughing, still crying. Connie stood and pulled the Boston rocker close and sat leaning forward and asked, "What happened? Was it Mother?"

Like a child sprinting homeward of a hot summer afternoon and sidestepping the basking blacksnake Leah said, "No. No, no." Connie's eyes appraised this and let it go. Leah went on, unable, unwilling to check, as if in rupture. "No," she said again. "I'm not what she wanted or expected and I can understand that. I can even understand that she don't have any idea how to deal with me. She can't set across from me and just carry on a conversation but gets all fluttery and curt, as if her mouth opens and her brain chomps the words off before they get out. I can understand that. I don't mean this like maybe it sounds but I forgive her that. Because I couldn't tell you how I'd be if I was her. It's awful easy to think you know how somebody else should be but you ain't them, never. Maybe I could've done different with her too. But I don't know how and clearly she doesn't either. So I understand that."

"Most times, I think, it's hard between a woman and the mother of the man she marries." Connie's eyes off a little distance. Then, "And Norman her only boy. With Father gone I wonder if he could've married any right girl. Just so you know."

Leah nodded. "Mother-in-law's the price every girl pays. I heard that said."

Connie smiled. "You don't have any friends here though."

"Norman's my best friend."

"You're lucky there perhaps. But—"

"I never had friends even when I was a child. My mama kept me away from the other colored children. Kept me separate. And the white children, they the white children. Didn't have the time of day for me. At least until I was old enough to be something they wanted to have time for."

"What do you mean?"

"I mean four white boys, big boys, sixteen, seventeen years old, got ahold of me one day. I was twelve years old."

"Good Jesus."

"I think that's maybe why I've had such a hard time keeping a baby."

"Oh good Jesus, Leah. Did you tell Doctor about that?"

She shook her head hard.

"Why ever not?" Connie slid back in the rocker and crossed her legs.

"Why not? Why not? He's a white man and he seen me most naked. It's not something I wanted to put in his head."

Connie was quiet with anger. "The bastards. All of them. It's not just you, you know. Whoever the man, there's that horn of evil upon him."

"Now you're not talking about any man that's been coming round here to see you. Must be that Manchester man."

Connie not moving, abrupt, alert. "What Manchester man?"

"One Norman told me about."

"Norman didn't tell you a thing. He doesn't know a thing. There's nothing to know."

"Said there was a man behind why you were so willing to come back up here."

Connie snorted. "I was ready I expect. Sick of that town. Sick of that old mill."

"No man then? No Manchester man?"

Her legs still crossed, her hands cupped over the upper knee. Eyebrows raised. "Not worth the telling."

"You fall in love?"

"I thought."

"So?"

Connie stood from the chair and went back to the sofa and took up her knitting. Leah sat watching her. The needles flared and cracked against each other. Leah sat with her mending loose in her lap. A short time passed. The long blue and purple winter dusk was gaining. Other-times, Leah would have risen and lighted the lamps. Now she only sat, letting the pale window light suffice. Connie worked until she came to a pause, counted out stitches and then began to finger out loops, backing up. Finished with that she held her needles flat in her lap atop the infant blanket and said, "First day in that mill was the most terrifying thing you can imagine. The racket of it. The size. The machines. All the people. I was determined not to be the country girl I was. I worked so hard at it. I think it was three months before I took a breath I didn't think about. I worked so hard at not being a country girl that I didn't even see him coming. I believe he had my number before I even knew he existed. Jack. Jack Lavin. He was a lovely man. I should've noticed that. He took me out. The opera house. Sunday picnics. Such a gentleman. Found out where I was from and got me talking all about it. Began talking about coming back here and opening a shop of our own. As if each one of us doing the same thing over and over a thousand times a day made us experts about clothing, dry goods. Brought me a cup of ice cream one afternoon and I got all the way to the bottom when I found the ring in it and Jack up against me breathing in my ear about how there would be a better one as soon as he could afford, how this was just a token thing against what he intended. Well it had me in a swoon I tell you. June evening. We walked out through the town to the old cemetery and by then it was dark but oh so warm. We lay out there among the dead until the dew came down and he brought me back to my boardinghouse wrapped up in his coat. And we did that for three–four weeks. I got so worried but he assured me everything was all right. Nothing to worry about. Well, I don't know why but I was fortunate. After five days of his not showing up I skipped my lunch, so sick already to my stomach, and walked down through the lengths of the mill buildings until I got to the rooms of the looms where he worked and found a foreman. Oh, Jack, he said. Jack married that Quebec girl and went off with her to the Gaspé where her people had a bakery. Said Jack told him he'd grown up in a bakery and knew bread like the back of his hand. Foreman said to me, You was lucky dearie, them Frenchies aren't gonna know what hit em when Jack Lavin breezes in and out of the old Gaspé. Might likely leave some flour behind but whatever cash and coin they stuffed in cans under the hearth will grow feet like that. And he snapped his fingers. I said I was just asking for a friend. He put his hand on my shoulder and said to tell my friend she was a lucky girl. So I went back to work with the sweat pouring off me and sweat like that two weeks until my monthly came. Just another dumb-cluck girl I guess. Like I said, Not worth the telling."

Leah put aside her held mending. It was too dark to see the needle passing. She stood and lighted the lamp on the side table and crossed over and lighted the one on the end table next to the sofa. Standing there, near Connie, she said, "You and me both know the bad of men. But there's good too. There's Norman."

"Well, yes, there's Norman. But I shouldn't care to share even if you would." And screwed her face up goggle-eyed at Leah. Idiot face. Both women laughed. Fell silent. The room fluid with lamplight. Tentative flickering warmth. Outside in blue dusk Norman crossed to the purple shadow of the barn. A hanging hook of moon over it in the eastern sky. Leah ran her hands over the hard nut of her belly. Connie wrapped her knitting and set it aside and stood. Leah said, "Time to get supper on."

"I'll help Norman with the feed-up."

"I think," Leah said, "he can manage all right."

Connie paused, then said, "What I'd like, is some tea."

"We got that pine-bark tea your mother sent up." They moved, not quite side by side, down the short hall to the kitchen. Connie said, "No thank you ma'am. I'll make that mint tea you like."

"Sounds good to me. I'm about sick of that herb tonic Marthe Ballou brought over for me. Build my blood, she said. Well, my blood's built enough this one day. Drinking it makes me jealous over that pine-bark."

"Maybe that's what I need. A little build-my-blood."

Leah looked at her. "Sounds to me your blood's doing just fine."

Connie shot her brows. "Being home's not so bad. Except for the shortage of men."

"There'll be a man. Soon as you stop looking, one'll jump right around the corner and scare you to death."

"Think?"

Leah filled the kettle under the spring-fed line. Connie had the flue and firebox open, pokering the stilled fire back to life. Leah set the kettle on the stove and said, "It happened to me. Happened to me, could happen to anyone."

Connie added sticks from the woodbox. Shut the stove door and straightened up to face Leah. "Except for the worry," she said, "I liked it."

Deep winter January. It had been sometime before Christmas since daytime temperatures rose over zero. Days still of air with light glittering off the hard-crusted snowbanks. Nights thirty to forty below and lying in bed wakened by the gunshot crack of trees bursting with the freeze, Leah swelling and flushed with heat, as if her body were a furnace wrapped around her child. Over the covers her breath hung in the starlight like pale moonlight off the snow. Afternoons she'd venture to the barns, swaddled like a slow-footed bear to review the hens from the walkway between the pens, leaving the filling of feeders and waterers and stoves and lamps to Norman and Connie, feeling henlike as she made her way in the fecund warmth. There were few eggs to gather and the brooder house was closed down. She'd go from there into the horsebarn, colder there, the windows rimed inside with a thick burr of frost, and slowly run a brush over each of the geldings. As a child she feared horses but this team of light drafts were different from saddle or fancy driving horses, capable of sustaining a light even trot on the cart or democrat wagon but happier with the steady step of daywork in the woods or fields. Heavy-footed and round, thick-necked with large proud heads, eyes the size of her bunched fist, eyes of a density and depth she'd known on no other creature. Tommy and Pete. She talked to them while she worked over them, inhaling the sweet rich horse dust rising from them as if inhaling something of their spirits or souls. She had no doubt they had souls. She told them everything about the child in her belly. She told them about summer. She knew they remembered summer. She'd carry each a handful of shellcorn, the great soft lips against her palm. She stroked their noses. Small beads of frost chained along their sparse coarse whiskers. She'd warm their noses with her hands and breath and then leave them. They were in her dreams. She felt them to be protectors of her child. She told no one this.

* * *

She passed the benchmark of where she'd miscarried the winter before, marking it with silence. The weather had softened enough for several new inches of snow over everything, wiping clean the bootmarks and ash trails laid down on the paths, the scuffs of cinders, chaff and bark rubbish blown down off the hill. The world a new morning. There were times she felt she was living in another country. Not the winter or the place. Times she felt she was another person observing her hands at work over some piece of task. Times she would hum a low soothe that vibrated throughout her and would take her away to nowhere at all; only when back did she know she'd been gone. This could happen alone or not. As if she went away not out but deeply in, far below sense of sound or sight and she would lose everything around her and have only the deep surge of her own bloodstream, the dynamo of pulse a hum in her ears. For minutes at a time. And then resurface abruptly with no sense of having been gone but for the unfamiliar around her. At the supper table, Norman was saying, "Be mid-March now is my guess. Happens like that, it'll be heavy."

"Means we'll be up day and night for a couple of weeks," Connie agreed. "But I like it. That excitement."

Leah kept eating. Her baby was due mid-April. She didn't need to but she counted backward and forward again. About to speak, to correct them, when Norman went on. "I've by Jesus never seen a winter without a thaw late January early February. Just cold like this. Bitter cold. But its going to make for a good sap flow. You'd think it less exciting you slung a yoke and trudged the wet snow with sap buckets either side of you, instead of tending the boiling. But you're right; I look forward to it."

Connie said, "I could I'd match you in the woods bucket for bucket, and you know it too."

Norman shook his head. "Yuht, you would. It'll be on snowshoes this year too. Good for me I guess. Get hardened up for the summer."

"That's right. You been lazing around up to the sawpit all winter."

"Yuht." Grinned at his sister. Then serious again. "I don't want the thaw now anyhow. I hate that stop-and-start sugaring. But Christ it could soften a little. I've got lambs coming any night now. Hard on those little buggers, this cold."

Leah stood and carried her plate to the sink, clattering it down, and turned back. Both sitting watching her. Norman said, "You all right?"

Leah said, "I've got vinegar pie. Still warm but set up. You all want some?"

Norman nodded, studying her. She'd tried to explain herself to him days before but only managed to confuse and frighten him with her telling him she didn't feel herself and then found herself reassuring Norman instead of the other way around. Since then, times she felt his eyes on her as if to fathom where she might be. That was fine. Let him keep an eye on her. He said, "I like that vinegar pie."

Marthe Ballou came down on snowshoes late one bright morning, wearing the heavy green woolen trousers of her husband and a red and black mackinaw. She filled the kitchen with the dense scent of wood-smoked unwashed old woman, sitting with Leah and Connie and drinking coffee, two cork-stoppered bottles removed from her coat pockets before she sat down, the bottles clear glass with the murk tonic within: suffused wild herbs and the tender stripped inner bark of some half-dozen trees. Putting them on the table she said, "You steady now. Thought two see you through. You need more send that man up. Liddle spoon mornings all you need now, lest you got a taste for more. Me, I take it from first snow till dandylions out. Up to you." Then sat silent drinking her coffee and refusing cookies while the sisters-in-law made chat of the cold and the three thus far new lambs until they ran out of things to say and fell quiet alongside Marthe. Marthe ignored Connie but kept her eyes on Leah throughout. After there had been steady silence for some long moments Marthe looked to Connie and said, "Come to see this one. Leave us lone, hey?"

"Well I—" Connie stood. A short pause with her fingers fluttered before her. Then said, "Gabbing like old geese. There's work waiting." Shot her eyes at Leah: sympathy and outrage, the hurt of a child cut free of a game. Then went into the entryway mudroom and deployed herself with deadly silence, getting into boots and winter wraps and went out, letting in a waft of chill air. Marthe seemed to wait for the chill to lose itself into the warmth of the house and then scraped back her chair, staying down in it but pushing out from the table. She said, "Stand, you."

Leah raised herself using both hands on the arms of her chair. Upright she faced the old woman: gray greased hair worn loose onto her shoulders, her face lined and charred to a texture of dried root, her nose a small smudge of lumped flesh set beneath great black eyes. Her mouth drooped and chapped to a rough red flake. Leah saw that as a young woman she had not been pretty but beautiful. Did not wonder what had caused her to join life with the half-wild man in the half-wild outward reach of the small gore. Anymore than she would explain herself and Norman. Marthe studied her midsection and then raised a hand, extended it open to its full reach before closing it upon itself and drawing it back toward her. As if bringing something in. She said, "Step close."

Leah stepped to stand over her, breathing the aroma no different from the tang of fresh-turned soil or the ammoniac of manure or the bronzed bolt of Norman's armpits the end of a summer day, smells all rending of her childhood and carried forward as if the movement of life itself, and Marthe reached and unbuttoned her dress from below her weighted breasts to her pubic arch, the belly moving outward easily as the fabric slid back against the protrusion, the navel distended. Marthe placed her hands on the abdomen and ran them over it slowly, moving from the center out to the sides and then back in again, a gentle round motion that touched deeper than it felt. Leah stood looking down at the grimed hands seeming to feel and draw something from beneath her own skin. Kneading as if the oldest most fragile loaf in the world. Wordless, worldless. Just hands and the belly under them. Going back once to where there was a slight movement, her hand again not probing but reaching somehow deep under the skin. Just a whisper she said, "Right foot." Then reached up and opened the top of the dress so the swollen breasts were freed and took each in a hand and held them, weighing them or just letting their weight fall into her hands. Then ran her hands down buttoning the dress and only then did she look up at Leah.

"This baby, she fine. She gon' be just fine. You fine. Beautiful, you."

"She?"

Again Marthe put her hands on the belly, covered now. As if explaining she ran her hands again. "She spread around you. Out wide like this. Boy-child be bunched up, high, cutting off you wind. Men start like that, makes it hard to blame them, them not knowing how to stop."

"A girl." A whisper. "A little girl."

Marthe leaned back in her chair, her eyes now bold on Leah. "Most likely. She start coming you send that Norman up after me. Don' let him get that Hurdle man in here. That man no good at all. Kill a woman bringing out a child. Don' let that Norman give you no guff. You gon' have this baby just fine."

Norman on his knees with one forearm slid into the ewe; a set of gelatinous feet lie along his wrist. Connie kneels at the front, cradling the lowered head with both arms, light comfort coming from her lips, holding the sheep still and upright. The ewe wants to lie down. Her bleats have broken to rasps, her breathing harsh in the cold night. A lantern hangs from a rafter overhead and a hinged two-sided gate leans against the drystone wall. At the other end of the sheepshed is a boulder half the height of a man, broad at the base and flattened at the top: too great to remove when the foundation hole was dug. Leah leans against it, overwrapped in one of Norman's greatcoats. The lambs born the week before are awake with the lantern light and play king-of-the-mountain on the boulder, butting heads and flying on and off the rock, missing Leah neatly and avoiding the end of the shed where Norman and Connie work. Norman seems absolutely still but Leah can see the muscles of his bared arm flex as he works his hand inside, moving in fractions of inches. He's silent, letting Connie croon to the ewe. Then, there, the ewe groans and the lamb slides out, Norman's hand coming with it, under it. His arm thick with blood and mucus lays the lamb on the bedding and clears its mouth and nose of membrane and raises its head and the mouth sucks open and draws air. Norman wipes the lamb dry with burlap sacking and while drying brings it to its feet. The ewe has twisted her head to watch. Connie still holds her. Norman gets the lamb upright against the ewe's side where it butts against her until striking the soft udder it finds the teat. The bit of tail works. The ewe groans again and a second lamb slides out just as Norman was raising his arm to go back in. He clears this one also and when it's up and feeding he cleans his arms with the sacking and stands. "Sometimes, with twins, the first one pops the cork." Leah steps forward to take the lantern while Norman and Connie pen the ewe and lambs with the folding gate against the corner wall. They all three stand side by side a moment and watch the lambs nursing. Norman takes the lantern and checks the other ewes still to lamb. They then go out into the hanging night, the moon great in the sky like the burnished skull of a long gone beast. The snowfields and hills with etched trees and farmstead buildings all softened, fantastic, substantial. Leah pauses a moment behind the brother and sister, watching the world. She loves this as much as a June day. Sometimes wishes at full moon she might sleep through the day and spend nights walking. Walking out in a world the opposite of the one she lives in, a world in reverse. A place where her spirit might be freed, truly freed at last. Freed from the burden of herself. A world that doesn't exist. She goes on. No lamps are lit in the house, just the faint glow of the lantern where they wait for her at the entryway.

By midmorning he'd be done with what the barns demanded and then he'd file his saws and grind the double-bitted axe and using the heavy harness with brichens he'd hitch the team to the sledge, load in the skidding chains and whippletree and a pair of nosebags with rations of oats and head up to the woodlot. At the sawpit he'd unhitch the team and leave Pete to stand while Tommy followed him, Norman carrying the saw over one shoulder and the axe on the other and together they'd make their way up the broken trail into the woodlot. He'd fell a tree, selecting not just for the thinning but also for a clean fall. Each site held several right choices with twice as many wrong ones. He wanted no hung trees. Down, he'd limb out the log with the axe and saw through either the tip or midsection depending on the size. Most mornings he'd cut two trees, some three. Then Tommy would skid the log out to the pit. Tommy was a skid-horse; stepping off with Norman's word and going on his own, needing no driving. Would be waiting with the log always just a few feet shy of the end of the skidway when Norman would catch up to him. So Norman would have to say "Step up there" and Tommy would ease the log up. Then Norman would slip on the nose bags with feed for both horses, step into the pit and pull back the old buffalo robe that covered over the peaveys and canthooks and heavy iron bar and using these tools roll the first log out onto the timbers over the pit. And begin sawing twenty-inch chunks from one end then the other of the log, the timbers over the pit set to act not just as guides for size but to keep the log stable until it was down to the final cut. Then it was down into the pit, the fresh sawdust spread sweet on the crusted old broken snow and frozen clotted sawdust from the days before. The pit not a hole in the ground so much as a cave manmade, with the south side open to level ground. Here he split the chunks into stovewood.

As a child with his father, this work took forever. Mornings were endless cold feet and hands and ears. Now alone he could load the sledge in a morning, often unaware he'd taken no break until the sledge was filled. At noontime he'd hitch the team again and take the load down to add to the lengthening cords stacked tight as drystone in ranks behind the entryway woodshed. Water and stall the still-harnessed horses, feed them down with hay and go in to his meal. In the afternoon doing it all again. He could look down from the sawpit onto the backside of the house and see next winters warmth in the gray stacks. Coming in at dusk or later to the kitchen steamed with food, fatigue a pleasure over him like summer sun, smelling himself as he washed for supper, the sweat and sweet sawdust on him as the skin of a day's work.

The danger stilled his mind. Danger only started with the felling. Then ran on the bright edge of the axe as he walked the downed tree, limbing. Then the log itself, in motion or containing motion all the way to the pit and then by hand up the skidway. Motion to crush a foot, a leg, a whole man. Then the axe again, rising and falling, quartering the rounds; the axe oddtimes glancing, and always throwing the chunks up to fall about him. And danger in the repetition: letting himself drift to the chickadee working the sawdust chips in the spruce boughs, the snort or thick plash of urine from the geldings, the bay of a hound over the ridge. His right arm pushed outward a small ache during the splitting from the old sabre wound, the ache serving to tether his attention to the bright slice of the axe.

Some afternoons the sledge was loaded and he knew by the lightfall he was early. As February spread evenly before and after, the cold held but the sun climbed and on this south slope he could pause, warm with work and the false cheer of the sun on his face and sit up on the timbers of the sawpit, his long legs dangling, his trouser cuffs filled with sawdust riding up to the top of his laced boots and there with the danger not so much gone as back up in the woods waiting for the next day his thought would idle and drift. Beyond what was at hand. Sometimes to the house below and sometimes beyond that. Oft to the hope of the child and as many times to his own shortcomings as a man. He felt as if his father was nearby. Just beyond sight in the rump of spruce running uphill one side of the sawpit.

"Father was proud of you, Norman." His mother's final words to him before she clamped a hand on the shoulder of the boy driving the rented democrat wagon and told him, "You're not paid to sit here daydreaming." The wagon then went clattering smoothly from the dooryard down the track, the back loaded with the chests and sets of drawers and cartons of clothing and personal items of Cora Pelham and daughter Constance, his mother refusing from pride or bitterness or both to allow Norman the same job done for free. As if in her desire to not upset his new life she found the one final way to make clear how badly she wanted to do so. Connie turning to wave at Norman, the boy driving wedged between the two women. Norman raised his hand to his sister and stood the brief moment until the wagon crested the rise of land and dropped from sight. And stood there still with his mother's benediction or condemnation or both still fresh and seared into him for all time. As if that was what she wanted. One final spring of doubt passed on with final authority from beyond the grave. Who better to know than she. Who better to choose the careful clipped neutral tone that left room for all meaning to fly in and settle on the sear, like crows onto a sown field. So he stood there until he heard Leah come from the house and then he started up and went away from her to the barns, wanting still to be alone. Without blame for her remaining inside while his mother departed but not willing yet to grant that lack by waiting for what words she might add. Went and milked the cows and swore that by the week out they'd be gone save the one fresh heifer for their own use. October home from the war.

Now legs dangling above the sawpit, already in the shade of the spruce the winter evening spreading like inkstain but him with the sun on his face. The team, not restless, slipped weight foot to foot. The sledge full. Chimney smoke rising from the house below in a thin vapor. A cloudless sky. Paused for his father's voice to come down from the spruce. It never did.

What child remained in him walked side by side with his father. Where affection came from the man in even reprimand tonicked with dried humor. A man with two daughters already, too pleased with a son finally to expect perfection, and so was to know the boy. His eye sharp as a raptor upon Norman's back always gentled when the boy turned in confusion with the bent nail, the flung tool, the short-sawn board. Never once he could recall praise; something made right was made right. Otherwise, the job remained. At ten he first rode the sledge to the village pond one January to join in cutting ice. They pulled up short and surveyed the men already out, sawing and using great tongs to lift the blocks, the dripping pond water freezing as it fell. After watching a short time his father stepped down, wrapped the lines on the left upright front pole of the sledge and took out the saw and their own tongs and looked up at the boy. "Question is, which of us takes the bottom end of the saw. Flip a coin?"

He believed his father would've liked Leah. He liked to think so. As if his father, freed from life, would also be freed to see all of her that Norman saw. Not only the beauty and courage that to him were evident as drawing breath but also the lesser fragments that made the whole: the temper and guileless smile; the pluck beyond even thinking; the decision then, the end product of that same pluck, given over to intense focused scrutiny as if she more than most knew clearly how one step leads inevitably to the next and not some other. Her gentle humor, less prod than tease, and the sudden way her face would bloom as if her skin gave off light when Norman would fumble or misstep. The containment of herself, so ferocious as if her skin were a moist sacking over whirling conflict and contradiction. Just the sight of her walking barefoot in a meadow amongst throngs of buttercups and daisies, black-eyed Susans. Or her face lifted and half buried in a spray of lilac. Or by evening lamplight leaning over the round reading table in the parlor, her elbows holding down the spread pages of the Randolph newspaper as she read the week's news. Or now filling with his grandchild. Whom Norman intended to name James after him. Norman sat on the timbers of the sawpit and thought his father might know all these things. Might not only approve but applaud. Thinking this because he thought the dead may know all things and not just what each action might mean to them: freed of that concern. For in truth he wondered if his father had been living would he have brought the girl home with him or taken her to some other place, an idea unknowable to the boy who had held the farm against his thin chest over his heart throughout the battles and long deadly pauses of march and tent and march again between the battles like other men carried lockets with the likeness of a wife or sweetheart next to theirs. Even wondered if he might have left her there in Washington and rode the rods home with the others, content with some good deed done, carrying with him always that passion and fear of the what-might-have-been. Because it was all very simple. The farm became his when he married, the parents to make partnership with the son and new wife. At such a time as he was able and all parties willing he might purchase it for market value. The sole clause being in the event of his father's death Norman must provide either home for his mother or a third share of the market value. As most are the will written with the intent of living decades past the dating and signing. Never dreaming of the mare's hoof anymore than of a star fragment piercing the night sky and his own head. And so made way for the boy to bring the girl home. And gave to Norman the bitter hidden secret of some relief in his father's death. As if he was freed by the death. As if his father gave him not only all of his own life but all of Norman's as well; do as you please. His father became sealed always to what had been and only informed the present by the convenience of recollection. Not only is to recall or not the choice of the living but also how and what to recall. The father became more echo to his own desire than a man full-blown. As a knife lost in the garden over winter loses its edge and the handle rots with the spring. How well it used to cut. As with his mother's words: Father was proud of you.

Norman let himself down by his hands on the timbers until his boots struck the sawdust in the blueing dusk. He went to the team and lifted their feet, cupping one mitten under each thick hoofwall to hold it against his knee as he scraped out the packed snow and ice with his pocketknife. The horse breath now hot steam in the cold. Stepped the team to the sledge and lifted the pole and hooked the neckyoke to the collars and then down the pole to attach the tugs by trace chains to the doubletree and evener. Then took up the lines and walked to the back of the sledge and stepped up behind the load. The saws and axe already wedged in on top. He gathered the lines in one big double loop in his right hand and held each line taut and looked down the backs of his horses. The evening star was up over the eastern ridgeline. The horse's nosebags dangled from their outside hames. He was cold now and felt the day's work in him. The woods were dark behind him and he felt a vicious thing not of the place, an intruder in his own life. Some rot. Some weakness that allowed the woman down the hill to be his reason for all things done and not done. As if he lacked something essential other men had or might have. He did not know. There was no reason to think his father would be proud of him, living or dead. He spoke to the team. "Get up now, boys."

The last Sunday in February the weather still had not broken and Leah was growing large, settling into and rising from chairs and the bed with effort and strained groans. Connie came back up the hill after church with Pete trotting hard between the shafts. She had not gone to dinner with her mother at Mrs. Breedlove's but come straight on. Once in the house she filled the copper boiler and lifted it onto the range and opened the flues. Rushed up the stairs and back down with clean undergarments and a dress over one arm. From his seat in the parlor Norman saw it was the dress she'd traveled home in. He hadn't seen it since. He glanced to Leah sitting with the family Bible open on her lap, wedged up against her belly and held from beneath by both hands. She would spend an hour over a page. Time to time a noise would issue from her mouth, a sipping sound as if taking something in or a more clear louder chirp of doubt. She met his raised eye and cocked head and only shook her head, a gesture emphatic enough to shame his questions. Connie closed the door to the kitchen and was in there some minutes before she came into the parlor to stand hands on hips and announce, "They make a reservoir now clamps to the side of a range by the firebox and allows for hot water all the time. None of this having to wait. Seems a small luxury in a house with a baby coming." Then turned and went back into the kitchen, the door sucked to by her passage.

Norman spoke. "Now, what was that."

Leah raised eyes hooded down like a turtle. "Seems to me she has a point. Those things are cheap. Simple too. Something a man handy could take on I spect. Hot water takes forever. You'd be surprised the difference. That lye soap raises up a nice sud."

"I recall bathing in hot water one or two times. You want something for the house then speak up. I'll not deny you, it's not too dear. But what has her to a boil?"

Leah ran her hand over the open page, her hand flat as if smoothing the thin paper. Then said, "You're thick in the head, Norman. The woman wants to wash herself and dress up. Likely not for you or me, either."

Norman was quiet a moment. Then said, "What're you reading in?"

"Job."

"Now that was a rare bugger."

"Nothing more than the rest of us."

"I can't see that."

"I always took it to be the point."

"That right there is the definition of faith."

She leveled her eyes now on him. "No. It's not. I don't know what is."

"That's fair. Tell you what. You find out, let me know."

She looked long on him. Through the kitchen door they heard the splash of water and small sighs of pleasure. Even with the door closed they could smell the scent of soap and rosewater on the steam runneling through the house. Leah said, "I don't spect it in this life anymore than you. You know that."

Connie came into the room, her face flushed with scrubbing, dressed fine and already wrapped for the outside. "We're going to skate on the river," she said, "I just hope my christly ankles hold up. Skating, they always fall out on me. Always landing on my bum. It's not the fall I mind, it's the being helped up."

It was the eldest Clifford boy came to claim her. Came in fast with a swept-back sleigh drawn by a fancy pair of black light trotting horses, each with a fine white blaze. Norman was amused and did his best to not be, feeling the smile tic the corners of his mouth. The boy—now young man—whose father owned the livery with teams and single horses to let, along with conveyances. Also a cartage business. The same boy then who five years before drove Norman's mother and sister away from the farm. Now come calling. Or rather to take the girl skating. Norman wondering how many years his sister had fired in Glen's mind.

How many long Sundays over the fall and winter it had taken him to reach this point. Glen took his hand firm and called Norman sir which pleased him and then went on to lament his being too young to do his part with the late war which Norman was gracious enough to only nod away. Glen promising Connie home not too much after dark, adding the dangerous explanation of a bonfire. Snuggle up to it was what Norman was thinking but only said, "You watch out that team. There's ice where the road's packed." And turned to grin at his sister, not caring if the boy saw this. And Connie then came forward and leaned up tiptoe and kissed his cheek. Glen taking his hand again and then nodding with a great and real gravity to Leah and speaking to her for the first time in taking leave. "Ma'am." The word ripened like sun-gorged berries with respect.

The two gone, Norman took his chair again. Leah watching him. Norman said, "That just made me feel like old folks."

Leah smiled, a hand over her belly and said, "Just wait, you."

The second week of March brought a sudden deep thaw that Norman declared to be brief and was: three days and nights above freezing with the days arching into the mid-forties. Then six inches of wet snow and the wind shifted and all froze hard again. Still that thaw was enough for Norman to carry the stacked sap buckets from the hayloft to the basement where beside the old milk cooling well he filled them in regimental rows, letting them sit with water overnight to swell the staves tight within the hoops. From the sledge he scraped out the layer of ice mixed with bark and sawdust and rolled the gathering tank into place. Set in the gathering yokes and buckets and took the team and sledge once again up the hill past the skidway to the small sugar house, just a roof on poles over a chimney and bricked hearth with a firepit underneath and the heavy boiling kettle set into the bricks. There unhitched the team and roped together the buckets in bundles and hung them over Tommy's back and let the horse follow him as Norman broke trail on snowshoes through the sugarbush, stopping at each of the rock maples to bore holes and hammer in spouts and hang buckets. Back down at the sugarhouse he shoveled out the drifted snow and pulled canvas tarping from the year-old woodpiles extending off the north side. He filled the boiling kettle halfway with snow and made a fire underneath and waited for the snow to melt and then scrubbed the inside of the kettle with a stout limb with a gobbed head of burlap sacking on the end. The sugarhouse was raw and bleak, more so with the winter snow cast out and the floor bare earth but he could see it already as it would be in a week's time or two: steam flaring off the kettle, the firebox running day and night with smoke hanging in the limpid air, the sweet scent of the woods rising as each boil-down ended and the kettle was tipped to pour off the syrup into the filters. Connie even now down to the house washing the squares of red flannel and spreading them on racks to dry tight-sided in the kitchen. Then he went down the hill, stopping at the sawpit to load the tools from there. He spent one afternoon in the barn wiping them down with grease and hanging them for the summer. Weather aside, he was done lumbering for the year.

A week later, a gray day, the cold still like toothache but a wind out of the west-northwest and Norman over breakfast stated winter was over. Then with nothing else to do went to the barns to gather eggs and fill the stoves and check the brooder house. Even with the cold lingering the hens were laying with the longer days and steady heat. Near twenty gone broody over fleets of eggs in the boxes in the brooder. No chicks yet. Looked in after his ewes and lambs. Easter dinner for those in Boston who waited for their Son to rise before going home to eat lamb with mint jelly. As if eating spring and resurrection its very self. All this though, for Norman, little more than escaping the house and his own idle hands. He tasted the cold drab air, sniffing deep for the change he was sure was held far down in that wind somewhere. Out over the Great Lakes, Canada, somewhere. Coming.

The women in the kitchen, Connie floured and up to her arms in kneading bread dough, the oven already thumping and crackling with heat waiting the loaves. Leah sat at the table, cutting dried apple rings to quarters and dropping them into a bowl of sugar water for the filling of the pie that would follow the loaves into the oven. She watched Connie's back and arms, already knowing the bread would be dense and stiff from the hearty pumping and soft thumping sound as she turned the knead over. Finally cleared her throat and watched the back stiffen and the arms pause and then continue, slowed, as she waited and Leah spoke with direct emphasis.

"So?"

Connie darted her face back so her chin grazed her shoulder, looked at Leah and turned back to her work. Her voice muffled as if buried in the dough said, "So, what?"

"You've been a busy girl."

"Umm."

"Having a good time?"

"I am." Emphatic, snapping her words closed like a box.

"I'm poking my nose."

"Oh no." Connie turned and swept back loose curls, leaving flour trails against her forehead. "I didn't mean that. You are, I don't mind. I'm having fun. Been back to Randolph six months now and I'm having a good time. I think I'll keep right on doing that."

"Sounds good to me. That Glen, he a nice boy or just a convenience?"

"He's nice enough. Maybe a little young."

"What, two maybe three years?"

"Two. Two and a half. But you feel the difference."

"Well, Norman and me, we're four years apart."

"It's different with the woman older."

"I guess. Does he, does Glen act that way?"

"Not one whit. Always has the right idea."

"And him younger than you."

"Exactly."

"And you been to Manchester and all. Experienced."

Connie shook her head. "I've no interest in a reputation."

Leah cut the string from another loop of apples and sliced. Watching her work, said, "No reason to think that'd happen."

Connie came forward and sat, picking up one of the dried rings and chewing like worrying over it. "But God, he's a well-made man."

Leah smiled at her. And said, "You're holding back."

"Well, for now!"

Leah nodded. "He's young."

"Some things, it seems to me age don't matter on a man."

"He strikes me as steady-minded."

"Any boy can mind his manners waiting on dessert."

"Is that what he's after you think?"

"By Christ I wish I knew. He talks a serious streak and so do I and then we're all over each other and it's Katy-bar-the-door. What I like about him is he's got big ideas but not too big. It all sounds right and fits with who he is but I still get antsy. Like jumping out my skin. Other times we're just having a grand old time and I don't think about a thing. I don't know what to trust: him, me, the both of us."

"Sounds like your Mister Jack Manchester man gave you something more than what you recognized."

Connie looked at her, one side of her lower lip pulled up between her teeth. Paused, thinking. Then made a small nod. "Thing is, how do you know?"

Without pause Leah said, "When you can't help yourself. When it's all beyond you. When thinking just doesn't even happen."

"Sounds like ten times a night."

"Then maybe it is. Or maybe not. One these days you're going sit across from me and bold as brass tell me what your future looks like. Could be him, could be not him. Could be somebody else. Could be tomorrow. I don't know and you neither. Hard as it is, that's how it should be. It keeps things, interesting."

Connie nodded. "Things're interesting enough I guess."

"Now that's good. All you can ask for."

"I want to know."

"Uh-huh."

"Stupid."

"Not hardly. But that don't mean you get advance notice."

"I worry I'm not around as much as you need. Both you and Norman. I made a promise to him and doing that, one to you too."

"You're round enough just now. Time comes we both know you'll be around more. Norman worries about the sugaring and I worry about this." Patted her stomach like a guest arriving. "Time you're shirking you'll know it. Who knows, maybe that Glen'll even come in handy."

Connie burst breath through her nose. "That'd be a fine day." Then said, "How'd you ever trust Norman?"

"I don't know. But, the time I met him, I knew I had to trust or not. It didn't mean I didn't leave my doors open. It just meant I wasn't going to use em less I had no choice."

Connie nodded, her face lowered toward the table. After a bit she said, "All I want is to climb up all over him. All the time."

Leah was finished cutting the apples. She needed to pee. She needed to all the time now. Both hands on the table she pushed up and stood, Connie now watching her. Leah rocked and steadied herself and said, "Your bread's ruined." She went to the entryway and pulled on a shawl and overcoat, wrapping herself easy for the outhouse. She looked back and Connie was watching her. Leah said, "Of course you feel that way."

Connie stood from the table and said, "I punch that loaf down and let it rise again it'll be fine. Won't hurt it a bit for patience."

Leah nodded. Turned for the latch into the woodshed and without looking back said, "Bread's not all will rise you wait a little."

They'd been sugaring day and night a week, the sap daytimes seeming to pour from the trees so both Connie and Norman hiked in the woods with the yokes, the snow shrinking each day so the trails became quickly packed enough to walk without snowshoes. The south side of each tree spread a small stage of bared brown leaves outward. They brought up the second older and smaller gathering tank and placed it on a scaffold beside the sugarhouse to empty the gathering tank into so when dusk fell and the wind dropped and temperatures fell they had two tanks' worth of sap to boil off. One of them would take the team and sledge down to do evening chores and eat supper while the other fired the kettle and began boiling. The first would climb back after dark with a cake tin of supper wrapped in towels.

The two would work into the morning hours, stoking the fire to keep a low rolling boil, skimming off the surface with a paddle and then plunging the paddle in a downward twisting turn to keep the thickening sap even. When it would froth too high they'd drag a lump of lard on a long string through to settle it. A long-handled dipper would pour forth a thin apron when it was syrup, a thicker sheet when it was ready to sugar. As a kettle finished they worked fast to pour it off into the long sugar molds. Then the kettle was refilled and the fire pokered up and there would be a brief time before the fresh sap came to a boil. Norman had a demijohn of cider and would pour out a couple of drams into the sugar dipper and sip at it until it was gone, Connie taking it once or twice for small swallows. Both too tired to talk. Norman would go outside and look out over the starred valley of the farm, his back to the sugarhouse. Then return to the work, the short chimney sending up a straight white plume while steam from the kettle broke out under all sides of the roof. They would finish by half past two or three and be back up in the woods by eleven the next morning. The soft spring air itself invigorant to the work.

The night the ice went out it was Connie came down for the evening feed-up and to eat with Leah and carry supper back up to Norman. Leah moving slowly around the kitchen now, cooking one-pot meals that would carry well and furnish the long nights. Connie was famished with work and mopped up two plates of pot roast with carrots, parsnips, onions and potatoes, the vegetables all showing wear from the long storage, while Leah across from her ate slowly and with tired method, as if the food were no more than sprite fuel atop an already filled stomach. Before she went off up the hill again with Norman's food Connie stopped while wrapping the cake tin and stepped forward and said, "You look peaked. You feeling right?"

Leah shook her head. "I'm wore out. Wore out is all. Nothing's comfortable anymore. Everything's a job of work."

Connie touched a hand to her brow. Held it there and lifted it off and touched her again. "I guess for a hot kitchen you feel all right. It's much to ask, you working down here for all of us."

Leah shook her head again. "Cooking's all. I haven't lifted a broom or dustrag since I don't know when. I'm fine. Nothing like what you two are up doing. You forget, I've done it years past. I know. All I am is a fat tired woman gonna have a baby. Poor little old me."

Connie grinned at her. Leah went on. "Go on. Get food up to that man 'fore he drinks too hard at that cider."

With Connie gone Leah washed up, using hot water from the new tank on the firebox side of the range. Then swept the kitchen and filled the stoves, here and in the parlor and the one in the front hall, the ceiling of which was punctured four times along its length with cast-iron round registers to let the heat upstairs. Then back to the kitchen and the luxury of warm water to wash herself and finally up the stairs in the dark, undressing and pulling the soft washed flannel nightdress down over herself and letting herself slowly down into the bed on her back. The second-story windows free of frost for the first time in months.

She was not sleeping when the ice began to boom. Perhaps she'd slept some earlier; she could never tell. Then she was lying in the bed and hearing it. The ice over the river a mile away in the valley, grown thick through the winter, began to come apart in great torn shreds the size of boxcars and barndoors, softened from the top by the warming days and strained from underneath by the feed of snowmelt from the hill brooks. It was a sound unlike any other. She imagined it to be like a very slow train wreck that went on for hours. Or maybe some bent memory Norman might hold from a great distance of artillery fire. She'd never seen it go out but had seen the remains the day after: the blocks and chunks and sheets all jumbled along the shorelines, caught up in stacks like huge spilt cards in riverbends or where the bank had caved, leaving a three- or four-tree clump half into the water for the ice to layer up behind. The central channel open and thick brown, roiling white on top with current, paddies and cakes of ice sailing along with tree limbs and other trash. So she lay in bed listening to the air-softened destruction of winter and seeing the aftermath of it in her mind, seeing also the slowed low river of summer spilling over the ledges and boulders of pools and shallows and then felt without pain or cramp or other warning the soft warm flow between her legs and reached down and knew what it was even as she lifted it to her lips to taste.

She rose in the dark and made her way downstairs to the kitchen where a single lamp was lit, hiked her nightdress and reached again and checked her fingers. Like admonishment her first and index finger were coated with blood. She stood what seemed a long time looking at it. And deflated said aloud, "Oh God damn it." Then went out through the entryway woodshed with the meager stack and took up a length of split wood and continued outside. Barefoot into the caked hardened mud of the yard to the weathered silver post where the dinner bell hung—the bell never once rung since she'd arrived, some thing left over from other days—and began to beat the side of the bell with the stovewood. At first just a low hollow tone and then the clapper broke free of the rust seal and at counterpoint to the stovewood struck the side of the bell. So there was the hard low metal *thrang* followed by the crisper tone of the ring. Beating it like beating herself.

Up the hill they'd just poured off into the molds and refilled the kettle with new sap and were awaiting the boil, standing outside listening to the ice going out. The night was still and Norman was pulling it in with small gasps, tasting for the turn of the wind to the south and the warm air to follow, not finding it but sure it would not be far off. The warm air would end the sugaring. They passed a dipper of cider. They both heard the sound at the same time and both said nothing but strained to clarify it from the percussions of tearing ice. They spoke at the same time.

"That's a bell," Connie said.

"Is that a fire?" Norman scanning the skyline ridges and blank depth of darkened valley beyond the farm. Saw nothing save for the faint light and rising steam and smoke from distant sugarhouses on the far ridge. Then again, both at once.

"That's our bell, that's our bell." The tones now clear, sharp rising from the farm.

"Oh my Christ." And Norman threw down the dipper and began to run, his boots sliding in the mud of the track, going then off the side into the snow, his arms pinwheeling for balance as he went. Connie stood a moment, watching; then the full implications of the bell came over her also. She started after him, then turned back, running to the sugarhouse to throw open the firepit door in the brick arch and, leaving it open, took up the old spade and ran in and out after shovel loads of snow, casting it on top of the freshened fire until she was satisfied the fire would die. She could hear Norman crying out for Leah. Connie blew out the lantern and left it there, running after her brother in the dark.

She fell twice going down and in the farmyard found her brother already with Tommy out, the harness thrown up over his back unbuckled and Norman trying to fasten harness at the same time he mounted the shafts of the high-wheeled cart into the fittings. She was breathless, panting, sore up her back and right arm with her clothes soaked through. She went forward and settled the hames to the collar and tightened them closed and stepped around her brother to lean and catch the bellyband and buckle that. He saw her as he tightened the trace chains and his voice choked. "She's bleeding. I got her back up to lie down." He pulled the looped lines free of the hame ball and stepped up into the cart, still speaking. "I'm going after Doctor. Go set with her." He settled into the seat and gathered the lines and took up the whip from its socket and said, "Keep her quiet if you can. It's not even a month early. She'll be fine. I'll get Hurdle up here and she'll be fine. Get up, you bastard!" and laid the whip across Tommy's back and they went out of the yard and down toward the lip of the bowl in the dark, the thick wheels sucking at the mud, the hooves pulling up smart with the slog, the cart lurching as it went through the mired ruts and pools that once were a road.

Connie went quick to the house thinking Mud like this it's an hour to the village, time to rouse the doctor if he be home, then an hour back if he don't kill the horse, and went into the kitchen and stopped, frightened. Her breath still ragged from it all. The house was very still. She stood in the kitchen trying to get her breath back, scrubbing her hands under the gravity line. Opened the draft of the stove and set the copper boiler atop the range and filled it with water. Filled the reservoir also. Then pulled the tea kettle forward, lifting up a range plate so the kettle was over the open flame of the firebox. Set out cups and saucers and teapot on a tray and stuffed the strainer with mint and dropped it into the pot. Spooned in fresh sugar made just the day before. Checked the kettle and saw she had time and ran down cellar to the small cask of applejack and popped the bung to pour out a scant half cup. The applejack made from freezing a barrel of hard cider and then siphoning off the small unfrozen core of alcohol. Ran back upstairs and poured the applejack into the teapot and then filled it all with water, the kettle singing now. Replaced the stove lid and lifted the tray and went down the hall and up the stairs, the camphorate odor of mint, maple and apple rising into her nose as she went. Her clothes still wet, clotted with mud, sticking to her.

She went along the upstairs hall. The bedroom door was open, light like orange rind coning onto the hall runner. She was terrified. The youngest child, she'd never seen a newborn. Certain it would come with Norman gone and the doctor not there. Such a small child, so early. She had only vague ideas of what to do. Her wet clothing chilled her, as if death walked with her. She paused before the door, out of sight. She could see the foot of the bed, the slender tent of Leah's feet. She dreaded what lay above them. The feet were spread apart. It was very quiet, no moans or the cries she'd expected. The tray an awful weight in her hands. The muscles in her forearms ached, holding it.

From the room, Leah's voice. "That you, Connie?"

"I'm coming," she called, her voice scraped, oddly gay.

"Get in here quick. I need you girl."

Connie went in with the tray. Leah was propped high on pillows, her face composed, calm, set. Connie set down the tray and poured out tea into the two cups, talking all the while. "I threw this in the pot coming up here. That mint tea you like, fortified up a tad. Norman's already gone for Doctor so you just rest easy there, he'll be back in no time, you'll see, and everything'll be just fine. Here take this, you look good, you look fine, are you all right?"

Leah took the saucer in both hands and brought it up to breathe in the tea, then set the saucer on the nightstand. She smiled at Connie. "I'm all right. I guess I'm going to have this baby. I don't know. I'm bleeding a little. It mostly stopped. Nothing else has happened, not yet. Look at you. You're a mess."

"We came running, both of us."

"Well. I was scared." Took up the cup, blew and sipped. Wrapped her hands around the cup and rested it against her covered belly. "I'm still scared but not so bad. I need you to do something you're not going to want to do but you have to anyway. For me you have to."

Connie drank from her tea. Immediately regretted the applejack over the cider she'd already had. With no idea what was coming. Swallowed a little more and set the cup down. Leah raised her cup and sipped again and looked at Connie, waiting. Connie said, "What's this thing I'm not going to want to do?"

Leah grinned and said, "You're just like a little bull calf sometimes. Put your chin down against your throat looking like you're ready to dig in your feet."

"What is it you want?"

"I want you to go up and get Marthe Ballou for me."

"Oh no. I won't do that."

"Yes you will."

"No I won't. I promised Norman I'd set with you. He's getting the doctor and you're going to be just fine."

Leah sat silent. Leaned back against the pillows. As if running something long and complicated through her mind all over again, to render it down to the simple flat statements needed. Connie saw all this and felt something waver inside herself, some weakness she'd never before guessed at, or named, or done more than dismissed before. And rose up against it still silent, all the while feeling the rally as something false, something not true to herself. And knew then she'd do what Leah wanted and knew also it was her duty to not acquiesce, to drag forth all argument. And felt behind this all men, the simple fact of manhood and their great abiding, the gift they held and also the curse. To see things simply with resolution determined when all life was trial and guess. At best.

Leah spoke. As if explaining elemental process to a child yet with bold straightforwardness not to be denied. "I'm bleeding a little bit. I don't know what that means. It's most nearly a month early. My water's not broke and I've got no cramps. Not yet anyhow. All of that I guess could happen any moment. Or a week from now. Or three like it should. Or I might be set to lose this baby. All those things. And I don't know which. Won't until I do. What I know is this: Norman went and did what he felt best to do. Didn't ask me but told me. Now, that shaken old man called doctor ain't so much as going to take down these covers and probe me. It just ain't gon' happen. He might do all that and be right with what he has to say but I ain't got trust with him. Not one smack of trust. And I do trust Marthe. So I want you to go get her. It's simple as that."

Connie felt all her wind wrapped tight in her throat behind her tongue. She said, "I can't, Leah. I promised Norman. I can't do it."

"Ask you something. Who's having this baby? Norman? Or me?"

"I know that. I just can't do it."

"Whyever not?"

"I said, I promised Norman."

Leah spat air.

"Even I was to, time I got up there and found her and got back down with her, Norman and the Doctor would be back long since. There's no point."

"I thought about that. What horse'd Norman take?"

"Well he took Tommy. Tommy on the cart. Only thing would go through the mud."

"It's simple then. Put the bridle on Pete and use a set of lead ropes for reins and ride the booger up there and carry Marthe back down here."

"Pete? Pete don't ride."

"Girl, Pete rides like he was born to it. You get out those clothes and dress up warm, get on a pair of Norman's wool trousers and belt em up tight and cuff em high and you'll ride like angels."

"You've rode that horse?"

"Rode him all around the place summertimes. With just a looped rope around his lower jaw."

"I won't. I won't do it."

"Course you will. It's me lying here with the baby asking. Course you will."

"No."

"Yes. Oh, yes you will."

And as the ice from the river it all broke free of Connie, she feeling it on her tongue as it spilled, hating it and loving it all at once. "What do you want with that dirty old woman? Old hag, wood's whore, all grimed up and greasy and smelling like skunk long dead or something dug up out the ground? Old bitch lying up there spewing out her get like a wild creature, like an animal. Christ you got no idea. Things I heard about her. Came down out of Quebec all on her own no more than thirteen and already more willing than the men she serviced. Dirty woman. Dirty stinking bitch of a whore. Why you think she knows so much about the ins and outs of babies? How many maybe you think she's carried? Just those odd half-dozen boys in and out of the woods? What about those others? What about the times she rid herself of them? And how about those other girls, those girls in trouble, mostly French girls, some not, would come miles to find her? Go up the mountain with trouble in their bellies, come down with trouble in their hearts. You know about all that? Anybody told you this about your great friend? I guess not. I guess not Norman. I guess not herself. I guess not one solid soul before me."

"You surely hate those Canadians, don't you?"

"I don't hate a living person but for one. But those people make a choice, they have the choice, they sink to one end and stay there. Like creatures they live. Like dirt their minds work. I can't change that. I can't change that."

"You don't know nothing about it."

"I know every goddamn thing I need to know."

"You don't know nothing. What you talking bout is niggers. Just niggers. Just some people you don't know nothing about but think you do. And you too stupid to know what you think's part of what they is. Just niggers. Niggers like me. Stop your silly schoolgirl friendly with me, girl. I just a nigger too. Just a fat little nigger woman bout to have a child the best way she know how. And nobody, no one, not you, not Norman Pelham, gon' tell me how to go about that. This my body holding this child, not his, not yours. Most not yours. Just this nigger woman's."

"Jesus Leah. Stop it." Connie hot with it, the heat all through her, burst like sunburn over her face. Shame, pride, anger, some fear, some sickness. Shame.

"No. I ain't stopping nothing. Choice is simple here. My mind is set like granite. Somebody gon' ride that horse up the hill around the mountain and fetch her down here to look over me. Only question is, it gon' be you or it gon' be me?"

Save for a time or two as a little girl when her father set her up for a brief amble she'd not been horseback in her life. So she led the giant from the barn with the blinkered bridle and makeshift reins, feeling at odds with the job and the strange constricted movement of the heavy belted-up woolen pants. She led him to stand beside the granite block with the iron ring on an eyed rod for hitching, and pushed the horse up against it and went around him to balance atop the block and holding the rope reins tight with handfuls of mane slung herself up the side of the horse, her right leg stretching and catching the broad spread of his back and her arms then pulling her up so that suddenly she slid evenly onto his back. The horse did not move. She pulled up on the rope reins and drummed him with her heels. He did not move. "Shit, you," she said. She slid her right hand down the rope toward the bit and drew back on it, pulling his head around and slowly he stepped off, following his head. She tapped him again with her heels. As if afraid of getting his hooves wet or slipping on the hardened mud he walked gingerly across the yard toward the uphill trace, responding more to her reining than her heels, his back arched, as if at any moment he would quit this. She pulled him up short and they stood motionless. She thought about quitting it with him but not for long. She said, "Dammit Pete, we got a job to do here. Now get your ass up." And took the long rope reins tight in one hand and backhanded with the ends to quirt him one shoulder and then the next and raised up her heels for a sharper jab and yelled loud for him to get up. And he went from standing still into a long floating gallop up the hill track, his body rolling forward with great weight as if he'd divined her intent and she somehow kept the reins as she fell forward, stretched along the high curve of his neck, both hands buried deep in his mane, her fists tight-curled into the long hair that raised otherwise to whip her face. Her legs clamped not around but against the great barrel of his sides. Not until they reached the upper leveling of ground and passed the sugarhouse at a slowed canter did she realize that her mouth, only inches from his bright bowed ears, was still pressing him to Go go go.

Through the night woods beyond the reach of the sugarbush trails the horse went on, now at a walk, now at a trot or canter, following the rough path of mostly frozen mud but for several points where the great spruce grew close both sides where the hardened dense shrunken drifts still lay, through which he floundered, sometimes up to his belly with Connie's feet scraping against the deeper of the drifts. She did nothing more than hold the reins loose; the horse did not so much know the way as discern the only track there was and went forward along it. The night was dark here with even the rotting snow a dull shade of the darkness. Above the containing bowl of the farm hillside the distant roaring of the ice going out was almost lost, more a disturbance in the current of air than actual sounds. Then they rounded the shoulder of the mountain and the only sound then the suck and scrape of Pete's feet as he moved over ground that stride by stride changed degree of freezing. Still he trotted more than walked. Once one forefoot struck rock and he lost footing and regained it before Connie even felt herself began to slide, the horse making great thumping bursts from his nostrils.

She smelled the woodsmoke before she saw light from the house and then saw the light from a distance off. She pressed the horse to canter. The bear and catamount hounds Ballou kept chained roared. Connie began to call out for Marthe Ballou and the door opened as she drew near, throwing a splay of light onto the frozen mash of the dooryard. Ballou stood in the door in his long underwear, holding across his chest a rifle and wearing unlaced boots on his feet. She pulled Pete up a dozen paces from the door, just at the edge of the light. The great hounds strained. The horse sidestepped back and forth, snorting nervous air.

"Looka that," said Ballou. "Pelham girl in long pants 'stride a plough horse. Me, I always thought woman look second best the back of a horse."

"I need your wife, old man."

"Any girl come galloping up here middle of the night, she need my wife. Days now at least. Time was, not so long pass, had to wait learn was me or Marthe she be after. Not no more. But maybe so hey? Maybe you just thought Marthe be your cure. Maybe you truly be needing old man Henri to fix you scratch, hey?"

Connie raised her voice, calling the woman's name.

"Aw, pipe down, she hear ya. Heared you comin fore them damn dogs even start up. She getting dress is all. How that chicken do this bitter time?"

Pete was dancing from the dogs. She took the reins tight and wheeled him to face Ballou, letting the man view more horse than her. She said, "The chickens did fine."

Ballou slid the rifle down to dangle one-handed, the muzzle toward the ground. He slipped his free hand between buttons of his underwear and rubbed his belly. He said, "Come time, she won't take no pay for nothing she done. But you, you send a brace fine young roasters up with her. Awful lean the venison and pa'tridge come this time of year. So send up a couple fat chickens, hey?"

Marthe appeared around her husband, without touching him causing him to step back inside the door. One hand carried a basket filled with bottles and bundles all wrapped in cloth. In the other she held the smallest pair of bearpaw snowshoes Connie had seen. She wore a plaid mackinaw over thick layered woolen skirts. She came straight to Connie and said, "That baby coming?"

"I guess. I don't know. She's bleeding."

Marthe nodded. "Bleed. What else?"

"Nothing yet I guess. She said not."

"Bleed heavy or light?"

"Oh Jesus I don't know. Light she said, I think. But that was a while ago. It could be anything now. Norman went after Doctor Hurdle and Leah bid me come after you."

Marthe said nothing. Nodded once and handed up the basket for Connie to take. Then sat on the ground to strap the bearpaws to her boots. "Carry that stuff down. Me, I be right along."

"Get up behind me. We can get there quick. Pete did fine in the dark coming overhill and he don't lack room for two."

Marthe stood, shuffled in her snowshoes and buttoned her mackinaw. Grinned. "Not for gin or gold, me. You see you, I run on these. Ever thing crusted fine an I just fly. Me, I go up and over, not all the way round. Could even be I beat you down."

"She hoped to get you there before Doctor."

"She just bleeding a liddle that man can't hurt her much. Sides, I tell you, I beat you to her." And turned and stepped into the darkness of the woods, a luminous figure against the gray-stained old snow. Walked a step or two more, paused, rocked side to side as testing the snowcrust, walked again and then skipped out into a spread-footed short loping motion. Connie heard the slap and cut of the snowshoes against the snow. Going uphill the old woman seemed to lose nothing of her stride as long as Connie could hear her moving. Then she was gone from earshot. I soured that, Connie thought. Then aloud, "Pete! Let's get to home." Wheeled him hard about and clapped her heels to him and loosed the reins. He jolted forward as if released. The dogs began to roar into the night again, Ballou calling after her about chickens.

Her head still ringing from the downhill scramble of the horse she came into the kitchen and found Marthe washing her hands at the sink. The bearpaws thawing crust from their lattice to puddle the floorboards and her mackinaw flung over the tabletop. She set the basket of tonics and herbs beside it. Marthe took up a towel and dried her hands with the precision of peeling an apple and spoke before Connie might.

"She fine so far. Liddle bleed. Nothing more, not yet." And poured water from the copper boiler into a washbowl. Crossed the kitchen as if it were her own and took a stack of worn washed sacking towels from a cupboard, draped them over one arm and took up the bowl. "Least you got plenty water ready. Most likely won't need but still. I'm gonna clean her up some, set with her, me. You make up some coffee so's ready them men when they get here. They be runnin a liddle late, hey?" Grinning at Connie, teeth like amber shards. "Then come up you, tell her about you ride."

So Connie was still in the kitchen, still in the oversized ballooning wool trousers, still flushed and animate from the marrow out, leaning over the range with a spit of crushed eggshell in her palm, waiting for the coffee to come to a boil so she could drop the shell in to settle the grinds, when her brother came through the entryway with the short stout doctor following, the doctors cleated bootheels reporting against the boards in perfect counterpoint to his ragged wheeze. Connie dropped the eggshell in and pulled the coffee to the cool side of the range and turned as Norman spoke to her.

"What's that Pete horse doing dragging a pair of lead-ropes around the yard?" His face splotched red and white with cold and wind and anger rising already from knowing something somehow was done without his plan or guidance: knowing of action beyond him, behind him. How he'd see it, she knew. And before she could speak he went on, the anger rising even more clearly now and she understood it was fear as much as any other thing and she wondered if he knew that as he said, "Why aren't you up with her? She all right?" His eyes scanning the stovetop, the hot water, the effects of Marthe.

The doctor was coming out of his overcoat as if from a tight embrace. His pince-nez were steamed and his vest was stretched over a great tight ponderous stomach, the watch chain a line of gold links fine as sutures. "The girl's upstairs." It was not a question. "I'll want hot water, strong soap and old clean quilts or blankets for when her water breaks. Or whatever mess we face. She's far enough along we should get a baby out of it. But we'll know that when it bawls. Also, that coffee, and applejack if you've got it; not, cider'll do. He had a handkerchief out to wipe his lenses clear and dab at his face, now throwing out a fine sheen of sweat. He loosened the knot of his bowtie and the collar of his shirt and lifted up the snap-top bag of cracked leather. He saw the basket then on the tabletop and prodded it with his finger. "What's this?"

"Marthe Ballou's. She's up with her." She looked to her brother. "She made me go after her. She's fine; she's all right just now. She threatened to go herself if I'd not; I had no choice." She ran eyes toward the doctor and back. "She knows what she wants."

"You left her." His eyes not hatred but swollen bright as an animal's. She feared him.

"You've made a grave error." The doctor lifted his bag and looked to Connie, his swollen features monkish, jowled, purulent. The veins of his eyes a red lichen. He said, "A hard job multiplied without need. I'll want the brandy with the coffee. Not in but alongside. A woman bearing or in labor is not within reason. You'll learn that firsthand yourself one fine day." And strode to the hallway where his bootheels diminished on the runner there and then resumed up the stairs and fell away again meeting the upper runner.

Connie took up the coffee and poured out a cup and then a second and handed one to her brother. He'd not turned his outrage from her while the doctor spoke. She said, "Marthe says she's fine now. Nothing going on at all. I didn't know what to do. She was lathered up but the bleeding had stopped. It seemed best to do's she asked, to calm her. It was a risk. There was no one here but me and she said Jump. I did. I'd dare you do otherwise given the same. And you know she don't like that man." Glaring hard to meet his stare, her whole body trembling.

Norman balanced the cup and saucer on the smooth worn rim of the soapstone sink, his fingers deliberate, trembling just away from the cup, still burning her with his eyes. "I trusted you. Trusted you to do's I asked." His teeth set, the words coming through them.

"Do as you asked." She mocked his words back at him. "You think to ask what anybody else wanted? You think to ask what she wanted?"

"Goddammit!" He swept the coffee into the sink. The rupture of cup and saucer as a physical blow to Connie, running through her. Norman said, "I did what I thought best."

"You! Always you! I know you. You came running down the hill and scooped her up and carried her back to bed and raced off after the doctor. Didn't pause for a minute but racing around like you know just the right thing. The first simple thing comes into your mind, now that's the right thing. And expect everybody else to agree with it, not question it. Just like you're God or something. But I'll tell you what, Norman. You was God you wouldn't have had to run after that doctor. You would've known how to stay right here and make things right. Maybe even, you was God, you'd have had those other babies too. Maybe everything you ever thought or did would've been perfect, right as rain, instead of hit-or-miss like the rest of us. That's how it'd be, wouldn't it? Tell you what, you think about that." Was shaking, her mouth twisted, anger contorted around the words. Her lips wet as if the words were the liquid gush of her fury.

He stood gazing at her, his head quivering with anger, his color like new brick. He parted his lips to speak and shut them again. She faced him. The room smelled of wet wool, sweat, fear, coffee. After a long moment he turned his back to her and began picking up the broken china from the sink. Then he stood like that, not moving. After a moment one hand lifted from the sink heaped with shards. He piled them carefully on the drainboard. His back to her, he said, "So she's all right?"

"Go see yourself. Take up whatever it is that fat man wants and see your wife. She's fine."

He then turned, his face now thoughtful. He nodded. "She knew what she was up to. She'd asked me, I'd have been hard pressed." He paused, glanced toward the hall and went on, "She strike you as being not within reason?"

Connie smiled. "She's ferocious all right."

"Yuht." He would not grin back but said, "So how's that Pete ride?"

"Kind of broad but wicked smooth. Why'd you lose your hurry to get upstairs?"

"Thought I'd let things settle out with the three of them first." He shook his head. "That Hurdle's a pushy little son of a gun, idn't he?"

"More a popgun than anything else."

"Well," said Norman, "I'm going upstairs."

The doctor had lighted a lamp in the upstairs hall and was tilted back in a straight chair there with his heels up on a rung. He scanned them as they came, his face wrung in smirked disgust. "I'm no use here. The colored girl won't allow examination or cooperate otherwise. The hag Ballou sits in the rocker chirping laughter like a squirrel. A pair of monkeys the two of them."

"Shut that."

"You'll carry me back overstreet."

"I'll carry you nowhere right now." Norman opened the bedroom door and stepped in. As he did the doctor said, "My fee's the same I sit here or deliver the child."

Connie looked down at him as she passed into the room. "Thank goodness for that," she said. "We can all rest easy now."

Marthe had the lamps down and the room was golden. She sat in a corner working a cat's-cradle, her hands up before her with spread fingers, the geometry of strings taut and everchanging as her erect fingers dipped and lifted, her hair a waterfall onto her shoulders. The room redolent of her wood-smoked woman and the stale mint tea and underlying all that the faint taint of blood. Leah was still up against the pillows, her head back deep into them and her arms spread over the covers in ease. On the night-table the washbasin stained in a swirled stream. A clot of damp cloth also stained beside the door.

Norman went to the bedside and stood over it, looking down. She looked up at him, her face relaxed, without expression. As if waiting for him. She said, "Hey there, Norman."

"I went to hell's half acre and back."

"I'm sorry bout that."

"You might've told me what you wanted."

"It wouldn't have done no good, I did."

He nodded. "It was a waste of time, still."

"Not my fault. Wasn't me in a panic."

He looked off across from her to the far wall. Cabbage roses faint and faded on old paper. Each seemed with its own shadow from the lamp. He looked back to her. "I was afraid of losing you."

Without smiling, her face lit with humor. "It'll be more than this gets rid of me."

He shook his head. "You oughtn't have been alone though."

She studied him a moment as if making up her mind. Then, her voice lowered for only him to hear, "I wasn't."

He took his hands from his trouser pockets and ran them together before him, his fingers muscled and swollen with work. As if he wanted to touch her. As if he wanted to take something up and hold in them. As if he wanted them available, visible, capable, before the unknown of the room. The cabbage roses almost an audience of dim worn past faces. He assumed she was speaking of the child in her belly but did not want to know if it was otherwise. She watched his hands and he watched the depth of glow in her eyes on him. Thinking she understood everything his clumsy hands were reaching for. She reached a hand then and covered his knit fingers with her own: long supple slender hand that gripped hard once and went back down onto the quilt beside its mate, both resting over the heave of belly. Norman turned then to speak to Marthe.

"Snowcrust must've been iced up pretty good in the woods tonight."

She tilted only her head in shrug. "Them bearpaws cut the ice pret good. Sides, it kept me movin.'"

"What do you think about this woman lying here?"

She continued working the cat's-cradle, her eyes off it and on Norman. "A liddle hard to say. What I think, that bleed just a liddle—what?— false nothing just to scare you. She go through the night fine I bet she go rest the way. Maybe she done something more she ought to. I bet she go just fine. But we wait the night to declare that. Dawn come then we can bet she go the last two, three weeks so fine. But she be stay in that bed even then, not up moving round, caring for you, hey?"

Norman nodded and stepped close to her. "Anything I can get for you, Marthe? Anything you need?"

"Me? I'm just fine. Tell you, what you need to do, get that man out the hall something to drink. I sit here, can smell the need coming off him even worse than his fear. It settle ever thing down round here, you do that."

"I can do that. I was inclined to deny him."

She shook her head at him. "Naw, don't do that. He suffer, we all gonna suffer."

"I'll do it," Norman said. "I need to put those horses up anyhow."

"You seen the ice busting out the river?"

"Yuht. Godawful big chunks shelving up atop each other, riding and jamming the channel broken in the middle."

She nodded. "Been years I seen that. Used to love I was down to see it. Don't get round like old times, me."

"I appreciate you made it down to here. That horse would've rode double, I bet."

"Less far to fall, them snowshoe." She grinned at him. "Get on, put you horse up and fix that doctor, him be hurtin pretty good by now I bet."

"Yuht. I bet." He turned to the bed, Leah watching him. He felt awkward, oversized in the room of women. His sister in the straight chair by the washstand. She'd gone out while he was talking to Marthe and was back in her skirts. So he only settled his gaze serious upon Leah and said, "I'll be back."

She said, "I know."

To Connie he said, "I'll take care of your horse." As he went out Leah asked Connie about the ride uphill. Then he pulled the door shut. The doctor was missing. Norman went downstairs and found him in the kitchen standing over the range with a fresh cup of coffee. Norman pointed to the door to the cellar steps and said, "Down there's a piddly cask of applejack. Cider in the barrel's not bad too. I got to care for my horses; then I might join you in a tipple." The doctor raised rheumy eyes upon Norman and gazed at him hard, the look of a man caught between being found out and deliverance. He sighed and slowly twisted his cup in the saucer, his motion deliberate, calibrated. He pursed his mouth and relaxed it open. "The girl is fine?"

"She is."

"I feel I'm no help here."

"You're here come help is called for."

"That's right." The doctor twisted the cup a final time and let go of it. "You need help with your horses?"

"No," said Norman. "Go on down cellar. Could be a jolt'd do us both good. I'll be only a couple of minutes." Thinking, Let him go ahead and satisfy himself without being watched and then catch up to him before he's too far gone. Thinking that inside himself was the same dweller owned the doctor; thinking his fields and woodlot and numbing round of work was not so different from the sweetened bite of drink. He wondered what it was for the doctor. And wondered if he'd grow to know his own more as age came to him. Hoped it would not be so. And saw no reason to believe that. So he scooped up Marthe's bearpaws to set in

the entryway where the webbing would stay cold and coatless went out
into the night, leaving the doctor to himself.

In the yard Pete and Tommy stood head to head, the one still in the
cart shafts and the other trailing rope lines as if tied to the ground. Both
swung heads to regard Norman as he came forth from the house. Steam
rose from their nostrils and light ice lay prickling their raised coats. It
had gone cold. The breaking river was a distant thing in the cold-stilled
air. Norman was ready for the relentless deep thawing of April; ready
for April altogether. What it was bringing. He went to Pete and lifted
off the bridle with the makeshift reins and set it over one of Tommy's
hames. Freed, Pete went for the barn. Norman dropped the cart shafts
from Tommy's harness and went to the head of the horse and rubbed
his bristled nose with one hand, breaking off the ice beads and warming it. He tilted his head back to look at the constellations: Orion overhead but swinging now to the south as well as the west. Wherever heaven
lay, he doubted it was out among the stars. He didn't know where it
was. He didn't touch the bridle but laid his hand along the muzzle of
the horse and said "Step up" and took his hand away. The horse followed him to the barn.

The lamp wick was guttered and the chimney fouled with sooted smoke,
the room weaving with shadow seeming to crawl the walls and sprawl
away on the ceiling; the contraction that woke her was a hard stab that
broke a gasp from her, waking her from a dreamsleep of contractions
and constrictions, the feeling of not being able to get her breath and
immediately as bad as they were it was better to be awake. She had slid
down the pillow bolster and sideways and so righted herself quietly and
squirmed to a body comfort. The room was empty of people but for
Marthe who sat collapsed into sleep in the corner rocker. Leah lay in
bed silent, taking long steady breaths against the next building pain, not
wanting to wake Marthe or anyone, not yet, wanting to be alone with
this while she could. When they came the pains were of such violence
that they seemed to seize her and each left her with long moments of
tear-eyed breathlessness. Then she would calm and gather toward the
next. She thought to herself it was like having fatal hiccups and almost

laughed aloud. It was nothing like that but the idea brought out a half laugh.

And then was lonely, not the loneliness of a child or the aching want of love felt when meeting Norman but the sharp desire for her mother, needing her mother there and then in the room with her, that need a brittle ache, a gorge in her soul: her mother. And that ache magnified with knowing nothing of where her mother was or how, even trying to see her, to envision or conjure something of her face. She would be a young woman still; for the first time Leah realized this. They knew nothing of each other. If there had been a way to send word someway she would've but there was none. Not even a letter. It had been as if in fleeing the old life she'd fled all the way into herself. Alone. How else to judge yourself and measure what distance covered if not through the reflected lens of parent or sibling? All this gone from her. And the wanting, the desire, was as if attempting to send a letter to a younger self. And so this left Norman. She felt a great fear of him, never once expressed and never would be. How could she explain that what she loved terrified her? He would understand and seek calm for her and so misunderstand completely. What she feared could not be reassured. The ones that can so simply destroy can never know they hold that power. Told to his face he'd laugh it away or at most watch her as a stranger for a day or two before falling back to his old easy rhythm with her. She knew his life too was shaped by hers but his was of solid construction: of granite rock, hardwood, black-turned earth. Hers was not even spiderweb but the dew-beads strung there on a summer morning.

And thought then again of her mother, birthing Leah at fifteen or sixteen, younger even than when Leah left home, birthing her in the small rank cabin alone with only the old woman Rey for aid. Rey probably all the help she needed, looking at Marthe Ballou sleeping in the corner, her mouth sagged open. Those old women always around someway. Witches, nearly. Knowing more than is good for them to know until you need them to know it. And wondered how her mother must've missed her own mother then, the little girl having a baby alone far from home. And was less lonely then, as if seeing all this stretching back made more sense for where she was lying and how. As if someway her mother was there with her. Knowing she would want to be was as if she were.

Leah held her hands up over her face and between contractions wept silent into them. Oh God she wanted her mother.

When she took her hands away Marthe was watching her. Not moved in the chair but for her eyes open. A faint gray light smeared the window and the room was cold. Leah wiped her nose with the back of her hand and felt the pain reach and sear deep in her and went through that all the while looking back at Marthe. When it was done for this time Marthe leaned forward in the rocker and said, "You all right there, you?"

"I guess so. Seems like this baby wants to be born."

Marthe stood. "I thought maybe so."

It was a gray day. Dawn brought vain thin color to the underbelly of low rolled cloud and the wind turned and it was warm. Time to time spits of rain or sleet fell. Norman and Connie did morning chores together and in silence, each with their own aches from the night before and each with their ears strained, leading their whole bodies through the work, listening as if striving toward the silent house. The faint *ping* only of rain on the tin barn roofing. A little after nine Glen Clifford arrived in a high-wheeled gig to fetch the doctor for a man with both legs crushed during the night when he slipped standing too close on the heaving riverbank beside the bridge in Randolph, the man trying to watch out for ice lodging against the bridge abutments. Glen back in an hour without the doctor, who found the man dead and repaired then to his home to sleep away the night's long nurse at the applejack, sending message with Glen he'd come if needed. Glen and Connie sitting at the kitchen table drinking coffee while Norman sat and fiddled or stood to pace, the house holding so easily the drifting down of drawn groaning and small choked-off cries. Midday Connie warmed food that none ate save for Norman, who ate a whole loaf of bread sliced and spread with butter. Then terrible cries rose and rose until they seemed to be only one long-drawn pitch of a soul fighting to escape itself and Norman bounded the stairs to the room where Leah drove him out with her cursing of him: God damn you Norman What'd you do to me Goddamn you. Marthe catching him at the door to stroke his arm, telling him to pay no mind, it was the pain of it; she needed that fight; it would pass. He went back downstairs through the kitchen to the cellar to draw a pitcher of cider but when he carried it back to the kitchen Glen was gone again and Connie was over the range, pushing back and forth the copper boiler and the big kettle and several smaller pots all filled with water, as a commander keeps all craft standing to in formation before a stout wind. All she sought was each at a constant simmer. He sat alone with a mug of cider but could not stand the cries and rose and carried the cider with him to the barn, where he sat in the small shop room on the south side and sharpened tools and watched out the window at the spring weather rolling in. And so missed when Glen returned carrying Mrs. Pelham with the fey Breedlove woman as familiar or shadow or simple reinforcement but when Norman stepped forth from the barn midafternoon he saw the livery's best covered carriage, the wheels caked with mud and the underside coated above the axle, and knew then not only who had arrived but also that Glen would one day soon marry his sister. The carriage was no vehicle for weather thus. He wondered if the use of it had been approved by Clifford the elder or if the son had taken it upon himself. Either way the meaning of it was clear. And went to the house to find the women silent in the parlor balancing cups of tea on knees drawn together, each listening not only to the rising and falling of life searching up the stairs but also to their own memories or hopes. Glen twisted from his stance at the window to duck his head at Norman. Norman spoke to the women and left them there, taking Glen to the kitchen to pour him cider. Now on the stove alongside the simmering pots was the great lard kettle, bubbling. As the men sat silent Connie came in and began to turn doughnuts into the lard and out again with a wire hook. She piled a plateful and carried them into her mother and Breedlove. Norman and Glen stood beside the stove and ate them as they rose and were drained on brown wrapping paper, the grease on them scalding the roofs of their mouths. The broken open sweet steam rising of sugar and yeast.

Norman felt as if each of his bones and joints and muscles were weakened to breaking. As if he'd been holding himself upright against a descending sky. Almost as if back with the long marching. His eyes ached and brimmed red. If not careful, his hands would shake as he reached for one thing or another. The cider helped only in that he no longer felt as if he'd fall down. It had been a long night with the doctor and at some point during it he'd failed to anticipate the day. Believing she'd hold out the short weeks left. Now he felt a sickness through him, not of his own making but as if he'd failed her some way. Some way he could never call back. Never do over. Her cries overhead had gone off now, had faded to deep grunts and body-drawn groaning. He had decided she would not live through this. He had decided he could forgive no one. Least himself. His revulsion was complete, near to panic. He stood eating doughnuts.

Then the house was quiet. He walked the kitchen. Connie came down and using thick rags lifted the copper boiler to carry up. He offered to take it and she looked at him and said no and went out. He listened to her footsteps up the stairs. Then quiet again. Then the single cry: high, torn, slicing keen as a razor, new. Raging into life. As if thrust from the womb and also torn from the breast of a greater, kinder mother. As if knowing no kindness had been done it. Furious rage. One raw gulped-out cry. As if knowing all the souls within the house straining to hear that cry knew this loss and so welcomed her joining them. Or had forgotten they knew it and so welcomed her as surrogate to themselves. That cry then: new, and very old.

Norman went upstairs to view his wife and daughter as soon as both were washed clean and swaddled, the child in lambskin with the fleece still on and Leah in a fresh nightgown and with the bed changed and the room cleared of the bloodied and soiled linens and toweling—Leah still sobbing and shaking, holding the child to her opened plump breast—and he went to the long narrow closet built-in and drew out an additional quilt and spread it over the bed, drawing it up close under the infant. Then Leah raised the child from her breast and the girl was silent as Norman held her, down before his chest as a small fragile piece of firewood, gazing into the puckered face with pinched closed eyes, holding her thus and feeling nothing, a small scrap of fear only and nothing more. The fear then nothing more than fear he might drop her or not hold her right. He'd expected something other than this but could not say what it was. So he only held her silent and read her features and looked to Leah and asked what they might call her. And Leah spoke her name, not as a question, not as a possibility but as an arrived-at thing and he shortened it and so it was done. Then he handed her back to her

mother and Leah slid her gently sideways until the nipple brushed her
mouth and the girl took it. And Leah, no longer sobbing but still racked
with shaking, turned eyes up to him, eyes hooded with a bliss he'd seen
before there and that seeing now ran a tremble through him, as if seeing something he ought not to. Leah smiling, her face etched with light
over the long drain of fatigue, telling him to leave them then, telling
him to send his mother up. And he looking down at her, his body and
brain jangling, still had the moment of himself to bend and press his
cold lips to her hot forehead before righting himself and agreeing he'd
of course do that.

And so descended the stairs to find his mother at the parlor door, her
face wary and soft at once, a small woman lined and frightened and
radiant, close to tears. He touched her and told her it was a girl and for
her to go up, and heard her tread the stairs, her steps tentative and gaining as she went; not the first time in six years she'd been in the house
but the first time she'd climbed those stairs her feet knew as her own,
and he swung out into the kitchen thinking there was all too great a
pain in this to make sense of, too great to hope to change and yet no
different than it could ever be. It was all he had and it made no sense.
In the kitchen Marthe and Connie and Glen sat at the table, too high-
spirited for him to understand and he went past them, saying nothing
but what he had to, refusing Glen's help as he worked into his chore
coat and went out into the young dark for the barns.

He fed and watered his stock and loaded the stoves in the brooder
house and the laying barn and left the egg gathering for the morning,
working through what should take near two hours in half that time.
Working as one who gets the job done quickly not only for the stilled
mind while doing it but to return to the tremble run through him as
soon as he could. As if the brief time away was needed but nothing more.
And came out to stand in the dark, the warm night, the clouds boiling
overhead before a three-quarters moon. There was no sense to his life.
He'd thought the child would bring it, that glimpsing her would run a
charge through him and clarify his faults and gains. There was none of
that. He supposed it would come, someway. He supposed he would love
her. He guessed there would be a time he'd cut his arm away from him
if only for her to use as a club to batter him with. But he felt none of
this. He felt that love was only one more weight working to drag him

bit by piece down into the earth. He kicked the toe of his boot into the soft deep mud and wondered why since he knew his destination anyway he couldn't savor what came before. He wondered was he selfish. If melancholy was just selfishness. He looked overhead. The sky was a turmoil. There was no mirror there. The sky was its ownself.

His mother came out of the house and found him. Stood before him a long beat, studying his face as if reading all of him there. She did not touch him. He gazed back at her, not caring how much of what she saw was true or not. After a while she reached and touched his arm. She said, "You've got a lovely baby girl." She paused and then went on. "She won't have an easy time of it. But what a time you'll have with her."

Named Abigail, they called her Abby. Eighteen months later the second girl, Prudence, called Pru, was born. Then twelve years would pass and they no longer cared or strived for another. And so the boy was born, named James for Norman's father. But Leah would not call him Jim or Jimmy. His sisters raised him as much as his mother at first; later instead of her. It was they who named him Jamie. He was as beautiful as Abby. He was a nightchild and would not work. He craved sensation of all sorts.

Three

In the late summer of 1890 the
Randolph Fair featured the African Behemoth, a six-foot-five deeply
muscled man who at thirty-minute intervals would step onto a low stage
in a darkened tent lighted by gas footlights, wearing just a loincloth, his
body freshly oiled, and for ten minutes lift an ascending series of weights
while the standing crowd passed hand to hand a two-foot inch-round
iron bar that would then be handed up to him. He'd take the bar by both
ends and in slow strain so that each muscle of his legs and torso stretched
and jumped bring the two ends together, the bar forming a loop. Ad-
mission was a nickel. In a box by the barker were the bent bars, available for a dollar. The real event was at night, in a barn or a clearing in
the woods, depending on the town, where for ten dollars all comers could
step into a ring with him, throwing down their ten dollars against a five-
hundred-dollar pot to last three minutes. Again, depending on the town,
this was advertised or not. The fee was high to discourage all but the
confident. The fights were bare-fisted, with disqualifiers of the gouge
or bite. Some men he'd fight slowly, with great patience and skill, holding them off and striking only to slow them down. Others he'd approach
and dodge their first or second strikes to come up and hammer them
with one great closed blow behind their ear or the base of their skull
and end it. His choice was not a reflection of their ability but also did
not seem arbitrary but rather some reaction to the man, some reading
of him that had nothing to do with ability as he stepped into the ring
made only by the pressing of the watchers. The African man did not
speak during this; only from time to time would a grunt or suck of wind

come from him. When his man went down he'd turn and walk to the low stool next to his manager, who was his barker by day, sit on the stool and wash his head with water from a bucket, drink from a dipper and stand for the next. Almost always the last contender of the night would be the local strongman, often the smith. He'd treat these men with great respect, grinding on through the never-ending space of trod earth and blows given and received and turned aside until the bell was close and the crowd grown silent. Then he'd slip his right in under the squared-off sparing stance of the strongman and bring it up hard to the jaw and watch the man's eyes turn as if searching something far back in his mind. While this was occurring he'd swing his left around to clout the side of the man's head and step back then, waiting, while the man would go to his knees and sometimes struggle there a moment before going all the way down. If he was in a town three or four nights he'd face many of the same men twice but almost never the last one of the first night again. It got easier as the nights went on. He knew his opponents. Immediately he knew which were drunk to face him again. He watched always with the repeaters for the flash of a blade; only once had he been cut. He broke that man's eardrum. Most often, though, he did nothing more than what each man called for. His back was laced with raised scarring, as if a badly made fishing net had been buried under his skin. He shaved his head and body hair each morning. He received a quarter of the take, day and night. The five hundred dollars had never been paid out. He had a small cone-type tent he pitched in the relative safety of the fairgrounds or deep in woods at times he divined to do so. His manager called him Ben, the man's corruption of behemoth. No one knew his real name.

He'd seen them before in the small scattered towns of the deep north where chance or circumstance had washed them up and left them and so the second afternoon in Randolph he knew more about Leah than she could guess when he looked upon the small crowd as he faced them, hoisting the weights more slowly than he needed to, and saw the tea-skinned woman flanked one side by a beautiful girl of eighteen or twenty and the other by another beautiful child, a small boy of five or so. He knew she'd married a white man most likely during or just after the war and come home with him. He knew it was probable that he was the first Negro she'd seen in a long while, if not since leaving wherever it was she came from. By her dress and manner he knew her as a well-off countrywoman who held herself at a remove from most of the whites around her. He was reasonably sure her husband was not among the crowd and wondered if he'd been at the fights the night before and guessed he'd not. With his eyes vacant and unfocused he watched her as he bent the rod and saw the satisfaction come over her face, as if they'd done the job together. He knew she would seek him afterward to speak.

Outside the back of the closed humidity of the tent where the light was rose-infused, the afternoon was bright late summer, hot, pellucid. He drank from ice water and without swabbing the oil from his body stepped into the red silk pantaloons he wore between appearances but left his chest and feet bare. His job now for twenty minutes was not to mingle but be seen. Long since he'd lost fear of being attacked in daylight by a man defeated the night before. The time or so it had happened his response had been rapid and effective and he knew he was better not thinking about it. He enjoyed these brief saunters through the crowds, his great bulbous head rising above those around him and the space that didn't generate from him but the white countrypeople who surrounded him. In its way this was when he was most free. Both his upper front teeth were gold and he enjoyed baring them in a soft almost kissing smile to any who'd meet his eye. He enjoyed the confusion this smile would create. He was forty-two years old and had eight thousand dollars in a bank in Brooklyn and wired more each week. He wanted ten more and already knew the building he'd buy with a good hardware store on the first floor and living quarters above. He needed to own it outright and the rest of this season and all of the next would do that. He knew always there was a risk in what he did, the risk of being cut or shot, but believed this would not happen for no good reason other than it would not. He paid great attention to the men he fought and made extreme effort to humiliate none while still delivering what they needed. It did not matter if they understood this or not at the time. He'd learned long ago that understanding almost anything was what happened later on.

So he stepped into the crimson pantaloons and tied tight the drawstring waist and bent then to tie the cords that brought the billows tight to his ankles and had just straightened from this when she came around the back corner of the tent. The beautiful girl was not with her but the young boy was, and he was not disappointed by this. He'd had enough of young women in small towns and the mother up close was pleasure enough. Still, he wondered why she'd not wanted to meet him.

As she came around the backside of the tent the woman said, "Scuse me." Her voice pitched and gay, nervous and off. He turned to her. The little boy back a pace, led by his mother.

"Well, hey there," he said, giving nothing but still grinning at them.

The boy said, "You're one blacker-than-soot nigger."

The woman protested. "Jamie."

The man ignored her and squatted, still not down to the boy's level but close. He said, "Jamie. You're mighty high-yellow yourself."

The boy pulled back against his mother, frightened, the words meaning nothing to him, not reassured by the kind tone. The man went on.

"You're just a little boy. Plenty people think, Little boy like that, he don't know when he's wronging somebody. They let it slide on by. They think he don't know no better. But he does. He thinks, I got away with it once, I can again. Maybe so. But someday, somewhere, be someone won't let you get away with it. And you'll be thinking, I got away with it all that time, why this person get so upset now? And you'll be thinking, Must be his fault not mine. But you'll be wrong." And reached out before the boy could shrink further and took his small shoulder in his hand and gave it a gentle squeeze just strong enough so the boy understood the message if not the words. Felt the boy quail before the touch and then push into it. And stood and addressed the mother, speaking to stop her apology before he was even all the way up. "That sounded like a lecture ma'am. Didn't mean it to. Just trying to warn him off."

Her features were alight. On a white woman would be a blush. "He knows better."

He nodded, grave. "I'm sure he does." Then, again without waiting for her, he stuck out his hand. He felt like a caretaker. "Name's Ben. Unless you want to call me African Behemoth." Grinned at her with the absurdity of this. Now more glad than before that the daughter wasn't there. Wanted nothing before him to diminish or compare this woman to.

She took his hand, her own as strong and calloused as he expected. She said, "I'm Leah Pelham."

"Missus Pelham." He dropped her hand. "Picked a pretty day to come out see the show." He waved his hand as if indicating not only the surrounding fairgrounds—the livestock tents and permanent exhibition buildings, the small neat grandstand above the harness-racing oval and the clawed field of the ox-pull, the thrum of the afternoon crowd, the smell of food fried or sugared or both, the giddy quaver of children's voices set free, the cries of stock and fowl from the tents—all this but also the day itself, his hand rising to include the sweep of sky, the dry hot air of late summer. As if it were all that and not himself she'd come to see. As if he were ancillary, even merely an accident.

"I heard you was here," she said, not diverted. "I haven't seen another colored person since eighteen and sixty-five. I know there's a family down to Grafton and some others up round Burlington. Likely some I haven't heard about. But I haven't seen a one of em. Where you from?"

"I seen you out in the tent, figured you wasn't just after watching me bend iron. I been doing that the last year or two. Before that, Brooklyn, New York."

"I mean before that."

"Uhh," he said. "Down home." He spat. They began walking along the backside of the midway, the tents of the freaks, among them Siamese twins which were nothing more than a pair of Holstein calves floating in a tank of liquid in eternal embrace. Stepping around tent pegs, chairs with the seat caved or gone where the performers rested or took air or privacy between appearances. They hadn't talked about it, they just walked, walking as they did the slow outer perimeter of the fair, the hidden backside. Once moving the boy loosed himself from his mother and went ahead, staying in sight but darting in and out of the ropes, up close to the freaks before veering away, not looking back but seeming to know his range.

Walking, she reached and touched the roped scarring of his back. "Seems to me, you too young to have that."

His voice still almost amiable he said, "Some of us, ain't never too young. You, you left there and likely think everything changed overnight. And look at you. You was in the house. You was in the house all right."

She said, "We was town people. Wasn't but four of us, colored anyhow."

He looked down at her then. "Your mama must've been a pretty girl."

"They was evil everywhere, town or farm."

He nodded, walked on a few feet and said, "South Carolina low country. Rice, some indigo still then, cotton on the higher ground. I was in the field time I was six–seven."

"My people come up from the same place, North Carolina. I never seen it but down along the coast. Big rice country there, the home place."

"Your people."

She looked at him. "Both sides. All the same thing, comes to me."

"My daddy was on one of the last ships come into Charleston from Africa. 'Twenty-three. Wasn't legal then but that didn't stop em. He was a great big man; next to him I ain't but a shrimp, so I hear. White people so goddamn stupid. They bred him out, all over the place. I got brothers and sisters I never heard of. Making bigger and stronger niggers. What they expect gonna happen? White people so goddamn stupid."

"You got outa there."

"Oh I got out all right. I got them Union men to thank I spect, same as you. Thing is, it wasn't like they was happy what they was doing. It didn't have nothing to do with me. Those soldiers, I never met a one didn't hate niggers as much as the next man."

"Maybe not all of them."

He looked at her and shrugged. "I spect not for you."

"You no different than anybody you talking about. Everything lined up according to how much you high color or low."

"I ain't stupid."

"You and me be as wrong about people as any white person. You know that's true."

"I never met a decent white person till I got to New York."

"You met one there or every one?"

He walked beside her awhile. Then said, "Sure is a lot of snow up here."

"I like the snow. I like that weather."

"That man of yours. He treat you good?"

"He's the best person I know."

"Uh-huh." Walked side by side, almost touching for a bit, Jamie out before them, ranging like a tethered wild thing. The man said, "You look like you done good."

She deflected. "I worked hard."

They'd come all the way around to the dirt track. The drivers had the standardbreds out, circling the course in loose clumps at a slow trot, warming the horses, the sulkies small low-seated benches over hard rubber wheels. The drivers with legs stretched out along the shafts, boots against braces. The horses straining, held in. Time to time one or another driver or horse, impossible to tell which, would break loose from the clump and surge a brief spate before cooling back to the pack. The races would be at sunset, cool for the horses with enough light for the crowd. Jamie was up on the white board fence, holding the top, his ankles stretched down for the bottom board. When he heard them behind him he came down off the fence and turned away from the horses to watch them come as if he were interested only in his mother and the man.

They stopped there. The horses long-legged, beautiful. She put her hands on the top board and held it. She said, "You got somebody down there in Brooklyn New York?"

"No." Not telling the truth for the same reason he wouldn't reveal his real name. Not for any reason but his own.

"That's too bad," she said. "You deserve someone there."

"Time comes."

"Why you keep fighting these white men?"

He watched a horse and driver. Rubbed his hand over his pate. Weary now of this northern country colored woman. Sighed. "It makes me the money. And it's what they want."

"What you want too."

He shrugged. She looked at him then, the first time since they started walking. Sizing him, he felt, knowing something of his deceptions, what he was leaving out. She said, "You ever been to North Carolina?"

"Been through."

"Place called Sweetboro?"

"No, ma'am."

"Just wondered." The boy was watching the horses again.

"That your home?"

She was silent. Then turned to him. Stretched out a hand and without waiting for him to take it said, "Been good to meet you."

He nodded. "Leave it be," he said. "Don't mess with it. Whatever it is, it ain't gonna be what you want or hope. Sit right here and raise up that wild child." Then took her hand, her hand right then for that moment all of her, and it wasn't just his idea but her clear beaming through. And he felt she'd taken something from him, he couldn't say what. The same or worse than sleeping with her.

She said, "I'm not going nowhere. Nowhere to go. Just curious is all. Stupid curious." She snorted through her nose, contempt at the notion. Then curt and he knew it was all done. "Good to meet you. Watch out yourself."

"Watch out for that boy." The child was back on the fence, half through it. She turned toward him. The man called Ben walked away then. He'd missed one of his tent shows. Docked pay. For nothing but to fill some stranger's vague desire for a touch of something long gone. Nothing to do with him. He held the anger of this inside his chest, wrapped there like a single thread around a ball of threads. Walking away, he saw the daughter watching him from the shadow of the oxen barn, her face not a scowl so much as contempt. Her arms crossed over her breasts, hands holding her upper arms. The same long curly hair as the hair of the little boy, shining like crow feathers. Keeping his course he passed twenty feet away from her, giving her no smile but a glance flicking her away. The girl arched one eyebrow.

She lied. She lied to herself when she first heard about the man at the fair and again when she saw him. Beyond that she didn't know how long the lies had been occurring. As if a small phial secreted deep within herself had twisted open some long time since, releasing a vapor that ran all through her, tainting her blood and coloring her vision over everything, so everything became a needle-click off-center the way a compass will fault close upon a certain mass of particular stone. But lied to Norman when she declared no interest in going to see the colored strongman and only knew it then, knew also she was going, would go, the next day. This way discovered she'd been lying for a long time. And could not trace it, could not attribute it, could not even offer specific charges against herself, no instances, no examples, no small disguised misdeeds, but rather as an aroma rising off of her so long it had become familiar as if indeed her skin gave it off rather than her mind. Or her soul. She thought it likely it was her soul.

And so that morning driving the phaeton with the light team of fine pretty sorrels into the village and beyond to the fairgrounds with the somber Abby and solemn-pitched Jamie she knew already she'd made a mistake, knew it was more than bringing the lie to life but once done she'd have no choice but to follow it back to the source, to let it drain her as a blown beaver dam drains a spreading new-grown marshland and reverts it to meadow. And drove forward, her stretched arms directly linked through reins as extensions of her own drawn tendons to the arch-necked prancing horses. Driving someway toward herself with no excitement but the prickling of inevitable fear. Fear delicious over her as a rupture.

So tied the team in the carriage shed and hung net bags of hay for them and then with great elaborate gravity toured with her children the livestock sheds, the swine stretched on their sides, some with suckling young, the pens of ewes and lambs and the single great curled-horn rams, the teams of oxen, the dairy cattle, which barn ended with a half-dozen stout high-sided pens for bulls, the plough and dray horses, the barn beside the track with the racing horses some of which had arrived in their own railroad cars and finally the barn layered with stacks of wooden coops keeping fowl, the hens and roosters and a handful of fancy feathered and to her mind useless birds. She went through this last with greater speed, already knowing what the countryside had to offer. There were none of her own birds there.

They went out then, passing the buildings of foodstuffs and handi-works and onto the carnival edge beyond the racetrack. Here she fed her children but did not eat herself until they came to the ice-cream vendor, where she took up a paper cup and wooden spoon and ate peach ice cream. She hadn't tasted a peach in years. The chunks of fruit fortified with sugar and folded into the frozen sweetened cream churned flavor that ran over her tongue and down her throat straight to her heart and she could not finish it. Her eyes rimmed wet in the dry rarefied air. She thrust the cup to her young greedy son and without meeting the eye of her elder daughter hurried beyond the tents to the privies set there, locking herself inside standing upright, blotting her eyes and nose with a handkerchief, with great effort making no sound. She wanted water to wash her face, to flush her eyes, but there was none. She emerged and passed around the waiting line and found her children. Wordless still she took each by a hand and led them onto the midway. They found the barking voice of the white man outside the tent and she more than the children gazed up at the broad strip of canvas with a terrible African depicted, a grotesque, breaking horseshoes with his teeth. She paid the fee and they went inside.

Afterward, after she'd talked with him, she stood there by the rail with light dust from the circling trotting horses raised up in a thin pall over the track, the fingers of one hand tracked onto Jamie's back to hold him there against his desire and impulse, her eyes lifted off to the hills beyond. It was a curious moment. Her mind was still, without thoughts, yet she sensed profound change, as if her mind would not yet allow words to what her body already knew. Her soul. As if arrived at a point neither guessed nor glimpsed but inevitable once there. And not as if directed from any source outside herself but a small persistent pip burst free of her core. She felt calm, enjoying the calm before the welter of thought and doubt. It was a peaceful moment there in the sweet heat of the end of summer with her hand upon her youngest child's back, both watching the flashing horses and the silk-jacketed men driving them, the land lifted around as known to her as the boy's body, the air holding them in perfect stillness and lucidity. It was the last peace she'd know and a part of her knew that too, knew at least that it might be. And still when Abby came behind them Leah knew she was there and turned before the girl reached them and said, "Let's get on to home. I've seen enough, if you have."

"I never wanted to come but for you."

"Well yes, you did your good deed then. And without killing you. But you might take the frown off that pretty face."

Abby scowled. "What'd you want with that pathetic man anyhow?"

"Umm," Leah hummed. "Just to see him, talk to him."

"Everybody else seen you talking to him too."

"Sooner you stop worrying about what everybody else thinks, the happier you'll be."

"I don't care spit for what anybody says. Never did, never will." Contradicting herself and not caring. Not even seeing it. A blazing heat coming off her.

Leah wondered if she and her mother would ever have reached that place together. Likely. Sudden tight focus with all peace gone, Leah said,

"And there was plenty odd about that man, plenty frightening to the truth. But not one thing pathetic, not that I saw."

"Mama, he's a sideshow freak."

"Oh, no." Leah shook her head. "Not to me he's not. Not to him either."

"I was flat humiliated, watching you two stroll and chat."

"No, you weren't either. What you were was scared to come talk to him yourself."

"I'm supposed to want that since he's a Negro?"

Leah shook her head. "No. I guess not."

Abby deflected, turning the criticism back at her mother. "I'd been more useful staying to home and helping Daddy and Prudy with the hay. You didn't need help from me."

"It was good to have you here. But you're right, its time for home."

Jamie's hands wrapped and locked around the top rail. "I want to stay. I want to stay and watch the fast horses."

"I spect you do." Leah unwrapping those hands finger by finger, closing one of her own hands around his as she freed it. "But we're going home now." Abby already trailing off toward the carriage shed, a long figure in a white dress tight at the waist and dropping close around her near to the ground, small ruffles at her shoulders like wings breaking through, the sleeves then skin tight down to the wrist. Leah steered the boy after his sister. She said, "Those horses'll be back another day."

She drove the team south back through the village emptied for the fair and on along the river another mile before turning off for the farm road, passing the scarred cellar hole where the Doton house had burned the winter Jamie was born. The hole was already grown up with sumac and black-raspberry canes, the big shade maples still standing and the burned-back lilac clump once again vigorous. She recalled the bent-over old woman who walked with two canes and who'd made no friendly effort toward Leah until the children, the two girls, had been old enough to pour down the hill and snare her with a child's natural grace and ease. She remembered, too, the adolescent girls at her funeral service following the fire: Abby sitting erect, the only movement the slow glimmer of tears tracking one at a time down each cheek, and Pru hunched into the pew as if her grief were a thing dragging her toward the floor. Pru then and forever after held by abject terror of fire, the nightmares that followed only subsiding with time but never gone, not even when Norman placed sap buckets of water in the corners of the girls' room and also beyond in the hall. And Leah driving home from the fair past the still-black foundation stones seeing this of her two girls as if holding a kind of photograph of each, some measure complete of each. Not an image as much as a sensation: each held not just as child or young woman but all of life, a totality of each. She could not say the same for the boy-child beside her on the seat, his hands over hers on the lines, his bow mouth chirping the horses on. It was not the simple definition of his years. She feared for him.

Going up the hill to the farm she knew she was going back. Not home, which spread around her, running deep from the earth like streams into the air and through her each day with husband and children and livestock and livelihood; not home then, but back. Back, back, to a place not so much of memory as of the scrambled fraught dreamland of the last twenty-five years, back to seek sense of that jumble, back to unthread and reweave that nighttime fabric that often as not left her upright in bed re-skinned in sweat and a patina of terror ill defined or all too clearly marked out. Back to reclaim all this and make it her own. Back to learn fates, not least her own. Back to learn who was living and who dead, who was remembered and who forgotten, who remained and who drifted to dust. Who perhaps was sought and if so who was left to do that seeking. And to what purpose. And so to learn herself anew. Coming up into the dooryard of the farm looking over at the bright proud hurt daughter of herself already older than she was then, looking as if to see if a hint was there of how to compose herself for this trip. And there was. And there was none.

Knowing this effort to learn herself again might be empty, hands raked through cold coals. Knowing also it might prove disaster lying content these years until she returned to face it or be snared by it. Knowing this was the same risk and danger central to her life in the same way she followed the wounded Union soldier boy who proved to be Norman for days through the countryside of Virginia and then finally, with no greater proof than the notion she must, descending to find him again to see how and in what way he recalled her. And clearly calmly understanding that this one success held nothing toward a second. Which was in its own way more reason to go than not. Everything at risk. Everything to be lost. Which she knew was not the same as failure or mistake but rather the thing essential to being allowed each day to draw air into her lungs and put one foot before the other. Walking out from house to barn of a warm summer evening was a simple thoughtless thing, at worst offering up a dead hen or sick ewe or a bare foot glued with chicken manure. Walking out there in the midst of a January storm drawn inland off the coast lacked even the vague premise of reaching the gone-to-shadow barn. Each had to be done, the way every fall forkful of turned-up potato soil has to be hand sifted for the small buttons and larger caked clods to reveal the unbroken smooth-skinned food underneath.

Back, then, and back to what. It was not a childhood longed for. But her mother first. Her mother surely. It seemed plausible Helen would be right there, if not in the rank squalor of Mebane's slave cabin then somewhere close by. A colored section of the town. Some small simple place of her own. No longer a young woman but maybe to have gained a husband and even a family of her own. Leah knew it possible her sudden arrival might bring pain, the past made vivid. So be it if it came to that. For all of them. Also as likely, there might be no trace of her. All Leah knew for sure was one way of living had been swept off and in that sweeping surely people fled, went off wordless into the night as she had. Her mother perhaps among them and perhaps even to well and good. And knew too it was more than Helen; wanted also to see what had happened to the town, to the place itself, to the white people. Wanted to see the Mebane house still four-square or broken to rubble as the cellar-hole just passed. Not even sure she knew which would satisfy her. And beyond all that, less precise and yet also in an odd intangible way, of considerable and terrible weight, wanting to know again something of the place she came out of: Beyond the people, otherwise from circumstance, to regain the place and so give form to the vague imagery of dreams. Be September and still hot, pale skim of redclay dust over everything, dulling even the leaves on the trees, the big oaks of the Piedmont pastures and the live oaks and magnolias of town streets all dulled with dust, only the loblollies and white pines shedding it but their needles still pale in the heat-shimmer. Lawns burned back. The midday breeze hot moving hot, the evening air stilled, the sun grown huge, the color of split peach as it dropped to the horizon smudge. September, she thought. People working in the tobacco fields at dawn, figures of clothing in the green waist-high fields with morning mist already burning away from the grinding sun. Children back to school, the streets empty even first thing in the morning. A good time to come in quiet and quiet as she could learn what there was to be learned. The span of summer lengthened out before the fall with people slowed almost without hope for the first cool day. Nobody even likely to pay attention to one strange colored woman off the train. What she hoped for. The advantage of being unexpected. Surprise.

She let Jamie drive the last five hundred feet to the barns. The sorrels quickened with the barn in sight and immediately she let him have the lines he stopped chirping for speed and held back the team, his feet propped against the dashboard and his legs straight, using his body weight to hold the team in, calling to them, his voice high and serious without excitement or fear. The horses' hooves clipped up off the dark packed earth like sticks off a drumhead, the geldings swinging smartly in the dooryard to come up before the carriage shed beside the horsebarn. Jamie sinking back slowly onto the seat, still talking to the team.

Leah sat a long moment on the carriage seat, not long enough for her daughter to look up from unhitching the team but time enough for the sudden sharp recognition of her boy—that whatever streak of doubt and tremble ran through her had made its way into the boy redoubled and been born a new thing altogether, a coiling anger that he held tight to him as another boy might a penny found. Held secret and deep until it was needed. She knew Jamie gained this from her and knew also that neither his sisters nor his father recognized it yet. But they would. She was confident and sad near to weeping that one day they would.

She could not bear to imagine what it might mean for Jamie, what it would bring to his life. Not yet gone, she knew he was what she would leave behind. What would remain of her. What was most true.

Norman and Prudence spent the afternoon putting up the first of the last cutting hay of the season, he on the ground and she on the wagon bed, the black Percheron mares drawing the wagon along the rolled-up windrows, undriven, their lines wrapped loose around one of the front uprights, the mares knowing the course by the length of the windrow, walking at the precise pace it took a man to fork up hay. It was hot and airless in the meadow below the barns and Norman worked bareheaded with his shirtsleeves rolled halfway up his upper arm. Pru on the wagon in a loose dress and barefoot with a wide-brimmed straw hat with the edge of one brim sheep-chewed. Norman felt a piker and delight at once, ambling and lifting the forkfuls up to her where she dipped her fork to take his hay and lay it into the load, building the load around and under her as if making a many-layered shingled roof, laying each forkful down in tight crosshatch to the next. The method let her finally stand atop the high mounded load as they drove secure to the barn, where she would hand down the forkfuls in reverse order. She wore the hat against the spray of cinnamon freckles that lay over her body top to toe as scales, barely letting her skin the color of dry tangerine rind show through. Her hair a soft brown as if sifted with ash. Her eyes wide and deeply set and beautiful like her mother's, the color of broken shards of pale green mason jar under water, flecked close to the pupils with gold specks only visible with light reflected in the right shade if you knew when to look. She was a short-bodied young woman, thick-waisted and thighed with upper arms strong as a man's, reminding Norman of his younger sister. He knew she pretended indifference to her looks and did not like herself. He knew she placed great distance between body and mind, a distinct opposite to her sister. He knew her heart was laced with despair and loathing. They'd never spoken of this.

They talked as they worked.

"Sister's about driving me up the wall with her mooning around. Everything's a production of sighs and sheep's eyes. Sits gazing off daydreaming and then hissy-fits I ask her to help with something. Then, just like that, she's mean as an empty purse. The other day, yesterday it was, she turned on me all the sudden. We were washing up after supper and I said something bout how fun it'd be down to the fair today, all the boys she'd see there, something like that, and she brought a hand up all wet with suds and thumped me right here"—touching the end of the fork handle to her breastbone—"and said, 'I ever say anything about getting married, ever, you whack me over the head with a stick.'

Irked me, I tell you. I wanted to say, It bothers you so bad stay home and make hay." Her face frustrated and amused, wet with sweat, stubbled with stuck chaff. She moved with the rocking track of the wagon as on a rough slow sea.

Norman, walking and lifting the forkloads over his head now, had less wind. "She got her heart broke. That's not easy, ever."

"Huh! I told her."

"Well girl. Told's one thing, knowing's another. One fine day you'll learn that firsthand I'd bet." Sweat burned his eyes each forkful lifted up.

"Me? I'd know better. All last winter I told her. I said, Have your fun but don't be making plans out of it. That Dan Martin's eyes wander too fast too far. Horizon he sees don't begin to rest on these piddly hills. Shoot, I told her, it don't even start there. She said, Yes, Daniel has ambition. I said, Ambition's not the start of it. He dreams on things you and I can't hardly imagine. You know her, placid little spitfire turned on me and said, Don't be telling me what I can't dream of too. So I shrugged that off. And besides that, what I didn't tell her was her lovely old Dan didn't mind wasting his time running his eyes on me. Think about that. But I tried. Tried to tell her."

"She's learned it I'd speculate."

"Not any too fast, seems to me."

Norman walked along, forking up a bit. They came to a windrow end and paused while the team rounded the headland and then started down the field again. In the bright afternoon light the windrows seemed rich rolled bundles of summer standing against the shorn pale stubble. Dark and fragrant, each with its own small shadow running alongside. Norman began to fork up again. The load was growing, the lift greater. He said, "Don't make too small of it. Love's a wondrous thing. Most honest people, it's almost all keeps them going. Otherwise you get pale imitation, some business scheme, some meanness to other folks, maybe bypassing it all and handing it up to Jesus. All that's good I guess, I mean maybe not good but necessary. But you love someone, find someone loves you back, that can't be beat. Now it happens, happens often too, one loves more than the other. Maybe all the time it's like that. Just depends on how great the gap is. Your sister—well, she found too big a gap. Like I said, that happens all the time. Mostly, all it does is teach us better what to look for."

She was high over him now, a figure backlighted by the lowering sun. "That happened to you? Some girl? Before Mother?"

Slow and thoughtful he said, "No." Then a pace or two along he said, "It might've. But that age, all I had was a war to worry over. Then I met your mother."

"Yes." She laughed down at him. "The rest is history."

"History to you."

Fast back she said, "You bet. At least part." And was quiet then a bit and finally spoke again. "Well you don't have to worry about any of that with me. I plan to stay right here and die of old age."

"Think so?"

"No man'll be coming around chasing after the likes of me. I'm nobody's fool." Wiped her face with the back of her hand. "But I spect I'll make a fine old maiden aunt to Abby's babies. And little firecracker's too, his time comes."

The back of Norman's head ached down into his shoulders from the sun and the lifting. He guessed she knew herself exactly and the ache in his head ran through him for her. Light and swift he said, "Ten dollars is what it'll cost you, the day you come singing a different tune to me over some boy."

She grinned down at him, her teeth a flash in the dark halo of hatted head. "Fine with me. Just don't be trying to pay no taxes with it before it comes."

Evening dusk of late August. Not the long soft dusk of summer but the short blue cool twilight of autumn. Where the fall began. Still the girls were out on the lawn playing croquet, the passion of Abigail learned the summer before and not abandoned the evening in June she came home and announced she was through with Daniel Martin, the only information she shared. As far as Norman knew, with any of them. It was possible Prudy knew more, either directly or through her divination but as could be expected she would share complaints with him but not intimacies. Nothing from Leah either, and here he knew it was because she lacked any more knowing than he held. He held anger toward the boy but useless without specifics, the same rage as when Abby came home tearstained from her first day of school. He sat now in the comb-back rocker by the window and watched them: Abby intent and serious, deadly with her mallet, Pru careless and idle between turns, watching the bats slipping from the barn eaves, her mallet held over her shoulder like an axe. Before him on the carpet his son belly-down up on his elbows over a magazine. Norman did not know the extent to which he read but knew he spent a great deal of time page by page. Beyond the boy Leah sat on the sofa, hands holding each other on her lap, her knees drawn together, back up, her face alert, curious, determined. Also, alarmingly, kind, as if holding great patience toward his final understanding. He was wasting his time, what that look told him.

Because of the boy he was congenial, conversational in tone but the boy lay away from him and so Norman was free with his face. He scowled at her and mildly said, "No."

She lifted both eyebrows and said, "Didn't ask yes or no from you. Unless you weren't paying attention."

Again he said, knowing already he was saying it to hear himself say it, to know he had done that much at least, "No."

"Norman."

"Well it's a crazy idea. Craziest thing I ever heard. All these years worrying and watching out and then like that—*bam*—you're wanting to go back there. Now you tell me, how does that make sense?"

"Good lord, I stopped worrying about anybody chasing me down years since. Don't tell me you're sitting there and been worrying on it every day since 1865. You know's well as me that time's long behind us."

"I worried about it. I thought about it. Truth to tell, with the years and these children and just plain getting used to having you around, there've been times it bothered me more than it ever used to. Just the thought of it. Thought of losing you. So don't sit there and tell me what to think."

"I'm not telling you what to think. Just telling you what I'm doing. What I got to do. You think about that. Put yourself in my place."

"I can't do it. I can't make sense of it. Some things, it just seems to me, have to be let go. You have to look around at what's here, here now, solid and sure. Ask yourself, Can I risk all that?"

"I don't believe I'm risking much. It's twenty-five years and I'm just going in and out. You got to recall, I'm not going to stick out there like I do here. Plus, I know what I'm looking for and what I'm not looking for. I know that place."

He heard the creep of uncertainty there and did not move in the rocker but to take up his pipe and tamp it and strike a match. Sucking, he looked out the window. It was a purple pane, with the lamp reflected in waving duplicate. Still, beyond he could see the girls. Playing on until dark. Like the young, he thought, to ignore night when it came. Again, and he sensed it would be the last time, he had the poor pleasure of saying, "No. You don't know anything about it. Whatever idea you have is bound to be wrong. That much time, what they been through, it's all changed. It could be worse, even worse. You don't know."

"Norman. I'm talking about my mother." And on this last her voice came up and then down hard, hard enough so the boy looked up from his magazine to study his mother and glance over his shoulder at his father. The both of them sat through this. When his head went back down Leah went on, her calm and tone regained. "You could understand that. I made problems for you and your mama, no denying it. And you wanted you could blame me even for her choosing to be distant from you, from all of us, right here, her right in this same town. But Norman, it was you went down the hill to be with her that time she was so sick. You could do it. And it was you that next spring who carried her up here to see the little boy named after your father. And was you helped shoulder her coffin from the church and stood there while it rained down onto her open grave. I don't know and never will what I cost you from her but I know I never cost you those things. Never once cost you what you had to do. So allow me the same."

Norman pulled on his pipe. The girls were in the kitchen now, eating something. Smoke like fluid ran out into the room, curling around the heat-draft from the lamp chimney. The world had just tilted a degree off true, everything etched vivid, precarious, delicate. He felt it in him precise as sorrow. Already knowing she'd deny and all the reasons for it, he offered a final quiet amendment. "I'd go with you."

And knew then the true reason for the kindness in her face, knew she also felt that sorrow. Her smile broke him. He felt held static by everything—her need, the children there around them, everything surrounding him. As if all conspired to hold him there motionless and voiceless, unable to change a thing: unable, finally, to help her. She smiled sad and kind. "I know you would. But you can't."

It had been a hard year. A hard winter and spring, a spree of events that seemed to Norman at the time to conclude by coincidence in June with the failure of Abigail's year-long courtship to end in engagement. At the time he was disappointed for her but not displeased; the young man struck him as the type as likely to rack a string of failures as to succeed. Now it seemed the summer might become merely an interlude of peace, perhaps even bittersweet, as clearly as he saw disintegration ahead. Some lying there waiting for him to notice and some coming surely with Leah's journey. Graduated, Abby talked of finding work as she drifted through the summer and he knew she would soon, either in the village or farther away. He did not know her mind. And Abby would not be long without a man, he was sure. Even Pru had just a year of school left and for all her talk of staying on the farm he mistrusted this also. With her, he knew at least a part of her wanted that; it was the other part of her he suspected might spring to wild and sudden flight. And hoped for that even as he hoped against it. So the summer hadn't even truly ended yet and already he was feeling it as the pain of a long-lost tender time slipped away forever. He thought he might be growing sentimental with age but knew better; he'd always been that way. And wondered if it was truly sentiment that allowed him to recognize the small reprise of grace after the sour and frightened winter.

Which began late in January when Hiram Howell became turned around in the depths of the small gore behind Mount Hunger in a snow squall while tracing a gut-shot deer. The storm was sudden and brief, lasting no more than an hour, but whited him out and left all backtrack or blood-spoor lost in snow cover, left him in the steep reach of the gore already gone to twilight even as the sky above streamed with mare's tails bright in the winter sunlight. Fearing the night and the cold that would split trees, he took fast bearing off the feathered clouds, the way the sun struck them, and made the choice to climb the steep east side of the gore with hope to reach before dark the low Ballou house tunneled back into the mountainside. Norman knew what that climb would be like, in waist-deep snow going near straight up all the way; even with a good crust to the snow a man would break through where the spruce grew close or the granite outcropping above held briefly to reflect the mid-day warmth. He knew the temptation to panic and move too quickly as evening fell and so risk footing on a boulder ice-cap and go down to fracture anything. Giving up, as the cold slipped a sleep over you, a gentle sleep sweet with relief.

But Howell didn't slip and made it up onto the blessed shoulder of the mountain just as night came on and found the track and Ballous' almost right before him, as if he'd been led there. For, as he told and retold, when climbing from the gore he had no certain notion of where he might come out and worried all the way up how to make the choice of right or left to find that shelter. The house was dark and the chimney cold but as he said it didn't concern him at first for with people like that you could never count on them being or doing any one thing at any given time like anyone else. He knew also that no one, perhaps least of all these wood-folk, would mind a lost man at dusk coming in to warm himself and spend the night, to even eat what provender might be had. At least, he'd told himself, pausing by the shut door, there would be tea to warm him and, as likely, something harder than that to heat him. So he lifted the latch and pushed the door open and went into the dark house from the dark woods.

Even with the leveling effect of the deep cold he smelled it as soon as he stepped into the dark house. Smelled it and yet, as he seemed to enjoy telling over and again, was not overly paused by it, thinking it just a condition of the dwelling, the aroma spread of those who lived there. So got his mittens off and dug through his opened coat to his waistcoat and found his match-safe and struck a match to find a lamp and took up the grimed chimney and twisted up the wick and lighted it. And there, then, in the slow flickering spread of light began to know he was not alone. In the low rope-strung bed lay Marthe Ballou, face up and, strangely, atop the covers. It was only when he lifted the lamp and went close that he saw the blown hole in her forehead, twisting up her face as if in protest, the hole ringed with a ridge of crusted frozen blood. One arm thrown up backward as if it once had grasped or tried to grasp the newel post of the headboard. The skin of her face odd to him, strange in lacking the ambered cast he knew to contrast with the splay of white hair spread around it, the hair, now as always, waxen and coarse. Instead she was pale as if drained finally of the taint turned upon her, her skin like apple flesh married to high-winter twilight blue. He stood over her a long moment before he understood that the white was frost settled upon her, raised in fine rimes along the hairs of her upper lip and eyebrows. Bedecking her nostrils.

What he did then he did not tell but was easily and correctly parsed: He turned from the dead woman still holding the lamp and returned to the table, where amongst the squalor was a demijohn of applejack. When he heisted it, it proved half full. He was chilled through, tired, shocked. He shut the door left open and keeping his back to the dead woman made a fire in the stove. Then sat at the table, his back still to Marthe, and let himself warm as the stench rose. During that he worked at the applejack. The woman was dead and so nothing could be gained by rushing things and more importantly he felt himself if not near-death then terribly fraught with his afternoon and the climb out from the gore. So he sat and drank and then, head down on the tabletop, slept. To wake in a scant few hours with his head a miserable thing, sitting atop his shoulders with all the malice and panic of a carrion crow. Suddenly and acutely aware not so much of the absence of Ballou himself as his presence. He poured a kettle of thawed water into the firebox of the stove and stepped out into the winter night lighted vague but clear enough by a sickle moon to lift his narrow long Green Mountain snowshoes from the snowbank he'd stuck them in earlier and set off. Leaving behind his own hunting rifle, which was free of incrimination by being one of the newer lever-action .30-.30s and so clearly not the murder weapon. And made his sick puking way around the mountainside breathing all the way not the frozen night air but the stench of death that rose off him clear as his own vomit, all the way around the mountain until finally he came out on the far side and there was able to pause and breathe deep the keen fresh night into himself. And decided he was done with deer hunting. Then made his way downhill toward the valley until he came to the first farmhouse, where he beat on the door and roused Leah first and then Norman. His panic so acute at that point that he sounded reasonable and calm, as if relating events happened to another.

* * *

Much later, in those bleak endless days of early November when with a fervency never known Norman wished he was out of his head, that all that had passed was a midday recollection of a single nightmare image, when he would once more try to unravel the unknowable down to a single thread or moment where his doing or saying something other than what had been done or said would've reshaped the world to come; then he would trace back and come down to that midnight clamor of Hiram Howell, the news he brought. He could go no further back, could not allow himself that, could not allow the jump back to before he knew her and she him, because to do that was to make clear irrefutably some meaningless measure she'd attached to the twenty-five years side by side. So he determined, once and forever after, that it was the murder of Marthe Ballou that turned something in Leah, something sinister and unknown, something greater than any simple human hope or desire or struggle to live, the bit unraveled that brought the whole net to collapse. As if she were to blame for Marthe.

    It was Abby drove the sleigh on the hard snowpack to carry Hiram Howell with his tale to the village constable, Pru left at the house with the sleeping Jamie, while Norman followed Leah up and around the mountain on snowshoes, Norman carrying his deer rifle. He finally getting ahead of her as they approached the cabin, quiet and dark, the door open to the night. Norman lit the lamp and Leah went to Marthe. Norman stood over the table a long moment, then swept his eyes over the dark reaches of the cabin and, without speaking to Leah, went to sit vigil outside, squatting against the dark side of the house, away from the lighted door. The table had been swept clean, a rubble pile of dishes and debris on the floor to one side, only the applejack jug and Hiram's .30-.30 left tabletop, the rifle balanced upright against the jug, pointing at the open door. Not the work of Hiram Howell. Norman sat with his deer rifle across his knees, letting his eyes roam the reach of light and dark—snow lying between spruce and hemlock, the stark boles of hardwoods, the darker upthrusts of granite—watching for movement, the simple flex of a treetrunk or boulder as his eyes passed over it. He had no distinct sense of being observed yet knew Henri was out there, perhaps out of sight of the cabin, perhaps not. After a while of seeing nothing, his leg muscles began to cramp and he rose and walked a long loose semicircle before the cabin, once glancing back at the door and then advancing steps into the woods before standing still. There was no noise, no scent, nothing. He spoke into the dark. "It's Pelham, Henri. Just me and the wife. Others'll be up soon though. You might's well come on in and set and wait. No sense staying out there. No need carrying this any further, is there now? Come on and set, Henri."

Stood like that. Knowing his voice, even low, carried well into the woods. Feeling the cold settle through his bare neck. There was no sound, nothing at all. He had no idea if he'd been heard or not but felt he'd done what he could. He turned and went to the cabin, pulled the door shut and dropped the inner bar into its brackets, to wait then for those coming from the village. He sat at the table, his back to where Leah sat with Marthe. Coming in he'd seen her, sitting the edge of the bed, holding the dead woman's hand between her own. He sat facing the door. Studied briefly again the arrangement of rifle and whiskey and then took Hiram's rifle and laid it flat on the table, pointing away from the door. It was bad enough without that flaunt of malice. With no idea why he was covering anything for Henri. So sat and waited, listening to the monologue as conversation occurring behind him.

"I knew something was wrong up here, Marthe. Something terrible wrong, the last week, ten days. Told myself it was just my imagination. Thought it was too cold to hike up here to see you. Thought you'd come if you needed. I did all those things you do, except to come up here to see after you. Selfish me. Just selfish. Told myself any afternoon, any one of those sunny afternoons, you'd come swinging down the hill all bundled up to see me. Always me. Sit the kitchen with you and drink coffee and watch you tease the girls, fuss over that little feller like you done. So all my knowing, that was nothing next to what I wanted. All I wanted was you. Birthed each and every one of my children. And you, old woman, damn you, always seemed to know just when I needed another soul to come on in my kitchen and set and talk. So old selfish me, never once gave thought to what *you* needed. Was always you had the answers to my stupid problems. Stupid. Unhh." And Norman sitting at the table facing the barred door heard behind him his wife strike herself and did not turn but could see her leaning low over the dead woman, still holding the near hand between both of hers, could hear her sobbing. And did not turn. Or speak. Because he knew she would not want or welcome him then.

And heard her, the same words low, over and over, "Marthe, Marthe. Goddammit."

Quiet then. Norman still at the table, still not turned. Listened to his wife breathing, sobs dry, free of moisture, hard and wracking. Lifted the deer rifle from his lap and placed it along the table edge, parallel to him. And placed both hands over it, one high up on the stock below the barrel and the other low on the butt. His hands loose, just resting there. Waiting in the night for the sound of approaching men.

Henri Ballou was not found until late spring when a fisherman stumbling through a swarm of blackflies in a small bog at the steep head of the gore stepped into the stench and followed it forward to where a brook emptied down the mountainside into the bog and there wedged between two boulders was all that remained of Ballou. Sweet ferns uncurling their heads between his legs, rotten clothing falling away showing the blackened flesh dropping putrid from the bones. A pair of great jet northern ravens rose rasping against the intrusion. The assumption by that time largely placed him thus or fled north to Canada. But the weeks following the discovery of his murdered wife had been otherwise: Ballou was everywhere and nowhere, a goblin of the woods and night. The search parties found nothing or, worse, maddeningly confused sign: a careful scatter of hemlock branches laid to a pattern none could read in a clearing of fresh snow empty of track or trail. The men searching, nervous and gun-happy at first, soon grew languid, half-hearted. None truly wanting to be the one to round a bend and have Ballou step from the evergreen screen. As word went out after Marthe was brought down to the vault, awaiting spring burial in the paupers' corner of the town cemetery, the grown sons drifted into town and out again, singly and in pairs, none helpful or willing to be for finding their father. None in the town though doubted they saw him. When the last of them went, the youngest and next to oldest, the cabin on the backside of Mount Hunger burned with none there to see the flames. Norman smelled the smoke but resisted going up to watch the blaze. Snow still lay heavy in the woods and the fire made no threat to anything. It was good it was gone.

Within a week they began to lose chickens. Young prime birds gone two and three a night. Norman was amused by Ballou's fine taste and light touch and alarmed by not so much the proximity as the level of stealth, a sharp danger in the silence employed. Even the mastiff dog belonging to Prudence slept through those first visits. He couldn't place the man directly as a threat but also knew he didn't understand the madness of murder and the following winter woods-life but felt there was something too finely pitched in the obvious delight Ballou took in the failure of his pursuit: those hemlock branches laid to a pattern none could read but unmistakable as made by a man. They locked the dog in the barn overnight and at dawn found him moved to the sheepshed, uninjured and happy to see them. Leah was raging and Norman felt played with. That evening just after dusk, when he could no longer be glimpsed from the high ridges, he carried his rifle and a jar of coffee to the main henhouse and sat watch on an upturned crate in the far corner that faced both doors. The gas lamps were off for the night but the stoves were going and he was comfortable. Just after midnight he heard the soft rasp of a latch lifted and brought his rifle up as the door opened. Beyond the door was thin starlight on snow and a figure stepped into the door and paused, sensing or knowing someway something off. Norman spoke. "You step inside the barn I'll shoot you, Henri."

No response. The figure didn't move in or out of the doorway.

"I don't grudge the food. Woods are lean this time of year. But it was my wife sitting here, she'd of pulled the trigger without a word to you. She was friend to Marthe."

Thought he saw slight movement at the mention of the name. A light twitching head motion. Still silent. Still not in or out. As if both accepted this neutral area. Or testing. Norman was calm, the rifle steady, his elbows easy as if he could hold the weapon so forever. His finger light with tension on the trigger.

"I could wingshoot you right now, Henri. Kneecap you or shoot you in the guts and haul you to town and hope you lived long enough to answer the questions. Don't even know why I haven't yet. You stand there long enough I guess I likely will."

Still nothing. The figure had relaxed, or settled as if accepting something. Not giving up but given up. Norman not mistaking this for fa-

tigue or acquiescence or least of all a moral weight. At least not the same
moral weight would welter him if the two were reversed. Someway
curious was the best Norman could believe. Ballou as if not cornered
but looking upon a new situation. Wary without fear. Norman thought
of him as a wejack, a fisher-cat, a wolverine. And then felt the tension
creep his upright arms. Knowing that Ballou was armed, even without
the figure showing it. Began to feel he was the one naked, caught and
obvious. So he used the only thing he had, no longer sure if speaking
was his own set snare or the invisible loop he plunged toward.

His voice was level, what seemed a normal tone. "I've thought about
it. A terrible thing, Henri. And now, even for someone's keen to the
woods as you, it must ride hard on you. You can go on as you are, a long
time likely. Forever even. But it won't go away. Seems to me, you turned
yourself in, at least you'd have the chance to tell your side of things. I've
thought about it as if it was me." This was not true. "Seems like, even if
you weren't believed, or as much as you'd like, you'd at least have it told.
Out there for all to hear and make up their own minds to. Not all tamped
down inside. It's the part I know would devil me. Right now, all that
stands is that you shot Marthe. No one knows the rest of it. And of course
there is a rest of it. A thing like that, why any man knows you must've
been provoked something wicked. In't that right?"

In the doorway a scrape and sudden flare. Norman nearly shot him.
Ballou held the match to his pipe and pulled, the flame rising and falling, showing his face, a map of shadow. Ballou took his time. Norman
saw the lifting wreaths of pipesmoke, after a moment smelled the sweet
tobacco drift. Then the voice, with staccato lifts and trills, as a voice used
to ravens and hemlock, strange near to lost for human register. "You
don't know nothing, Pelham. You think you do but you one idiot man.
Thinking, Them dirty Canucks, they all the same. Fuck, fight, breed,
eat and die. Same as you, yes? Thinking you got that old truth. But what
you got? Provoke? That's a woman's job, come to a man. Ain't you
learned that? So. Marthe and you woman, they friends. You ever think
about that? Sure you do. Thinking, They same as each other. They the
odd ones here, this place. The strangers. So they come together. Nothing odd about that. But Marthe, see, she don't like women. Never did.
Think about that. All them girls, ones come to her with the little same

old problem, they think they find a friend. But they not there the house after they gone, not there she turn to me and say, 'Look there old man, there go another whore for you to rut on. That girl she good for nothing now but to whore.' So, provoke you say. That ain't true. Long time gone I come to peace with her, who she is. Fine I say. Live and let live. But this winter all that changed. Man, I think I be lose my mind. She witched me. First time I understand why we never had no girl babies, raised up all them boys. Me thinking it be what a man-jack I was. But no. One night, still long November, woke up to the ring and clatter of little bones dancing round my bed. Oh. All them children. And the old woman, sitting in the chimney corner, working that cat's-cradle, fingers flash like sparks of hell, smiling that soft worn-down smile of hers, singing them same lullabies put those boys to sleep years gone. I tell you no lie, me. Wake up, think I'm having a bad dream. But lying there in the bed, them little girl-baby bones still clattering on. Not just girl babies either, but all them little babies she stop come into this world. I didn't see nothing, no. But that sound. You rattle bones and make a sound like nothing left in this world. Light shake and tremble. But with a gaiety to it. Like they enjoying themselves. Sound like the deer-mice got to the liquor and be dancing reels. Strange a thing as that would be, me, I'd of welcomed it. But she was calling them out. Them old French songs. Oh man. All them little babies. And the old woman sitting there smiling at me like a challenge. Nothing friendly in that smile, I tell you friend. And me, not able to move limb from the bed. So it go like that, you know, off and on, until New Year.

"Ignorant me. Just didn't think that one out. Man, I put her right where she want to be. House got lively then. Two–three days of that was enough. I got right out of there. Couldn't do nothing with her anyhow. Ground bound up like iron. Didn't change even when that moron Howell found her and she got carried down and vaulted. House still going like a wedding party day and night. So I burned her out. Took care of that, yes I did, me.

"Now, you be thinking, man gone off his head. Well, maybe so, maybe no. But I tell you what you don't know: I was twenty-seven years old, working the lumber camps up the Connecticut Lakes when she come down from the townships wasn't only fifteen year old. Already knew more than me, and me, I thought I knew the women upside and down.

But this girl come into Colebrook and was like she looked the men over and saw me, walked up to me and tapped my chest and just like sheet ice went in wrapped around my heart. And me young fool thought it felt hot. And you thinking, So young Ballou fall in love. But it wasn't ever no question of that. Huh. Maybe I didn't have no love in me to give. Maybe that's what she saw and knew. Point is, even then, the heart was long gone out of her. Ask me why, I couldn't tell. Something gone on up the townships likely. Maybe just her nature. Maybe the way she born. Who knows, maybe she even some mistake. I don't know. She learned that business somewhere. So. And she liked woods living well enough or tolerated it or maybe it even suited her. And she left me to my own ways much as I wanted and still enjoyed the bed well as any woman and so for long enough I thought what man could ask for more. Hey?

"So I had to get old, slow enough, maybe even stupid enough to understand wasn't anything about me. Me, I was just convenience. Just a way for her to finish up, or maybe just carry on, what was all started behind her. Like this: She seen me that first time and knew someway I was a man dead to love and so suited her fine. Because she not just dead to love her own self but wanted it torn away from everbody else. And figured I was too dumb to see her doing that or too ignorant to do anything about it if I did. See, I don't claim no sainthood, me. Me. I got no regret, Pelham. Seventy-two years old and I lay claim to three free months, three months all my own. Whatever hatred ran her bile, whatever meanness ate her, ate me too. So. This ain't the story to tell nobody in town is it? Fuck all. Tell the truth, woods ain't that lean. Sick of chicken."

And did not step back but was gone from the doorway. As if he stepped aside without moving. Norman sat holding the deer rifle that had come down sometime into his lap. Imagining the figure dark against the snow gaining up the hillside toward the dark of the hemlock and spruce. Or perhaps not even visible from the moment it went out the door. After a time he knew the weight of the rifle and laid it across his knees. There was a draft from the open door and he rose and closed it, not looking outside but to glance once to the house. He had no fear of Ballou. He stoked the stoves and then sat a long while in the dark. He had nothing to report to Leah. He'd not lied to her but in small ways and so determined to spend several more nights in the henhouse and could thus allow that Ballou surely sensed his presence. The chickens were safe. He believed they were all safe if the delicate webwork of day to day could be trusted and there was nothing else he could do. He had nothing to report to Leah.

He had nothing to report to anyone.

So on a wet day the second week of September he drove her, just the two of them, to the Randolph station early in the morning to catch the Boston & Maine that would take her to New York and the Atlantic Coast Line's Florida train. She'd said goodbye to the children in the daybreak kitchen: Abby sleep-eyed with pretended distraction; Pru erect and stiff within her soft body, worrying over the stove and packing a lunch for her mother; the boy not understanding beyond his own circuit and the gaping maw of mother gone, alternating sullen turned-down face with shrieks of demand to go too. Then they were gone from there in the covered carriage, Leah holding an umbrella tilted to her open right side to catch splash from the road. She was best-dressed in dark violet over white, her hat brim a sinuous drape enfolding the shape of her head. Her dry boots shone as wet. She had three hundred dollars in new bills from the bank in her purse and another hundred in tens folded under the lining of her right boot. They started out the drive with small talk about the children and the farm but this fell away worthless before they even reached the Randolph road and they rode silent. The rain was light and steady and the backs of the horses dappled slowly to deep doeskin red and the world was close. The road was still hardpacked from summer heat and the horses' hooves clapped a fast tattoo, sounding to Norman something like the drivers of the train they approached. He wanted some fine intimacy with her, some slight tender touch there in those last moments before the town and station. He had no words for it, knew there were none. He took the lines tight in one hand and reached his other hand and laid a single finger against her hands twined together in her lap over her purse. She did not look at him but took the finger between hers, her hands folding palms around the bole as if taking him in. Her hands were cold, moist, then grew warm around his finger.

She would be gone a week, perhaps ten days. Longer only if she found her mother and needed more time. In that event she would telegraph.

The town was early morning quiet and the station was not, as if the town had realigned itself and poured its life down through the streets to this one place. At the north station end the freight dock was beaded with wagons backed in while others waited as the farmer men lifted up their crates of late-season corn and onions and early potatoes and cabbage as well as crates of eggs and others the tall cans of milk to the men above who loaded dollies and handtrucks with the stuffs and wheeled them around the side of the station out of sight to the waiting cars of the B&M morning freight to Boston: this familiar to them; even just the day before Prudence had driven down with the weekend's worth of eggs and eighteen crates of young roasting chickens to the same end.

Behind the station, down along the tracks, visible, was the locomotive, spewing a low roil of black coke smoke and periodic spurts of steam from the brake valves, the engine a juggernaut of great beauty in the odd way of an ugly thing grown used to, beauty and terror also; just two winters before a train had derailed over the White River near Hartford in February, going off the bridge and crashing onto and then through the ice a hundred feet below to drown people in the frozen waters and the other cars collapsed onto the ice and caught fire and the people there were burned to death. Both Leah and Norman thinking of this as he swept the team into the upper end of the station from the freight docks, here the area clear with only a hotel livery and two private buggies in the ample gravel spread for the travelers. The stairs to the platform were ensconced with wrought-iron railings and at the top were twin gas globes, squat, onion shaped, the glass the color of milk with vines of balanced slender iron embracing them, holding them in place. Norman was not shy but saw in the eyes of the drummers and sample-case men dressed in their cheap fancy suits and spats the same old quick glances between him and Leah, back and forth and then skimming over him and dismissing him in his rusted black wool suit-clothes before settling on her as she came down out of the carriage. So he stepped quickly around to her side, trusting the team to stay nosed-in as he lifted down her valise and let her take his arm to climb the stairs and so pass the clumped smoking and coughing men, who up close were pasty and

tremulous and turned their eyes down or off to one side before his raptor gaze, and so together they passed through them to the station doors,
Norman greeting them as a group: "Must be early in the morning for
you fellers. But don't rouse yourselves. I buy no gimmicks nor waste time
with spiels. So save the garbage for the unwitting down the track." He
felt their hatred upon him as the doors closed and regretted speaking,
wondering already which one of them would avenge himself upon Leah
with chatter and innuendo for the trip south, his consolation knowing
they were all bound for the next town, or at most the one after that. It
was the best satisfaction he could expect of the day.

The stationmaster took Norman's money and passed the ticket back
through the grille. A small man with a fierce weave of white eyebrow
that knotted over the bridge of his nose. He cleared his throat. To
Norman the sound of a man spending too long indoors. He spoke. "Now
Missus Pelham. This is coach to New York. There you have a sleeper
to Goldsboro North Carolina. There you have coach through Raleigh
to Sweetboro North Carolina."

Leah spoke. "Yes."

The man reached his left arm to drive up the garter on his right sleeve.
"In Virginia you may lose the sleeper and have to ride coach the rest of
the way."

"But I have a sleeper ticket all the way through."

"That's correct. You do."

"So why would I lose it?"

"I can't say you will. That'll depend on the train. How busy it is. Even
I guess who's working on it tonight."

"I don't understand this. I have a sleeper ticket. A Pullman berth."

"Yes ma'am."

"And you're telling me that in Virginia that may change."

"It may. May not."

"I see." She was quiet a moment and then said, "But this ticket, it's
the same railroad. Isn't that right?"

Sometime during this conversation he tipped his head down to fill out
forms. Now he raised it again. His face was streaked, purple and reds
blotched high against his skin. "State by state," he said. "It's the same company. State by state. All I meant was to tell you that. Do you understand?"

"Oh," she said, "I do. I do."

"Probably," he said, "it'll be fine. Just the odd case; I didn't want you to be surprised."

"All I'm trying to do is go home."

"Yes ma'am. And I wish you the best with that. Me. I'm Randolph born and bred and to speak the truth, I been trying to do the same since I was about thirty-five years old. So I wish you the best, ma'am."

Leah took a step back from the counter. She had the ticket in her hand. Back, she said, "Thank you. I appreciate it."

"I just wanted you to know. And anyhow, you'll get there."

"Oh," she said, "I know that."

She stepped back again and turned and took Norman's arm and they went out the other doors onto the platform and she kissed him and mounted the train and he stood watching as she made her way down through two cars and found a seat by the window and sat without looking at him. Her face was taut and he felt the fear in her he'd been avoiding in himself and he stood there, watching her as the other passengers boarded, and still she did not look out at him. Then he watched the train pull away, watched her pull away. For a very short time he could see her and then could not. She was gone. Gone off within steel and coal into the depth of America. Gone off away from him and far back into herself, gone into the American South, that place to him of blood and gore, bones, all now gone to dust he guessed. He could see no pleasure in farming a crop out of ground fertilized so. Down the valley the whistle sobbed as the train went through Bethel. It was raining. He went out of the station and drove his team home.

Late Friday afternoon of the same week: Norman and Prudence had spent the day shoveling wagonloads of litter and manure from the henhouses and spreading it over the cropped-back hayfields and, finished with that, were lounging outside the main haymow open door, sitting on upturned egg crates, their clothes layered with the fine pale dust of the henhouse, their boots gummed with droppings. On the hillside above the house Abby and Jamie were digging potatoes, a small basket just for supper, but even at the distance Norman saw them turning it into a game, a keep-away with the girl leaning forward, her arms spread wide to try and capture the boy holding the potato high as a trophy, the boy dancing back and forth in the potato ground as she advanced on him, a stooped spread-legged ogress, swaying at the waist to reach for him, her face low and jutted forward. Shrieks came down the hill.

Norman took his pipe from his vest pocket, stirred up the bowl with the blade of his pocketknife and clamped the stem with his teeth. From the same pocket he drew out a match and leaned to strike it on the granite foundation wall behind him, his free hand up to cup the flame: a habit even with the air settled, motionless. His cheeks bulbed and loosed jets of smoke into the yard where they hung and fell apart. As of Wednesday morning, when her train schedule had her in Sweetboro, he'd lost track of her. For twenty-five years he'd known always where she was. It was as if a part of him were flayed away. The children felt this also, each to their varying degrees of understanding. The need of her. He sat smoking. There was a rage in him, held in place by the three children and by his own ineffectual ideas of where it belonged. It was general, directed everywhere but at no one thing and so finally nowhere but himself; he was a man helpless to everything beyond the simple containment of himself before his children. As if his directionless anger were a pustule buried under his skin, running the length of him. He held the pipe in the cup between thumb and first finger, the digits splayed back along the shank of the briar, the bowl hot against his callus. The smoke went off into the afternoon.

Father and daughter sat watching the two on the hillside. Norman did not know if it was the pellucid air or his worked muscles relaxing or even the bowl of tobacco but it seemed to him that the boy's cries grew and his movement over the potato ground increased—antic, agitated— even as his sister's approach of him became more grotesque, exaggerated, her torso now almost parallel to the ground above her spread legs, her arms groping, her face protruding, straggled with hair.

"She keeps that up, he'll pee his pants." Pru had a piece of split shingle from the barn siding and was scraping chicken shit off her boots, slowly peeling the smeared droppings away, her leg lifted and crossed at the calf over the opposite knee. One eye to the job, the other to the siblings. "That's a little feller delights himself with terror."

"Most little chaps do."

"Unh." Not committing herself. Then said, "Big ones too, seems to me." Cutting her eyes at her father.

"No," said Norman. "It's not so much habit as what gets hurled your way."

"Me, now, I think she's trying to impress on him how fearful women can be."

"That right?"

"Yuht."

"Boys don't ever believe that."

She grinned at him. "Have to learn the hard way, huh?"

"Why sure. Old lady nature wouldn't stand for it any other way."

"It sometimes strikes me as pretty pointless."

"That's just because you think about it, that's all."

"And sister?" She gestured up the hill. "You believe she doesn't think about it?"

"I believe"—he pulled on his pipe—"Abby is prepared to wrestle life right down to the ground and pin it there if she can."

"And me? What do you make of me?"

"Why like I said. You think about it. You ride that river, now and again notice the bank slipping by."

"You think that? You think it's wrong?"

"Oh Lord, don't ask me about the rights and wrongs. Everybody's got their own way they have to live and not really so much choice in it as they sometimes like to think. That's about it, for me."

"I pity the man she marries."

"Abby?" He spat in the drying dooryard. "She'll make a fine wife."

"Oh, she'll make a fine wife, no doubt. I just wouldn't want to be the husband is all. I expect any man's just going to get in the way of her doing her job of wifing, that's what I think."

"Careful now," Norman said. "Times we end up getting for ourselves what we think of others."

"You're pretty worried about her, aren't you?"

He looked at her. "No. She'll get over that boy just fine."

"I'm talking about Mother."

He tamped the pipe bowl down with his thumb and put the pipe in his vest pocket. "Not so much. She's capable." He paused and added,

"I fret not knowing where she is moment to moment but that speaks more of me than her. But your mother, I've not seen her faced with a situation she hadn't already figured out." And knew he was lying but could not think why just then. He said, "She'll be fine. She's fine."

Pru was not looking at him but nodding her head, which he knew meant she'd heard at least the hesitation if not the lie itself. After a moment she said, "What's it like, that country?"

"Where she's from?"

"North Carolina, yes."

"Can't say. You know I spent the war in Virginia and only met her as she was coming north. Virginia now, that was freezing mud in the wintertime and hot summers like wearing a boiled blanket. Other than that, what you could see beyond the war was pretty enough I guess. But I wasn't sightseeing and the local folks you must recall were doing their best to kill me. So I might not have the best impression of the place. There was times though, little gaps in it all, where I could see it was a fine place. I recall thinking, Why, bring in a batch of Green Mountain boys used to plowing granite and hoeing gravel and turn them loose on this and their sheer wonder at the ease of the soil would've ended the whole shebang. A fertile place. But then perhaps that's half the problem. The easier things are the more people just want, want without thinking; gratitude it seems only comes from wrestling something good from something hard."

"Sure. Like the way Abby just takes her looks for granted."

"Well, they were granted. She did nothing to get them. She's not to be envied. She knows that and I thought you did too."

"Doesn't mean it's not hard."

"Yuht. For now. But time's just an old idiot locked away in a closet when you're young. But the rascal doesn't stay there, I promise you that."

"I hate that you'll-understand-all-this-years-from-now talk."

"I know it. But that's just the thing. You will."

They were quiet then. The figures up the hill had gone back to work, the small boy beside the young woman, who bent as she pressed the fork into the ground with the arch of her foot and turned it up with a studded clod, the boy's arms darting to pluck up the food. Then Pru turned on her egg crate so her body was front to her father and reached a forefinger and laid it upon his temple. She said, "Showing all that wisdom, right there those silver hairs."

He turned to her touch. "Well, you noticed. I thought they added a nice touch, myself."

She nodded. "It suits you. Me, what I hope for is to get old. With white hair and wrinkles I won't no longer care. That's when I figure I'll be all me. Able to relax and stop chasing myself around. The same time, my plan's to stay just the way I am. I can't imagine feeling any different about things. You don't fool me, I know you worry over me. For no good reason I see. Maybe I do ride the river but I know I'm by Jesus in it."

He nodded. "That's as reasonable plan's I've heard."

She grinned again. "I think of it more as an experiment."

"Maybe you should take notes."

Her eyebrows folded up upon themselves and she studied the ground before her a moment, then looked at him. "Actually I do. Every night I write down what happened that day, maybe a little of how I felt about it. So it's there."

"Do you?"

"Uh-huh."

Now over the western ridge was a single high anvil of cumulus, blown there by winds far beyond their knowing, the edges of the cloud scalloped black with the body swollen like a dozen lumped breasts. He said, "Times, I wish I'd done that. Wrote things down. But then I wonder if the words would get in the way of the memory, replace the memory. But of course memory's nothing but what some part of you chooses. The problem with you and me, people like us, is we want to hold on to it all. We can't let none of it go. But it goes on and goes, all the same."

She was quiet and then said, "Oh. You're a melancholy man today."

He waited also but less time than she had and he said, "I've always been that way."

"I think it's a terrible way to be."

"I guess maybe so. But it's the only way I know."

They were sitting to supper in that same evening dusk turned cool when the muted polyphony of wheels and hooves came clear as a vehicle crested the hill into the farm. Norman heard it first and stood to the window and then the boy was beside him, grasping the window ledge to bounce up and down as his father peered down at the hotel livery approaching, struck still with the apparition of some news, a telegram, something vivid, worse than he could know. So he could not see what was simply there. Behind him he felt the weight of the girls at the table watching him, both held torpid with their own sense of disaster. Only Jamie was free then to cry out, "It's Mama. Mama's back!"

She would not speak of her trip and stopped the clamor with firmness. "I'm back; that's all. Don't pester me." She sat to eat a small plate of the fresh potatoes and a single slice of cob-smoked ham and Norman saw she was near trembling, each motion slightly adrift with tremor. She would not meet his eyes but once, this a chilled beseeching for solitude. She watched her plate, working knife and fork constantly to carve and maneuver the food into slight portions that from time to time she'd lift to her mouth. She told nothing and asked no questions and the room fell silent around her it seemed without her noticing but as if the silence extended out from her. Only at the end of the meal did she take the small boy briefly between her knees to press him against her and stroke his head and then her hands fell easily off him when Abby came forward to take him up for his story and bed. Prudence began to wash up after the meal and Norman rose from the table as was his custom, going to the parlor to smoke, and, standing, looked to Leah, expecting she would rise also. She sat at the table, her eyes still on the cloth before her, her hands lying on their sides on the table, thumbs and fingers forming crude cups, as if dropped there. He stood looking down at her. Her clothes were smeared with dust, ill-fitting with travel, slumped upon her. She did not look up at him. At the sink, Pru worked quickly, very quietly, her back straight with tension. She washed and rinsed and left all in the drainboard, not drying with a cloth to place things away in the cupboards and drawers but left them to air dry and rinsed her hands under the gravity line and left the room, her eyes scanning her mother and father both in one swift roll. Norman stood a moment more, the sound of the door closing a stubborn sigh in the kitchen, as if the air there were inhaled and held. Then he sat at the table again, took out pipe and pouch, filled the briar and smoked. Waited.

She sat without moving, not watching her hands on the table before her but some space well beyond them or far closer, he could not tell which. After a time she sighed, nothing more than breath gone out of her but he felt it as a vibration, a rippling out of not just her lungs but the muscles and fibers of her body, the sound more a gathering of herself than relaxation. She stood and lifted her valise from the floor and placed it on the table, undoing the clasps so it spread, a squat hourglass animal. She went then to the sink and with her back turned to him stripped to the waist, letting her clothes fall, the heap ragged and stiff with travel. She washed herself with a coarse cloth meant for scouring pots, spending great time on her face and hands before abrading her upper body. Then still avoiding his eyes she dug into the valise and brought out a cotton nightgown and pulled it over her head. She reached under it and dropped her skirts and underclothes and lifted the nightgown to bunch with a rude knot about her waist. Used the same cloth to wash herself below, a furious scrubbing, finally lifting each foot to place on the grillwork edge of the range to wash it, thrusting the cloth between the toes and working it back and forth as if to clean away the ground covered, the miles traveled. Norman watched at first and then averted his eyes but still watched, not sure if this private act displayed before him was confidence or indifference. When she was done she loosened the knot and her gown fell around her. Then she bent to gather the fine rumpled sour suit and without ceremony pressed it hard down into the valise, snapping shut the clasps to cover it all. As if it were gone from her. Then she looked at him, her eyes wide, flickering, not steady. He saw them filled with troubling, with fear. He didn't believe this to be directed at him but knew no other target. The eyes reminded him of a young horse, raised wild without human touch, now confined, smelling the upright creature approaching.

He said, "You got that over with quick." Overhead there were footsteps, murmured voices, then quiet. The supper split-wood settled in the stove firebox. He could hear Leah breathing, little rags of phlegm in her throat.

"There wasn't nothing." Her voice rough, as if her throat were scarred or skinned over, as if bark grew there.

"Nothing of your mother? No word, nobody knowing anything?"

She shook her head. Again, her voice quivering, a spent arrow shaft, she said, "There wasn't nothing."

Confused as much by her as her words, he said, "What do you mean, nothing? No town? No people there at all?"

"No, no," she cried. "Just there wasn't nothing."

"Leah." His voice opening out around her name.

"What do you want of me!"

He sat back in the chair, turned his feet out from the table and crossed one knee over the other, his sock-foot dangling. Again he thought of the wild horse, the way when touched the muscle under the hide would ripple, the sensation of being able to touch fear. He said, "Why, nothing. I can see you're wore down. You don't have to tell me about it. Not now, not anytime, you don't care to. I'm glad you're back is all. Safe and sound."

"I don't know," she said, "why you should be."

She slept thirty hours and the rest tiptoed as if the house held sickness. At half past four Sunday morning she rose and dressed in the near-dark. Norman woke also and lay silent watching her, a dim figure against the predawn panes. It was cold in the room and he thought Frost on the Hubbards to sweeten the meat. If there'd been lamplight he'd have seen his breath. He lay watching her assemble clothing from out of drawers and draw it on and this familiar everyday reassured him. He considered speaking to her but something in the way she stood before the window made him not: nothing so clear as an attempt on her part for stealth but more complicated, as if she drew clothing onto her with a focused distraction he felt more than saw. He lay in the bed not as if sleeping, knowing not to hope to fool her, but as if sleep lay still heavy over him. Once she was gone from the room he listened to her tread in the hall and on the stairs and then rolled onto his back, fully awake. He heard her in the kitchen, could smell woodsmoke as the range came up to life and sometime after that began to feel the creep of warmth. Then, as the panes boldened to stippled dawn and he was just short of rising, heard the backdoor clap lightly shut, the sound of a held-back door eased to. He guessed she was out to the barns and stood then from the bed, feeling all was well, was sliding back to old ways and counts and he dressed simply in wool trousers with a checked shirt drawn down into them, his braces snug and tight over his shoulders as if affirming the rightness and roundness of the world.

There were four loafpans of bread rising on the counter and she was not in the still-dark barns. From there, as the day came on, he saw the clear trail breaking the frost on the meadow grass above the house leading up into the woods. She had gone for a walk, was all. He went back to the house and ate a meal of bacon and biscuit, a thing learned from her. He drank a single cup of coffee; years recent his bowels could not stand more. He smoked his pipe and went to the outhouse and resolved again to consider indoor plumbing. He waited for his children to rise on their weekly lazy morning and waited for his wife. He sat reading the days-old paper, sitting in the parlor to have no view of the hillside, not wanting to watch for her.

Midmorning Abby baked the bread which they ate with beans at noontime, still with Leah gone. The bread was without salt, lacking savor and texture, tasting not so much of flour as nothing at all. Without speaking of it, after the meal Abby took the remaining bread to the yards and broke it apart for the hens and returned to the kitchen to turn up a fresh sponge. Pru hitched a single sorrel to the high-wheeled cart and took Jamie to town for ice-cream sodas. Norman sat in the parlor a brief time, his stomach rumbling from the rough lunch. His pipe held no pleasure. After a time he went out and stood in the yard, surveying the hillside for movement. Beyond the small flock of sheep there was nothing. He went into the house again, to the scarred rolltop long since forgotten to have been his father's and sat to his accounts and after a time the afternoon fell before the trickle of pencil markings into columns. In the kitchen Abby roasted a chicken for dinner, also halved squash, baked onions, the last of the tough old snap beans boiled down with salt pork as her mother made them and also turned out a pie from the select first few ripe Pound-sweets. After a while Pru and Jamie came back from the village and Norman rose and did the chores, Pru joining him after changing clothes. They did not speak. She went on to the house ahead of him with the baskets of eggs. He stood a long while in the blue dusk, running his eyes up the hillside, trying to recall just where her track had broken through the frost that morning. There was no sign of her. He thought to go up after her but knew she could be anywhere, knew also she would scorn him should he chance onto her. She was out where she wanted to be. He recalled how she'd rambled odd hours and days when they seemed cornered to be childless. He went to the house and sat to Sunday dinner with his children. The bread was rich, the chicken fell from its bones. Jamie was restless but someway that afternoon Prudence had impressed him and he made no complaint, did not call out for his mother. Perhaps he was simply sated, tired, content. Norman did not know. Then the meal was done with and the girls worked fast to clear the table and take the boy up, leaving Norman alone to smoke his pipe. And wait his wife. He woke from dozing at the table sometime before midnight to scrub his face with the fading warm water from the reservoir and went out into the moonlight to scan the hills again and smoke once more. There was nothing to be seen. Scant high thin clouds. A halo around the moon. He wanted to call her name. He tapped out the pipe bowl into the air and watched the embers flare toward the ground and die. Heard their faint hiss against the frost already down. His stomach wrenched, torn, as if the midday beans worked their way back up. There was nothing he could do. Finally, he knew he was not a man to trust anything to return to how it had been. He went up to bed and lay there cold and sleepless. Still, she woke him when she came in before dawn, woke him with the chill of her backside pressed into him. He did not speak. He knew she knew he was awake. She did not speak either.

It was not that she would not talk to them. After her long sleep and long walk the days patterned again to a resemblance of what had been but she fooled none of them, not even the boy. She was brisk, never brusque, blunt with her statements, directions, admonitions or corrections. There were no odd misplaced sighs drifting from her mouth mid-meal or mooning empty eyes glazed off into a distance only she might see. There was none of that and yet she was not quite there. As if she moved with an invisible glass of water balanced on her head, the water perhaps the liquid of all the cries, the withered shriek, the discharge of her soul, that she believed hidden from her family. Even when she raised her voice there was no emotion to it but simply a rote thing: the child spilled milk, command him to clean up after himself. Less walking through motions than some vacancy at the center of herself that all the outer layers could not completely shroud. This lack in her spread out to those around her, and the days tightened with the nut of anger drawn up a shaft of despair. The sisters fought bitterly over small things out of earshot of her and then subdued, worked with a frenzy visible to their father but not their mother to accomplish what must be done and even what might be done before she might notice it. As if their action might assuage her, ease her back, perhaps even just cause her to notice how deeply wrong things were. Jamie went through a rough patch, clinging and tearful, and his mother would take him up, hold a handkerchief to his nose, command him to blow, wash his face and utter her soothe, the same words that worked only months before, but she would now set him free and not see his eyes working over her, as he sought to find the mother he knew in the familiar form turned inside out. Or outside in. Sometimes Norman thought the boy knew better than all the rest of them what was wrong with her. More than once felt the impulse to draw the boy off, take him up to the sheep pasture with the hope someway that what the boy knew might come clear to him.

Norman with an anger swinging loose and wild and tamped down, all at once. What conversation he held with Leah he grew quickly to hate. There was nothing there but a perfunctory response. He felt played with. He felt it was not her doing the playing. But did not know who else it might be. His anger was selfish also; he felt too old for this. He was trammeled, bludgeoned, wrought to a fine spin. There was nothing he could do. He admired her skill. He blamed everything, most of all himself. For what exactly he did not know. She did not so much continue to refuse to speak of her travels as ignore his questioning. There was nothing to be said. The world was a short squat globe, tiny, that daily peeled away more and more of itself, as a vast endless onion of fine incalculable skins. Smart to the eye, right up through to the brain.

She reminded him over and again of the wild horse. A strawberry roan, bunchy little mare, got from his brother-in-law the summer Abby was six. The Pete horse was grown old and Tommy too. And there was this mare who just needed gentling. So she came. Portia, she'd been called. And what he remembered now was not her fear of mankind, which he understood and shared; and not those fine moments when her fear grew so great he felt ensnared by it, almost a rapture, as if each treaded a circuit known only to the other; and also not when he finally made enough gain with her to know he'd make no more and determined, hard as it was to admit, he was not the horseman to calm her or, easier, she not the creature to have around two small girls. While all this happened, what he recalled in those weeks after Leah returned—and this he'd forgotten for years for it had been one bad afternoon and nothing more—was the time she tried to kill him. It was that simple. Now he saw how clever she'd been, the cleverness nothing more than an animal suddenly flaring or perhaps even choosing her moment. He'd hitched her to the single-row cultivator to run through the hilled potato drills and they'd gone up the hillside above the house and went down the first row and halfway up the second, the dark dirt folding up soft and flaking like flour under his feet, the thick-leafed potato plants to either side seeming to grow even darker as the soil turned up between them and he'd fallen into the steady walking mesmerism of the job when the mare bolted: her hindquarters hunkered as she sprang away, the cultivator handles jerked from his hands, the machine tipped sideways tearing through the drills as the mare sprinted for the open field, Norman chasing half-assed behind, the looped and knotted lines around his neck and they went on that way until they came into the tall grass of the field and the cultivator tines caught and the machine flipped and he stumbled against it, still drawn forward, and fell, the back of his neck snapping hard when the lines drew tight, smacking his head against the ground. Even as he struck one hand was up getting the lines off his neck. His eyes spangled. He fought to gain his feet. The mare then turned and came onto him, raising her forefeet off the ground just inches to lunge, her lips twisted away from her broad snapping teeth, her eyes rolling huge with whites surrounding them in the sockets, the whites blared with bursting veins. She was over him, one hoof grazing his shoulder and the other concussing the air beside his head as his hand bunched tight and shot forward and he punched her hard in the soft tip of her nose. He broke his middle two knuckles and felt the gristle between her nostrils crumble and spread under the blow. There was a long time, perhaps a second, when his fist was driving hard into her and he twisted it to do as large a damage as possible. Then he sat down. The mare retreated a dozen feet and stood blowing, watching him. He rubbed his hand and only then cried out with the pain, only then knew it was broken. When he cried the mare's ears came forward, first one, then the other, then both flickering before centering forward. He cursed her. She was gone. Already gone. A canning horse. She had no way to know this. She watched him sitting in the grass, the harness askew on her, the cultivator upside down to one side. After a moment she bent her neck forward and blew again. Great gobs of excited snot feathered out onto the grass. Then she dipped her head and grazed through the timothy to the rich clover below.

He lost his temper with Leah only once that fall and nothing was changed by it although for a couple of days he felt a great relief, as of an emptied vat filled near to bursting, and also a timid embarrassment, as if he'd taken advantage of someone smaller, weaker than himself. And within three weeks would have the opportunity to rework the episode endlessly to carry as another man, in another time and place, might have carried a many-lashed short-handled whip to cut himself across his own back with, walking barefoot in thorns and nettles, hatless under a white burning sky.

He'd been on the barnfloor, cleaning the ciderpress. The cider was made, down basement in barrels, and he'd washed the tub and leaned it to dry in the sun. He'd taken out the metal workings of the press itself and these he washed and dried with sacking and then worked in a fine coat of machine oil, the oil flowing onto the metal and enriching it, the parts taking on a rich patina. Even the small pits and faults on the outside nothing more than inevitable: the abrading of time. And Norman then dropped the larger of the two gear wheels and it fell against the press-plate and two of the cog-teeth on the gear broke off and with no more effort than that the gear was junk, a thing graceful in its utility and beautiful in its simplicity now scrap. And cast scrap, not even something to be reforged or made to some new purpose. He sat looking down at it. He looked at it a long while and then sat looking out onto the farm. The press was only forty years old. He could order a new part for it but this was not the point. It was a good thing ruined through carelessness, through not paying attention. It was not an accident. He felt his mind overloaded and, feeling it, knew it to be true. He felt the stiffness in his shoulders and arms and twined through his bowels as a heat and down again into the muscles of his legs and all of him ached. It was not work. It was not age. He spat onto the chaff litter over the floorboards and cursed. A short vile spew of language meant to purge but was only coal oil on his burn. He looked again out onto his farm. Prudence was gone, in school for her final year. Abby and Jamie were up to the orchard with a single horse and the stone boat with plank sideboards, filling it with the last bruised windfalls to bring down and parcel out daily to the sheep before they rotted. High on the trees the last remnant apples clung in the wind. Some would be there through snowfall. Partridge would fly in at warm midday in November to eat them as the sugar fermented and then the birds would spin off down hillside in crazed drunken flight. Last year they ate a brace that crashed into the barn and lay dazed on the dooryard. He rose and bent to lift the broken gear and placed it with great care on a ledge of framing on the inner barn-wall, broken teeth gaping up, where he knew it would remain for years. He already wanted to save it: as reference to his anger, as reference to the day. He went to the house. His gait a stalk. Each footfall hurt and drove him forward. He felt extraordinary: taut, wakened, shrewd, elaborate, guileless, enraged, simple. Righteous.

She was in the parlor, on the year-old sofa covered in blue-black velvet with a raised floral scroll of navy. She was sitting with knees together, hands in her lap, head tilted back against the rest. Not sleeping but with her eyes closed. He sat in the peg-back Windsor opposite, feet apart, elbows on his knees, chin cupped. He waited but not long and his voice broke into the room. He liked it, liked the way it filled up the room that for weeks now had seemed to him shrouded with fragments and whispers and held-back sighs, with her lackened to a pulse just able to carry life, not even forward but maintaining a stasis. His voice brash as hammered piano ivory, he said, "You made an effort, maybe you could tell me just how long you expect to go on like this. Then I'd know, we'd all know, how much more of this horseshit's piled up ahead. Seems to me that's fair to ask. Since you cannot or will not tell me. Maybe just don't want to or don't even know whatever it was bound you up tight as a bandage on your little trip back down home. And I guess that's your business. But there's a family right here in front of you that each one wonders where it is you've gone. Even that little chap wonders where his mother's got off to. You thought about that? How it is for him? Little boy doesn't know first thing about any of this at all. All he knows is Mother's a stranger to him. Me, I never saw you the sort to let your own misery spill over onto somebody else, least of all some helpless little feller like that. Not to mention the rest of us. The rest of us can go to hell I guess. Seems like that's how you'd have it, at least."

He paused then, took breath, considered if his anger was out of him and it was not but surged again.

"You won't talk to me. All right. I don't like it but I can live with it. Maybe someday you will. Nobody there, you said. Well. I'm not an idiot. So. What you learned was not what you'd hoped for. Maybe even worse than what you'd feared. I'm guessing. Guessing since that's all I can do. Goddammit Leah, I'm tired of this. I never once stopped you from doing what you wanted or thought was best and more times than you might think another man would have. And most all those times you were right on the money. I give you that. But I'm here to tell you. Right now. I will not live like this. I cannot see the way to live like this. And I won't do it and I can't see what to do about it. So. You. It's your turn. You've got to tell me something and I don't know what it is. But you do. So."

Partway through, when he spoke of Jamie or just after, she opened her eyes, gazing up at the ceiling. Then closed them again. Her features spread evenly over her face as if calm. Or held down placid under urgent control. Or a slackness of fatigue so complete as to create a vision of composure. Or a resignation almost chemical in her, chemical if the soul were made of compounds and elements.

Her eyes still closed she said, "That boy be fine."

His voice low now, through his teeth. "Jamie. I'm talking about Jamie. Not some boy."

One eyebrow stirred, settled, a fine etched arch. "You all. You all be fine. Leave me alone, Norman."

"No. I left you alone a month now."

"You keep right on." And her eyes still closed she lifted one hand and made a throwing-away motion. "You doing a good job at it."

"No," he said. "I'm done with it. Done with humoring you. Done with watching these children try and do the same. Time you got a hold of yourself."

She opened her eyes and looked at him. She smiled. Terrible as a skull. Her eyes flat with anger, hatred. Far worse, pity. "Oh, a hold of myself. Mister you got no idea how good a hold I got. The rest of it, you be done with whatever you want. It don't change nothing with me. You, you need to learn to be satisfied with me. That's all you get. It's a terrible thing over me, ain't nothing to be shared with nobody, not nobody here. So, you think on that. Think maybe you all spared some things. I ain't hurt you; I ain't hurt them children, don't matter what you think, all of you. I ain't hurt none of you." She closed her eyes again.

He stood and, standing, did not know why he was up. He made a step toward her and stopped. Turned, looked out the window. Nothing there. Same as always, each thing of outside broken by the sixteen panes and fluid with the old glass. He looked back at her. His hands itched and worked before him, wanting to take something up, rend it, shred it, peel it off away down to a core. He looked at her and imagined striking her and felt in his chest the heat of satisfaction and his stomach wrench up with disgust. He said, "You're hurting each one of us, every day. Hurting yourself too."

"Oh Lord," she said, speaking not he felt so much to him as out into the space around her, as if it were not vacant but filled up, peopled. "Ain't hurting nobody, ain't hurting nobody no more. Can't be done, can't do worse. All I do is hold on tight and not hurt nobody. You got no idea. You can't even begin. You know it and I know it too; Lord Jesus and his Father they got more in mind than little piddly you and me and what we like or can't stand. I was lifted up, thought I was lifting myself, dropped down longside you thinking I'd been made new. No not made. Given. Thought it was what, salvation? Reward? No. No, no. I wasn't never that stupid. Thought maybe it was the chance to do right, do good, do what I could all my own. Thought that was enough. Thought that was a blessing. Didn't think it so much as knew.

"There was a before and after. One time, one place, one me. Another time, another place, some other me. Stupid bitch. That's what you ended up with. Stupid bitch. Don't go feeling sorry for yourself. Don't shrink from the truth, Norman. Stand up to it like a man and stand there, watch it tear you down, bit by piece. Like them old stone buildings blasted by the sword. I always saw that happening like a thunderclap, lightning strike. But you know something? It wasn't never one like that I bet. It was all that fine old rough stone falling apart crumble by crumble, each little chip torn off by some fool passing by. Not even knowing they doing it, all wrapped up in theirselves. Not even notice the dust and chips fall behind they pass. That's how it is. That's all they is." Her eyes still closed.

He crossed to her now, his boots inches from her shoes. He did not trust himself to bend and touch her. He wanted to strike her, smack the side of her face. Open her eyes. Make her open her eyes. His voice soft like cat's-paws, he said, "It can't be as bad as you make it. All pent up, that's half of it. Or more than half. You got to tell me. You tell me about it, it won't be as bad as you think."

She opened her eyes and looked at him, briefly. Then cut her eyes to the same window he'd looked out earlier. "Trouble with you Norman is you ain't got the nerve to tell how you feel. Or see how things are. You think it's all just you and me. It ain't that at all. It's people after people, each one nothing to the next. You don't care bout me Norman, you care bout you. Even them children you worked up over, that's all just cause they look to you. Otherwise, they some children over the hill somewhere, you wouldn't care nothing. Don't rile on me, you know it's true. Man, woman, we all just a fake thing. Carry on, great importance, nothing. Simple as that. Nothing but grime under some other body's toeprint. Nothing but waste. Everthing, it come down to nothing. Nothing at all. We just fools, otherwise. Old brother Jesus, maybe even He the biggest fool. Maybe took Hisself a little too serious. Maybe His Father, He still sitting holding His head in His hands over what a fool His son was. Maybe He don't even care about what we all think, He so caught up in grief over how His child turned out. You ever consider that? You look at it that way, you got to wonder. How else could it be?"

Norman said, "Shut up with that. Shut that kind of talk."

She perked. "What talk that be? You Jesus working on you?"

He turned without even thinking he was doing it and swept a blue milk-glass vase with a single clump of late-season asters to the floor. The glass shattered fine and disappeared against the carpet but for the small spread stain of water. Here and there in the stain the late-afternoon light caught reflection, shards invisible, fine slivers to work deep into the hard callus of a bare foot. Her eyes glittered as if struck by the glass.

She said, "Oh. Nigger talk. That what you mean, ain't it? Nigger talk."

He stood over the stain, his boots planted wide, his voice a great labor as if under a lost freshwater sea. "Your pain delights you, delights you more knowing I can't understand, you knowing that before you even try. And you sit there, carrying the burden, to keep us all safe. Now what I see, it's as if that pain owned you. As if it had made you its own. Everything else is you just fooling you. Nobody else. That's all."

She nodded as if understanding. Then her voice pitched to the familiar, the first time he'd heard it in weeks, said, "Well, Norman. You married me. Cheap little rings in a midnight river and nothing better. Cause you too much a coward to do more. But me, I don't hold that against you. You knew what you was getting. Nigger girl, nigger woman. Right through, all the way. You done yourself proud. Even if you don't know nothing. But that ain't your fault. I mean, I coulda told you, but then, why you listen? I don't know nothing more than you. Never did, never will. But, Norman, tell me this. You think you was marrying a white woman? You think I was gonna be a white woman someday?"

He stood on the carpet. Before the front drape of the sofa, just beside her left foot, lay the thick bottom of the vase, lying on its side, flanges of glass extending each separate and fragile, as an ill-made crown. He stepped forward so he was far up over her and looked down at her, waiting for her to look up, knowing his bulk could not be ignored, not then. After a time she did. Her eyes wide, wet, shining. Without fear at all. Almost calling for pain from him. Or something he could not read, could not understand. And hated her for this. He reached his right boot forward then and slowly brought it down on the glass, grinding the boot. The glass fell apart slowly, the dry sound of it the only one in the room. Then his bootsole scrubbed hard into the carpet. He did not look down, at the floor or the woman. He walked to the door and turned back only when he was already through it, holding it back from closing behind him. He said, "I know who I married. Always have. Self-pity's a terrible thing. I never thought to see it in you." And let the door close.

In the kitchen their elder daughter and son stood, backed against the sink, Jamie with his head turned into Abby's skirts, his face buried against her thigh, his hands clenching the fabric in strained bunches. Abby held a small basket of windfalls against her other thigh, the apples pocked with rust but firm, hard, the color of dried blood. Her eyes wide upon him, hard dark nuggets of confusion and fear. And some wild elation. He passed them without speaking, feeling the heat of his face, not wanting to stop moving or try to speak, not wanting them to see him trembling. He went on through the entryway and outside. Went to the barns and sat and smoked a bitter pipe. Knowing he had lost an argument, one with a form and function unknown to him. He fed his animals and did his chores. Prudence arrived home from school and wordless, joined him. He felt her watching him and did not speak. Together they went in the dusk to the house and he sat in the kitchen with his children to eat a supper. Leah had gone to bed. Later when he went up he found her sleeping deeply, on her side, her breathing a deep rhythm almost not there. He lay beside her a long while. Once she murmured in her sleep and he leaned close to hear what she would say but she was silent. He lay on his back, up against the headboard, and reached one hand and laid it on her jutted hip. After a time he slept.

Three weeks later on a drear November morning of drizzling low sky she dressed in workaday clothes and took herself up through the sheep pastures beaten down by frosts and into the woods to the spot where the granite outcroppings were jagged upthrusts with sodden moss-backs slick to a bootheel, the rocks overhung by a pair of ancient scarred maples, the northern one that marked a boundary line for the farm running back to the original deed with the same tree, and there with a length cut from the coil that Norman turned into lead-ropes and rope halters for the horses hanged herself with a simple slip knot run up to the maple limb above and a second slip knot for her own neck before stepping off the rock. She left a couple of feet of slack, enough for a hard jerk, and although her side was smeared with moss and mud where she slapped against the granite her hands were clean as if even in the last brief spasmodic effort her body continued to obey her will.

* * *

He found her midafternoon. He knew her absence in early morning, knew it was all wrong but felt hampered, harnessed by her two months' distance. He fretted through to noon, his heart a black node in his chest, a swollen painful thing. There was a moment, climbing down a ladder from the hayloft into the sheep pens when he lost himself, was overcome, dizzy, nauseated, his eyes dazzled with floating motes of light against a red field. Later he would conclude this was the moment she stepped free of the rock. He'd been forking down hay through the trapdoors and it was sometime then that he'd determined to search after her and perhaps it was nothing more than his rushing with resolution through the job and then too fast down the ladder. Still, there would forever be that long moment he clung to the simple rungs built into the barn wall, sick, weak and blind.

There was no trail to follow in the soaked November fields and then the woods, all dead flattened grass and leaf-litter already sinking into itself toward decay, toward humus, and he needed none. He knew where to find her, and he climbed up through the misting rain and as he went higher the dropped clouds, passing through ghost-boles of trees with their stripped heads waving slowly in the rocking air, those heads denuded and lost in the cloud come down to earth.

He had brought her here that first fall after the war, before even his mother had moved herself and his sister off the farm, climbing up here, Leah following Norman's extended long stride, chasing after him. He carried a basket dinner of sandwiches made of cold beans and bacon and sliced onion, apples, a piece of cheese the white of the moon and a jug of fresh cider just starting to harden. Behind the granite boulders was a spring, a stream-head; sunken earth around a clear pool with beds of ferns upright around it as if trying to hide the sweet water. In the center of the pool bubbles rose slowly and whole, to pock the surface as they broke, new water and ancient air rising from the earth. And they came here and ate their dinner, sharing an apple with carved cheese and then crushed the sweet ferns into the moist soil around the pool. And had come times after that. And then, without speaking of it, had stopped coming. As if each trip there diminished the strength and clarity and pureness of the original. Norman recalled lying on his back in the ferns, wetted with a sheen of exertion head to toe after that first time, the old maple-head rocking overhead in a wind he couldn't feel and knowing as absolute fact that something of his father squatted on haunches in the woods above and watched them, intent, approving. He knew that as sure as he knew she was all he would ever need.

No sound came from him that he would ever remember when he cleared the last ridge and came into the boulder field and saw her, an object off the ground, peaceful, not moving, her head tipped down to rest against one shoulder. The mist was not rain then, just wet air streaming against him, wet air that he moved through. The dormant woods, the tree bark, the clotted leaf-duff, the moss on stones, the texture of the stones' surfaces: all were bright-colored with the wet, each texture distinct, separate. As if to prove the relentlessness of life. Red and mustard-yellow lichens, bright as stains. The warning bark of a squirrel. Her clothing was soaked dark with water and her skin was the dull purple of blackberries dried on the stem with August sun. Going toward her, he could not hold breath. He was wildly angry with his sobbing, a mean, puny indulgence before the sight of her. Nearer, she stank of feces and urine. He took her waist and lifted her with one arm and sawed at the wet rope with his pocketknife and could not cut it. The knife was dulled. He'd not owned a dull knife in his life. He tried again and she turned against him and her face fell against the top of his head and he could not cut the rope. Finally he climbed the stone beside where she swung and took the rope in a hard turn over his elbow and held her weight and gazed off at the higher part of the maple trunk as he reached high and slowly cut it through. Then lowered her to the ground, as close as the short rope would allow. The rope end went through his hands and she dropped and lay crumpled, folded over herself. He slid down the rock face after her and picked her up and cradled her against him, her face now against his, her body held to him. He took her down the hill.

After the graveside service, when the pine box Norman had built and sanded and polished through one entire night was lowered by ropes into the earth and the Congregational minister said his last few spare words, Norman bent and took up the first handful of clumped wet soil and dropped it onto the box where it made a hollow sound loud to the hushed craned necks. Norman stood then at grave edge, wavering a moment, studying the spread clot on the honeyed wood before he turned and took up the spade and drove it deep into the mound that seemed so much greater than the small hole it had made. At the moment that he flung down the first spadeful and swung back toward the pile, his body absorbing the job of work to be done, Jamie broke free from where he'd stood framed by both sisters, a small still figure near alone but for some cousins opposite the grave amongst the adults. Jamie appeared to see no one around him throughout the brief reading of the twenty-third psalm, but at the moment his father took up the spade the boy saw his father's face black and sagged with anger and grief and tore his hands from his sisters and fled. For a brief moment the family, the minister, Connie and Glen and their children, the small number of neighbors and village tradespeople, the even smaller number of veterans, all lifted their heads from the coffin in the hole and watched the slight figure tear raging across the hillside slope away from the burying plot, his arms flailing for balance in the tight black suit, his voice one long endless wail of rage coming back to them in the still air. The sun was shining on them all, a pale washed thing before the stiffened chill wind out of the northwest.

Norman looked after his boy, then at his daughters. They looked one to the other and did not speak. Abby reached quickly to take and drop her sister's hand and then turned and walked without haste after her brother already gone from sight down over the hill. As if she knew she had to find him and knew also it would do no good. She stepped through the gap in the stone wall enclosure of the dead. There was no gate, only an opening with a pair of flanking upright granite posts with old holes drilled into them for a gate long since rotted away. The sheep grazed summers between the blackened granite stones. Off in the southeast corner an old rose had grown wild, now a thicket of bare canes crabbing together in the wind. Above the plot in the edge of the sugarbush a hundred or so crows had chosen the afternoon to caucus, their cries brilliant, jagged in the air, pitched as if to lift the short hairs on the backs of necks, the flesh on the arms, of the people gathered below. Norman watched Abby until she dropped bit by bit from sight on the incline down to the farm. He did not wait for her to come back into sight in the farmyard. He didn't look at the people around him. He turned back to his shovel. But the moment offered by his son had stopped everything in him and he bent to his work with the clear notion that this was the job of his life, that everything else had only one way or another pointed him to this. He shoveled easily and slowly now, not wanting it to end.

They filed down the hillside following Norman and Prudence, the sky hazing so the sunlight fell on them with the vapid color of old beech leaves, the wind up. In the house they stood in random odd clumps and pairings, standing up eating off plates of the funereal food carried in on platters and in canning jars and beanpots and baskets of baked goods wrapped in clean toweling. The minister, his slender work done here, stood in a corner leaning over his cupped plate like a palm tree, his hair windblown, leaving his skull shining as if polished. Norman sat at the table in the kitchen with his children, drinking coffee. Abby had Jamie on her lap, one of her hands running constant back over his face with a damp cloth napkin. He'd sobbed and screamed himself into a narcosis of grief. Norman had looked at him and at Abby and back to the boy and Abby shook her head and he nodded at her. She'd tell him later. People drifted through the kitchen to lean and speak to Norman and the girls. He watched their mouths move and their faces work and did not understand them and so mostly nodded and took offered hands, trying not to watch their eyes, loaded as they were with stark strata of pity, dread, surprise, animation and fear. Connie came, finally it seemed, and pulled a chair close to tell him she'd take Jamie for a couple of weeks.

"No. But thank you. I want us all together."

"Think it through, Norman. You can't understand him right now anymore than these girls can. Or me. He's got three cousin boys all ages surrounding him and those four can parse death in ways none of the rest of us can begin at. I'm not offering you anything; it's him I'm think- ing of. What he needs right now is diversion and people that speak his own language and he's not going to get any of that in this house for the time being."

"I'll not turn from him for convenience. His mother would not for- give me."

"There. You've made my point." Her eyes on him were delicate, bright-veined, dry. "Her forgiveness isn't something to be concerned with."

"He won't want to go."

"What he wants right now he can't have anyway."

"That's cruel."

"Norman. I'm the least cruel person you'll ever know in your life." Then she paused and he saw the hurt smirch her face. She said, "I never once truly doubted you Norman but this time I know best."

And he turned away from her, the intent and focus in her too bright to believe, all that lost to him. And turned to see Abby gazing wide-eyed at him and then to Prudence with her swollen face squirmed up with pain and through this she was nodding at him. He turned back to his sister. "All right then. A week, ten days. If he wants home before then, you'll bring him."

She nodded and laid her hand on his arm. People were leaving, and he wanted them gone. Wanted the house empty, wanted the quiet for the vacuum of his heart to spread out and join together with that other vacuum cringing back already and always in the shadows and corners of the rooms, wanted this last marriage of solitude opened to him, not to dwell in grief or memory but to live within what was there now: the vast array that he believed would number his days in a polarity to those of his life ended when she cut the length of rope, when she took the train home, when Marthe Ballou was murdered. When she stepped off the granite.

So Norman and the girls went round the house and farm and what work needed doing each day for most of a week, each tender and withdrawn into themselves, aware of the others and each also aware nothing could be offered. Odd moments the girls touched their father, he stood with their brief caress and could not touch them back, as if laying hands on them was too close to touching Leah; they accepted this or perhaps with their own swept-tight sorrow feared his. Perhaps they merely understood it. The day he drove to the village to go over legal matters with the lawyer Sutherland and meet with the banker to consolidate accounts the girls cleared the closets and drawers in his room of her clothing and effects, which he noted that evening and winced before the loss and thanked his daughters without speaking, aware his new habit of stepping into the closet before bed to lay his face among her hung garments was not a thing to be continued but a small indulgence best done with.

It was Prudence who first sought him to speak. Norman in the parlor, pipe clamped, a newspaper spread open on his lap as if any moment he'd take it up to read. A fire clucked in the grate. Through the closed door to the kitchen the sounds of Abby washing her hair. Even with the door the sweet woman-scent of soap and wet and steam. The mantelpiece clock dragged its hands up and around and down as if weighing a judgment upon him. A jurist clock. The newsprint before him only so much of everything that didn't matter. Time, after all, was not made up of small things but a spare handful of events after which the world was changed. He'd thought he learned this in the war. He'd learned nothing. Or he had to relearn the same thing over and over. Which made him doubt that any of it mattered. Of what use, the life of ignorance. The question was central, could not be avoided, could not be answered. After all, he knew it was either a small mind that found solace in the day to day or a thriving mind that found purpose. He could not say which. All he knew was he owned neither. And then heard her steps coming downstairs, pictured her before he saw her, the navy high-necked dress spread evenly with a pattern of frail fine white ovals, her feet bare, still corned and calloused despite the early snow and the chill of upstairs, the mass of uncared-for pumpkin hair, her splotched skin spread over features broad and rough and true, her body beneath the dress the duplicate of his sister. He even knew by something purpose-filled in her downward tread that she was coming to him. That she had something, some message, to deliver. And he smoked his pipe and tilted down to the paper and waited for her.

She said, standing over him, before him, her gravity keeping her from sofa or chair, "Got something to tell you."

"What's that?"

She scowled, her lips pressed. "I should've told you before now."

He slowly folded the newspaper and placed it on the side table. Palmed his pipe and laid that hand in his lap. "What should you've told me before?"

She shook her head. "It's nothing what you're thinking. Nothing to have changed anything."

"Did she talk to you? Tell you something?"

"No. It's nothing like that. No, she didn't talk to me." Her eyes flat and squarely upon him now. And he knew she was not lying and knew she was not quite telling the truth either. Guessed she held some information intuited or overheard or guessed at, arrived at in some fashion she either didn't completely trust or didn't feel was hers by right to tell him. A right she'd concluded and so was staunch by. He admired this of her as much as it frightened him; wondering what in life would wear this thin for her. Sooner or later, most everything.

He said, "What's your news then?"

"No news. Just something I got to tell you."

He waited, then nodded.

"I hate it," she said. "Hate telling on myself. Hate that I have to. Oh boy, I hate it like hellfire. Me and my big pride. Honest Prudence. Prudent Prudence. So much pride, pride like my big fat foot in my mouth. And that's what happens, isn't it. You always get found out. Little thing like a nettle gets under your skin and just stays there, burning away at you. Like a botfly dug in and festering up till the worm crawls out."

"Honey." He interrupted her. "I don't have any idea what you're talking about."

"Oh, I know it. See? Here I am, so brave, talking stupid circles."

"Why don't you just sit and tell it. Get it over with."

She drew herself to. "I'll stand. I'm not proud of this."

"I can see that." He lifted his pipe and deployed tobacco smoke to signal he held no prejudgment and was inclined to forgiveness. He was curious now, almost wondering if her design was to draw him forth. And if she intended this, how he'd respond.

She said, "When Mother caved for me to get that Scupper dog; that was—when—five years ago, six, the spring. You recall what a big rough clumsy fool puppy he was. All over everything. Couldn't stand next to a person without treading on top of their feet. Like he didn't know his own size. And lord knows he's still the same way but he's grown up some. And Mother laying down the law about his staying in the woodshed, I guess that helped him some. Although maybe its just his getting smarter, older. And to tell the truth, long as I'm confessing, there's been many a night I've slipped down to lead him up quiet to sleep with me. I always knew when he felt too left out of things. Or maybe even it was just when I needed him more than other times. But I always got him out before daylight. He's a good dog, all I'd ever ask for in one. And I think I know my animals.

"What I'm trying to tell you. That first year, when he was still a pup, Mother took one long look at him and told me. Said, You go to the barns close the door on him. Don't take him up there with you. Don't let him in. She didn't care how much I thought I had him trained or how much attention I'd pay him. Told me, That dog, you let him in the barns, he'll get in the runs with the birds. It don't matter what you do or think you're doing. You open a pen door just that much, he'll be in there. A dog's nature, was what she called it. And I did what she said. And he seemed fine with it. I mean, he'd lie outside the barn door, blowing down snow at ten below; he'd just lie there and wait on me. And I thought, Oh he's a good boy. So one day that next spring after getting him I took him in the barn with me. Thought he'd just follow me or maybe trot up and down the walkway and look at the birds. And I went to change the water in the young birds and just like she said he came right under me through that open door, barking and bouncing, all frenzied. To this day I don't think he had any idea what to do once he got in there. And of course I set down the waterer and got hold of him and dragged him out of there. Wasn't but five, maybe ten seconds. But it was enough time for them young birds, eight-week fryers was what they were, to all pile up in a corner on top of each other. Time I got him out of there and got back in to pull the birds apart there was ten or so dead at the bottom of the pile. Just suffocated by the panic. Not a tooth mark on em. And what I did then, I took those dead birds into the horse barn and laid them in a hay manger in an empty stall. And next morning, first light, I slipped out of the house and got a spade and carried them up into the woods and buried them. And I never said one word to anybody. Not anyone. Not that I put it from my mind. I always thought I'd tell it someday. Always thought I'd tell Mother. But Daddy, there just was never that right time. Since when you get right down to it I'm a coward. And now she knows it, knows it and knows I never told her. It's an awful thing. I feel like I'm found out, all of me. I can't stand it and don't know what to do."

"There's nothing to do," he admitted. "You already know the wrong of it, from start to finish."

"I know that much." A sheen was on her. "I've taken it apart one side to the other and back again. I'm seized up with it, can't get out of it. I thought telling you might help, but it won't I guess. It's just something I'm left to live with. There isn't ever any absolution, is there, Daddy?"

He wanted to tell her having children of her own would provide that. Instead he said, "If there is, it comes awful slow. But then, those chickens, we knew about them."

"You did not."

"You think Mother would've lost birds and not known it?"

She looked away from him now. He took pause, trying to guess what she was looking at. Her own reflection in the windowglass, the lamplight a pliant brass worn down from the rag. He said, "It was fourteen little fryers. That's a hole even in a bunch. And there hasn't been a child come or go out of this house odd hours we both didn't know of it. I didn't even trouble to look for the grave of them. But there were those feathers in the manger. Not to even talk about how the dog slunk for days, your eyes sharp onto him. Not to mention you slunk some yourself. So. You see."

She put her chin toward her left shoulder, her eyes still off him. "It doesn't change my not telling."

"No."

"It doesn't change her dying without my telling."

"No."

"It doesn't change much then."

He paused hard. Looked at the clock. Bedtime. Bedtime for somebody. The old life. It made no difference. What's taken for granted is not the same as what's granted. He tried to imagine himself a year from now. Five years. He imagined himself come to terms with it all. Come to accommodations. He couldn't do it. And knew it would happen, some way. He thought maybe he was the sort of person who held less and less of themselves, peeled away until there was nothing left. Some husk. The image of an old man out of his head railing before death. Again, he thought, self-pity. He said, "Only for you. Your mother, she knew and forgave you long since."

"In its way, that makes it worse."

And through all this had been the red anger lying in his belly waiting to sprout out his tongue. Which he did not know was there until it came. "Each and every one of us is alone. In the beginning and at the end and everything else in between. Anything else is just pretend. Just a moment here; then, gone. Don't fool yourself thinking it's otherwise or even that it should be. Sooner you learn that, the better off you'll be."

She gazed at him. "You don't believe that." Her eyes wet shining.

He hated himself for it, scarring her with his eyes, enjoying the doing of it. "What about your mother? What thought she put into what she did? Whatever her reasoning was, it lacked all of us. It was all about her, every bit of it."

Now her eyes changed, taking measure of him. It was an odd thing, had never happened before between them. He was less now to her and gratified for it. She said, "Why, you're angry at her."

"Of course I am."

"And you're doing the same thing you just accused her of."

"You're angry at her too. You've reason."

"No. I'm sad. Terribly sad. Sad so hard my chest hurts, I wake up with it aching. Sad for her being gone and sad she took herself like that. And I can't tell you where the one lets off and the other begins. And yes I am angry. Not like you though, not at her. I'm angry at whatever it was took her there, led her there, drove her there. Whatever it was left her no choice. I'm not so stupid to think she didn't consider all of us. Which leaves me, what? Leaves me thinking whatever it was, was a horrible hard thing you know far more about than you'll let on. So I'm angry at you too. Angry that you won't tell me about it. Angry that you didn't do something, anything. Something more than what you did. You were the one with all of us sitting watching her those last months; you were the one might've changed things, done something. So. Yes. You're right. I am angry. But angry at you. My own father, such a coward."

"Don't you talk that way to me."

"Oh I guess I will. Talk anyway I want if there's truth to it." And stood there, her head high, chin aimed at him, arms across her chest. Collected, abrupt, launched. "Look at you," she said. "all wrapped up in your own grief. Or sorrow, regret, remorse. Whatever it is. Like you're the only one with all that. Oh," she said, "you make me ashamed of you."

He sat still. His hands in his lap. A bolt in his chest. He did not take his eyes from her. He said, "Is that all?"

She looked at him, her eyes cornered. "That's it."

"You're done?"

"Yes sir. I said what needed to be said." Crying now, silent, tears tracking her face. There, he thought, you made her cry. Still believing it had to be done.

"Sit," he said.

She looked at him but did not move.

"Sit," he repeated. "I'll tell you what I know. But it's not going to be one long clean straight line that starts here and ends there. Even if I knew all of it, it wouldn't be that way. And there's more gaps than you might think in what I know. But you want it, I'll give it to you. After all, you're right; it's yours as much or more than mine. If I'd meant to spare you and made that choice wrong I'm sorry. You'll forgive me. Or not. So sit. I won't talk to you looming."

She took a handkerchief from her dress pocket and blew her nose and cleaned her face. Wiped her eyes and cheeks and then her forehead. Not watching him, taking her time. Put the handkerchief away and looked to the mantelpiece clock, as if to make her decision upon something beyond them both. Then stepped eighteen inches and swung around and sat on the sofa, sweeping her dress against the backs of her legs as she went down, landing without effort and leaning forward, her elbows on her knees, her eyes back to him.

"All right," she said. "Here I am."

He told her of Sweetboro, of where her mother came from. Not the version she'd grown up with but the version that was his. At least told her what he would of that. Told her what happened to drive her mother north those last months of the war, named the people and told her as much as he knew, as much as he remembered, as much as he fathomed of it all, speaking of emotions flared and those tamped back; attempted to explain the ties of blood both active and violent and those refused, insidious, ignored. And so again attempted witness: to make location vivid and actual, true as could be made with something he knew nothing of but knew as well he felt as his own simple surround of hills and woodlots and livestock. Except that he could not come to any comprehension of her final short journey and so only left that there, in the air between himself and his daughter. Knowing that his telling of the old was enough. Knowing that she'd accept if not understand his failure to know more than he did. And he told it slowly, with great attention and care, backtracking over and over as small details slipped up from memory to skate the surface. Giving almost everything he had of it, not for absolution or mercy or grace or even any forgiveness of his faults or failures but simply to have it out, to have it shared and so owned by someone other than himself. And the only part he would not share, the only fact withheld, that he would not allow her, was the burden that her mother had murdered, that somewhere—not at the beginning, the true beginning, but that which propelled her mother out finally—was this act. Which he would not lay upon the daughter. Saw no gain made by such a burden. And so kept it for himself. When finished he was wet with sweat through his underwear and shirt beneath his arms and looked over his girl's shoulder where she sat with sunken head and saw by the clock his telling had taken less than twenty minutes. And did not know if that mattered or to what degree. A span of time to hold another span within. And waited some minutes for response until he knew there would not be one, not then, perhaps not ever. And so knew she would rise before she did and watched her cross the room and turn at the door to tell him goodnight, her voice nearly not there. A voice lost of itself. As if, he thought, she did not believe him. As if she sensed something left out. And left him there then, a creature hunkered, hunched and broken upon himself, raw to a flaying, his hands troubled knobbed things helpless and useless in his lap, his spine and feet aching, his mouth dried, bitter, decayed. There was nothing he wanted.

In the kitchen Abigail sat in a robe with her hair bound up in a towel long after the conversation in the next room had ended and her sister had gone back up the stairs. Sat with her hair dried and knotted within the towel. Sat with the words of her father, not just the story, only parts of which were new to her, but his reaction to it all. His anger of life. As if she'd found a poem of a dozen lines that cast calm over turbulence, that made succinct the indistinct. As if a puzzle had been laid together before her and she was not surprised by the picture made, had even expected the picture, but was surprised by the hands doing the work. And understood those words to be part of a continuum for her own life, an understanding of how things are. Knew the acuteness of her own

details were the only measure of herself she'd ever have. If it was a bitter rind, that was fine; she wanted it all.

She waited long enough for her father to have followed her sister
upstairs to his own bed if that was what he was after and when he did
not go she waited some while longer in a courtesy she'd never before
felt or needed to feel for him and then rose and shook out her hair and
laid the towel over the rack by the range to finish drying and went to
him, went bearing the one tale she had that she'd share with him, the
one splice that overlaid their lives. And came into the living room where
the lamp had guttered so he lay slumped down sleeping in the armchair
in a sooted light, his mouth slack and open, his face collapsed with fatigue, his broken knotted hands resting on the arm grips of the chair as
if laid there by someone other than him. And she stood watching him
sleep only a short time before she went to the chest behind the sofa and
took out a woolen Johnson blanket and spread it over him, slipping it
up against his throat and using the edge to wipe the bead of drool from
the cleft of his chin. Then she cupped the chimney and blew out the lamp
and went up the dark house to her own bed in the room where she kept
the floor grate closed year round and the window open to sleep. Some
mornings there would be a fine peak of blown snow on the sill or the
floor beneath it. This night there was no snow, just the thin starlight of
early winter with no moon. She lay on her side with a pillow between
her thighs and both arms up under the pillow beneath her head. From
here she could see the upper sheep pastures and the hillside woodlot
cresting up against the few stars. She lay a long time without sleeping.

Next day midmorning under a dense low sky folded upon itself like
beaten tin, holding snow, Norman was out around the barns when he
heard the hard chuck of buggy wheels rising toward the farm and before it cleared between the dull barren trees he had one of those moments where he knew not only who was coming but why: more than
guesswork but as if it had happened before. And so met them in the yard
and lifted his son down, the boy with his head turned down and away
but not so much that his father did not see the blackened eye and blood-
crusted nose and Jamie fought against his father's lift and so broke open
the scabbed nose and stood then on his own, glaring up at his father,

blood running down over the etched thrust lips with his hands curled to fists at his sides as if ready to fight again, making no effort to wipe the smear clean from him. Norman stood looking down at him, not yet looking to his sister at the reins and said, "I expect the other feller's marked some."

"There was three of em."

"Unhh," Norman said. "That's a bunch."

"Bastards." The boy turned then and walked toward the house. Most of the way there the entryway door opened and Abby stepped into it and watched what was coming on steady toward her and only when he drew close did she stoop and spread her arms and only then did he break stride and run into her. Six years old in six weeks.

Norman turned to his sister. The woman he loved so dearly, with least encumbrance. Only, he thought, because they held enough remove between them. Which started with the war, that absence that allowed them both not to know each other in ways that would lead to less than cherishment. She was wrapped in wool with her lips and cheeks chapped. He said, "You beat the snow at least."

She looked down at him. "Boys are vicious creatures."

"Yuht."

"I feel to blame. I raised them to know better."

"I know it."

She studied him. Paused with that. Then, "I did you know. Maybe I would've anyway but what caused me to, was you. You and Leah."

"I know that too."

"But it didn't do any good." Her eyes like stone still hot out of the ground.

He nodded as if agreeing. "Boys run to a pack. Nothing so much as like good house dogs run off and joined up with one another. The ones'll run deer in the winter just to hamstring them. Boys don't know what they're doing. But they get older you know. Life moves them along, like it or not. Seems to me it's too soon to say if you did any good or not. I expect you did. Why, just bringing that little feller back here this morning, taking him away from them, I bet they already learned something."

"Goddammit, Norman. I meant to do a good thing when I brought him home. Not just for you three here but for him too. I didn't want more hurt onto him than he's already had."

He nodded. Then he stepped up to the buggy side. Steam was coming off the horses in the cold. He reached a hand and placed it on top of her gloves holding the reins in a tight bunch. He said, "Lately, I've come to believe we can't know which will end up as which when we do it. All we can do is try. That's all we get."

"You're entitled to it but that's a terribly sad view of things."

He took his hand away and nodded. "The view from here."

"I wish I could tell you it'll get better."

"Oh," he said, "maybe that's the saddest part. I know it will."

Now she reached and touched him, her hand on his shoulder, laid onto him a long moment before she took it away. He looked off to study the sky. She said, "I so wish I could help someway."

"There's no help."

"You'll see," she said. "You're too much a man to stay like this."

He looked at her now. Her anger so clear, contained, poured onto him. The great endless anger of love. He smiled at her. "That's half the problem right there. Being a man. I don't even know what it means anymore."

She kept her eyes on him until he looked away. Then she chirped up her team and swung the buggy around and went out of the farmyard and down the track. He watched her go. Before she reached the hillcrest one gloved hand came out of the buggy to wave at him. Crooked at the wrist like a bat in the gray air. He knew she would do this. He knew she'd know he'd be watching. He waited until she was out of sight and then turned to the house.

So Abigail waited with her story. She felt no urgency, was almost languid with it, as if emerging into a deep and true calm as to a condition essential to her nature. Took the boy inside and cleaned his face and packed it with last year's remnant ice and slowly allowed him to tell his story, the same old story just fresh and bright with pain and realization for him, listened to this and soothed him as best she could. And then sat and listened to her father try and do the same thing, the rough texture of his tenderness making the one low flare of burn in her that she could almost see, a dim knot of washed-out orange sputtering in endless neutral darkness. Something that if she could reach she would lift up and set away from her, the hands that might do that reaching thick with scar tissue, impervious to the dilute caustic acid of it. And instead rose up and began to put supper together over the stove, simple fried pota- toes with onions and bacon, tomatoes stewed and put up by herself and her mother the summer past. And Prudence home then from school and so the whole thing over again with its new variations and then the three left for the barn, the evening chores, and left her alone with the supper. And if she was not happy she felt herself well past sadness. She was an engine, stilled but not stalled, running a long track that looped over it- self again and again, circling always back to herself because it was the only where to run. She alone owned her life and was not cold to it; it did not matter how others saw her.

So she waited through three more days. She did not expect her story to change anything as much as to have everything that could be known available to her father. And herself. And no longer believed in perfect moments so only waited for something easier to spot: quiet, the two of them alone, a breadth of time. So Thursday evening sat alone in the liv- ing room, her sister and brother both in the kitchen, Prudence using the table for her homework before the warmth of the range and Jamie working over the sheets of addition his sister wrote out for him and then corrected and handed back to him. He had short patience with it and Prudence alone could ignore this and simply keep him work- ing. Norman was in the small office down the hall doing his weeks books, and after a time she rose up and went down through the dark- ness to the line of light under the shut door and knocked and waited his command to enter and did, shutting the door behind her. He waited wordless, as if knowing something of why she was there, and she lifted the stack of ledgers off the single spare ladderback chair and dusted the caned seat with her palm and sat. And with her sitting Norman laid down his pen and pushed back from the desk to turn his chair three- quarters to face her and laid one knee up over the other, tipping the chair back onto its hind legs just enough to give him the appearance of ease. And she knew he too had been waiting for her. She needed no preamble.

"I came upon her talking to herself. Not just mumbling. Like she was answering somebody. Or more like she was making an argument."

"You mean like there was somebody there when there wasn't any- one but her?"

"No. I mean like after something's happened and you figure out what you really could have said at the time but didn't."

He nodded. "When was this?"

"After she came back up here from going south."

"Yes," he said. "I figured that. I meant when after?"

"I don't know."

"I want to know," he said, "if it was recent."

"You mean just before she hanged herself."

"Yes."

"Why's it important when?"

"I'm trying to learn her state of mind."

"You think you can understand it then?"

"Perhaps. When was it you heard her talking?"

"I think it's more important what she was saying. It was maybe only a week or two after she got home."

"I see. Where was everybody else?"

"Out the house. She had no idea I was around. And I didn't show myself. I just listened."

"You weren't trying to sneak around other times hoping to catch her at it?"

"It was an accident. And just because I didn't tell her I'd heard her going on when there wasn't anybody there doesn't mean I was being a sneak about it. I thought it was private to her. Also, it a little bit gave me the willies. And I don't understand all these questions. It's like you think you already know what I've got to tell you. But I don't believe you do."

He looked at her, a level gaze. Then took his pipe up, filled it and scratched a match against his bootsole. Worked at the pipe a moment to get it going and then said, "No, I don't expect I do. I asked those questions because I want to know as much as I can about what was around your story before you tell it. Do you understand that?"

She shrugged. "None of it's going to change anything."

"Nothing that matters."

"Nothing that matters."

"All right. Tell me then."

"On one condition."

"What's that?"

"You tell me how what I've got to say fits with what you know. I heard you talking to Pru the other night. And I knew some of that before. But some of it, some of all what I know, doesn't square with things I heard you talking to her about."

"I won't promise anything. Seems to me perhaps you spend too much time overhearing other people."

She shrugged. "There's nothing you can protect me from."

He drew on the pipe and clouded the room. He nodded. "No," he said. "I guess there's not."

She said, "I don't trust my memory to repeat her word by word. And it would get all jumbled up, even more than it was. So all I've got is what remained with me and what I've made of it. It's the best I can do. But I've got a pretty good memory."

"Memory's what you make of it."

"I wish," she said, "for once you'd be quiet."

He nodded and laid his pipe in the thick cast brass tray he kept for it on the side of the desktop. They both sat silent a time. From up the stairs came the thin sounds of Prudence putting Jamie to bed, going to bed herself. They had not come to speak goodnight, even at the door. Abby did not confuse this with respect, for privacy or any other thing. Norman put his thumbs under his braces and studied the floorboards. After a while she knew he was done, was now truly waiting for her.

"It was two of them she was talking to. That's what confuses me. Because with both it was argument, like I said. But the tone was different. Like the one she was adamant with, clear with hatred, and the other almost as if cajoling. Or pleading. That's a better word. As if explaining herself away, some guilt. I felt she was talking about the same thing, something that happened. Something bad it was, too. And I felt she was talking to the one person it happened to and the other that caused it to happen to the first one. All right? I felt like she was speaking to a dead person and one still alive."

"Yes." Norman interrupted. "The dead person would be her half brother, a white man. The other I guess would be her mother. Your grandmother."

Abby shook her head. "I don't believe so. I think that's wrong."

"Why's that?"

"Because both people were men. I'm sure of that. What was the half brother's name?"

"Alex. Alexander Mebane."

She shook her head. "No. The dead person she called Peter."

He fingered his trousers over his thigh. "Peter," he said. "You sure of that?"

"I'm sure."

"You know who Peter was?"

"Yes. That old colored man helped her when she ran away."

"And what did she call the other one? The one you felt to still be living."

"You. She called him You. She never used any name."

"All right," he said. "Now you've got me confused. Tell me what she said."

"Best I can do. The first one, the one she wouldn't call by name. She lit into him, up one side and down the other. I never saw her mad like that. And it took awhile listening to even know how angry she was. Because her voice was calm, way down calm, and flat. Almost as if the thought of the person she was talking to sickened her and made her furious at once so the only way she could speak was calm. But more to it than that. It was as if she was before something evil and small both. Scorn, that's the word I'm looking for. She scorned the person before her, in her mind, in her mind's-eye she didn't fear him. Although I think she once had. All right. She was telling him he'd known better and still allowed things to happen, caused those things to happen. That he took the revenge intended for her and poured it onto someone else. Because she was not there but more than that—because he could, because he had the power to do those things. Evil things, that he knew in his heart were evil and still allowed. Caused. Likely celebrated. At the time it happened and all the years later when he told her about it. Told her smiling. She talked about that, how that smile wasn't anything. Because she knew the truth of him, knew it then and had known it always. And she told him he knew it too—knew what sort of man he was. Said she had no pity for him but hoped with all her heart that the knowledge of himself ran around in him all the time, never leaving him be but working on him all the time. She spoke of that as being like a low fire always burning, like a fire of greenwood in him, in his guts and heart. In his soul.

Told him all he had for a soul was that burning. Told him she was glad
to see him living, hoped he'd live on forever and ever, each day and night
a torment on him. Said she wasn't fooled by the smile; she knew the smile
of a dead man when she saw it. And told him finally that she wasn't the
only one to know this. Told him each person in his life knew it of him,
every one, including that old man who saved his life and whose life got
taken in thanks. And that this was with him always; all she wished for
him was for it to be with him always, for that knowing to eat away at
whatever passed for his heart like fruitflies at a big rotting peach. Told
him in this life that was the best he could hope for. It was," Abby said,
"like she was making a wish as much as a curse. Exactly like I said earlier—as if she'd gone over and over something she'd not got right the first
time but had it right now." And she stopped then, waiting for her father.

His lower lip was pulled up between his teeth. His head nodding
slightly, thinking, not agreeing. After a moment he said, "I'm confused
here. Except unless you got the one thing wrong. But let me wait with
that. Tell me the other part. The part of her explaining herself, what
she felt guilty over."

"The Peter part."

"I guess that would be it."

"It's hard, Daddy."

"Harder than the other?"

"Lots harder."

"Why do you think so?" The room now very still around them, the
whole house somnolent with winter night, with solitude, with the lives
within settled down to just this pair, the fire in the small freestanding
stove almost silent but for brief sounds as a bird turning in a nest, the
rest of the house even absent the nightsounds of settling jamb or frac-
tional easing of a nail in a stair tread or the weight of generations of
ghosts clambered together up attic against the cold as if the house itself
had surrendered to the recent violence or even just made peace for the
night against the ferocious and dreadful calm passing between the two
in the small office—that room vibrant—the two each etched with blue
color before the worndown brass lamplight, etched around as fine tuberous electricity given off as both sat facing the other, both knowing
this was no picking of a recent scab but as if both joined together to dig
the hole that would hold them there once dug as surely and everlasting

as a grave. So both calm before it, the young woman and the middle-aged man, not so much father and child, now or any longer, as much as cohabitants of an island country built out of the night. Launched and stranded at once, forever. The blooming nightflower, not seen again. The two plantigrades, now forever after walking hard on their heels as if not trusting the earth.

Abigail said, "It was what she was saying that was so hard. And the way she spoke. There was no calm in her. She wasn't loud. But her voice was wild, that wildness of an anguish beyond control. There wasn't any of the certainty, the bitterness, when she was speaking to the other one. This was all torment to her. She was telling him that he'd known all along what he was doing. That he was trading himself for her. That she hated her ignorance not to have seen it at the time. That she knew better. And wondered if she had just not allowed herself to know. Or that she had hidden it from herself, had told herself she was leaving a life behind and making a new one for herself. That this was courage. That this was what people did. But it was cowards finally who believe they can lay down one life and pick up another and not have them meet again. Told him perhaps it was the Lord who allowed her to do that only so when she came back she would stand revealed before herself in the full glory of retribution. That no punishment could be greater than to find in herself that all the rest of her life, that new life, all that was made from a lie. Lying to herself. That the Lord knew she could undo nothing and yet could not go on as before. And so was stranded in her hatred, was left to hate herself and all she'd made for herself. With no escape. Beyond escape. Daddy, the way she said his name, not just once but when she called him it was over and over, like beads on a string. Peter Peter Peter Peter. The way that one word each time carries everything in it that can't be said, that hasn't got a voice. You know just what I mean."

And paused then, her eyes blunt upon him, waiting, until he nodded understanding. Then she went on. "Then she told him that however awful, however unbearable, it was for her, whatever she endured, whatever she allowed, she could never know what it was like for him. Not ever she told him. Not unless she was led out by a group of men and taken to stand tiptoe on a block with a rope around her neck and doused down with coal oil and set afire until she danced off that block.

Said it made her sick. Sick of herself. And sorry for herself. Told him that was the part of herself she hated most—that feeling sorry for herself."

Abby stopped then and turned her eyes from her father in a slow scroll over the room behind him without moving her head. Then looked to her hands lying flat in her lap. She was quiet, finished but not done. They sat silent.

Norman inclined his head so it rested against his breastbone. He closed his eyes and sat motionless a long time. There was no movement but still she felt the tremors rise off him with his breathing, breathing so shallow she could not see it. After a while he raised his head with his eyes open upon her, those eyes bright with recognition, a resignation beyond grief. After another while of indeterminate time he spoke. "That man Peter. It wasn't just that he helped your mother run off. It was what she was running off from."

She waited.

"It's the part of your story that confuses me. The other man she was talking to. The half brother. The one you felt she addressed as if living. He was not. But I can see how from what she was saying you'd think so. Blaming him for what happened to Peter. Because in his way he surely caused it. But see, he's dead too. In fact, he's been dead longer than Peter. Though likely not by much."

She shook her head. "If you'd heard her."

"You're not paying attention. It was on account of the half brother, on account of his death, that she had to run off in the first place. It was because of that death that Peter helped her."

"She killed him? The one called Alexander?"

"Yes."

"Why?"

"Why do you think?"

She studied his face and then looked away. Took her lower lip between her teeth gently, as if cradling herself in that one soft curl of flesh. Looked back at him and now he saw the hard shining glint of grief in her eyes, sorrow free of self, sorrow not for the mother but for the woman, now greater within her than before and also, although he didn't think she knew this yet, lesser.

"You didn't tell Pru that part."

"I didn't see the need for it. I was thinking only to save that grief from her, from the both of you."

She was quiet a time, looking off. Then she looked at him and nodded, her voice low and said, "It scares me. It all just scares me. That idea of what happens to people and how they live with it, go on, go on so long and then have it come all the way back around on top of them. And take them over, just like it was yesterday. Twenty-five years ago. She killed herself over things happened twenty-five years ago."

"There's more to it than that. Although you're right. Funny how time collapses on us. That happened to her when she went south. I almost said home but it wasn't ever home to her. I think not. I think this was her home. I think those twenty-five years meant something to her. So I don't think it was home she went back to but where she came out of. Sometimes there's no difference, others it's all the world. But there was something happened there. I'd like to know. I wish she'd felt she could tell me. She always told me everything else. Far as I know and I think I know pretty good. But there was something, somebody. It wasn't just whoever told her about that old Peter man, although it could've been the same person. But it was something more than that telling. I'm thinking, if she was talking out loud to ghosts what else was there then that was so bad she wouldn't talk out loud about it? Or maybe not a ghost to tell it to? Or both? Maybe neither. I wish I knew."

"You thought about going down there?"

"No. Even I found something out, learned something, it wouldn't give me more answer than I've already got."

"It might."

"No."

"Because it wouldn't change anything."

"That's right."

Then both quiet. The room quiet, joined now back again to the rest of the house. The one small eight-over-eight window laid in above the desk whickered against a sprung-up northeast wind. Both not moving, looking at each other as if newfound, without curiosity but as if cousins long separated but met now and knowing one another without even the burden of a handclasp. And for the only time in his life and he old enough to know it both eyes poured over with equal hearts-aching to one another. And elastic time stretched and he thought he

might die of love and thought that would be fitting. And in that moment his life as a melancholy man ended although none who knew
him would ever know it or be able to claim it for him. But there then
he left all that and began a new life, no less sad or sorrow-etched than
the one before and so invisible. But he turned his back on God altogether and if any god noticed there was no way for Norman to know.
Nothing was to change and all things were as they were before but he
was to regard them from some minor and key distance from within
himself. With the tolerance of knowing nothing may be changed and
that what pattern lives does so outside of human desire or effort to
afford change. He did not seek but still found pleasure in this and if
no smile ran over him again it was because he needed none. All that
fell around him was perfection and all that occurred was not. He expected nothing and so was pleased with many and diverse small things.
Sitting that night in his small inconsequential office with the wind
rising against the panes and his elder daughter across from him he
sensed all this. And perhaps it was not this yet at all, perhaps it was
only the first time in months that he found himself sitting fully in his
chair, simply tired. Perhaps that, then, was enough. After a while he
broke his gaze from her and took up his pipe and held it cold in the
corner of his mouth and spoke to her.

"You ever going to tell me what happened with you and that
boy?"

She cocked her head at him. "No," she said. "I don't believe I
need to."

This time he did not nod. Slowly he struck up a match and drew on
the bowl. Then he said, "Well. There will be other boys."

"No," she said. "There won't be."

He said nothing.

After a time she said, "I'm a colored girl. Pretty and smart, but still."

For longer this time he had nothing to say.

Finally she stood from her chair. She went to the window to study
the blank squares and turned back, raised her arms above her head and
stretched herself, then dropped her hands to join before her groin, the
fingers laced. He sat wrapped in smoke, she at the edge of it. She lifted
one hand and ran it across her brow as if wiping sweat or fatigue away.
She took breath, as if she hadn't had any for hours. Then said, "There's

maybe not much I can control, what happens to me. But I can control myself. I have every intention of doing that."

He released smoke once more and laid down the pipe. "It's late," he said, and stood. He did not doubt her and could not wish her otherwise.

"It is late." And she held the door into the hallway open while he bent and blew out the lamp and they went one after the other down the dark hallway, she turning at the newel to climb the stairs and he continuing on into the kitchen to draw on boots and mackinaw and out then into the night, to check the barns, the wind raging through his hair like a summer meadow of tall timothy. Finished, he stood a long moment with his head tilted back, his eyes wide to the maw of night. Then turned to the dark house.

Part II

Bethlehem

Four

In a predawn early in the summer of 1904 Jamie slipped from the house while the others slept and went down the hill wearing his best clothes with forty dollars of his own money earned hard and saved over three years and another sixty dollars stolen from his father during the same time. He caught the milkrun train north through the valley fogged thick with mist off the river. He rode looking straight before him, meeting no eye and not watching out the train window as the train ran through the blank morning. At nineteen he was small-limbed with thin muscles, lithe, with a sense of motion about him even when still. He was attractive to women while most men did not like him on first meeting. Something ethereal in his honey-eyed skin and large dark eyes, prominent above high cheekbones and a head of soft dark curls. His fingers were long and slender with nails clean and pink. His mouth was sharply defined as if cut out from his face. He was priapic and intent, clever but lacking just enough confidence to be charming. In one coat pocket he had a folded straight razor, in the other his cash in a money clip. The sun was up now, a burning ball of rose in the mist. When the train came into the Barre platform he got off, not James or Jim, still Jamie, but otherwise ready for all things new.

He went through the station yard as if he'd seen it all before—oxcarts of six and eight yokes with crated monuments and some with loads of faced and unfaced building stone, draft teams with wagons of coke and coal for the furnaces and others of pig iron for the forges and foundries that ran day and night to support the quarries; loads of goods and foodstuffs for the city; overhead strung with the wires and lines of the new

191

century, electric and telegraph and telephone; outside the passenger depot canopied hotel wagons with boy drivers and other boys in sandwich boards strolling the crowd crying out for restaurants, rooming houses; men working in shirtsleeves or threepiece suits and from them came the filter of unknown tongues—and he passed through this with rising excitement, as if he'd found a place where he could begin.

On Merchants' Row he found a tailor and bought a readymade nine-dollar suit off the rack and paid two dollars to have the alterations done while he waited. Once the pinning and chalking was done he crossed the street and bought a pair of shoes with a hard bright finish and went then to a barbershop and had his hair cut and was shaved, knowing that thus far nothing had been finer than the hot towels laid over his face and the smooth sweet brisk strokes of the razor and the deft shears, the fingers working pomade through to his scalp, the final whisk of the powdered brush against the back of his neck. Then he claimed his suit, bought new socks and carried out his old clothes and shoes tied up with string in a paper bundle. In a paper sack he carried two additional collars and two sets of cuffs. He dropped the bundle inside an alleyway on a pile of rotting debris.

He walked up through the town and came into the row of old river-side tenement houses with small restaurants and even smaller sundry stores, pawnshops, junkshops, and barbershops on the ground levels, the buildings interspersed with scrap yards and rag-pickers sheds. He took a mean yellow room three flights up for three dollars a week, the room with a sprung bed and stained mattress and a straightback chair and a washstand with a chipped pitcher and bowl. He paid for two weeks and went immediately back out. By now it was early afternoon and a quiet of sorts was over the street. Flies worked in swarms over offal in the gutter and a pack of five- and six-year-olds swarmed by him, boys and girls both. A woman leaned from a window and hung laundry on lines strung between buildings. His stomach ached now with hunger and he walked past three cafés, unsure of what to eat, how to order. More than anything he did not want to be the fool.

He only thought he wanted food. He found what he truly needed right away. Later he realized she'd found him. She was old, at least twenty-five, perhaps thirty. She had thick ropes of black hair to her waist and her breasts were large and low beneath her simple white blouse.

She was everything he wanted and he ached against the scratch of his new trousers. She simply walked to him and brushed her hand against him and said, "You need help with that?"

She named a price and he offered half that and she took his hand and led him into a doorway and up a flight of stairs and even as he followed the intentional flounder of her skirted buttocks and hips he'd already learned something. At the first landing she stopped and ran a hand down the buttons of his flies and took him out into her hand and he thought she'd misunderstood. Then she turned and lifted her skirts, leaning forward to grasp the railing. He'd expected a room, a bed, her face, and so stood understanding but not, looking down at the puckered breadth of her rear, the thrust of rasped hair rising into her cleft. She looked back over her shoulder at him once and then turned her head away again but reached back between her legs to grasp him hard and bring him in. He stumbled against her and a cry of pleasure or pain came from her and she pushed back against him and he came just as she was raising her voice again. When she realized he was coming the cry stopped, her work done. She stepped off his steady erection and smoothed her skirts down, turned and pressed him back into his trousers, doing up the flies. She patted his crotch and said, "You remember me." Then she was down the stairs, leaving him there. When he went back down onto the street she was nowhere in sight.

He went away from the way he'd come. Two doors up on the top step of a stoop was a girl his own age wearing a navy waisted dress with white piping at the collar and hip pockets and hem. She sat with her knees together and her hands over them, watching him come. She had the same thick black hair, this time wound around her head in a loose blur but her skin was very pale, bright white against the dress and her hair As he passed she grinned and cocked her eyebrows at him and shook her head. He nodded at her once firmly, dismissing her, not shamed, and turned his head. At the corner he went into a café and ordered spaghetti only because he'd heard the word earlier. He'd not seen or eaten a noodle in his life. The meatballs tasted strange to him, but he ate two platefuls and mopped it with the hard crusted bread. It cost him a nickel.

Back outside his penis was stuck against his trousers. He turned back toward his room. The girl was not on the stoop. At his room he carried the pitcher to the pump and back upstairs where he stripped and washed himself. The room was hot and stank of urine, sweat, blood, rotting wallpaper, cheap plaster, decay. He forced up the window and the air over him was hot, fetid from the street. All around him in the building and out was the sound of movement. He lay naked on his back on the mattress and laid the wrung washing cloth over his eyes. He spread his arms and legs wide, spread-eagled against the heat. A contentment came over him. He was not happy but did not yet expect to be so. The contentment was that of an animate stone finally dislodged and rolling downhill. After a time he slept.

It was dark when he woke. He dressed and went out. Far uptown he could see the bright flare in the sky of electric streetlights. Along this street the only light was what came from the steamed murked storefronts but the sidewalks were clumped with people, some strolling, some moving with purpose. The stoops were also filled, families and single men and women motionless as the night threaded away at the last of the day's heat. Up the hill above the town the great lights of the quarries bloomed and he felt the rumble of machinery through his feet and body as much as heard it. He was hungry again and went along the street toward the restaurant where he'd eaten earlier. Tomorrow, he figured, he'd branch out.

A woman approached and spoke quietly to him. He didn't believe it was the same woman from earlier. It was not the girl from the stoop either. He told her thank you, no, but she'd already read that of him and moved away. He didn't look after her.

The restaurant had thick paper shades rolled down inside the windows but was lit within and he saw figures move silhouetted behind the dirty yellow paper. A man sat on the one-step stoop, his knees drawn up near to his chin. He wore a small-brimmed derby hat and was smoking a thin cigar, the smoke a rancid twist in the air. He watched Jamie approach and then caught his arm and spoke to him in Italian.

"I'm just looking to get food. Eat." He made motions with his hand toward his mouth and stepped around the man as he opened the door and went in. The man came in behind him. Unlike earlier the room was full, each small table ringed with men. There were no women. No one was eating but the tabletops were filled with small squat glasses, most empty but for one before each man. The empty glasses were separated each clump from the others to make a record. On a table at the back of the room were carboys of glass covered with woven straw and racks of glasses. The man who had fed him earlier crossed the room even as Jamie was entering with his escort. Thick-bodied and with gray strings of hair wrapped over his skull he followed his belly, speaking not to Jamie but the man behind him, who answered back. Up close now, Jamie grinned at him. The man did not smile back. He said, "What you want?"

"Something to eat."

"We don't serve no food. Private club."

"I was here earlier. Had a good dinner. Was looking for some kind of supper."

The man was shaking his head. "No food. Lunch only. Private," he said. "Private facility."

"All I'm looking for. Is a sandwich or something. I know you got something to eat back there somewhere." Then for the first time took his eyes from the man and panned the room. He said, "Or maybe even a little something else. Something else to fill me up." And grinned.

The man frowned at him. Lifted one hand and wiped it over the top of his head, smoothing the oiled-down hair or wiping away sweat. At the same time he did this two men at a nearby table stood, both in suits with chains and fobs spread over their stomachs. The only men besides Jamie in the room not dressed in rough workclothes tattered over with granite dust, the only men with eyes not brilliant red from the same dust. They stepped up to one side of the proprietor. Who spoke once more. "I told you. No food. So. Time you go."

The two men stepped forward and one caught Jamie by the shoulder harder than he'd expected and spun him and then the four hands came over him and lifted him by the arms and thighs, their grips deep into his muscles. The pain was near euphoric in intensity. They carried him forward. The doorman held open the door. They carried him just to the door and then threw him up and forward. While still in the air he tensed himself and landed upright, swayed and caught his balance. Someone on the sidewalk clapped. He turned. The door was shut. The man in the derby hat stood outside watching him. When Jamie turned the man grinned at him, the thin cigar still clamped between his teeth. Jamie set his clothes back right upon him and approached the man.

"You little fucker," he said. "You'll see more of me."

The man reached and took the cigar from his mouth, holding it between his thumb and forefinger. He made an odd dipping salute with it, the red end describing an arc in the night. Then bit back down on the cigar and sat as before, his arms around his knees, gazing out down the street away from Jamie.

He crossed the street to the opposite sidewalk and went on, ignoring the gawking, the one who applauded. He passed a billiards parlor and the smell of fried meat but it was brightly lit and full of men and youths and he felt leery and strange, without his pins straight beneath him. He went on uphill away from the river and closer toward the main street and found a small café with a sign in English and sat at a bench-laid table and ordered a plate of beans and ham from the woman and ate it with sliced loaf-bread. Then went on filled and more at ease into the brightly lit central part of the city and near the opera house found an open drugstore with a soda fountain and he loafed there awhile, leafing through magazines off the rack and eyeing people at the counter. They seemed to him much the same as Randolph people and he made no effort to join them or even to sit at the counter. They all knew one another and he knew this was not where he belonged, knew he'd find the like of them everywhere and each place would be the same to him. And knew there was something else running through this town and all others where he'd fit and flourish but did not yet know what it was. The youth behind the counter was watching him now and so was an older man behind the cash register. So he walked to the counter and purchased a pack of Chesterfields and a box of matches and tipped his forefinger to his forehead and went out into the night.

Back in the neighborhood of his rooming house he slowed down, watching the movement and flow on the street. After a time he went up an alleyway where others entered and came right back out and there bought a pint of whiskey from an old woman who sat in a rocking chair in a darkened doorway while three younger men sat at a table behind her smoking, their faces blank as she took his money and reached into a rag-covered basket by her feet for the pint. On the table before the men was a cashbox with iron straps, a coffeepot and tin cups, a young puppy sleeping on its side and a baseball bat. He put the whiskey in his coat pocket and sat on the steps of a rooming house two doors down from his own and broke open the cigarettes and smoked one slowly. From time to time he dipped his head down to his coat and sipped at the whiskey. After a time he went up the sidewalk to the house where he'd seen the girl in the navy dress. There was a family out on the stoop but she was not among them. He tried to talk to them but they had no English. The woman was suckling an infant and she turned her head away from him and it seemed to him her shame was not her breast but something of his query.

He went to his own rooming house and into the back for the privy and then pumped water to drink from his cupped hands. He stood out in the dark and smoked another of the cigarettes and then went up the backstairs to his room. He laid his clothes out over the straightback chair and brushed the dust from the trouser legs. He sat crosslegged, naked on the bed in the dark, listening to the low folds of sound rising from the street below, the eventide of it broken only now and then by a man calling greeting to someone, a woman calling the names of children. After a time he laid his folded razor under his pillow and stretched out on his back.

He woke midmorning to a lemon light burning through the last haze off the river, the room already hot with flies spinning against the ceiling. The street below was quiet, dried slop and churned dust. What he took to be three whores lounged in an opened doorway across the way. Neither the woman nor the girl of the day before appeared to be among them. A ragpicker made way up the street, the horse a broken-down gray with a low roman head and patched and poorly laid-on harness fittings rubbing eternal raw welts into its hide. The ragpicker cried his way, walking alongside the rough-loaded cart. A woman came forth from one of the entrances opposite with a bundle. He'd not seen the whores move but they were gone. The woman stood with the bundle hugged against her as she argued with the ragman, finally handing it up and taking one by one into her palm the coins he counted. He went his way, crying out again. The woman still stood, fingering through the coins as if their number might grow if she only looked again.

He washed from the basin and dressed and went out. The sun hurt his eyes. He went to the café where he'd supped the night before and

had coffee with cream and sugar and read through a newspaper bought
off a boy on his way in. The job listings weren't discouraging although
there was nothing he was interested in. He already knew the work he
wanted wouldn't be found that way. He still was unclear what that work
would be but knew he wanted money and that money wasn't made
standing on the rail platform blistering his lungs to drum up trade or
some such. That was some other feller's money. He drank his refill and
thanked the woman and left a dime for the nickel cup and went back
into his own neighborhood and there was shaved in a storefront shop
with a rough-painted pole out front. There was a single chair and a foxed
mirror but the towels were hot and the razor sharp.

He went to a pawnshop and spent a long time leaning across a flat
glass case of knives. Asking for first one and then another to be brought
out. Until he settled on a long thin-bladed doubled-edged stiletto with
a vine-and-leaf motif etched into the blade, the handle fine wood the
color of old rose petals with inlaid straps of brass running up to the boss,
which was a delicate knob of solid brass with an oval of the same wood
laid into the flat top surface. The knife was balanced and keen, the
sheath of fine thick leather supple to the touch. There was no strap; the
knife lay inside the sheath like sex, firm and grasped, but slid into his
trouser pocket and reached for, the blade came out of the sheath without friction. Finally he took out his razor and laid it beside the knife
and looked at the man behind the counter, a tall bald Jew with a beard
golden and long, the gold stippled with silver. "How much," he asked,
"the one against the other?"

The Jew touched the razor but did not pick it up. "Garbage," he said.
"The knife is five dollars."

"That razor's whetted to a fine edge. A lot of use still in it."

The Jew looked at Jamie. He wore a fine shirt with a real collar and
cuffs. After a bit he blinked slowly and said, "In the gutter allover are
empty bottles. You take one up by the neck, smash off the belly against
a lamppost and what you got left cuts just as fine as your razor. So. You
want style, you want substance, or you want both." He shrugged . "I care
less."

"Four dollars."

"Five."

"Four with the razor."

The Jew sighed and took up the stiletto and placed it back in the case. Pushed the razor across toward Jamie. "You come back when you don't waste my time."

"Jesus Christ."

The man crossed his arms over his chest.

"Four fifty."

He shook his head.

"Seventy-five?"

"Look at me," the man said. "You think you can wear me down?"

"It come with a guarantee?"

"Of course. The guarantee is that whoever you cut-up with it, I never saw that knife before in my life."

"Five dollars," Jamie said, no longer quite a question.

The man did not nod but waited.

Jamie went back onto the street with the knife in his pocket. It made a nice weight against his side. Comfortable. The brass boss lay just above his pocket seam, covered by his coat but easy to reach down and pull free. There was no one he wanted or planned to cut. There was no one he would be cut by.

He went the length of the street twice, cutting across where it died at the river to come back the opposite way, strolling, his pace easy. The coat was hot on him in the sun. His shirt was wet under his arms and down his sides and stuck to him and he knew he'd have to buy another shirt, maybe two, and find a way to have them laundered, socks also. He was looking for the girl but did not see her. Yesterday he'd thought the girl's look held invitation in it but today wasn't sure. It might have been only mockery or pity. She was nowhere. He'd've guessed her as itinerant as himself but for her knowledge of him; that had not come from arriving fresh off a farm somewhere. The way she perched on the stoop also had spoken of some knowledge, not so much of the place itself as the kind of place it was. And of her place in it. And so he ignored the obvious whores, as if this chastity might renew him in the eyes of the street and someway be communicated to her. He believed she would know it of him, were she to see him.

A shift change took place in the works on the hill above. First men began appearing from rooming houses and quarters wearing clean rough workclothes and carrying pails or sacks stained with food as they made their way upstreet to where the trolleys ran. After this men came down the other way, sagged, stooped, ragged, even the young among them. The fine dust of stone lay over them as if the earth they emerged from followed them home. For a time the shops and cafés were busy with these men and their women and then as the afternoon heat settled the dust and the air in fine waves over the street it became quiet again as the men went inside to sleep or drink or lie with their wives. Jamie went back to his own room during this time and sat with his jacket and shirt off, the shirt spread uneven over the ladder of the straightback chair to let it dry and air in the unmoving heat. He drank a small spot from the pint of whiskey and smoked one of the cigarettes. After a time he felt better and drew his clothes on and went back out on the street. He was hungry and eager to face the man from the restaurant of the night before.

The girl was on the same stoop two doors up as the day before. Again in a navy dress but this one with white dots the size of pearls. She held up against the sun a small white parasol that seemed fine but as he came near he saw was slitted and ragged, a shade of ash and tallow from age and the bituminous sift the air carried. Her legs were stretched before her to the bottom step, crossed at the ankles and her hair was a loosely bound aurora about her face. She did not watch him come but he felt tracked, not only each step but every fiber and thought of him. When he came abreast of her she swung her face up at him just before he paused, looking at him seriously a moment.

"Well, slick," she said. "I see nobody chased you off yet."

"It's a pretty day, idn't it?"

"Go on. I'm too expensive for you."

"I don't truck with whores."

"I'd smack your face, it wasn't too hot to stand. I'm no whore, I'm in the entertainment business. What, were you upstairs preaching Jesus to that wore-out old woman yesterday; was that it?"

He folded his arms and tilted his head back to study her. "Seems to me, an expensive girl like yourself don't have much ambition. Can't be much trade for an entertainer along this stretch. Makes me wonder why you're not uptown. And an aberration don't make a habit."

"I've heard more ten-dollar words than you can imagine. Likely more than you even know. Any man found out always claims it was that one-time only thing. I'm surprised you don't try and dress it up like it was her that lured you in there someway. I work nights up at Charlie Bacon's Supper Club which I doubt you've been to or got into yet. And you know, bud, I don't think it's going to be me to invite you."

"No," he said. "I wouldn't guess you'd want that."

"I've heard sarcastic before too. Why don't you go on before you put me to sleep?"

"Sure," he said. "I'll git. But you still haven't explained why I keep seeing you down here, this part of town. You so high-class and all."

She looked at him a long beat, her brows drawn, deliberating. Then shook her head, more a quiver than any motion distinct. He felt he wasn't meant to see that. She said, "Some days I like to get some air, see the sun, before I go on to work. Uptown, there's always some feller who's seen me sing and comes on pestering me. This place, no one bothers me. At least, it used to be."

He blinked at her, both eyes slow. Looked at her as if making up his own mind between disregarding her rudeness or her altogether. Then said, "I'd ask you to lunch but I'm meeting a man about a bit of work I've got in mind. Perhaps another time."

"Dishwashers are a dozen to the dime this town. And I wouldn't want to strain your pocketbook anyhow. At least not being trapped across a table for an hour with you. Fact is, more I see of you the less I think there's anything of me you can buy at all."

"You're a smart little cookie," he said, and tipped two fingers up against his brow as if he were wearing a hat and stepped away from her. "But you're not as smart's you think."

"A course not," she called to his back. "Not a one of us is."

He went on. Ten paces she called out to him. "Joey."

He stopped and turned, looked back at her, scowling. "That's not my name."

"It's mine. What I'm called. Now don't be telling people you're a friend of mine. All I'm being is polite."

"Joey," he said. Walked halfway back to her. "That's a odd name for a girl."

"*Joie,*" she said. Then waited and when he waited also she went on. "French for joy. What I was named. I wasn't ever Joy though. Never brought joy to no one. So, the time came, I changed it to Joey. It suited me."

"Joy," he said.

"No." Emphatic. Even, he thought, a flair of distress. "You can forget I told you that."

"Sure," he said. "Joey. I kind of like it."

"I wasn't concerned you liked it or not. It's my name is all."

"Sure," he said again. Then felt clear it was time to leave. This would happen over and again in his life and he always heeded it; this still did not explain the times the warning failed to occur. He grinned now at the girl and said, "I gotta go. I'll see you around, Joey."

"Maybe," she said. "You never know." Then she grinned back. "Be careful around those guineas. They'll do you worse than pitch you on your butt in the street, you don't pay attention."

Now he stopped smiling. "Where'd you hear that?"

"It's a little town. You might not think so but it is." She paused and studied his anger and added, "Don't get worked up. Everybody gets some story or another told about themselves. Now you got one, you watch out for yourself, you won't need another. See what I mean?"

He was quiet a long moment, then nodded. And looked her over, more bold than before. And she met his eyes with her own and then looked away and he said, his voice tuned down a pitch, "You could use a new umbrella."

She took it down before her and looked at it. Then propped it back over her shoulder. "Sure I could. I could use plenty of new stuff. Show me someone who couldn't. Show me one person in this town who doesn't need and want."

"Oh," he said, "I guess there's ones pretty well satisfied."

"Don't you think it. There's no fools so well off they still don't want and want. Want theirselves to death. Some new trinket, some new toy."

"Maybe I was wrong," he said. "Maybe you're smarter than I thought."

She said, "Don't you forget it."

It was the middle of the afternoon. Some few high mare's tails had broken and spread to haze the sky and the air was swampy. The storefront restaurant's paper shades were up with the windowglass fogged with grease. Inside the front room was empty but for a girl with deep wide dark eyes sitting at one of the tables drawing with a pencil stub on butcher paper. He seated himself at the same table he'd eaten at the day before and waited. The owner came from the back, dressed now in shirtsleeves and a stained high apron tied just under his arms. His face did not change expression upon coming through the half door.

The man stood over the table, stinking of sweat and redolent of kitchen, a sharp pungency. Jamie looked past him to the menu, a handlettered cardboard stuck on the wall. The writing was Italian or could have been English translation; it didn't matter which for it meant nothing to him. He looked to the man. The man seemed to be waiting for this. He said, "So, you."

"I had lunch yesterday. I never had nothing like that before. It was good. So I came back for more."

The man looked at Jamie. His face did not change. Without nodding or making acknowledgment of any sort he said, "All right. Spaghetti then."

"No. I want something different this time."

The man's head tilted just off-center. "What different?"

"Well I don't know." He angled an index finger toward the cardboard. "I don't know what any of that means. Just so you know."

The man broke in. "What you want then? What you want here?"

Jamie nodded as if admitting the problem of the question. Then said, "Bring me something good. Up to you. Bring me what you'd want, you hadn't eaten since yesterday, what you'd fix for yourself. How's that sound?"

Now the man frowned at him. "You want something different. Not everyday. All right. But, if you don't like."

Jamie stood fast and put out his hand, too fast for the man to more than draw up to himself. "My name's Pelham. Jamie Pelham. Now, I wasn't thinking on my feet last night. Wrong maybe but it's no crime. Most folks do it one time or another. What I'm saying is you done right how you tossed me out. I was you, I'd have done the same. Just so you know I understand."

The man looked at him, looked down at the hand. Then took it up. "Victor Fortini. Victor to you."

Jamie said, "You know your food. I don't. So bring me what you'd eat, you was me. I like it or not, that's my risk. What I think, you don't take a little risk here and there, you never learn anything."

The man dropped his hand. Still studying Jamie. After a moment he said, "It'll take a few minutes."

"That's all right. This afternoon, I'm in no particular hurry at all."

Some time passed. Jamie sat without moving. Victor came from the kitchen with a platter of food, short flat noodles twisted in the middle mixed with bitter greens and tinned and fresh fish, the fresh cut in strips and rings, all in a sauce—white, not red—and spread over with finely shaved cheese. A loaf of hard crusted bread. Left all this with Jamie eating it and went again into the back, not waiting for any comment. Reappeared as Jamie mopped the platter with the last crust and took it up and placed down a plate with a chop of meat on it, the meat covered with a thin pale brown sauce and some kind of mushrooms. The meat was not pork and not beef and Jamie had no idea what he was eating but he ate and it was good. And finally Victor came back again with another platter, this time of pickled vegetables and slices of meat and cheeses and he removed the plate with the chop bone on it to the next table and set the new platter down and then sat across from Jamie and helped himself to food. And Jamie was not sure if this was Victor's food or if he was meant to share it so he sat back and placed his napkin on the tableside and his hands over his belly. Victor looked at him and gestured to the platter and said, "Antipasto. Try some with me."

Jamie took some up with his fingers and ate. He liked it and said so. Then both were quiet until the platter was empty. Both sat back. Jamie raised his hands up and locked his fingers behind his head. He said, "That was good. All of it. Now, I bet that was a two–three dollar meal."

Victor lifted both hands into the air, fingers spread. "No charge. On the house. I got no work for you. I got nothing needs doing. No sweeping up, nothing to wash, nothing to carry off. Nothing needs nothing."

"What makes you think I wanted work?"

He shrugged as if it was obvious. "You got nothing to do. Around all the time. Knowing nothing. Going where you don't belong. Nice clothes but so. The food, that is for your curiosity. And walking back in here after last night. Either stupid or brave and maybe both. So, I give you the food. Maybe you learn a little something. It's a favor to you."

Jamie nodded. Took the money clip from his inside coat pocket and without ceremony or show stripped out four dollar bills and laid them flat on the side of the table. "I pay my way Victor. What you think of me, you're only right so far. I did come back because of the food. And also because I want work. But I'm not talking about swamping this joint out or scrubbing up after you. Now, the thing is, you know what kind of work I want and I know you've got some of that going on. And those two things don't add up to a job for me just like that. And you're right—there's plenty I don't know. But I got a couple things going for me, things you consider enough you might find a use for. One, I'm quick to learn, to put the pieces together. Two, I'm new and don't look like the kind of fellow'd be working with you. So. You think about that."

He spent the remainder of the afternoon in a building across the street, led there by Victor down a cellar bulkhead to a cool stonewalled room. There at a small table with a kerosene lamp the two men of the night before sat, one laying out slow hands of solitaire while the other read through a newspaper or racing form, he couldn't tell which. They paid no attention to him at all and only spoke to one another from time to time briefly in Italian. Two walls were lined with wooden casks and from these he drew out wine to fill crates of empty bottles all of a uniform size but free of labels or other markings and then stoppered them from a box of corks and repacked them in the wooden crates until there were eight such crates loaded. It was dusk when again he went to the restaurant where he sat with the young daughter as she drew maps for him on butcher paper, labeling each street and then marking more carefully the alleys that ran up between them. He felt slow and stupid beside the bright sure intelligence of the child but paid careful attention at least until the end when she handed over the maps and told him, "Don't worry—you can't get lost unless you try and drive the horse. Just hold the lines loose and he knows where to go and where to stop. I've done it myself."

The wagon had raised sloped shelves that rose to a peak in the middle and the shelves were lined with empty peck baskets. There was room behind the seat under the shelving for the cases of wine. The horse was an old bright bay with heavy feathered feet and strung between the hames was an old set of cowbells on a thong. The clappers of the bells were abraded to tender thin strikes of iron against the greened bronze and so did not ring out but rather chimed in the moist stilled air as if delight muted.

He held the lines loose as directed and the weary horse drew the wagon up through the alleys sprawled against the hillside over the town, the alleyways' hardpacked dirt just wider than the wagon itself and edged with homemade fencings of wire or upright planks each of a different size and length and each set with a likewise gate and as they went along people, usually an older woman but several times men of different ages and thrice children, were waiting to step from the gate to the wagon with a peck basket or two filled with vegetables mostly but sometimes breadstuffs and always each a washed empty bottle identical to those in the crates. The baskets were not always full but regardless each was exchanged for a bottle of the wine and the people bore those away inside empty baskets. All of the people nodded and spoke briefly to Jamie and he nodded back but made no effort to speak. There was no exchange of money and no record-keeping for he drove the route as marked out and the baskets were loaded in order front to rear. Once he clearly saw a small tight square of folded money stuffed down the side of a basket filled otherwise with new lettuces and after seeing this he did not look, did not want to see any more. The system struck him as elaborate and beautifully simple.

When he returned he unhitched and unharnessed the horse and stabled it in the small shed behind the restaurant, forking hay into its manger and filling the tub with fresh water pumped up in the yard and carried in by the bucketful. He rubbed the horse down with a piece of old sacking. Outside now was humid and rancid and he dragged out an old patched canvas tarpaulin from the wagon bed and covered tightly the baskets of food. Then he went into the kitchen of the restaurant which was still, clean and empty but for the girl. She was eating a plate of bread fried and dredged with syrup. She was ten or eleven, very pretty. Old enough to study Jamie carefully and not quite old enough to know why. He sat across from her.

"What's your name?"

"Loredona. I already know yours."

"You cook that up yourself?"

She looked down at the plate and back up to him, embarrassed. As if he'd caught her out someway.

He said, "Your father out front?"

She nodded. As if she could not speak to him. No longer the absorbed self-important child directing him over maps hours before. She almost made him angry. Very gently he said, "Loredona. Please run ask your father to come here a moment when he gets a chance. Tell him I'm back."

And watched her go through the swinging door to the front, her pretty hair down her back and her legs bare below her knees. When she passed through the door a low surge of voice and thronged presence filled the opening. He knew it could be Victor coming back or the two fuckers in cheap suits from the night before. But left his knife where it was in his pocket and reached fast across the table to cut the slightest wedge from her fried bread with her own fork and smear the wedge through the syrup before taking it into his mouth and swallowing it, pulling the fork back slowly through closed lips. Set the fork back on the plate, turned the way it had been.

The girl came back with her father and with a hand motion Victor brought Jamie away from the table to the yard where they peeled the canvas back and Victor went around the wagon, touching each basket with the first two fingers of his left hand as if counting but Jamie knew it was something more than inventory. Then they replaced the canvas and Victor paid him. It was more than he'd expected. There was no talk of the work done or the morrow. Victor gave him a loaf of bread. And went back inside.

It was near midnight; the air was close with rain. He went uptown. People moved under the electric lights, each lost in the crowd but each distinct upon passing, features highlighted in a way daylight would not proffer. The opera house above the city hall was emptying out for the night. The street was filled with gigs and buggies, the sidewalks with people dressed for the show. He was going the wrong way and so turned and drifted with the crowd. Finally he fell into the backwater of a streetlight post and leaned against it, putting one foot up behind him on the post. He lighted a cigarette and waited and caught the arm of a passing man and asked where Charlie Bacon's Supper Club was. The man paused and with deliberate delicacy lifted Jamie's hand free of his arm and dropped it and told him to follow his nose.

After a time he found it, two blocks off the main street. The entrance was canopied and gilt lettering spelled the name against polished wood over the entire front. There was a small crowd waiting outside. He went close to the windows and could see nothing more than tables filled with men and a few women. Waiters in high aprons over white shirts and black trousers with ribbon down the sides glided back and forth. He could see no entertainment. It was a restaurant was all. It began to rain, a poor spittle of soft summer mist. He went across the street and smoked again. After a time he saw that men also passed by the building to turn down an alley along its side. Few came back out onto the street. He finished his smoke and went down the alley and came to a single door overlit with a bare electric bulb. He went up and rapped hard on the door. When it was pulled back he could see only a hallway but could hear music, voices, a woman singing. He said, "I'm looking for Joey."

The man behind the door said, "Wrong place pal. No Joey here."

"She sings."

"Thought you was looking for a Joey."

"That's right. She sings here."

"You been fed a line. Ain't no Joey here, he or she. Ain't nothing here for you." And the door was shut. Jamie stood and then knocked again. This time there was no response. After a time a couple of men came up behind him. They stood and he felt them watching his back and after a moment one said, "They won't let you in, they won't let you in. Don't be an asshole, step out the way and give others the chance."

He went back across the street and watched the alley. It was only men that came and went. The men leaving were in high color, laughing and filled with themselves. Some too drunk were helped by friends. He watched one lean, holding his knees, being sick over and over. He stood and smoked. After a time the rain grew strong and fewer and fewer men came up the alley. The sky paled with a thin dawn through the rain. He was cold and his last cigarettes were falling apart in their paper package and he was wet all the way through his clothes. He went back down through the streets to his room. Men were out now going to work. He stripped off his wet clothes and draped them over the chair and the bedstead. Then lay on the mattress and for the first time pulled the rotting blanket over him and lay shivering, his teeth monstrous with cold. The rain had come in his open window and the mattress was wet beneath him. After a time he slept.

He did this work for four days, rising at noon or later and getting shaved and drinking coffee and reading the papers until late afternoon he'd go to the restaurant and be fed before crossing to the cellar-room and bottling wine from the casks. There were two routes and he alternated nights with them. He was not charged for his food and ate well but not like the first day. He did not see the girl Loredona again and decided this was by design. He also could not find Joey in the brief freedom of his afternoons. He learned some things. The one wall of slightly smaller casks held grappa that Victor poured off into crockery jugs or tin buckets, diluted with water and flavored with caramelized sugar and a small amount of vinegar poured from a jar packed with hot peppers, and these were sold to people who would rebottle it and sell it as whiskey. He also learned he'd be paid once a week, Monday afternoons. He wasn't sure he liked this, even if it felt like a regular job. Still, he had no choice but to trust. Nights when he finished work he'd walk uptown and patrol the streets until the early summer dawn lightened the east like river water rising to drive him to sleep. He bought a paper shade for his window. He sat one night at quarter of one in Charlie Bacon's and ate a steak and palmed a five-dollar bill to the waiter and asked about the back and the waiter thanked him and gave him directions to the bathrooms. He did not try the alley entrance again. He bought a new shirt and had the old one scalded and ironed with starch. He washed his socks in his room with handsoap. At night he'd flatten his cuffs between the pages of a magazine and slide it under his mattress. Not counting the new clothes and shoes but adding in what he'd been paid his money was holding steady. Except for the steak. With what he was owed he was ahead.

Sunday there was no work. When he woke midafternoon and walked uptown the place he had his coffee was closed. He was able to buy a paper at a newsstand and a package of cigarettes and sat on a bench reading and smoking. Some few people passed, on foot, in buggies and gigs. It

was only with a report as a gunshot high on the hill over the town that
he realized the quiet was also the stilled quarry works. He put the paper
down and listened as the sound came closer and rounded a corner onto
the street, a small two-seater automobile with brass fittings, balloon tires
and no doors. Once on the level the backfiring stopped and the machine
accelerated and sped down the street, the driver wearing goggles and
cap and the woman beside him muffled in white muslin gauze. He stood
watching them go. It was only then he realized everyone had been traveling in the same direction. He followed down to the south end of the
street and crossed over the river and came to a park. There was a grandstand and a trotting track, both empty, the track only bearing the beaten
pocks of the night before. But people were eating picnics on the grass
and there was a game of baseball. Along the river in the shade of elms
men were fishing and boys in dark tights were swimming. In the
shadow of the grandstand was a small cluster of concessions and he
bought a pasty from a ginger-haired old woman with blooms of color
on both cheeks who grasped his shirtfront and pulled him close to smell
his breath, declaiming in a thick-tongued Scottish accent she'd sell none
of God's good fare to drunkards. The pasty dough was tough and still
raw inside and the stringy meat and chunks of potato tasted old to him.
He lay on the grass midway of the picnicking families and those watching the ball game, supporting himself on one elbow to survey the game
and the crowds of people. It was all slow and stagnant. Watching, it
seemed to him everyone was only defined by their others, as if their
chatter, their animation, their display was all for those observing. He
knew there was reason for him to be out among these people. He felt
himself in motion, not unlike the small boys swimming in the river.
Pulled along to where he'd end up. He lay on his back and watched the
thick-bellied summer clouds, vaulting against the pitched sky.

Monday he woke early with a terrible hunger and went down onto the
street. It was nine in the morning and the men had been three hours
gone to the quarry, first shift of the week. The street was quiet, with
women already stringing washing. He wanted breakfast before anything and decided since he was up early he'd spring for a hot bath as
well as being shaved. So he turned upstreet away from the barbershop

and toward the common-table restaurant and so did not see her sitting on the stoop two doors down from his own. But heard her feet on the cobbles and her small cries of his name and turned and she stopped then, feet away from him, her head turned up at him, chin tilted to one side, defiant and cocky, saying nothing. Showing him the purple and black plum that was her right eye and the crusted black blood around her nostrils. Her dress the color of raspberry jam dirt-caked and one sleeve torn free. In the moment they stood looking at each other before speaking she lifted one hand to pluck at the torn sleeve, trying to press it back into place.

He got her upstairs to his room without being seen and left her, carrying the wash pitcher down to the back where he roused the woman proprietor and purchased hot water and carried it back up. She was out of her dress, sitting on the bed in a chemise and knee-length knickers trimmed with lace. Her upper arm where the dress had been torn was bruised peach and blue in thick horizontal bars, the flesh-shadows of fingers. He left her to clean herself and ran up the street and bought four fried egg sandwiches in a paper sack that turned transparent with grease and a can of coffee and a pint bottle of milk and then to a druggist for three paper packets of headache powder. And thought also of the raspberry dress thrown off into a corner of the room and sought a dry-goods shop and bought a cheap ready-made dress off the rack, using his hands to outline her height and shapes. And then stood, feeling stranded, while the clerk folded the dress and wrapped it in paper and tied it up. Finally the package was before him, and he paid and swept it up and went out toward her.

She was crosslegged on the bed, wearing his extra shirt buttoned up with the tails covering her in front and behind. She watched him with her eyes cut sideways as if doubting her decision to come to him. He put the dress parcel on the chair and the sandwiches on the bedstand and handed her the coffee and milk and then fished the powders from his pocket and held them out, saying, "These should ease you a bit."

"I'm making trouble for you." She drank down half the milk and refilled the bottle from the can of coffee and tipped out two of the powders on her tongue and washed them down.

"That old bird downstairs is deaf as a post. You don't have to worry over her."

"Shoot," she said. "You could murder somebody in one of these rooms and wouldn't anybody care, long's the room's paid up. That's not the trouble I've got in mind."

He took one of the sandwiches from the sack and left it open on the bed between them. He said "Help yourself" and bit into the bread and egg and then said, "So what happened to you?"

"Not what but who," she said. Then, "You never made it into Charlie Bacon's did you? Seems to me you didn't try very hard. But they told me, Mike told me, said,'That slicked-up boy what's hauling wine for the guineas is outside asking after you and I run him off.' I'd thought you were the persistent type."

"I hung around a couple nights thinking I'd run into you leaving."

"I never leave there by the front or even the side, just to avoid the moon-faced boys and men. At least I try and avoid them."

"You want one of these sandwiches?"

"I'd just puke it up. My stomach's awful sore. He worked me over pretty good."

"You look a little rough but those bruises'll fade out. I never seen a woman beat up before. It would be one sick pup would do a thing like that."

"Good God. You don't just not know a thing about women, you're stupid about men too."

He took another bite of sandwich. "All right. I'm ignorant. Who did all this to you?"

She shook her head, not denying him but as if he were hopeless. "I already told you I'm an entertainer. What that means is I wear outfits that make clear there's a girl underneath and five or six times a night I stand up there on Charlie's little stage and sing. Songs like 'If You Were a Kinder Fellow Than the Kind of Fellow You Are' or 'The Man Was a Stranger to Me' or to slow em down a little things like 'Don't Go Out Tonight Daddy.' You wouldn't know it to hear me talk but I've got a good voice. Between numbers I have to circulate, work up the crowd. Keep em buying drinks, let em buy me drinks—which is always nothing but cold tea. Keep the money flowing. That's what Charlie says he sees you hanging around the back, Get out there girl and keep the money flowing. Sure some of it flows to me. Fellows tip you for a song, you flirt a little bit, they tip some more. And there's some who'll get a crush on a girl and bring presents to her, give her money that sort of thing. Charlie doesn't allow his girls to hook but that doesn't mean some of the girls some of the times don't make arrangements to meet men outside of the club. What they do then is their own business unless they get arrested and then they don't have a job. Now, the thing about that business is you have to pick and choose. Because what you want to do is keep the fellow coming around, both to the club and on the side. So you have to work them along, maybe giving a little but mostly putting the idea always in their heads like they're getting far more than they are, or like they're just about to. Some girls can keep a man going for months like that. There's others who don't bother with it but pick their men carefully, usually older men who long since gave up ever seeing a young woman with her clothes off again. Now those fellows, you choose the right one, the faster, more eager you are, the longer you've got them nailed. I've not gone that route myself. Although there's more danger in the tease-squeeze-and-run. Mostly I've been lucky."

"You feel as lucky as you look?"

"Pretty much. I've been whopped on a time or two before. You try to avoid it but it's like anything else—there's hazards peculiar to the work. Like I said, it's not so much the what as the who."

"Which is?"

"Which is the brother-in-law of the mayor."

"Married to his sister or his wife's sister?"

"Sister."

"I don't see the problem. Man's not going to run to his brother-in-law complaining about some entertainer girl who wouldn't do as he wanted."

"That's exactly the problem. That's where you're wrong and where I got into trouble. See, Mayor Townsend, he bet his brother-in-law twenty dollars that he wouldn't be able to bed me. And the fellow, Michael Heany is his name, he's been trying for a month, being a sweet little lump of cash growing in my pocket. And last night when he lost his temper with me I went right on like I can't help myself and laughed at him, telling him on top of everything else he was out twenty dollars to Townsend. That's when he took hold of my arm and started in larruping on my head."

"Still, it seems to me he'd be the one worried, what he did to you."

She nodded. "It's a game, see? The rules ain't written down but everybody knows them. A girl can take a boyfriend and everybody knows about it and it's all right. And all the men think that's what they want. But if a girl just sleeps with the men, takes their presents and cash and sleeps with them, well then she's a whore and nobody else wants to chase after her. It's all the chase, see? It's all in trying, not getting."

"I still don't see the problem."

"Pride," she said. "Mister Michael Heany made the mistake of talking about how head over heels he was about me and Townsend made him the bet. That took it outside the rules, see? It wasn't any longer a game but a competition. But the thing is, now it's over, the one who has to lose, lose finally and all the way, isn't Michael Heany. It's me. And it's not just Charlie will be rid of me, it'll be the whole town. I have to get out of here."

He studied her. After a time he said, "You going to drink the end of that coffee or could I have some?"

She shook her head. "Those powders are working. I don't need anymore."

He took up the can and drank what was left, cold. Then said, "It all makes sense but for the last. He already beat up on you. What more could he do?"

She took a bite of the cold sandwich and shuddered and put it down. "That's how I know you're fresh in town, Slick. Because Mister Michael Heany, he's just a numbnuts clerk in the city hall. But his brother, he's the chief of police."

"It's not such a great thing."

She put her hands on the mattress behind her and leaned on them and looked at him. "Being chief of police?"

"No. Knowing all the ins and outs of this little burg. It's not that great an accomplishment. You shouldn't feel so superior over it."

"Stop looking at my thighs."

He was quiet a moment, then said, "They're right there."

She did not change position. "The smart thing is for me to get out of town. The problem is I need to wait until dark so I can go back uptown and figure a way to sneak into my room and get my stuff. I've got two valises of clothes I'd rather not give up and a roll of bills in my closet that I need pretty much to go anywheres. If nobody's found it yet."

"You think someone's gone through your room?"

"Could be. I'd bet a dollar there's at least some young beat-cop camped out in the hallway waiting for me to show up, probably hoping he can get a blowjob before he hauls me in anyway."

"I wish you wouldn't talk that way."

"Facts of life bother you that much?"

"No. You don't need to impress me. I figure you came here because you thought I could help. I'll do what you need done. That's all."

"I came here because there was nowhere else to go."

"Isn't that what I just said?"

"Not really." She looked away from him. And then back. "I'd have come down even if you wasn't here. This is where I grew up." Then she stopped, as if having said already more than planned.

"You don't look Italian."

"I'm not."

"You got family here?"

"No."

They were quiet. Finally he looked away from her to the window. It was afternoon but still early; the light fell into the room at a slight angle.

"What're you thinking?"

He didn't look at her. "Trying to figure this out."

"I know I'm trouble pretty much all the way around." She said this flat, her voice old and bereft of anything.

He looked at her. "Hey there, Joey." Reached and touched her bare knee. The round cup of knee seeming to him an eye opened onto the world.

She drew her legs up and stepped off the bed. Went to the side of the window and looked down on the street. Reached up and touched her broken nose and then the bunched eye. Then turned and pointed to the package on the chair. "What's this?"

"A dress." Watching her.

"For me?"

"I figured your other one wasn't any good anymore."

She took the package up and looked at him. Then opened it, dropping the string and tearing off the paper with quick movements and he felt he was seeing her, that she was showing herself, for the first time. She shook the dress out and held it up before her, facing him. "It's yellow."

"I thought it might look good on you. I always seen you in those dark colors. It's just to get by."

"Don't apologize you did something nice."

He didn't say anything. She laid the dress on the chair and unbuttoned his shirt and took it off. She turned sideways to him and lifted the bunched dress over her head. The chemise top lifted to show her stomach, the small perfect shadow of her navel on her belly-rise. The sunlight was enough so he could see the rest of her through her underwear. Then she brought the dress down over her head and fitted it onto her shoulders and hips with her hands. Came to the bed and turned for him to button the back and then turned back to face him, her hands still smoothing it. She said, "How's it look?"

"Good."

"I never owned a yellow dress." Then, "How'd you size it right?"

Without even thinking he raised his hands off the bed and once more described her to the air.

She put her right hand flat up over her mouth and stood looking at him a long moment, her eyes bright on him. He sat and looked back at her, feeling as if his face could peel from him and fly through the air onto her. Without taking her eyes from him she reached behind her and unbuttoned the dress and stepped out of it and laid it over the chair. She stepped toward where he sat. "How come," she said as she pulled the chemise over her head, "it seems like you've got so much more clothes on than me?" And sat beside him on the bed a moment and then lay back and said, "Take them off. Take my bottoms off."

Sweat-slick he took his weight up onto his elbows. Her neck to her breasts was mottled pink and white, the spray of blue veins like something grown under the sea. He stepped off the bed and went to the window and stood looking down at the street and smoked. It was afternoon, sometime. He couldn't say better than that. When he turned she was as he'd left her, sprawled and open on the bed. One of her hands was down light between her legs.

"Jesus Christ."

"You never saw a naked woman before, have you?"

"Not rightly."

"This your first time, idn't it?"

"You know better than that."

"I'm not talking about whatever you did with that old woman the other day. I'm talking about proper right loving."

"Well, I guess so."

"Lord look at you."

"Sometimes it just won't go down."

"Come over here." And reached for him.

Later he lay on his back beside her. The afternoon light was gone altogether from the room but lay against the buildings across the street, giving the crackled paint and weathered wood a tone of softness not there otherwise. She was turned on her side away from him, sleeping he thought. The dense small knots of her spine descending to the small of her back and then the swell of her hips thrust back at him and he lay looking down the length of her and thought everything he'd ever seen in his life could be found there. Fruit of all sorts, the lay of land: pastures, meadows, turned ground. Hillsides rising up. The structures of bark replicated in the patina of interlacing skin tones, one flowing to the next. The knots and ribs of tree branch and root overlaying one another. Her hair wild marsh grass and wind blowing through hay and the bundling high fleet winter clouds. The parts of her never touched by sun newfound snowbanks hot to the touch. The salt of her skin. The furrow of her backside turned earth. The small pasture spring unseen from any distance at all but always there, the moisture seeping away to disappear into the surrounding ground. Her teeth a feral ivory. Her breath mist off a river.

It was dusk when he woke beside her. It was only then that he thought of the Italian's waiting wagon, the bottles of wine. It seemed a distant place, unreachable from the small reserve surrounding him in the room.

There was no remorse but the sense he'd made a trade of sorts and the
lost job now appeared to clarify and he wondered just how long it might
have lasted otherwise, if he'd perhaps even someway saved himself.
Everyone it seemed knew more of what he was doing than he did. So it
was well and good. Time to scoot, he thought. There was still the question of money owed him. Other questions also. He sat up in the bed and
smoked, sending trails toward the soft gasp of heat out the window. Joey
rolled onto her back to look sideways at him. After a time she said, "Now
what?"

"I'm thinking on it."

"I'm wicked hungry."

"Yuht."

"Aren't you?"

"Yuht."

"Well don't strain yourself thinking."

"I'm just trying to piece it all out. What comes next."

"You were supposed to haul hooch for the guineas weren't you?"

"Uh-huh."

She got off the bed and started to dress. "You sit there thinking. I'm
dying here. And I've got to figure some way to get my clothes and stuff.
And then what."

He stood naked and took her arm. "Hold on," he said. "Let me go
out and you stay here. Let me do a couple things and I'll bring us back
some food. Then we can work on your problem and how to get out of
here."

She looked at him. Drew the chemise over her head and took up
the dress and held it. Then said, "What makes you think I want your
help?"

"Well I don't," he said. "It just makes sense we work on this together."

"Sense to you maybe. I've steered clear of involving myself with
men."

He nodded. "And you've done fine I guess. But it wasn't me showed
up on your doorstep bloodied and out of places to go."

"I don't want to owe you nothing."

"You don't. Free and clear. All right?"

She sat back on the bed. She shook her head. "I know what kind of
heart you've got."

"What's that supposed to mean?"

"Nothing. Nothing. Go on. Go do what you want to do. But bring me something to eat. And don't tell nobody I'm here."

He washed his face in the stale water left in the pitcher and slicked back his hair. He smelled her over him as he dressed, as if his skin was suffused with her and this distillation ran through his skin and throughout him. Dressed, he turned to where she sat waiting on the bed and said, "Get dressed and wait. Lock that door after me but be ready you hear me coming up the stairs."

He circled the long way to come upon the back of the restaurant. As expected the horse and wagon were gone from the shed. He stepped into the kitchen and there was no one there. He went then fast across the street to the backside of the opposite house. The brass padlock was off the hasp and he lifted one of the bulkhead doors and left it open and went down the steps. He kept his eyes steady and down as he came into the cool dripping room. Victor was behind the small table, his back inches from the rivulets seeping from the granite foundation stones. Even here a braid of sweat worked against his forehead. Across from him sitting out in the room was one of the other men. Jamie nodded to him and the man turned his eyes away, a broad sweep across the room. On the table was a lead and brass cashbox and the table was spread with stacks of banknotes and as he approached Victor laid one hand each on the end stacks and pulled them all together and lifted them and placed them in the box. Jamie all the time with his eyes on Victor's as if the money wasn't there.

"I fucked up."

Not even a nod. "So why you come here?"

"You owe me something for what I already did."

Now Victor smiled. "You stupid or what?"

"No," Jamie said. "I don't think so."

Victor nodded. "You think you know something could hurt me." The other man, beside Jamie, with his head tilted up now to watch him, rolled the fingers of one hand on the tabletop.

"I'm pretty sure I'm the one would get hurt. But still, I did work for you and need to get paid for it. It's no big complicated thing."

"Everything is complicated. Most things bigger than you can know. And you so dumb and also young. So. I always do the right thing." And lifted then a hand from the cashbox and took a banknote out and passed it flat onto the table before Jamie. It was less then he'd been paid for the first single day. He looked at it a moment and then took it up and said, "That's it?"

"That's it."

"Well shit. I guess there ain't no room to discuss it."

"No."

"I didn't think so."

"Don't be coming round here again."

"You know what, Victor? I don't guess I would want to."

And turned as if leaving. Took one step forward and leaned down even as he pivoted back around, swiping up from the caked floor the wooden mallet used for driving bungs and came around with it not only already up in the air but descending hard into the forehead of the scornful-faced man with the busy fingers who was rising up from his chair, his eyes flared with swift surprise, rising as if to help Jamie meet his forehead with the down-swinging mallet. The noise identical to the crack of bat against ball the day before in the park. The man sat back down and took the chair over sideways with him. Victor still had one hand flat on the table where he'd laid the banknote but his right hand had come off the cashbox and snaked toward his vest. Jamie dropped the mallet the moment the first man went down and now had the stiletto free of his pocket and drove it down through the hand that still lay on the table and this stopped the right hand, which paused mid-air, wobbling, then moved toward the left pinned to the rough boards. And Jamie reached slowly and took that right hand gently and held it in both of his and said, "Don't touch anything Victor. Just set still." His own hands trembling slightly. Victor leaned his head back to rest it against the wall behind him. His eyes rolled up and back again into his sockets and then up white again. The whites shot with blood as if he'd been cut there.

"Easy now. Pay attention here, Victor." Still holding the limp free hand, Jamie opened the cashbox and counted out notes until he had what was owed him. "Pay attention, Victor." He reached and struck the stiletto with the flat of his hand, driving it a little deeper, moving it a little side to side. "All I'm taking here is what I'm owed. Not even a bonus for having to collect it like this, see." He fanned the notes and then added one more five. "Now this here, this is to pay for the knife. That's what it cost me. I don't see a choice but to leave it with you."

Victor yellow, pouring sweat, his mouth clamped upon itself. Eyes insensible, gone, eggs of the soul turned inside out. Not moving. Jamie laid the free hand on the table beside its pinned mate and took up the money and stepped around the other man on the floor and then quickly went up the steps and was outside. Suddenly cold and soaked with sweat. No sound yet from the cellar but that wouldn't last. He closed the bulkhead door, searched in the dark and came up with a heavy brass padlock and this he snapped shut through the loop of the hasp. Then walked to the back corner and stopped and saw no one and began to run down the back alley along the river. His legs grabbing the ground like the dips and bursts of swallows. At some point running he lifted out the empty knife sheath and sent it sailing out into the river. His mouth wide, lungs gaping. His footfalls faint slaps echoing the pump and thrust of his chest.

"You didn't bring me nothing to eat?" Still in her underwear, the rank tallow stub in the bedside saucer lit.

"Oh boy. Oh boy." Went to the window and stood to peer down into the street. "No, I didn't bring you nothing. Get your clothes on."

"Jesus I'm dying."

"Shut up. Get dressed."

"Don't you talk to me like that."

He turned and said, "I'm sorry. You got to believe I am. It's just I figure we got two minutes maybe only one to get out of here. Fuck oh fuck."

"What'd you do?" Already with the dress over her head, her hands behind her back for the buttons.

He went on his knees and dragged out his valise and danced around the room, picking up his belongings. Remembering the extra set of cuffs under the mattress.

He took his money clip from his trousers and counted out what was left there and handed most of it to Joey. Still feeling the slight heft of the other money in his jacket pocket. "I ain't got the time for it right this moment. What you need to do is get yourself to the station. Do it quick but don't cause notice of yourself. Look at the schedule and give me half an hour. No, make it closer to three-quarters. Get us a pair of through tickets to Portland Maine."

"Maine? Portland Maine? I'm not going to Maine."

"Just do it. I'm not going to Maine neither. And don't mess around with food or nothing like that. We'll get something on the train, we're lucky enough to get that far. Just buy the tickets and sit somewhere quiet and don't talk to people. Try not to let anybody see how banged up you are. But just be casual, like it's just what you're doing, nothing else. You know what I mean?"

She bent to his valise, snapped it shut and leaned to blow out the candle stub. In the dark she said, "You don't need to tell me how to act. But I got to get my stuff, we're going to run."

"That's what I need the time for. I figure better me than you. Won't be anybody expecting me there. At least I hope not. But you got to tell me where it is and how it's laid out."

She stood silent in the dark a moment and then said, "I got no reason to trust you."

"It'll save us time and trouble, we go on what we got right here. Outside of that, there's nothing I can say."

"It's a pile of money."

"It's not your money I'm after."

"I guess I know that. I guess that's what bothers me."

He picked up the valise and knocked it against his knee. "Maybe," he said, "for right now you just got to have faith. The rest, we can sort out later. But I figure we already used up the time we got. So, are we going or what?"

"Boy Jesus, I hope I'm doing the right thing." And stepped against him and held the top of his head with her hands and kissed him. Still holding him she told him where she'd lived and described the house inside and out and how her room lay regarding the streets front and back and the yards that grew around it and what to look for when he got inside and what to ignore. And how to go from there rough and quick to the station. Then both stood silent.

"I better get going," he said

"You just make it to the station quick as you can."

"I'm not going to run off on you."

"I'll see you there then."

"Don't even worry about it. Comes time to board, I'll be the one right behind you, my hand in the middle of your back to help you up."

"You better be there."

"I'll do her."

She reached and took his head again, this time slipping her fingers deep into his hair and then turning and twisting them to raise him on tiptoes even as his knees swooped. Blood in his eyes, tears breaking onto his face. Her face close to his, that breath clean hot over him. She said, "You don't make that train, I'll hunt you down and shoot you."

"I guess you'd have to stand in line."

She kissed him. "Don't you fuck with me."

He found the house up the hillside and scouted it, walking once along the opposing sidewalk. Lights were on in different rooms and boarders sat out in rockers and gliders on the porch. He went up a ways and cut through into the backyard and stood in the shadow of an old paper birch and studied the back. He counted the second-story windows and found hers. The light was on as she'd left it the night before. A clump of lilac grew up the building, the upper branches obscuring the lower part of her window. He crossed quickly to the base of the lilacs, paused and found the way into their heart, a thin path opening into a small chamber walled round by the woven gnarled growth. He tipped his head back and studied and then went up quickly and paused again. There was no one in the room and it seemed undisturbed. He boosted himself onto the sill on his stomach and wormed his way forward and down. Then was all the way in and rolled onto his back with his knees pulled to his chest, not moving. There was no sound. The room was full of the smell of her. He found her two bags in the closet and went back and forth to fill the bags from her drawers and from under her bed and what was piled atop the bed and then standing in the dark rectangle of the closet to lift dresses down from pegs. Wrapped the three dresser-top bottles of cologne in a blouse and settled them down deep into the already packed clothes. And finally went back into the closet to squat and feel along the baseboard and found the loose lath behind the broken plaster and dug out the tin canister and opened it. It was packed with rolled bills.

Then, on impulse, reached again into the hole and drew out a small velvet bag with the heavy weight of coin. She had not mentioned this to him. It was a curious thing. Not the sort of thing she'd forget. Did she know him well enough to know he'd probe deep like that? He put the bag in his inner jacket pocket and the canister in among her clothes and fastened closed the bags. Then surveyed the room. There were more belongings but he had what she'd told him to take from there. He hefted the bags. There was no possibility of going down as he'd come up. He turned out the light and opened the door. He took up the bags and pulled the door shut with his wrist and went down the carpeted hall and the front stairs and out the front door where he turned and strolled down the hill.

The station was quiet, some few dozen people waiting on the benches with their luggage at their feet. A boy with a wooden tray on a strap around his neck for hawking cigarettes and sweets was curled sleeping in the hard shoulder of one bench, his cap pulled low to cover his eyes. Jamie set the bags on a bench empty but for an old countrywoman in black, her chin dipped into the wattles of her neck. He scanned over the small group. Joey was not among them. He stood and read the board and figured there were fifteen minutes to the next train running to Montpelier. And from there east. He went to the grillwork window and stood waiting for the clerk to finish reading the evening paper.

"I'm looking for a girl. Dark hair, wearing a yellow dress. Would've come in here the last half hour or so. Would've bought a pair of tickets to Maine."

The clerk studied him. "That right?"

"It wasn't me that knocked her around like that. I'm just trying to help her get to her aunt over there in Maine."

"I bet."

"You think what you like. She did come in here and buy a set of tickets. And that other ticket wasn't for her little sister to join her."

The clerk looked hard up at him. Put his visor back on and took up his paper and from behind it said, "She's on the platform."

He went back to the bench and took up her bags and headed toward the doors onto the platform. Beside the doors was an old man with a bald dome and long hair growing behind his ears down onto his shoulders. His legs were gone at the knees and he sat on a wood plank with wheels at the four corners, his trousers pinned neat and tight under him. Even in the summer night over his shirt he wore an old greatcoat with epaulets and the vee stripes of a sergeant on the arms. Wedged firm between his knees was a tin cup with seed coins in it. He held a stout short stick in his hand to propel him over floors or cobbles or dirt, the one end capped with an iron spike, the other with a sewn leather pad. When Jamie paused the man spoke out, his voice near song. "Help a man, stranger. I fought the war and luckier was the man what died."

"Where'd you lose your legs?"

"In the Wilderness, son."

"That was a bad one, what I heard."

"No man can imagine it, no man can repeat with words how it was."

Without taking it from his inner pocket Jamie opened the neck of the drawstring velvet bag and drew out a ten-dollar gold piece and leaned and dropped it in the cup. The old soldier heard the sound, different from the thin chink of coin and his hand scrubbed inside the cup to lift the piece up where he turned it in his fingers, then ran it between his lips for his teeth to try. Then the hand with the gold disappeared into the folds of the coat and Jamie stepped on toward the platform. The man called out a thanks as Jamie went through the doors without looking back.

Joey was on a bench most of the way down the platform, away from the pool of light under the overhang, sitting alone with his valise between her feet. He could hear the train off away down the river, the sound coming through the night like the mighty roar of a band of angels. He set her bags down and sat beside her and said, "I gave one of your ten-dollar gold pieces to that stump-legged man inside."

She was silent, looking ahead of her, the paper folder with the train tickets held in both hands on her lap.

"I'll pay you back. There must've been some left after buying the tickets."

She looked at him. Her face cut up and bruised with shadow so all there was to see of her was her loveliness. A face he might have dreamed if he'd known enough to. She said, "You think the train'll beat the guineas here?"

"I hope. I hear it coming."

"You wouldn't hear them."

"I know it."

"That gold piece wasn't yours to give."

"I'll pay it back. He's blind. Wouldn't know one banknote from another. I wanted him to know what he had."

"I don't want it paid back."

"You didn't even mention that bag, telling me what to get."

"I knew you'd find it."

"I can go get it back from him."

"No," she said. "Let him have it."

They rode the Boston train to Montpelier and waited an hour and
caught a local east to St. Johnsbury, where they would wait again for
the Maine Central eastbound toward Portland. He had been stiff and
silent during the first layover as they sat off again down in the shadows, able to see the statehouse dome lighted against the night sky somewhere behind them, and she sat without speaking as she had on the
train, her head tipped a little to one side as if to conceal her marking
but also as if to leave him be. He thinking all through that first layover that a fast man angry enough could make the distance from Barre
during that hour. Once back on a train this lifted and she responded
by relaxing enough to lean against him and sleep. So they came into
St. Johnsbury in the long pale thin summer dawn, the town this early
only ghosts of structures within the river mist and empty but for a stray
handful of dogs teamed up to patrol the streets, and once a glimpsed
milkwagon, the canary yellow paint blunted by the dawn but still
brilliant, as if a voice speaking, calling some name down the empty
streets. Here they got out and went away from the station to a nearby
place where they ate red-flannel hash topped with fried eggs and
toasted loaf-bread and then he reached across the table and she sat
looking a long moment before she reached out and ran her curled
fingers down the back of his hand. Except for small words of excuse
or reassurance neither had spoken to the other since the evening before. But still they went away from their breakfast back toward the

train hand in hand, as if for the moment God had paused and turned away, lingering elsewhere, content to let these two be the life of the world, their sweet unspoken understanding all the judgment ever needed.

They rode east less than an hour and left the Portland train in Littleton, New Hampshire, the train filled with families and groups traveling on into the White Mountains on holiday excursions. It was only drummers and salesmen and local people returning home who got off with them at the depot, the town west enough from the mountains to miss the splendor and air of the resorts just miles to the east. Instead there were mills and tanning sheds and leatherworks and shoe factories spread along the Ammonoosuc River that ran out of the mountains. They ignored the trolleys and trudged east from Main Street and followed the bow of the river past the leather sheds and found a cheap rooming house where the woman looked from Joey to Jamie and back again, her eyes bright with contempt for both but her wash-scalded red hand took his money paid out for a week.

Mornings he went out and bought hard rolls at a bakery and meat and cheese from a butcher and brought them back to the room where they had breakfast and then she made a sandwich and wrapped it up in the bag from the bakery and he stuck it in his pocket and walked to the depot to catch the train. This way he spent his days in Bethlehem and Twin Mountain and Fabyan and Bretton Woods and Crawford and Franconia, making his way around the high-storied white-colonnaded hotels, each one a thing imperial, seeming to him as magnificent and self-contained as ships upon the calm waters of tended sweeps of lawn, all overhung with the mountains close, upswept, delineated in the rarefied sharp-edged air. He studied the men playing golf and lingered near the tennis courts where men and women both played on the packed red clay surfaces. He made his way to the rear buildings and there talked with men in the stables and dairies and women working in the laundries and kitchen and dining room workers on breaks. He was offered work and each time he turned it down. He decided they had come to a very good place.

Late afternoons when he returned to the room she would be silent, angry, impatient as her face slowly lightened down the shades from purple black to reds and yellows over the days, as her skin transformed slowly back to its own tone, with only the impressions of watery proud-flesh around her eye, and the broken vessels of her nose healed and the small crusts appearing daily around the flanges of her nostrils grew smaller and then fell away altogether. And after the first day he learned to wait to tell her of his journeying. In the long summer evenings she would brush out her hair and with it loose and wild around her face they would go out to find someplace to eat. Sit silent eating the rough good food as around them men whose arms and faces were stained the color of walnut sat eating and speaking low to one another in a patois of French and English, a smell rising from them that was not death or putrescence but a mixture of lye and tannin and the sharp tang of some chemical compound—not so much the smell of dead cow or the waxen gleam of calf-leather but rather some crude shadow of the creature in between. And from time to time he'd look across to her and see her head tilted a way that made clear she was listening and following the jabber beside them. And he did not ask what she heard. They did not eat two nights in a row at the same place.

After eating they'd walk slowly back to their rooming house through the bat-slung dusk where they would sit on the bed and smoke his cigarettes, both of them barefooted, and he would tell her of his day, of what he'd seen and where. Of what they might do and where when she was ready, and he held nothing out as absolute as if he was not the maker of plans but a simple scout for her authority. And as he talked he would always find the point to reach to her and begin to make his way through her clothes, still talking and she still listening, and sometime after this her hands would come over to him until they were both naked in the settling dusk when the words would stop, sometimes petering out as if a trail lost and other times clamped away with speed and violence.

Later, in full dark, they would lie side by side on their stomachs with their heads lifted up to the window and one's hand laid smooth on the sweat-slick bowl of the small of the other's back. One would smoke and hold the cigarette to the other's mouth. The air already cool enough to chill delicious their sweat. And it was then she talked to him.

* * *

She could not remember her father. There had been a photograph so she knew what he'd looked like and she recalled sensations that matched the figure in the image: great roughened hands that enwrapped her body, the coarse bristle of his mustache, huge shoes, a shadow over the grass. She remembered being lifted and tossed up above his head while he stood, his hands up to catch and toss her again, over and over: Quebec. She remembered the trees on the lawn of the place in Saint-Camille and the bright whiteness of the house and the sailing summer clouds, all these things as she was thrown wild into the sky; but she could not, in her memory, make herself look down at that face looking up to watch her. All she remembered was the trees and the house and the sky. And not even the hands that caught her, only the moment of safety those hands made before they freed her again into the air. Marc LeBaron. "I got my mother's hair," she told Jamie. "His was blond, that thick blond hair that falls in waves not single strands."

That next winter one hundred and twenty miles south a winch cable snapped in the Millstone Hill quarry and he was crushed by a four-ton block of granite being lifted to be worked into elegant monuments for other men. She did not recall the telegraph arriving but an afternoon dark from the early winter twilight when a neighbor woman bathed her in a washtub in the kitchen while her grandparents and uncles and aunts sat in the small parlor with the heavy curtains drawn and a lamp lighted, the only sounds the drawn raw wails that would rise from time to time from the bolted room upstairs where her mother had been for a day. Those sounds became the death of her father and the twilight colors on the snow her memory of him.

On a raw bright day the following spring with the ground thawed he was buried under high blown clouds down off the St. Lawrence, the shadows moving over the land like the hands of God, leaving her face intermittent with heat and chill as she stood beside her mother head to toe in black. Two days later they rode trains south from Sherbrooke, her mother following the trail in reverse of the letters that arrived over the winter from an attorney in Barre city offering attractive services in a suit against the quarry. Joey later came to understand her mother was traveling not only after the promise of money, some restitution for the life envisioned, but also fleeing from under the roof of her in-laws, the small village gossips and the glances of the single and married men of Saint-Camille.

For six months they lived in a modest hotel and ate cheese and day-old bread that Claire brought home from the bakery where she worked as a counter clerk. Leaving Joey then still Joy with a hump-backed woman with a small cottage set apart among the derelict rooming houses and failing shops along the riverfront, the woman who would slap Joey when she spoke French not English, cuffing her shoulder or the back of her head. There were a dozen other children kept thus and the older ones boys and girls both tortured the younger. It was there she learned that pain inflicted directly upon a penis immediately changed male behavior toward her. The girls were harder, more clever in cruelty. Joey watched them all, sure that watching would reveal how if not to please them at least to imitate.

Upon occasion known only to himself the attorney McCarson would arrive of an evening carrying a paper sack of licorice whips and horehound drops for Joey. He would consult quickly with her mother and then leave, to wait on the outer stairs while Claire quickly brushed out her hair and changed to her best dress and left Joey alone with the sack of candy. She would eat the licorice and feed the horehound one drop at a time out the small dormer window, watching the lozenge slide down the mossed shingles to lodge in the eavestrough or bounce clear into the street. For a couple of days after these nights out her mother would be pensive, her forehead working in quick bursts of thought, then after a little time would relax. And her chin would again tilt up and her eyes quicken leaving each day for work. As if, Joey told Jamie, she had again seized the future.

The suit failed. McCarson sent a clerk reading law in his office with this news. A week later himself arrived, a vast man of fine suits and a constant sheen to his face, florid, with a pouched neck. An eater of beef and pork and game. An appeal was proceeding. The key was not to despair. He knew these men. It was much like chess but Claire did not know chess. It was much like devising a new recipe, knowing the ingredients and knowing the end result aimed toward. You do not stop once you've begun. Where would any of us be if we did that? There was the question of his bill to date.

She would lie listening to her mother's cries, pips of birdsong as if broken out of her. Then long silence. She would not listen to his chuffing, his entreaties. Then again, finally, the pips blown out full, terrible cries of unbearable pain. Pain Joey could not imagine but felt appropriate and did not know why. After she heard the door close after him she would wait some more and then go out through the blanket curtain to her mother, who would be settled back against the bedstead or sitting up at the table in her robe, her face slack, her eyes open without seeing and nothing beyond this to explain the torture. As if it had left with him. With nothing to explain the ways she'd taken part.

"In a way those were the good times," she told him. "That first year, year and a half, when she still had hope. But somewhere in there she allowed herself to see what that cocksucker lawyer was up to. Maybe she just learned it bit by bit. But she wasn't the only stone widow in that town so she might have heard things more directly. And then things kind of came to a head with me and she made some choices and changes."

"What happened with you?"

"I got into some mischief. She moved us out of the hotel and into a rooming house down there near where you were staying and worked a deal with the landlady to sweep and clean the slop jars and such each morning and then went off to work up at the bakery. Evenings she did piecework in the set of rooms we had fourth floor up under the eaves. Broiled in the summer and froze in the winter but it was cheap. And part of the deal was the bitch owned the place was to watch out after me. She and me came to understand one another real quick over that; she didn't want to do it and I didn't want her to. I went my own way and whatever I did it was up to me not to let Mama hear of it."

"What was the mischief you got into in the first place?"

She rolled onto her side to face him, both still lying to watch out the window but with a blanket pulled sideways off the bed to cover them over. "I pooped in a sack and carried it uptown along with some farmer's matches I'd gotten somewheres and climbed the stairs to Evan McCarson's office and set the bag alight there before his door and then rapped on the door so someone would come out—him, I thought—and stamp out the fire."

"That's an old trick."

"I guess so. It was new to me. And I made the mistake of standing watching and waiting."

"You didn't run off?"

"I wanted to see the look on his face."

"How'd that go?"

"It wasn't even him but someone young and quick enough to grab a bucket of water kept inside the door to pour out the fire and still chase me down the stairs and grab me before I made it to the street."

"You get whipped for it?"

"What?"

"Did she thrash you for doing it?"

"No." She looked at him, a look he thought meant she failed to understand him. He would learn this look meant he'd failed to understand something of her. She said, "She never put a hand to me. Not then or ever." She paused, watching out the window. He left his hand on the swell of her hip, not moving. After a time she said, "She worked like that four years. Until she had the money she owed him. She wouldn't pay him piecemeal. The evening came she had it when he arrived. I was ten years old. Sitting at the table doing my homework. I think about it now and wonder what that knock on the door meant to her. How she'd waited for it. What she thought at that point was happening in her life. How she let him in as always and poured him a cup of tea while he sat at the table. He no longer brought me candy or such. They'd long since stopped any pretending. Although he always took her out for the evening first. Myself, I think that was just to show her off on the town. Something he owned, what was his. But that night she poured tea for herself instead of slipping past the hung blankets to dress. Sat across the table and took the paper money from the can where it had been rolled waiting on the table for him for two-three weeks. And counted it out to him, down to the last dollar. And how he stood then, not counting the money over like I bet she'd hoped he would but folding it and disappearing it into his vest pocket. Then told her he'd forgive the interest. Took a ten-dollar gold piece out and laid it on the table. And told her to get herself dressed. Told her he was hungry and said by the look of her she was too. Told her to recall prostitution was a crime in the state of Vermont. But a gift between friends was nothing more than that. And then took out a cigar and trimmed the end of it and lit it up, his fat mouth sucking around it, and dropped the dead match on the floor and went down the stairs to wait for her. The room filled up with the smell of the match. And she stood there looking at the door. She was still young. I only realized that this minute. And then she went behind the blanket and I heard her dressing herself and she came out without looking at me or speaking goodnight or nothing. Went down the stairs. I sat there listening to her go."

"Let me ask you something."

"What."

"Was this the same fucker roughed you up? When we ran?"

"I already told you who that was." Impatient. "No. He never messed with me after one time I was home alone and he undid his buttons and tried to stick it in my mouth and I bit it."

"You bit his dick?" Felt himself shrink against the mattress beneath him.

"Oh yeah."

"Bit it off?"

She rolled against him and spread her mouth and razed his shoulder with her upper teeth. "Of course not. But I left marks. He yelped and slapped my head."

"So what happened?"

"What do you mean, what happened."

"After you done that."

"What do you think? He left me be."

"Yuht, I bet so."

Picking up where she'd left off she said, "She talked about going home. Quebec, I mean. Not Saint-Camille. Talked about going to Sherbrooke, even Montreal. Saving her money, thinking she'd buy a little bakery somewhere. Every second Tuesday she went out to meet McCarson and those gold pieces went into that sack. I never saw but the first one. She of course thought they were a secret to me. I didn't care about going anywhere. I'd listen to her when she talked about it but I never had any enthusiasm. Canada! You know how people hate the Canucks around here. It was the last place I wanted to go."

"I always try and take a person for just how they are."

"Huh. That's what you think. What you like to think."

"Why do you say that?" He'd rolled onto his side, reaching over her to the sill for the cigarettes. He propped on one elbow, trying to read her features in the streetlamp light.

"You've got fevers of hate in you." She paused, not moving, her stillness a perfect thing—the slope and craft of her nose. And added, "Like any man."

With his thumb and first finger he popped the cigarette in a high arc out the window and did not wait to watch the glow trail down out of sight but rolled onto his back. His voice soft he said, "I expect you're right about that." Still mild he said, "What happened to your mother?"

She hadn't moved when he did. Still on her side looking out the window. He couldn't see her now. His eyes lost on the ceiling, nothing there but the dark of a water stain. She said, "You're bound up tighter than a secret. Just so you know, we're not going to get anywhere like that." Then she went right on. "I hated school. It was a fight to make me stay there long's I did. The only part I liked was the recitals and commencement pageants and the plays. I was always the one to find a reason for some little spectacle. For parents or just for classmates, it didn't matter to me. George Washington's birthday. Lexington and Concord Bridge. Ethan Allen. I'd figure something out for it. Plus the dramatic society. I'd stayed I'd of done good with that. She found me a voice teacher. I wanted to take lessons on a piano but I'd as quick gotten an elephant as a piano. So I ended up with just my voice. Which the way it worked out was good luck from bad."

"Be a pickle, we was trying to haul along a piano right now."

"Exactly. She was a horrid little old woman with a mustache. Hungarian or Polack, something like that. She made me stand on a stool. Told me it would keep my back straight. Taught me how to breathe, how to sing. Stood there before me with a pencil lifted in one hand, beating time while I did the same exercise over and over. She'd poke me in the chest with the stub end of the pencil when I was getting tired and say, 'Lazy girl, lazy girl.' I didn't like her but I liked what she taught me. It was enough to keep me going back. I didn't need prodding from my mother, although she kept it up. I think she'd figured out before I did that it was the only thing would save me, would maybe make me a life better than hers. She knew I didn't have patience for most things. I've always been that way, hate to wait for a thing. She had a cancer. In her parts. For how long I don't know. The time I learned about it, it was all through her. She didn't tell me until she had to."

She was quiet then. After a time he asked, "How long ago was that?"

"Three years."

"That's a long time."

"I've done all right. I've got a talent."

And he lay silent still gazing up at the mottled spray of the plaster wondering how many other times she'd lain so, naked beside some man as she spoke of her life, the parts she'd pick and choose to offer up each time somewhat different and knew he would not ask her, would not only not want to know but whatever she told him he would not be able to believe, even were they to lie so through a thousand nights to the numbered dawnings and her tellings adding layer to layer as her soul clarified itself before him; even then he would know there was something not told, something held back, and he admired her for this.

He rose from the bed and stood looking at her. In the gaseous yellow from the streetlamp her body was pale, the color of old riverstone bleached by sunlight against the furrows of the sheet, her legs running out from her as water flows down from above, her hips meeting the swelling in his brain and chest and then the concave fall of her waist and the thin rise and spread up to her shoulders, the knobs and raised planes of her shoulderblades, her head and arms akimbo hidden under the dark spray of her wild torn hair. The underside of her heels resting at bed's edge made to fit exactly his palms if he were to step forward and lift them up. He rubbed his face with his hands and then ran them down over his chest.

"Joey," he said, "we can do whatever we want. There's not a thing can stop us. We're orphans, both of us. We're free."

She rolled over and sat up, pulling the sheet around her waist. Her back to the window, her face a blank mask, she spoke from within the tangle of knotted hair. The tips of her breasts as eyes out of a void. "I had you pegged for a runaway farmboy."

He nodded, not confirming or denying. "I killed my mother. Getting born."

She sat silent with that a moment. "You never knew her."

"No."

"Like my father."

"It was just Father and me," he lied. "My father was off in his head. You weren't even right about the farmboy business. It might once have been a farm but all I ever saw was it grown up to puckerbrush and the shingles going a little more each spring. He fought in the war. The Southern Rebellion. Had some kind of wound to his head. Just didn't much care about things. That legless old man back there in the Barre station, that's why I gave him that piece of your money. Father was like that, but some ways worse. He had a pension from the army but mostly lived on money made by selling off bits of land. He was a fair hand to cook and would have supper on the table for me every evening but that was about it. Sit there watching me eat it. Told me stories but they were all about the war or before and the same ones over and over, mostly a jumble of things. The way I grew up, it wasn't so different from how you did. Left on my own, I mean. It's no brag that I was a hellion and a fair one at that." He paused then and looked away from her and then went and sat beside her on the bed, no longer looking at her. "I wasn't even really a bad kid. It's just that people don't like peculiar things and the two of us up there on the hill was peculiar to the rest of them. So I ended up getting a little toughened up too. Which was good I guess."

After a moment she reached and ran a finger down from his ear along the line of his jaw and held the tip of her finger against his chin and stroked him there and then took her hand away. He waited a moment more and without turning his head reached behind him for the cigarettes and leaned to hold himself upright with his elbows on his knees. He said, "It wasn't nothing but a chimney fire. But I wasn't to home and so they tried to pin it on me. Once a person thinks you're a certain way, that's the way you stay in their minds. It doesn't matter what happens. That was March of this year. I guess it'd been a couple years since he swept the flue. Burnt the house to flinders, what was left of it anyway. Pretty much all what was left was the cellar hole filled up with charred timbers. So the minister took me in. He and his wife didn't have any children and I guess they had hopes for me. I got a decent suit of clothes out of it. And I waited until the last bit of that land was sold and I had a little cash and came north. Went to Barre because that's where the train was going. But maybe, I figure, I was going to meet you." And sat still and did not look at her.

"That's some tale."

He could read nothing distinctive in her tone. So turned his head just enough to look at her. "It's the truth," he said.

She said nothing.

So again, his voice gentle and low and sweet, just only a prod, said, "We're orphans, you and me. We can do anything."

She leaned toward him then. Her voice also low, urgent, some taint of threat. "I make my own way."

He looked at her. Wanted to touch her and did not. "You really sing?"

"Like a bird to break your fucking heart."

He nodded. "Tomorrow, we'll take the train and tour around. You'll see, this is a different place. We can do anything we want here. We can do it straight. There's ins and outs to figure but all that is, is a little time. It's a good place."

"I don't believe that. For a minute."

He nodded. "Tomorrow, you'll see."

She leaned closer and ran her hands over his head. Her fingers turning furrows in his hair, stroking through to his scalp. The fingers already telling him what he wanted to know. And he knew the trick was never to reveal that he knew a thing before it was announced otherwise. So he sat under her touch.

"If you fuck with me," she said, "I'll cut your throat."

He pulled away from her hands and lay back on the bed again, his feet still on the floor. Looking up at the ceiling. He said, "I know it."

Five (interlude)

They'd rise midafternoon long after
the morning fog burned away and the sun was beating through the
hemlock and tamarack stand surrounding the house, the air still and
resinous of soft-needled duff, waking slow with the dawn blankets
thrown off and the sheet twisted to a rope between their legs, slick and
slow with sleep. Green-backed flies beat against the screens and
thrummed against the ceiling, the song of afternoon. One or the other
of them would make coffee and they'd carry this, wearing only robes
with towels slung over their shoulders, out through the redolent canopied evergreens where chipmunks trilled at them, into the sheep-shorn
pasture with ledges of clamshell-colored boulders thrust up in the full
bake of the afternoon, down the worn path to the Ammonoosuc. They
sat on flat-topped boulders the size of boats and drank the coffee and
then swam in the hole made by the riverbend, the water in July or August a cold shriek that shrank his scrotum and lifted her nipples and
gooseflesh laid over them. Awake, hangovers gone with the current,
they'd stretch on the boulders' backs with eyes closed and hands under
their heads to doze and brown in the sun, the quavering myriad river-
tongues cleanly filling their minds with nothing beyond precisely and
minutely where they were. Sometime later while the northern summer
sun was still distinct but the folds of the riverbank had gained slight
shadow they would go back up to the house and there bathe and shave
and dress for the night, eat a breakfast of eggs and toasted bread and
she would drink a cup of tea with honey and lemon laced with whiskey
and he'd take a small fruit-juice glass of the whiskey neat. Then in the

long lovely twilight they'd drive the three miles west into Bethlehem and he'd drop her off at the Casino on the grounds of the Maplewood and then continue a mile farther west to the Sinclair where he began his night, a shift of five hours managing the lounge there, hiring and firing and taking inventory and stopping left and right all throughout that time to make fine kind relaxed talk with anyone not in his employ who happened upon him. Around midnight he'd leave there to run up and down the long main street and the few short sidestreets where there was reason to go, pulling up to backdoors in the thick shadows of summer night and making deliveries from the backseat and trunk of his automobile. Sometime between two and three in the morning he'd go from where he finished to the illicit after-hours club on Swazey Lane where most nights Joey would already be before him, sitting on a stool on the small raised platform beside the piano player, no longer having to work the room or pose and stretch but able now to just sit with her knees together and sing, the room swathed in layers of smoke and blue from the low lights and the people allowed in would be content with their stupor and fatigue merely to sit and listen to her. Here Jamie did not work so much as make contact: a man easing up to him and while maybe looking away mention the name of the place or the name of a man met in the place and the threads of a deal would be laid. Jamie never agreed to anything. All things were tentative, not even so much as implied. He'd listen and at most nod his head, not in complicity but simply as if indicating he'd heard what was being said or asked. Then he'd go away and think about it, or not think about it but let it settle within him and a few days later he'd know if it was right or not. He made no promises, except to himself. And those had nothing to do with greed. Mostly he sat back in a far corner and watched her sing and sipped whiskey and waited. When she took breaks he'd join her outside to smoke and breathe in the night, not even really speaking but in short bursts of coded language, fragments of speech. Other times he'd stay seated, seeing she was at work, crooning to someone, leaning forward off her stool, her eyes without distraction, milking the one ripe fruit in the room about to fall. Then he'd leave her be. He trusted her. He'd learned he had to. She drew money from men the same way he filled the hole in them; it was what they wanted. It was not that he thought people were stupid about love or whiskey or sex. It was that he knew all men were tigered. Each had the chink, the soft spot. The only ones he liked were the ones it was hard to find. He'd not yet met a man where it wasn't there. The thought of that was the one thing he feared. Finally there would come a time when the piano player didn't return to the keys and the room was empty but for the two or three unwilling to go and Joey would be slumped with her arms spread around her drink on the table and the sound of birdsong from the lilacs and elms and rosebushes outside would break through into the basement and he'd reach and touch her arm and he'd say "Home" and she'd nod. This was summer.

Five

It had been the skeletal accordion-limbed piano player who saved them. Scully. They'd flown through that first season of summer and fall five years before heedless as children, living in a cramped basement room and sharing a cold-water bathroom with a dozen other hotel workers, Joey from the start working at the Maplewood as a dining room waitress and singing from time to time in the small clubs that sprang up and disappeared, while Jamie went through a string of jobs not from an unwillingness to work but a restlessness that drove him distracted from place to place as if intent on unraveling the workings of the entire town as quickly as he could. Both of them not oblivious so much as in some dream-trance of summer and so disregarded any signs or indications that they should make preparations of any kind until the wet cold third weekend of October when the leaves stripped from the trees and Monday morning the trains were filled leaving and shutters began to go up over the tiers of windows as if the hotels were closing their eyes against the sudden damp chill. Not even the few rare clipped mornings earlier in the month when all had gazed off at the snow topping the Presidentials, the glaze of white brilliant against the sky—this had seemed to them nothing more than a moment, a flare to the festive quickened life around them. Their summer wages: new clothing hung from a strung wire across one corner of the room and the memory remnants of whiskey-laced summer dawns, the etching of color as an electric current promising the day only hours of sleep away from them. And all either of them needed then on those foot-soaked dawnings was not to sleep or eat or even think of the work that waited once more

241

but only now to be alone one with the other and let loose the creature they made together, the loveliness of tongues and skin. Walking from wherever they were to the small basement room, holding tight one to the other, their heads together, the smell of each sharp as must to the other's nostrils, staggering up that long swooping main street of Bethlehem, not even noticing or when they did laughing back at the tight pursed glares or purposefully turned-away eyes of the other early morning walkers, the guests—middle-aged women in pairs dressed in long white frocks and white gloves and with their hair up under wide-brimmed hats or older men in full suits alone out walking for the mountain air and striding along away from the sluggish downward spread of their own bodies and the pull of the earth made all the keener for the sotted sex-wraithed stain of youth passing them by—and Joey and Jamie knowing this hatred and knowing it did not apply to them, that it was a bitterness not of their making. "You gotta wonder about it," she told him once. "All anybody needs is a good drink and a good fuck. What's so hard about that? What's the big fucking deal?" He couldn't tell her otherwise. And he knew the sorrows layered behind her words. The only thing to do, the only thing that mattered at all was to steady her with his one arm and hold her cheek tight against him with his free hand and take her near earlobe between his teeth. Hear her breath freeze up in her throat.

And so to the late October Monday when as if from a sleep they stood with a cold drizzle against them and the town shriven around them. Workmen on ladders up and down the street unlatching the black or dark-green painted shutters and folding them over the windows and screwing them in place. The train platform a stew, classless now with end-of-season vacationers and fleeing workers all clumped under the sparse awning. Steamer trunks piled in lumps against the duffels and straw or rattan suitcases. The freights going through thoughtless now to the suddenly small town. No one arriving.

They went to the Casino. It was not yet noon. They were the only custom. No one paid attention to them. A pair of men were taking inventory. The floor was mopped under their feet. The room was dark and it grew darker as broad shutters the size of barn doors were laid one by one at long intervals over the windows. They sat huddled at the table, not talking, not bold enough to demand anything from anyone.

After a time the barman brought over a pair of glasses and a stoppered half-bottle of something which he left on the table before them without a word. They knew it was without charge. They drank from it slowly. There was nowhere to go and they did not speak of it.

Scully found them there, crossed the room as if he'd known this was where they might be. In a rusted black suit with cuffs and pantlegs too short for him, hollow-chested with stretched thin skin over the bulb of his skull, the lank paste of hair the color of a worn coin, fingers stained with nicotine dangling off the knobs of his wrists, his fingers even in movement composed, as if they alone of his parts knew their competence. He seated himself, a limberjack of angles and lines. A slender ankle hooked up over the other knee.

"I thought you two might yet be around."

Joey said, "Where's everybody going off to?"

He shrugged. "Boston. New York. Some go south: Florida, Georgia, North Carolina. Where there's work."

"It might be nice," she said, "to be somewhere warm for the winter."

Scully nodded. "I've done that. You have the train fare?"

Jamie said, "I'm going nowhere. Make my way whatever way there is to make."

She looked at him, said nothing.

Scully said, looking more at her than Jamie, "There's ways to winter. It takes two—three things all run together at the same time but it can be done. Sometimes lean, sometimes fat."

Joey turned her glass in the wet track on the table and looked at Scully. "You've heard me sing."

"Why yes I have," he said. "That's the easy part."

That first winter they lived together in Scully's four-room house in Littleton down the hill close by the railroad tracks where the freights rocked their sleep and the whistles pierced their dreams, the house with the close-layered reek of a man alone a long time, the front room filled with an upright black piano scuffed and chipped but precisely tuned and stacks of sheet music on the floor and scattered over the burst-spring sofa and the spindle-legged chairs. The small room off the kitchen where Joey and Jamie stayed was layered with alligator-hide instrument cases mired with dust and frozen broken latches, the cases in all shapes and sizes as if a mad leatherworker had been building anatomies. "I don't play a one of them anymore," he'd told them. But I can't help but hold on to them."

"Maybe," Joey said, "I should take up the ukulele. Give me something to do but sit there between verses."

"Don't do it," he warned. "Your audience don't want a thing between you and them."

That first winter Joey and Scully traveled the north country, mostly on weekends to North Conway and Fryeburg, Colebrook and Saint Johnsbury, even Dixville and Berlin to opera houses and house parties and a handful of winter-pressed swelled-bride weddings and wherever the money took them. From ten days before Christmas until the day after the New Year they slept on trains and worked every night and arrived back in Littleton with pouched black eyes and a thousand dollars between them and had their own small celebration then. Other nights they worked barn parties and skating parties around the western ridge of the Presidentials and made little more than their fare. As if the musicians existed for no purpose beyond that moment back off in the corner spinning out what was needed. "We're preachers to the blood," Scully told her. "They need us there but nobody wants to figure out why. It's a good time is all. If they're having one, we should be too. It ain't talent so much that makes it a business as understanding what exactly's provided. Don't confuse it with anything else."

"I was raised by a whore. I don't spin pipedreams."

He'd looked at her then. Somewhere on a daylight train. Through the window sunlight on their laps like summer. Beyond the glass, snow plowed back off the road so high the banks went out of sight overhead, the direct look out the window into the bluewhite snow. So fine and cold that the lips and furrows of the banks tilted and held in place, not moved even by the passing train. Scully said, "A bit of dream won't kill you."

He was a man without women. Had clearly at some point indeterminate abandoned the idea of them in his life. His hands worked up and down the ivory and ebony keys like a lover finally at home. Always, even after a ten-minute break, with the attention of a long absence.

It took Jamie longer than he liked to learn this. It was a hard winter. Through the first part he found no work and spent his days in the house, most often alone, or idling in the newsstand or barbershop upstreet. Sure someway he'd lost her. Taking each phrase she passed to him, even those in lovemaking, and turning them over and over in his mind, finding the rot there that he wanted. And still she came back. Then in January Scully and Joey responded to an offer of three weeks' work in North Conway and he saw them off at the station with flitting eyes, unable to focus clearly on either of them or on what she was saying to him, and he did not wait for the train to depart but walked out along the frozen river to the tanning sheds and shoe works and took a job in the gluing room of one of the factories, knowing he'd squandered his summer and seeing clearly he was less well off than being back on the farm but was determined to grit it out, to wait the spring and pay attention this time. The only alternative was to steal the gold and go but he had to believe she'd come back and knew he wanted to be there when she did. In an odd way he did not care what he had to do, did not care about the work if she was not there to see him doing it. So he worked three days in the gluing room and left the first two nights sick to his stomach with his head aching and his eyes red-rimmed and weeping tears that froze on his cheeks as he walked back through the early January night to the cold house and a cold supper. And at midday of the third day he found his supervisor and quit, only shaking his head when asked why. The other glue workers were imbecilic, misshapen, enormities of oddity and he was without interest in learning if they were born that way or came to the condition through the work; he would not remain there and felt this answer to be obvious. And so ended up on the large open floor of the factory, seated at a stitching machine sewing precut tongues to uppers over and over, but the room was warm and the windows looked out over the river and a rank of spruce beyond that and he found he could do the work and still cut trails through the spruce in his mind. And so he made a living and was without pride about it; even when the musicians came home he would still be at his machine each morning at seven, hungover but awake from the thirty-below mile walk to work. He made no friends there and wanted none. This was a time in his life he'd never repeat and would never revisit. As a child kept in after school writing *I will not*s on the blackboard he sat at his machine, stitching leather to leather, his right foot working up and down in a smooth steady pump, the sound each beat the passage of time, each shoe a shoe closer to summer.

When she was away he did not try to avoid thinking of her, of where she might be and what doing, of where, halfway through his workday with the sun on the icicles outside the factory windows like blades; she might be waking and the countless faceless men all beside her or at least all those each night wanting to be. And he never questioned her of any of this. There was nothing he wanted to know. Twice, as winter ground on through March with slate skies pressed low for days on end and the cold damp now but with nothing yet of spring in it, he walked girls home from the shoe works and both times sat talking with them until he saw they were bored with him and then excused himself and walked to the dark house, where he helped himself under the stiff cold blankets, thinking of what he could have, should have, done. Imagining those girls and others as well but never once Joey for his pleasure. As if excluding her kept him removed from all guilt. When she was away he never assumed she'd return but let the fever of his soul, the turmoil of his blood, call her back. It was a winter of holding breath.

So in May when the snow was rotting under the spruce outside the shoe works windows and while the river ran high and free of ice, and Scully and Joey were far down south in Portsmouth at Wentworth where some semblance of a season was already under way, he collected himself and quit his stitching post. Daily he rode the train to Bethlehem where the great hotels still wore their shutters and the grass was matted brown in packed swirls left as shadows of the snow on the lawns and the golf courses but where also some few of the hotel men were back in town, camped in basement offices next to wood- or coal-burning heaters and going over their books from the season before, walking out each noon to stand on the empty porches to gaze east and gauge the snowmelt on Mount Washington, which stood at a far distance away down the main street. And some few of these men, he learned, would also come out of an evening with a glass of whiskey in their hand to stand in the same place and watch the snow-crest of the mountain turn pink against the crystalline sky as the sun sank behind their shoulders and on some of those evenings they came out in their shirtsleeves. And he came to know them all by first names and learned something of their histories and families, and so in mid-June on a Friday afternoon when the first guests of summer disembarked the trains out of Boston, Jamie was assistant to the bar manager at the Sinclair, a position he was qualified for simply by proximity and persistence.

And his winter of eating day-old bread and hard cheese and green bacon fruited as he spent his savings renting a small green-shingled house with three rooms just off the Whitefield road north of the center of Bethlehem and it was here he led Joey when she came back north from Portsmouth with a summer tan from the ocean beach, her hair stiff from the salt breeze. That first night he ate the salt from her body as if he'd had no seasoning for months, she curling up under his tongue. Later he propped on an elbow to watch her sleep. He felt back in the race. The temptation to take her by the throat and beat her head against the wall was momentary. He let himself out of the house into the June night, standing naked on the thin grass sprouting around the heaved-up elms. A frail moon was caught in the new tender leaves.

Summer was once again upon them and this time he saw it clearly for what it was—a short pause for all, guests and workers, an interlude aside from the hurly-burly drag-weighted span of days. His intention was to pick apart that summer's draw of days to learn a way to inhabit that place, not to become a hotel man—he'd seen enough of them already to know that was not a route for himself—but some other thing that would be his, in the same way that Joey and Scully had made their pleasure their life. He had no doubt it could be done. And it was not that he was too young not to see what this had cost Scully; he simply didn't believe it would happen to him that way. He believed in luck. Not the ordinary luck that comes to all in runs of good or bad seemingly out of nowhere but luck searched out, sought in the corners and back rooms and cobwebbed recesses where no other might think to look. Luck, then, earned someway. And luck that summer was an unlikely man.

Binter was a Boer. Or Ukrainian or a Pole. Jamie was never sure and did not care. What mattered was the farm he had in the Easton valley south of Franconia in the swale meadowlands of the Gale River, a mixed farm of dairy cattle and sheep he grazed on the rock-strewn uplands rising toward Sugar Hill. Five years before his sheepshed had burned and he'd left the timbers charred and collapsed over the foundation hole and built a new barn and used the old site as a pit for his winter's worth of manure, a steaming mound even in the hardest freeze of January. In the ruined cellar he built a small room of brick roofed over with the jumbled burned timbers to create a chamber in a place where none should be. And in this he established a distilling kettle and worm and space enough to draw off the raw mash into small kegs and keep it there for some few months before he determined it ready. The pale fumes from the still rose up through the manure piled over it and there was nothing to indicate a thing beyond what was seen: a steaming pile of shit. He purchased loads of corn to feed his dairy cattle and alternated that with freight cars of potatoes from Maine, which made an excellent sheep feed, and so ran off batches of mash and something close to vodka: both spirits clear and raw, each little different from the other but the variation in materials was just enough to evade suspicion. He had great numbers of both cattle and sheep. He had little incentive to part with any animals. His English was excellent, fair, or gone altogether, depending on circumstance. He was a tall droop-shouldered man with thick hair and a mustache once blond gone white and he wore full suits with a vest and fob chain to milk his cows in. Under the speckles of manure and sawdust bedding, his shoes held a full daily shine. His custom were loggers and woodsmen from the upper Connecticut Lakes and local men that he knew. He did not lack ambition or greed but had the immigrant's wise and excessive sense of caution. That summer Jamie made three trips to see him before Binter would speak English to him. Jamie was happy with this. And patient. He already knew what he needed to know about the man.

One evening in July he arrived at milking and a just-freshened heifer was belligerent, balking on the runway behind the stalls. Binter as usual ignored Jamie until he stepped behind the cow and with one hand to guide her neck used the other to screw the cow's tail up over her back and like that she stepped up into the stall and Jamie went alongside her and pulled the stanchion closed against her neck. Her head went down in the trough, eating the soured leftover mash. Binter crouched at the flank of the cow beside, his fists wringing jets of milk to strike the side of the pail, the sharp *ping* giving way to a more hollow *thump* as the pail filled. His head turned sideways to rest a cheek against the belly of the cow. Looking at Jamie. And for the first time Jamie smiled at him, knowing the deal was already done. Jamie waited. After a time Binter turned his gaze back to the filling pail, his hands working slowly now, stripping the hindquarters and then the fore teats of the cow. Done, he looked at Jamie. The old man had a wen at the tip of his nose. He rose and stepped across the gutter and set the filled pail on the walkway. Turned his head to hawk into the gutter and looked at Jamie and nodded.

"Cash on the barrelhead. Once a week, no more often. Come chore time, morning or night. Never on Sunday. You want it bottled, bring your own glass. But you, you have the automobile. So you'd prefer by the cask. Do your own bottling. The casks you can bring back. That way too you don't have to worry about underestimating your needs. Because"—he raised a finger in the air—"I am very serious about the once-a-week only."

"I thought about that," Jamie said. "Give me a couple weeks and I should have it tuned so I wouldn't bother you but every two–three weeks. Best for both of us that way."

He enjoyed his work at the Sinclair. Each afternoon the black trousers and starched white shirt with new cuffs and a new collar and the silk brocaded vest limned in black with a paisley motif in dark gold and jade across the back would be on hangers in the small office behind the bar, sent up fresh from laundry, sometimes still warm when he pulled them on. He was a fine hand with the ice pick and small mallet and could continue conversation while his hands worked beneath him to fill a glass with hard shavings from the block of ice. He talked while polishing the silver-topped seltzer bottle behind the bar, making it look as if he was only keeping his hands busy while wiping away the smudged fingerprints so once again the tops of the high-necked bottles threw off perfect reflections from the gaslamps that in this room alone of the hotel had not yet been replaced with electric lights. He was studiously slow with a match for a cigar or cigarette, waiting a long beat clocked from an eye's corner until he was sure the guest needed such and then was there with his hands cupped around the match as if to fend off some unknown breeze. He would not forget a man's name even if three or four days separated the first and second meeting but he might run across the same man the second morning on the porch or striding Main Street and would not speak to him, only nodding if the eyes came his way. Understanding that the bar was sanctum sanctorum for some men on their holidays. Understanding that some men needed refuge from the refuge, that some men's lives were complicated to the point where their families were further impediments. They tipped him well. Even that first summer, in the logbook on the small table next to the front desk where departing guests wrote comments on their stays, his name was mentioned several times. Shown this, he was deprecating. Still, some evenings after the bar had closed he would linger around the front desk before going off in search of Joey. Leafing through the pages of the guestbook, looking for mention of his name. Those blotted scrawled entries revealed his presence, rooted him, placed him in a way his own eyes and heart never could. He hated that he read them.

The bar manager was a Scot named Oliphant with red-gold close-cropped curls gone silver at the temples, a stout man who rose only to Jamie's shoulder but whose eyes followed him as if not trusting him. Jamie liked him. Oliphant slipped him a sheet of paper with the name of a printer in Concord and Jamie took his day off to ride the train south and make arrangements for labels. The bottles he ordered directly from a glassworks in western New York State. It was understood he'd do no trade where he worked. The distillation of potatoes he diluted by a quarter and held in glass carboys for three weeks with a cheesecloth bundle of juniper needles suspended in the liquid and then decanted into bottles with gin labels attached; the corn liquor he bottled straight with a coloring of caramelized sugar and this was his scotch. The labels were not copies of any in existence but they looked right. He sold only to men he knew and then in case lots; he sold nothing directly to guests, of his hotel or any other, but to desk clerks and dining room managers and headwaiters and barbers and stablemen. He sold to the small underground nightclubs. That first summer he would not sell to local men not associated with the hotels but during the next winter he slowly expanded and so met Wells and Terry. Brothers by nature, stature and inclination but not blood; both woodchuck-faced, hard-muscled men going soft from no longer working in the woods; both with the tang of woodsmoke and bacon grease year-round to their clothes. Strong yellow teeth showing black rot along the edges. Terry the larger and taller of the two, Wells with his temper riding him like a bull thistle down his shirtfront. Together they traveled the north country from Island Pond in Vermont east to Millinocket in Maine, servicing the lumber camps and mill towns, once every month or six weeks coming through Bethlehem with their heavy wagon drawn by a six-horse hitch of big-barreled roan Belgian geldings, year round. Jamie trusted them. They knew what they were doing and did it quietly and without pretense or show. Jamie distrusted flair.

By the summer of 1909 they'd been there five years and their lives had taken on a pattern of satisfaction and accomplishment. He was now bar manager. And he had the liquor business. The local and state police were his customers. The federal men were farther north along the border and he had no interest in going to Canada for cheap liquor. He had no need. Binter was wrapped like a Christmas present; he bought all the farmer could produce. He drove a T-model Ford new off the line the winter before. He'd bought the small house in the tamarack stand the year before, the house with eighteen acres along the river, the sheep pasture and an old meadow grown up to alders and poplars and briars and young birch just beyond the sway-backed barn where he kept cases of liquor under a mound of rotted hay as well as a team of hot bay trotting horses and a sleigh for the deep winter when the Ford was no good at all and a high-wheeled gig for the brief weeks when the frost went out of the ground. In the early afternoons which were his mornings he would stand before the mirror shaving and remind himself that he was small-time. No Diamond Jim. He liked doing this. It was true but also somewhat of a joke. He had just started. He was in good shape and happy. He hadn't exceeded his expectations. He was twenty-five years old.

An evening in late July. The Ford running smoothly, along the avenue of maples lining the road leading along the slow swell of grade toward town, the grounds of the Maplewood already along the north side: the sand traps and greens and the taller roughs. He wore a driving coat, leather gloves, a visored cap and goggles. Beside him Joey was wrapped in a duster buttoned at the neck and spreading down around her to cover even her shoes, her hair covered with a wide-brimmed hat with flags of gossamer that tied under her chin. At her feet a satchel of gowns and slippers, costume changes. They turned into the long drive of the Maplewood and he took the fork for the long way around to the Casino. It was still early.

"I'm cooking in this tent." Dust the color of ash lay over her cheeks and nose. This was a routine conversation warm summer evenings.

"It'll likely storm later. That'll cool things down." To the east the crown of Washington was outlined shale gray against a welter of thunderclouds, lightning like small jets of gold cutting the dark from time to time. It was too far away to hear. The late sun angled against them.

"I'd rather it was to storm, it'd do it earlier. Pretty evenings like this, they all stay out till dark, hiking or golfing or playing tennis. Half of them just want to eat dinner and soak in their baths and go to bed."

"That's right." He nodded, then added, "But there's always still enough to go around. It's never dull this time of year."

She was quiet then. People in groups and couples and some alone walked the roadway edge, all with the practiced remove of the guest not bothering to glance at whoever was arriving by motorcar.

He knew her thoughts. She worked now with the hotel orchestra. Two nights here, then one at the Fabyan House, one at the Mount Washington, sometimes at the Profile House in Franconia Notch. It was later after the ballrooms closed that she'd be cut loose to the small after-hours clubs where he'd always find her; then alone with no orchestra. Just the piano player, sometimes some sideman from one of the orchestras tailing her to sit in. Some horn player. And her schedule was no different from her desire to have every available person in her audience, each night, at whatever place, each time. It was a greed, he thought, the greed of talent. At best three and a half months, thin-stretched to four in good years, when she had the audience she felt herself worthy of. With the proof. The rest of the year was makework. But for now she was only herself, some purified rare creature in footlights and the single spot when the stage lights went down, a length of velvet or satin or late at night sheer contours limpid on a stool or prowling the small stages. Her eyes innocent and hooded, turned down toward herself and bold yet still; thrust up with a jerk to find the one man five tables back who had not succumbed—who thought her a lovely voice but trite, too contrived, not quite making the mark, not grand—and she would drop her raised eyes on that one man and sing half a line or part of a chorus and then turn her head back down and he would be finished. Jamie knew how she worked.

They came around the side of the hotel where the spired tower of the Casino was ahead and he notched down the throttle and the Ford backfired with a tight neat puff and they slowed. The air over them was still, free of dust, and she began to remove her wraps. They came to a stop before the Casino. He was airy, jubilant, seething and joyous for the night before him. He said, "Here we go. Another night to clean pockets and unstuff shirts. Give everyone a taste of what they want. God, I do love these people."

She stepped out of the car and removed the duster and folded it and set it in on the floorboards. Untied her hat and took it off and placed it atop the duster. Lifted out her satchel and placed it on the lawn behind her and brushed her dress: a dark violet satin, the color of moonlit midnight. Her buttoned boots blood red, saddle leather. Her eyes turned off toward the tennis courts. She said, "No, you don't. You hate them all."

He could barely hear her. He shut down the Ford. Thinking, Here we are again. He said, "I wouldn't want to be a one of them. But that doesn't mean I hate them. At least, not more than most anybody else." And grinned at her.

She picked up the satchel. Then turned back to face him. A clump of guests were coming up behind the stopped car. He was keen with awareness of them. She said, "It's not necessary you stay up so late every night to see me home. I can get rides."

"I bet so. I bet that cornet player would be happy to give you a lift. Thing is, I guess he'd lose his way, get lost. I bet he'd do that."

Her eyes on him. "I know the way."

"That's what worries me."

"He's just a musician. More pecker than brain. You don't have to worry about me. I just feel a little cornered is all. Roped in. It's not that

I don't like seeing you setting out there. It's just maybe sometimes I'd
like to have to work it all out myself."

He nodded. "You bet." Knowing they were both lying now. He said,
"Well I'll leave you be then."

"I'm not telling you to run up there and screw some girl working
laundry."

"I never thought it. Unless that's what you mean."

"Don't twist me around like that."

He got out of the car. Went around the front and lifted the crank
down and inserted it. Paused then and looked at her. He said, "I'm not
twisting you one way you didn't set out to have me do."

She swung away from him, the satchel striking her thigh. The violet
dress slapped tight against her. Without looking back, she said, "Don't
be an idiot."

He twisted the crank until the flywheel clicked tight. Then stepped
back and clipped the handle one more time and dropped his hand. The
engine turned and caught and the handle came to a stop. That first flip
could break an arm. He got back in the car and pressed the throttle
lever up and drove around the Casino, raising dust in the airless dusk
and scattering guests as he went. The storms over Washington held and
he guessed there would be no rain this evening. Or perhaps late, when
the sheet lightning came down broad in strokes of orange and green,
purple and blue. He liked those storms. I'm maybe an idiot he thought,
but I'm sure as shit not stupid.

At the Sinclair he spoke to his bartenders, sat in the small office and
wrote out a beer order and another for cigars and cigarettes. Read
through the notes in the bar ledger. Studied a single time card. Went
out to the service end of the bar and leaned there until a particular
waiter came up, a man older than himself with damp drooping ovals
staining his shirt under his arms, his tray wet with beer froth. Empty
glasses.

"Evening, Mister Pelham."

Jamie nodded. "Henley." Then, "Problem last night?"

Henley had red ears that stood out like exit lamps. "No sir. Not much.
Had to ask a man to leave."

"A man to leave," Jamie repeated.

"That's right. He was bad drunk, stinking. Mad at the world. Didn't like the beer, didn't like the cigars, didn't like the whiskey. Didn't like anything. Sitting alone there in the back. The gentlemen around him, I could see they were uncomfortable with him. And he poured a beer on me."

"That right?"

Henley nodded. "Said it was skunk piss. Asked me how I liked the smell of it."

"And?"

"I asked him to leave."

Jamie inclined his head toward the bartenders. "You get Jake or Stanley involved?"

"No sir. I didn't see a need."

Jamie nodded. "So you asked him to leave."

"That's right."

"And he left?"

Henley wet his lips. He was still holding the tray out beside his body, the arm supporting it beginning to vibrate with the effort. "He did leave. I had to assist him some."

Jamie nodded again, as if interested. "What was that?"

"Mister Pelham?"

"What sort of assistance did you provide?"

"I took him by the arm."

"And he left then?"

"He wanted to fight me. Broke away and put up his fists."

Jamie smiled. "That right?"

Henley smiled back. "It is."

"What happened then? You don't look scuffed up."

"I told him he touched me once I'd pound him into the ground."

"You told him that."

"I did."

"And he left then?"

"Took his hat up off the table and put it on, the rim soaked with beer, and shook his finger at me. Told me he'd hang my rear out to dry and left."

"Ass."

"Sir?"

"It was your ass he said he'd hang to dry. Not rear."

"I was trying to be polite." Henley's eyes now floating, drifting away from Jamie.

"I wish you'd thought of that last night. Mr. Arthur Shipley of Schenectady New York. With wife, two teenage daughters and a younger boy. Arthur junior I believe. Two maids. Three rooms, two baths plus the maid's lodging. The full month of July. This would be his third year in a row. He enjoys golf but stops here instead of the Maplewood because his wife likes the view off the back porches and the flower gardens. Set that tray down before you drop it. And stand here two minutes while I figure your time and I'll have Stanley cash you out of the register."

"Mister Pelham."

Jamie reached and took the tray and placed it on the bar. Then placed his right index finger on the waiter's breastbone. "If the man had stood on his table and pissed in your face I'd expect you to get off work and go home early and take a bath. Get a bottle of whiskey from Jake or Stanley for your troubles. And that's all I'd expect. Now you wait here and then we're done. He pulled his index finger back a couple of inches, curled it at the knuckle and rapped hard, once.

In the office he rewrote the schedule for the next two weeks and under-lined the changes in the red crayon he knew to be an alert to his em-ployees. Wrote a note to the hotel accountant diverting Henley's back wages to the bar till. Rolled a pencil back and forth on the smooth blot-ter and silently said To hell with it and unlocked the bottom drawer of the desk and poured himself a drink. Dragged the tall standing tele-phone onto the blotter and took up the earpiece and leaned to speak into the mouthpiece, asked the girl at the switchboard to get him the Maplewood and waited, then asked the girl there for the casino and waited again. Then Gurnsey was on the line, his counterpart at the Maplewood. Each man chipped, inferior to the other. Gurnsey had the plum, the best hotel. Jamie had the liquor business, independence. And so odd equals. Intimacy of respect and isolation; each to the other what no other man was. This didn't mean they liked each other.

"Eric, things slow down there for you tonight?" Over the rough oceanic quality of the line he could hear the fluid yammer of a crowd, the strains behind that of the orchestra. Pressed the earpiece hard to try and pick out a vocal, a woman in song.

"Shit yes like a cemetery. I stop to consider it's the end of July already and I'm a dead man. Just doesn't seem like there'll be a season this year. I can't even bring myself to look at the reservation book. And I got help quitting left and right."

"Don't hire a man called Henley, he comes looking."

"Had him last year. Couldn't haul freight. Slow's it is, I rather chat of a morning. You need me to run a case of something up there?"

Jamie rolled the pencil. "No. No I don't need nothing." Paused again. Gurnsey said, "What is it, Pelham?"

He wet his lips, remembered Henley doing the same thing. Almost said nothing but his need was greater than the desire of his pride. His voice dropped a register, he said, "Who is it this time, Eric? Is it that horn player?"

Another pause, this one on the line. The burble of static, of distance. Those few miles. Then Gurnsey said, "That cornet man is just a pup. Big sloppy eyes and a grin he can't get rid of. He's smitten bad but he's no problem. For christ sake don't whop on him like you did that boy last fall. It's hard enough to get these fellows up here for a three-month contract."

"I never touched that man last year. I talked to him was all."

"Jamie."

"It's true."

"You could step back a moment and see it how it is, you'd find some pleasure in it. She reels everybody in, one way or another. Jesus, Jamie, it's what she's paid to do. You have to expect some dog-eyed men along the way. It's just part of the deal. And I do believe she knows that."

Jamie was nodding. Worked the key in the bottom drawer again even as he leaned into the mouthpiece. Brought the bottle out and set it on the blotter beside him. The label was his own and tonight gave him no pleasure. He said, "You're jacking me around here, Gurnsey. We're not just talking about some moon-faced boy in the band here. She's working somebody, we both know that. It's what she does. I'm not coming up there with a pissed fit. I just want to know what it all is. This is a woman we're talking about. She travels around me with whatever she wants to say and when I begin to catch on looks at me like I've just shit my pants. A hundred times a week it's her job to ruin men. All I want to know is what I'm dealing with when there's one's got to her. A professional courtesy, Gurnsey. That's all I'm asking for."

"I don't think I can help you with that problem."

"I understand that. It's a high roller, I know that much. If he's gotten to her, he long since left you creamed your pants."

"It's your woman. You're the one should know. You're good, Pelham, but you're not good enough to dirty everyone else with your personal problems. None of us is. Maybe you should remember that."

"Eric, you're right. I stepped over the line here. It leaves me in a quandary. I can forget all this. Or I could ride up there and see for myself. It's not what I want. All I want is the who part. Just so I know. You can understand that."

"You're an asshole."

"Don't we both know that."

"I swear, Pelham—"

"Save it, Eric."

A long pause then. Jamie pulled the corked stopper from the bottle and turned away from the mouthpiece and drank. His ear still flattened hot to the earpiece, waiting. The liquor was pretty bad but he drank it because it was his. He felt the day he stopped drinking it was the day he would stop selling it. Then the noise over the line grew muffled, went away. For a moment he thought Gurnsey had hung up. Then realized his hand was over the mouthpiece. This was not good. He waited. Maybe it was not good. After a brief time Gurnsey came back on.

"It's a sporting goods man from Providence. He's at the end of the first of two weeks. I understand his wife and kids are at the shore. On the Cape. So he's just another lonely old fart. Nothing to worry about. She's just doing her job."

"What's his name?"

"I don't know his name."

"Don't fuck with me Eric. I'm not coming up there anyway. But I won't be a fool."

Another pause, this time with all the noise. Gurnsey then said, as if breathing out, "His name's Sloane."

"A Jew?"

"Not here."

"Sloane." Turned up the bottle once again. "What's he look like."

Gurnsey sighed. "Like an old man. Forget it, Pelham. Its nothing."

"What's he look like?"

Gurnsey said, "There's men would be happy to shoot you and have you gone. You know that, don't you?"

"Fuck off, Eric. What's he look like?"

A long pause then. "He's fifty. Maybe fifty-five. A little bald but in good shape. Well-dressed, well-mannered. Like I said, sporting goods man. Hikes daytimes. Has a chest of guns with him. Hired a caddie to toss clay pigeons for him. In the early evenings. Every day. He can double if the caddie is fast enough. A fisherman also, up in the mornings. A drinker at night. But not so he doesn't tuck into his food. That enough?"

"I guess maybe so."

"Jamie?"

"I'm right here."

"It's just her job."

"I know that."

Again, quiet. Then Gurnsey said, "Anything I can do." It was not a question, not quite an offer.

"Not a thing, Eric. Not a fucking thing."

"It'll pass, Jamie. It's just a thing."

He didn't go home. He didn't go looking for her. When the lounge closed at half past two he fired up the Ford and drove over the hill to Franconia and out to the Notch where he found a waitress at the Profile House just getting off work. Together they went the couple of miles north to Echo Lake, where they sat on the sand beach and drank from the bonded bottle he'd lifted from behind the bar and lay back and watched the stars wheel up in the slender wedge of sky between the narrow cleft of mountains and talked about how men and women couldn't seem to help but do each other wrong and how things should be. Later, when it was too cold to do it, they stripped off their clothes and swam briefly in the lake. When they came out of the water he lifted her and carried her to the picnic table and set her down facing him and took her ankles in his hands and spread her legs and with her saying no he entered her and stood thrusting with his face turned up to the sky and when her arms and legs locked around him and her voice changed from words to other sounds it did not matter. He lifted both hands to cup her head to him and called her darling and sweetheart and love and then came in her, she rising off the table as he came. His hands hooked her buttocks and he carried her around the beach, the soft sand slopping and grasping at his feet. Some nightbird called out from across the lake. A fox barked up in the hills. The stars were still. A lightened sky in the east. Pale, almost no color at all. He stood and watched the girl dress. She was clumsy in the sand, standing on one foot and then the other. He smoked a cigarette. She was slow and he was cold.

Joey was not at the house. It was past dawn and the sun had been out as he came over the hill between Franconia and Bethlehem after taking the girl—Alice was her name—back to the dormitories behind the Profile House. She'd been teary and he was too tired to do more than drive the car. He just wanted to be rid of her. It was nothing to cry over. Before he dropped her off he held her a moment, patting her shoulder, wondering if anyone he knew was spying him out. Then he drove over the hill with the low-spread sun an angled pain running through his eyes to the back of his head. Out of Bethlehem down toward the river he drove into the dense river fog and it wrapped around him like a bandage. And Joey was not there. He'd been prepared to find her sleeping or even sitting up, still dressed from the night, eyes red-shot and her face choked with anger. He stood in the kitchen. The dishes from their breakfast the evening before still in the sink. There was no sign she'd been there and yet he felt she had come and gone. He went through the house and it seemed everything was there as it should be. The only things gone were what she'd taken last night. Too tired to make a fire, he poured day-old cold coffee into a cup and filled it to the brim with whiskey and sat on the small front steps and listened to the fog drip from the trees. His neck ached as if it had been beaten with an iron rod. He finished his drink and went into the house and stripped and washed himself with a cloth and cold water from a basin. His fingers smelled of sex and tobacco, the soap only a thin layer of perfume over the deeper scents, as if those smells were coming from within his skin. He went to bed.

She came in early afternoon. The house smelled scorched, a faint odor of mouse scat and dead flies. She'd slept only a few hours but was restless not tired. She looked in where he lay sleeping on his side, his knees curled up and his hands between his legs like a boy, his bottom lip pouched and slack, a dark spot of drool on the pillow beneath him. She looked at his clothes dropped on the floor and for a moment thought of picking up his trousers to smell the crotch but didn't. There wasn't anything she wanted to know. She built a fire and made coffee and then undressed, her clothes stiff and creased with wrinkles, slept in. She took an old shirt of his from the laundry basket and wearing that carried her coffee down to the river. She sat on a boulder and took the shirt off and drank her coffee while her body alternated hot and cool with the clouds sweeping over the sun. Her hands were shaking. It was the coffee she thought.

Her life felt in pieces. Not that she expected otherwise, everything she'd learned tuned her to expect this. But those pieces seemed slight things, fragments too dear or fine to hold. Water ever-passing around the mute boulder shoulder beneath her. She saw herself clearly, in ten years, maybe fifteen, her voice a tailfeather of what it had been, her body grown thick and stout, sitting somewhere, always sitting somewhere, waiting for the night and those few moments when her old self might rise out of her, where again she could stalk some small shabby room, sitting waiting, drinking something. In five years she'd stopped believing in the savior, the one man out there who would hear her and take her to New York or Boston. She was good but not that good. She was good for where she was. And for the time being. Time being, what? Today. Tomorrow if she was lucky. Her mother learned this the hard way. Joey was determined not to find the hard way. The question then was what was the alternative? Trust some man? She spat in the river but didn't even see her spit land or float or merge. Just gone. Clouds moved off the sun and she was hot. Making the best was what she had. Men could be turned she knew but only for so long. How long she didn't know, couldn't say. She didn't know how an honest wife did it. Perhaps men changed. Perhaps they made accommodations. Perhaps they only learned more contrived elaborate lies. Perhaps they loved their wives and children and went on being men. Perhaps the women even understood it, someway forgave it. She didn't know. She could see the house across the sheep meadow and through the evergreens. She didn't know who it was lay there sleeping. The noonday clouds had thickened, the anvils lowered, the towers higher. It would storm by dinnertime. She had an hour, maybe two. She slid down the side of the boulder into the cold water and swam there, fast back and forth against the current, diving down over and over so her whole body was under the surface. She clambered back onto the rock and stood there shivering, the sun out. Herself then as tight and high and young as she ever had been, as she'd ever be again. She stood on the stone to warm but didn't and finally bent to take up the shirt and carried it up toward the house, walking naked across the pasture and then through the tamaracks, the water drying fast as she went, the stippled flesh still abrupt, erect. Her feet light on the duff.

She heard him before she saw him. *Thock*. Then a pause and the sound came again. Then she came through the trees. He was sideways, his back to her, dressed just in trousers, barefoot and bare-chested. He had a bucket of golf balls and a driver and was driving the balls one at a time in a high sailing arc out of sight into the puckerbrush behind the barn. He didn't play golf but bought buckets of balls from the caddies at the Maplewood and time to time would come out with an old driver he'd found somewhere and send the balls one after another into the woods until the bucket was empty. She stood back and watched him. The twist in his back as he drove the ball and his arms followed through with the driver up over his head was a beautiful thing. His body not the boy she'd met five years ago, not so much changed as confirmed, wired muscles taut and lean. His bones and limbs fine as if carved from wood. He would, she guessed, look much the same in twenty years, thirty years. She put the shirt on and as he leaned toward the bucket she stepped from the trees into the small opening of sunlight where he saw her and paused a moment and then set the ball on the tee and drove it off into the woods, watching it go from sight, his head tilted back. Then dropped the club by the bucket and walked to the steps and took up cigarettes and lighted one and smoked, the smoke dribbling from his nose.

"The fuck you been."

She made a small shrug. "I made it back in one piece."

"Be hard to tell you wasn't."

"What's that mean?"

He spit tobacco flecks off his lips. "Don't be pissy at me. You tell me you'll find your own way home and then come crawling in the middle of the day. What do you figure I'd think?"

"Think what you like."

"That's it? Think what I like?"

"Jesus, Jamie." She shook her head. "Some of us went to a party out toward Whitefield. Some Canadians there playing fiddle music. Reels and jigs and such I hadn't heard in years. People dancing like they meant it. I had fun was all. I didn't have to do a thing but have fun."

"And you couldn't've done that with me?"

"Listen," she said. "I'm sorry about saying that last night. Sometimes I just feel like I'm all cornered up. I'm sorry."

"I don't want to corner anybody anywhere."

"Don't do that. I didn't even know about that party until after work and things were winding down at Laird's and Godchaux was the one had heard about it and brought it up so we all went. That's all. I don't know if you'd have liked it or not. That kind of music. But the people were all drinking your whiskey so you'd probably have liked it just fine. But you weren't there and I wasn't about to hold things up trying to hunt you down at three-thirty in the morning."

"He the cornet player?"

"Godchaux?"

"Yuht."

She nodded.

He waited, then said, "So who's we?"

She looked at him. "Just Godchaux and Scully and me. Godchaux drove us over there and then Scully and me home. Wasn't anything more than that. I slept in a chair there at that house a couple of hours." She shook her head. "You don't need to worry about that Godchaux. He's just a horny boy which is the last thing I want. Think about it a second.

Though he plays that horn sweet. From New Orleans, Louisiana, if you can imagine. Everything to him's ragtime or barrelhouse, stuff like that. I can't figure that music out myself. But I like listening to it. But that's all. I believe he's got some nigger blood to him also; you look at him, you have to wonder. Skin like a lemondrop. Maybe he's just unhealthy. There's fevers down there in New Orleans I hear."

Jamie pinched off the cigarette head with his fingers and let it smolder in the needle duff, sending up a fine trail of smoke like an incense. He flicked the dead butt off into the mint patch beside the house, then stood looking down at the little flame running along the needles a moment before he stepped onto it with his bare foot and ground it out. Looked back up at her. "He was colored he wouldn't be working here."

She laughed. "How could anybody tell? He's never out in sunlight. What'd you do last night, yourself?"

"Me? Nothing."

"Nothing? Come on."

"Stayed away from Laird's because you'd told me to. Rode out to Franconia and drank a bottle of whiskey and went for a cold goddamn swim and rode back here. Went to bed alone. Had a fine old time."

"I bet you did."

"Did what?"

"Had a fine time. You likely didn't even know you were enjoying yourself, riding along getting drunk. Feeling sorry for yourself. I bet you had a grand old time, doing that."

"I wasn't feeling sorry for myself."

"Of course you were," she said, grinning at him. "You wasn't feeling sorry for yourself you'd of been chasing after some girl somewhere. Don't think I don't know you a little bit."

He tipped his head and squeezed his nose between his thumb and turned-back forefinger and said, "You think so?"

Then she said, all the gaiety gone from her, "You thought, in your heart, I was off with someone else, the first thing you'd do is get laid. Yes I do. I know that."

He looked off, over at the bucket of balls and the dropped driver, then off into the tamaracks where the sun had gone, leaving them standing in a cool shade of cloud cover. While he looked a burst of wind picked the boughs and flopped them hard and then was gone. The air was still again. Cooler. It would soon rain. He said, "I never hurt you."

"Not yet," she said. Her eyes on him. "I need to take a bath. A long soak. I'm too wide awake to sleep but it's going to hit me hard later on." She went around him up onto the steps. Stopped there and leaned to kiss the top of his head. The smell of him the oldest constant thing she knew outside of herself. She said, "It's going to rain. There's not much to eat. Why don't you put the top up on the Ford and when I'm done we can ride up early and eat some supper somewhere. I could eat a real meal. A bucket of steamers maybe. Or a beefsteak. Something like that."

Then, the wind whipping down through the boughs again, flapping the tails of his shirt around her thighs, she went in through the screen door. He watched her go across the kitchen and out of sight into the bathroom. The sky was suddenly low and dark, the way storms dropped here. In minutes it would be raining, pouring water, the sky torn purple with lightning. He heard water running in the house behind him. Then it began to rain hard, slantwise. He walked out through it to the barn and put the top up on the car. Opened the passenger side door and looked around the seat and floorboard to make sure Alice had not dropped or left something. Removed a single long blond hair from the seatback. He was a little ashamed and angry at being found out without being found out. As if her innocence was worse than any knowledge. And did not trust her innocence either. Did not trust much. Was glad he had held on to Sloane, had not mentioned the name. It would've been easy. Not yet, he thought. The blond hair was wrapped around one finger. A thin ring of gold cut into his skin. Patience was the best weapon he knew. He unwrapped the hair and dropped it on the barn floor where it was lost in the old hay. He was hungry and liked the idea of going somewhere to eat before work. The bucket of steamers would be good. Little butter-soaked cunts. The rain was lashing in the door of the barn, thunder now right atop the trees, flattening the world. He thought of Joey in the bath, knew she'd have a candle lighted against the sudden dark afternoon. He advanced to the barn door and stood looking out, getting wet. His driver and the bucket of balls were still sitting, a puddle around where the bucket had filled and was overflowing. He took his trousers off and wadded them under one arm and ran naked through the iced snakes of rain toward the house. Up the steps and inside. Wet and cold. He dropped the pants on a kitchen chair and went into the bathroom. His skin prickling, tight. His prick out before him.

It was no trick finding Sloane. He left the Sinclair the next evening just about dinnertime and walked the slow two miles east to the Maplewood, the main street rimmed with red light from the westering sun and people in slow promenade with the day's heat broken and Washington sitting neat as a cutout at the end of the street, the small jets of black smoke from the cog railroad rising from the slope as if the mountain breathed. He walked down behind the hotel, past the farm buildings and stables and beyond the kitchen gardens to a stretch of rough field studded with outcroppings, following for some time the reports of a gun. He perched up on the top rail of the old-fashion stile set into the fence and sat watching, smoking, making no effort to hide himself.

A hotel or stable boy was heaving the clay pigeons, snapping his arm in a flat motion of elbow and wrist to throw the small discus. Cradled in his other arm against his body was a stack of the pigeons. A crate of them sat on the ground. The boy tried to get another into the air right after the first so there were two sailing through the air at the same time. Only then would the gunner, Sloane, raise his shotgun, the motion a swift smooth upswing as his body remained still but seemed to crouch and spring forward at the same time. The pigeons were thin black slices in the sky until hit and then they blew apart in a scatter of fragments. Jamie sat watching. There was a clear satisfaction in it, he could see. He'd thought it would be the sound of the gun but as he watched he guessed that Sloane didn't even hear that. It was the spattered clay he was tuned to.

Sloane shot with a thoroughness, a tenacity of spirit and concentration evident even from this small distance that Jamie recognized immediately. It was the calm certitude of a man centered exactly in the world, one whose shoes owned each piece of ground they fell upon. The clay pigeons that broke apart were not so much appreciated as expected. The others, those few that fell in a long glide into the grass, were dismissed, not worried over. Not as if they hadn't existed but simply they were gone. He was moving along to the next set, ready for them, the double-gun broken open and the brass and paper cartridges ejected still trailing smoke to land in a litter of other shells behind him as he slipped two new shells into the gun and then held it, ready before him, up against his chest, alert and relaxed. Jamie sat smoking, the tobacco mixed with the sweet-bitter waft of burnt powder from the shot-shells.

Sloane finished while the hotel boy still cradled a stack of pigeons, just left the gun broken open over his arm and reached into his pocket to hand the boy a tip and turned and stalked up through the field toward the fence. The boy restacked the clays in the wooden case and then bent to gather up the spent shells. Sloane walked toward Jamie, not looking at him on his perch, just walking up out of the field with the gun held like a child in the crook made by his left arm while his right hand passed a handkerchief over the length of the barrels and the wood of the stock.

Jamie watched him come: a man of medium height and build, full-fleshed but not fat, his features birdlike, replete and avaricious at once—a hard brow and nose falling to soften with a full chin. Hair the color of old silverware, cut as if it were a utensil. Jamie watched the fingers of his hand running over the gun, concentrated, meticulous and unaware at their work. Sloane came up to the opening in the fence and glanced up at Jamie and his eyes slid past to the hotel beyond as he turned himself sideways to come through the stile, his eyes going off Jamie as if he were a bush or shrub, some ornament set out by the hotel. A sundial. A weathercock. No one he needed to know.

And because of this Jamie spoke to him. He hadn't planned or wanted to. He'd wanted to be the stranger out of place. An observer. Instead he felt like a boy. So he said, "Good shooting."

Sloane then paused and looked up at him. He said, "You a hunter?"

"Not so much anymore," Jamie said. "For a while I did. And I've been thinking about taking it up again."

"Well, you should. It's what a man is. Most directly and without dressing himself up. Everything else we do, that's just for show. Don't waste your time young man. Don't waste a bit of it." His eyes already turned away, toward the hotel, the lowered dusk, the dinner formed in his mind. Jamie sat rocking on his buttocks and heels, both sharp against the fence rails, nothing to say as Sloane stepped through the stile and walked up toward the hotel, not looking back.

He walked back to the Sinclair and spoke with both bartenders and again lifted a bottle of bonded whiskey from the shelving behind the bar and went out into the night. He drove out of town, this time taking the back road to Franconia, the long way around the shoulder of the mountain, the road washed and gullied and ripped by boulder-backs even in the dry pack of summer, driving slowly, at times idling the car by inches along the broken and spavined crust of roadway, drinking from the opened bottle held between his legs, the headlamps pale illumination as the car rutted its way. A mile or more above Franconia he came out into a brief meadow that broke the treeline sufficient to show Mount Lafayette in the moonlight, the cleft between the flanks of the mountain clear in the night air. He rolled the car to a stop and shut it down and got out carrying the bottle with him and walked into the meadow where the hay had just been mown and lay in long swaths. He sat there with his knees up, working at the bottle and smoking cigarettes, the moonlight over everything faint and brittle as the crisp sugar of the drying hay.

He was doing what Joey had thought he'd done two nights before. In a way this made him feel more honest. Sometimes other people get the facts wrong but the intent correct. She had said nothing of Sloane. Even if her account of the night of Canadian fiddle tunes was honest there was the omission of some detail, some way that Sloane fit into the night for her. Even if he was not there. The problem, Jamie had long felt, was not that people weren't capable of telling the truth; it was that they weren't able to understand what they were hearing. The truth was not a line from here to there, and not ever-widening circles like the rings on a sawn log, but rather trails of oscillating overlapping liquids that poured forth but then assumed a shape and life of their own, that circled back around in spirals and fluctuations to touch and color all truths that came out after that one. So a thing was not one thing but many things. A fact many facts. He understood this perfectly and understood also that with the first words out of his mouth this understanding would collapse to a small mean thing, a target to be driven home toward. There was the sensation of being trapped, caught between who he was and what could be explained. He lay back in the hay, his hands behind his head, fingers laced, the moonlight spread around him, the bottle upright, nestled in the stubble beside him. The summer nightsky, the Milky Way, was a broad smear of light overhead. Except for the Dipper he did not know the stars. As a boy his father had tried to show them to him and he would strain to follow the broad thick finger and nod his head but could not discern shapes or patterns in the great blot of distant lights. He wished he knew them. It was one of those understandings people seemed to have of the world that he could not grasp. He strove to ignore them but he knew his lacks.

He sat upright suddenly, waking, hay in his hair. He did not know where he was. Some time had passed. The moon was gone, the sky more pitched, the stars brilliant. He found the whiskey bottle, his cigarettes. Stood and drank, wavering. Retched and leaned and spewed a vile stream onto the hay. It backed up into his nose and he hawked and spat. Drank from the bottle once more and then once again. Spat and walked a ragged circle against the heavings of his stomach. Lobbed the bottle off into the woods, where it fell into the underbrush without the satisfactory crack and splatter of glass. Smoked. He felt unspoken between them was tacit understanding that screwing for gain or leveraged compensation was private, business, something that lay outside the slender artifact each returned to the other for; he did not expect purity from her anymore than of himself but only fealty of her heart. Hers the same as his, damaged goods, an ill organ beyond hope of repair or long life but known to the bearer and so something to be trusted. He felt her his twin, so deeply mirrored as to be a sister sent over from some world running side by side with this poor one, some part of himself missing now found. He believed this, of himself, of her. He trusted her.

He did not trust her. Up in that lost midnight meadow of hay standing with his neck bent back toward the sky and his eyes pinched tight he saw her vivid astride a prone Sloane: the slow wet glide of her with her back arched, her head bent back as his was now so her loosed hair was a down-strewn broken piece of night-river with her face lost in it, her arms and shoulders and collarbone forged twigs, her breasts pulled up by the curve of her back, the nipples greedy, his hands covering them.

Sloane in turgid satisfaction, some part of himself watching this young woman work over him, some part of him expecting this, some part deserving, believing he deserved. A shooter of clay pigeons.

He started the Ford and backed around in the meadow and rode through the woods again back to Bethlehem, where a lone horse stood between the shafts of an empty gig, the horse jumping sideways and shaking the gig as the motorcar passed, the broad street otherwise empty. He stopped at the Sinclair but the bar there was closed and empty save for an old man with a bucket and mop scrubbing the sticky floorboards. Drove on then to the after-hours club with bricked-up basement windows in the house of a man, Laird, that Jamie did business with but did not care for, the two of them each puffed and tight with the other, speaking in jokes and barbs indirect and circuitous. Here a couple of motorcars and a couple of buggies were edged up in a clump under the sugar maples behind the house. One of the cars belonged to the one-man police force, a Spanish-American veteran, a captain, a man called Haynes. Jamie sat outside, squatting in the dark near the bole of one of the maples, smoking and watching the black rectangle of shut door. If she wasn't there he didn't want to walk in looking for her.

The basement walls were stone and mortar foundation eighteen inches thick and he couldn't hear anything, music or voices. He might have been the only man in town. The horses at the buggies next to him stood each with one foot cocked up, sleeping. From time to time one of them would briefly rouse and shake the harness or grind teeth on the bit and then go back to sleep. His cigarette smoke drifted and lay about him in the night. After a time the door opened and Scully came out and shut the door behind him and stood without moving, taking fresh air, stoop-shouldered near to a hunchback from the cumulative years bent over the keys. As if his body had become a functionary of the instrument.

Scully looked past him a little when Jamie came up. That was all right. Jamie said, "She's not here, is she Scully?"

Scully thought about it. "She was tired. Went on to home I think."

Jamie nodded. "I'd guess she'd be tired. You too, after that carouse the bunch of you went on last night."

Scully looked at him then. "It was a late night."

"I wouldn't ask you anything you'd have to lie about. You know that."

Scully looked away again. "I never covered up anything for anybody."

"I know it." He paused then, looking away also. Wanting to be gone before anyone else came out the door. He said, "I'll get on home myself I think."

Scully nodded. Then said, "You ought to marry her, you know."

Jamie grinned at him. "I don't know, Scully. I don't know she'd have me. I thought about it but I'm not sure either of us is the marrying sort, her or me. Seems like all it might do would make bad things worse and chip off some of the good in the process. You know what I mean?"

Scully nodded again, the dome of his head pale-bald in the darkness. "I always thought of marriage as a way to death. But then it's not such a grand thing, being alone, you get older."

"I'll think about that," Jamie told him. "Like I said though, I have doubts she'd have me. Right now at least."

Scully was kneading the fingers of one hand into the wrist of the other. Sore, wanting to play, to get away from Jamie. He said, "Right now's probably the best time for it, you ask me."

"Think so?"

Scully looked at him. Shook his head. "What do I know? I'm the least expert."

She was not at the house. He lighted a lantern and carried it to the derelict barn and loosed the two driving horses from their straight stalls and followed them to the trough by the pump and pumped water until the trough was overflowing and listened to them drink, the long knotty gurgling pipes of their throats working. Once, he'd liked horses. It would not be so many years though and the motorcars would function year-round. Roads would continue to improve, the cars too. Sometimes the future lay open like a staggered deck of cards. If you were not bound to the past. The smell of horses, the sweet and sour of their coats, the dried sweat turned to dust rising off a smacked flank, links of a chain cut through and through but unbroken still in the small hidden glands working memory. He carried scoops of sweet feed from the bin to their mangers and they turned from the water and came back eager to their stalls and he fastened them to the manger-chains. Carried forkfuls of what remained of the good hay to them. He needed to buy hay for the winter. It was growing light and he went to the trough and picked up the lantern and went to the house. Other times no soul could say what the morrow carried.

He did not see her for three days. He did not seek her out. Wherever she was she had new clothes. It was the only thing he could say for sure. He spent time in the office behind the bar in the Sinclair and went over everything so the business could run on its own until the end of October or burn down before then, he did not care. He attended to his liquor business. On the third day he left work early in the afternoon and drove the long slow thirty miles north to a lumber camp up near the Connecticut Lakes where there was a man who owed Wells and Terry money that they owed to him. It was not a thing he had to do. They were competent in collections. The man was a Frenchman cook at the camp and Jamie asked for him by name and stood out in the sawdust-strewn yard with the hot summer sun against his back, his shoulders strained already as he called the man out of the long low cookhouse, a big man but fat and soft with a face puffed and red from his ovens, his thumbs up in his red suspenders over his naked sweating chest. Jamie stepped forward and explained why he was there in a simple declarative sentence as he stooped and came up with a broken canthook handle that he laid across the face of the man and as the blood blew forth from the Frenchman's nose and as he came forward and down Jamie stepped back and brought the handle deep into the Frenchman's belly and the man crumpled onto the ground and Jamie left him there. Driving the miles back as afternoon turned down to evening he stopped the car and was sick. He hadn't eaten in days. He could sit in his office behind the bar and order a full meal off the dining room menu and some girl would bring it back to him. He wanted oysters. A salad. Some roasted joint. Potatoes. The small puffed steaming rolls. Butter. Pie.

The fourth day he was up early, midmorning. All he was doing was going to work, coming home, not staying up. He wanted to see no one. Whatever was being talked of had not reached him and he understood this absence of gossip as a gauge of the problem. He had been a very small boy last he wanted to cry. Take her by the shoulders and shake her until her head lolled and her eyes turned up. He built a fire and waited and threw a handful of grounds into the boiling water and set it aside to settle. There wasn't anything to eat in the house not spoiled. He wasn't hungry. He burned his hand pouring coffee into the small cracked cup with the wild roses running just below the rim that she always drank from. Drank it burning and puked in the sink on top of a pile of crusted crockery. As if his stomach wanted out.

He went from the house to the barn and took up a shovel and walked out into the thin woodlot grown up with alders and young birch, where fall mornings timberdoodles would rise up straight to tower over the young growth and hover a moment before planing off, leaving scattered over the marshy ground the whitewash of their droppings. He could maul a man, eat a chicken, discharge old men from their last hope of gainful employment but he could not shoot a bird. It was not an event of purity. Another lack. Fucking Sloane. Carrying the spade he walked out past the spots where he had paper money buried in coffee cans and mason jars with dome lids and rubber seals, farther into the pucker-brush, and once there he did not hesitate but sank the blade of the spade and turned up the black wet soil he already knew was undisturbed but still found the tea canister of gold wrapped in burlap sacking that he hefted and then reburied and smoothed over the ground, scattering gathered trash of twigs and finger-raked leaf mold back over the scarred ground. It was hot. Sweat ran into his eyes. He backed out of the thicket and stood and deerflies were over him and he swatted at them and re-alized he was naked, that he had left the house without dressing. His body flecked with blood from the bites and smeared with mud-prints from his hands. Stood looking down at himself so. A savage. Some kind of man. Deerflies in his hair. On his thighs, his rear. His back low where he could not reach. He danced, swatting himself with his free hand, and then stepped down on a berry cane and was stabbed and at the same moment stung on his forehead and he swatted himself between the eyes with the other hand that still held the spade handle. The sunlight through the leaves and trees swelled and burst. He stooped in a crouch, leaning on the spade. He began to cry.

Up on the road out of sight of the house an automobile came to a stop, the cylinders popping like single drumbeats. He strained but heard nothing more. Then came the clap of a car door being shut. Still holding the spade he began to run. His idea was to make the barn and go from there to the river and swim and so clean himself and come up to find her already in the house, composed however she would be, himself as any other morning. Well, he practiced silent, it's a pretty day isn't it.

Into the backside of the barn, panting, streaming sweat, he laid the spade against the wall and stepped toward the front door of the barn and saw her coming down the sand track through the tamaracks into the clearing, striding loose-jointed, easy, a posture he hoped. Still wearing the same white dress piped with black satin as four days before but holding up pretty good he thought for four days' wear. He scrubbed the streaked tears and sweat from his face with muddy hands. It would've been easier if she'd strolled in wearing a new outfit—he saw she would not lay a thing out before him. Her containment a full measure.

There was nothing for it but to walk out and greet her and she looked him up and down, her eyes cut with laughter and fear. A flick of concern, one of victory. "What happened to you?"

"I was out in the woods."

Her eyebrows arched. "Wrestling what? A catamount?"

"I wasn't wrestling anything. There was some dogs barking woke me up and I ran out there and chased them off and fell down and got the shit stung out of me by deerflies. I was just going down to the river to swim. It's awful early in the morning for you to be up and about. Your boyfriend kick you out?"

"No," she said. "My boyfriend did not kick me out."

"Well. I don't want to hear whatever story you made up and got ready to tell me. I guess maybe you don't feel so cornered anymore. That's good. I'm happy you knew you could go off for however long you wanted and do whatever you wanted with whoever you wanted to do it with and get yourself uncornered. And know you could traipse back on in and I'd be falling-down-glad to see you. I'm glad you knew that much. But I don't want to hear the first word out of your cocksucking little mouth right now because I'd split your lips open and lose you some of your teeth and feel pretty good about doing it. So I'm going to go swim. I figure you either came back or come to pack your trash and get out. I get back up here from the river and you're here, then forget about whatever you had all rehearsed to tell me. You understand me?"

"I heard that about you."

"Heard what?"

"That you'd taken to larruping on french canadians."

"I don't know what you're talking about."

She scanned him again up and down, most clearly not liking what she saw. "Old men and now women. It's a sad place to come to, Jamie. I saw Estus Terry; he told me how you broke up that old cook's face."

"How'd you see Terry?"

"Told me he'd already got the money you were after. He was spooked, Estus was. Said he paid the doctor for that old man from his own pocket. And a fit of dentures as well. Told me he couldn't see how you'd go off like that."

There it was, he thought. Her hair a jumble like she'd risen from bed five minutes before or worse didn't care about it and in clothes rumpled and dusty but still too fresh for four days of living, walking in like any morning, her eyes clear and large and it all turned back on him. He could not help himself. "I'll settle with Terry. And that Frenchman business was about a lot more than him. Estus knows that. He was working on you was all. Where was it you said you saw him?"

She shook her head. "I didn't say. But he was at Laird's two nights ago. Looking for you. All I could tell him was you hadn't been in."

"I guess that's right."

"You hadn't. I don't know what you were hiding from but it didn't need to be me."

He looked at her. "Estus Terry knows where to find me otherwise."

She stepped forward then and ran a finger over a point on his chest where a deerfly bite had crusted, her finger taking away the crust and then daubed again in the slim rivulet of blood that seeped, lifting the finger to her mouth and cleaning it between her lips. "I guess," she said, "he'd tried to find you. I guess that's why he came to talk to me. I can't see any other reason for it, can you?" Her eyes open on him now, great blank reflections empty of everything but himself.

"Whatever Terry told you about that Frenchman, he knew better. Terry's got no reason to be frightened of me."

"Oh Jamie." She sighed. Then looked around the clearing, at the house, the barn, the stand of hemlocks and tamaracks as if sweeping for an answer or merely confirming what she already knew. She said, "He's asked me to go off with him."

Imbecilic, seeing himself so, his mouth stretched grotesque around the words, "Estus Terry?" As if his brain was determined to keep with the old order, the other conversation, not to move forward the step she had already taken. And her look of naked pity as if viewing a spine-broken chipmunk, some creature she could not help but love.

She shook her head and said, "No."

"I know," he cried out. "I know."

She was silent, her head in a small shake, not to refute him but to make clear some way he could not know, could not understand. A gesture beyond her control. He saw all this.

"Fuck. It's that fucker Sloane you're talking about isn't it?"

"Edgar," she said.

"What?" He hadn't moved, was breathless.

"His name's Edgar." She looked away then, as if giving away something she'd not intended. He thought there might be a balance there, some teetering point he might nudge or slip into motion or challenge or change.

He stepped back away from her and stood running one toe in a circle in the sand and needle-trash and again realized he was naked and crossed his arms over his chest and said, "So what're you going to do?"

"What do you think, Jamie?" Her face tilted back at him.

He shook his head. "I knew I wouldn't of asked." Paused and added, "You look like you're afraid of me."

"I been afraid of you since I first ever saw you."

"You and me," he said, "I thought we were kind of partnered up."

It was hot in the clearing there before the house. A sheen of sweat over her face. Her eyes flared, wet. "We had some times," she said.

"Some times," he repeated, the center of him opened, heart, soul, a knife thrust neat from septum to sternum. She knew she was shredding him and still she would do it and now for the first time in those five years he felt the heat of that engine turned against him, the peculiar force she emitted as if it did not belong to her, as if she held no responsibility for the low moan that came forth and entered into the dried heart and bitter soul of the man listening. "Some times," he said again. Then without pause said, "So, he just going to move you in with his wife and children?"

"It's so small-time. You think you've got your hand in everybodys pocket, don't you." She shook her head, a small contempt. "It happens he knows men, in Providence and Boston both, men in the entertainment business. And I'm not talking about music halls and such but theatre, real theatre. He knows I've got a talent, Jamie. All he wants is to help me. It's not always about how much cash or how much ass. I know you don't believe that. It's no sure thing, I know that. But this is a chance, a risk I've got to take. Could be the only one I get."

"You're stupid. All he's going to do is stick you away in some cold-water flat somewhere and pay your bills and give you enough money to live on. Maybe turn you out to some little work or another so you feel like the gold ring's just around the corner. And come by to fuck you once a week. Just turn you into your mother is all he's going to do."

"You asshole."

He went right on. "Maybe that's the right thing. I mean, maybe that's how it works. We can't ever learn a thing. We just keep doing the same things over and over. Not even intentional. Like we can't help ourselves. Like it's who we really are. That's it—we spend our lives just becoming what we already someway know we are."

"I hate it here," she said. "I hate the winters, all cooped up, frozen. I hate the summers too, the same people, year after year, the same little diversion I make on their summer trip. I hate saying the same things over and over, singing the same songs over and over. I hate it. I do! I can't stand it anymore."

"You think that's really going to change? Say, even all the things you think you want, say those happen? You don't think it'll someway come down to the same thing? Pleasing people you couldn't care less about? People who don't give a shit about you, people you're just a ornament to. You doubt that? It comes down to it, it don't matter whether you're fucking Mister Edgar Sloane on some cold winter day or trailing around in a fine gown with a glass of champagne and five hundred people all dressed up pressing your hand and kissing your cheek; in the end, the end of the day, they all go off and leave you alone with yourself. And where's that leave you? Where do you think? Just right there alone is all. Just right there with your own self and nothing else."

"That's just it," she cried. "You think that way, you won't ever find anything else. I'm sick of it. I'm just sick of thinking that's how it's going to be." Her face strained, turgid, the gape of a turtle snapping at air. So lovely.

"Well fuck," he said. His energy gone, unfocused, shriveled. As if he'd held her in his hands as long as his words came forth and then with them gone she also fled back into herself. Wherever that was. Not here. "Fuck it." He began to walk a circle around her, stalking, his feet churning the sand, his motion a tightening of his pitch. "I never did a wrong to you. I never trailed after you. I let you go your way. Maybe that was my mistake but it's how I have to be, how I have to live, whoever it is. I gave you everything that's mine to give. I never wanted anything but you. I trusted you. Trusted you with me. Stupid fucker, right? Stupid fuck good only until something better comes along. Stupid, stupid, stupid."

Her voice small when he was behind her. "I never thought I knew you. Who you really was."

He struck, grasping her shoulders and turning her to face him and he leaned close so he could smell her and she him, drops of sweat flung from his face to hers. "All right. Fuck it." And he sprang away from her and ran the simple feet to the Ford and tore loose the crank and jammed it home and twisted it tight and looked then over his shoulder at her still standing where he'd turned her and called to her. "Let's go then. Get whatever it is you come back for and let's go. I'll take you where you want. Let's get out of here."

"Jamie," she said, advancing a step toward him.

"What is it? He up there on the road waiting for you, is that it?" His body crunched down against the front of the car.

"Jamie." Stopped now, her face torn apart before him.

"So you don't know me. All right. Let's go." He twisted the crank and let it go and the car popped and churned and died and he raced around the side of it and adjusted the magneto and the gas lever and then ran back to the front and again spun the crank.

"Jamie." Her voice up, calling him.

"What? What do you want? What do you want from me?" Words like birds breaking their way free, splintering his breastbone. Still leaned at the crank.

She beat her thighs with her fists. Cried out, "I don't know."

They did not speak words again until later when they were down at the river both naked then—after he'd come those few steps forward from the Ford—forever after not able to recall how he traveled that distance and their mouths struck together so their teeth broke through their bloodied lips as they suckled and fed upon the other's mouth before he picked her up and carried her into the house, the two of them already a one-formed creature lumbering through the kitchen knocking over a chair and down the hall to the bedroom where he threw her down upon the bed, driving the wind from her lungs as a hole in her his soul might fill, she lifting her legs and skirts toward her chest as he knelt and tore the knickers from her and there was language there in the room but no words. After that first brief wild spiral when she rolled him off of her and stood without looking at him and removed the fragments of her clothes, her breasts already bruised and raw from his lips and teeth, bending over to take him in her mouth until he was full and strained again and then over him in a hard wild flail that had him arched from the bed in a beaded bright pain far beyond his command or desire to stop, he helpless before her driving, even his vision swept red and he could not tell in that not-darkness where he left off and she began; a liquid-gripped pair of fists connected them and the sea of red over his eyes pulsed with the blood of both of them, driven each time in perfect time with the cries breaking from her mouth hot against his face.

And still not speaking as they lay apart on the bed gathering their wind back and each benumbed and someway still joined and already each alone, the afternoon light through the windows where the sun fell over the floor, the room hot and still enough to hear the settle of the other's limbs against the mangled sheets. They lay a time like that, on their backs, just not touching, neither willing nor wanting to speak, and then he stood off the bed and she followed him and they went back through the house and she gathered up towels spread over the backs of

kitchen chairs to dry from days before and they went one beside the other
along the path they'd made through the thick boles of the widely spaced
evergreens, across the sheep meadow and over the fence, down along
the river to the bend where they always came. She sat up on the ledge
of rock and watched him swim and then came in after him so they both
came out of the river at the same time, hair slicked back and bodies tingling and for just a moment shining with heat and water like spun honey
before the air began to dry them and even then they were still silent but
lay back on the towels spread on the boulder.

For a time he lay thinking there was no need for words, that the last
hour had flung off the shroud fallen over them, between them, during
these days just passed, that they would rise up from here at some point
and go on as they always had or not even that but in someway not yet
known to them, and he lay believing this until enough time had passed
and she had turned with the heat from her back to her stomach and he
began to believe this long wordless gap was a point that neither could
rise from and carry on as before, that the gap itself was all he needed to
know about it. And then he lay for a time more, aware that once he spoke
or even likely moved there would be an end to all this. He heard a ewe
bleat for her lamb in the pasture above them. Beyond that the snip-
ping worry of a chipmunk. The river. The sound of the river where
he wanted to live. Over the surface of the far back pool of the riverbend
a green damselfly moved, its wings a translucent blur against the brilliant body. He watched until it was out of sight in the shadow thrown
down by the undercut bank. Then he stood and roughed his head with
the towel, looking away from her although he could feel she'd sat up,
was looking at him, at his back. He took a breath and let it out and took
another, her eyes against him. He looked off at the far side of the river
and said, "I'd marry you tomorrow, you wanted."

His words hung out there and fell away and he'd already stepped
down off the granite and was climbing the sharp bank to the sheepfence
when her words came but he didn't need them and didn't want them,
the wait long enough to tell him all he needed to know. Gripping the
post and feeling the wire cut against the hard sole of his foot as he stepped
up onto the fence to swing his leg over. Too late for that. She guessed.
Walking alone, scattering the sheep, he wondered why she had to guess.
Fucking women. Trying to be kind. Running through the woods to-

ward the house, his sobs ratcheting for breath, wanting just to gain the house and clothes and leave from there, to be gone. Sure now her guess was a kindness, some gentle setting down of him. He wanted out of there. She'd been beaten before and he thought it likely she'd be again. But it wouldn't be him. The morning's fear of him in her eyes. It would not be him.

She sat in the sun until she heard the sound of the Ford leaving, perhaps half an hour. She sat watching the river run by. She guessed she would be nostalgic for this place but sitting waiting she would not think of it, just sat watching the water. She waited until she could no longer hear the car and then waited ten minutes more before she stood and walked up to the house. She did not know how she was to get where she was going. She'd refused to make a plan until the moment unfurled because until it happened she'd not been able to say for sure what she would do. Then the moment came and she told him it was too late for that, the words coming out of her almost as random choice. She failed to trust Edgar Sloane as much as she'd wanted Jamie to believe. She was absolutely without belief in love. She had eight, maybe ten years to trade upon, was what she believed, and what occurred during that time would set the course for the rest of her life, one way or another. It had not been so much a career singing she'd implied when she spoke of taking the risk. And Jamie. Jamie would not be alone long. Beyond his looks plenty of girls would peel out of their skins for that taint of danger he carried, that spread out from him like a sun-basking snake. She did not fear him and did not know why she'd told him that. Because she knew it was the one threat he could not counter. It was true that she did not know him, as true as how she felt of herself. She did not trust anything, least of all herself.

At the house she dressed and brushed out her hair and considered the closet and took out only a small valise that held another pair of high-buttoned boots and one of slippers and three dresses and a single gown and changes of underclothing and then a small box of earrings and bracelets and her one single strand of baby pearls that had once been her mother's or perhaps her grandmother's. She was not discarding but being practical. This time of day there would be plenty of traffic on the meager highway running from Crawford Notch up into Bethlehem and she had no doubt of catching a ride. With the summer vacationers the odds were against being picked up by anyone she knew but she did not want to appear a burden to anyone or make memories. Just a girl with a grip trying to get to work.

She went to the barn and saw he'd been using the spade and knew what for and went out into the woods and dug up not the gold but one of the mason jars of rolled banknotes, money as much hers as his, and she left the hole dug up with the empty jar beside it and went back into the house and buried the roll down into her underclothing. She did not want the gold. She knew she could leave it here and it would stay here. She might live to old age away and Jamie marry some woman and raise children and die and she knew the tea canister of gold pieces would stay right where it was until the canister rotted away in the ground and there would only be the ancient thick wafers of buttery gold lying out there unknown in the leaf-mold. It was better than a bank. It was better than taking it with her.

Then she was done and meant to walk right out the door with the valise and up the sand track to the highway. Instead she sat at the kitchen table. The summer smell of kitchen garbage, fetid dishes in the sink. The odor of decaying wallpaper paste. She recalled the morning she'd left Saint-Camille with her mother. The trains south where there was no choice but to go. The lawyer McCarson. Edgar Sloane was no McCarson. And who precisely had her mother thought McCarson was that morning they set off on those southern trains into another country? The balm of sun and riverwater gone now and only the ache of sex left, her thighs stretched and her breasts tender within their coverings. Her mother died, finally. She'd become a whore and life had whored upon her. Joey knew the difference between them was that her mother considered herself accidental. As if life had conspired against her more so than anyone else. Not fate but some abuse from God. Some way she'd abused her God and He'd responded in kind. A grand fearsome kind her mother thought she deserved. When all it was, Joey believed, was every one has good and bad to them but no one is willing to face the bad head-on and take it as part of themselves. There might be that bravery somewhere. She might have it. She might have a little. Edgar Sloane might have it. He was precise, focused, nerved-up and steady. A man in his fifties. Perhaps it was that. His confidence came off him like aftershave. But it remained that he was on vacation. And there was only the one way to know him otherwise.

She sat at the table and cried a little. For a short time she cried because she had to and then because she thought she should and when she knew that she stopped and dried her face on one of the towels and stood and found a box of cigarettes and lighted one, intending to smoke it and calm herself before walking up to the road, to let her eyes dry and lose whatever swelling might be there but as soon as she had the first smoke in her lungs she couldn't stand to be in the house any longer so she lifted the valise and walked out into the afternoon up the track and smoked as she went and when she came to the highway she walked west toward Bethlehem, waiting for a ride.

Jamie stopped at the hotel to speak with his nightshift bartenders and the hotel manager and went on to Littleton where he took a room at the Thayer, paying for a week and ignoring the aslant eyes of the desk clerk, a man he knew from somewhere but could not say how. Things would proceed fine without him, the time short or long. Offhand he could name a dozen men eager or willing to try to take his place. So he'd gone as far as he thought wise. He sat in his rented room in an armchair throughout the remainder of the afternoon and watched the slow northern evening come over the town and then dark and still he sat. He had no appetite for food or drink. He sat smoking.

For the five years since the night they fled Barre he'd always one way or another been able to place her, to locate her, in his mind if not some actual structure. He'd always been able to imagine her. And now he could not do that. She was gone. Anything he thought was a warped thing, an approximation: she and Sloane in bed at the Maplewood; eating dinner there; already on a train south in the dining car; in a Pullman; in his motorcar, something better than the Ford with maybe even a driver while Joey and Sloane sat in the deep cushion of the rear compartment eating something out of a wicker basket and drinking champagne. He could see all this. He could not help but see it. And all of it, however close, he knew was wrong. He sat smoking. Like the man-jack felling trees who gauges and understands everything about the tree and then finds himself pinned beneath the fallen trunk, his legs crushed and dead already but holding the rest of him down into the snow to die slow. He did not understand how he had come here. It was all clear—this had led to this—but it made no sense.

By midnight he could not endure it. He walked down and in the quiet weeknight cranked the Ford and drove with enough moon to not need the headlamps along the spread valley between the mountains to the Profile House in Franconia where the waitress Alice refused to speak with him, where the bartender served him a single watered drink before the bar closed and occupied himself counting the till and had no inclination for conversation. And Jamie then went back to the Thayer where the night clerk was sleeping sprawled forward in his chair so Jamie slipped his knifeblade into the kitchen door and worked the lock and had cut slabs of ham and was frying them up with eggs when the clerk stepped into the kitchen and Jamie turned and waved a free hand indicating what was cooking and told the clerk to put it on his bill. The clerk backed out of the kitchen nodding his head and reaching behind him for the door and was gone before Jamie realized the hand he waved still held the knife he'd sliced through the ham. He held on to the knife and used it to slide the ham—and then the eggs on top—onto a plate before setting the knife on the counter. Wiped it first with a rag. Tore a large heel from a loaf and sat at the butcher table and ate the food. Three-thirty in the morning. Wherever she was she was twelve hours gone. He wondered if the rest of his life would be like this.

It was ten days before he went back to the house. He mostly stayed in the room at the Thayer, taking his breakfast in the hotel dining room. Before that he would go out and get shaved. Then long hours alone in the armchair next to the window of his room gazing down onto the street without making note of any passing thing. Each night he would drive out to Bethlehem and spend a couple of hours at the Sinclair locked in his office going over the books and writing out orders or amending those already made and reviewing time sheets and suchlike. He would send out an order for a dinner to be brought to him and he would eat it there alone with the office door locked after the girl had brought the plate of food. Whosoever knocked upon his door otherwise would only be one of the nightshift bartenders or the hotel general manager and these times few and the problems brief and minor but someway needing his approval or words of confirmation. And any of these men would meet his eye while speaking and then look away from him and he did not want to know what the talk was, what was being said, what people believed of him or did not believe. Finished with that he would drive back to Littleton and the third-floor room where he would wash his face in the basin and turn off the hanging single electric light bulb, watching the filament burn a slow orange disappearance in the dark and would lie in the bed, sleeping or not, dreaming or not, all through the night. He rose each day not rested but further abraded as if the sheets and the hours in the armchair worked at the thin layer of skin over him that was daily nothing more than a sack to hold his stranded heart.

He ignored his liquor business. If men ran short they would only appreciate him the more when he reappeared. There was no other ready source, not for a few days of dry. They could buy it bonded like all the rest meanwhile. But one afternoon he left the Thayer just after lunch and went looking for Estus Terry.

As much as his character would allow admiration for a man he felt it for Terry. If a model might exist, not for means and methods but for essence of a nature it would be Terry he'd look to. He did not believe Joey's telling that Terry was displeased with him. But he wanted to be in straight with Terry. Who he knew understood the beating of the Canuck cook. That was the business.

Terry owned a one-story single-room house free of civilization built by a hermit called Bliss in the decade before Jamie was born in the untouched forested land north of Bethlehem where the Ammonoosuc turned north in a big bend. Surrounded by stacks of uncut firewood piled tepee style. The sides of the house year round summer and winter banked waist high with raked-up leaf mold and woods trash and the whole anchored in place with cut hemlock boughs stacked one over the other intertwined. Like a burrow with not a piece of windowglass set into it. A single rotting stovepipe rising askew like a hand waving for help or goodbye. The place an indication not of economic condition but of the soul. A place no woman had ever walked.

There was no reason to expect Terry to be there in the peak of summer with the traveling he did—he covering the lumber camps of northern Vermont and New Hampshire while partner Aaron Wells did the same for the vast lonesome tracts of most of Maine. He bumped the Ford slow down the track rutted deep by the teams of heavy horses and the giant wheels of stout freight wagons, the wood's growth on either side of the way running overhead and so closeby that the motorcar was swathed. He came into the clearing where midday summer no smoke rose from the pipe but the front door was ajar and a pair of big roan Belgian horses with speckled rumps grazed free on the spare grass of the yard like a pair of watchdogs, the horses without halter or tether, neither one bothering to raise heads at the sudden loud approach of the car. Road-broke.

A small-framed man, Terry showed himself in the doorway and stepped back into the gloom briefly before coming out into the yard. In that brief half-lit moment Jamie saw the dark length of a rifle barrel down alongside Terry's leg. The weapon gone with the man out in the sunlight, Terry in gray wool woods-pants and a boiled white shirt too bright it seemed to have come out of that house. He went to one of the horses and stood with his hand on its withers while Jamie shut down the car. The horse lifted its head and lipped the pants-leg beside him and then dropped back to crop the grass.

"Pelham." Terry had several days' growth of a white speckled beard but his hair was combed, slicked back off his high forehead.

"Estus. Didn't mean to sneak in on you."

Terry spat. "I heard you coming. It's not many would risk a shiny thing like that machine to this road."

Jamie grinned. "Federal men maybe."

"Federal man can't find his ass with both hands, I tell you what."

"You need to get yourself two–three of these rigs, Terry. Get out of the horse business. Speed things up."

Terry worked his hand on the horsehide. "Not come winter it wouldn't. Although that day'll come I expect. But it'll be a younger man than me. I'm used to the pace of a team."

"Don't talk like a old man. You change with the times; there's always an easier way to get things done."

Terry shook his head. "Tell you what. There's always some younger fella coming around with some faster smoother way and it's them you need to watch out for. Times, those fellas can be too fast, too flashy. I got some money for you." He snaked a purse on a chain from a front pants pocket.

Jamie put his hand up. "I don't want it, Estus. I heard you got him doctored. There wasn't any call for you to do that."

"Shit boy, he'd already paid me what he owed when you thrashed him. That's what there wasn't a call for."

Jamie shook his head. "Last I'd heard, he owed. And even not, it's not a good idea people think they can be slack. With me. Or you."

"There's a difference between making a point and meanness. What I saw how you left him was plain meanness. I don't like it." Terry looking now full at Jamie, his face hard cast like something from a furnace. Terry went on. "He was other than who he was I'd cut you loose. Liquor's like spring water in the north country, you know where to look. You get over sure of your importance you'll fall flat. Or worse will happen. You got to keep in mind there's far more people aware of you than you might care to think. Once you get outside the lines you got to walk it straight and tight. You got to remember you're not the first pup with a bright idea. Not the last either. You keep that in the front of your head you'll be all right. Now here, you take this and we're square and we go on from here." And unzipped the purse and counted out banknotes from a roll and held them out.

Jamie stood very still. "No. I screwed up it shouldn't cost you money."

And Terry stepped away from the horse and came very close to Jamie and reached up gently and slipped the folded notes into Jamie's shirt pocket and leaned his face close and said, "You fuck with me I'll pound you into the fucking ground you hear me." And then stepped back and locked his hands behind his back, studying Jamie.

Jamie stood a long moment his eyes on Terry's. Then looked away. Took cigarettes and a box of matches from his trousers and lit one and blew the smoke off into the yard, aside from Terry. Then said, "It's a pretty day."

Terry said, "I heard your piece of tail run off on you."

"Well. She's gone."

"Chasing bigger fish I hear. Well, you're better off. They're fun when they're young but they get older they turn into one bit of nuisance after another."

Jamie nodded. "She tell you she was going?"

Terry looked at him again, his face opened now. "Me? I haven't spoke to her. Haven't seen her since I was last out to your house there

on the river. Back in the spring. May, wasn't it? Blackflies terrible bad
I recall."

"That's right," Jamie said. "It was May. But it was her told me you'd
paid to repair the French Canadian. Said you'd told her."

Terry shook his head. "It wasn't me. She just heard it around I guess.
She's the kind that hears things."

"I believed her," Jamie said. Not contradicting Estus Terry.

Terry said, "A woman'll lie as it suits her. It must've suited her. Now,
I got some bottles of beer lowered into the springhouse. That sound
good?"

He resumed in the liquor trade—acutely aware it was summer where
the bulk of the year's profit tallied. He made his rounds as usual with
the exception of Laird's after-hours dive where he had no desire to see
anyone or be seen and so went there afternoons on his way to the Sinclair
when Laird was still puffy and distempered from sleep and skull-
rockets. He called upon Binter, hanging around after his business concluded to make conversation that was little enough, and so oddly and
sweetly just right. A place free of associations. With motion once more,
he could not understand his just-ended inaction. As if he had lost himself. What was frightening was he'd acted far different than he'd have
predicted for himself. Drifting. A thing undone.

He went back to the house one midnight. The sheep farmer Flood's boy
was paid to daily water and feed the driving horses. Still he went first
to the barn to see them and stood there in the summer dark talking to
his horses, old everyday words issuing forth as undirected encompass-
ing love, a croon of self without content and fraught with meaning. And
heard himself, heard his father, his sister Prudence also, and stopped.
His father would talk to horses as if they were the god who happened
to live next door, easy terms and reverential at once. And his sister talked
to all creatures as if they might die without the sound of her voice and
she there just to reassure. He stood in the dark barn. The horses restless
now with his uneasy presence. He stroked them, not speaking.

*   *   *

The house was rank with absence. He sat in the pale filtered starlit yard and smoked and drank a small glass of whiskey. Then went through the dark house to the bedroom and lighted a lamp. The closet doors stood open as she had left them. He stood before them and gathered together an armful of her hanging dresses and thrust his face into them. Laundry soap. The closet smell of mouse scat, pale ancient cedar, a floral thread that might have been from her or might have been only the clothing itself. He blew out the lamp and undressed in the dark and got into the bed. The sheets musty, smelling old.

He woke during the night or half woke in another state altogether. He rolled off the bed onto his knees and crabbed across the floor and found her torn-off clothes from that last afternoon and he took them up wadded against him and lowered himself onto the mattress and humped against the balled clothing and then rolled over onto his back and with his left hand held the mess of clothes against his face, pressed to his nose and mouth as if he meant suffocation and with his other hand masturbated with a furious tight clench. Then slept again.

His first three years of school he frequently arrived home bruised, bleeding from his lips or nose, his eyes swollen. His knuckles broken and raw. It came in spates, days in a row or weekly and then weeks with nothing at all and then it would begin again. He would not speak of it, would stand silent, helpless tears on his face as one or both sisters ministered him. It was Abigail took the buggy to visit the teacher at Riford School but came back with nothing, her face a sneer of undirected anger. Nothing happened on school grounds. The Clifford boy cousins denied all knowledge, their eyes running over Jamie as if memorizing him. Aunt Connie squatted and took him by the elbows and naming them one by one asked if her boys tormented him and he denied it. After this Prudence laid claim to the job of driving him to school and picking him up afternoons but he would slip out of the house while she was in the barn harnessing a horse and go fast across the meadow into the woods and down to where he could come out and cross the road to the school. Afternoons if she was sitting waiting for him he'd bolt past the back of the gig and leap the ditch on the far side of the road and be off into the alders and popples in the springy damp ground there. And yet there in the woods they found him also and once found he would not run but turned to face them, one or five, and stand shaking before their taunt—of himself, of his father, of his dead mother, of his sisters: of them all. Not as simple as his skin or that of his mother or how she died but all of it mixed together in the animal cruelty of boys, the real with the imag-ined or conjured, the words' meanings not even understood by them or him but the cut and thrust of them clear enough, the indecent giddy pleasure of making pain. Until he would charge them, silent, clench-fisted. The boys: not just his cousins Clifford but the Polk brothers, Jimmy Potwin, Dennis Dowd, Bill Bartlett, Duffy Smith, the Morgan brothers. Sometimes others. He would always fight them. He knew if he quit they would also and knowing this made him all the more fero-cious, wild and ineffectual as they bloodied him and he would not quit. His father knew this, both these things, and he would sit nights wreathed in pipe smoke explaining aloud what the boy already knew. His father gentle, puzzled, remote and tender, his wearied recognition not aid but a balm as if together the two of them understood the pointlessness of the anger of the two women—that it was not the blood or fists or even the words but some other thing altogether that could not be stopped, checked or changed.

When the boy began his fourth year of school not only bloodied but with a dislocated shoulder that the doctor clenched and brought back to place with the first yelp of pain from the boy any of them had ever heard, it was then his sisters determined to take him from the school and so also from the town and their neighbors and educate him at home. Once seized upon the sisters held to this with the righteous fervor not of the convert but of the veteran. As if they might save the boy this way. And what that boy knew but could not ask was to save him for what? To raise up and so walk alongside them a monk to their nunhoods of carving the earth and cutting wood and the pervasive husbandry of live-stock that was all they allotted themselves? They had found him as their project, their wellspring of devotion. And it was not even love but thrall that kept the ten-year-old from explaining what could not be explained to his sisters. He was sure they knew. And so he learned that ignorance is not always stark deficit but can be so clearly and simply a denying of what is known. So they removed him from the battle. And so he never once won, never once caused harm or true fear in his opponents. And in this way those tormenting defeated him through the agency of the women who loved him more than any others ever would or could. And those women did educate him but they did not make him. He was already made.

He woke in the morning beside her ruined clothing stiff with semen and crushed where he'd rolled onto it in the night. He felt he'd fouled her someway. He carried the balled mass out to the stone-lined pit where they burned paper trash and poured kerosene over it and set it alight. Back in the house he gathered the rest of her clothes off their hangers and drove to Littleton to a laundry where he left it all to be cleaned and starched and ironed, telling the woman to pack the items for storage. The sun was well up now and he was hungry but wouldn't stop to eat. At the house he made a fire in the range and filled the copper boiler for wash water and began to clean the house, starting with the dishes clotted together in the sink. He found a rag and wiped down the furniture and then swept and after this found more rags and poured vinegar into a bucket of warm water and washed the windows, inside and out, with the sun hot now on his bare back and his stomach a hard knot consuming itself. Back inside he found a stiff brush and so was on his hands and knees scrubbing the floorboards when a motorcar came down the dirt track and he ignored it for his work and so Scully walked in and found him so, the knees of his trousers sopping from the scrub water, his chest and arms wet from his work, his hair slicked down, and when he raised his head to greet Scully the sweat ran into his eyes.

Scully drew back a chair at the table and seated himself to watch Jamie work. Scully in his rusted black trousers and white shirt and black jacket, his derby hat off his head on the table, one ankle over the other knee, his elbows out from his sides as his hands fiddled together on the tabletop. Bringing to mind a great awkward bird. With his hat off his thin hair invisible across the dome of his head, his skin stretched tight, a color like the crust on butter left too long in the air. From the folds of his coat he drew out a pint bottle without a label, stoppered with a cork and set it on the table. Lighted a cigarette. Drew hard upon it and coughed and drew again. Jamie thought There's me, thirty—forty years I don't watch it.

"Once you get it neatened you got yourself a problem. You can either scamper around trying to keep it all just as it was or you can watch it slowly pile up and fall over itself again. Either way, it's not a pretty thing."

"It's summertime," Jamie said. "A house needs a good cleaning once a year."

"Spring cleaning is what you're talking about."

"I guess the spring got away from me then." Jamie sat back on his haunches, let go of the brush and leaned against the cupboards. His hands were swollen and sore from the lye soap. "How long'd you know she was leaving?"

Scully shook his head. Uncorked the whiskey but didn't lift it. "She never even said goodbye to me. Other than that, I thought it was only a flirtation. The way she can look at a man and size his bankroll and all the time have him thinking it's his peter on her mind. You know that about her."

"I always thought it was shuffle-and-dodge. I never thought she'd run off. It irks me though. You had to have seen what was going on. I thought we were friends, Scully."

Scully took up the whiskey. "Friends, Jamie? I don't believe I know what that even means. Seems to me friends are people useful to a body. I'm losing what use I ever had and I know that for a fact. But say I had thought this time was different? And had remarked on it to you. What would you have done? That would have changed her mind?"

"I know it."

"I told you to marry her."

Jamie stood then, pushing off the cupboards and feeling his knees crack as he rose. Took up the cigarettes and the matches. "Say I had. Even a year ago, before this Rhode Island sportsman came along. You think that still would've stopped her?"

Scully nodded. "She's a peculiar strong girl."

"She's a whore, what she is."

"No." Scully didn't ponder this. "That's your heartbreak talking. She's just a girl turned loose in the world with only herself to count on.

Trying to figure out each step which is best. That's what seemed to make you two such a fine pair, maybe, but on the other hand wouldn't it be natural for her to grasp hard onto someone who knows the way? And that sameness in you both, it could be, she wouldn't see that as attractive as you do, might be even she could worry over it. This make any sense to you?"

"What do you want, Scully? What'd you come down here for?"

"Why, to check on you. Make sure you were all right."

"I'm not going to blow my head off, if that's what you mean. Other than that, I couldn't tell you how I was."

"I guess not. But I hadn't seen you."

"You expect me to just drop by like old times?"

Scully drank now from the opened whiskey. Offered it over and Jamie shook his head. Scully said, "There's people want to see you maybe. Out and about."

"Ones that want it bad enough know where to find me. I don't need to chase after anything."

"Maybe it's just to be sociable."

"I don't feel that way right now."

"Maybe that's the best time."

"Could be, maybe not. You got some new girl singing with you yet?"

Scully shook his head. "It's just me and them other boys. It works I guess but it's not the same. It's a sad act right now."

Jamie took up the bottle and drank a little bit from it. It wasn't what he wanted—he was ready now for coffee and some food—but had no desire to eat lunch with Scully. He wiped his mouth and said, "I've got no interest in being a part of it."

Scully spread his arms to indicate the empty house, the housecleaning. He said, "Alone this way is sad too."

Jamie shook his head. "It's private is what it is. The rest, sad or happy, whatever, is just other people's ideas."

Scully stood then and replaced the cork in the bottle and the bottle back in his coat. "Well then." He looked off at the shining clear glass over the sink, the sunlight prismed there in the small bubbles in the glass. Then back to Jamie. "Don't be a stranger, boy."

Jamie nodded, then stepped forward and took the old man's hand. And said, "All right."

* * *

The summer rolled on, July into August. He retrieved Joey's clothing from the laundry, the dresses and capes and winter coats packed in long thin cardboard boxes with tops that opened like wings, held together with a pair of hard paper buttons bound one to the other by string. Loaded in the back of the Ford he could not help feeling they were a sort of coffin. Of love or trust or both. He brought them home and stacked them in the unused spare bedroom. Shut that door soft but with a strong pull to hear the latch click to.

As August advanced the nights held a foretaste of winter and he began to leave the house afternoons with a fire laid in the range and a lined overcoat folded on the backseat of the motorcar. He bought hay from the sheep farmer Flood and ordered oats and stacked the sacks in the granary of tight-joined oaken planks. Nights, fires were lit in the public rooms of the Sinclair, one in the bar as well, and the vacationers would cluster in their summer clothes and Jamie raised his bartenders' pay by a dime an hour simply because they had to make the same remarks about the weather over and over. The guests were all on summer holiday but the season had turned and the hotel workers felt it and it laid an edge to them. Jamie sat in his office or sometimes perched on a stool at the bar sipping ginger ale and for the first time could see how this worked—the quickening of tempers and emotions, the sudden quittings, the ends of love affairs or the beginnings of new and unlikely ones, the workers slightly slower in response to the guests, the afterhours parties more tainted with futility and so bearing harder upon the partygoers so more waiters and laundresses and liverymen and kitchen scrubs and bellboys showed up later in the mornings or if on time more hungover or both. For him, all it did was make him sad.

He brought girls home with him. In between times, it didn't seem very often but when one was there with him there would always come a time, usually before he roused to drive her back to where she needed to be but a couple of times when he woke in the morning and found her there beside him, he felt like it was just one after the other with a different suit of clothes to take off and high or low breasts and waists wide or slender and different teeth and cries coming out of them or not. And with each he was tender and murderous, wanting while he lay with them nothing but their pleasure and caring nothing for his own but once both were done, once both had taken it as far as it might go he wanted them only gone. He would rise up at four in the morning—when all he wanted was sleep—and make coffee and carry it in to the bed and nurse her from sleep and approve of her sitting up and sipping at the coffee, her face puffed and tender, the sheets and blankets pooled in her lap as she sat, his mind already out the door cranking the Ford.

He woke from dreams of Joey leaving him where he would sob and beg, clinging to her, debasing himself. Would come awake in breathless agony—the look, touch, feel and sound of her fading away. Some days a dream-image would return brilliantly later in the day and he would stop what he was doing to bend double as from a cramp in the middle of him.

And then it was September and the families were gone and it was older couples and maiden aunts and bevies of old women and groups of men; hiking or outing clubs come to the mountains. Some young women traveling in pairs. The occasional solitaire, a man or woman of middle years wrapped in a sheath of loneliness hardened like a cerecloth about them, features set in an ever-distant glare. "Oh, Miss Blake!" one of the older ladies would call from a group at the card tables as the woman hurried down the corridor, away, away. He had not seen Miss Blake's face; she could be his age or twenty years older, plain or pretty, severe or timid, poised to flight. But he felt he knew something of her, nothing like whatever the women at the card table were discussing. And the Miss Blakes in their rooms gazing out a window endlessly creating and re-creating what might have been.

He anticipated the winter with the mute dread of a falling dream.

His managing nightshift bartender Stanley Weeks was overeager for the end of October. One night counting receipts with Jamie he spilled over. "That Florida's the ticket come winter, I tell you what. Clearwater's a sweet town. Winter there's like this place turned inside out. You ought to shed this north country. Why you'd walk in there and own the town. And that Mexican Gulf, you've not seen nothing until you set your ass down on that white sand and watch the sun set over that blue water. Swim all the winter through. Custom's good too, some of the same Yorkers that summer here, plus you got the leftover rich Southerners. Some sweet gals there I tell you. I mean it J, you say the word to Oliphant and he'd write you a letter would have you sitting pretty anyplace in Clearwater. The rest of the state for that matter."

Jamie lifted one by one the rubber-banded stacks of banknotes and slid them into a yellow envelope and bent back the metal clasp. Dipped his pen and wrote the amount and date on the outside of the envelope and flourished his initials beneath. Then said, "I believe I'll sit tight, Stanley. I've obligations."

"You could farm it out. You should do it, at least one winter, just to see. It's a different place. It ain't just the weather, it's the attitude. It's all easy. Now, there's the Jews; you got to put up with them. They take to Florida like it's the promised land. But on the up side there's the coloreds what do all the grunt work. I'm serious J, a good man's golden there. Write your own ticket."

And Jamie wrote the date again and the amount once more also in the narrow columns of the ledger book in his small tight hand and closed the book and slid it into place and stood and crossed the room to place the manila envelope in the open floor safe and spun the dial and heard the tumblers click softly. He sat a pause with his hands on his knees and then pushed himself upright and went back to the desk and stood behind Stanley and reached one hand to hold the bartender's shoulder and for just a moment let his fingers slip deep to a grip past touch but nearer caress than pain. He said, "Help yourself to a bottle of something, Stanley. Just make note of it."

Mid-September one weekday morning with the hardwood leaves up near the peaks already changing he walked into the office of the Sinclair and found centered on his desk blotter a penny postcard with a lighthouse scene, beachgrass on dunes, the sea with a smudge of breakers.

On the back her scrawled handwriting without break or punctuation: *If you want to come see me Id like that.* Below she'd penned a box with an address in it. He dropped the postcard back on the desk and went to the office door and locked it. Took up the card and studied it again. His hands quivering. Tore the card in two and then those halves in two again and on until it was bits that he let fall from his fingers into the empty wastebasket under the desk. He took up his cap from the desktop and turned for the door without a clear plan but to leave, get outside, drive somewhere. Then turned back and knelt on the floor and took out the bits and pieced them together and still kneeling copied the address onto a sheet of hotel stationery. Folded that and put it in his inside jacket pocket. Took up the bits of postcard and carried them out through the bar to where a fire burned in the hearth and scattered them onto the flames, ignoring the handful of guests seated there. Went down the main hall and out the front doors and walked around the building to where his motorcar was parked, going the long way rather than back through the bowels of the building, avoiding anyone he knew. Anybody that worked for him would know about that postcard. If you want to come see me. He couldn't trust his hands, not on her or anyone else. If she'd turned the corner in front of him he couldn't have said what he'd do to her.

What he'd imagined, when he allowed it or when he couldn't help it, was her showing up unannounced and unexpected. Maybe walking into the Sinclair one night off the late train. Or even come whistling down the track to the house some morning, scuffing her feet in the sand, that cheap valise banging against her side, her hair down over her face, her eyes glinting onto him, her mouth set firm against the smile wanting freedom there. But that *If you want to come see me Id like that* was a rock lobbed hard out of the sky, from behind a tree he'd already passed, from a hand unseen. Striking the back of his head.

He cranked the Ford and drove out along the main street without plan or intention but found himself turning off beyond Mount Agassiz to circle the long rough backroad around the broad shoulder of mountain that escarped the land between Bethlehem and Franconia, passing the small farms and then into the long stretch of woodlands until coming again to the small meadow where the night back in the summer when she hadn't left yet but he'd known she was going to, he'd come drinking and fallen asleep. That looked out onto Mount Lafayette. Now with a thin cap of snow on the stone-rubble summit. The snow beautiful in the heat of the early fall day. He parked in the meadow, now grown up, not be to mown again until the next summer. Browse for over-wintering deer. He didn't get out of the car. Left it running.

It seemed a short time he was there although he felt the sun pass over him and watched as from a distance the small shadows pass from right to left. At one point he beat his hands upon the steering wheel, the fists popping up and right back down but it was only after a time doing this that he felt the pain slip up his arms into his back and from there his neck into his head, where it resounded. The bitch of nerve. What she gave him. Someplace where he must step. He knew it when he saw the postcard on the desk. How many ways may a man despise himself. Most all, he guessed. Maybe even—and here he'd quit beating the wheel and held his wounded hands in fists to his mouth—ways never guessed at. Ways not known until presented. The return address. What the fuck was she doing in Massachusetts? He gave credit—she knew how to write a postcard.

When he finally put the Ford into gear and drove a wide circle around the meadow back onto the road to return the way he'd traveled he saw the snow was gone off the mountain. Couldn't have been much of a snow. It was afternoon. He guessed he'd run out of gas before he got back to town. He thought the walk might do him good.

What he remembered of his mother was hearing his father come into the kitchen and running in from the front parlor to see his father standing by the stove holding his mother in his arms, her head lolled down and turned back, her face swollen, the bruised purple-black of a blackberry. Then his father seeing him and his voice booming, fractured and frightened at once, yelling at Jamie, Get out of here, get out of here. And Jamie just standing, staring without words at the face of his mother. Then he did not remember what happened. If he fled. If one of his sisters came in and took him out. Or something else altogether. He did not remember. And he could not call up her face any other way. There were tingling fragments of memory: where she was a presence, a smell, a view of some piece of clothing in motion. He remembered her holding him but could not recall her hands. He could remember her reading stories to him but not the sound of her voice. When he dreamed of her she was monstrous, frightening, most often angry at him for something he had done or not done but even when he woke from those dreams it was not as if he had seen her, the way he felt when waking from dreams of Joey but more as if he'd been in another country, some other place that never was. But once out of the dream there was no lingering sense of the real. Except the feeling that she was not happy with him. Only that remained.

He rode the slow night train to Portland. He watched himself in the windowglass. Another man would have cast her off, crumpled the postcard and discarded it and excused her from himself as a few good years with some fun there, in his youth, and gone on ahead and perhaps have found another woman or not but have lived with himself in some measure of totality. Have held a line of pride and self. Even have held out so long and then with the postcard cursed her for the impudence of it and let her go. But he felt he knew her. And that card was no impudence, implied nothing beyond what he could do if he wanted. And he was on the train. With a through ticket and twenty-five dollars in his trouser pocket and his wallet pinned inside his jacket with twelve hundred dollars cash money. Because he knew he needed it but didn't yet know why. In Portland rode an express through to Boston and did not believe he slept—his brain too boiled for sleep—but long patches of time swept away as he gazed into himself again in the windowglass and at some point the land began to spread around the train in a ghost of dawn as he came into Boston.

At the station he began to understand why he'd brought so much money with him. He held a misunderstood conversation with an old man behind the ticket grate. Finally ended up with a local ticket to Plymouth and a two-bit map of Cape Cod. His eyes burned and his body was stiff and he felt off-tilt, precarious, and could not afford appearing what he was, a countryman lost and not knowing how things worked, even something as simple as transportation. He did not want to put himself in another's hands. It was as simple as that. He would not ask directions. He felt he should be able to go anywhere and know what to do and how to do it. People fled left and right and back and forth around him and he felt little more than a huge bruised knuckle they must walk around. He knew this was himself and not them but he could not change it. And would not give in to it. Whatever he found where he was going he was determined not to wash up there like something haphazard and helpless.

And so he got off the train in Plymouth raw and confident and walked three blocks and unpinned the wallet from his jacket pocket to count out eight hundred dollars for a new Ford ready to drive away and thought if it turned out to be an extravagance then the entire trip would be so. The man he bought the motorcar from had a livery and forge and was reserved and delighted with the paper money. And so Jamie felt easy asking again, this much closer, about Truro.

"Truro," the man repeated, just correcting pronunciation. "Well, now, you're driving up to there you'll need to let some air from the tires. Them roads all turn to sand."

"For cash money," Jamie said, "I guess the tank's full."

"It'll be full, you pull to the front."

"A sandy road, that's hard to travel."

"You let them tires slop down some, they'll be fine."

"Thing is," Jamie said, "I got to be there by noon."

The man nodded understanding. He said, "You pull around to gas it, I'll deflate em down just right. You'll be good then."

Jamie glanced off at the sky. "It's a pretty day, idn't it?"

It took until the middle of the afternoon to make Truro. The last hour and a half on boggy sand roads that was not like driving in mud or snow but more like dreams of running with heavy limbs, the car wallowing steadily forward. It was not bad driving once he got used to the idea that the conditions would remain constant but it was slow. The air was warm over him and heavy with the reek of the ocean and the salt ponds and the bay. The lower cape was a discernible landscape of small villages and farms but once the road turned north onto the long narrow neck of land he felt the disorientation of the unfamiliar. And he was fatigued. The houses were low-slung with long roofs and he imagined winter storm winds passing over them as if they were not there. He passed a man mowing with a scythe in a meadow that Jamie would not have taken to be fodder of any kind, a tall rough spare grass. From time to time on one side or the other the slight sand hills fell away or opened up between for glimpses of water—little more than a pale gray smudge out to the distance where he could not tell where the sea ended and the hazed sky began. He felt peculiar, out of place. Not without excitement. People looked at him as he passed. There was little other traffic and only one other automobile, coming south. He passed a cart drawn by oxen, an old man walking slow as the cart carrying a long goad. The cart heaped with nets, rust red buoys like bullets. He hadn't seen oxen since Randolph.

Truro was a scatter of houses. Picket fences with sand blown through like the teeth of a comb. Some scabby late-season roses. From the post-card he half expected a lighthouse but didn't see one. There was a single mercantile flying a flag and a post office shingle hung under the eaves. He parked before it and went in. It was dark after the light of day. A woman with gray hair drawn back tight and wearing a cable-knit sweater sat behind the counter and she did not greet him when he entered but watched him. One end of the counter had a couple dozen pigeon holes for mail and there was a brass-fitted slot for letters. He prowled the short aisles. He took up a tin of sardines and a handful of crackers and a package of Sen-Sen to clear his breath and laid them on the counter and then asked what he had to.

"I'm looking for a place called High Tide. A house I guess."

Her eyes rested on him. She wet her lips and said, "That would be the Sloane cottage."

He nodded. "I guess that would be right."

She waited then, not as if she mistrusted his intentions or doubted he should know of the place and not even as if she were making some judgment otherwise. She just made him wait. Then told him where to go and what to look for. And he thanked her and gathered up his food-stuffs and went out the door. That moment he would have beaten Sloane the sportsman to a savage death with the crank off the front of his pre-posterous new car if he had appeared.

He drove to where she'd told him and parked when the sand began
to bog around the tires. He sat in the car and ate the food. He wished
he'd bought something to drink. He got out of the car and scrubbed the
fish-oil from his hands with sand. Brushed the front of his vest free of
cracker crumbs. Opened the Sen-Sen and chewed one. Ran his hand
through his hair, thick with the salt air. His face seemed to have a layer
over it. He lighted a cigarette with the match cupped against the wind
and then went forward, walking up through the sand toward the gap
in the dunes before him. Seagrass hanging from the dune tops either
side of him. Then was up on top.

It was nothing like the postcard. The beach was broad to the water
and stretched either side of him to nothing. The ocean was a miracle—
such mass that he immediately saw it and allowed it but could not comprehend what he saw. The breakers three or four long lines of upturned
white never stopping and never the same as if a tangible upthrust fist
from what made them. The air and wind now over him as if to hold
him in place.

He went down to the packed sand of high tide and walked the way
he'd been told and watched up the dunes to the occasional house for one
to meet the description but mostly he watched the water. The waves
exhausted ran up in flanges like the small shorebirds that raced ahead
of the water. The sun poured over him, diffuse and not immediate like
in the mountains but as if from a great distance. There was no one else
on the beach. Out in the water, what he decided was a short distance,
was a boat working, short and stub-nosed. Far out he saw a bigger boat.
Against the horizon. A ship he realized. It was warm, more like midsummer than mid-September. Then he turned back to look at the dunes
and saw the house described to him.

She was up on the screened porch seated crosslegged on a daybed and
even with the warmth of the day the air moving on the shaded porch
was cool and so she sat with a quilt wrapped loose around her, down
off her shoulders but over her lap. Her hair was gathered behind her,
heavy and coarse with salt. There was a hogshead cistern on a trestle
behind the house to gather rainwater off the eaves but otherwise no fresh
water and she swam daily in the ocean but barring this left herself be.

The hair that escaped the binding ribbon and sprang out in coils around her face was of a different density than she'd ever known and she liked it. There was no one to see her anyway. When she walked to the mercantile in Truro on off days the old woman there took no notice of her, and whatever she might think was not Joey's concern.

She saw him when he was still far up the beach. Too far at first to be more than a figure she nonetheless knew was him. And only when she saw him did she allow herself to know how much she'd counted on his coming, as if the days spent walking the beach or sitting in the dunes or here on the porch or her solitary evening swims had consisted of something else, had been that time spent thinking things through that she had claimed to need. And now him walking so slow down the beach toward her, she knew this was what she'd been waiting for even before mailing the postcard. And for a moment wished he'd not come so soon. To sustain somewhat longer those days now behind her of walking and sitting and waiting. To continue those evening swims in the dusk when the land and sea and sky merged and she would swim out in the water still warm with summer. A woman alone at the edge of the world. And Jamie now coming. And whatever he came with and whatever he went away with, even if she were left here still, that other time before he came was ended.

Watching him now peering up at the house she knew she had wronged him. She felt ready for whatever that meant. She could take nothing away from what had happened and would promise little but honesty. It was a slim straw and she tried not to attach overmuch importance to the simple fact of his being there. And within all of this she felt calm. Whatever happened it would be worth it to feel this way.

He went up through the trodden declivity in the dunes and could see now the dim figure of her within the porch. His stomach roiled and he had another Sen-Sen and wondered if the sardines had been bad. It was improbable his being here and yet he could not imagine not being here. The sun was low over his left shoulder and the front of the house was lighted and he walked up to it feeling he'd made a grave error coming directly here, that he should have come down and stopped the night somewhere first. He felt rough-limbed and awkward, as if he lacked the language spoken here. He went up the two steps and opened the screen door and stepped in. Joey looking at him wide-eyed. At first he was not sure it was her—this was not only her absolute presence but the fragility of himself before her.

And then thought she looked frightened and he grinned at her. And said, "It's nothing like I pictured Rhode Island to be."

"No," she agreed. "I didn't end up where I thought I would."

He nodded. "That took less time than I'd thought." And knew this to be cruel but could not help himself. He went on. "It's not bad though. Pretty. Be cold come winter I'd guess. This place's not built for winter, seems to me. And lonely too. But maybe he comes up here weekends to see you."

"You have to do that?"

"Do what?"

"Start off that way. With what you think you know."

"It wasn't me that ran off."

"I didn't run off."

He tossed up his head. "You didn't? What do you call it then, what you did?"

"I don't know. Maybe I went off a little bit. Something."

He nodded. "Sure. And you're better now. And want to come home."

"I don't know what I want. You acting this way is helping me sort things out."

"Me? It wasn't me sent that postcard."

She was quiet a moment. He was swaying. Then he realized she was not going to say it, not point out his presence; that she was trying to stop all this. After a pause she entreated. "Jamie."

He looked away from her. Through the door into the house he saw a plain pine table with a brass hurricane lamp on it and behind that a rough-mortared fireplace of round seastone with a stack of driftwood for burning to one side of it. He looked back at her. "You have anything to drink? I bought some lunch but didn't get anything to drink. I'm about dried out."

She stood, stepping off the daybed and out of the quilt at once. She was wearing a white dress tight across her breasts and to her waist where it opened then in loose folds to her ankles. A little short for daytime, he thought but this was the beach. And there wasn't anybody else there.

Right then, he reminded himself. She said, "There's some bottles of beer but no ice. The ice wagon only comes along the beach summers. And I didn't have a way to carry any out here. You're overdressed to be walking on the beach anyway." And turned then without touching him and entered the house and glanced back at him and he followed her.

"What I'd like is a drink of water. And I didn't know I'd be hiking on a beach when I got dressed to come down here." He said this to her back, the sprigs of hair showing at her nape beneath the bundled mass of the rest of it. He wanted to put his nose there. He wouldn't reach for her, the familiar stranger.

They sat at the plank table with a tin pitcher of water drawn from the cistern and a pair of mismatched glasses. The water was warm but sweet. Moving from porch to house something unspoken had been settled between them, not so much truce as acknowledgment that both stood precarious. Without speaking toward it, or touching, some tenderness between them had risen. Emerged from wherever each believed it hidden.

Jamie removed his jacket before he sat and rolled up his sleeves. Without thinking removed one shoe to empty the sand and then caught himself and looked at Joey across from him. She grinned at him. Those small perfect teeth. "Go ahead," she said. "It's a beach house. Sand's in everything. So how've you been, Jamie?"

His shoes and socks off he drank down the glass of water and poured another and said, "Why am I here?"

"I'm not going to dance around it. I want to come home. If you'll have me back. There's complications."

"Is that right? Complications for you? Or complications for me?"

"I understand those questions. I'll answer whatever you want with the truth but I won't apologize for anything. How's that sound?"

"That's the high road all right."

"It's the only road I've got."

"I guess. But it puts me in an odd place."

"How's that?"

"Well, whatever you say, it makes it hard to doubt it or get angry about it. Sounds like a discussion between a pair of angels what you're after. We're not either one of us that, so how could it happen? Seems to me we'd be better off letting it lather and spit and if there's any pieces to be picked up after, why then we'd know what we were left with at least. I'm here, doesn't mean I'm not some pissed off at you. Part of me doesn't even know why I'm here. Why now, I stop to think about it much at all, I couldn't tell you."

She nodded. "That's fair." And again left hanging unspoken where he was.

He said, "So what happened up there, over there? Wherever Providence Rhode Island is from here. I don't even know where the hell I am."

"I'm going to have a baby."

He stood up from the table and walked barefoot across the room past her to where a screened door let out onto the back of the house. Stood there and lighted a cigarette. The smoke broke through the screen and curled away. The rain cistern was out by the back small ell of the house. Past that just sweeps of dunes braided with the air flowing through the beachgrass. Late-afternoon light. With his shoes off, his pantcuffs scuffed the floor. He stood there by the door and finished his smoke and tipped open the door enough to flip the butt out onto the sand. Then turned. She was still at the table, her back to him. She hadn't moved. Her shoulders and neck and head were stiffly held. He wondered if she expected him to strike her. He walked back to the side of the table and looked down at her and said, "I guess that's the complication you spoke of."

She looked up at him. Her face in pieces, as if he couldn't bring all her parts together in his eyes. Or all those parts stricken and fierce at once on their own, independent of him. She said, "I didn't ask you to come rescue me."

"Is that right?"

Then those pieces all were one. If that was him or her he could not say. Then knew it was her. She said, "That is right. I don't need you to raise up a child. I've seen it done alone firsthand and know it can be done. And I know what it takes, what it costs. And you do too I guess. I'm not talking about me here. All I know about me is what it takes is what I'll do. But I'm thinking about how it was for me as a child and how it was for you. One of us the mother gone, the other the father. I'm not saying we turned out wrong—truth is I think we're both pretty smart because of it. But it's a smart we had to fill out as we went along, a smart to make up for something not there to start with. And I'm thinking maybe we could avoid that, this time along. I'm thinking, we wanted, we could do some good together."

"Jesus shit," he said.

As if life just disguised as a woman had sat up and told him that a structure is in place before you even begin to think and it reveals itself not when you want it to or think you've keyed it but when it wants to, capricious. And for no good reason thought of the brand new Ford motorcar maybe a mile up the beach in the dunes and was ashamed of it. As if it were everything wrong with him drawn up into one machine.

He said, "I'd guess you're parked out here in nowhere because your friend Mister Sloane wanted to ease you on out without you making trouble for him. I guess you saw that handwriting before he even opened his mouth and already knew what was the best angle for you. I bet you thought That Jamie, he's a stupid son of a bitch and I can work whatever I need off him. I bet you've got more money on you than you ran away with. And I even bet you already thought of everything I could say before I even knew there might be a reason for me to say it, and had a answer cooked up ready to serve me. And here I am. Feeling like the chicken just looked up to see no it's not shellcorn but the old woman with the axe."

She looked away from him then. Down to the table where she spread her hands flat and studied them. Without looking up she said, "It's our baby, Jamie. Yours and mine."

"Why, of course it is." He backed a step away from the table and jammed his hands down in his trouser pockets. "You wouldn't have called me down here to ask my help raising up another man's child, no. Not at all. You, you're a straight-shooter. You're not a girl chases opportunity down whatever rathole offers up. Not you."

She pushed hair off her face. Turned her head as if she was tired. "You say anything you want. You won't get a fight out of me. Go on, spout all you like. It's you made the trip down here."

"Could've saved me that trip, you'd written more than a single line. It wouldn't have taken much. Could've just asked if I wanted to raise up a bastard child with you."

Her eyes cut in half. "You wouldn't have come? You really wouldn't have come?"

"Even an animal, given the chance, won't lay down in shit."

The water glass burst against the side of his head. His shirtfront was wet with the sprayed flung drops of water. He'd closed his eyes before the glass struck and against his closed lids could see like moving pictures the black and white of her snatching up the glass and hurling it. Not ducking. Closed his eyes against the splinters of glass. Then the image of her was gone and the pain swept through him. It was more hurt than he expected. He thought it would be like a slap. He leaned forward and shook his head, getting rid of the glass splinters, trying to shake his head free of the pain. He opened his eyes. One hand up, trailing fingers through his hair to pull away the glass. His fingers came down bloody. Then heard her. He thought she'd been speaking right through it.

"Get out," she said. "Go back. Get out of here. Get away. I was wrong about you. I thought there was a man behind that little-boy mug of yours. Sitting down here I thought maybe this is happening because it's what needs to happen. But I could be wrong. Being wrong, that's something you don't know the first thing about. But I can be wrong, I know it. So just get out. Go."

"Jesus, you got a rag or something? I'm bleeding."

Then she threw the water pitcher at him. This time he ducked and heard it ring out a hollow gong as it struck the wall. Bent over he saw her rise and take up the chair she'd been sitting in and come around the table toward him, the chair held up over her head and he thought he could take her down with a body block and thought of her being pregnant and paused and then she was too close for him to do anything and he scampered sideways away from her, one hand crabbing for his shoes with the socks stuffed in them and then she broke the chair over his bent back. He went down. The wind out of him. A sharp pain in his side. Could have been a piece of the chair run into him. Or a broken rib. He got his wind back and came up onto his hands and knees and slowly stood as if unfolding. His side hurt when he moved. Breathing hurt. There was blood on his face, in his eyes, from the cuts in his scalp. He was still holding the shoes.

She held out his coat. "Get out of here." Her voice a livid hatred of him.

* * *

She picked up the ruins of the chair and set them atop the stack of drift-firewood. Swept up the broken glass. There were a few sprayed spots of blood on the floor and she left those to dry and be swept away with the sand. The pitcher had a dent in it and she set it back on the table. The damage would give the Sloane wife something to ponder next summer. She went out on the porch and took up the quilt from the daybed and wrapped it around her shoulders. Through the screening she could see him. He'd gone maybe a quarter mile up the beach the way he'd come. He'd rolled his cuffs high on his calves and was carrying the shoes and his jacket over one arm, walking down on the wet packed sand just above the waterline. Walking slow. The impatience she felt toward him she knew was toward herself more truly. To have sat waiting for him. An idiot. All making more clear why she'd left New Hampshire that summer past. Now she had not much but to get on with things. Watching him straggle along the beach she only wanted him gone. So she would be freed finally she understood to sit in the house that night with a fire burning, the driftwood throwing off blue and green sparks of burning salts as she determined what came next. For this day, it would be motion enough to do that.

Then while she watched he stopped. He didn't turn back to look at the house but walked up to the dry sand and bent to set down his shoes and spread his jacket and then he sat on the jacket, facing the ocean, his knees drawn up before him, his arms wrapped around his knees and his chin down atop them to gaze out onto the breaking water. If anything she'd expected to see him arrest himself and turn back with intent purpose. He looked small. She could not watch him. She reached up behind her and took the ribbon binding from her hair and shook her head and then worked her fingers through her hair. It needed washing. She would never know what he was thinking sitting there but she recognized the configuration of him; it had been hers the first week she'd spent here. She pulled the quilt tight around her and went across to the daybed and sat down on it, drawing her feet up under her with her knees angled and then draped the quilt around herself. With her hands inside it, laced over her belly. The sun low enough now so it came broken through the screening into her eyes. Waiting for him.

*   *   *

The world had gone amber when he came back through the screen door of the porch, still barefoot, his jacket again over his arm. He opened the door and looked at her and stepped in. She saw he'd left his shoes somewhere and wondered if he even knew that. He laid the jacket on a porch rocker and said, "What I was thinking was, maybe one of those beers wouldn't taste so bad."

"Is your head all right?" There were streaks of dried blood on his cheek and she could see where the hair was clotted.

He grinned at her. "No, my head's all fucked up."

"Beer's in a crate on the floor in that little pantry off the kitchen."

"You want one?"

"No," she said. "I don't believe I do."

He came back in with the opened bottle of beer and a saucer to use as an ashtray and sat crosslegged on the floor before the daybed and sat looking at her waiting and she watched him and decided the spleen was out of him and that he was curious and now she was frightened, not of him but of herself; the central fact was out between them and fail or not everything else was up to her. So she sat and told him how it had been, that it had not been what she'd hoped but neither what he'd predicted. That Edgar Sloane had taken her from the Providence station not to a rooming house as she'd expected nor to an existent apartment as she'd feared but to a narrow three-story brick row house with a slate roof and a brass knocker in the shape of a swallow and delivered her into the hands of Virginia Reeves, a woman of Sloane's age, well-kept and formal, simply and expensively dressed in white and black, her straight black hair unstreaked and pulled back to a tight French braid, who spoke briefly with Sloane before leading Joey into a parlor with a fine grand piano where the woman played a series of scales before nodding to Joey and together they went through a couple of music hall numbers and then the woman paused to ask Joey what song she'd sing if her life depended on it and Joey replied "If I Could Tell You" and the woman played it in a slow tempo, softly, with her head tilted away from the keys to watch a point across the room as Joey sang. When the

song ended the woman trailed a few final notes into the room as if wanting them to linger there and then ignored Joey but turned to Sloane and
said, "Where did you find her, Eddie?"

So Joey came to live with Virginia Reeves. Through the rest of July
and the month of August. And did not ask and did not need to be told
what lay between the woman and Sloane but could see it for herself that
first afternoon and later the one or two evenings a week he'd come to
the house at a quarter past five on his way from his sporting goods store
to his home where his wife and children waited dinner upon him; stop
as Virginia prepared a gin rickey for herself and Sloane would pour
himself an inch of scotch into a tumbler from the decanter on the side-
board and they would sit then, the three of them, and pass the time of
day. Joey could see them as they were when their younger selves first
came to the grand collision that would not be enough to draw either of
them from the course each had already set but strong enough to alter
that course and so create the taint of sadness in their pleasure of each
other. The pleasure Virginia Reeves and Edgar Sloane created was received and bestowed measure for measure effortless but at great cost.
And she watched them together and knew she was being allowed a
privilege few others had. Watching them, her skin hurt.

Daytimes she sang scales and exercises until her stomach muscles were
a hard band and her lungs pressed outward within her chest. Drank
chamomile tea with lemon and honey for her throat. They worked
through Joey's repertoire as song by song Virginia Reeves discarded all
but a handful and she learned new ones, some new to her and some new
altogether off sheet music arrived from New York. Afternoons they had
tea with frail cookies baked by the Irishwoman in the kitchen and served
by an Irish girl and the tea would turn to drinks and then they would
eat together a meal again prepared and served by the mute help and
afterward would sit in the parlor alone on the nights Sloane did not stop
and play mah jong or listen to opera arias from the Victor gramophone;
they would sit when a record came to an end with the haunt of sound
lingering until one or the other would finally rise to lift the bumping
needle and place the heavy curved arm back in its rack or sometimes
start the needle at the beginning to listen once more to the recording.
What conversations they had beyond instruction and manners were

slight, as if the Reeves woman in her silence was not only maintaining privacy but allowing Joey the opportunity to discern the full import of a mantle of discretion.

But with this reticence, perhaps because of it, Joey learned things. As simple as tracing the past by walking slow down the six turns of landings from her top-story room to the ground floor and studying the photographs framed on the walls along the way. Some framed newsprint. By dates, clothing and the slow-changing face tracing thirty years in the woman's life. From music halls and revues onward to be a single figure in concert halls and extravaganzas. And Joey decided Virginia Reeves was older than she looked and then decided she looked as old as she was, and so learned; life was not always a flattening press but might also be a conveyance toward a stretching-out into something she might call dignity. Self-possession. An attribute, she determined, that come what would she'd locate within herself.

Then Virginia Reeves began to have people in for dinner: small parties of four or five, at most six guests, men her own age or older, some with wives and some alone or with younger women companions, actresses one and each. The wives regarded the actresses with cool appraisal. Virginia Reeves paid no attention to this but while appearing to include equitably each of her guests it was with the men that another coded language was spoken, all at the table aware of it and no others trying to take part. At the end of each of these evenings Virginia and Joey would sit together and Virginia would instruct her in who each of the men were—what theatres they owned or which entertainment companies, what their political positions were and what that meant within the frame of greater Providence, what sports teams or ball clubs they owned a share in, what their other business holdings were, how devoted each was to their own particular pursuits, as well as which ones drank too much or were frivolous with the actresses. When Joey asked when she would sing for them she was told the men knew well enough why they'd been invited, and something of who the strange dark girl was, simply by her presence at Virginia's table. "We will let them think about you a little bit, let them wonder just who you are. It's good for men. Let their imaginations work before you even open your mouth and they will be lovestruck. You'll see."

August then and she missed her period and fretted but chalked it to excitement or the strange place when she thought about it which she didn't as best she could. At first thought that wanting to sleep, needing to sleep all the time, was only a way to avoid that panic, to close her eyes against it. She was not sick but allowed Virginia Reeves to think she might be as explanation for her fatigue and so although not sick found herself mealtimes staring down at the food on her plate as upon heaps of strange matter, some alien forage that even as she minced into small pieces and lifted to chew and swallow she could not believe she was doing so. And felt the eyes of Virginia Reeves upon her not just at those times but all others as well. And the panic would break through its fine web and flush through her. As if the panic was an advance guard of the truth she would not face.

One afternoon in the middle of practice Joey bolted from the room down the hall to the bathroom with her hand over her mouth to stop the uprush of soured chamomile tea and stood leaning over the basin with the water running, feeling her stomach clench as gorge rose again, thinking, It's supposed to be in the morning, and then washed her face with warm water and stood looking at herself, at the hollowed and bruised and bulging face, unknowable, gazing back at her from the glass and was at sudden peace. Went on steady feet back the long hall into the music room and announced to the woman still seated on the piano bench what the woman already knew but had been clearly and patiently waiting for Joey to reveal. And Virginia Reeves spoke briefly of an acquaintance, a doctor who quietly tended to the actress demimonde of Providence and when Joey refused to even allow discussion of this the Reeves woman rose from the piano bench and stood a long moment, regarding her with eyes of ferocious sorrow and then wordless left the room, her back erect as always. Leaving Joey to consider the not-very-broad array of cause for that sorrow. Even while hearing the low tones of the woman down the hall at the telephone table.

She sat alone in the music room for an hour and a half until Edgar Sloane arrived. Although it was still late afternoon he took her out to a restaurant that was dim and cool with ceiling fans and dark polished wood. It was the first time since New Hampshire they had been alone together. Sloane was poised and calm and gentle and she sensed a tremendous tension within him and guessed he felt himself in some danger to be seen with her and his taking that danger unto himself touched her and she was very formal with him. They sat over food neither wanted and he asked her what she intended to do and she told him she did not know. And he asked what she thought her options were and she told him, having spent the time alone in the music room with those same options revealed to her as simply as a tight fist opening to reveal a spare handful of pennies. She knew what she would not do. And she knew that continuing with Virginia Reeves was not a possibility. And she would not ask and did not expect anything from Sloane either. She outlined to him what she saw her choices to be, the words not as brave or clear as the thought behind them but she did not apologize for the paucity of her opportunities. And again, he asked which of them she felt most likely. And again she told him she did not know. He then lifted his napkin and pressed it to his lips and folded it and laid it aside on the table and told her what he could do.

Early next morning he called for her and she was waiting, slipping out the door in the late-summer chill dawn with only the cheap valise she'd left New Hampshire with, not having seen or spoken with Virginia Reeves since the afternoon before. Joey had written a note of thanks and regrets and then folded it small and carried it away with her in the pocket of her dress, believing Virginia Reeves would view the gesture with contempt. They traveled east by train to Orleans, sitting side by side and not speaking. What his private hopes for her had been she did not know and so could not read if he was reconciled or relieved but either way she knew he was engaged now in an action called for not so much by the fact of her as by some theory of conduct, a notion of comportment. She knew his action was enough, a measure of some devotion or passion mute in his soul.

At Orleans the summer coaches were still running and they rode north again in a cluster of strangers. If there were any among them that Sloane knew he did not speak to them and no one addressed him either. At the store in Truro he bought a stock of groceries without consulting Joey who trailed him along the shelves and then went outside to stand on the porch and wait for him. When he came out he stood silent a moment before explaining the groceries would be delivered with ice later in the day. Then he took up her valise and led the way out through the dunes to the beach and they trudged south more than a mile, she trailing him to watch the water and the sky and the birds skittering along the waves' froth. At the house he went through it quickly, explaining the water system and the small cookstove and the icebox and then hat in hand he stood before her and told her to stay until she knew what she would do or the weather drove her out, told her then also that if she needed anything more, anything at all, to contact him at his store and he left a card for the business on the table and then they stood looking at each other and she knew she wouldn't see him again and guessed he knew it also—guessed he understood her well enough to know it was true. So she stepped forward quickly and kissed him and as she took her mouth away a small groan of anguish came from him. Then she stood on the porch and watched him walk away down the beach.

Finally, without preamble or apology she finished by explaining that since she'd left New Hampshire she'd fashioned herself Joey Pelham. That she had taken his name long since.

The day had gone into pale blue and slate twilight. From the sound she knew the tide was coming up. He'd sat on the floor without moving through her telling, the bottle of warm beer untouched beside him. With his bare feet and pants rolled up he shivered from time to time as the porch breeze came off the water. She wondered if he'd brought his shoes up somewhere into the dunes or on the steps; if he'd left them on the beach they were gone. When she was done he sat some time without moving or speaking, his face confused and strained, soft as a young boy, she wrapped in the quilt, wanting to go down to him, to touch him. After a time he spoke.

"Did you screw him?"

"If I told you yes or no would that change how you think?"

"I don't know."

"If I told you no you'd always think I was lying. If I told you yes you'd use it on me, always, come a hard time. So, you sure you want to ask?"

"I guess I pretty much already did."

"What do you think?"

"I don't know. I don't know what to make of you."

"All right," she said. "So you want me to answer? You want the truth?"

"I believe I do."

"Up home. This summer. He wanted me bad. And he talked such a clean honest idea of what he could do for me. It wasn't like most fools. So the truth is that if it had come down to it I would have. But most men, most all their lives except maybe once or twice it's only the one thing they want and then they lose interest in anything else. And I wanted what he was holding out. So I made him wait. And I was right about him. If things had turned out different who can say? But they turned out the way they are. And here I am. Your short answer is no but I would've if I'd had to, if it'd come to that. You live with that?"

He was silent. The twilight had gone all slate. He looked away from her, around the confines of the porch as if at floor level he'd discover something sought. Then he looked back at her. "You're going to have a baby."

"It looks that way."

"My baby."

"Both of ours."

"What do you know about babies? I don't know anything about them. Never been around one much now I think about it."

She grinned at him then. "I never was either. I guess you just have it and then one thing comes after another."

"Seems there's more to it than that."

"I guess there likely is."

They were quiet then. It was near to full dark. A piece of moon hung out over the water, making light there and throwing a pale thin gray light into the porch. The wind had fallen off and it was not as cold, the air heavy as if charged or someway filled by the presence of endless ocean. After a time he spoke. "So you want to come home?"

"Yes," she said. "I do."

He stood then, coming up smoothly but he did not come to her, turning to stand instead at the screened side of the porch, his back to her. He stayed like that some time. No longer shivering. Finally he turned. She had not been waiting for him but watching him, knowing he was

sifting and sorting, allowing all things to align within him—she sure
his answer was known sometime before to him as well as her. He said,
"It's awful pretty, isn't it? The times I imagined the ocean wasn't ever
anything like this. I guess you couldn't imagine a thing like this, not
really. You think?"

"Not until I saw it I couldn't."

"You want to take a walk down along there? As long as I'm here, I'd
like to see it some."

"You lose your shoes?"

"No. They're out the front of the house. But I'd go barefoot to walk
the beach."

She came up then, off the daybed and stretched herself, her arms up
over her head. Then brought them down and hugged herself. "Let's go
walk."

He took a step toward her. "You're sure it's all right? For you?"

"To walk?"

"Don't laugh at me."

"Jamie, I've been swimming naked out there every night until this
one. I can't see a walk would hurt a thing."

"Swimming in the dark?"

"Swim out and ride the waves in."

"All that water," he said. "It's fearful."

She went toward him then, did not touch him but went past to the
door and opened it and stopped and turned. "It's delicious. It's fear and
everything else all at once. You'll love it. Come on."

"You want to swim out there?"

"I want to swim out there. With you. I want you to see what it's like."

"Go swim naked out in all that?"

"Yes," she said.

"Aw, Joey," he said.

"It's not dark out there. You won't believe how much you can see.
And what you can't see you don't care about. See the moon? Come on."

He stepped toward her then and she turned and went down the steps
into the swells of sand atop the dunes and turned and looked back at
where he stood on the top step, his hands in his trouser pockets as he
looked down at her. He said, "So you called yourself Pelham."

"I did."

He nodded, his head in the moonlight a dipping luster of face then salt-torn hair. He said, "People hate a French Canadian, don't they?"

"I was trying to be smart."

"Pelham's a stout old name."

"I wasn't trying to take anything from you."

"Oh no," he said. "Whatever good it did you, you're welcome to the use of it." He came down to stand beside her in the sand. She could smell him again, an odor she couldn't recall away from it but couldn't place herself apart from when he was there. "Mostly," he said, "people are cruel, given the chance."

"I know you think that."

"I know it. You do too, good luck aside."

"I guess maybe I do."

"Tell you what," he said. "Let's walk a ways."

She wavered before him a moment, then took his hand and turned and led him down through the dunes to the sea.

Foster was born the next March during a storm that began with a foot of wet snow before turning to frozen rain that glazed over the snow and then the temperature dropped and three more feet of fine soft powder fell and on the third day the sky cleared and the world was white, crystalline, placid and heaped. Somewhere during those three days there had been a terrible eighteen hours with no hope of help and Jamie stood at one point in the kitchen beating his head with his fists as the thought came that he should reenter the soiled awful room and choke her with his hands to end it all. Then went back in and knelt for some period of time and took from her bloodied thighs and bedclothes a wet child into his arms also soaked with blood and a clear slime and the child cried once, only a soft mewl, and then went happy to suck. And Jamie then washed Joey and cleared the bed and slipped under her fresh bedclothes and went to the kitchen and used the last of the heated water to clean himself. Finally at the end of that day stepped outside, forcing the door against the piled snow and stood gazing at the storm around him. From the barn he heard the hungry horses and thought he could do no more and turned to go back to the house and then turned back and went through waist-high snow to the barn, each step breaking through the hidden crust and bruising his legs. By the time the storm cleared, the next day or the one after, he was never sure, he no longer wanted to go anywhere, wanted nothing more than to stay right where he was.

Foster was named for no one. It was a name they liked. She had suggested only once his father's name. Then days later out of the blue asked how he liked Foster as a name. Three years after that a girl was born to them. Without question or conflict they named her for Joey's mother. Claire.

Six

For a time in the summer of 1919, following the winter of influenza that left the two of them alone, he left the boy at home and paid the youngest Flood girl to walk over each day and tend him. Jamie thought this Sharon competent to watch the boy. Perhaps even felt he was offering her something in return beyond the small wage. Some refuge away from the reek of dung and constant bleat of the sheep, beyond whatever hand it was she shrank from. And she was convenient. Until the afternoon he returned to the house and found the boy halfway up one of the hemlocks, spraddle-legged on one of the big limbs, his back against the trunk, his feet dangling. The girl Sharon seated on an upturned crate, a bar of handsoap clutched like a Bible. She told Jamie, "I was frying up slabs of that cold pot roast for his dinner. He was pestering me to eat. So I told him take the pan off the stove and set it on the table while I cut bread. And he grabbed hold the pan handle and burned his hand. Then he said a bad word. I told him not to speak like that around me. He said I wasn't his mother, he could speak as he pleased. I told him I was paid to mind him, and he'd mind me. I told him foul language can't come from a clean mouth and I took up the soap. He ran out here and climbed the tree."

Jamie stepped to the base of the tree and looked up at his boy. "Foster. Come down here."

"No sir. Not with her waiting."

Jamie stroked his chin, still looking up. "Come down here. Let me see your hand."

320

Foster looked from his father to the stout girl, weighing things. Then came down the tree. Jamie heard small gasps break from his mouth as his hurt hand caught against the rough bark. Then he was on the ground and turned silent to hold out his hand. Grimed with pine tar the pink spread of fingers showed a broad band of yellow sear, the burn hard. It would be days before it would fill and blister.

Jamie said, "What happened?"

"She told me put the pan on the table. It was moved to the edge of the stove. I didn't have any idea it was still so hot. It hurt, was all."

"What else?"

"Well. She wanted to cram that soap in my mouth. I wouldn't stand for it. She chased me out of the house. I climbed up this tree here."

"What else?"

"Sir?"

"What did you say? Made her want to do that?"

"I said Shit. When I grabbed onto the pan."

Jamie took up the offered hand and bent to study it, with both children watching him. Then he let go of the hand and said, "Go on to the house. Wash that sap off your hands, put some butter on the burn. Go now."

The boy would not be alone in the house. The world was changed and most nights now Jamie was home but the few he was called out he took Foster with him, the two of them in the Packard Twin Six, the boy for the most part riding silent. Sometimes he would hum, snatches of tuneless sound. Sometimes short phrases of songs his mother would have once sung around the house but never did he sing the words but only offkey humming, a high child's rendering. Thoughtless. As if the phrases were some part of him unconnected to anything else. Sometimes the humming would drift off to nothing. Other times it would stop mid-phrase. These times Jamie would glance over. The boy might be gazing straight ahead out the windshield into the night. Or his head turned to the side window. Or lolled down sleeping against the door upholstery.

Now with the Flood girl gone Foster rode along daytimes as well. At least for the remainder of the summer. The two of them in a world unmoored.

* * *

The previous November the four of them had driven to Littleton for ceremonies marking the armistice signed in Europe. After the false armistice something arose in them and prompted an urge to celebrate that might otherwise not have occurred. For the war itself had been more hindrance for Jamie than anything else—the hotel trade had fallen to some token resemblance of its former self—and while he was close-mouthed about it outside of the house, inside he so often said that like everything else it was all about money that Joey would sometimes mock him by finishing lines he'd just begun. Still, that November day was bright and warm, with the new snow shrinking already when they departed the house midday, the winter birds, the chickadees and jays, darting with evident delight as if winter was not just held back a day but coming to a close, and there was a spell of adventure over them as they drove to the festivities. Later, Jamie would attempt to attribute the unease he felt to some premonition, some foretaste of knowledge.

The Littleton streets were frothy with autumn mud, leached of frost by the day, farmers with their wagons and teams moving easily to the side to allow a sputtering churning flivver to make its own rough way. The big Packard went through the mud as if rolling over a lawn. Flags flew on staffs angled over the street every twenty feet. The opera house had a great swoop of bunting across its front for the event. It was filled with people dressed in winter clothing against the late-afternoon trip home. The building was overheated. People rasped with the dry air. Behind Jamie a man punctuated each segment of the ceremonies with wet blasts into a handkerchief. The choral society performed "Over There" and "It's a Long Way to Tipperary" and "When Johnny Comes Marching Home." A state legislator made remarks. No active-duty soldiers had yet returned to the north country but a veteran youth with a finely trimmed mustache and a slim cane made sly remarks about the Huns and Paris and the old home town. A lovely girl swathed in layers of a gossamer cloth with her hair piled atop her head and a silk banner of red white and blue sang the national anthem as the men removed their hats and strained to discern the shape of her breasts beneath the swathing. A reverend minister spoke a prayer for all who had suffered and died, for all those maimed and unfortunate, for the loss of homes and destruction of cities, for the boys on troopships coming home, for

the mothers and fathers awaiting them, for the continued munificence
toward the great nation, for the state of New Hampshire, for the people
of the town and finally for the state legislator. As prayers went Jamie
thought it was similar to those few others he'd heard: too long. Still his
unease was gone. They went out into the falling dusk of midafternoon
and the sharp chill and drove home toward the leafless mountains with
the rose wash of sunset over them. Joey was ebullient, flushed. He
watched her cradling Claire asleep on her lap. Joey saw him watching
her and said, "That girl was lovely, such a pretty voice." He thought I
need to get her out more often. Figure out how to do it. She was too
willing to allow the children to be an excuse. He thought, We can do it.
It's not such a big thing. Just some weeknight out. Go to the pictures
for christ sake.

Three days later he was dying. He sweated the sheets through and
after she stripped them and turned new linens out under him he would
lie clenched with cold, his body racking and his teeth in a hard staccato
ratchet. His lungs seemed to droop and grow small in his chest, as if they
no longer could pull air in. Sputum always at the back of his throat, the
taste in his mouth of putridity, of decay. As if he were rotting. The bedroom was kept dark and she piled blankets on him regardless if he was
sweating or chilled. She would not listen to him. Later what he would
remember most clearly was her seated on the side of the bed holding
two fingers of one hand against his lips and telling him to hush, to hush.
He would wonder what he'd tried those times to tell her that she would
not hear. She'd draped a silk shawl over the bedside lamp and with the
windows covered day and night all was dim, a blush of light. Time went
away. Most often it seemed she was pulling him upright and forcing
broth in spoonfuls into his mouth. More than once using the thumb and
forefinger of her free hand to force apart his jaws. As his father or sister
would do with a horse unwilling to take the bit. Other times the walls,
the room itself, grew fluid and fell away before the fever. Not dreams.
Visitations. His father. His sisters. His mother. A girl whose name he
could never remember screaming silent at him, blood running from her
nose and eyes, her hair matted with mud. Or dried blood or shit. His
father kneeling, weeping, bent in prayer. As he'd never seen him. He
thought. His mother laughing, dissolving, back again, turning her back
to him as she opened her dress, telling him she would show him some-

thing. Racing ponies. Horses on a dirt track. The colors brilliant beyond life. His little girl, Claire, her voice high and plaintive but with some excitement at the thought also, outside his door, asking if Poppy was going to die. He could not hear the answer.

Then three weeks where he was not dying but wished he might. The fevers now just a chill and ache in his bones without the diversion of nightmare frescoes. Time returned. Lengthened and stretched; days of bedsores and racking coughs, nights of the same cough and spitting wrenches of sleep. Now also he was able to fear for his wife, children. He'd read the accounts out of the Boston papers of the hundreds, the thousands, the tens of thousands dying. Most in days it seemed, if you could believe what you read. He lay recovering in the downstairs bedroom listening to the children playing games upstairs as December shut down around them, lay with the windows no longer shrouded so some days it was bright and others dull. Lay those dull days thinking he could not only see but hear the snow falling outside. He'd not been sick like this before. Some afternoons he would rise and wrapped in a robe go to the kitchen and sit by the stove while the children whirled hectic indoor games about him. Joey tending him with hot tea. Fresh bread. Trying to hush the children. He'd flap his hand at her to let them be. He wanted to hear them.

Then, finally, out again. Christmas Eve day all bundled into the car for the trip through falling snow, fine blowing flakes dancing as if each pellet were unsprung upon its own single course of air. To Littleton where Joey shopped with the children and Jamie wrapped in a greatcoat and muffler, still coughing, his legs still spindly—a strawman— went to the Thayer Hotel and spoke with the desk clerk and made half a dozen calls from the public telephone and then down the street to the barbershop for a haircut and to collect some money held there for him, making arrangements as best he could. A month out of it and his trade was falling off by half. He made promises he wasn't sure he could keep but had no choice but to make. Then small shopping of his own: matching mother-and-daughter lockets on fine gold chains and a twin-bladed pocketknife for the boy. Back to the car where he ran the engine for heat and sat sipping from the leather-covered flask out of the glove box. Watching the figures moving up and down the street in the dim gray of falling snow. Waiting for those three. Smoked a cigarette and killed his coughing with a taste from the flask. Saw them then, Joey carrying Claire against the piling snow, packages in her other arm. Foster beside his mother, both arms around wrapped boxes. The red paper and green ribbons framing the boy's cold-red face. Then all of them in the car, Joey's breath warm against him as she leaned to touch her cold lips to his face.

So they had Christmas. Snow kept falling. Late in the day he forced his way out to the barn. The horse stalls empty the three years he'd owned the Packard. He sat in the cold on an upturned crate and smoked, not even bothering to gaze at the moldering pile of old hay, not needing to envision the eight crates of bottled whiskey buried there. A fraction of what he needed. Which meant the long drive out to Binter's farm and then to the rented basement in Bethlehem where he would bottle the whiskey. Then the deliveries—at night now, with the wartime prohibition still in effect until demobilization and the Anti-Saloon Leaguers boiling over the country like a hot tar. Volstead was inevitable. All which meant hustle. Hustle and duck and dodge. What had been more sport than effort now held a weight and he was tired when he could not be, weak where he could not afford weakness.

Two nights later Claire crying woke them. The two small bedrooms under the eaves were unheated save for what came up from below but she was hot to the touch, sweating and twisted in her bedclothes. By dawn she was very still, lying as if sleeping, her breathing a wet suck, the small cup of her lips smeared. Joey sat on the bedside, dipping cloths into a basin of hot water and pressing them onto the girl's forehead. Jamie going up and down the stairs with fresh water to replace that which cooled almost as fast as he brought it. Downstairs keeping the stoves at full force, moving the pot of broth from the hot side to the cool side and back again to keep it warm. Barking once at Foster who sat silent at the kitchen table, commanding him to watch the soup, the firebox, the supply of water in the boiler. To carry in more wood from the shed. The boy rose silent and frightened; for a brief moment Jamie saw him trying to move five directions at once. His eyes keen with some anger across his father.

By afternoon Joey was abed also. For the rest of that afternoon and through that night Jamie did not know if it was worse now than it had been for him because there were two of them or because the influenza had sharpened someway or just that he was on the other side now. He wanted to believe the last. He carried Claire down the narrow stairs and put her in bed with her mother. He could not feed them. They were hot, insensible, beyond him. He could do nothing for them because they could not answer what they needed. He switched the forehead cloths from hot to cool. He leaned over them, one or the other as the afternoon fell short to listen to them breathe, to seek breath. Down close, the gurgle of their lungs. Claire now mostly still, gone very white. Joey at times in throes, her face blotched as with a passion, her tongue out running round her lips.

At three in the morning he ran up the stairs and roused Foster from the bed where the boy was not sleeping and sent him out with a lantern to dig a path for the car to the road. The snow was stopped now and the winter starlit night was low and Jamie set the boy to the job although he knew that the road was as filled as the driveway track. He wanted evidence of some effort. For whom he could not say. With the boy out of the house he cradled the swathed girl and strode back and forth with her in the kitchen. As if waiting for something to arrive. Hours later when a pale purple predawn slid over the snow under the tamaracks he at last set the girl down in the bed with her mother and went out to find the boy. Foster a hundred and fifty feet up the driveway with a shoveled path ten feet wide, the lantern guttered out, the banks of snow reaching either side far over his head. Crying as he shoveled. His nose and mouth chapped with frozen snot. Not stopping when his father took his shoulder. The clips of snow feathering up off the blade. The boy's body shaking when his father took the shovel away from him and drew him tight against him, the boy's face turned away as if looking back at the job not yet done.

The Christmas lockets hung around the necks of the dead. In the few minutes he had alone with the two of them he used his pocketknife to saw a snip of hair from a hank jerked out tight from his head, then divided the hair and placed half in each locket. Would have cut into his own chest for pieces of his heart if he could have done so. And bent and kissed the cool gold. It was the only thing he could think of. Would not kiss the cold faces. This, days later.

* * *

Joey had said of Foster, "Must've come from your side. LeBarons were all stout-built close-to-the-ground people. Mama's side too." Jamie said nothing but it was true, the boy was longlegged and longarmed with a high spread ribcage and shoulders like river rocks. With a stiff hard brush of hair, the shoeshine black of Joey's but without her softening curls. Or Jamie's. Eyes the remote blackness of a night creature. For all his length he was not awkward but a child who moved with delibera-tion, as if each motion however small had been meticulously considered and arranged before execution. What little he had owned of a child's exuberance died with his mother and sister. After this, the enthusiasms he would display appeared slight, almost superficial, as if he did not care one way or the other. In fact, Jamie was sure these few things deeply mattered, mattered so intently the boy was ready to deny them rather than admit their importance. He was quiet.

That winter had groaned on, storm following storm. The snow did not shrink but settle. A thaw in March and then winter again right on into the first week of May. So much snow the trains stopped running through the Notch for a time. That in February. Foster out to school when he could, Jamie running whiskey when he could. As much as he could he did during the daylight. The boy would not be alone in the house. Those few nights they rode together, the dark packed snow of the roads in the lights, the rising banks of snow either side and the black night lost above. The snowbanks higher than the headlamps' reach. During that time, Jamie did not like having Foster with him, felt the boy had no place within those things even if all the boy did was ride or wait in the car. And that first winter, that non-spring, what Jamie liked least and would not allow himself to examine too closely was the idea that his boy was protecting him. That Foster was more guide than passenger. That in some way the presence of the boy was a talisman, a ward against chance or misstep.

Summer came without benefit of spring. And Foster's hand was burned and Jamie sent the Flood girl packing, watched her go down the track between the trees with the sunlight sifting light over her slow even pace. Jamie paid her, his voice thick as he thanked her and told her she'd be wanted no more. There was nothing else to say.

Summer. Sunlight so etched, winter could never have been; even night itself seemed remote, a vagary of the mind. Foster's fingers stained purple from black raspberries. The two of them at the riverbend, on the shelf of boulderback. Jamie in black swimming trunks, the boy naked as a trout. Brown as syrup. Jewelweed hanging over the bank.

"Poppy?"

"What's that?"

"What do you think about heaven?"

"Well. It's a nice idea. I guess I wasn't ever sure what to think about it."

The boy nodded. Was quiet a moment. Then, "Me neither."

Jamie sat with his knees up watching him. Foster looking off somewhere—the trees across the rivermeadow, the high summer clouds. Into the jewelweed. Then looked at his father. "At least there's both of them. They've got each other there."

A doctor in Whitefield called Dodge bought liquor by the case from Jamie for his own use and for those of his patients that were the better for it. He owned an English setter bitch who that spring had whelped a litter of nine puppies and Jamie bought one for Foster, feeling it a transparent and ineffectual thing to do but something tangible, some diversion, companionship at the least. Dodge wanted to make a gift of the puppy but Jamie wouldn't have it and the older man nodded with gravity and folded the bills into his vest pocket. Inquired then mildly about Jamie himself and without pause or thought Jamie said, "The piss and vinegar's gone right out of me. I need to be looking sharp and I just don't care. I can't shake it, it'll get me hurt or killed or jailed. And seems like nothing I can do about any of it." The doctor said nothing to this, studying Jamie. Dodge was not a young man and there was little of kindness about him but Jamie knew he was silent because there was nothing true to be said, no remedy to be offered. Then Dodge reached and touched his sleeve, a quick gesture as if lifting something away and told him for Foster to call if he had any questions about the puppy, and to bring the boy and dog by sometime and let him see them.

For that one moment when Jamie brought out from under his jacket the twelve-week-old squirming puppy an illumination appeared in his boy's face, a brief slide from shadow as the world made new. By the time Jamie spoke the words "She's for you," the boy was already reaching for her with his face once more grave, very serious, as if all the implications were understood and accepted, the responsibility assumed and undertaken. The puppy laved her tongue in hard quick curls over the contours of Foster's face and briefly his eyes closed with pleasure. Then he got both hands firmly around the puppy and held her down against his chest and looked at his father. "I'll call her Lovey," he said, "because I love her."

The speckled pup and the boy. Out gone and lost in the woods through the long summer afternoons that tipped into evening before both would turn up, a pair of sweetly fragrant hungry tired pleasured small animals. Sleeping one next to the other in his bed upstairs. Jamie would wake before dawn and hear the puppy crying and then moments later the boy coming downstairs to let her out. Evenings sleeping on the floor of the kitchen, in the small parlor, the radio playing, the puppy stretched prone, the boy wrapped up to her, his knees drawn tight against her with his arms loose over her. The two of them wrestling in the hemlock duff afternoons, the boy sitting on his knees as the puppy bolted tight figure-eights around his outstretched arms. For a while every small object in the house torn or shredded or punctured by the fine driven points of her teeth. Jamie would sit a morning with his coffee regarding his shoe left out the night before and admire her work.

And still he could not leave the house alone. Starting the Packard was all that was needed to bring boy and pup out of the woods or house or river or even some hole in the ground for all he knew and the way they looked both piled together into the passenger side of the seat. Streaked and dirty and intent. The pup lying on her back with her four legs spread out between man and boy, her head resting on Foster's thigh, her eyes locked on Jamie. Foster with a hand on her belly. Never asking where they were going. Not even looking at his father. His eyes already slipped down, half into himself, half waiting for the car to slide into gear, for motion to retake him.

So Jamie became the bootlegger with boy and dog in tow. Most of his clients were people he knew well, men who'd been buying in bulk for years now. Many from the hotels: a desk clerk or bellcaptain or stableman or whoever else it was for the thirsty guest to see. Others: railroad men or lumber bosses or area barbers or druggists. Some called Foster by name and would stop by the side of the car to reach in and fondle the puppy. Others ignored these passengers the same way they ignored any indication of knowing the details of the winter Jamie and Foster had just passed through. Some few, new men who'd tracked Jamie round the slick whispers and had the right name to mention to him, some of these looked strangely upon the boy or Jamie or both and to these men Jamie would always speak up easy—"It's my boy Foster. Shake hands with the man, Foster"—His eyes on the stranger a slick glint like the side of a new coin as he made the introduction.

During her fevers there was much she said that did not make sense and there were other things that he would not hear at the time and would not remember. After the fevers passed, when she lay very still, her eyes bright, wide, dry, her mouth gaped for air her lungs could not receive; then, when the girl abed beside her was already a corpse although he did not think she knew it, she twice spoke to him. She said, "I'll never have to"—and then a long pause as she coughed and gagged and sucked and finished—"have to sing that song again." And later one clear sentence to hang out in the grasped tight air of the room: "Goddamn you I'll never screw you again." A lament. It was these twins of weariness and regret that he allowed himself of her. Each a summation he could hold within himself that would unscroll all he knew of her. Each the trail end of a knotted set of interlocking dense-corded nets. The only sure memory of her voice. He could hear her.

Late July of the year Binter arrived one morning in his T-model Ford with the rear-end cut off to make a truck of sorts. Jamie didn't even know the farmer knew where he lived. But he heard him coming, the engine missing on one cylinder, the backfires popping off as if the truck

were engaged in small warfare with itself. Jamie out on the short steps
to watch it come down the track from the road. Binter did not step down
from his rumbling farting machine but sat behind the wheel until Jamie
went over to him. The old man, his hair gray but bleached as if streaked
with urine, said, "Chew need to know I'm done. This batch working
now, she's the last. After that, I'm out. Retired."

Jamie stepped close, leaning down to spread his hands over the doorframe, to bring his head closer to the old man. The sound of the Ford a
mortification in the summer afternoon. This close, the smell up out of
the car of unwashed man. Grayed woolen underwear a grimed circlet
above the open collar of the man's shirt. The black jacket rusted and
wormed with moth holes. "The fuck you telling me?"

Binter looked at him. Slowly, with regret and distaste, his eyes ro-
tated away, back to the lap below him. Then up to the windscreen.
"I'm out," he said. Then put the Ford in gear and drove a circle around
Jamie in the soft soil and back up the track to the road, the Ford popping as it went.

He drove Foster and the puppy into Littleton, to Scully's small house
where the old man now sat most days in a padded rocker by the small
coal-burning range that gave what heat there was to the place, even now
in midsummer a small fire chuckling in the grate, Scully with a blanket over his knees. A stack of magazines one side of the chair, a box of
dime westerns the other. Scully twisted always a little sideways, his arms
and legs angled sharp and hard with arthritis. His hands curled claws
that palsied as he held his reading matter. Jamie explained himself.

"Boy's always welcome. His creature too, it don't shit the house. If
he'll listen, I'll tell him tales. The old days."

"Don't let him pester you."

Scully ignored this. "Somebody should tell him. He should have
something of her. I know you won't speak of her."

Jamie looked around the house. Lovey sniffing crumbs along the
counter edge of the sink. Then to Foster. "You be all right?"

"Yessir."

"Be useful. Fill the coal scuttle. You could scrub up some too."

"Leave the boy be. He don't need to cart after me."

"I won't be but a couple–three hours."

"Yessir."

Back to Bethlehem then to track down Jeeter Carrick, watery-eyed sometime dishwasher errand-boy loafer rounder-of-the-town, whom time to time Jamie employed to bottle liquor out of the casks and could not be trusted but he was in to you. At this time he was in to Jamie for a couple hundred dollars, the loss of five cases of liquor fronted to Carrick for a sure-thing deal, that as Jamie had told him when the liquor was gone and no money to show for it, wasn't sure at all but was quite a thing. Found him sprawled in alcohol narcosis in a cheap ground-floor rented room and kicked him awake, hauled him down the hall out into the yard and pumped water over his head, holding him by the neck with one foot up on his backside until Jamie was satisfied that he was as alert as could be hoped. Then stood him up and slapped him a hard roundhouse blow the side of his head and stood waiting for Carrick to pick himself up from the soft mud surrounding the pump. And stepped in and held his shirtfront and slapped him again, this time just enough to focus the anger out of the boy's eyes and then told him how it would be. How a debt was to be paid. How good would come of it.

The two of them rode then over the hills to Franconia and down the long valley of the Gale River with the farms spread out either side between the dark high ridges, both silent, Carrick settling himself with small hits from the leatherbound flask out of the Packard's glovebox. The farms to Jamie like Sunday afternoon although it was a weekday. The smell of mown hay. Mixed herds of Jersey and Guernsey cattle in meadows, some lifting heads to watch their passing. A pair of big bay Belgian horses standing in the shade of an elm, their heads drooped somnolent, their tails whisking for flies. Even the smell of the barnside dungheaps was sweetened, distilled out into the afternoon air. Willows and elms.

Carrick bumming smokes, head turned to the open window, flatulent.

In Binter's dooryard they stopped. The house and yard still, silent. Some red hens dusting in the sun against the side of the barn. Jamie stepped out of the Packard and looked back at Carrick. "Wait," he said. "And think it through so you got it straight. You try to go around me, go out on your own, I don't care how small-time or peckerheaded a deal it is, I wipe you up like crap off my shoe. I been thinking, riding along, for you it'd be a red poker up the ass. Think on that. And stop drinking my fucking whiskey."

The Binter woman had no English but left the kneading bread to come around the kitchen table in a floured fury when Jamie came through the screen door, her arms up and hands spraying white flour dust as she gesticulated, her face a harridan of hatred as if she recognized unwanted fate in the form of a single man when she saw it, her mouth old dry lips stretching out from yellow teeth, her tongue clacking against the roof of her mouth, the language Dutch or Ukrainian or Polack or something else, Jamie had never learned what. He went the opposite way around the table from her, ignoring her protest, the small hammer of her fists on his shoulder and back. She was small, big-breasted, her hair a tight bun, the color of dulled gunmetal, no gray. Now she had hold of the back of his jacket, pulling to stop him and he twisted free of her without turning toward her. Had no interest in silencing her, happy to let her quacking bring Binter out. He'd not till then been inside their house yet turned easily in the hall off the kitchen and down to the first door on the left where the drapes were pulled to block the light and the furniture was dark wood, carved with scrolled arms and clawfeet, dark-green-velvet upholstered. The walls a dense dim floral paper nearly covered with prints and photographs in silver- and gold-painted plaster frames. Binter rising from a single-ended settee of the same velvet, his trouser waist loosened against the bulk of his stomach for his nap. His hair flown. Buttoning his flies. The wife had stopped at the parlor door as if giving up. Or witness.

"Get her out of here," Jamie said.

Binter ran a hand through his hair, his fingers crabbed as if not caring, the gesture without intention or thought. Studying Jamie a long moment. Then spoke in their tongue to the woman.

"I got a man's going to live with you. You teach him the liquor making, front to back and back to front. When I'm happy with what he's doing I'll take it all off your hands. Not until then. Meanwhile, you can use him however you want. He makes any fuss at all about anything let me know. That's how its going to be."

Binter looked at Jamie and said, "It cannot be."

"It already is. He's here, in the car. There ain't no choice in this."

"No."

"Listen old man. You want to retire there's only two ways to do it. This is one of them. This is the best one. You comprehend that?"

Binter took breath, weary. Again: "It cannot be."

Jamie shook his head. "You should've of thought this through all those years ago when you started in. Once you fill a need you can't just quit in this world. The same way I can't let you just quit me. It's not just you and me, it's a whole line of people. But then again it is just me; you're what I got right now. And I won't let you go just because you got tired. Why, you look at it the right way, it's not so bad. What am I talking about, four–five months?"

"I sold the cows."

"You what?"

"I sold the cows."

"What was all that I saw driving in here if they wasn't cows."

"They're sold. Once they're gone I got no excuse for all that corn. Same man's wanting the sheep."

"Well fuck."

"Just right. Like you say, I'm tired. Also, things have changed. People, they watch different now than it used to be."

"Well fuck this now." Both then quiet a long moment. Jamie looking around the room, Binter watching him. After a time Jamie looked back at Binter and said, "You sold your stock, how come it's all still here?"

"He give earnest money."

"Sure." Jamie nodded. "I see. How much?"

"A head?"

"No the whole fucking lot of them."

"Chust the cattle or the sheep too?"

"Oh my christ all of it. The whole deal." Digging around behind him and pulling out his wallet. Unzipped it and took out the roll of bills circled with a rubber band. The roll he'd never once let another man see. Hoping he had enough. Knowing Binter could well mention any figure at all and he'd have no choice, no gauge, no knowledge. Cows and sheep. Fucking farmboy.

"I'm too old," Binter said. "Too old for this work."

"Like I said I got a man for you. All you got to do is tell him what to do, how to do it."

"A man to live here?"

"That's right."

"Who pays his board?"

"Well christ. I figured he'd earn it."

Binter shook his head. "The kind of man you'd bring, I'm thinking, will be more work than doing it myself. However much he learns."

Jamie considered Carrick. "How much board then?"

"Twenty a week."

Jamie paused counting the bills, looked at Binter. "I'm buying the cows, the sheep, be buying the feed too. And you want twenty a week to board my man?"

"Yuht." Binter smiled.

They walked out through the pasture that bordered along the Gale, stood there with the summer sun hot on the backs of their necks. The river a small oxbow a dozen feet across, the water five or six feet deep. The opposite shore heavy in shade, beds of fern smelling sweet and cool, the smell coming off the water like a breeze. Carrick kicked one foot toefirst into the ground.

"Nope. I'm not milking a bunch of shitty cows. And I'm not shoveling shit for him either. That wasn't the deal. I won't even tote pails of milk for him. That smell, milk and shit all mixed together, it makes me want to puke just thinking of it. Told myself I wouldn't ever do her again."

"You're off a farm?"

"Little runt-ass scratch of rocks and stones up to Lyndonville. I've not looked back and don't think to commence now."

"It's not but a couple months. Look sharp how things work it might not take that long."

"Then what? Move the still somewhere else? All you got then's a piece of machinery. How you aim to account for the raw materials?"

"Tell you what. You work off your debt, let me figure out the rest of it. That's why we're standing here, I'm good at figuring these things out."

"You got my ass in a sling is what you mean to say."

"You're looking at this all wrong. You put a little effort in, you're going to be valuable. You following me?"

Carrick shook his head. "I never ought to've tried the liquor business. I had a bad feeling about it, even when I was thinking I was going to skin those birds."

"You got to make mistakes, starting out. It's how you learn what to do right."

"Shit." Carrick turned away. "Let me meet this old fart."

Crossing back over the meadow Carrick stopped of a sudden. Took a smoke from Jamie and lighted it, crushing the match into the grass. Blew out smoke and looked at Jamie.

"Back there, I'd said no and stuck to it, what'd you'd have done?"

Jamie studied him. Finally said, "You've got an interest now. See?"

Carrick nodded. "I'd be in that little river with my head stove."

"Well, you're not going to be running around flapping your mouth."

Carrick looked off, somewhere else. Then back at Jamie. "Shitty fucking cows."

What Jamie saw, everywhere: women with children. A woman in spring snow on the street of Bethlehem bending near to a squat in her heavy overcoat to tighten a muffler across the face of her child. A woman walking with a pair of children, a boy and a girl behind her, each carrying a sack of groceries. A woman in a sailor blouse on the lawn of one of the hotels playing croquet with her teenage daughters, a group of four intent and serious, hair wisping sweat-soaked onto their cheeks, one of the girls looking up to glance at Jamie as he passed by, then immediately back down to her game. The young woman teacher at Foster's school, outside of a May noon with the children at recess, a flock of children around her. All seeming to radiate out from her, small planets in steady irregular orbit to her sun. A young woman stepping down onto the train platform, holding an infant out from her hip, her head tilted back slightly as she scanned the small crowd for the man they both were meeting. The settled certainty of her glance, contentment. Central to the world. And smiled then, a brief eclipse upon her face as the young father come north ahead of them stepped forward. But mothers with daughters, little girls. These he would look at and look away, afraid they would one or the other glance at him and read something of his wanting in his face and misunderstand it. Or understand it. One summer afternoon in Bethlehem heard Claire's exact cry—"Poppy!"—and stopped where he was, not looking, not wanting to see the child caught up by her father. Another evening followed fifty feet behind until they turned into the Maplewood a man with a young girl up riding his shoulders—the man from behind could have been himself, the girl Claire—Joey's hair, the small dress, her father's hands up to hold her in place by her knees, her arms wrapped around his head, her chin riding the peak of his hair. When they turned he looked away, kept walking, not wanting to see their profiles. As if he carried a pair of small river-smoothed pebbles in some pocket cut into his heart. He thought he might inhale some particle of air that had once passed in and out of their lungs. Scully was right; he would not speak of them to Foster. Even as he was sure variants of the same things moved someway through Foster. But neither of them owned a language for these things. Jamie did not believe anyone did.

One morning in late August when a single small maple along the river burned a lone fire of the season turning, the doctor Dodge drove in unannounced, his setter bitch sitting upright on the passenger side. Jamie stood on the step with a cup of coffee and watched as his boy and the pup Lovey ran outside, the puppy galloping and barking excitement, dancing around the motorcar. Foster, Jamie knew, spoke to Dodge time to time over the telephone. Dodge got out, wearing knee-high gumboots and wool trousers, a green and black checked woodsman's shirt. Jamie walked over, the sand cold and damp under his feet. The setter bitch jumped over the side of the door and nosed her puppy, then swarmed her with an attack of teeth and savage snarling. Lovey cried and crawled away a dozen feet, peeing as she went. She stopped there and turned to crouch and watch. The doctor was tamping a pipebowl of tobacco. The bitch lay at his feet, her eyes on the men. The doctor was talking to Foster as he got his pipe going.

"You've had her out?"

"Most every day."

"Got her quartering for you?"

"She works back and forth pretty good. I haven't had to do much."

"How far out?"

"Depends on where we are. Thick woods she stays in close enough most of the time. The pastures and orchards she'll get out of sight on me."

"Uh-huh. She's young. You worked on that Whoa business?"

"No sir. I couldn't figure out how to do it."

"It's easy enough. Teach her around the house. Before you open the door to let her out, before you let her eat. That sort of thing. Teach her when she'll do it because she wants to. That's the best way to learn. She'll still bust birds but it'll sink in after a time." Then to Jamie, "You look healthy, Pelham."

"I'm all right."

"What I thought, you didn't mind, I'd take this boy off your hands for a day. See if we couldn't scare up some young partridge. See what kind of a dog she'll make for him."

Jamie looked at Foster. Without need he asked, "How's that sound?"

"Sounds good."

"You behave yourself. Pay attention to what the doctor tells you."

Dodge said, "He'll be fine. I've got a sack of lunch made up. You have boots, boy?"

"Yessir."

"Well go get into them. It's best we start before all the moisture goes off and takes the scent with it." Then with Foster run off to the house, Dodge turned to Jamie and said, "He needs something, might as well be this. Somebody got me started once. Some debts are long."

"I don't know what kind of summer he'd have had, it wasn't for that pup."

Dodge nodded. "I ran into Estus Terry the other day. Asked after you. Told me I ran across you, for you to come see him."

"How is Estus?"

"He'll outlive me."

*   *   *

Estus Terry still lived in the hermitage set back in the wildlands north of Bethlehem in the big northward loop of the Ammonoosuc. He was out of the business, retired three years since his partner Aaron Wells was disemboweled by a logger in an Allagash camp and as Terry told Jamie at the time, "You got to quit when you can't go in behind your partner. I got the news first thing occurred to me was four–five years ago that sonofabitch wouldn't have even thought to pull a skinning knife on Aaron and if he'd been thick enough to try anyhow would have been him sitting on the ground trying to stuff his guts back inside himself, not Aaron. How does a man know when the time is come to say enough? You can't trust your nerves, or we'd all have quit long since. So a sign comes. If it'd been me, I guess Aaron would be shacked up with some wore-out old whore in Bangor or Augusta. Someplace like that. I'm sorry it happened but I'm glad it was me was left."

The big horses were gone. Where Terry went now he went on foot. The house was much the same, but for a new stovepipe replaced the old one rotten to an angle. Terry was out in the yard awaiting him. Jamie had brought a pair of bottles of bonded whiskey and stepped out of the Packard with the bottlenecks gripped together in one hand. Terry spread-kneed on a chopping-block: green Johnson wool pants, a white shirt, black vest buttoned over the shirt. Hair straight back flat as if a wet comb had just passed through. He grinned a black-rimmed greeting.

"Pelham."

"How're you keeping, Estus?"

"Just fine. Except I ought to've come over the spring when you buried that girl and the children. I'd like to tell you I was puny or didn't hear until too late but the sad truth is I just wasn't up to it, not the trip but all the rest. I never been one for such things. Ceremonies."

"That's all right, Estus. It was a quiet little thing anyhow. I wasn't up to having any big todo over it all myself. And it was Joey and Claire died; the boy, Foster, he never even come down with it. Sailed right through."

"I knew it. Not about the boy but I'm glad to hear it. The rest I mean—I knew you wouldn't want a show. Maybe it was that left me feeling I ought to've made the effort. I liked that girl."

"It was only getting something taken care of at that point. They'd been dead and waiting four months. It was a wet day, Estus, there wasn't much to it. She always liked you too. I brought these along for you." Jamie laid the bottles down in the grass growing up through the chips around the chopping block.

"Now that was thoughtful."

Jamie took out cigarettes and matches, looked off. Smoked. Then said, "I got a setter puppy for my boy off that sawbones Dodge up to Whitefield. They're all out woodsrunning today."

Terry ran his hands up and down the tops of his thighs. "I heard you got a new setup."

Jamie went down on his haunches, still smoking. Looking at Terry. "You heard what?"

"You got a new setup."

"Nope." Jamie shook his head. "Same deal it's always been."

"Don't shit me."

"Shit you? I'm shitting nobody. Same deal."

"Pelham?"

"What is it?"

"How far is it to Whitefield?"

"Whitefield?"

"From right here."

"Jesus, Estus, I don't know. Twelve–fourteen miles?"

Terry nodded. "Close. Now tell me why I'd walk all that way. And back. Most of a day. To ask a man to ask you to come see me."

"You're saying you think I got a problem of some kind."

Terry spat into the grass.

"That Jeeter Carrick's not worthless as he seems. There's a streak of gumption to him, just needs to be nudged along. And I already know he'll get ambitious on me and he already knows I'll take him down however many pegs I feel I need to, the time comes. Which it will. I'm no fool, Estus, I know it will. But I can manage it for a while. I don't see the way Carrick could get around me. I'm years away from losing my quickness, I do believe. And he was available, with some advantage to me. Sometimes the right thing happens that way. And I think he's not so stupid as to not see that."

"Well yes, I guess that might be right."

"Binter wanted out. I had to move quick."

"A course you did."

Both quiet then. Nothing resolved. A chirp of tension rising in Jamie, reaching around in the dark for something he wasn't even sure was there. Not unlike those times he'd waked of a sudden, middle of the night, reaching for Joey, not understanding why she was not there, where she could be, not even sure where he was.

Jamie stood and walked to where the horse trough still stood, the water full and clear, running in from a spring-fed line, the overflow a small worn vee in one end of the trough where the water ran off into a small stream. He cupped his hands and lifted water and drank, twice, the water sweet, cold to ache against his teeth. Turned back to Terry then and said, "But Jeeter Carrick's not why you walked to Whitefield and back."

"It's a nice walk."

"I suppose. This time of year. I expect there's folks you could thumb a ride with."

"I like to think I walk everyday then the odds go up for a quick death. Something sudden. I can't stand the thought of lingering."

"Healthy living. I wouldn't've guessed it of you, Estus. What happens you miss a day?"

Terry grinned at him. "I try not to. Even bad snows I can go to the river and back and not get lost. It's not but a mile each way. Not much of a walk but it gets me out of the house. Patrick Jackson was talking about you the week last he came by to see me."

There we go. Jamie dried his hands on his trousers. "What was Pat Jackson doing over here?"

"Why he brought me a bottle of bonded whiskey. He likes to come around and talk time to time. I imagine he feels he can say whatever he likes with me and most everybody else is watching to see what side of a thing he's going to come down on. Everybody else has an interest in what he does. He knows it. I think he likes to come by here and blow off steam. And don't kid yourself, he's as confused about this prohibition business as the rest of us."

"I never had trouble with Jackson or any of those Federal men."

"Patrick's sound. He's got no soapbox. And like before, those Federal boys are mostly concerned with the border, what's coming south.

The problem he's got to deal with is availability, see, now the legitimate business is over with here in the States. You understand? There's people think this prohibition bullshit will work. And like everything else, there's people who'll be watching out for any little way to grease their own skids."

"I already got a dozen envelopes I stuff with cash every month. I don't see what else I can do. I got everybody covered that will let themselves be covered. Those others, all I can do is steer clear."

"I think what Patrick was concerned about. His boys are pulling a big quota off the Canadians. They got no problem with that. Plenty gets by them and they know it. That don't really matter. As long as they haul enough so it looks good. So maybe he was thinking you might see an opportunity, a hole to try and fill. And was saying let that hole be. Stick with what you have, what you know. You do that, you should be fine. And it looks to me, what you have is enough. Is that right?"

"Maybe I should visit with Jackson."

"No. Patrick's the rare thing. He doesn't get caught up with fashion. He knows the nature of man. And he's not one of these small-town shitsuckers looking to line his pocket wherever he can. What I think, you're best leaving him be."

"Well, I don't have any big ambitions but to keep what I got rolling along."

Terry nodded. "You or me, we could predict the future, we'd have different lives anyhow. Any man would. But I'd hazard sometime, might be a year or two, there'll be new faces around, trying to tie up the market. You understand what I'm saying? I'm not talking about honest men like ourselves, just trying to make a living. This'll be a new breed is what I think. But I think there's some time before we see them much. Until then you should be fine."

"You think that? Is that the feeling you got from it?"

Terry shrugged. "Like always. Watch your back. Keep your head down. All that's changed is there's more people keeping their eye out."

"I believe I'm good that way."

"But there's complications behind you now as well as out front."

"I know it. But I got reins on Carrick pretty tight. I believe I'll see it coming he tries to slip the bit. And he knows what I have in store for him, he takes a mind to. That's enough for now. Everything else, I wait and see. The biggest problem with him is I got him milking cows and tending sheep."

Terry smiled. "He thought he was off the farm."

"What I thought was I'd nose around the hotels. Find some girl waiting tables or working in the kitchen. Some big strap of a girl homesick for the homeplace. One just good enough looking so Mister Carrick's little head takes over for his big head. One thing I know: A smart woman's smarter than a lucky man."

"There's no end of people looking to get back to where they came from."

"Those are the ones made us the wealthy men we are, Estus." Jamie grinned at the older man.

Terry did not smile. After a moment he said, "I was curious also about the farmer. And his wife. They can't be happy with the arrangements."

Jamie nodded. "The money's good for them. And the work is being done, someway at least. It's not his worry anymore. I think I got him cornered up pretty good. For now at least. It's a slippery time, is what it is. I'm jumping from rock to rock. But I know it."

Terry stood, stretched his arms up toward the sun. Gray wet ovals under his arms on the white shirt. He bent, took up the whiskey from the grass, held a bottle close to read the label, his eyes pinched. Then looked at Jamie. His eyes still pinched but the focus changed. Something near to affection. He said, "Even an old rat, caught in a barrel, you'd be surprised how high he can jump."

Throughout the early fall when school let out Foster would come through the house shedding some clothes and adding others, sitting only long enough to eat a slab of bread while he laced up his boots and then would take up the silver whistle on a cord and loop it over his neck and be out the door into the afternoon, the puppy Lovey dancing around him in a steady bob and weave and lather of tongue. Both boy and dog over the summer had sprouted, spindles of arms and legs, both clumsy-gaited and agile at once. Foster already shoulder high to his father. Jamie had not felt so small since he was Foster's age. And some afternoons felt himself near anger with the boy, as if he could give up his mother and sister so easy as this. And steadied himself, recalling he had no clear notion of what went through the boy's mind. Anymore than the boy did his. What frantic urge took Foster off into the woods, into the bleak beautiful mystery of the world? He did not know. He did know there was a tremble in himself, an uncertainty that had not been there before. Was this circumstance, or growing older?

Other things did not change. He still could not leave the house of a night without the boy. And the puppy. They could be sleeping and he would not even have the car cranked and they would come out the door, ready to go. As if the door itself, opening and closing, was all that was needed to rouse them. He considered it but in the end could not forbid them.

The doctor came three more times in September, Saturday mornings, to take Foster and Lovey for the day. Those evenings, when they were returned to him, Jamie asked nothing of their days, the fatigued pleasure so clear in both boy and dog that there was nothing more he could know, no understanding available to him. One of those afternoons he decided he should feel some jealousy. But there was none in him.

As if the boy were already gone from him. As if he might only watch manhood overtake his son.

In the Stodd Nichols store in Littleton he allowed the clerk to probe more personally than he'd allowed a man in years. And so came away with a single-barrel .410 shotgun and two waxed cardboard cartons of shells. The gun, he understood, perfect for partridge and timberdoodles, up close, the right thing for a boy. Make him work for it now, the clerk had said, and he'll only like everything else better as he grows up. Also, the clerk made clear, a boy could only do minor damage with the small-gauge shotgun, if mistakes were made. Jamie wasn't worried about mistakes. But he liked the idea of the minimal start. Of giving something that implied a beginning. Of working toward a passion. He could not kill a bird himself but he understood the rest of it. And stood with the new gun in a case under his arm, leaning against the glass countertop studying the small array of pistols, revolvers— he didn't know what they were really called. And would not ask. A couple of little numbers flat without the bulge of cylinder. He liked those. Something for a pocket. And for a moment looked up at the clerk who was watching him. And Jamie felt known. Not at all like a father buying a first hunting gun for his son. He pulled his right elbow tight against the long case and spoke to the clerk. "You've been a help. Nice day." And walked out of the store.

Foster ran both boxes of shells through the gun with nothing to show for them. Coming in afternoons with his face set, grimly carrying his failure silently. When the shells were gone Jamie went back to Littleton and bought this time half a dozen boxes and then spent an afternoon in the sheep pasture tossing up tin cans for the boy until like a singular magic the blast of the gun sent a can spinning hard away from its arc. Foster shot up three boxes of the shells, with the last box hitting near as often as he missed.

"I can feel it," he told his father. "The instant I pull the trigger I know I got it."

"Maybe we'll have partridge for supper one night then. Once they're empty, these cans don't make much of a meal."

"What it is, is just looking at the can. Nothing else."

"Is that what it is?"

"It's my brain stopping, is what it is."

Jamie ran his hand quickly over the boy's head. Said nothing. The short autumn afternoon gone to evening. Twilight. The leaves of the trees along the meadow edge a soft glow in the half-light, the maples like coals in a fireplace.

Early October, the middle of the night, rain like warfare, the telephone went off like the end of the world. Jamie in the hall in the dark, one hand holding up the mouthpiece stand, the other pressing the earpiece against his ear, listening. Even with the line static and the storm he heard the shrill rise in Carrick's voice. And so responded with a deep calm, his voice easy, saying, Yuht, and Sure, sure. This calm against the screaming little-rat-bomb going off inside his own head. Finally said, "Sit tight. Don't call another soul. I'll be there half an hour. How's the old woman?" Listened. Then said, "Of course she is. Listen: make her some tea, put some liquor in it. No, fuck that. Just give her a little glass of liquor. Not much, just some. You understand?" And did not

wait to hear what Carrick replied but had already hung up, was going
back up the hall, pulling off his pajama bottoms. Heard the rustle of
noise at the top of the stairs. Boy or dog. Likely both. Snapped up the
hall switch for light.

Two reasons for gratitude: Binter died if not in his sleep at least in
bed, sitting up with a racking motion, waking his wife, both hands
first gripped tight to his chest as his voice rattled broken out of him,
then his hands reached out, groping, before him. And so there was no
culpability upon Carrick. None to be laid at least. And this: the surprise that the Binter woman, that angry figure hovering for the past
near-dozen years whose job it seemed was to glower at Jamie, this
woman of garbled gibberish actually spoke American at least as well
as her husband had.

When he came into the farmhouse that night out of the rain with
his boy and the dog shut out in the car the woman had come to him
and held his elbows with her hands and studied his face and then she
crinkled; her face folded into itself and she moved in and laid her face
against his chest and held him and wept. As if he were her son. And he
stood there holding her, patting her back, ignoring the eyes of Carrick,
seated at the kitchen table with the open bottle of whiskey before him,
the pair of glasses. The woman shuddering against him. He looked
down at the top of her head. Her hair loose for the night, down over
the shoulders of her nightgown. And he stopped patting her back and
slid both hands around her back and pulled her close to him and she
tightened against him and they stood there, holding each other. His chin
in the furrow of her hair. Her chin a small sharp jab into his breastbone.

Later, after Jamie had telephoned the Franconia doctor to drive down
and complete a certificate of death and telephoned a telegram to the new
widow's sister and family in New York and then carried a heavy basin
of water up the stairs so the woman could wash her dead husband, pausing a moment beside the bed, Binter in death smaller, composed, calm—
after all this Jamie sat at the kitchen table and took up the woman's
untouched glass with three fingers of whiskey in it and drank it down
and looked at Carrick, who had been waiting for him.

"So what do we do now?"

"Do? We don't do anything. I'm going home. I don't need to be here for the doctor or when the neighbors start coming in. You're fine; you're the hired man."

"Not what I'm asking."

"I guess it depends then."

"On what?"

"On how much you managed to learn these three months."

"I know it. Start to finish. He was good that way. Slow, explaining things just enough but not too much. I'm set. I'm good to go."

"Where's things stand?"

"We got a run barreled off and a new one just started."

"Well, we'll see then."

"See."

"How it turns out."

"It'll be fine."

"I'm glad to hear it."

"Pelham, you're fucking with me."

"How's that, Jeeter?"

Carrick spread his arms wide. "I'm talking about all this. We don't need this setup anymore."

Jamie shook his head. "What I'm going to do is, wait a decent time, a week, maybe two. Then make her an offer. And you, you've learned your business, then stick to it and do it well. Not fuck with me. You'll be able to pay me off for the farm, three maybe four years, you look sharp to things. It'll be gravy then. Pure gravy."

"Aw shit, Jamie. These shitty cows. I can't stand it."

Jamie leaned forward across the table, his forearms flat on the surface. Looking at Carrick. "Wake up boy. Never again in your life will anybody offer you something as good as this. Pull your eyes out of your asshole and look around."

They were driving, Jamie and the girl, a weekday afternoon, Foster in school. The first thing she told him, going out the long uncurling drive of the Mount Washington in Bretton Woods, was that she liked children. A plainfaced girl with a soft mouth, redblond hair, not pretty but for her youth, something reptilian in the beak of her nose, her arms soft, freckled—they would thicken quickly—Amelia Hewitt. Amy, she liked to be called. Finding her had not been so hard as he'd feared. He'd gone to Bretton Woods, where as far as he knew Jeeter Carrick was unknown. It was October; everyone was thinking of what came next. He told her, "And you'll have a raft of your own one day soon, I'd bet. But all I've got in mind is a nice drive on a pretty day. I'd like to tell you about a friend of mine. That's all."

She looked at him quickly. This was not the same look she'd given him earlier, that one a variation on the look women all the summer season had shot over him: some skewed blend of carnal sympathy, as if the death of his wife eliminated some intermediate steps. As if he were a vessel abandoned, ripe for captain and crew. Now though she was appraising the situation quickly. He liked that. When he'd talked to the dining room manager at the Mount Washington the man had known right away the girl Jamie was looking for. Now, he thought, he'd find out if they were both right.

"I wondered why it was me you singled out."

He said nothing.

"What's wrong with your friend he can't find a girl on his own?"

Now he looked at her. "Jeeter? Why there's nothing at all wrong with him. I'd guess he'd be fighting them off he was out in circulation."

"Jeeter? What christly kind of name is that?"

"I don't know. A nickname of some sort maybe? I never gave it a thought." At the end of the drive he turned east toward the tight gap of Crawford Notch.

"What's wrong with him, he's not in circulation? Is he locked up?"

"In a way I guess. To a man like me he is. I always thought you had to be either desperate or have it someway in your blood to farm."

"What kind of farm?"

"This and that. Milking cattle. Some sheep. I don't know. A farm."

"What kind of cows?"

"Brown ones."

"Jerseys."

"And some splotched white and brown, reddish brown."

"Guernseys."

"I guess. Cows." Some part of him thinking someday likely he'd pay for this pretense of ignorance.

"Seems to me odd some neighbor girl wouldn't have snagged him, he's such a fine catch."

"Could be one will. But he doesn't know many folks, I guess. Not even so many of the neighbors." Guessing with Binter dead that would change and hoping not too much. He said, "He's up from Vermont somewhere."

Now she shifted, turned away from the open window and slipped her back against the door, twisted on the seat to face him. "Where's this farm at, anyhow?"

"Down to Franconia. Out Easton. You ever been out there?"

"No," she said. "But I know it's opposite of the way we're going."

He pulled off the road into the parking area at the head of the notch. To the left the auto road dropped down from sight into the deep narrow gorge of the notch; to the right the rail line ran along the side of the southern flank, a sinuous break descending into the trees, the sides of the notch rising sharp and steep, as tight and precise as if cut by a lightning bolt. Other motorcars were parked here, some vehicles from the hotels. People stood against the rail, gazing east.

They remained in the car. She said, "He's from Vermont, why's he got himself a farm here?"

Sharp enough, he decided. "Him and me are kind of partnered up."

"I figured that someway. But, a farm?"

"Well, there's more to it than that."

"I guess likely."

"Whatever you've heard about me's likely only half true. But. Anybody'll tell you, I'm straight. What I say is what I do. What I thought is we could sit here and talk a little. Then, you wanted, we could ride down to Easton and see the place. Meet the fellow, you cared to." When the fast cloud-shadows moved over the car it was cool, then warm again with the sun. She looked away from him, watched the tourists gaping at the notch. For a moment he thought he'd lost her. Then she turned back.

"It's not my business and I'll not say it but once. You're more in need of a woman than some young jasper's probably still needing to look close each time to decide which edge of the razor to use. How it strikes me, anyhow."

He was quiet a moment. Then said, "I've got no urge."

"Didn't say you did. But want and need, now that's two different things."

He looked at her. Big blousing girl. Looking right at him. After a time he said, "I've got this boy. He's the only need I know."

She reached and touched his arm where his wrist lay over the wheel, her fingers just grazing him. His skin lifted under her touch. Then her hand was back in her lap. The cool of clouds ran over the car. She said, "I don't like sitting here like a gawk. We rode over to Easton, you could tell me what you wanted to. Since we're out for a drive anyhow."

November. The world gone gray. Some wet dull mornings the brightest things the paper birches luminescent among the other trees of the woods, the mountainsides. Jamie already feeling the pull toward the holidays, the first year passing. As if with his head tipped back to take scent off the air. Some taint of dread. Trying to measure himself and Foster, the year of the two of them against what might have been for the four of them. Unfathomable, as if trying to chart out a different life. Empty hands.

He'd paid fifteen hundred dollars cash money for the hundred and eighteen acres of pasture and meadow and small plot of bottomland along the Gale River, the steep rising sheep pastures up the ridge toward Landaff and the woodlots above that. He drove the Binter wife to the Littleton station for the train taking her to her sister and the family awaiting her. Some other life. She worked her hands together in her lap, her face straight ahead as if not seeing, not wanting to see any of it, for the last time. He wished he could do her a kindness, say something. The best he could do was be silent. He sat with her in the station until the train came and stood then on the platform as it pulled away. Not watching the windows for her face, lifting no hand. Just standing watching.

Bottling in the rented basement room in Bethlehem with Carrick. A single electric bulb, the window boarded over inside and out. Daytime, with Foster in school. A four-by-four dropped into angle-irons against the oakplank door at the bottom of the dormer, the dormer doors closed and padlocked from the inside. Jamie tense as could be, always during this operation. This part, this setup, he felt the weak link. The distillery was good, proved. Carrick was in check, thus far. His contacts, his ability to read them, he felt confident about. Making the runs, the deliveries, was dicey only for the unexpected development—the flat tire in the wrong place, that sort of thing. It was only here where he felt vulnerable, and no talk, no grease, could change how it was, how it would appear. To the wrong eyes. And no way to know where those eyes might be. So he worked with a tin funnel and a box of corks and the empty wooden crates at one side, a pile of straw to stuff in around the bottles as the cases were filled. His upper and lower teeth moved back and forth in a small sliding motion, a faint click in his jaw, running up into his head.

Carrick said, "That Amy. She's a pistol."

Jamie said nothing. Working.

Carrick said, "A firecracker, that's what she is."

Jamie sighed, let himself be heard. Said, "That right?"

"You know it's right. You must've known."

Jamie didn't like this course. "Seemed a sensible girl. Head on her shoulders."

"Oh she's sharp enough I guess. A little pigheaded even. Blunt. But I like that. Says what she means."

"Yuht."

"But I tell you."

"Jesus, don't."

"I mean it. My ears are dried off and then some. I've had my share. You know how these hotel girls are."

"I guess."

"Most of them anyhow. They want it, you know. Now that was a surprise to me."

"Sure."

"But this Amy. Jesus."

"Well, I'm glad for you."

"She does this thing. I never been done like that."

"Jeeter."

"What?"

"Leave it be."

"What I keep thinking is, how did she learn it? How did she know?"

"It's just men and women, Carrick. They didn't figure out how to make each other happy, maybe none of us would be here."

"You gotta tell me."

"Tell you what? Nothing to tell."

"What she does is, she takes me with her mouth. Now I've had that before and never did mind it, I tell you. But this thing she does, when she's got me most all the way there—"

"Stop, Carrick. I don't want to hear it. You understand that? It's not of interest to me."

"You never had this happen to you? When she knows I'm right there next to it she drops her mouth all the way down and bites me. Real hard but quick. So it's come and gone before I know what she's up to. Jesus man, it's like my balls blow up. Tell me. You ever had that?"

Trying to recall. The shitsucker lawyer that had Joey's mother bottled up over there in Barre, Vermont. McCullen. McCarson. McSomething. And Claire. Two Claires now he would never know. That lawyer. Recalling Joey tell of biting him, biting his prick. She a child, little more than Foster's age. Three years perhaps. Not, he knew, that this mattered. But he wished there was someway, any trade at all he could make, to get to that little girl, pick her up, carry her out of there. As useless as any other what-if and so the one he preferred. Something pure. Something he'd not known.

And wondered if that twelve- or thirteen-year-old girl, if when she bit the prick of the lawyer, wondered if he'd come in her mouth then. Could see thick suet fingers wrapped tight in the child's roped curls, lifting her scalp.

She had never done him that way.

Less and less could he sleep. Even less wanted sleep. Could not stand returning out of those short brutal dreams.

In later years, Foster would recall his boyhood in three distinct levels, phases as sharply delineated as the separate stories of a house—with the first, the lowest, a place of murk, broken images, memories of his mother and sister, but also of something else, some sense of continuity, as if life briefly assumed a guise of sense. He suspected this was true of all childhood and he merely owned an abbreviated version of this falsehood. Still it lay within him and by adulthood it was not the melange of imagery that would provoke him but some ordinary thing, something everyday that for a moment could seize him and hold him with its own inestimable sadness: a certain windless hotday drift of pine resin, the berry scent of jam spread on toast, a certain winter twilight, the smell of someone passed by in a crowd, the first breaking of the peel of an orange. Freshly washed woman's hair. Whippoorwill at dusk.

Then following were the three or four years where he was unowned. Where the first of the dogs came into his life, the dogs he grew to trust more than any other creature. More than people. Where he was woodsbound, always, each day someway even if only at a school desk watching out the window the heavy flakefall and seeing clearly how it accumulated and lay in this or that part of the woods and meadows and old overgrown orchards he knew as his own. Knowing how the snow would drift around the trunk of a certain tree, leaving one side open bare down almost to the ground. How on sunny days in February small enclosed south-facing enclaves would melt down to the ground and he'd bend close on hands and knees and smell the wet earth, study the dried stalks of weeds bared. The world, the dog and the woods, and himself out in it all. The dog leading the way no more than he did, just each of them always knowing where the other was and where they both were. Never lost. And the presence behind him of his father. If the dog and he were magnets to each other then his father was the greater magnet that would draw him in. Even those nights when ghosts walked the house and he would not sleep but lay in his bed curled tight to the sleeping dog, always there was the comfort of the hugeness of his father asleep right under him, separated only by thin floorboards. On those nights he'd hear his father rise and he'd rise also, pulling on clothes in the dark, the dog already up, and then the both of them down the stairs and out to ride along. Hurrying always, even after he understood with nothing said that his father would wait for them, would not leave without them. Expected them. Riding through the night, sometimes sleeping, crunched down in the seat with the dog, almost always before waking knowing where they were, even the odd places—the little haymeadow carved out of the woods above Franconia, the swamp road up toward Whitefield, the pull-off near Twin Mountain where once waiting they'd seen a bear— in those places meeting a man or men, impatient, hurried, polite. Almost always, pausing to speak to him before they opened the rear door and unloaded out of the backseat. Other things also: the rides home, summer nights with the top down, the sounds of peepers rising from the passing roadside ditches, or the winter nights when the snowpack was high with a moon out, the road a clear dark-laid ribbon before them, where his father would turn off the headlamps and they would drive for miles in the dark as if it were a secret way to journey. His father pounding the wheel of the car as if there was not enough speed in the world for them. Throwing a cigarette out the window to shower sparks behind them. Lighting another. The world all gone, belonging to them. As if they would not, could never, stop.

Then the last part. He was fourteen, fifteen years old when it began. Or when he became aware of it. And even while it was new to him, he believed there was no surprise in it for his father. As if his father had seen it coming. Or expected it. Or expected nothing less. But it was later that Foster understood this much. Because what he had learned in the woods was that everything new is only a shift in what is already known. Some shift of the familiar. A new pattern, nothing more than that. The world was knowable. He knew that much. He was fourteen. He had smoked. Drank, more than once. A good afternoon he could go out and come home with a couple–three partridge. Some timberdoodle. The dog Lovey was a part of him. The world radiated. He'd not yet been laid. But he had ideas about that, also.

Estus Terry died the winter of 1927. Someone, Jamie never knew who, had hiked in during the March thaw and found the corpse, already well gone. Terry had broken a leg, hauled himself back to the house and lay there in the bed and starved to death or froze to death or both. There were signs about the house that he'd tried to make do. A rude crutch fashioned of a branch. Some utensils strewn. Empty meat and bean tins lined alongside the bed. The woodbox empty. A hundred unreachable feet away a dozen cords of wood stacked inside the unused horsebarn. Mice or a weasel had been at work on his face and hands, through the socks over his one unbooted foot.

Jamie drove his year-old Chrysler the first day of April to Whitefield for the service. A Congregationalist minister spoke not of Terry—whom he'd not known—but vaguely of the dire condition of man and the glory of God. He read the Twenty-third Psalm. The service was concluded. There were not quite a dozen people there, among them the Federal marshal Patrick Jackson. It was a billowy day. Spurts of rain lashing the clear-paned windows of the small church. Then bands of weak light lying across the pewbacks. Jamie sat wrapped in his overcoat three pews from the back on the aisle. Jackson's broad back stretching tight his own overcoat, upright, unmoving through the service, seated in the front row alone. Jamie watched him and Jackson did not bow his head for the concluding prayer for all their souls. Jamie wondered if he watched the minister or the plain wall behind him.

The group milled briefly in the stiff mud before the church and then broke apart. As if they would not speak to one another willingly. All knew the others and all had known Terry and someway each wanted to be private and alone there. Except for Patrick Jackson and Jamie knew it and did not wait but approached him first.

"Jackson." Followed the name with a tight nod.

"It's a crummy day for it, idn't it? Not that Estus would've cared. I don't think there was a weather he didn't like. Never heard him complain winter's too long, mud's too deep, a summer day's too hot. Know what I mean?"

Both holding the other's eyes. Neither hostile nor friendly: regarding, taking measure. Jackson was a big man. Jamie felt someway that was to his favor. He said, "It was what he feared. Dying slow. Laid up."

"It's what we all fear though, don't you think? Any of us had a choice in the matter. It wasn't likely so bad; the cold would've got a pretty strong hold of him. Not that he hadn't plenty of time to know it was coming. But still the cold'll lift the worst of it away from you. Is what I hear anyhow. He was fond of you."

"We got along. I didn't see him all that much. Maybe not even as often as you got out there."

"Yes," said Jackson. "I'll miss those visits. But christ it was a trek in there."

Jamie made a slight smile. "That road."

"Wasn't a road, man. That was a footpath with ambition."

"I'd guess you see plenty like it."

"Well yes. But those others you don't pay so much mind to. Too busy keeping an eye on where it might end. You're the invisible man these days, Pelham." As the humor rose in Jackson's voice his face compensated, growing more grim.

"I've got a quiet life."

"I'm glad to hear it. Wish there was more men content with quiet lives. But then, if there was, maybe I'd have to pay more attention to them."

"To read the papers, seems like you're busy enough."

"We keep at it. Border country's big with every little river or woods road a highway these days. And it's not like it used to be—some fella just trying to save a few dollars on the tax. There's organization to it. Twenty men working for every one of mine. It's a big business."

"I wouldn't know."

"That's right. The quiet man." Jackson tilted his head, scanned the broken skies. "Well, Estus Terry. We'll not see his like again. You run across a man named Pompelli in your travels?"

"Can't say I have."

"I've not yet either. I don't know what he is, a greek or a wop or what. But he's the little kingmaker is what I think. You keep running up against the same name and you haven't got a face to put to it, most likely he's your man. He could be in Boston for all I know. Could be he's just the money behind it. But I'm thinking, that was the case, he'd have a man standing up for him, local. There's plenty men working but they're the roughnecks. Somebody's in charge. I'd be curious to meet him."

"I'd guess you would."

"Well now," Jackson said. "Mostly if I can manage it I like to stay around the house on a Sunday. You're ever up to Colebrook of a Sunday stop in to visit. Anybody around can tell you how to find the house."

"I know where it is."

"It's the hard thing about this business, Pelham. Remembering to look over your shoulder time to time."

"Estus said much the same to me once."

"Is that so?" Jackson's face opened a little now, faint surprise. "Tell you the truth, I was talking about myself."

Driving away, raining once more, Jamie thought Now what the fuck was that? Another warning? An offer of some sort? And who the fuck was Pompelli? The only thing he knew for certain was there hadn't been a single thing Jackson said by accident. There were large amounts of bootlegged whiskey being run through the area out of Canada. He knew he'd lost some trade because of it. But he'd thought most of it was not stopping but going south to the cities. And when he lost custom he let it go without the fight he'd have waged ten, even five, years ago. Whatever loss he had he still felt he was holding his own. All he wanted. And Carrick: Carrick was quashed both sides, front and rear, Jamie content with how things stood and Amy Hewitt, Mrs. Carrick now, knowing her husband well enough to know Jamie understood the business in ways Jeeter never would. And they had three children. These and the farm were Amy's fortress. Jeeter like a rabbit in May clover lacking any sense of the hawk spiraling overhead. And Jamie, driving, wondering now where his own unseen hawk floated.

For a time, several years after Joey and Claire died, he would bring home a woman or girl after a night of careful lighthearted venturing in the small backroom and basement clubs of the north country. That stopped a couple of years ago one summer morning when he rose late and lay in bed listening to voices, laughter, coming from the kitchen and went down finally to find his son in shorts and an undershirt and the girl wrapped up in one of Jamie's old shirts sitting across the table from each other, drinking coffee. The room dropped to silence when he came in, as if he'd stepped somewhere he shouldn't have. And in the moment it took to recover himself and walk to the stove for coffee he realized the girl was closer in age to his son than to himself and that she was the last

he'd bring home. And could admit then that there was no joy in it anyway, felt relief as if letting some part of his life go. He recognized himself, in that moment of decision, to be a creature hunkered. One that
had always been such. Some comfort in that recognition.

Foster had spent the afternoon after school with Andy Flood, hooking a
ride with the old cedar-ribbed canoe out to Twin Mountain where they
put in and floated down the river, hoping to jump-shoot early spring
ducks. Lovey curled up against the ribs, pressed against Foster's knees for
support as they worked their way downstream, keeping to one bank as
much as possible, letting the current carry them, using the paddles only
for direction and to prod off boulders, the canoe bumping softly, scraping its way along. The spring flood was behind them; in another month
the river would be too low for the canoe. It was a fine afternoon, sifting
spraying rain in their faces, the underbrush along the banks red with
spring growth, buds swollen on overhanging branches. When the sun
broke through it was the color of honey. They put up a small raft of mal-
lards, too far off for any shooting. Then a single male wood duck, a knave
of color but they just sat watching it, Foster holding a streamside branch
with one hand to keep them in place. Not many wood ducks. They didn't
even have to talk about it. He liked Andy for that. They weren't out for
ducks anyway; it was the float they wanted.

   At the deep riverbend below the house they took the canoe out and
carried it up to the barn, each with one hand up to steady a thwart, the
other hand carrying their shotguns. The dog, gone from sight, home.
She would only tolerate a boat if Foster was in it.

   They set the canoe upside down on a pair of sawhorses in the barn,
the smell of wet wool from their jackets and caps fresh in the must of
the barn. Out the open barn doors the Chrysler gleamed with beading
rain. Andy Flood scuffed a boot-toe in the old hay. "Thought your old
man was off to a funeral."

   Foster nodded. "Some old rascal I never knew. I guess they got him
in the ground all right."

   "I'll get to home then."

   "You shouldn't take it personal. It's nothing you did."

"Well he sure don't like Floods."

"He doesn't like much of anybody I think."

"I'll get on."

"All right." They walked out the barn doors together. Foster could see Lovey hunched against the door at the top of the steps. Andy turned up the track toward the road, looked back, "That wood duck."

"Yuht."

Inside his father was over the stove in his shirtsleeves, his tie tucked into his shirt, a floursack apron tied around his waist like a waiter. The windows steamed over. Something boiling. Food smells. Foster hung his jacket and cap on pegs to dry, took a small wooden box from a cupboard and sat at the table and broke down his shotgun. His father looked over at him.

"You're wet through."

"I'll dry. What's for supper?"

"What's for supper? I don't know. What'd you bring?"

Foster grinned. "Nothin."

"Nothing?"

"Saw a wood duck."

"Woody's good eating."

Foster had a small rag smeared with oil, running it over the parts of the gun. "Was too far off."

"I stopped to Bethlehem and got some chops. That sound all right?"

"I could eat a chop."

"Two?"

"Maybe so."

"Irish potatoes. Tomatoes stewed out of a tin."

"You're getting me hungry."

"You were hungry before, just hadn't stopped to think of it."

"Could be." Then paused and asked, "So how was the thing?"

"The service?"

"Yuht."

"Not much. At least not much to me. But I'm glad I went."

"Howcome?"

"Oh, Estus was one of the old ones. I'd like to think he'd of known I was there. I'd like to think, the time comes, some few might crawl out of the woods for me."

"You feeling old, Pop?"

"Not old so much, just. Nothing."

"Not so young?"

"I been that a long time. No. It's nothing."

Then both quiet. Foster finished with the shotgun, wiped it down with a clean rag and put it back together. Stood and put away the box and set the shotgun up in a corner. Then said, "You want me to scrub the potatoes?"

"They're already cooking. You can smell them."

"I wasn't sure. Just want to help is all."

"You can't help. I already got it. But you're honest at least. I raised an honest boy."

"I've not lied to you."

"Not yet."

"Pop?"

"What's that?"

"Stop."

"Stop what?"

"Just stop. I can't stand when you get like this."

"Like what?"

"Nothing."

"No nothing. Like what?"

"Just antsy and all. Nerved up. Ready to pounce on something."

"I'm making supper is all. It's my turn, isn't it? It's my turn."

"I made it last night."

"That's right. See?"

"I made it the night before too. But you weren't here so that doesn't count."

"I wasn't here? Where was I?"

"I don't know."

"Where was I? Jesus I don't know."

"It's all right. What kind of chops?"

"Beef-rib. That all right?"

"That's good."

"Rare?"

"Real rare."

"That's right. You're the wild man."

"I just like it tender is all."

A pause. Then, "How's school?"

"Fine."

"Fine?"

"Fine."

"What I'm asking is, how're you doing. You keeping up?"

"Pop. I'm fine."

"You've got to pay attention. Think ahead. It's not enough to plan out what you want and try and make things fit that plan. You've got to figure out how to fit yourself to that plan. You understand?"

"Just stop. All right? Just leave it be."

After a bit: "Pan's hot. One chop or two?"

"How many'd you get?"

"Three."

"One."

"I'll only eat one myself."

"One."

"All right. I'll cook the three and we can fight over what's left."

They ate. Foster handing down strips of fat and lumps of potato under the table to the dog, who took the food off his fingers with a moist swipe of her tongue. They split the last chop. It was good beef, the layers of muscle run together with sweet braids of fat. The kitchen was warm with the range, the hot scent of foods, the bodies there. Quiet but for the chink of flatware against the china. Budroses around the plate rims, the color faded from wear. Jamie pushed back from the table and lighted a cigarette. Blew the smoke up toward the overhead three-globed lamp.

Foster said, "Talked with Doc Dodge the other night. The night you wasn't home. He's got a young stud dog. Lovey'll come in heat sometime in May. I want to breed her to that dog of his."

"What for?"

"Puppies."

"I know puppies. Why do you want to have puppies?"

"She's coming eight. I'd like to keep one from her. Other than that, just to have them. Keep one, sell the rest."

"Going in to business."

"Not really."

"Keep one, huh? What happens, you can't stand to get rid of any of them? Then what, we're stuck with a raft of dogs?"

"Pop. Setters usually whelp eight or ten, sometimes twelve pups. I know what I'm getting into. All I want is the one."

"Jesus Christ. Eight or ten dogs running around the house."

"She'd have them in the summer. I'd want to whelp them inside, make a box for her, get a big carton and cut it down. But once they were a week or two old they could go out to the barn."

"You've got it all thought out."

"I wouldn't talk to you about it I didn't."

"Ask."

"Sir?"

"You're not talking to me about it. You're asking me about it."

"All right."

Jamie looked at him, crushed out his smoke in the ashtray. Made a small close-mouthed grin. "You turning into a hardcase? Giving lip to your old man?"

"No. Didn't mean to. It's just, it'd be a good breedback."

"What's that mean?"

"The stud dog, Trice, he's out of Lovey's dam by a dog called Copper, who is half brother to Lovey's granddam. So it would be a good breedback. That's what it's called."

"Sounds to me like one of those old swamprat families where everybody's married to somebody they're already related to."

"It's like that except it's intentional. You're breeding for traits and characteristics. You can't do it all the time but you do it just the right time, the right dogs at the right distance or closeness to each other and you can do pretty good with it. Get some pretty good dogs. Doc Dodge thinks his Trice dog and Lovey'd be a good go for it. Me, I'd like to see what happens."

His father sat, gazing off over the table one side of Foster. Foster waited, then stood and cleared the table, ran water into the sink and began to wash up. Behind him his father said, "You ever imagine what it'd be like, your mother and sister were still alive?"

Foster turned. His father hadn't moved, wasn't looking at him. His head tilted a little sideways as he studied a spot on the far wall. Foster said, "I think about it time to time. I can't imagine them any older than I remember them."

"You can't?"

"No."

A pause then. A crinkling sound in the stovepipe as the flue cooled. Foster rubbed his hands together.

After a time his father said, "You start chasing after girls, you remember you had a sister. One that might've grown up, had to contend with boys like you. You remember that. You understand me?"

Foster was silent.

A shorter pause this time. Then his father turned his head to look at him. "I asked you a question."

"I heard you. I just don't know what you want me to say."

"I want you to say Yes, I understand."

"I don't really."

"Shit." His father stood. "Don't mind me. I've got a foul mood on me tonight. I didn't even see it coming and then there it was. Must've been that funeral. Never mind. I've got to go out. You want to ride along?"

"I've got homework."

"Time was, you wouldn't stay to the house on your own."

Very quiet Foster said, "I don't mind it so much anymore."

Jamie tugged his tie out of his shirtfront and smoothed it down. Began rolling down his shirtsleeves. Foster stepped along the counter to the stack of schoolbooks. "Go on," his father said. "Have your puppies."

Pompelli. How to seek after a name you would not utter since there was no way knowing what interest the one queried might own? Only by listening. Listening more intently than you already were. Which he believed was not possible. So, listening with a bent focus, something, keen, tuned to the sound of the name. And the danger in that: Watching thus for the one thing meant the possibility of missing something else. What was he missing?

                              *   *   *

Spring into summer. The hotel season opened and accounts still dribbled away. Nothing swift, nothing to be confronted, just men needing a little less. Naw, two cases'll do me fine till Thursday. Truth is, make that Monday. How you doing Jamie. How you doing Pelham. How's that boy? Growing up, idn't he? Even the timbermen, some not even showing up, others cadging, buying a little bit. Those, Jamie thought, were just milking what was coming through their woods. And it was this vagueness that chased him around, nights. Then there was Carrick, backstocking barrels of ready whiskey in his hayloft, trying each time Jamie came by to take him up and fork away the hay to display it all, Amy Carrick watching him throughout, then rushing up before he drove away with a pan of bread or a sack of eggs or something out of the garden that she'd press upon him. As if she needed to take care of him. What frustrated him most was time to time in the hotels running up against men, strangers, men he knew at first glance were not guests but draped in good suits, who would scan him with their eyes and gaze past him as if he were not there. He'd sidle in closeby and hang back and try to listen to them. Talking about baseball, sometimes politics in a grandiose simple fashion, pussy in general, local pussy in detail, fragments of more personal speech that he could not follow, as if it were in code—which he knew when he heard. And as he heard this he saw himself again as the man on the outside. The one who doesn't get it.

   And nothing, not once, of Pompelli. As if he were chasing a blankness down a blank road that led to nothing. It occurred to him more than once: Was Patrick Jackson trying to set him up? Except there was no reason for Jackson to do this. Some nights that summer driving he would feel his hands slip upon the wheel, the sweat coming off him in the cool night. Too cool for sweat.

The middle of a night late in June, Foster woke to a wet bed, Lovey by his feet with two puppies out and a third on the way, the bitch curled to clean her firstborn with her tongue, the puppies palm-sized, blind, ears small and pressed tight to their heads. He took a case off a pillow and began to clean the puppies as they emerged, stroking the straining bitch, lifting the pups one by one to sex them and then nudging them together

along the row of swollen nipples on her belly, the pups white mostly with
faint traces of color, lemon or blue, dark noses, tails sleek thin stubs. Ten
in all, one born dead. Nine puppies, three females and six males. The
dead one was a female. He took up the dead puppy while the bitch was
still in labor and wrapped it in a pillowcase and set it up high on a shelf
in the closet. With all that was happening to her she would not miss it,
he was sure. Foster felt he knew death well, felt it was a part of him,
that he recognized something others his age did not yet know. But for
all of this he'd not, until those early morning hours, been a part of the
beginning of life. Had not seen it from this end. It was unbearably tender. So an answer formed to the question that he hadn't even known
was in him: What keeps it rolling around and around?

After dawn he went down the stairs and found his father up, drinking coffee. Foster took a cup and filled it. His father said, "I heard you
scrambling around up there."

"She had her puppies."

"I thought the plan was for it to happen there." His father indicated
the cut-down carton lined with old shredded blanket to one side of the
range.

"That was the plan."

"What do you do now?"

"Carry that box upstairs and put em in it and bring em down and
hope she takes that all right. I'm betting she'll just come along and jump
in. I'm betting she doesn't care anymore where she is, as long as she's
got her pups."

"How many'd you get?"

"Nine. Three bitches, the rest dogs."

"It's a girl you want to keep isn't it?"

"Yuht."

"Cuts your choices, just the three."

Foster finished his coffee. "It's enough," he said, and went to take up
the box.

As the summer season went high business picked up, as it should have
done, as it always had, yet Jamie could not rid himself of thinking that
it was being allowed. As their orders increased men became easier with

him, more comfortable, as if they were no longer disappointing him. And yet there it was, the peckerhead of doubt. As if some word had come down: Give Pelham some rope.

The Carricks too were easier. He told himself it was not just the increased volume, the diminishing hayloft backstock, but also the midsummer drift, the brief time when the seasons seemed suspended. Mostly, he knew, Amy Carrick was happier, less snappish. Her children were fat and she too seemed to gain solidity each time he saw her, not so much girth but more a radiant certainty that spread around her. Her youngest was almost two and she took clear delight in hiking him onto her hip and lifting her blouse to give him suck, her breast white as milk but laced with blue veins, the nipple an engorged blood-dark rosehip. Without it ever being said, smelled or witnessed, he understood that she consumed careful regular amounts of the whiskey. She would never, he guessed, be so drunk as to be found out. But there was that constant meticulous inhalation against the world's edge. He'd seen this before and understood it himself. He also thought it a dangerous thing, more clearly in a woman than a man. Why that was so he could not say, but he knew it was true.

One evening late in July he'd just made a delivery to the Forest Hills above Franconia and was on the road home over the highland toward Bethlehem and he came around a curve to a place in the road where the land opened up on both sides, the woods fallen away for a beaver pond. The last of the sun was striking low. He stopped the car and sat in the redwine light. He smoked. For long moments, he was relaxed for the first time in months. As if he were all the way back inside himself again. He drove away, thinking it was possible again. And even thinking that, the action of thinking such a thing was clear cause not to believe it. Not to trust it.

Summer mornings he'd sit on the steps and watch across the yard where Foster had the puppies loosed from the barn, the pups' coats growing out, their legs overtaking their bodies as they galloped and chased through the hemlock duff, their markings, more a roaning than spots, coming out on them. Long streaks of color in their ears and tails, the lemon or blue truing up. One of the males a tricolor, with a black mask and dark bay streaks on his legs. Foster sat on a crate tipped back so he could rest against the side of the barn, his legs sprawled out before him, the puppies over them like a steeplechase or using them as logs to hide behind for ambuscade. Foster near inert, only leaning time to time to pluck a pup away from embedding its teeth too deep into his ankle or to unravel a mess of them from his legs. As if the motion, the turmoil of the young dogs, soothed him. Less often, Foster would throw himself off the crate onto all fours into the duff and sand, swatting out with his hands in gentle swipes to bowl a puppy, the hand hovering as the pup righted itself and sought around itself, spying the hand overhead and attacking it. Sometimes Foster'd be down on his back, the puppies mauling over him, the boy's laughter a bright rippling shatter to the held morning.

He'd turned sixteen the March passed. His father watched him: the boy and man piled up one atop the other inside the single gangling form. Something coming to an end. He would sit those mornings and try to determine what came next.

Late July there was an incident, what the papers called it, a calamity, far above the Connecticut Lakes in the rough unroaded border country. Something middle-of-the-night that left two federal marshals and three other men dead. A wrecked set of cars bogged to the axles with loads of Canadian whiskey. The Littleton paper was shrill. In the article Pat Jackson was quoted as identifying the three unknown men as being members of a "criminal network not locally based." He had nothing else to say. The dead marshals were local men with wives and children. There was a service with overflow attendance. The Littleton editorial called for stomping out the blight, for cutting its head at the source. It failed to locate that source.

The doctor, Dodge, took his stud fee in the tricolor male. Afternoons Foster would take the gang of pups down to the sheep pasture along the river and sit on one of the boulder backs and watch them play. In the late afternoons he'd shut them in the barn except for the little bitch he called Glow and he'd walk out through the swampy puckerbrush with her fighting to keep up with him. Sometimes he'd get far ahead, out of her sight, and he'd hear her begin to cry. He'd sit then and wait. She'd find him. Sometimes it took awhile. Learning how to use her nose, to let her nose direct her head. He was happy to wait, squatting in the damp, holding back all urge to speak her name or utter a low whistle, anything at all. And then she'd lift her head from where her nose was drenched in his scent and spy him, coming at him then with the unleashed passion of one come to love. And he would take her up so, pressing his nose into her coat, the sweet puppy smell of her wrapping his heart.

Foster sold three of the pups through Dodge, both available females and one of the males. It was hard to accept the money, six dollars apiece, and then the men drove out of the yard and the money was in his pocket and Glow chewing at his cuffs and he felt all right about it. The last males he sold through an advertisement in the paper. This was harder yet, the people rank strangers. Without caring what the people would think he lifted each pup and kissed its head and without words wished it well before handing it over. Then it was done. Lovey's coat began to grow back. She returned, something forever shifted in her but the old dog back. Aloof and demanding, pressing up against him at night. Turning her head away when he'd reach to stroke her. And there was Glow. A strident urgent puppy. Sometimes, in the woods, stopping so suddenly on top of some scent that she'd topple over her own legs, her nose down in the soft dirt, her eyes already turned up to scout her next move.

The way things happen. As if a gap, a hole in the world, is only waiting to be filled up. And not passive waiting but gravitational. Just after midnight, the fourth of August, the Perseids streaking the sky, Jamie at an oval polished table in the general manager's office of the Forest Hills, above Franconia. This room a small lap of luxury left in a diminishing industry. A private sitting room with a fine daytime view of the Notch and the mountains around it: the Old Man. The manager an old hotel man called Harold Shelton. Jamie sitting there drinking whiskey through the evening hours with Shelton, both of them passing time trading stories and laments, Shelton pausing to lift the telephone in response to the bell, settling a problem without moving. Watching him do this recalled to Jamie something familiar, where a man made order in his wake. He could look clearly at Shelton and see a man out of time, a man not only of an old order but of one passed by. Who did not know that yet. Or more likely, as Jamie sat and sipped, who knew it well and was simply riding out whatever was left to him. Shelton a lean stringy man with a trimmed ginger beard and manners matching the manicure of his fingers. His hair white-patched over his temples, the white fading back in sublime fine disintegration as if a sign painter had done the job. On the wall a round electric clock, an audible click with each minute passed. A neat stack of stationery with the hotel imprint on the top of the sheet. A fountain pen and well. And the telephone. Nothing else between them but the bottle and the glasses and a pair of cork coasters. Late, and quiet in the room. Shelton turned his glass on the coaster, watched the revolution, looked up at Jamie. Jamie touched his own glass and then looked at Shelton.

"There's a man, Pompelli. You know him?"

And watched Shelton's face change to a set of composure, a long-practiced face laid over him, his problem-facing face.

"I don't know him," Shelton said. "I'd of thought you would though."

"Why'd you of thought that, Harold?"

"Well." Shelton looked away from Jamie toward the nightblank windows. "You're all in the same business."

"I've not laid eyes on him."

"Is that right?"

"What is it, Harold?"

"I thought you two were doing business together."

"What gave you that idea?"

Shelton shook his head. "What I heard."

"Where'd you hear it?"

Again Shelton shook his head. Paused. And Jamie felt it before the older man even spoke: betrayal, not in the room but flooding over him like an electric current. Shelton said, "Now I can't say that I did. Just, how things go around."

Jamie breathed out. A useless question but he asked it. "You know where he is?"

"No idea. You know I'm not even in that end of the business any-more anyway. It's other fellows now. But they, men that work for him, it's hard to miss them. That's maybe why I thought you'd know him." Now also an alertness lay alongside those fear pinpricks, the globes of his eyes bright, the lids lowered by half.

Jamie sat silent a time, twisting his drink. Sat long enough for the silence to communicate fully to the man across from him. Then qui-etly, looking off as if addressing himself or some other presence alto-gether, said, "These days it seems a man can't know what direction a thing's coming from."

Shelton nodded. Said, "It was me, wanting to find someone like the man you're looking for, I'd start in my own backyard."

Half a mile south of the Carrick farm in the Easton valley there was a pull-off in the woods with a trailhead for hiking paths up into the Kins-man range. Far enough from the farm so he could drive another mile, turn around and come back quiet with his headlamps off and coast into the pull-off and sit and no one at the farm would know he was there. The first night he drove there at half-past two from the Forest Hills and sat until just before dawn when a cold fog rose off the Gale and spread over the valley floor. From a bend in the river or a pond nearby he heard the cry of a loon. The farm silent, sleeping all night as he sat. With the fog the dawn chill went through him and he started the Chrysler and drove past the farm where the cows were lined up at the gate from the nightpasture waiting for the barn. Drove through Franconia and on to Littleton where he ate breakfast at the diner. Washed his face with hot water in the restroom. At nine o'clock he went down the street to Stodd Nichols and bought one of the little flat automatic pistols and a box of .32 caliber cartridges for it and was patient and quiet while the clerk demonstrated loading the clip. Paid cash and drove home, the gun loaded, slid up into the springs under the seat where he could reach down while driving and find it behind his feet.

Foster was eating sunnyside eggs and toast, his legs scissoring back and forth in satisfaction and for the faint rub of his penis against his trousers, thinking of Judith Beebie who this moment he was sure still lay sleeping in her bed in Bethlehem, the all of her in a loose nightgown. He could not imagine that she might sleep without clothes of any sort as he did because he could not quite imagine what she would look like without clothes. What he liked to think about was getting her to go for a walk in the woods with him and Glow and Lovey. He was pretty sure she'd like Glow; he could not imagine anyone not. He couldn't see a pretext for inviting her for such a walk and so he left it to chance, thinking if he spent enough time in the woods perhaps maybe he'd come across her. Sitting on a log because she liked it there. Maybe gathering wildflowers. She was a year older than he was, a galaxy. And he was left alone. Some skewed community knowledge of what his father was and what his mother had been and even the way he lived. Some distinction that set him apart. Possibly he was simply odd. A personality that would not fit in. Waiting to find that one who felt the same way about things. Ways he wasn't even sure he could articulate but thought he would not need to. With the right one. Which brought him back around to Judith Beebie. Not that there had been any sign from her. What he thought was She just doesn't know it yet.

He heard the car come in. He stood and moved the coffee over onto the hot side of the range. His erection subsided. He sat back at the table and mopped the eggstains up with toast. His father came up the steps into the kitchen, the screen door a weak slap behind him.

"Morning, Pop."

His father looked at him. Jamie was beardstubbled, bloodshot, his frame soft within the wrinkles of his clothes, his movements slow, deliberate, slightly quaked and wavery. He looked around the room, back to Foster. "Why aren't you in school?"

"Pop? What month is it?" Foster studied him.

His father ran a hand up over his face, pressed it against his eyes. "It's August," he said. "Only August."

"You want something to eat? Some eggs? There's coffee."

Jamie shook his head. "I ate."

"Maybe you're not so old after all. Up all night." Foster paused and then said, "Hope it was worth it."

Jamie came halfway to the table fast and then stopped. Looked at the boy, the grin on his face still there but apprehension flared up in his eyes.

Recalled the first time he took the boy swimming, Jamie on his back at the riverbend: holding the child over him and then lowering him slowly onto his chest, the boy kicking and squealing. Terror and delight and then abrupt absorbed silence as the water came up cold around him as he lay prone on his father's chest. That same boy now watching him. Some fear in his eyes. A sprawl of a boy. Jamie cut his eyes away and went to the stove and poured out a cup of coffee he didn't want. Drank some of it and set the cup down on the cooling ledge of the stove. He said, "Whatever your plan is today, I want it quiet. I need to sleep."

"Sure."

Jamie tipped his head, cracking his neck. He said, "Jesus."

"You all right?"

"I'm tired is all."

Foster stood and took up his dishes and passed his father to the sink. Began to wash up. Without looking he spoke. "Anything I can do?"

"Just let me sleep."

"Beyond that?"

There was a long pause. Foster got the plate and cup and cutlery washed and rinsed and then scrubbed out the skillet with clean water and put it back on the range to dry. Feeling his father behind him, the strength and tension of him a magnet to turn to, to resist.

After a time Jamie spoke. "No. Nothing but that."

Jamie woke in the long lowering summer twilight, not sure of where he was. For those first few seconds thought he was a boy on the farm in Randolph, time to rise and help with morning chores. His body rolled effortlessly as a child and he came up on an elbow but there was no window where there should be a window and then he was all back. And then groaned. Thinking of the night behind him and the night ahead. Wondered how many nights it would take to prove him right. And felt a twinge of fear turn over inside, wondering if he was too old for this.

He bathed and dressed and, shaving, could smell and hear dinner being made down the hall, his boy talking to the dogs as he worked. He paused then, his face half swathed in lather, the razor cutting broad clearings through it. He was young enough. Those fuckers. The man in the mirror had bright unwavering eyes. Foster's laugh came to him. He smiled at the sound.

Calves' liver with onions and bacon. Black-seeded Simpson lettuce dressed with cider vinegar. Bread-and-butter corn. A bowl of radishes and scallions. He liked a scallion dredged with salt. The corn was first of the season, sweet, bursting with milky pulp.

He said, "What'd you do with your day?"

"Helped Floods put up hay this noon. Washed the chaff off me at the river. Read some."

"Floods can't get their own hay up?"

"I know you can't stand em. But that Andy's all right. He's a pal. It all gets shunt onto him anyway. So I was just helping him out, really."

"I bet old man Flood loves to see you over there busting your butt."

"Then I took the Chrysler to Bethlehem."

"That right? Took the car to town? Just like that?"

"Somebody had to shop. It was either that or wake you before the store closed. Way you looked this morning, I'd not of been surprised you slept straight on till morning."

"So you went to the store and came home."

"I wasn't out sporting around." But did detour slowly down through the late dusty afternoon streets to pass the Beebie house and looped the block to pass by again all without sign of the blond-bobbed Judith. The answer, however you looked at it, wasn't a lie.

Jamie shrugged then and said, "You're old enough to want to get out and about. We'll have to work something out, times I know you'll be able to use the car."

Quiet a moment. Then Foster said, "I'd like that."

"Boy oh boy, that corn's some awful good, isn't it?"

"There's more to the sink, I can drop in the pot you want."

"No, this is good, this is enough."

Then both quiet, busy with the food. And for Jamie, those moments recalled to him the many days he and Joey would sleep until late afternoon and rise then to begin the night, another lifetime but one that still ran threads through him and one big strand sitting across from him, and for those moments he was calm and easy, a simple partition of grace from the rest of time. And so he finished his meal, buoyant, confident of the night's work before him. He smoked and tilted back in his chair and looked at his boy. Foster sitting watching him back. The puppy Glow working the room, back and forth between the two, waiting silent for them to notice her starvation.

Jamie said, "What would you say, we quit all this and tried something else. Someplace else."

"What're you talking about?"

"I don't know. I was just thinking, maybe we should cut out of here. Things aren't what they used to be."

"See there." Foster grinned. "I told you you were getting old."

"You're happy?"

"Happy enough." Then, "What were you thinking of?"

"I don't know. Out west somewheres maybe. New Mexico."

"Live with the red Indians?"

Jamie smiled back at him. "California?"

"Be in the pictures."

"Sure. You could do it."

"It's handsome fellas they're looking for, I hear."

"Most likely they always need somebody to stand around and make a crowd."

"Not my fault I'm so much taller than you."

"Point."

A pause. Then Foster said, "You're halfway serious, aren't you?"

"Well. You're about grown. Maybe a change of scenery would do you good."

A longer pause. Then Foster said, "What's going on?"

"Nothing's going on. I was thinking was all."

"I'm happy. Happy right where I am."

"I can see that. But you given any thought to next year? The year after that?"

"Not too much. Some. I want to get the pup started this fall. Maybe, she works out, I might try raising some more of these setters. Maybe keep a few of the best ones, get them started, sell them that way. That's where the money is."

"Be a dog-man."

"I don't know what else. I haven't got that figured out."

"That's all right. There's time."

Foster blew air through his lips. "New Mexico."

Jamie grinned. "It was just an idea."

Quiet then. A long pause. Then Foster said, "You heading out somewhere tonight?"

"A little business. Might be late. You want something, want me to drop you somewhere?"

"No. I'm fine to stay home. You want me to ride along with you?"

"No. It's no big thing."

"I'll ride if you want."

Jamie shook his head. "There's no need. Like I said, it could be late."

"All night maybe?"

Jamie smiled. "It's not what you think. Tell the truth, I wish it were."

"It wouldn't bother me you had a lady friend."

"Is that so?"

"It wouldn't."

"Well, then." Jamie stood, ran his hands up under his braces to smooth his shirt. "I'll keep that in mind."

It was well past dark when he left the house but he felt no urgency, driving away with the same easy calm over him the supper had brought forth. Focused and steady. Came up into Bethlehem and thought of Foster earlier in the day, no doubt cruising the small streets as lord of the way, and with this bemusement fresh over him he recalled the little snub-nosed automatic tucked up under the seat. He reached down and felt for it, his fingers against the crosshatched grip, thinking still of Foster. It wasn't fear of Foster finding the gun; the boy had known, without ever being told, not to poke anywhere, to leave things be. It was the fear of needing the gun. A complicated, essential fear: that he might not be able to protect any single thing, come down to it.

A dank mood and a rank mind. Hotel guests were out walking the lamplighted streets of Bethlehem. He drove slowly. Not looking side to side but straight ahead.

He took the long way over the hills to Franconia, the back way, the rough track. It was still early. He stopped three quarters of the way where the small meadow opened amongst the trees. He left the car running and took the automatic out from under the seat and got out. The gun heavy in his hand. A good thing, that weight. In the headlamp beam he studied the safety lever and moved it up and down, on and off. Then pointed the gun out ahead of him down into the ground and clamped his right index finger hard back against the trigger. The noise an abrupt rupture in the night. The gun leaped in his hand. As an echo to the concussion of the firing heard the deep *whomp*s as the soft-nosed bullets drove into the ground. Saw a faint spatter of dirt and torn grass rise. Satisfaction. He was a little bit restored. He knelt in the pale tangerine light and reloaded the clip and shoved it home. Another click of satisfaction hearing the snap of the mechanism grasp the clip. He left the safety off and got back in the car, now setting the gun in the glove box.

Down into Franconia, over the bridge, down the Easton valley. At the Carrick farm a light burned in the parlor window. He went on past the farm for several miles and turned and came back north and drove into the trailhead pull-off and shut down the car. Sat in the batwing dark a long time before the silence of the night settled and came alive around him. The light was still burning at the farmhouse window. And he decided it wasn't that early after all. He sat waiting.

Then, just like that, like he'd already seen it happen, a little after midnight an automobile came down the road and turned into the farmyard. He watched as it backed around in the yard, dousing its lights as it slid behind the barn. He'd done the same thing himself many times. Still he sat. Only moments passed and the parlor light went out and then there was the bob of a lantern being carried from the house toward the barn. He waited until the lantern blacked out going into the barn. He fired a smoke and smoked it down and then started the Chrysler and pulled onto the road with his headlamps off and drove slow until he came to the farm drive and as he made the turn in hit the gas pedal and reached to the dashboard for the lamp switch and so came in fast and hot to pile up beside the strange car, Jamie already out of his door with the heavy little gun in his hand as he raced around the Chrysler past the other vehicle, a big Dodge touring car with the top down, its engine running also. He kicked open the barn door and came into the pale circle of lantern light.

Carrick and three other men. Heads up. Cases of whiskey in a stack on the barn floor, right out in the open. Waiting.

Jamie had the gun up, jerked the trigger once and remembered to
let go. One case in the stack splintered and jetted. Jamie cried, "That's
it, boys. You all hold on now."

The three strange men turned very slowly toward him. He was outside the circle of light. They moved as if practiced, their hands swept
away from their bodies, young birds contemplating arrested flight.

One of them said, "What's this?"

Carrick said, "It's him."

"Jeeter, you fuck."

Another of the men said, "It's Pelham?"

"Shut the fuck up! Jeeter, I'm done with you, you fuck."

The first man said, "Calm down, friend. Mr. Carrick here might be
surprised but we been expecting you. Just calm down."

Jamie advanced halfway to the circle. Swinging the gun in an oval
over the men. "You don't expect shit. Shut up."

Carrick said, "It's nothing off you. I been straight with you."

Jamie made another step and leveled the gun off at the first man. "I'm
not hard to find, you wanted to. How long you been expecting me?"

The man smiled at him. Took his hands down from their winged-
up stance and rubbed his face. "As long as it took you to wake up."

"I'm awake right now."

"That right?"

"You Pompelli?"

The man laughed. Then looked up into the darkness of the overhead
haymows and studied them. Back at Jamie. "You only think you're
awake."

What happened then he thought as it was happening that later he
would look back and see he'd missed something. The softlight footsteps
onto the mowfloor chaff. A pivot turning in one of the men's eyes. Some
sense of something coming behind. All this ballooned in his brain the
instant the hard round double end of a shotgun struck into the nape of
his neck, the base of his skull. And from behind she said, "Toss it off.
Toss it off, shithead."

And in that moment between when she spoke and he understood,
she did not wait but pulled the shotgun back away from his head and
drove it forward again so the barrel ends struck him hard this time,

knocking him forward and off balance even as her message came through and he let go of his gun, throwing it into the thick layer of last year's chaff before the mounds of new hay. His head a bright brute flare of orange and clear-white pain. Then he was down on the floorboards, the rough uneven planks of the mow. Jeeter said, "There's Mother now."

The three men gathered Jamie up off the floor, all with little guns out like Jamie's that one collected from the chaff and put in a pocket. His head a continual echo of pain. Amy Carrick in a housedress and open sweater holding across her front a shotgun more as one would hold a broom. One of the men went to her and lifted the shotgun away from her and she let him take it. Jamie could not see Carrick, he was behind where they made their group on the barnfloor but Jamie held no hope for Jeeter's help anyway. That much he'd known before he tossed out that last cigarette and drove on in here.

They lashed his wrists behind him with a piece of lead-rope. He stood for this without moving or speaking. The one who'd first spoken was the leader of the three, not in some way overt but by inclination, the sweep of personality. Perhaps he was the most calm of the three. When they were done tying him the first man said to Jamie, "Like I said, you been expected. You want to see Mister Pompelli, do you? Well now, nothing so bad as he's wanting to see you."

Jamie said nothing to this.

The man stood regarding him a moment and then did a very odd thing: reached out and with one open hand lightly stroked Jamie's cheek.

Then he turned and spoke to the Carricks. "You two follow us. Bring his car too. I don't want it sitting here. Drop it off in Franconia, one of the hotel lots, and then follow on."

Amy Carrick said, "I'm not leaving the children—"

He cut her off. "I'm not asking a favor here."

Jeeter said, "Mother."

The man said, "That's right, Mother. Listen to your husband."

Jamie spoke then. "I don't see the need to leave my car at Franconia. Just carry it on to where we're going, I can take it home from there."

The man smiled at him. "Well, there. That makes sense. But Mister Pompelli don't like too many cars cluttered around his place. He don't like the attention."

*   *   *

They drove in caravan up the Easton valley, one of the men driving the Dodge, the other two with Jamie between them in the backseat. Some distance behind followed one of the Carricks with the Chrysler and behind that the other Carrick driving their old Ford. His brain working now, trying to settle, seeking the angle, the hook to spread for Pompelli. He didn't have much: Pompelli already had Carrick; this left Jamie with some distribution. Not much, given that Pompelli could easily, might already, be duplicating it. His local contacts, those glad-handed receivers of monthly cash, Pompelli would have those also. Pat Jackson. There was nothing he could give Pompelli of Pat Jackson. Jackson would get him killed he guessed. So what he had. Not much. Just to wait and see. See Pompelli.

In Franconia they turned east and he began to think they might be headed south through the Notch, down to Lincoln, North Woodstock. Some part of him had always guessed this might be where Pompelli was. Only because he did not go that way much himself. He'd always worked north of the Notch.

Then they turned again and went up the hill toward the Forest Hills and it was here that they idled roadside while the Carricks left the Chrysler in one of the lots but then they continued on, going toward Bethlehem on the Agassiz road. And Jamie knew he knew nothing. There was a bad moment when he thought they might be going back to his own house where there would be others waiting. With Foster. And then stopped thinking. He tilted his head back a little to watch the sky. His arms hurt and his wrists were sore behind him. He wanted a smoke but wouldn't ask for one. The August summer sky a sheet of light, cut by the bright sudden flare of the meteors. Leaving a faint trace on the eye, the reverse of a shadow.

Right under his nose. Into Bethlehem and then north onto the White-field road but off again almost right away onto one of the side streets, before pulling into a yard of old hemlocks. He knew the house although he'd never been in it. Only a few years old, a one-story bungalow done up camp-style with cedar shingles and green-painted trim. There were already four or five automobiles nosed in off the drive. The three men unloaded him and flanked him as they went up the short steps and into the house without knocking. The house all lighted up. As they went in Jamie heard the Carricks' Ford cough and die outside but he didn't expect them to follow in and they did not. Inside was a big room with a stone fireplace with a fire in it and electric fixture lamps from the ceiling and twig-style furniture with deep cushions. The four of them stopped there and the man whom Jamie thought of as the boss went on alone through a wood-paneled French door. The other two men stood just behind Jamie, one to each side. Jamie watched the paneled door.

The doors opened and a couple of men came out and left the house without looking at him although he recognized both of them, two of the men he'd become aware of over the past year. The door remained open and one of the men behind him shoved him gently. He shrugged the best he could with his hands done up behind him and walked through the doors. His minders came after him, pulling the doors shut.

A nice room. Leather upholstered chairs. A broad desk with a deep shine. The desk maybe a little too big. Deep green heavy drapes pulled over the windows. Polished hardwood floorboards with a Persian carpet over much of it. Electric lights but not too bright. A man behind the desk in a good crisp suit, better than any Jamie owned but not flashy. He'd expected a middle-aged man, someone heavy, jowled, thick-lidded. This man was a good half dozen years younger than he was. Maybe close to ten. Tight shave. His hair oiled, straight back flat against his head. That head cocked just off center, watching Jamie come in. The other man, the one who'd brought him from Carricks', sat far down in one of the leather chairs off to one side of the desk. Looking at nothing. Enjoying himself.

Jamie went a third of the way to the desk and stopped.

"For chrissake Sammy, you got him tied up? You don't need to treat him like that. What's wrong with you."

From his chair Sammy said, "Take the rope off him Lester."

One of the men behind him undid the rope, working at the rough knot. Jamie waited until it was all the way off and clear and then slowly brought his hands before him. Wanted to rub them together but did not. Just let his hands rest before him.

The man behind the desk said, "Come on, come on." Waved his hands at Jamie. "Sit down. Pull a chair up and sit down."

Jamie said, "You Pompelli?"

"Yeah, I'm Pompelli. Vincent Pompelli."

"Well, Vincent. I'm all right right where I am."

Pompelli straightened his head. Looked at Jamie. Then looked at the man slouched in one of the chairs beside the desk. Looking at him, he said, "I'm just asking you to have a seat, we can talk, face-to-face."

The man in the chair, Sammy, stretched one leg out and caught a leg of an empty chair with his foot and slid it over the carpet so it was right up against the front of the desk. Across from Pompelli. As he did this the two men behind Jamie took him by the shoulders and moved him forward and around the chair and began to press him down into it but he lifted his hands to them and touched them both, still watching Pompelli and they stood back and he sat. As he sat one of them moved behind him and eased his chair up tight to the desk like a waiter. He let that happen. He joined his hands and laid them up on the desk surface. Still looking at Pompelli.

"There now," Jamie said.

"Aw, Pelham. Pelham."

"I don't see the problem, Vincent."

"No?"

"No. All I'm doing I been doing a long time. But I'm small time. You know that. You already got my man. My market too, as much as I can see. The way I see it, all that's just a tittle to you. You can shut me down, sure. But, I'm thinking, that's what you wanted you would've already done it. Not waited for me to figure it out. So, I serve you someway. Just by being here. Some way that works for you and is best I don't know nothing about, best for you and best for me. You're a young man. And you've got this deal pretty well greased, that's clear. So we can talk. Just don't think I'm some old fuck you can jerk around. Things'll work. Or they won't. How's that, Vincent?"

Pompelli nodded. As if agreeing. But he looked down into his lap. As if not sure of something. He took his hands off the desk and put them down into his lap. Seemed to be turning them over, studying them. As if to find an answer there. Then looked up at Jamie, not raising his head but tipping his eyes up. Almost a flirtation. Running his eyes over Jamie. Then he spoke.

"You think we can work together?"

"It could be."

"No. I got to know. You think we can?"

"I think," Jamie said, "we stop fucking around, we can likely work something out."

Pompelli nodded. As if thinking this through. He smiled at Jamie. Straightened again in his chair. His voice still soft said, "Give me your hand."

Jamie looked at him.

Pompelli lifted his left hand up from below the desk, made a reaching gesture with it. "Come on. Give me your hand." Reached across the desk, halfway, his hand open, the fingers loose. Still soft he repeated, "Come on."

And Jamie raised his right hand and extended it over partway and then thinking it was the wrong hand to shake a southpaw started to take it back but Pompelli had snaked his open hand past Jamie's and grasped tight his wrist and came up out of his chair as he pinned Jamie's hand down, open palm up, on the desk and as he rose his right came up from under the desk and flew forward and down and back again with the thin silver slice of a razor in the lamplight and then Pompelli let him go and sank back into his chair and Jamie looked at his hand lying flat on the desk with the cut a broad deep sideways swipe across his palm from the ball of his thumb to the base of his little finger and as he watched the swipe filled with blood and then his cupped palm like an ill-made vessel. Then his knees jerked up and struck the front of the desk and his bloodslick hand bounced once on the desk surface and flew back and he held it with his other hand against his shirtfront that was already hot and liquid and moving against him, his hand a hot hard thing as the rest of him spread and spewed. The room and the lights suddenly hot and bright. His spine curled. A voice came out of him: "Aww shit." Looking at the pool of his blood left on the desktop, so much of it so sudden.

The pain a meteor trail that blew open inside and ran all through him. An orange split open with blood juice and pulp. The crotch of his trousers dampened and warmed. His eyes blinking, trying for focus. Far back of them his brain stilled, absolute, silent, refusing to work. Shutting down to try and save itself. The lambent light and air of the room suddenly charged, a faint sound as if some insect was working within.

"Sammy, get a towel." Pompelli turning the razor over in his hands, his head tipped down to study it. Ignoring Jamie.

The man Sammy threw himself up from the chair and with no particular speed left the room and came back moments later with a soft peach handtowel and handed it to Pompelli who used it to sop the blood from the desk, turning the towel over for a dry portion to lightly buff the wood. Then he balled the towel and threw it across where it struck against Jamie's wrapped-together hands. Jamie took the towel and opened it and wrapped the cut hand in it. His other hand doing this job as if it was the right thing to do. He could see now and, as if he knew this, the man Sammy did not return to his chair but came and stood by Jamie's shoulder, one large hand spread out over the back of Jamie's head like a careful cap.

Pompelli still turned the razor over, looking at Jamie again. "His hand, you know, is like this." He lifted his right hand and opened it partway as if grasping a small glass, the thumb crooked in toward the fingers, the fingers evenly spaced, not touching one another. "Victor Fortini. The kids call him the Claw. Vic the Claw."

"Jesus." The word out of Jamie air out of rotten bellows.

"No, He ain't gonna be help to you now. Now, Vic Fortini, Vic, he's one of those long slow fires, nothing slick or flashy about him, just one step after another. Hey listen, I know the man; he's my father-in-law. One thing you got to understand, Pelham. He's known where you was for years. Years and years. Think about that. His hand all fucked-up frozen and he just waits quiet and patient. Most of us, we think, There's an opportunity in front of us, we better take it before it goes away. He could have come after you long since. So what do you think? What is it gives a man the confidence to sit back and wait? It's something to ponder. I watch him myself, thinking maybe I'll learn a thing or two. Shit, Pelham, I don't know. But you got to look at the facts. All those years he waits and then here you are tonight. Like he knew this night was coming for you. What he told me was, Wait, Vinnie, let him come to you. He will, he will. That's what he told me. And look, here you are."

Jamie said nothing. Nothing to say. His mind now a bright clear empty shining star. A small pith in absolute darkness.

After a minute Pompelli said, "It's funny, how something stupid sometimes can work in your favor. You, you'd gone farther away, gone to New York or Jersey or someplace, he probably wouldn't have been so patient. Might have thought you could slip through and away. But you do something stupid, go—what? a hundred miles? So he knows right where you are. He keeps track of you without any effort at all. And you, I bet you worried for what—two, maybe three months? Looking over your shoulder. Bet you even thought you were laying low." Pompelli paused and finally set the razor down, placing it on the green blotter before him. A pale rust of blood on the slice of moonlight blade. Looked back at Jamie. "Well? You got anything to say?"

Jamie sat silent. His hands down now in his lap, the clotted towel a rough wrap over the tender flaring hand, the other hand wrapped over it all, all resting on top of his wet crotch. The tang of urine the only clear scent in the room to him.

Pompelli said, "Sammy?" As if asking an opinion.

The hand on top of his head gripped hard and drove down so Jamie's forehead struck the desktop. Shattering the glass star. Shards red and silver emptying into the dark. The hand in his hair jerked him back upright. His eyes seemed to be bleeding.

Pompelli said, "Talk to me. Tell me. You think it's too much maybe? All those years walking around traded for this? But you got to remember that hand all fucked up. Kids laughing at him. Calling him names. Men too, laughing. Not out loud but the way men do. That hand, it made him a little less. Not to him. Never to him. But how people that don't know any better, how they see it. You got to hand it to Victor. Think about it. All those people: for them, yesterday is just like today. Today just like tomorrow. No difference. The only difference at all is Victor; he'll know. He'll know. And you. I guess you know. But that don't matter. Does it? Come on. Talk to me."

And Jamie, thinking at last, still silent, Let them. Whatever was to be extracted. All of it was theirs to take. Given over. All he wanted was Foster left be. It was all he asked. There was no answer. The world, the heavens, the universe were silent. As always.

Pompelli pushed back from his desk, leaned back, his forearms down on the arms of the chair, his hands hanging loose over the curled ends. Jamie thought he looked tired. But then everything was tired. Pompelli frowned at him. As if disappointed. And for that one fine moment Jamie wanted to please him. His worst moment. Then Pompelli focused again and his face grew smooth. He said, "So nothing? No little thing? A small signal of remorse? A message I can pass along? Consider it: he might be moved. He might feel contrition. He's an old man. Anything is possible. He could pay for a mass."

Jamie was silent.

"Fuck it." Pompelli stood out of his chair. Crossed the room and pulled back one of the drapes and looked out into the reflection of himself in the glass. Let the green fabric go so it covered what he saw. Turned back into the room. No longer looking at Jamie. He said, "Get him out of here. Give him a ride."

He could not stand. As if the messages his brain was sending were not being received. Nobody home down there, limbs sluggish, tired, running under water. The man Sammy did not touch him but the other two, Lester and the nameless one, helped him come upright out of the chair, their hands on him alert but relaxed, as if moving an animal. They turned him and steered him out of the room. His legs working now, one going before the other. They went out and down the steps and over the rough uneven yard to the big Dodge convertible where they put him into the backseat. Down the drive, parked by the side of the road, was the Carricks' Ford. Jamie turned his head, spots going off behind his eyes, to face Sammy, still outside the car. He wet his lips, his tongue a thick rough thing. He said, "Save you the trouble. I'll catch a ride with them."

Sammy leaned down, his hands on the doorframe, his face close to Jamie. Pleasantly he said, "Shut up."

Then he left Jamie seated in the car, Lester beside him, the nameless man again behind the wheel as Sammy walked down the drive, where he conferred with the Carricks. Then he walked back, slow and easy, and slid in beside Jamie. Without being told the driver put the car into gear and turned back toward Bethlehem. They went up the main street, empty, nothing moving, the summer shadows thrown by the streetlights deep and unmoving. They turned onto the Agassiz road and downshifted for the sharp climb out of town. Jamie shaking with the cold, unable to stop himself. They passed the last few houses, all dark, and then swept along, the bordering woods dark and soft and deep, the slip and ping of gravel flying up behind the car.

Sammy, next to him, spoke into his ear. "You must be feeling pretty shitty."

Jamie said nothing. His knees jerking, his teeth a loose shaken bowl of bones.

"That's all right," Sammy told him. "You'll feel better after a bit."

The man Lester spoke up. "You remember what he said? When he came in with his little gun? Hold on boys. Ha-ha. Hold on boys."

"Shut up," Sammy told him.

They wound down the other lesser side of Mount Agassiz and onto the broad tableland stretching toward Franconia. The road here straightened. Far behind them, the pale lights of the Carricks' Ford came after them. A long straight stretch. Sammy spoke up. "Give it the gas, Bishop."

There it was. It seemed important to Jamie, learning this missing name. As if something were completed. As if named, he might know these men. Odd, he thought: Sammy, Lester and Bishop. Wondered what it was about the driver that kept him on that slight remove, the lacking first name. Some measure of respect perhaps? Maybe Sammy wasn't the boss of the three after all. Perhaps the silent man. Jamie felt he'd missed something crucial here.

The big Dodge raced down the road, gravel spewing, the headlights a soft wash of color, the color the only warmth in the night.

Sammy put his left hand up, ran it across Jamie's shoulders, rubbed them through the coat, not roughly. He said, "Pick it up a little, Bishop."

Then, as the car jumped forward, he grabbed a hard big-twisted handful of Jamie's jacket and pushed forward, sending Jamie's head down toward his knees. At the same time Lester did the same on the other side and both men used their other hands to grasp Jamie's thighs, underneath, just back of his knees. All this in one furious motion that continued as they lifted him up and threw him out of the back of the car.

Face up, in the air. The stars still, distant, a moment suspended. Then down hard to bounce on the back of the Dodge, something in his back or shoulder cracking, and then down harder face first into the road. The diminishing funnel of engine sound from the Dodge the last place he traveled.

*   *   *

A great horned owl high up in a hemlock one tier back from the road had been watching a vole in the high grass the other side of the road. When the automobile broke through the night the vole shrank tight against the earth and the owl tipped up on its talons, the muscles tensing where the wings lifted from the back. Then the automobile was gone and the owl lifted off, a long dive swooping silent that with a single wingbeat carried it over the road and the strange bundle below and on into the grass where it seized up the vole and again a single beat lifted the bird back into the night. Up to a new perch.

The Ford came to a stop fifty feet down the road. The man and woman got out and walked up the road to where he lay. As she passed the front of the car the woman stopped, stooped and lifted out the heavy elbowed crank and carried it with her. He was on his side in the road, one arm torn off his jacket and a splinter of bone showing through. Bloodfoam seething around his lips. A hand lying open on the gravel as if waiting for something to fill it, the hand a broken thing with a broad wound crusted over. Some feet away a stiffened towel. The turned-up side of his face was cut and scraped away where he'd struck the gravel and then turned or rolled over with the momentum. The man leaned close, his hands on his knees. Leaned and then stood quickly. Speaking, the peak of bile rounding and thickening his voice.

"He's done."

With the voice the head seemed to bounce up, the other arm raised away from his side where it had laid slack, the arm led up by the hand a short distance into the night, the hand opening and closing as if trying to grasp the night and draw it back.

The woman said, "Jeeter, he's not."

The hand fell back down.

"I guess maybe he is."

"No," she said. "We won't risk the chance. Someone might come along." She tried to hand him the crank.

"No Amy," he said. "I won't do it. The man is dead. Can't you see?"

She looked at him then. The both of them shaking a little with the night. She hated him for the shaking, his and her own. She said, "You're piss-poor of a man." And she stepped the final step and raised the crank with both hands and brought it down once and then a second time on the head of the man on the road. Each time feeling the skull break and the crank pierce through and stick before she wrenched it free. Each time she brought it down and felt it first break into the skull she said Oh.

The middle of the afternoon Patrick Jackson turned off the road and drove down the dirt track through the hemlocks and tamaracks to the house, another marshal following behind in the Chrysler found in the parking lot of the Forest Hills, empty of gas but with a small patch still reeking in the sand below the gas tank where someone had siphoned it out. One of the details he was choosing to overlook. The sky was piled up with clouds, the sun bright. The clouds would continue gathering as the heat built and sometime around nightfall it would storm.

In the yard a pair of bird dogs trotted out to greet the cars. Jackson drove straight up before the house and stopped. The other marshal parked the Chrysler by the barn and came and got into the passenger side of Jackson's car as Jackson got out. The boy was already out of the house, standing on the steps, watching all this take place. The younger of the bird dogs twisted in, tail working, to greet Jackson and he paused and ran his hand over the dog's head. Looked up at the boy. Tall and lean, muscled the way his father had been, without bulk but strength in the ropy muscles. A rough-cut head of hair, black shining blue in the sunlight. His skin olive like his father's but with a red cast beneath. A man that would appear suntanned year round, inside or out. His eyes dark, deepset, wide on Jackson.

"What happened to him?" The boy standing on the step above Jackson, looking down at him, his hands loose at his sides. The bird dogs had come up and were sitting each to one side of him.

Jackson took out his badge and spoke his name. Did not try to shake hands, knowing the boy didn't want it, would resent it of him later. He said, "It looks like he ran out of gas and pulled off at the Forest Hills. We guess he was walking the Agassiz road, maybe hoping for a ride. It must've been pretty late. Somebody ran him over."

"Somebody ran him over?"

"The way it looks. We think, maybe he'd been drinking, maybe was out in the road. If it was late, you know. And whoever came along, we're thinking maybe they'd been drinking too, going too fast, maybe not even seeing what was in front of them. There wasn't any skid marks."

"They didn't stop?"

"No, son. Not that we know."

"He's dead then, you're telling me."

"I'm awful sorry."

The boy didn't say anything.

Jackson said, "Listen. I never had any problems with your father. You understand me?"

The boy was silent.

Jackson said, "I got to ask you. Was he having problems, anything you knew about? Guessed about even. Anything out of the ordinary lately?"

The boy's eyes did not go off Jackson. After a moment he shook his head, slowly.

Jackson said, "Clark there filled up the Chrysler with gas. You drive?"

"Yuht."

"You got any family, anybody I can get ahold of for you?"

"Nope."

"Anything at all I can do for you?"

"Nope."

"I knew your mother a little bit. Always liked her."

"Where's he at?"

Jackson told him. Then said, "You think of anything, anything at all you want to tell me, you know how to get ahold of me."

The boy's lips were a tight line. Then he said, "Am I safe here?"

Jackson said, "I don't know. You tell me."

"I don't know."

And they stood looking at each other for some short time, each knowing the other knew more than would say, would be gotten out. Then Jackson said, "It was an accident is what we think. You shouldn't have to worry. I'm sorry about your father, I truly am."

"That's all right," the boy said. "It wasn't your fault."

He sat that night with both downstairs doors locked and barred with furniture pushed up against them, sat upstairs on his bed with both dogs

with him in the dark as the storm blew around the house, on the bed
his pair of shotguns laid out both loaded; the little .410 his father had
bought him years ago and the sixteen gauge L.C. Smith side-by-side he'd
bought for himself the year before. After the storm sat listening to the
water drip from the hemlock boughs, his window open. Some hours
before dawn the sky cleared and it grew chill and then as dawn came
on fog came off the river and filled the woods. He took the dogs out the
backdoor, carrying the side-by-side, whistling them close with short soft
chirps, watching around him in the fog. There was no one there. When
they were done he took them back inside and barricaded the door again
and fed the dogs. Then called them upstairs and left the window open
and slept a few hours. Still dressed, blankets pulled up tight. The guns
either side of him, the dogs at his feet. When he woke the sun was burning through the fog.

Four days later he sat and walked and stood through the service and
burial as if asleep although he'd not slept more than a handful of hours
since his father's death. The minister spoke words that he did not understand and that had nothing to do with his father. He sat alone in the
front pew because that was where they put him. Left alone, he would've
sat at the back. The number of people there surprised him, although he
recognized most of them. When somebody spoke to him he answered
them back but would later not recall a single word said. It was hot at
the afternoon burial, the sun splintering off the polished wood box as it
sank down into the hole. Somebody handed him a spade and he set to
work until someone else took the spade away from him and he understood he wasn't expected to finish the job, just start it. It seemed to him
they ought to have left him alone to do it. It seemed to him it was his
job to do. Afterward there was food that people had brought that the
minister's wife laid out in a room behind the church but he went in and
saw the people standing and eating and talking to each other and he went
back out. It was no place for him. Outside Patrick Jackson was squatted on his heels in the small shade of the Chrysler and Foster was not
surprised to see him.
    Jackson said, "People need to do it. They need to honor the dead but
then they got to get on with things. It always seemed to me to be too

fast but I never could figure out what would be the right amount of time. What would you do? Still, I can't see eating a ham sandwich."

"No sir."

"You have any trouble, down there by the river?"

"No sir."

"You all right then?"

"My father's dead."

"I know it," Jackson said. "Mine too."

Two mornings later a Littleton attorney called Ewert Morse drove in and if he was surprised or alarmed to find Foster seated on the steps with a shotgun laid across his knees he did not show it. He wore a finely woven straw Panama and sweated mildly in the morning sun. He had with him the deed to the property and explained to Foster that two years before his father had changed the deed so it was in Foster's name. The deed was on heavy paper folded three times and tied with a ribbon. Morse opened it to show him.

"What do I have to do with it?"

"Do with it? Why you don't have to do anything. It's just, it's yours."

"What do I owe you for bringing it out here?"

Morse shook his head. "You don't owe me anything. It's part of the service that your father already paid for."

"Can you hold on to it for me?"

"I can."

"And what will that cost me?"

"Won't cost you a cent, until such a time you want to do something about it."

"Like what?"

Morse shrugged. "If you wanted to sell it."

"Then what would it cost?"

"Only the nominal fee for the transfer. Likely the new owner, the buyer, would pay. That's how it works."

"I don't plan to sell."

"Well then. I can just hold on to it for you. Or you can keep it yourself. It's up to you. It's yours."

"But it would be better off you held on to it." Not quite a question.

"It would be in a fireproof safe."

"All right. And I don't owe you anything?"

"No. Now. That's it for the estate. No bank accounts, no loans, no liens. But, back in July he brought me this, asked me to hold it for you." And reached into his vest and brought out an envelope. Handed it to Foster. He took it and looked at it. His name was on it, in his father's fine loopy script.

"You know what this is?"

Morse said, "It was sealed when he gave it to me." Not quite an answer.

"All right," Foster said. "I owe you anything for this?"

"No," said Morse. "Nothing."

In the envelope was a hand-drawn map of the area of woods just behind the barn. Landmarks were indicated with circles and in each circle was a number. On the side of the map the numbers were repeated, each with a figure after it. At the bottom of the column was a total. There was no note, nothing else.

Foster took a spade from the barn and dug up the mason jars and coffee cans, all eleven of them. Some of the cans soft with age. He'd known they were out there, just had no idea there were so many of them. He carried them in armloads into the kitchen and took out the tied rolls of bills and flattened them out on the table in separate stacks. And sat and counted through it and then counted again. Then checked his father's addition on the map. Off somewhat. Foster thought about that. It wasn't like him. Counted the money one more time. A little more than fourteen thousand dollars. He divided the money into five-hundred-dollar stacks and rolled them and tied them with string. Then stacked them into a shoebox, the best thing he could find. The odd hundred and eighty-three he folded flat and put in his wallet. Then he took up the shoebox and walked around the house with it. Finally he put it down at the bottom of the woodbox and stacked kindling over it. Summertime, it seemed like a good place.

Far out in the woods, not marked on the map, down in the ground an old tea canister had rotted away. The tin melted into the humus.

The old gold pieces nestled in the soft earth like precious lustrous butter pats.

At night he wept. With both dogs upright beside him, both faces intent upon his as he sat with his hands over his face, the all of him racked up in his throat. Over and over saying, "Poppy, Poppy, Poppy," the name bubbling out of him. For hours until he was sick, aching, exhausted. Wept even after he realized it was self-pity as much as grief. Until he suddenly and vividly heard his father's voice commanding him to stop. "Stop it." Just once. He took his hands from his face and looked around. There was nothing and the sound did not come again, just the echoes of it. He looked at his dogs. They looked back at him.

What he'd missed at the time and what he could not stop thinking about now was the absence of Jeeter and Amy Carrick from the service. He did not like them, never had and knew his father had not either but still. They should have been there. What bothered him more was he was sure Patrick Jackson had noted their absence also. And said nothing. Which meant he was also turning them over in his mind. Or he was accepting something. Foster wanted to know which. But would not contact Jackson to talk about it. He could not say why. Maybe nothing more than an echo of his father reverberating within him. But one night he went to his father's bedroom where he'd not been in years and tipped open the door and turned on the light. He went to the small rolltop desk and sat and went through it, all the pigeonholes, all the drawers, all the loose papers scattered over the surface. He did not know what he was looking for but knew he would know it when he found it. Confident that willing or not his father had left some message for him. What he found was nothing close to his thoughts. One of the small drawers pulled out hard unless lifted up in its track. He got the drawer free and went down on his knees and reached back in and pulled out a small packet of letters bound with a rubber band. At first he thought they might be old letters from his mother to his father and was excited by the idea. But the most recent postmark was little more than two years old. He went back through them. All the same return address, an Abigail Pelham of

Randolph, Vermont. The same handwriting. Postmarked every couple or three years. Each and every one addressed to his father but at a distant post office, General Delivery. Wells River. Conway. Berlin. He sat for a time, holding them in his lap, knowing he held something that would forever change what he knew of his father. From a box on the desk took one of his father's cigarettes and lighted it and decided that some part of him would forever be trying to clarify that knowledge. And so opened the most recent of the letters and unfolded the single sheet. Pale ink gone brown on the page it began:

March 29, 1926

Dear Jamie,
Father has passed. . . .

Part III

Sweetboro

Seven

What surprised him first was how
close it was. On the roadmap it seemed a vast distance. But the final
day of August he'd left at sunup with Andy Flood coming over at
dawn to eat a breakfast with him and go over the care of the house
and see him off. A little after two that same afternoon he'd parked on
the main street of Randolph Vermont, watching the people walk by
him. Thinking that even among them might be one with some fragment of his own blood. During the time since he'd found the letters
he'd reconciled to the notion that his father had a past and had been
silent about it. Foster could not say for sure that at some point in the
future he'd not do the same. Everything that had happened to him in
his life this far seemed impossible to describe to any other person. He
suspected that any telling would diminish the actuality of it, that such
a telling would replace memory and lock events and persons into some
simple single line of reference, some reduction enacted both upon
himself and the persons recalled.

He ate a sandwich and looked out upon the mild weekday throng.
Trying to feature some younger version of his father among them.
Studying the buildings, the streets. Watching the people. Parked at the
curb, he felt comfortable. The people seemed to him more workaday,
less worried over themselves than the people he was used to from the
resorts. Even the merchants seemed plainclothed; suits readymade without overdue fuss or attention. Himself bareheaded, in engineer boots
and corduroy trousers and a plain open-necked white shirt. He felt he
might step out and walk among them and be at home someway.

The man at the post office studied him carefully before issuing curt precise directions to the farm. As if examining him for intent. Foster thought Well, two old ladies living alone, I'd be cautious too. That was what he knew: Abigail, the letter writer, and her sister Prudence. And Father, his grandfather. Now dead. No mention of any others in the handful of letters.

What he knew: The first letter had been written a dozen years ago, clearly in response to one from his father and had been effusive, a quickly written three-page expression of delight, with an invitation for the four of them to come visit. More than three years passed before the next and either in response to the long silence or in something his father had written the tone had changed and this change was maintained throughout the remainder of the widely spaced letters. It was clear each was in response to communication from his father. One mentioned a postcard received. All after that first letter had been little more than updates of agricultural notes and the health of Prudence and Father. Abigail did not write of herself. Only the last letter, writing of the death of their father, had been sent to the same General Delivery address as any of the others. Foster believed she'd written it without any assurance it would be claimed. He could only assume that his father had not written a reply.

He drove south out of town and turned right where the postmaster had told him to and climbed in low gear the rough-packed road, a grade steeply up through close-drawn woods and then the land opened into a bowl and he saw the farm sitting ahead of him, the house and barns backed up against a hillside of pasture, the land below the barns spread in more pasture and hay meadows. The hillside pastures were studded with rocks and low circular juniper and a flock of sheep moved in the late summer grass. Below the barns in another pasture a herd of dun-colored cattle grazed, some ruminating in the shade of a pair of elms. Above the sheep the pasture gave way to woodlot that crested up over and crowned the ridgeline. Torn late summer clouds above.

He drove down the lane and parked in the yard between the house and barns and told the dogs to stay and got out and reached behind him to tuck the tails of his shirt back in and went up to the house. It had never been painted and the wood was weathered the soft buttery color of molasses. He skirted the back entryway where he knew everyone entered and exited and went across the small lawn past an old lilac and stood on the oblong block of granite set into the ground long ago as a stoop and knocked on the front door, his knuckles light at first and then harder, a crisp three raps.

The door opened in and an old Negro, a short stout woman in her fifties, stepped into it. She wore heavy serge trousers tucked into knee-high rubber boots and an old sweater darned many times. Her face deeply wrinkled, skin the color of cinnamon but heavily splotched with tangerine freckles. Green eyes. A fierce head of hair, once the same color as her freckles but now salted with gray. She peered up at him and said, "Oh, my."

"Oh, ma'am, excuse me," Foster said. "I must have got the wrong turn."

"Well I don't guess so," she replied.

He'd not seen a Negro but a couple of times and those from a distance. He stepped back off the granite onto the grass. "Excuse me," he repeated. "I made a mistake."

She stepped after him and snaked one hand out and grasped hard around his wrist as if to hold him there. Her hand hard knotted, freckled and calloused. "You look just like Father," she told him. "You're Jamie's boy, aren't you?" And then without waiting for an answer, without letting go of him she pivoted her head and called back into the house, "Sister come here look!"

And swiveled back to peer at him again and said, "You are Foster, aren't you? Foster Pelham?"

"Yes ma'am," he said. His voice coming out of him as from a great distance. Not understanding anything. Somewhere far back he cried out Poppy! Poppy!

And she looked down where she clutched him and as if understanding something of his confusion and even fright she let go of him and took her hand in her other before her but at the same time she spoke. "I'm Prudence Pelham. Pru or Prudy is what all calls me though. To you I guess I'm your Aunt Pru but that sounds strange don't it. Although I've thought of myself that way for years, knowing about you and that dear little girl also, your sister that died. But I never did hear or even speak the words out loud. So you call me what you like—Pru or Aunt or both or neither. Oh I can't tell you how you look like Father, your grandfather. Yes indeed, look at you. Those great wide eyes. You never seen anything like me I guess." And again she turned without pause to shout back into the house, "Sister you come look right now!" And back to Foster, still speaking. "I'm a shock to you, I can see that. So you didn't know what to expect. I'm not surprised by that. What's happened to your father, that you're here? What kind of trouble's he in?"

Foster rocked. When he stepped back he came to rest with one foot up on a small hummock of grass that othertimes he'd not of noticed. But now it had him off balance and his right leg was shaking, the knee beating like a wing. He looked at the woman, her wide mouth with stained teeth. He said, "He's dead."

"Oh my," she said and laid both hands up flat on the breast of her sweater. "Oh no," she said. Her face working then swift through changes. She said, "What happened to him? It wasn't good, was it."

And her pain so bright like focused sunlight over her face touched him and he took a step closer to her and his voice soft he said, "It was an accident was what they said."

She tipped her chin toward him and her eyes were wet but very clear and angry and she said, "But it wasn't, was it?"

What no one had said. And so it was easy to rock back and forth before this strange old woman and tell her. "No. I don't guess it was. Just made to look like one. And what I think, looking like one served too much purpose to too many people to find it otherwise."

And she took her hands down and said, "I feared for him. Always. Not a day went by in my life that I didn't. He was angry over everything, your father was. And he wanted everything also."

Foster said, "He was a good man. Was good to me."

"I'm sure he was," she told him. And again turned her head and cried back into the house, "Abigail!" A beat for each syllable and coming down hard on the last so that it sounded to Foster like two small preludes and a final hard chord. Prudence looked back at him and said, "He was tender, your father was. Always. But he never found a way to allow that part of him. Not that I knew. Now you're telling me he did." Her face working like some clockwork lay behind it, the works of sorrow as she spoke. "I expect you're right. You knew him much after I ever did."

Foster did not know he knew this until he said it. "I think all he ever wanted was to make things right. And maybe he didn't know how to do that. Or maybe he just had bad luck. But what I remember was that he tried."

As he said this he heard the tread of someone coming down the hall behind Prudence. He rocked forward to see past the splintered sunlight who it was. And Prudence seemed to rise a little as if alerted but was also bent sideways, craning past him, and then her hands flew up and she cried out. "Is that your dog after the chickens? Boy? Foster? Look there."

Glow had gone out the open window of the car and was stalking the length of wire runs off the side of the barn, stepping forward slowly, each step a cautious trembling motion, pausing to lock on point at the birds, so huge to her, so close—nothing she'd ever seen before. The young dog silent with her stalk. The chickens in mild hysteria, gabbling their alarm and outrage. Roosters swaying nervously between the hens and the wire. Lovey sat upright in the driver seat, watching her daughter, ears lifted. She already knew about chickens.

Foster went down across the lawn and passed the car, telling Lovey to stay, only to say something, to infer some authority upon the situation, and went over quickly but smoothly to come up behind where Glow was frozen, shivering, only her head moving in faint clicks as her eyes passed from bird to bird and back again, trying to keep them all under the pin of her gaze. Hundreds of chickens. He ran his hands over her sides, telling her to whoa, and took her by the collar and pried her around in a half-circle until she faced away from the birds and then he squatted by her and stroked her nose as she kept trying to turn her head back to the birds and he spoke to her in a soft voice, telling her no no no.

His head downtilted, his eyes cutting up to study the house, the strangeness there. Another woman had come out the front door, this one taller, in a dress. Standing talking to the first one. Abigail. Abigail and Prudence. Foster not understanding anything yet, except that everything was changed. And not even feeling this yet except as a veneer over him, a shiver of knowledge. Wondering if he might not just walk Glow back to the car and get in himself and drive away. Knowing he could not and angry with himself for even thinking he might want to.

Then the taller woman started down the lawn toward him and he rose, hobbling bent over with the straining Glow toward the car. Abigail coming around the front of the car as he opened the door and got Glow up inside and rolled the window up enough to keep her in and shut the door. And straightened then and turned.

The strangeness convulsed within him, twofold. The world unraveling and knitting itself together at once. The woman before him was some version of his father. Taller, in an old-fashion highnecked dress of pearl-gray, with her hair drawn back tight behind her head. But with his father's features. The same olive-toned skin tight over fine bones, high features, deftly sculpted. The same crisp lips, pouched and taut. The same eyes running over him and taking him in. The nostrils with a broader flare but even that flare delicate, arched out as if the tissue and filament of her face were built to taste the world. The second convulsion indistinguishable from the first—he'd not until now understood that a woman older than twenty-three or so could be beautiful. And this shock of recognition and desire rose in him together and he felt as if he were someway deformed and he felt this knowledge rise up hot over his face and he looked away from the woman, up the lawn toward the house to check and make sure the other woman was there also, thinking that if she was it would someway lessen his monstrousness. And she stood, Prudence, with fists on hips, watching them. He guessed she someway knew what he was feeling, had known it herself other ways all her life. And he felt tenderness toward her and looked again to Abigail before him.

She held out a hand toward him, the slender long arm encased in a dress sleeve with a flourish of lace rising to rim her wrist. She said, "I'd bet a dollar you were thinking you should just get in your automobile and scoot. Get away from all this. I'm Abigail."

He took her hand, thin bones, dry. "I found the letters you sent to my father."

"Pru tells me he's dead."

"Yes ma'am. He is."

She let go of his hand. "And you drove over here."

"I did."

She studied him. Then said, "You're what? Sixteen?"

"Just turned."

She nodded. "It's a lot, isn't it?"

"Yes ma'am."

She did not smile at him but he felt she wanted to. "Don't ma'am me. Are those his dogs in the car?"

"They're mine."

"They going to be all right? With that window up that far? It's a hot day. They have enough air?"

"I think so."

"Don't kill your dogs over some chickens gone off the lay."

"I wouldn't. I think they'll be all right, ma'am."

She did smile at him this time. As if caught out. Like his father. She said, "Leave them then. Come up to the house and we can sit. There's questions we all have."

"I don't understand much of this."

She looked at him quick then. Again like his father. She said, "That's not my fault."

Prudence crossed over the lawn to meet them and the women led him in through the back entryshed filled with tools on a bench one side of the walkway and room to stack firewood the other side and through a heavy door into the kitchen. They sat with him there, not in the parlor like a guest but around the pineplank kitchen table. Abigail filled glasses of water from a gravity line running into the sink and Prudence set out a plate of lacy-edged molasses cookies that none of them touched although Foster drank off half his water when first it was handed to him. Then he told them without being asked what had happened to his father, adding no conjecture but simply and briefly what was known to have taken place. What seemed to him all that was proper to say. All he was quite sure his father would want him to say. The women sat watching him and he looked from one to the other as he spoke. Prudence it seemed to him was most struck by this news, her face in a constant working tremble. Abigail sat up against the table, her hands flat before her. Several times he saw questions run across her face but she remained silent.

He finished by mentioning the property in New Hampshire, the deed in his name, that his father had left to him. He did not want these women fearing he expected anything from them. He could take care of himself. Then, as means of explaining his presence here, he mentioned again finding the letters from Abigail to his father.

"You knew nothing about us? He never spoke of his family?"

"Abby, wouldn't of been Jamie to've done such a thing."

"I was asking young Foster here, Sister."

"He slipped out that door the middle of the night and never once in his life looked back. You know it and so do I. There's no need to torment the boy."

"I'm tormenting nothing but your imagination. I was asking a question was all."

"Actually," Foster said, "Pop never said anything about family at all. But then I never asked. Although I seem to remember that he didn't have any family. That they were all dead. Somewhere back in my mind there's that."

Abigail interrupted. "Living and breathing the both of us as you can see. And your grandfather, his own father, alive and mostly hearty too until just two years this past March."

"The thing is—" Foster faltered. "The thing that's hard to explain is after my mother and sister died we just didn't talk about whatever used to be. I think that was a lot of it. Also, he worked for years in one of the big hotels over there, the Sinclair. Was a manager. But that trade's slowed awful the past years and there's lots of men without work. But Pop had a liquor business going. A pretty good one I guess. And it wasn't like people didn't know what he did. But still we kept close-mouthed. I think it was all just habit. And so no, he never did tell me about you people here. I didn't have any idea. And I still don't. I don't know a thing about what's going on here or who you two are or any of it."

He stopped himself. As if he'd gone too far and still not far enough. Both women watching him: Abigail detached, amused, his father's hawk eyes floating out of her head; Prudence back in her chair, slumped a little as if at rest, studying him.

Foster stood and went around the table and filled his glass again and drank it down and refilled it. As he did this Prudence stood and waited for him and told him to come follow her and they went down a hall to a parlor door, Abigail following. The parlor sofa was of old dark wood with a funereal blue-black upholstery. Heavy drapes of the same material flanked the windows. The rest of the furniture was even older: a spindle-backed Boston rocker, a set of slender-legged tables, a small dovetailed blanket chest, a newspaper stand by the rocker. Prudence took up a gas lamp from one of the tables and lighted it and carried it to the mantel behind a parlor stove with ornate fenders and sculpted legs. She set the lamp beside an eight-day clock and stepped back to let Foster come close. On the wall above the mantel was a double portrait in an oval frame.

He looked at the man first and quickly. Young, stern-faced to the camera, deepset dark eyes sadder than his age, a thick burst of dark hair. But it was the woman. Dark-skinned with a wiry rage of hair pulled back away from her face. A Negro woman. He could not tell her age but she was young. Even in the faded dunyellow of the portrait her mouth was a dark lustrous fruit upon her face, her nose hawked from the bridge down to her nostrils. Her pale-colored eyes reared up as if her gaze intended to travel far beyond that moment and wait—wary forever for whomever it might need to meet. Ferocious eyes, he thought. Then he looked back at the man and decided his eyes were less sad than keenly pitched also, as if he had determined to face the world squarely and then gaze beyond it to some world of his own making.

"What," Foster asked, still looking at the portrait, "are their names?"

"Norman and Leah Pelham. Your grandparents."

"Mother," Abigail said, "was a Mebane from Carolina. Her maiden name before she met your grandfather."

"That name don't mean a thing," Prudence said. "It was just the name of the man she ran off from."

"He was more than that."

"Hush that," Prudence said.

Foster lifted both hands and rested the tips of his fingers on the mantelpiece. Not ready yet to look away from the couple on the wall. Feeling sweat running down his sides with his upraised arms.

Behind him Prudence said, "He's the spit of Father."

He took his eyes from the Negro woman and looked at the man. He could not see himself.

Abigail said, "Father went off to the war in eighteen and sixty-two. He went, scared and frightened, swept along by what was going on around him until that became what was happening to him. He went because it was where he had to go. He was just a year older than you are when he set off. All he'd ever tell me, when I'd ask him about it, was that he felt he didn't have a choice."

Foster turned then and looked at her. Abigail standing back in the center of the room, watching him. He said, "I can understand that."

She smiled at him. "Oh yes," she said. "I imagine you can."

Prudence said, "He served right on from 'sixty-two until the end. Was wounded two times, the first at Gettysburg. They don't brag about it because they wasn't that kind of men but it was the boys of the Second Vermont that broke the back of that battle, the way I heard it. It was them tore into Pickett's flank when he made his famous charge and made a hole there and that was when the whole thing turned. He took a sabre wound to his right arm high up. It cut through the muscle right to the bone. He was in hospital with that but went right back after he got out. He could've come home. But he didn't. Second time was right there at the very end, the spring of 'sixty-five. They were down in southern Virginia chasing after the ragtag ends of Lee's army and some of them rebel boys threw some shots back at them, a couple rounds from some little artillery gun. Tore up a tree beside where Father was crouched and a piece of the tree struck right into his head. I don't know what happened then, he was never sure whether he wandered off and got separated or maybe was left behind. But he got lost. He didn't recall any of it. When he woke up there was a runaway slave girl taking care of him in the woods. That was Mother."

"So she nursed him," Foster said, "and he brought her back here."

Abigail snapped her eyes on him. "Something you must understand. What Father said about our mother. That she was the most beautiful woman he'd ever seen in his life."

He turned back to the portrait and studied the woman. Yes, he decided, he could see she was beautiful. And guessed also if a man saw her that way, living in the flesh, he would feel all sorts of other ways about her as well.

Prudence said, "That old sabre wound bothered him in his later years. Weather would go wet and cold, it would stiffen up on him. He could tell two–three days ahead it was going to change. That wasn't just his arm; all those old boys read the weather like a book. But he'd use the arm to explain it. Say, It'll come rain by Monday. That sort of thing. Now I think about it, I guess that wound bothered him right along, but as a younger man he wouldn't speak of it, wouldn't let it slow him down. Father was like that. No complaint out of him. Tough as ash-wood he was."

So Foster studied the image of the ash-wood tough man. That this old carrot-colored woman claimed he was the spit of. Seen on the street, Foster would not claim him as blood. Even as he peered at the image and began to see how someone could pronounce that he and this man resembled each other. All of this at the same time feeling the eyes of these two strange old women upon him. Taking all of him in, head to toe, in a way he could not do for himself. And he considered this, still looking at the portrait of his grandfather. Straightbacked beside the Negro woman. His grandmother.

The world, he thought, moves too fast. Oh Poppy. Daddy.

He turned back to the room, the two women, his hands swept behind his back where one hand clenched the other. "He died," he said, "just a couple years ago. What happened to her?" Caught on a slick boulder midriver in flood he launched out toward the next. Slick-wet mossback.

The women flurried. They did not move and even their eyes only cast for split seconds before landing back upon him. But still he saw the tension rise and sweep their bodies. As if they had been holding themselves some other way since first sighting him. It was Prudence who spoke. And her voice was kind and very sad. "She died a long time ago. Your father was just a little chap. I'd think her dying was most of what he might recall of her."

"He never recalled anything."

"To you."

"I was all there was."

Abigail said, "And the rest of us. That your father chose to ignore. His own father." Then she shrugged. "Sister and myself as well."

"She's angry about that," Prudence said. "But then she's angry over most everything."

"I see things clear-eyed is all. Unlike some."

"The world is a great huge stone that don't care how many times you hurl yourself against it. It just sits there. You might's well sit back and laugh along aside it."

"If I see fit I will shriek with my final breath."

"No one doubts it, Sister. No one at all."

Foster was alarmed. He recalled Glow's big worried eyes turned on him during his night-grieving over his father. He spoke, and even as he spoke he realized he was breaking into a long conversation started years ago and one in which both women took part perhaps without even being aware of it. A mold of language so old grown between them it served as conduit for other, more remarkable, less easily spoken words. But his own were out. "All I've done is upset everyone. I shouldn't ever have come."

The women went silent, very still.

Then Prudence said, "You did the right thing coming. I am upset. Years since I determined I'd not see or hear of my brother again until word of his death. But thinking that and this day are two different things."

Abigail said, "You shouldn't pay much attention to us, young man. Two queer old ladies living alone together so long when we're not arguing we're finishing each other's sentences and neither one of us ever noticing one way or the other. But you, maybe you're thinking you really hadn't ought to've come. You've got reason to feel that way. Because we're much more than the two old maiden aunts you must've pictured. Your father left more than us behind, left some part of himself as well. Because he could pass."

Prudence said, "You could too. You'd of done fine, away."

"No," Abigail said. "I could not have. Because I could no more step away from my people than you could ever change that ratty old hair of yours. But Jamie, he could float away from himself like dandelion floss."

The eight-day clock chimed four. Fine fluted bells peaceful, a minor beauty breaking the tension. Prudence turned her frown, her tightened mouth, from her sister to the clock. Then she looked at Foster and back to her sister.

"I've got cows want milking." And turned, her shoulders tight and broad in the old sweater as she walked from the room, her gumboots a soft slap on the hall runner.

Abigail raised her eyebrows at Foster. Her lips pursed in amusement, not a smile. She said, "What she means is that it's time for me to get out and take care of the hens and feed the horses and check on the ewes while she does the milking. As if I wouldn't do it if she didn't remind me. Because, you see, she loves doing it. She knows I do my share but there's no love in it for me; it's just what needs to get done. I warned you; two old ladies living alone, gone off a little queer."

Foster grinned at her. Crossed his arms over his chest. "Can I help?"

"Can you help? No. You cannot help. Even if you were farm-raised it's not for you to do. Pru and I each have our chores and we do them and walk together at the end of each one's work up here to the house. What I would do, I was you, is eat that plate of cookies sitting in the kitchen and then take those dogs cooped up in that fancy automobile for a walk up the mountain. Let them run themselves out so they won't worry over the hens. There's a rough lane, goes up through the sugarbush. Do that and come down and we'll sit down to supper."

Foster studied her a moment. Then said, "What did you mean, that Pop could pass?"

"Pass? Pass for white."

When he came out to the edge of the sugarbush he stopped to look down at the farm below, the two dogs mostly at heel, Lovey trotting in her steady over-the-ground pace and Glow worn down with exuberance, both happy to pause there with him. Late summer gold late afternoon light, the sky blue near to black. Some goldenrod stalks blooming in the tall meadow grass grown up at the wood's edge. Purple asters.

They'd hiked hard, not just up through the sugarbush but beyond that as well up through the spruce and hardwood ledges on the rough ground above the sprawl of the old maple canopies. Dogs pent up, released from the trap of the Chrysler into the wild unknown scent-land. The boy hiking hard after to keep up with them and to let himself just work. Then there were the birds. More pa'ts than he could hope for in a week over to Bethlehem. Young birds, still not fully broken up from the spring broods. He thought of Andy Flood: "A passel of pa'tridge." Glow had the right name, he decided, standing looking over the bowl of valley. She'd burned through the spruce and ledges in a constant back-turning series of figure eights, her tail a rotor that would only stop to arch when she locked on yet another young partridge. She'd forgot all about chickens, he guessed.

He'd come across an old platform for sawing logs, the frame still sound but the sawdust pile beneath low, sunk with rot and years of not being used. Young popples grew up through the frame of the platform. He'd stood there, in a small draw in the woods, big spruce surrounding almost choking out the old skid-trace, knowing this was something of his grandfather's. He stood there a long moment, thinking something might come to him of the man. But only the big mute timbers, notched together by axe, not a nail to the structure. And the considerable spread of rotted sawdust. Some kind of work he could not know. Some kind of man he could not know but felt flicker inside him. The spit of him, he thought. He'd hitched up his pants and moved on, whistling the dogs, thinking, We'll see.

Now he stood in the opening up over the farm. His body sweet with ache. His mind a sweet drink of water. Disturbed by the twin stones of the sisters dropped into it. Almost loath to descend the hill, to take them up again, to break the woods-peace over him. But even as he thought this watching one figure move outside the barns, driving slow-footed cattle before her. And wanted also to approach again, to walk down there and sit with both of them and learn whatever he could, everything he could. And not, he realized, because it was the only place to come to. But because it was someway all part of him as well. And he scanned the hillside below, the close-cropped sheep pasture with the sheep spread across in the last light of day, their heads down as they moved in one direction together. And saw the stone-walled enclosure set in the middle of the pasture with a single grown-wild apple tree against one wall and over the opposing wall a tangled joyous trove of roses also long since grown wild. And between the walls in the plain upright wilting late-summer grass the simple slabs upthrust as if determined out of the earth. Each with its own shadow.

So he laid a hand either side of him atop the heads of his waiting dogs and cut down across the pasture to pass through the granite gateposts where no gate hung into the small graveyard.

The stones all simple granite, the only deviation being some had rounded corners at the tops. Most were blackened and the chisel-work softened so that he had to at times lay his fingers onto the stone to trace out the letters or numerals. A full half of the markers were small, with the dates spread over short years, some even with only a single date. So many infants dead. Great-great uncles and aunts. The freshest stone, still bright clear-white granite with sharply incised engraving, was his grandfather. Norman. Eighty years of age. Second Vermont Regiment, Grand Army of the Republic. Beside that the other most recent stone was his grandmother. Leah Pelham. No birth date was listed but for the year 1848 and then the day in November of 1890 of her death. She was only forty-two years old. Below this was the inscription *She Could Not Stay*. He squatted there, studying this. Then rose and wandered through the remainder of the stones. James. Earl. Amos. Osborn. James again. David. Henry. A James who was clearly his great-grandfather. Died 1864. And women: Charlotte, Jane, Estelle, Ellen Ann. And beside his great-grandfather, Cora Pelham. Died 1886.

He lay on his side propped on an elbow, the late sun slanting over him, the air still and losing its warmth. The shadows long, flowing one stone into the next, leaving only aisles of light down the rows of grave markers. The dogs stretched out nearby against the heat of the earth. From below the bawling of a cow. She could not stay. His grandmother. The Negro woman. The same age at death as his own father. He tried to picture that, gauging his father against the unknown woman. He could not do it. Could only keep thinking, What does that make me? A question he had no answer for. Negro? Some part clearly but what part was that? How to know? And then, what to do with that. Pass for white. Pass for what? Pass? As if it were some kind of school. And then finally, growing cool as the earth itself cooled, back to She could not stay. Recalling those ferocious eyes in the plain front-faced portrait. She could not stay. Why not?

He stood and rubbed his hands together, then brushed the grass off him. The dogs up with him. The sun gone behind the ridgeline but with last rays sent up against the trailing pale clouds. The farmstead below quiet. The Chrysler parked square in the center of the yard. From here he could see it might be an intrusion, something dropped in from another world. What little else he might know, he knew that welcome as he might be he also posed some threat to the world of the two old women below him. He could not say precisely what that threat might be but was sure it was there somewhere within him. Some hurt he might bring. He stood watching as the thin heat vapor of smoke from the house chimney clouded and billowed and burned before slowing again. A shimmering. Someone was fixing supper. He was hungry and he went down the hill, the dogs trotting behind him now in the dusk. Below, he knew they were waiting for him. He went toward them, determined that best he could, he'd do no harm.

"We set a plain board here." Abigail, over the stove in her pearl-gray dress. "Not like the fine fare you're used to over to the resorts." And commenced filling the table with platters of slabbed ham, boiled new potatoes, sliced tomatoes, steaming sweet corn, bowls of yellow wax beans, small onions caramelized in cream and butter, parsnips, applesauce, pickled dill beans, cucumbers sliced in vinegar, yeast rolls, saucers of butter and jellies. Prudence came in from the hall out of her work clothes, wearing a button-front pale blue housedress. Her hair bound in a headcloth like the cartoon colored people he'd seen in the papers. Smelling of soap. She filled water glasses and moved a coffee pot to the hot center of the range. Foster washed his hands under the gravity line, the water cold enough to sting, barely raising a lather from the rough soap but his hands came away clean. He made slow work of drying his hands as the ladies took their places at the table and then went to the obvious place, where he'd been seated earlier. Lost amongst all the food the platter of molasses cookies sat untouched. He wished he'd taken some up into the woods with him.

"We ask no grace at this table," Abigail said. "But the grace to accept the workings of the Lord, mute and unknowable as He is in His wisdom."

"Are your dogs not housebroke?" Prudence asked.

"Yes ma'am, they are. But the young one can still be a handful. They're in the car. I was thinking maybe there was a shed or empty stall I could bed them for the night." He would not tell them the dogs slept with him.

"We'll set them up after supper. They'll be wanting some scraps I'd bet also."

He grinned. "They'd eat some I think."

"Eat," said Abigail. "I can hear your young stomach rumble all the way over here."

They passed the food around, filling plates. Foster was flushed, the heat of the kitchen, the surfeit of food. He'd been living on sardines and crackers, rat cheese and egg sandwiches, tinned meat, a couple of times hamburgers at the diner in Littleton since his father's death. He took up an ear of corn. The first he'd had since his last meal with his father.

"That sweet corn'll be tough, likely," Prudence observed. "It's late season. Would be better creamed I'd think."

"Saw you up in the burying ground." Abigail, dicing ham into small squares on her plate. "Would be more questions than answers for you there. Is that right?"

He chewed and swallowed. Took up the cloth napkin to press against his mouth. "It's a lot of Pelhams up there. That one James, he was my great-grandfather, is that right?"

Prudence nodded. "Father's father. Died while Father was at the war. Kicked in the head by a horse as he bent to pick up a dropped dime. Father said it was the hardest dime that man ever earned. He'd say that dry, like it was humorous but you could hear the sadness behind it."

"And that's who Pop was named for?"

"Pop," said Abigail. "That's what you called him?"

"Yes, ma'am. Mostly. Sometimes Dad. When I was little, Poppy."

"I can't imagine it. Our father was always Father. And mother Mother. But Jamie taught you your ma'ams. He knew the importance of politeness."

He looked down at his plate. Ate a little. Said, "It was just the two of us. Mostly, we were comfortable with each other."

"There, you see," she said. "Perhaps I'm jealous of that. Yes, your father was named for his grandfather. Us girls, we were just called names they liked. Which is better, do you think: to have a name that connects you to some past you don't know anything about or have a name that doesn't have anything to do with all those old dead people?"

"I don't know. I wasn't named for anybody that I know of. But my sister, she was named for our mother's mother. Other than that, I couldn't say." He felt he was being sized to some gauge he had no knowledge of.

"Don't sit there," Prudence said, "with your plate empty watching us fuss over our food. You want more, take it. Clean the table, it won't make us anything but happy. Try some of that yeast bread. Sister takes great pride in her bread."

"It's just bread. It's nothing but that."

"You see? I can't bake bread. It's just not in my hands."

"In your head is where it is. Bread is just bread. Unless it's wrong; then it's not bread at all but something else."

"Bricks or mush, that's what's in my head. But I gave up years ago. Why bother when it's good and right on the table each day? Take some of this." She passed the bread to him and he lifted out a pair of the rolls and then both sisters began to circulate platters and bowls toward him and he filled his plate again. The coffee was boiling on the range and Prudence pressed back her chair and without rising reached back to push the pot off to the cooler side.

Foster sat waiting while she did this. He split one of the rolls and spread butter. Cut ham and dished out applesauce. The tomatoes were salted and were a bitter sugar on his tongue. He looked at the corn but there were three cobs on his plate and he didn't want anymore. He took up half a roll and ate it. Then forked up a bite of ham dredged in the applesauce. Such sweet food. Then placed his knife and fork alongside the edge of his plate. Looked up, from one sister to the other. Both watching him. As if waiting. He could not be sure but it looked that way. He nodded.

"It's good bread. My grandmother. Your mother. She died awful young, didn't she? And that on her stone? She could not stay. What's that?"

Abigail scraped back her chair and roughly, swiftly, rose and left the room, the door into the hall closing behind her with the soft swipe of old smooth hinges. Foster was alarmed, watching her go. Then looked to Prudence. Who was not looking at him but was intent mashing a bit of potato together with a curl of butter. She lifted this to her mouth and chewed and swallowed. Took a drink of her water. Then looked at him.

"She blames herself for what happened. She's certain she could've done something to stop it. What was just a doubt in her at the time, over the years, has hardened into certainty. It didn't matter what Father said to her, what I said to her. It has never mattered to her what another person thought or felt regarding her, if it was contrary to what she knew about herself."

He nodded. Drank his own water.

"Now." Prudence pushed back her chair from the table the better to face him. He was done eating also. She went on. "I already told you Mother was a runaway slave girl. From down in North Carolina. She was just sixteen years old. That winter of 'sixty-four and 'sixty-five. That was a terrible hard time for those people, all of them. Mother used to say that the white people got the cream, the coloreds got the skim. That winter I guess it was more like the whites got the skim, coloreds the gravel. So things were pinched. And what happened was, the son of the man who owned her—you understand that? One person owning another? Like cattle or hogs or sheep?"

"Yes ma'am. I had my history."

"What happened was, that boy—and he was just a boy, a couple years younger than her and he'd already been off in that terrible bloody war and lost a part of one of his arms and got sent home again all so he and his kind could keep on owning people like Mother—what happened was he and she was alone one day that winter and he tried to force himself on her. You understand that?"

"Yes," he said, his eyes now on hers. Her arms crossed over her breasts as she sat reared back in her chair, regarding him. "I understand that."

"Not yet you don't. But it gives you more to think about. They was alone to the house and she laid him out; him just one-armed, it wasn't that hard for her. She grabbed ahold of a flat iron and swiped it into the side of his head and he went down, blood everywhere and she saw him and knew he was dead and she ran out of there. Got some help from an old man also owned by those white people and left that night, right then and there. In a pouring cold rain.

"She traveled alone, most times at night. Got help from people here and there. Someone would point the way, name landmarks. Give her a bit of something to eat. Think of that. A girl your age traveling alone in strange country when she hadn't been five miles from where she was born before. And every step of the way a step she wasn't supposed to take. That war was most of the way over and there wasn't any way but for most everyone to know it but that didn't make it safer for her; if anything it was the opposite. It was desperate times and terrible things were happening, could happen at any time. But on she went.

"Now the people she ran away from, the white people, it wasn't some big farm, plantation or anything. They was just town people, the white man a lawyer. So the colored people, the slaves he owned, were just that old man called Peter, the one who helped Mother get away, him and Mother and her mother, called Helen. And a very old woman. Rey. Rey was her name. Aunt Rey Mother called her but I don't know if that was blood or just because she was an old woman. Anyhow, it was just those four colored people. And she ran away from there and left not only that white boy dead but her own mother behind as well. Imagine that. Scared to death and full of guts, a wild girl running out of the only life she'd ever known and running toward something that she didn't have any idea of. North. That was all. No idea of where she'd land or what she'd do with herself once she got there. Just going."

She stopped then, still looking at Foster.

He said, "And she came across a wounded Vermont farm boy named Norman Pelham."

"That's right." Prudence stood. "At least that's the short way of telling it."

Abigail spoke from behind the hall door, her voice muffled. "She hanged herself."

Then she came through the door and stood beside her sister and gazed down at Foster, her face broken up with rage, grief, the skin shining, taut. Again she said, "She hanged herself. She was forty-two years old. November of 1890. She was the same age your father was, I just realized. She lived all those years here thinking she was hid out good from killing that white boy but what she hadn't counted on was not being able to hide out from herself. And all that time she couldn't stop thinking of her mother. She couldn't even send a letter. Didn't dare but didn't know where to send one either. But it kept working its way inside of her, chewing away at her. Until she couldn't stand it anymore. So she took the train down there and was back in less than a week and wouldn't talk about it. Not to us, not to Father. Not to anybody. But herself. I overheard her. We'd try to talk to her about it and she'd look right by us. Not like we weren't there but as if it was something that could not be spoken of. And then one morning in November without a word or note left behind she took herself up high in the woods and hanged herself." And stopped as if out of breath.

Foster, pressed into the chair, feeling the backslats cutting into him through his shirt. The room hot. The two women side by side, the one looking off, away from him, the other taller, leaning forward, swaying, the anger coming off her as a bright current that filled the room exactly to all its contours. Foster said nothing.

Then Prudence began to clear the table, slow deliberate motions as if she might drop something, lifting bowls and platters one at a time with both hands, her feet treading each step firm down onto the floorboards.

Abigail said, "Your father was a little boy. And he saw her. Saw her when Father carried her down out of the woods, her face all swollen, bloated up, purple-black, the color of a plum. He saw that. Five years old." The words chipping out of her mouth, spittle in beads as if broken from the edges of the words. "He hated himself, your father did. Hated what he was. Ran out of here and never would come back. Because he did not want to be what he was. The same way Mother thought she could leave her old life behind clean he did the same. But it does not work that way."

"I don't know," Foster said, soft.

She went on. "And then here comes you to tell us he was killed in an accident, run over by a car and also telling us he was a bootlegger. Had a liquor business is what you said. Well I'm not an idiot. I am not a stupid woman."

"I don't know," he said again. "It could've been the way they said it was. I don't know."

"Oh," she said, "I can tell you. However it was, it was not an accident. Even if it was, it still was not. Do you understand me?"

"No ma'am."

She leaned more toward him, her upper body over the table now. Prudence behind her, at the sink, her back to the room, not moving. Abigail said, "Your father was at war with himself. There was no harm he could inflict upon himself so he looked to the world to do it. When he was a boy, a small boy he was too, the other boys tormented him. Called him names, spoke of his mother. Cruel things, the cruelty of boys. And he fought them. Fought them, one on one or in groups. He never cared. All of them bigger and stronger than he was. But not a one of them tougher. He would not quit. They would leave off of him before he would quit. And he would not speak of it. Now, a boy like that, is he going to change as a man? Or is he going to go on mistaking the world for himself. For what he hates?"

"I don't know." His voice small against her. "He was always good to me. My mother and sister too, the best I recall. He'd tease me, but it was always kind."

She placed both hands on the table edge and braced herself on her arms, studying him. She said, "And all that time he was lying to you. If you want to learn anything about your father, what you have to do first is set aside everything you think you know."

Foster looked back at her. After a minute he said, "No. I can't do that. But I can add to it. I already am."

She pushed off the table to stand upright. "Well," she said. "Good for you."

Prudence had a pair of tin lard buckets filled with scraps for the dogs. He followed her into the woodshed entryway where they paused as she lighted a lantern and stepped out of her carpet slippers and into one of the pairs of gumboots lined against the wall and he followed her out into the yard.

He set the lard buckets on the roof of the car and let the dogs out. Glow raced in and out of the lantern light. Lovey came down off the seat slowly and stepped up to Prudence and sniffed at her and Prudence held down a hand and spoke to the dog and Lovey relaxed, letting her head be stroked. Foster whistled for Glow and set the buckets down in the circle of light and the dogs ate.

Prudence said, "It was Sister mostly who raised your father. After Mother died we were still a family but it was an odd little bunch, at sixes and sevens most of the time it seems now, looking back. It was Sister who worked so hard to make things as normal as she could for that little boy. Played games with him like a girl half her age. And later, when because of the fighting and torment we took him out of the school, it was her that did his lessons with him. Her that planned them out and kept up with them. Father would set him to parse sentences and then forget all about checking the work to see it was done right. It wasn't bad intentions; it was that after Mother died Father did not pay attention to things the same's he'd done before. But because it was Abby mostly who raised your father it hurt her bad when he ran off. Without telling anybody where he was going or why."

"I could see that."

"There was some bitterness in it too. She'd had some disappointments as a young woman and then, just at the time when she might of gone off somewhere, done something else with her life, she was suddenly left with a grieving father grown old and a wild little boy needed mothering. And so whatever ideas she ever might've had about anything else, they all got swept away."

"What about you?"

"Me? I never saw or wanted anything than to stay right here on this farm and work it like a man. I've done just fine, thank you." Her face wrinkled in the orange lantern light, serious.

He grinned at her. "I believe it." Then asked, "You said disappointments. That Abigail had? What were those?"

"The usual sort. Boys. She was some right sort of beauty as a girl."

"Still is."

"Umph. You're not so young as I thought." She went on. "But the disappointment was, beauty she might be but it wasn't a wife those boys were chasing. That colored blood. She was the berry everybody wanted to pick but eat right there in the field, not carry home with them. Stop on the way theirselves and wash their hands. And that was before Mother killed herself."

Then each stood silent regarding the other and the night around them. The dogs worrying the empty pails, their heads down inside as they scraped the flavor away with their tongues, the pails scooting against the dirt of the farmyard. Quiet, Foster asked, "Why'd she do that, you think?"

Prudence looked away from him a long moment. Then said, "Pick up those buckets; let's get your dogs some water. Then find then a nice place to bed them down."

In straight stalls in the horsebarn there were a team of heavy horses and next to them a team of driving horses and in a last stall a big stout pony the color of cream. The horses stirred and blew when they came in, one of the drafts stamping hard against the stall planking. Prudence took the buckets from Foster and dipped them into the iron-strapped water trough and set them down and the dogs, standing back, noses and ears up toward the horses, crept forward and drank. Then they went through a door into a partitioned sheepfold and the sheep also stirred, moving away from the light to the dark corners. At the end of the walkway was an open area with a pile of sawdust bedding and a stack of hinged two-sided gates used to make small lambing pens for individual ewes. Prudence took up one of these and swung it open and still holding it up against her hip kicked a thick layer of sawdust from the pile up against one stone foundation wall and leveled the sawdust with a boot and then moved the unfolded gate and without them even aware she was doing it cornered the dogs within the enclosure made.

"There," she said. "That should do them fine."

"They might cry some. A strange place and all."

"They'll settle down. It's warm and dry. And the sheep, it's a lot of company. It's a great calming thing. You'll see. Your dogs'll be fine."

"I know." And because he wasn't sure he leaned over the gate and stroked the two heads and as he did this behind him Prudence spoke.

"Who can know the amount of despair someone feels that they take their life? It's as much to ask what it's like to be dead. All I can imagine is you come to some understanding of having failed in some fashion that is so much a part of you that it is not endurable. That all other things grow small and pale by comparison. The people around us, the ones we depend on, and those that depend on us. Whatever sense you have of God, whatever idea you have of Him. That also has to fail. I'm not talking about a crisis of faith. I'm talking about all your life you hold what you think is a rock in your hand, even though you can't see it. But it is there, you know it's there. Then one day you look down and right there, clear as daylight in the palm of your hand is only a pile of dust. And maybe even as you look at it some breeze comes across and blows it away. And you're left with nothing. Just an old open hand. But that's not really what you asked, is it? You think there might be a code or a key that will help you understand."

"No." Foster said. "I think you might be right."

As if she had not heard him she said, "This is what we know. What she learned when she went back to Carolina all those years later. The old man, Peter, who helped her get away. She learned he was taken out by a group of men and killed. Tortured and killed. Abby heard her talking about it. Talking to herself. He was put up on a block with a rope around his neck and then soaked down with kerosene and set afire while the men stood around and watched him dance himself burning up right off that block so he died by the rope. But all the time burning he didn't kick away from the block until the last moment, until he couldn't stand it. Because a man will endure most anything to stay alive. And those other men, watching, waiting for that moment when he gave up hope."

"By Christ," Foster breathed out.

"That's what we know. What we can be sure of. But there's other things. More questions than anything. But they're still there. Some ways, they're bigger even than what we know."

"Did she find her mother?"

"No. Not that we know. The thing is, the time Abby overheard her talking—" Prudence stopped, gazing at the rough stone foundation, a soft jumble of surfaces in the lantern light. Then she looked at Foster. "I'm making her sound like a crazy person. But she was not. Even though she hanged herself, I do not think she was crazy. I think she was horribly sane, as if she'd seen something beneath the surface of the everyday. Now, I'm likely the one sounds crazy to you."

"No ma'am." Foster stood blinking at her. His dogs behind the gate curled into the sawdust, already sleeping, as if the strange woman was speaking a lullaby to them.

"I don't sound like some old woman going on in years with her head tilted by all this tragedy in her family? I don't sound that way to you?"

He grinned at her. "What you sound like is my dad. He had this theory that almost everything people do is not what they want but what they think the world wants them to do. He'd wonder what sort of world it would be, after things got sorted out, if everybody just started doing what they really wanted. And he would grin and say it would be paradise for those that survived the blood of it getting sorted out. I think he was talking about the same sort of thing you're talking about."

"It's the nature of a human to be vicious."

"Yes ma'am."

"But all any of us really wants, in our hearts, is that one long golden day."

"Yes ma'am."

They were both quiet then. After a time Prudence said, "Except for the part about Peter we do not know, any of us, what she found. Who she found. But there was nothing said that made us think she found her mother. But what it seems like, is the person she was addressing—we think it was the boy, the white boy she thought she'd killed all those years ago. We think maybe he wasn't killed after all. That he survived. You talk to Abby. She was the one there. Hearing Mother. She's told me but still she's the one for you to ask."

Foster nodded. Then asked, "The boy, the white boy, the one who attacked her? He was the son of the man who owned her?"

"Yes," she said. "Yes to both. But he was more than that. He was her half brother."

"Now wait," Foster said.

But she did not wait. "He was her brother. Because her father was the man that owned her mother. That owned her too. That owned his own daughter."

He sat up in bed in the dark room. The old house still but for night-sounds around him. The creak of a joist. A settling snap of a stairboard. The room of his grandfather. His own father's room had long since been turned into a sewing room by Abigail. He'd not explored the heavy old furniture, the fixtures of the room. But had opened the old valise that had once been his mother's to find a fresh shirt for the morning and turned back the covers and blown out the lamp and stripped down in the dark and got into the big old soft bed. Where his grandparents had slept. The mattress still heaved up in the middle to a soft ridge. And pushed himself up to sit. An unfamiliar dark room.

When he and Prudence had come from the barn to the house it was empty and quiet, Abigail gone from sight. The supper dishes finished, stacked in the drain to dry. Prudence had told him, "She's disturbed by all this. The news of your father. You. Everything."

Foster had nodded, studying the old woman telling him this. He said, "Me too."

She'd stood then, silent and awkward, looking at him. Then said, "It shouldn't have to be like this. I'd do anything for it to be different."

He could not say, now, sitting in the dark, which of them had moved. It seemed that neither had crossed those few feet between them. But he was leaning over this woman, this sister of his father, his face buried down in the headcloth wrapped over her springing hair, her arms around him holding him as if she'd been waiting all her life to do so. His own hands running up and down the span of her back, the hard muscles there under the thin housedress she wore. Both rocking. The smell of her. Woodsmoke. The sweet savor of animal, dung, bedding, milk, hay-must; the odors of cooking; the faint sour smell of old body, and underneath this a light floral scent as of a soap used long ago, perhaps, he thought, only this morning. Keening for his own lost mother and everything else lost. But for that moment mostly her. And understood the old woman against him was doing the same for a different mother. He held her tightly.

In the three weeks since his father died he'd been numb-walking, wild with grief at night, sleeping short dense hours before rising up into another day of the familiar grown strange. Now he sat in bed and knew he'd passed into another life altogether, where he'd look back upon the years in the White Mountains as the simpleminded innocence of a child. And knew his father was not dead, truly; he would haunt him forever— the man unknown, never knowable. What he told Abigail was only partial truth: he would not simply be adding to what he already knew, but fighting also each new fact along the way to hold intact the laughing ease of his father, the clear sense of the man he'd had until this day.

He sat in the bed, stiff against the old high headboard, wide awake. Breathing in the smell of the house. As if to add to the memory of his father. He slid down and lay flat on the mattress. Certain he would not sleep that night. He thought briefly of his dogs. Then did not fall asleep so much as pass into unconsciousness as if the day had struck him senseless.

He woke before first light exhausted with dreams and sadness. He woke to the smell of breakfast cooking. He hadn't done that in a long time.

He dressed in the dark. Because the room was chill he dug in the valise for the worn blanket-lined canvas shooting jacket that old Doctor Dodge had given him. And went out onto the landing and heard the faint riffle of voices from downstairs. He paused there and then, an invader, went down to the lower hall. Pushed open the door to the kitchen.

The women were bright, dressed both of them for barn work, chirping to him and each other. Behaving as if he'd always been in the house. He accepted coffee from Abigail, the cup a delicate porcelain thing with a winged handle, the heat seeping through as he wrapped his hands around it. Her eyes flashing over him as if noting his discomfort and dismissing it at once. As if some peace had settled overnight in the house without bothering to alert him. He was jangling. He refused breakfast, claiming first the need to see to his dogs. Taking the coffee with him. Feeling both sets of eyes on him as he stepped into the entryshed.

Outside was blueblack, a slice of moon and one big star low in the east. A planet, but which he couldn't say. He went to the Chrysler and set the coffee on the hood and took cigarettes from the glove box and lighted one and leaned against the car and smoked it down, drinking the coffee. He considered the case of bonded whiskey he'd dug up out of the ground in Bethlehem that was now in the cargo space hidden under the rear seat, alongside his shotguns in fleece-lined wooden cases. He wanted to crack one of those bottles, take a long drink from it. He watched the house. Those women would be out any minute to come to the barns. He finished the smoke and coffee and left the cup on the hood of the car and walked in through the barns to get his dogs. The first door he opened every creature within stirred and cried out someway. And he understood something of Prudence telling him that this was all she wanted or ever needed. Among this he heard the lowing whine of Lovey and the sharp cries of Glow. Through the dim barns, past the murmur and stamp of the horses, into the sheepfold where the bleat rose like water suddenly swept by wind, down the dark walkway to where the dogs heard him and came piling over the gate to greet him. The sheep went quiet. He took the dogs back the way he'd come, out the door into the now-blue dawn. The hills a soft charcoal against the lightened sky. In the yard he met Prudence and Abby, lanterns lit and swinging. Abby stopped beside him.

"Your creatures all right?"

"Yes, ma'am."

"You think you ever might just call me by my name?"

"I don't know," he said. "It seems an odd thing to do."

"I guess maybe it does. You want to eat alone, there's food there in the house."

"Thank you. I thought I'd take these dogs for a little walk first."

"I don't blame you. Get away from all this."

"It's not that."

"You and me," she said, "have a ways to go. But we understand each other, don't we?"

He said nothing.

She said, "Maybe you don't know it yet. But we recognize each other. You and me."

He looked at her. Then he said, "I don't know."

She waved her hand at the hills. A few thin streaks of cloud were over them now, showing pale color from the hidden sun. "Go on," she said. "Run your dogs."

The short cropped grass of the sheep pasture looked like an old man's hair, flat silver with frost. When he stepped down and lifted his boot the frost was gone, leaving behind him a wedge of trail. He went up to the family burying ground and hunkered amid the old stones. He thought to see if he might capture some feeling there, something brought up by the old bones but it was only silent and chill. On the far eastern ridgetop the first light angled up into the sky. A single crow flew over the bowl of the farm, its rough hoarse cry cutting the air above the land. Then it was gone into the trees, silent.

But then sitting there he realized that what his father had kept from him was not something as simple as the Negro grandmother (half-Negro? What did that make him? Was he going to learn anything following these lines?) but far more than that. Not only the two women at work below, his father's sisters whom he would now never see talk or probe or laugh or tease his father but all the rest of it: The old man dead two years when he would've been fourteen. The veteran of the War of Rebellion. What exactly had his father denied him by removing him from that old man? He would never know, would always wonder. What complicated levels of emotion drove his father not only to make the choice years before but to enforce that choice throughout all this time? He did not accept that it was as simple as Abigail made it to be, the notion of self-hatred. He sat as the sun came up to quicken the frost and the grass came back to life, the earth began to smell of itself and he warmed in the tender light. The dogs bouncing over the ledges and outcroppings, their tongues out, happy.

He rose after a time of watching the dogs and went down the hill, calm and resolute and undefined at once, much older than he'd been the morning before raising his hand in farewell to Andy Flood as he drove out away from the Bethlehem house. It may have been only the eggshell coffee but he felt prepared for whatever was before him. The only thing he knew was that he would shrink from nothing. His father had not been a coward; he knew this. But Foster was determined to face it all.

He stayed two weeks on the farm, with no timetable, no plan save to learn what he could. Following that first shock, what impressed him most, what he admired and desired for his own, and what he finally determined was not a thing that could be assumed but a way one was born and lived thereafter, was the way the women went about their days. There was no distinction between work and life but rather each day was an unhurried yet constant movement from one task to the next as if each woman followed a pattern that was old and worn into their very beings, that the work performed was not routine but life. They were grim but not dour, as if understanding that life was unrelenting but not ponderous. He'd seen enough sour hotel workers to recognize the difference. He only knew it himself through the woods. But as his father had reminded him, dollar bills would not be found in the moss or fern-beds of the woods. Be a dog-man, his father had joked. And he knew the world did not demand dogs the way it did butter or milk or eggs. Or meat. Or whiskey.

So he grew comfortable with the sisters. And found himself fond of them. Aware of this, he sought to contain it. Not sure he might trust fondness, the empty well in him. And they, mostly, left him be unless he spoke to them. Unless one would come upon him at some time the woman deemed to fit some schedule of her own in which she would speak freely to him of whatever was passing through her mind.

He did not presume upon their work. Instead he studied the place and so spent most mornings working with the double-bitted axe and the chopping block beside the stacked cordwood behind the house, splitting the wood to firesticks and carrying it by the armload into the entryway shed and stacking it against the empty north wall where scabs of bark and shreds of wood splinters on the earthen floor as well as common sense told him the winter stovewood should go.

Midmornings Pru hitched the big cream pony to a two-wheeled cart and went to the village with cans of milk and crates of eggs. It was often then, Foster at work with the axe, his shirtsleeves rolled high above his elbows, that Abby would come around the house with a glass of water for him and settle herself on an upturned round of wood and watch him drink the water and then continue his work until she would begin to talk. As if answering a question he'd not yet quite thought to ask.

"Look at you," she said. Then when he stopped in self-conscious confusion she laughed and went on. "So much of Father in you. I can see him as a young man. Is it any wonder Mother risked everything to help him when she found him so?"

He leaned on the axe handle. "How'd she risk anything, him being a Union soldier?"

"All those Union boys were not angels, son. Plenty were halfhearted about freeing the slaves; preserving the union was what most concerned them. And even those that were true abolitionists, a young man's principles might soften up or disappear altogether, they found themselves alone in the woods with a young runaway girl like that."

He leaned and lifted a new chunk to the block. "Well. He was wounded you said."

"Oh, he was more than that. It's part of what your own father missed out on, his losing his mother so young. But Sister and I grew up with them; they were everything a man and woman should be together. Whatever oddness had ever been between them, if there ever was any and I doubt there was, was long since gone. They were man and wife, ordinary and difficult as that is. In some ways maybe even easier for them. They'd already jumped the one big hoop; everything after that was simple."

He popped the chunk, turned one of the halves sideways and halved it again. "So however it ended, until then they were happy?"

"They adored each other."

He split the other half and kicked the pieces away, keeping the ground between the block and his feet clear. "It was hard for Pop, growing up, it sounds like. How'd people treat them, people in the town, like that?"

She went quiet then. He kept working. He did not think she had not heard him and so he waited, splitting wood.

After a time she said, "In a way it's hard to say. Grandmother Pelham was sweet to us girls but distant too. Always gifts at birthdays and Christmas, little things. Other times little treats. But would she have been different if Father had married some white local girl? I honestly can't tell you. She moved out of the house when he brought Mother home but she would've done the same for another bride. She was an old Abolitionist too. I know from Father telling me; she never would've. I know for a fact she did knitting and packed food parcels that were passed along to the people heading for Canada. She didn't harbor any, but I know the name of the woman she gave the parcels too. A Glover in Braintree. But was she happy when she met Mother? You can believe in the idea of a thing but that doesn't mean you want it in your living room. It'd be nice to think she was high-minded enough so she only saw that it would be difficult for them, that people would always stop and look, some say things."

He nodded, paused. Then asked, "Other people?"

"Your grandfather was respected. In an odd way though I think Mother commanded more respect even than him. Because she walked right up in the face of it. It was her built up the chicken-and-egg business. Time was, it was a regular little industry. Father now, he'd of been happy to continue on as ever before: a little of this and a little of that and it all comes out in the end with food on the table and no spare time. Mother though, was a businesswoman. She put money in the bank. And those same neighbors, they might not tell you what they think, but they respect someone hardworking and clear-headed. Myself, I never ran across any true meanness, except for rude men, and any woman comes across those time to time. After Mother died, it changed a little. There was a little more distance, a little greater gap that people left between themselves and us. Part of that was they did not understand it; we did not broadcast details. We retreated a little bit after that. But it was not shame. It was respect. For her. For whatever her reasons were, those we could understand and those we could not. Does that make sense to you?"

"It does." Thinking of his own father.

She went on. "But what you should do, you want another view of these things, is go talk to Connie Clifford. That's Father's little sister. Her own sons was some of those that tormented your father as a boy. They're grown men now with little ones of their own. She did not approve of what her boys were up to. But that does not mean she could stop them. Your great-aunt. She's overstreet to Randolph village.

Evenings after supper he spent in the kitchen with Prudence; Abigail retreated to the parlor to read the paper. Prudence busy without pause throughout the day save but to pass him by with a tease or joke of some sort. It was only evenings when she would grow serious. Times, he felt he had to coax her, as if someway his being there was enough to satisfy her. As if she mistrusted too many words. As if she knew they might not clarify but only confuse what was most essential. Other times she was blunt and direct.

"Is there family," she asked, "on your mother's side?"

"She was out of French Canada. Her folks came down so her dad could work the quarry in Barre. He was killed in a accident there. Her mother died sometime after that, I guess. Some years later. So Mama was an orphan time she met Pop. She was a LeBaron. I'd guess there's relatives somewhere up there in Quebec but I wouldn't know where to look."

Prudence nodded, said nothing. He could not tell if this answer pleased her or not. Perhaps, in the way it was for him, it was nothing more than information.

Another evening she queried him in detail about his father; wanting descriptions of how his father had aged, where they had lived, what Foster knew of his father's history, his business and work. And of how his father had been with his mother; what Foster recalled of the two of them, as well as friends, the people his father worked with. And also again not so much how he died but what it was like after that: the funeral, the people there. What was said. Where his father was buried. What that place looked like. And Foster told her everything he could and in the telling discovered more than he thought he knew and it all came out of him, a swift rush of words that would not stop even as he ate up the piece of vinegar pie she had placed before him, a combination so sweet and delirious that he was actually stopped, choked off for some moments gazing at her across the table where she sat with her head down on her arms, before he realized she was sobbing. And he sat looking at the rind of piecrust on his plate, knowing better than to rise and go around to her. There was no comfort, there. None wanted.

After dark he would go to the barns with Pru while she made her last check of the livestock by lantern light. When she was done he'd stand in the yard and watch her cross to the house, the circle of light bobbing roughly over the lawn. Then he'd return to the barns to release his dogs and the three of them would go up the hill under the stars and what moon there was. The dogs ranging out, loping in the starlight. Most nights they would go high onto the ridge in the woods until the dogs were tired. Twice having to call Glow off the chittering of a raccoon and once running his legs sore and his voice hoarse as she ran after deer. But most nights they would just go up through the woods and circle back down into the empty sheep pasture, the ledges soft shadows in the night and come to sit in the small cemetery where beside his grandfather's stone he'd nested a bottle of the bonded scotch whiskey and he'd sit cross-legged and take out a box of cigarettes and unscrew the whiskey and drink small sips and smoke. Considering his day.

As he had done evenings in New Hampshire in the time between burying his father and his leaving, sitting on the boulderback by the river suspended in the mesh of grief. Foster was no fool; he'd understood Patrick Jackson's message. Now he could see that when he'd found the letters from Abigail he'd glimpsed not only a place to study his situation from the safety of some distance but also the hope of some clarity, some wisdom greater than his own. Some method perhaps to decode more perfectly the message Jackson gave him. Instead he'd learned there was no method. And understood that a portion of what Jackson had offered was a threat, from the same forces that had swallowed his father as completely as the earth covered his body. He knew he would not be returning to New Hampshire, not in any time he could name. He would keep the house. Let it rot and fall down if it came to that. But, keeping it was holding a presence, a small cry against the dark. Even if no one noticed or heard.

So he would sit in the starlit September burnt-back grass of the small family cemetery that was partly where he came from and drink small swallows of the whiskey and consider the breathless beauty of the earth and the perfect precision of its ways, where he saw no action as random or uncounted, and try to understand this weighed against the workings of men, a world that had been moving silently to bring him to this time, to this place and moment in his life. It was a world that seemed to hold no place for him. It was a world he was not even sure he wanted part of, and yet a part of it belonged to him by the simple fact of his existence. And knew he must take up that part for himself.

He grew sentimental with the whiskey, profoundly sad and hushed before the terrible beauty of it all. His dogs slept beside him, shivering with the early fall.

He went to see Connie Clifford. He dug his best shirt and his black trousers and coat from the valise and amused Pru and satisfied Abby when he heated the flatirons and pressed his own clothes. It was only what he'd always done, his father too. Perhaps his mother had once done this work for his father but it was a time he knew nothing of. Bathed and shaved and with his boots brushed clean and buffed with an old rag, he shut his dogs in the barn and then used the same rag to wipe down the Chrysler, clearing a week's worth of yard dust from it.

Abigail said, "You took no such pains before driving in here and presenting yourself."

He looked at her. Her face was pleasant. He said, "I didn't know much, did I?"

She smiled and reached to refigure some minute way his collar. She said, "She'll be flustered by you. Don't pay any attention to that. You look wonderful; she'll fall in love with you and treat you like someone trying to sell her something."

The house was in the village, white with green trim, three stories under a pitched green tin roof. Behind what had once been a livery but now was a garage fronted with hand-crank gasoline pumps, the doors of the shop open where a man worked on his back beneath a T-model Ford. The man came up from under the Ford and moved slowly into the light of the day. In his forties, hard-muscled, with a slackness to his jowls and belly. His hands lined deeply with oilstain. He filled the Chrysler with gas and washed the windshield with a rag out of a bucket and dried it with another rag out of his hip pocket. Foster paid him and told him, "I'm looking for Constance Clifford."

The man looked at him. Blinked slow once and did not introduce himself. "That's Mother. She's to the house with Dad. Park your car by the garage and walk around the side, you won't miss it."

As if she'd been expecting him she met him at the open front door, stepping onto the stoop, a thickly built woman in her seventies, low to the ground, a button-front sweater open over a sun-faded light print dress. Her hair a snarl of silver curls. She greeted him. "Beginning to think we'd have to come up there and pry you loose." She did not smile. Her eyes the blue of winter water. "But you escaped all on your own."

He felt he might apologize. He said, "You heard I was here then."

"Prudy's a talker. Some excited, I can tell you. I'm sorry to hear about your father."

"Yes, ma'am."

"Come in the house."

Her husband Glen was a small person also, in a suit coat and vest with fob and chain and carpet slippers, who rose from his seat by the cold parlor stove and shook Foster's hand, then covered their two joined hands with his other. His hair a pale fringe gone but for a sharply barbered clip behind his ears. They all took seats, the couple in their flanking chairs, Foster on the edge of an old stiff horsehide-covered sofa.

Glen said, "Prudence was correct. He favors your brother."

"That's what they say."

Connie studied him. Then said, "You do take after him, it's true. Norman was gone to the war between when I was a little girl and grew up. He was a man time I got to know him. He was a sentimental man, Norman was."

"I'm afraid I'm that way too."

"It's not a trait to pity or fear. Perhaps it makes for sadness looking at the world. But that doesn't make it less true."

"Maybe I'll grow out of it." He tried out a small grin on her.

"Now there. That's Norman."

Glen said, "It was a hard time for your father, as a boy. The other children were hard on him, more so than they were with the girls. And it was our own boys, often as not, led the pack. I strapped them all in the woodshed over it, more than once. Boys always need something different, something someway strange from themselves. It's how they decide who they are. Your father was an easy target. I strapped those boys of mine even as I understood they felt if they didn't do the leading then they'd become that other thing as well. Times, even, I wondered was I making it worse for your father. You do what you can do, but not a one among us can say what that amounts to, what it brings down the road."

There was a short silence in the room. Glen and Connie looked at each other. As if he'd said more someway then either of them intended. Then, out of this, he went on.

"Aiden—that's our youngest who you just met out the front of the store—he heard you were in town, he came to me. Told me of a time, the older boys had got hold of your father up in the woods. After school. A pair of them had him by the hands and feet, stretched out between them. They was swinging him back and forth, getting set to dump him down the side of a bank. And Aid, he told me—just a little fellow, not big enough to do anything otherwise—he went roaring in, yelling at those big boys to hold on, to wait. That he wasn't done yet. So they held your father swinging there while Aiden waded in to kick up and down his ribs. Told me he wanted to hurt him, wanted him to feel as much pain as Aid could make. Before he went sailing down that hillside. Aid telling me how your father would not make a sound as he kicked him. So Aiden came a couple nights ago to tell me this. Not only because he knew you were here. It had been working at him these years. He came in, sat down, told me, asked me why I thought he'd done that. All I could do was look him in the face and tell him he didn't know any better. And he sat there, right where you are now, and told me that yes he did."

Foster said, "My mother and sister both died in the flu the winter of 'eighteen–'nineteen. If there was ever a time for bitterness, that would've been a good one, I think. Everybody here thinks he was all hatred and old regrets. I guess there was some of that in him. But it wasn't the man I knew. All I know is he never talked about this place here. Could be it was such a bad thing he wouldn't talk of it. But then, maybe, it didn't matter that much. I guess I'll never know the answer to that. You think?"

Quiet again in the room. Quiet enough so through the raised windows Foster could hear the low rumble of town. He locked his hands in his lap and looked down at them. After a time, Connie spoke.

"In some ways, it could be, your father wasn't so different from your grandfather. I've not thought of it this way before. But Norman was a quiet man. You didn't know him, you'd find him silent, even severe. But he was not that way. I think two things, the war and his love of your grandmother, left him feeling he was best off at the side of life. I think he saw the farm as a refuge—a place where what world was made was of his own making."

"Yes, ma'am."

"I recall as yesterday the morning he walked back up to the farm at the end of the war with that dark-skinned girl with him. It was September and we'd been expecting him some time. Most of the men had come home by the trainload. We hadn't had a letter from Norman since before the surrender. Mother was sick, worrying about him. Those men that came back, all we'd get from them was Norman had stepped up and asked to sign his mustering-out papers there in Washington D.C., that he wanted to walk the way home and see the country he'd just fought for. Now understand, Brother was the sort that had gone through the whole war with never a request of any sort, not even a complaint. When Father died he could've come home then, no one would've questioned it. But Norman was the type of man that once he took something up he saw it through to the end. So when he wanted to walk home, they honored that. I've no doubt there was men, officers certain but likely other men as well, that knew about your grandmother. But we didn't hear the first word of her. Just that he was coming along. The way he wanted. And it hurt Mother wicked. All those men coming off the trains and Norman nowhere in sight. She would not speak of it but she'd read the paper and the lists of names and the accounts of the homecomings. And of course he knew that. Stupid in love he might have been but Norman Pelham was not the kind of man to forget what the rest of the world was up to. So when he walked up the hill that September noon with that dark-skinned girl Mother already someway knew he had made a choice that did not include her. She was just a widow woman with nothing but a fourteen-year-old girl, trying to hold everything together, waiting for him to amble on in. A mother"—Connie glared at Foster—"is nothing but a tortured creature."

He returned her look. He said, "It must've been a terrible shock then. What she was."

Connie Clifford did not move in her chair but gathered herself up, her eyes pale, lively, snapping. Then she leaned forward and looked away from Foster a moment, her eyes lighting around the room as if seeking some proof of her conviction. She looked back at him and with her voice dropping down solid on each word said, "Leah Pelham owned herself."

He did not understand this at first and then did. Soft, he said, "Yes ma'am."

Her glare did not relent. "People would say it was Norman made that possible. They would be wrong."

He waited.

"She had known the worst people can offer up to one another. And walked away from that. With her head up square. And certainly she and my brother loved each other. As a young girl it was wonderful to see." She glanced at Glen, back at Foster. "But with or without him, Leah just ate the world up. As if, you see, she not only owned herself. But owned everything she could see. I'd never known a person like that before. A woman like that." And paused again and added, "Or since."

Quiet then. Foster looked at the floor, the sheet of bright linoleum stretched under the furniture, not reaching the corners of the room. It was not what this great-aunt had said so much as her pitch. His voice still low he asked, "What was it happened to her?"

And Connie Clifford sat back into her chair, her hands released from the arms into her lap where they lay gnarled and twisted over each other. Her face collapsed back to her age, the skin lying loose over her skullbones. She looked down at her toiling hands. When she looked back up at him her mouth was compressed. Her eyes dimmed, someplace away. "I don't know," she said. "She was my friend. Was what she was."

When he left there he did not return immediately to the farm but instead drove two blocks into downtown Randolph and parked nosed in to the curb. He wanted to be alone. So he walked among the people of the town and was alone there. It was not his father's town; he knew that now. But it had been his grandfather's. And his grandmother had made it her own. And now the recluse maiden aunts on the hill. The other people that were here he did not feel belonged to him. He would remain a stranger they were kind to. So finally, it was the not-so-long-dead old man and the long-dead dark-skinned woman that he felt might someway stalk within him as he walked slowly along the storefronts.

When he'd left Cliffords' and walked around the garage to where the Chrysler was parked Aiden Clifford had come from the darkness of the shop, coming up to Foster, rubbing his hands on a dirty rag, his moon face turned down. He'd said, "It's some car."

"It was my father's," Foster told him.

Aiden looked away from Foster. "Changed the oil for you. Looked her over good. Other than the oil, she's set to go."

"Well I appreciate that. Hadn't thought about the oil."

Aiden nodded. "Yuht. People don't."

"I keep an eye on the water and tires."

"Change that oil often enough, she'll go forever."

"I'll keep it in mind."

"Sorry to hear about your father." Aiden looking away, off across the street.

"It's all right," Foster said. He lifted his wallet from his hip pocket. "How much for the oil and all?"

Aiden looked at him. "Nothing," he said. "It's no charge for that."

Foster looked back at him. "They don't give that oil away."

"That's all right."

Foster paused. Then said, "You mean a kindness I suppose." He unfolded the wallet and took out a dollar bill and held it. "But Pop, he was a little more than a couple quarts of oil." He let go of the bill then. It sailed out, rocking in a small sashay toward the ground.

In a narrow empty lunch counter he ate a hamburger sandwich and a slab of pie made from tinned cherries and drank coffee thick with cream and sugar. In a hardware he bought a new collar for Lovey. Her old one was pocked and frayed from where Glow would lie against her and chew on it. He thought maybe Glow was over that now. The new collar was beautiful. Double-stitched fine supple harness leather with a brass buckle, it lay in his hand limp and soft, the weight of it countering the pliability: a thing that would last. He bought gun oil and a chamois polishing leather.

Back on the street he paused and looked around him. The light aslant with early fall midafternoon shadow, everything delineated. He was distracted, buoyant, restless. Himself. He felt confident that he could meet all things head on and remain himself. He wanted the woods. He recalled what Connie Clifford had told him of Leah Pelham owning the world. And thought perhaps this certainty was some small click passing down to him from his grandmother. And smiled with this idea. As if she had survived all things to come to rest within him. Why not? was what he thought. He was sixteen years old and bold as a rivet bolting together a pair of steel plates.

He filled the woodshed side of the entryway with split stovewood, five tiers running from the outer door all the way to the wall of the house where three steps led up into the kitchen, the tiers stacked to the shed rafters. So when you walked in you passed alongside a dense wall of wood, the smell fresh and sharp against the old must and machine oil of the shed. Not even a quarter of the stacked cordwood behind the house but all there was room for. The other side of the walkway, beside the workbench with the old tools oiled and hung each in its place on the wall, he sat afternoons to whet the axe bits on the grindstone, pumping the treadle, the stone whirling roughly in place as he held the bits against the edge, his fingers knuckled back to keep them from the wheel. The water in a slow drip from the thin spout over the wheel, the smell of wet stone and steel. The bit when he turned it over a fine bright crescent shaved down to a wafer edge. The day he carried in the last armload of wood to stretch up and cram in against the rafters he sat afterward and sharpened the axe a final time and with a rag spread a thick coat of oil over the sharpened double bits and set the axe up in a corner by the door, the handle against the wall, the oiled head resting off the ground on a block of wood. So whoever used it next would find it ready.

Using his grandfather's tools, looking around for the ways and methods for their care, finding what he needed, he was surprised by what he knew. His own father's tools had been few, ordinary everyday hammers and screwdrivers with no particular attention paid. Yet he possessed understanding of these older, more dangerous tools. As if it were passed down without language. He realized you might know something without awareness until the knowledge was called for.

This was not so different from the woods. Peering close at each leaf fall, each white bird-spoor splash on the duff, as at the same time hearing the wind move through the trees, seeing the angles of light change, imprinting without effort the terrain ahead; all these things marked the way you turned and walked, not only the direction taken but where you'd come from. Seeing behind and ahead at once. Because, when the hunting was done you had to find your way home.

Pru was up in the sheep pasture picking the early apples from the three old big trees and he hiked up to help her, the dogs loping out and back as he called to keep them close, to not worry the sheep, who were bunched together higher up, watching the dogs. She had a pair of round-bottomed bushel baskets and a yoke to carry them with. The apples were rust-red, scabbed, small, knobbled. Flesh bright white stained pink and sweet and crisp. He worked alongside her for a time. Ducking under the heavy branches hanging with still-ripening fruit. All they gathered were the early windfalls. It would be another week, ten days, another frost before the rest were ready. But Pru was after some cider, maybe even a pie.

He told her, "I was asking Abby about Grandmother. About her time down there in North Carolina. Not about when she went back there but before. Before she met Grandfather. Abby just waved me off."

Pru was bent after apples. She grunted, a sound of disdain. Her fingers worked through the grass, cupping one, two, three apples.

Foster went on. "Seems like, whatever happened when she went back down there, the key to it all had to be from the time before. What was the name of those people there?"

She straightened up, studying him. A breeze off the ridgeline ran over them, a freshet of air, tugging the short grass back and forth. She said, "Except for how she came to leave there she never talked about those times. Not even so much with Father, not that he ever told us. Not any stories that would explain anything to anybody. After she died Father talked some about traveling there to try to learn what he could."

"Why'd he not?"

She looked at him a long time. Then asked, "Why'd you not stay over there to the White Mountains? Try to unravel what might or might not have happened to your father?"

Because I was scared to, he thought. And said, "Because it wouldn't have changed anything."

She nodded. "That's right. Mother would still have been dead." She paused and then added, "Perhaps some part of him was afraid to go, also. Afraid of what he might find. When he was old, the last year or two, and not so spry as he'd been and his mind would slip around with him, times then he'd talk about it. How he should've done something, gone down there."

Foster was quiet a time. Then he stepped around her and still wordless bent to the work. Apples into the baskets. They worked until the ground was clean and then Foster hooked the harness ends into the basket handles and slipped the yoke over his bent head, reaching up to settle it across his shoulders. He turned to start down the hill.

She said, "People's name was Mebane. All I know's the boy she thought she killed, his name was Alex. Alexander. Mister Lex she called him. Mister!" She spat in the grass.

"Mebane," he repeated. Then, "Where?"

"Name of the town's Sweetboro. That's all I know."

"It's a pretty name."

She started down ahead of him, not waiting. Her voice came muffled with the breeze. "Nothing pretty about it."

Up in the burying ground under the starlight. Full of pie and boiled beef. A hard freeze coming down. The sky jellied with light. Little sips of whiskey. The old dog pressed against one thigh for warmth, the pup sitting high up on her haunches at the gap in the stone wall, surveying the star-soaked pasture for movement. An owl moaned mournful up on the ridge. Another sip of whiskey. Shaking his head. The owl not mournful at all, just an owl, the voice of night. Sitting with his head resting against one of the stones, some Pelham. He could see both stones of his grandparents. He no longer expected anything magical, any sudden burst of understanding. Because if those old bones told him anything it was that understanding was slow.

He wept. He missed everything of his old life. Not only his father anymore but the articulate parts and pieces of everyday. The things he had not even known he could count upon. It was beautiful weeping: quiet, absent of self-pity. He took it as a measure of rightness that his dogs no longer grew alarmed when he wept. They were a comfort except for the fact that he also felt they were clear-headed judges. His old dog took her head off his thigh and tucked it down into her own shoulder. Likely only cold. He reached down and stroked her.

There was a final cigarette in the box that had belonged to his father. He wanted it but did not smoke it. He sipped again and corked the bottle and slid it behind the headstone and rose to walk to the wall and gaze down over the speckled meadow as he peed, Glow leaning to sniff where his pee steamed. He buttoned his flies and traced his way along the rough wall, one hand running up and down over the uneven hard-laid slabs. Came to the gate into the pasture and looked down at the quiet farm. The dogs out before him, ranging easy in the pasture dark. He went down the hill.

Another afternoon he lifted out the backseat of the Chrysler and removed the L.C. Smith from its case, ran a rag with a fine smear of oil over the gun and put a handful of shotshells in his coat pocket. He hiked up the woodsroad through the old sugarbush and began to climb up through the mixed hardwood and evergreen draws, the dogs both out before him now, serious, quartering back and forth the ground before him, tails working, heads out like drawn bows. Time to time he could hear one or the other pulling air in great snorting bursts, eating scent off the air like food. As the cover thickened they began to bust birds. He waited until Lovey locked up a bird and Glow slammed up behind her mother, honoring the point. He spoke a soft warning to both dogs, stepping past them. The partridge went up, a sudden burst of speckled animation that hit a long going-away glide down the mountain and he passed the splendid moment where his mind left him and was all out ahead of him, pinned down only on the flying bird as the gun came up. Then there was a pinwheel of feathers and both dogs broke past him and he was back. He knelt and took the partridge from Lovey's mouth gentle as lifting an egg. He spread the tail: a young cock. He held it between both hands for Glow to bury her nose in the feathers. Only for a moment. Then stood, reaching behind him to put the bird in the pouch on the back of his coat. For a few feet Glow stayed behind him, bounding to bounce her nose against the bulge in the coat. He said nothing, just walked on. Lovey already back out hunting. Soon enough Glow went after her.

He came down off the mountain in a pale dusk under a sullen changed sky with three birds swelling the game pouch and a four-month-old puppy who thought she understood everything about the triangle formed of herself and the birds and the boy with the gun— the pup dancing back and forth in the sheep pasture, nosing the ledges, making half-assed points at mullein stalks or milkweed pods, stopping to gobble sheep pellets, her eyes rolling toward him.

Prudence was still in the barns. A pale shimmer of lantern light through those windows. In the kitchen he and Abby worked together at the soapstone sink, dressing and plucking the partridges. "Young birds," was all she said, an approval. Then sent him below the barns to the garden where by lantern light he cut the green leafy heads from young turnips. He came back and found the partridges cut into quarters, the pieces in a bowl of milk. Prudence was in from the barn then and the sisters worked together over the stove: Prudence whisking egg whites to peaks and slowly turning the whites into a bowl of cornmeal batter with the backside of a spoon, then dropping the batter onto baking sheets for the oven; Abby cooking cut-up Hubbard squash in a small amount of water at the side of the stove, the lumps of squash slowly softening and settling into a mass. She took the greens from him and rinsed them and chopped them fine and added them to boiling water. She cut a thick wedge from a side of bacon and minced the wedge to slivers and added those to the greens and covered the pot and moved it also to the side of the stove.

Foster sat at the table watching them, the broken-down shotgun over his lap as he cleaned and oiled it. Outside a wind had sprung while he was in the garden and now it was raining, water aslant driving hard against the side of the house. The dogs under the table, shivering with the smell of food.

Abby cut slabs from a brick of lard and melted them in a deep skillet. Prudence mixed flour in a bowl with dried herbs and spices shaken out of cans, adding and adjusting by bringing her nose close to smell the mixture. Foster watched them. He understood that his seat at the table, his dogs under the table, all of that was understood and accommodated within the pattern of their movements.

Abby turned and said, "Most times, we have this meal springtimes. When there's young roosters to spare. Then it's dandelions instead of the turnip greens. We never got in the habit of fall greens. The turnips are for the sheep, come winter. But it comes down from Mother. It's not a meal you'll have had before, I tell you that."

She turned back and lifted the quarters of partridge from the milk and dredged them in the flour and let them go into the hot grease. They sank popping and then came back to the surface, swimming with the heat as they cooked. When they were all in, she moved the pieces back and forth with a long-handled fork. Newspaper was laid out on the counter beside the range to drain the bird-parts on. Prudence opened the oven and lifted out the sheets with the high delicate corn puffs. Drained the water off the greens and added butter and cream to the squash. All this set before him. He rose and stood the shotgun in a corner and called the dogs out from the table into the woodshed. Then sat back down. The women seated, looking at him. Their faces bright, shining. He understood behind that love was a tremble, a quiver of expected rejection. And he was no longer sure of the night before him, not so sure he could announce himself. He took up a piece of partridge and his teeth broke through the hot savory crust and the sweet meat came off the bone clean into his mouth. He smiled at them. "Oh my," he said, "that's some good." And they got busy passing bowls around and he helped himself. They ate, all shy, not talking, eyes skittering away from the others. And he ate the lovely food with his heart hurting in his chest. All the way through the meal the two women throwing their eyes over him as if casting hopeful broken nets. All the time turning his eye to what he could not see, toward what he wanted to stand and walk to and study again: the oval portrait of his grandparents in the parlor.

Supper was over and cleaned up and he'd taken the dogs out, running bent over through the rain to the barns to lead them down to the sheep-fold and their bed and then back to the house where he stripped off his soaked coat and hung it on the back of a chair near the range to dry. The women were in the parlor. He stood over the sink and drank two glassfuls of water, then passed through the door into the hall and down to join them.

They'd laid a fire in the stove against the wet and he stood by the mantel for a moment with his fingertips resting up there as if he were warming himself as he studied again the man and woman in the portrait. And he believed now he understood the arch of their gazes; what he wanted to find was some fragment of the tender world they'd held between them. He turned to the room and held his hands together before him.

Abigail spoke. "Did you graduate your high school? Over there to the Whites?"

He'd been about to speak. He paused, knowing he was frowning a little in response. He put his hands in his pockets. "No, ma'am. I've a year to go."

Prudence said, "It's September already."

Abigail looked at her. As if reminding her of some agreement they'd made. Then she looked back at Foster. "You were a good student?"

"I guess I was. Got good grades."

"Well then. It's not too late. You'd catch up soon enough."

"Abby," he said. "I'll not go back there."

Prudence said, "No one was suggesting you return over there and live alone."

Abby looked at her sister. Prudence said, "I'm quiet."

"We agreed—"

"You'd talk. Why don't you go on then and do that. Me, I'm not saying a thing."

Abby held her gaze a little longer. Then to Foster: "Sister and I've talked this through. We don't offer this lightly. If you were to stay here, finish your high school in Randolph, then you'd be prepared to go on to college."

Gently he interrupted her. "The truth is, I've got most of my course work done. For a diploma. Mostly I'd be sitting killing time."

One side of her mouth tightened and relaxed. She smiled. "So you're a better student than you let on to be. There's nothing wrong with that. But still, it's too late for you to get into college for this year. So you might as well sit through that last year and get your diploma like everybody else. And perhaps spend some of that time thinking about where you want to go, what you want to do there. Now the university to Burlington's a good school, is what I hear. But it's only one of many. You could go anywhere you want. Down there even to Harvard College in Massachusetts. There's Dartmouth too, not so far away. Or anywhere at all. Anywhere you wanted. Off to California, you wanted."

"Well," he said. "I don't know. I hadn't thought about that."

And she heard his hesitation and went ahead. When she spoke he saw a triumph in her eyes, a fierce pride. "Mother knew the value of money. More than Father ever did. She knew that freedom is only a word without money. Freedom is assumptions but money is actuality. That was why she cared for it. Not for any everyday thing. Even though she was a woman could dress herself in style. But that was all going to town. Around here she was happy in wore-out old clothes. Barefoot frost to frost. It was two things she understood: that the only hope in this world was money. And education. You put those two together and the world opens up for you ways it will not, cannot, otherwise. The point is, there is money in the bank. Money and then some to send you to the best school you can or want to attend." She paused again and held up a hand as if foreseeing protest and said, "And it is not something you should feel is being given for free. A part of it is yours. A part of it always belonged to your father. The same way a part of this farm did, and so belongs to you. But you're no farm-boy. That's clear. Now, Sister and I live here and will until we die. But we've no great need for the money, not much of it anyhow. So. There is more than enough. For you to go ahead any way you want."

He was quiet a long time. Both women sat watching him. He reached up and stroked his nose with his thumb and bent back forefinger. He felt teary and would not cry and a part of him felt he was too close to tears too much of the time these days for it to be good for him. He wanted again nothing more than to be sitting in the house outside Bethlehem with his father, the two of them arguing in the amused not very serious way they always had over anything at all. He looked at the tall old beautiful-woman version of his father before him and said, "Pop was not broke. Besides the place over there he left to me, there was a pile of money. I've got money enough." And because he did not want them to doubt him, he said, "It's all rolled up in bundles in a shoebox outside right now. In the back end of the car."

"Don't you touch that money!" Abby's hands working together before her, over and around themselves. "Put it in a bank! Then, four—five years from now, you finish school, know what you want from yourself, you'll have something to start off with." She stopped and took her bottom lip between her teeth a moment and said, "Maybe then, that money'll do you some good. You'll see."

Foster felt his body swaying. He was hot by the stove but could not move. He looked down at the floor where the carpet ended and met the floorboards that ran under his feet. As if he could find purpose or reassurance there in the gap between what was covered and what lay under. Feeling the eyes behind his head blank out of the portrait. Wishing they would speak to him, those dead souls. But there was nothing but the blood booming in his own temples. Still looking down he said, "I can't."

There was no pause. "Can't what?"

So he looked up at them because he had to. His voice came from him broken and sad and soft. "I won't stay here. Not to finish school or go on to college. I guess someway I pretty much hate to tell you this but it's not what I need to do right now."

Prudence did not move but Abigail did. She sat back in her seat and crossed one leg up over the other, fluted fingers even as she moved plucking the fabric up and releasing it so the skirt of her dress settled over her crossed legs, all smooth. She rested her head against the back of her chair. "So just what," she asked, "do you propose to do?"

"Well, ma'am"—and he looked from one to the other before continuing—"I'm going to North Carolina. To Sweetboro. To see what I can learn."

Abby did not move. But Prudence leaned forward, her hands taking a hard hold of her knees. She cried out to him, "Oh, no. Why would you do that? Foster? Whatever for?"

He stood there rocking silent before them. Because there was nothing he could tell either one of them that they did not already know. And he knew they knew this.

After a time Abby stood and left the room, wordless. He stood listening to her going up the stairs to bed. When she was gone he looked at Prudence. She gazed at him until he turned to her. Then she turned her hands up on her knees and gathered her face into those hands and wept. Still he stood. Until he knew her tears were not short and were not for him alone.

It was still raining. He went to the barn and let loose his dogs and they went out together into the rain. He could not see them in the dark and could not hear them but knew they were beside him, close by. He went up the hillside in the dark to the burying ground where he stood hunched in the rain, not by any particular stone because now they were all his. He drank off the last of the whiskey from the bottle, his face upturned wet with the rain. The whiskey like nothing at all. From where he stood he could see nothing at all except from time to time the vague quick shapes of his dogs coming close. Below, a single pale lighted window. With the rain, it could have been a faint star.

Eight

"Whatever it is, I don't want any of it!" This from behind the dull shade of the screen door, far and close at once, as if the distance was not great but the traveling of it would be. The voice sincere, mocking of its own authority, as if calling out to someone not so much known or expected but as if there were no alternative. As if there could be no strangers. And then, in the deadstill end-of-September afternoon heat came the rising scuff of feet pressed forward, hard-working, accompanied by the metronomic offbeat pock of a cane. Through the screen, down the length of hall, a figure made its way up toward the door. Tall and lean, stooped toward his left side where that hand worked the cane for support.

Foster waited in the deep shade of the porch, sweating where he stood, the sleeves of his open-necked shirt rolled over his elbows. The car parked on the street under the live oaks, the small oval leaves dulled with a weight of rust-red dust. The car windows down for the dogs sleeping in the heat on the backseat. Three levels of ruined flower beds and rose arbors fell from the porch steps to the sidewalk. Even the cobbles of the brick walk were twisted up and uneven from the unchecked growth. Long spears of roses gone wild climbed above the clotted honeysuckle spread over the gardens. Here and there the dead spike of some flower or the rough foliage of a tuberous plant lifted out of the honeysuckle canopy in the way some memory of life otherwise gone remains more vivid than the present. Persistent in lone shorn beauty.

It had taken near two weeks to reach this place. In truth he was not sure of the day of the week. He had bought a paraffin-treated canvas pitchtent before leaving Randolph and from there had traveled west in New York State before turning south and so had driven down through the country inland from the seaboard and the cities there but had stayed out in the sparse broken-up land of small farms and woods along the eastern foothills of the eastern mountains, camping overnight and sometimes more than one night where he could find a place to, where the farmers did not care but to warn him of fire, or in the broad upsweeping reaches of woods where there were no farmers or anyone else to ask permission for the land. In the middle of Virginia he'd turned east, away from the mountains and fall and back into summer.

The night before, after a long day on roads that were broader than the mountain roads but also ankle deep in red dust that boiled around the car as he went, on either side of the road long fields stretched out either side and he saw crews of people working in those fields, bent among crops he did not know—the soft dull droop of midday tobacco and the green stippled heavy-as-if-with-snow spread of cotton—at the end of that day he'd stopped in the town of South Hill and rented a room in the railroad hotel and ate a hot meal in the dining room and bathed in a rusted tub. And was up before dawn to walk his dogs in the moist shrouded light that even at that hour was mild, not even cool. And without food from the hotel he drove on. Crossing into North Carolina as the sun hefted itself beyond his left shoulder, a red ball huge in the pale mist that hung between earth and air as if it were a final hope of the night. Then he went down a long gentle swoop of road and up again and the sun was out, no red ball but a blaze of heat coming through his open window. And he could smell the earth then, hot and sweet and fetid. He passed wagons piled with long burlap sacks stuffed full. Other wagons with the tender cradled layers of leaf tobacco. The wagons drawn by mules. Sorrel mules. Some the color of burnt wet wood. He'd never seen a mule before. All driven by Negro men in rough clothes who would not look at him as he drove around them. After he passed each load he'd lift his left hand up above the roof of the Chrysler in greeting and then watch his rearview but no man responded and after a time he just drove. He was hot. He could hear the dogs panting in the backseat even with the windows all the way down. That air churned, gritted with dust. Fouling his mouth and nose. He considered New Hampshire. A man at work there roadside would not pause to greet some passing stranger. So it was. Still, in the gangs working the fields there were children as well as men and women and some of those children close by the road would raise faces in fast dark flashes to stare at the car and he wondered what they saw passing them by, if he was some dream or some other vision altogether unobtainable.

He crossed over a river and then some miles later crossed it again, still driving south and east. The river a deep low dark sullen thing, with none of the bright flash and quick sparkle of the rivers he knew; this one cased between banks of low-hanging trees, its color not out of the air or reflected sky but as if sprung up from the earth, moistened by the wealth of foliage overhanging it. The water oily, without obvious movement. A deceptive stillness.

Tracts of pine woods. Small rises of land capped with hardwoods. Crabbed patches of cotton broken out between the woods. Other fields, larger and more level, of tobacco. Cattle pastures with burned-yellow grass, the cattle bunched up in the shade of a single huge-spread red oak. No barns that he could see but sheds of weathered wood everywhere, high and square and small on rough raised stone foundations. Some just standing on piled stones under each of the four corners. Some chinked tight with the gauzy air of heat over them and the faint tang of woodsmoke where tobacco cured. These sheds always with a colored man close by, lounging on a chunk of firewood or bent down some feet from the building, tending a low fire.

The land was not flat but seemed so. The sun high and spread overhead, the horizons far off. But as the road turned and moved over the land the land also moved, revealing itself to be pockets and small open spreads of space. Briefly it would flatten and the fields would grow larger but there was always a backing flank of woodlot, a stretch of pines, something to crease or fold the land. As he drove on he realized what that thing was: the river, which all the land aimed toward.

He dropped down and followed the river itself for some miles, passing under a railroad trestle, a tower of creosote-blackened crisscrossed matchstick high over him, and then the road graded up and he passed a metal sign, black letters on white for the Sweetboro city limits, and went on some distance and then came into the town itself. Along a residential street he dropped down in second gear and traveled slowly, the houses set back from the road, smaller than he'd expected but surrounded by land and flanked by trees he did not know. Then into the three-block downtown, mostly brick but some wooden buildings, three and four stories tall. It was very quiet, very small.

He parked in thin shade and found a lunch counter in a drugstore and drank a bottle of soda pop and ate a grilled cheese sandwich and drank another bottle of the pop. Only one other man seated at the counter, reading a newspaper, glanced at Foster once with frank open curiosity and then went back to his paper. The counterman a lank man with a purple birthmark over one side of his face like a burn. Foster paid his bill and left a dime on the counter and stepped into the telephone booth at the far end of the counter and folded shut the door after him and sat with the phone book. It was easier than he thought. Only one Mebane. Alexander: 61 North Main. Telephone 8459. He shut the book and put it back on the shelf.

He drove back out of town the way he had come in and spotted the house and kept on going. He drove as far as the railroad trestle and pulled off underneath where the ground was packed dark and bare. There was a ring of fire-blackened stones and bits of trash: empty soda bottles and pieces of cork painted red for fishing bobbers and tangles of fishing line and several flat-sided pint liquor bottles. He let the dogs out and they went down to the river and drank, wading in up to their bellies. He called Glow back when she started to swim out. He did not like water he couldn't see into. When the dogs had cooled themselves he put them in the car and without letting himself think about it turned around and drove back into town and parked under shade just down from the house he'd spied out.

"Someone has misled you. You have the wrong house." The old man stood with his bad arm leaning against the screen door to open it partway. His cane-tip poked out through the opening as a weapon. With his stoop as tall as Foster, in tan trousers and a white shirt, the sleeve of his missing arm folded up square and pinned under the elbow. The pin a little crooked as if done quickly, with long practice. Thin hair ragged over the dome of his skull. He added, "I can't help you. I don't know any woman name of Lee. There's no Lees around here that I know of. No family, that is. Now, there's plenty of boys called Lee. I wouldn't know them all. And there might even be a girl called that. It's a popular name. But I don't know of any. I can tell you this though. Whatever girl you're chasing is not here, not at this house. Someone has misled you."

Foster studied him. The old man was dry and cool in the heat of the day. The hand gripping the cane handle shook slightly with the effort of keeping the tip free for any sudden use. His eyes were wide with a taint of wildness to them, square upon Foster. Those eyes someway at odds with the speech just delivered. His lips were dry, cracked open over broad age-stained teeth. The teeth with gaps between them where the gums had shrunk back.

Foster looked down at the warped porch boards, then back to the old man. He said, "She thought you were dead. She thought she killed you. Brained you with a flatiron, was what she did. I'd guess that little ridge up over your ear there is what's left of that try. Her name was Leah. Not Lee."

The man said nothing. Rocking back and forth slightly. Then settled the cane tip and stepped squarely into the door. Not out of the house but with the door pushed open so he stood in it. Resting the cane before him with his one palm flat on the curved handle. Fresh-shaved, the scent of bay rum.

"Tell me your name again."

"Foster Pelham, sir."

"How old are you Foster Pelham?"

"I'm sixteen."

"And where is it you're from?"

"New Hampshire. Is where I grew up. But I just came down from Vermont."

"Is that right?"

"Yes sir."

"Well, how come, Foster Pelham? Leaving aside the question of this woman you're looking for, asking after, how come now? You, sixteen years old, chasing off across the country. How'd you get here?"

"I drove."

Alexander Mebane leaned forward a little and peered out onto the street and spied the Chrysler and looked back at Foster. "That's your automobile out there?"

"Yes sir. It was my father's."

"It was your father's. He's not with you?"

"I'm alone. My father's dead. That's how—I never knew his family. After he died I found two sisters over to Vermont. And it was them told me about things."

"What things would that have been?"

"That my grandmother was a Negro woman. From here. That her name was Leah and that the people who owned her were called Mebane. That she ran away from here at the tail end of the war. And that something happened and she hurt one of them, left him hurt, her thinking that person was dead. Somebody she called Lex."

"And you think that might be me."

"Yes sir, I'm thinking maybe it was. Said you were a one-armed man."

"Did they? It's what they call a distinguishing characteristic, isn't it? I was a boy when I lost it so I can't hardly recall what it was like to have both. Most days I don't even think about it. You're not a boy that takes things for granted, though, are you, Foster Pelham?"

"No sir. I never had the chance to do that."

"Still, you chased off halfway down the country after something what might have happened almost sixty-five years ago. Why'd you do that? What is it you think you might find? Other than a single old one-armed man?"

"She came back here. Came back down twenty-five years after she left. Came back to try and find the mother she'd left behind. Or find out what happened to her. It would've been September of 1890."

"That was still a long time ago."

"I think she saw you that time. When she came back."

"What in the world makes you think a thing like that? You think I keep track of every vagrant Negro that passes through this town? Why boy, on any given day they come and go at numbers I couldn't even guess at. If I wanted to. And why would I want to?"

"She was your sister. Your half sister."

Those old eyes slid over Foster, crackling bright, sly and flared at once. "My sister. Is that right? You're telling me that my daddy, that he laid down with a Negro woman? That he not only laid down with one but had get? My daddy? My old daddy dead these long years and not here to deny or laugh at such a tale. That's what you come all this way to tell me? That a man had a colored woman in his own house and that he screwed her? Why boy, get in that car of yours and drive around. Every two–three pitchblack faces you see you'll see at least one watered-down coffee-colored Negro. What you think made them that way? Laundry bleach? They're not related to anyone but their ownselves, their own kind. Black has all tones, low and high, but there is only one white and make no mistake about that."

"What about me?"

"What about you?"

"What am I?"

"A Yankee is what you sound like. Other than that, right watered down, I'd say. But listen here."

"What?"

"Who knows where you are?"

"Nobody. My aunts, I guess. My father's sisters."

The old man nodded as if making a point. "And where is it you plan to stay?"

"I don't know. There's a hotel I guess."

Mebane nodded. "All I have to do is step back inside and make a telephone call and you wouldn't have a place to stay. All I'd have to say is you're a colored trying to pass as white and you wouldn't have a room. Or, I make one other call and there's the law to escort you out of town while they offer up a little lecture about disturbing the peace. You following me all the way through this?"

"I guess I am."

"It's a problem though. If you were to go over into Fishtown where all the coloreds live, there wouldn't be a one would want to talk to you. You wouldn't find a place to stay over there either. In fact, you poked around enough, made enough people nervous, they'd do you as fine as our sheriff's men would. Maybe finer. I don't know what it is about Negroes but they like a knife. Maybe because it doesn't make any noise. Not like a pistol which would tend to draw attention. But those people, all they'd see is a strange white boy who talks funny and is poking his nose in their business. And it wouldn't even be you so much they fear as what you might bring with you, what might be traveling behind you, what you might not even know you'd be bringing with you. Because life over there works in different ways than you've ever seen life work.

And so you wouldn't even know who was watching you and what they might think about you. But those people, those colored people, they'd know."

Foster put his hands in his pockets. "When she came down here in 1890 she didn't stay very long. Went right back home—where she wouldn't talk about what happened, what she learned. But it was something bad. Because they heard her talking to herself about it. When she thought there wasn't anybody around. Then one day in November of that year she hanged herself."

For the first time Alexander Mebane looked away from him. Down through the porch railings into the long shade of afternoon over the ruined gardens, his eyes glazing there as if seeking something, his thin lips working, silent. His hand wrapped around the cane handle. He lifted the cane and thumped the tip hard twice against the porch boards. Then he looked back at Foster.

"Tell me one thing about yourself, Foster Pelham."

"What's that?"

"As a man, are you practical? Or romantic? By nature."

"I don't know. I don't know what difference you'd make between them."

"Well now. A practical man would be thinking he might get something out of all this. Might find a way to turn it to his advantage. A romantic man, on the other hand, he wouldn't care. He'd already know what he wanted out of it. His blood would be up. He'd already have featured it all out and would go along so it fit his plans. Some kind of revenge, some kind of reckoning."

"I don't think I'm either one."

"What is it then you want?"

Now Foster looked away. At the hot car where his dogs waited. Back at the old fierce man with the cane. "I just want to know what happened is all. That's all I'm after."

"I see. A poet."

"No sir. I'm just after the truth."

Alexander Mebane smiled at him then. He twisted the cane handle in his hand and the cane rose up in an elaborate loop, then back down. Foster did not smile back; there was a tremble in him that he was breathing over. Mebane lost his smile and ran his eyes up and down over Foster. The way a woman would. Or someone seeking some own lost self. Then he kicked the screen door back and stepped out to hold it open. He said, "Pawn captures bishop. I can't stand like this. Come inside."

Foster behind him, Alexander Mebane turned off the hall into what had once been a dining room, the table still there and the sideboards and the chairs lined against the wall but also bookcases built in between the sideboards and a pair of castered spring-backed captain's chairs pulled up to the table which was covered but for a small bare space with stacks of books and magazines and newspapers; also a green blotter on a leather pad and a stack of ledgers. The bare space held a linen place mat and a blackened silver napkin ring with a piece of dirty fabric stuffed through it. The mat and the smudged surface of the table littered with crumbs of food.

Mebane said, "There's no peace in this life is what it is. It's why we stretch out our hands toward heaven. But all the same, a man can't stop. Well now that's not right—plenty do. But it's not those ones we're concerned with here, is it Foster Pelham? It's the rest of you, that keep always hauling your way ahead, thinking if you get one more thing, one more bit of understanding, one more question answered, one more confusion cleared up, then maybe you'll get it here on earth—that peace, I mean."

And he turned sudden, quick, spinning the cane tip before him. Foster was close behind him to follow what he was saying. He stopped short, stepping back. Mebane smiled again at him, used the cane tip to prod back one of the rolling chairs and sank into it. He pointed the cane at the other chair. "Sit," he said.

The walls an ancient faded mustard with the teardrops of waterstains. A persian carpet worn down to a heavy corduroy crisscross of threads lay over wide heart-pine plank flooring. Thick drapes the color of moss pulled partway back to let in some light of the afternoon, the windows behind them shut tight, the glass discolored. A crane-necked electric lamp was lit on the table. The air in the room unmoving, smothered with so many layers of odor over so many years that it had become its own thing—soft not sour, near fragrant.

As if seeing the room as Foster would Alexander Mebane said, "For years and years I had a woman in every day but Sunday to cook and clean. Then one evening I was eating the dinner she'd laid out for me and her in the kitchen waiting for me to finish so she could clean up after me and I stopped eating, put my fork right down and got up and went into the kitchen and I asked her, 'Millie do you need this job?' She looked right at me and told me someone had to look after me. I told her it wasn't so. That I wasn't about to starve to death and the rest of it could fall down around me for all I cared but it seemed ignorant to be sitting in there at more dinner than I'd eat in three days while a woman ten years older than I sat waiting in the kitchen. She sat there looking at me while I said all that, not agreeing but not looking away either. So I asked her again if she needed the job. If she needed the money. And she told me she didn't. Since then I've done on my own, looked after myself. It may look poor and sad to you as it does to some others but I'm happy with it."

"Wouldn't she already have quit," Foster said, "if she didn't need the job?"

"The money you mean."

"Yes, sir."

"No, I don't believe so. Some people would have. But with her it was something else also. More than habit or pride too. Some part of her had come to know herself as the woman who worked for me. Of course she took the money home with her, spent some part of it too I'd guess. Most everybody needs more money than what they have. But that wasn't the point that night in the kitchen and she knew it too. All I was asking was did she want her time all for herself. And she did. I sent an envelope of cash over there every year at Christmas until she died three years ago but that isn't the point. It wasn't for me and it wasn't for her. And we both knew that."

Foster sat with his hands folded together in his lap. "You're saying she felt bound to you someway and you set her loose from that."

"See now, you're making a leap all the way from one end to the other. It's true that if I hadn't done that she'd most surely kept on working for me until she died or grew too sick to work. But all I can tell you is she realized I'd had enough. What she said that night when the dishes were done and she had on her coat and shawl for the walk home, was,

'You get sick of it, don't call on me.' She'd seen the mess a man can make sinking into his own self. Which is what I wanted and intended and she knew it. So don't confuse that with either meanness or bigheartedness on my part. It wasn't neither one."

"I don't know why you're telling me all this," Foster said. "Unless it's part of some complicated excuse for something else you've got to tell me."

Mebane looked at him, his old-man's mouth a dry purse. The amusement in his eyes dry also. He said, as if trying it out or as if it might even be humorous, "A man is the sum of his parts."

"Maybe," said Foster. "I don't know. Seems to me though, the last one who could do that sum would be the one involved."

"Who else? Who else would know?"

"I don't know. The ones around you maybe."

"No. Because every man is at least two men. One of those known only to himself."

"Maybe."

"Listen: The same time as Millie I had a yardboy. Great big man over six feet but he could work his way weeding through a flower bed as if he floated over it. Now, he was a young man, in his thirties. With a wife and family. So it was very much the money to him. Good lord, Fred Fox, hands on him like a set of hams and black as Piney Woods pitch. And he stood pleading with me when I let him go. But all that first season, an evening or two a week he'd come by and work on the flowers out front. Push the little lawn mower out back. Trying to keep things up, keep them right. Because he knew that was how they were supposed to be. I'd go out and tell him, 'Fred, if you keep working here then I have to keep paying you and I don't want to keep paying you so you have to stop working here.' He'd tell me he didn't want the money, just keeping things up. I told him I didn't want things kept up. Finally I warned him I'd call the police and have him picked up for a trespass. He just stood looking at me, brushed the dirt off his hands onto the front of his pants and told me have a good evening. That was the end of that."

"So letting those people worked for you go, that was just some way of making a change for yourself. Is that it?"

"Maybe." Alexander Mebane grinned at him, the same sly grin as earlier on the porch. "Maybe I was just running out of money."

"I told you I wasn't after anything like that."

"They's not any Mebanes left to speak of," the old man went on as if answering a question. "Now you get down around Wilmington, below on the Cape Fear, there's plenty of second and third cousins three and four times removed that have the name but they're nothing to me. They'd be as much a stranger if one walked in the door as you are. I haven't been down there since I was a boy, since before the war, and don't expect or want to go back there, not in this lifetime. My one brother was killed at Petersburg and both my sisters are dead too; one went to Raleigh and married there and raised up a boy and three girls but not one of them's a Mebane by name or nature and the other sister stayed right here and married a farmer called Pettigrew and there's children from that and children of those children but except for the one crazy one I don't see much of them either. It's a drifting falling-apart end of the line is what it is, here. My daddy somehow picked this little plot of nowhere to hang his shingle and drag along my mother who was from Raleigh and thought she was getting better than what she got. He snuggled in tight with the government during the war and was doing fine for himself but he was a man couldn't see around a corner that wasn't even there. When Lee quit and then Johnston my daddy had near ever cent of his money tied up in Jeff Davis bonds that went from being a wild hope to something you could light a cigar with if you was fortunate enough to afford a cigar which he was less and less able to do. After the war, men—and men with less connections and ability than my daddy—they had to make themselves all over again. When the Yankees and coloreds was running things just after the war he threw his luck in with what was left of the old ways and it went against him and then when the Yankees pulled out and left us to sort things out ourselves he made a stab at sidling up to the Negroes but by then it had all shifted around and his old cronies were on the rise again, except they'd watched him spin and they left him right out there. Dangling. Where he'd got himself. It wasn't anything he didn't deserve but it was hard on my mother. There was her house in Raleigh and this place here and that was pretty much it. After she died it took everything I could do to hold on to this place, settling old debts and such. There was more than one banker who looked the other way on her account. Out of pity for her, out of contempt for my daddy. Who of course in his sensible selfish way managed to die a good ten years before her. There was still a cigarbox of those old useless bonds in his desk we found after the funeral. But that was about it.

"Not that I've done much better. I read a little law too and did my best, as a young man. But my heart was never in it. The law is an ideal superseded by a structure. I just have never been much of one for finding my way around a structure. No sir, I was not much of a hand at being a lawyer. I was the one always taking on the cases without a prayer or a dime, those I couldn't win. Especially of course those are the ones can't be won. It doesn't matter if they should be or not. The law is not about should-be's. I counted up my pennies and spent two years writing letters pursuing a war pension. I had the luck to have an arm gone and even more luck that there was a hospital record someone finally found in Virginia and so after those two years I got that pension. Which I can't tell you in all honesty arm or no arm that I deserve. But money comes each month out of Washington D.C. and I take a small pleasure in that. As if it's some balance against my dead brother. Or it could even be nothing more than plain old everyday greed. Getting what I can get. I truly don't care, either way. But there. Just so you know. In case you were sitting up there in New Hampshire with dreams of some fine plantation, some life waiting for you. All it is, is a old bitter man in a falling-down house."

"I told you. All I want's to find out what happened here."

Alexander Mebane leaned forward, the mechanism of the captain's chair crying for oil. "What's the matter with you," he asked. "Don't you have any imagination?"

"No sir. Not the way you're thinking. All I know is, back behind my own father, and his two sisters, what happened in their lives all comes someway out of what happened to their mother. And nobody knows what that was. At least not much about it. Because it happened here. Not there."

"What kind of man was your grandfather?"

"I did not know him. My father left there young and never went back. I don't know if there was a problem with him and his father; I don't think so. I think his problem was his mother hanging herself. He was just a little boy. His sisters, my aunts, they admired their father. What I can tell, he was a good man. I know he loved my grandmother something fierce."

"Did he?"

"Yes sir, he did."

"There you go." Alexander Mebane paused and looked away from Foster. After a time looked back. "I remember your grandmother."

"Yes sir."

"Both from when she went away the first time and the time you mentioned. When she came back but did not stay."

Foster sat quiet. Mebane studied him, the thin eyebrows almost invisible above his large eyes, eyes set out in the tight shining skin of his head. The room was grown hot as the quickened early autumn westering sun slid down the outside of the house beyond the filmed windows. Pale bars, unsteady, aqueous, slid over the threadbare carpet, a deep glow on the old heartpine planks. Foster was tired, hot, his eyes and throat sore. He watched the old man across from him as if watching some new species rise up before him. Attractive and repulsive at once, a dense and self-laid pattern of traps, some set, some perhaps already sprung. Thinking this, he took his eyes away from the old man. He wondered what was in the stack of ledgers, the pens laid out in a stand, the ink capped tight. As if they were the only valued things in the room.

Mebane gripped his cane in a sharp sudden gesture and came upright, the chair rolling back some inches as he stood. As if the man and two objects were conducting practiced ritual. "Come follow me," he said and did not wait but crossed the room not to the hall but to a single door with no handle but a brass plate turned black against the heavy old wood. With Foster behind him Mebane turned his shoulder against the door to nudge it open and it floated back on old hinges and stuck open and Foster passed through and saw the door would open in either direction where the spring-loaded hinges would hold it open for a moment before it would slip silently shut again. They were in the kitchen. The door so people could go silent from the kitchen into the dining room and back into the kitchen again, leaving behind plates and bowls of food and then be gone.

They went through the kitchen. A big double-oven range, its cold top heavy with dust and stacked up with utensils and baskets and iron cookware and other objects. There was a square thick-planked table in the center of the room. This table was empty, discolored in places, scarred. On a counter by a sink was a small steel portable cooker with a pair of electric coils. The drainboard by the sink held a single glass, a single plate. An electric toaster was also on the counter circled by crumbs of darkened bread.

They went through an outside door and down short steps into the backyard. Ahead to the left was a square-timbered mud-chinked one-story building with a rock chimney at one end and a single window offset from the door let into the center of the building. There were no steps up but a single flat stone before the shut door. The building was raised on foundation ranks of stones at the corners. The other end of the yard stood a small two-story barn. The yard was flat here, not terraced like the front. A small garden patch with burned-out vegetables grown up with weeds. A rotting plank fence enclosed the yard, the fence overgrown with honeysuckle. As if the woven vines held the punked planks in place.

The sun a watery red egg huge in dull haze coming through the live oaks beyond the yard.

Mebane strode through the spindle grass, sweeping the cane before him, the stalks cracking as the cane-tip smote them. His gait rocking and steady at once. As if he moved in gravity unlike other men. Foster followed him up to the low cabin, the whitewash peeling off the timbers in curls and blisters. Mebane stopped before the door and lifted his cane and brought it down upon the door, right above where a hole was cut through the door, the hole worn into a teardrop from years of working a leather latchstring. The string was gone. Mebane prodded with the cane and the door swung in.

"Right here is where she was born: your grandmother. Right here is where she lived until she was sixteen years old. With her mother and another old colored woman. The three of them stuffed inside of here. Summer days it must've been a little on the close side. You think about it. My daddy coming out here time to time after his pleasure. Nights I'd guess. Summer nights. Hot and rank in these nigger cabins. It makes you think. He must've someway liked the smell. Can you imagine that?"

Foster off to one side, the old man turned at the waist to glare at him. His eyebrows working, a writhe on his forehead. His mouth twitching, some disgust fighting a smile. As a mock at his words, the situation laid out before them. Or only a pleasant hatred, extruded slowly as if long awaited. Foster did not know. The sunlight spread down the side of the whitewashed walls; the open door was a bare oblong of dark.

Foster said, "Can I go inside?"

Mebane took his cane-tip away from the stone below the door. Stepped back, rocking unsteady in retreat. As if what he could not see left him without balance. "Go ahead," he said. "Help yourself. The ancestral home."

The cabin was dark inside, empty, the air dull, smelling of mice and little else. The inside walls were not whitewashed but the timbers were dark with soot and old lives. The fireplace small, swept clean. The pale rectangles of a snakeskin on the rough stone hearth. A rough plank platform built into one corner, what had once been a bed. That was all. He stepped up to the fireplace and stood looking at the old rough-laid stones, the crumbling clay mortar. There was fire-stain and soot on the chimney stones above the fireplace. He stood like that, trying to close off the summer day and his own fatigue and the old man wavering outside, stood to allow the lives fallow in the old walls come out, to announce themselves if they would.

"She had that pretty bred-down skin like new saddle leather and the same green eyes as my daddy had," the old man called. Foster turned and standing back in the shadow looked out at him. "But what you haven't asked, is how her own mother looked. What she came out of. Where you've failed, boy, is thinking back far enough. There is no simple answer otherwise."

Foster came to the door and looked down at Mebane. The old man standing now with his feet apart, the cane planted between them. His head tilted back to look at Foster.

Foster said, "What happened to her?"

"Who?"

"Her mother. After my grandmother left here. After the war was over. What happened to her mother?"

"I don't know."

"You don't know?"

"She left here is all I know."

"Then what were you talking about?"

"Before. I was talking about before. Before any of what you even have thought of."

Foster ran his hand over his face. He said, "I tell you what, Mr. Alexander Mebane. All this is too much for me. I'm beat to pieces from the road. You're talking riddles around me. I got two dogs in the car likely near dead from the heat. I need to get them some water and find them a place to run. Then I need to get a place to stay and sleep. Think about all this some. All this is brand new to me and I'm trying to sort it out as I go along. You been sitting here sixty-some years waiting for someone to tell all this to. And I'm the one to do it to I guess. But right now, I'm about dead."

Mebane looked at him. There was no disappointment in the look. He said, "Pret much everbody calls me Lex. Or Mister Lex."

Foster nodded. "I'll call you whatever you want. I just need to take care of myself now. Maybe I can see you tomorrow."

"What sort of dogs are they?"

"Sir?"

"Your dogs."

"Bird dogs. English setters."

"Is that so?"

"Yuht. A mother and daughter. Good dogs. The one solid and the other started on partridge and woodcock. I thought, long as I'm coming down here, maybe I can find them some quail to work. Give them something new."

From the trunk of the car he lifted a tin can of water and poured out what was left into a lard pail and let the dogs out to drink. The lard pail was half full when they started and they might have wanted more but they left a half inch of water sudsy with drool that neither dog would take. They did not want to get back in the car but he coaxed them up onto the backseat. They drove out of town into the country, under the railroad trestle and then turning where Alexander Mebane told him to, onto a narrow road, a wash of red clay dust rising around them, Mebane sitting up square and straight talking as they went.

"My brother Spencer and I hunted birds all out through here when I was a boy. Little boy too because that was before the war. In most ways my childhood stopped when I was twelve and the war came and Spence went off. At least it seemed like it stopped, like it was something just hanging there waiting for when he'd come back. There would be those short sweet times when he'd get a leave and be home a week or two and we'd try and pick things up but it was all changed and we both knew it. So what I have are those sweet sweet memories of the two of us, Spence old enough to be good at what he was doing and so serious about it and because he was that way I tried to be too. We didn't have a dog because my mother wouldn't have a dog around the place on account of the fleas and ticks but some one or another of the boys Spencer hunted with always had a dog. Mostly big old hammerheaded pointers is what I recall. It's mostly still what you see around here. They's some setters but not many. They can't stand up to the heat as well as the pointers plus they get all wrapped up with burrs and thorns and such like that. But oh yes those fine days. Seems like most fine memories come out of dawn or evening, I don't know if that's just me or not. But some way even cleaner than the moment right in front of me I can see old Spencer in a stand of big pines with a covey of quail going off before him and what I recall is how he always took a little pause as the birds went up to watch them before he'd single out the one he wanted and then that gun would come up and go off at the same time like he wasn't even thinking about it."

"Yes," said Foster. "That's how it works."

"I was never that good at it. I was all right and if I'd kept on I probably would've gotten better. Although there were men, still a few here and there, lost arms like I did but kept on in the woods and fields like I did not and learned how to shoot one-handed. Always got their deer. Some birds. But it was not like that for me. I lost all taste for it. Wasn't the war so much because the truth is I didn't see much of that business. I can't even say it was some kind of grieving for my brother although if he'd made it back we would likely have picked up where we'd left off— but it wasn't just him either. It was both those things and more than that. Some men are on a clear course from day one; others make themselves as they go. Then there are those few others who drift along. In the world but just barely. Who kind of nudge their way."

"Where're we going here?" Foster said.

"Why, along a bit, just along a little bit. This is all Pettigrews' anyhow. My sister's boys' land. See that there, that stand of pine, it used to be real good in there when it was young but grown up like it is and choked out a man and dog couldn't hardly get through it. They get around to logging it out and it'll be some kind of good again though. Those birds they love that new young growth. There now, there's the house. No, no, don't pull in there, we don't need to see those people. Just go on. It's not far, the place I've got in mind. It's a cornfield and a beanfield with a little bottom between them, little creek there in the bottom. This time of day, that's where you'll find the birds."

The house they passed was set up away from the road under a pair of red oaks with low sheds and barns scattered around it. The house two stories four-square with a deep porch the length of the front, a stamped tin roof painted silver. An older hard-used Ford up under one of the trees. Fields of tobacco spread out either side of the farmyard with a scrub pasture running down to the road. All under the thin pale red-hazed sunlight, the land a muted charcoal with the light over it.

They went on past more fields either side of the road broken by pieces of woodlot; some hardwood bottoms and others pine plantations on the rising land between the fields. They went through a crossroads with a handful of unpainted rough houses with pumps in the bare dirt yards and dull-colored laundry on lines, dust rising up from the passing car to settle down over the clothes. A meager store with cracked yellow blinds pulled against sun. Opposite the store was a one-story-long building not much different from the shack houses but for its coat of white paint and the bright blue painted door set in the center of the front. From the peak rose a simple small cross of painted two-by-four. A handpainted sign: MOUNT OLIVE METHODIST EPISCOPAL CHURCH. Negro children stopped play to watch the car pass. A man in overalls stood at the roadside, watching the children until the car was past, and then turned to watch until it was gone from sight.

"What's that called?"

"What?"

"That place we just went through."

Mebane glanced over at him. Looked back ahead. Straight into the spreading diffuse sun. "Crossroads. Pettigrew Crossroads."

"What I could see. They all are colored."

Mebane shrugged, a small gesture of head and one shoulder. "It's all Pettigrews."

They went off the road over a culvert into the head of a beanfield and parked there, the rows of beans stretching down the fall of land before them, the hedges of the beanplants stricken with the light and the rows between dark shadow. What was left of the sunlight came filtered through the poplars and locusts and sweetgum growing up along the bottom. Foster took the silver whistle from the glove box and let the dogs out and the three of them went down through the beanfield, leaving Alexander Mebane sitting up in the car. The dogs raced quickly, leaping the rows of beans and then calmed and began to quarter, their heads up high in the still air for any feather of scent riding along there. Foster walked slow, his legs sore from the long sitting of the drive and the afternoon with the old man. He felt awkward and stiff, the man sitting up there watching him. He wished he'd saved some of the water for himself. He guessed whatever they'd find down in the bottom it would be no brook he'd want to dip water up from.

The dogs were working the beanfield now and he let them, although he guessed Mebane was right and the birds would be over at the edges or even down in the cover of the woods as dusk came on. Maybe even along the little creek down in there. But he wanted the dogs to learn something about where they were before they ran right into birds.

He did not like Mebane. And as he walked and loosened he understood it was at least part that he felt dependent where he had not expected or wanted to. And realized this was more than the vague threat the man had offered up to him earlier but was also some threat he felt from the place itself. As if he did not know exactly who he was or how to explain himself. In a place where clearly he would be expected to do so. And walking out then in that strange soft dusk that felt as if it rose right up out of the ground he felt lost, for the first time felt truly alone, missing everything he knew. He kicked his way through the rows of beans toward the trees with his throat and chest tight and he brought up the whistle and blew two short bleats and when the dogs turned, their heads popped up high over the beans as they arrested, he lifted his arm and signaled them down toward the woods and for a moment they both turned their heads to look where he directed and then they were gone, bounding over the rows to cut across in front of him and down into the woods and he loved them so.

The woodsfloor was strewn with thickets of berry canes and ropes of vines and twisted black-barked trees with spiked thorns and he made his way down to the bottom with the dogs around him, the white of their coats and their speed a flaring brightness in the ocher of the woods. Then he untangled himself from a last vine and stepped down a short bank and knelt by the small stream, the water unmoving but clear and he dipped up handfuls of it. It was warm and faintly brackish but tasted good, tasted of the place, and this simple thing, that he could find water to drink, made him feel better. As if he might be able to find his way around more than just the woods. He looked up then, still crouching by the water, and saw both dogs locked up with their tails flagged at the edge of the cornfield above him. He called out a low whoa to them and stepped up the bank and went through the last of the trees, learning how to part the brush with his shoulders and backside rather than his hands and came out behind the dogs and paused a moment. Both of them steady. Glow rolling her eyes back to try and see him, to urge him along. Her quivering. The sun over the cornfield was gone into beetroot haze. He stepped past the dogs into the low hummocks of grass that lay between them and the corn. The quail went up then, whistling and bursting into the air, coming up everywhere it seemed in a cluster and then breaking off into long gliding separate planes.

Glow broke and went off into the corn after the mass of birds. Foster too flushed to care, not wanting to call her back. Old Lovey still on point, waiting for him. Her whole body shivering. He went up to her and stood with her between his legs and bent down to run his hands along her sides.

They went out through the cornfield after the singles and Lovey found three and Glow one or perhaps others that she'd flushed but not pointed and Foster flushed one just walking by. They could have gone on from there but the dusk was fast and deep, the woods line already forming up into a solid thing. And he was aware of the old man sitting waiting up in the car. Who had brought them to this place, had given them this thing. And whom Foster would now understand he had no choice but to trust. Not greatly, not overmuch, but some little bit. So he walked the dogs along the edge of the cornfield to the road rather than fight back through the woods and stopped and waited in the dust where the stream ran under the road while the dogs went down to drink and then they went up the short hill where he could see the Chrysler sitting out among the beans. A shape up against the blueblack sky.

They rode back in silence but for Mebane giving directions. Still, Foster did not mind—he knew the old man had not run out of words and so knew the silence was for him, some small token. He decided he needed to pay attention to such things.

Coming into town Mebane spoke up. "What I was thinking was you should eat some dinner with me. There's not a place open to eat this time of day as it is. At least, no place you'd want to eat at."

Foster said, "I'm all right."

"No you're not. I know a hungry boy when I see one. And more than that, I think you should stay at the house as long as you're here. It's not like there's not room."

Foster had let the car slow way down. It was full dark, the windows still open, the air still warm. He said, "Well, sir. I appreciate it. But it'd be better, I think, I was to stay elsewhere."

Mebane had the cane planted on the floorboards, his hand capped over it. He twisted it a little bit but did not look over. "You're sixteen years old, is that right?"

"Yes sir."

Mebane nodded. "What you think, some boy like yourself he tries to get hisself a room? What you think those people going to do? With this great old fancy car? And that Yankee speech of yours. You think they're just going to leave you be? You think that?"

"I've got the money to pay. So far that's been enough."

"What about those dogs? You going to turn this car into a kennel?"

Foster let the car drift slow along the curb to a stop under the live oaks. Small electric streetlights at great distances threw poor pods of sifted light. He looked over at Mebane. Who was looking at him now. Foster said, "They're happy enough in the car."

Mebane said nothing.

The cicadas were up singing. There was no other place to go. After a time Foster said, "I'd be grateful for some supper. As far as spending the night, what I'd be comfortable with, is if me and the dogs were to stay out in that little cabin. Be out of your way."

"The slave cabin."

"Yes sir."

"We'd have to haul out a mattress for you. There's a feather tick or two could be spared. And you'd want a pillow."

"I don't need anything. There's a bedroll in the trunk of the car. And a pillow too. I camped my way down here."

Mebane nodded. "You'll need light. A lantern at least. Go on then, pull off from here. I'm about starved I don't know about you. What you want to do is go all the way past the house until there's a little opening off to the right, a little alley. You want to pull up there and that'll put us right behind the house. Now, that's a good place to park."

They sat squeezed by the stacks of papers and ledgers at the dining room table to eat a supper of tinned soup and saltines. Mebane had opened two cans of the soup and heated it in a rinsed pot on the electric coil of the hotplate and then just poured off a skim of soup into his own bowl and filled the one set out for Foster so that Foster had to use both hands and a slow stride to carry it without spilling in to where they would eat. A box of saltines under his arm. Mebane behind him, the cane hooked over his elbow as he carried his own bowl. Then they sat and ate. Tomato soup made with water because there was no milk but delicious. He made himself slow down for the last third so it would be enough. Mebane broke crackers into his bowl and stirred them and Foster waited a spoonful or two and then did the same. It was awful good.

Mebane said, "It's not much but it's what I have."

"It's just fine. It's good."

"I know how sad and thin most things are compared to what you expect them to be. I haven't answered the first question that you had. What answers I do have may not bring any satisfaction at all either. The thing is, what answers I have are my own. They're what you get. Anything beyond that, you'll have to look elsewhere."

Foster took up the last soaked cracker piece with his spoon and ate it. Put the spoon down in the empty bowl and looked at the old man. "I can tell you this. Time comes you're talking and I feel like you're holding back, I'll tell you."

Mebane said, "I guess you will. I guess most certainly you will."

He took the lighted lantern and tick mattress to the cabin and then went out to the car. He released the dogs and opened the trunk for the bedroll and blankets and his old withered valise. He went back across the dark yard into the cabin and set the lantern on the floor where it spread a small low pillage of light up the walls. He dumped his belongings on the sleeping platform and went to the open door where he could see the dogs, out roaming in the fenced yard, pale shades in the dark. There was an upstairs light on in the house and that was all. He wondered how the old man would sleep and wondered the same for himself. He turned back into the cabin and took the valise off the bed and spread out the bedroll and the blankets. And turned then to regard the snakeskin on the hearth. He only knew grass-snakes. This was bigger than he wanted to think about. He didn't want to pick it up, to touch it. He called the dogs in and shut the door. There was a latch, a bar on the inside to drop into a worn piece of angle-wood set into the timbered wall. He slid it to. The wood was dry and smooth under his fingers. He wondered if there had been nights it had been left off. Or how easily a penknife could slip in to lift it up.

The dogs circled the room, both inhaling deep at the snakeskin. They climbed onto the platform where he'd spread his bedroll and blankets. Where they could smell him. He undressed and folded his clothes over the valise parked beside the bed, a hand reach away. Then knelt naked to blow out the lantern. And when it was out wished he'd thought beforehand to check his pockets for matches. He had some. Somewhere. He felt along in the dark and got into the bedroll, pushing his feet and legs down past the crunched-in dogs who only shifted enough to let him in. Once in, he stretched and turned and the dogs turned with him.

"Hey. Hey!" The voice low, urgent, a whisper articulated into the night so it became a thing of the night itself. The words again repeated, calling out: "Hey in there. Hey!" A woman, a girl, the voice low in her throat but quick, breath filling the words, as if she spoke from some distance direct into his ear, as if she knew him and were calling him out as he turned waking, the dogs already alert, sitting up beside him, a low-throated growl rising from Lovey. Glow barked once and stopped when he placed his hand on her back. Then both dogs quiet. As if they did not know what to make of this new place. Foster sat up in the bedroll. The girl outside was rapping on the door as she called again, then rapping on the window, then back to the door. Silent he cursed himself for not having matches, for not knowing where they were, and writhed off the plank platform with the sleeping bag held up under his arms and hopped two-footed to the door. He leaned at the door, one hand sliding up the wall to find the wood latch. He didn't lift it but kept his hand there and bent his head close to the door and matched her own whisper.

"Who is it?"

"Who is it? You don't know who I am. I could tell you anything and it wouldn't make a difference to you. Open the damn door."

"What do you want?"

"Shoot. You going to play twenty questions or you going to open the door?"

He was silent, his hand on the latch. He felt he could feel her breathing, thought she must be leaned up against the door on the other side the same as he was.

"It's Daphne. There. Does that help?"

"I don't know any Daphne."

"Of course you don't. You don't know anything. But you opened the door, you'd know something. That'd be a start, don't you think?"

"I don't have any clothes on."

He heard her laughing. She said, "I don't recall asking you to get naked."

"I was asleep."

"Well, get dressed."

"It's dark in here. Do you have any matches?"

"To see you with?"

"So I can find my clothes."

"I'll tell you what," she said. "Why don't you open the door and for the two minutes it takes you to get dressed we can be grown up about it. How's that sound to you, Foster Pelham?"

He rubbed his hand over his face. Tried to scrub through his hair to flatten it down into a single piece. He could feel the silent dogs behind him. He said, "How'd you know my name?"

It was quiet a moment and then when her voice came back it was still low but for a moment all the humor was gone from it. "What do you think? I just fell out of the sky?"

"I drove by three or four times this evening and that big fancy car I'd never seen before was parked out front and then when I came by again and it was finally gone he was gone too and I didn't know what to think but it had caught my attention I can tell you that. So I rode around some more and went out to the house and had some supper and was on the porch and what did I see go by but that very car and I could see him setting up there beside you, him that never goes anywhere unless he's dragged and then not very far or for very long. So there wasn't anything for it but to come back over here and see what kind of business he was wrapped up in. I went up to the windows and watched the two of you eating one of his famous soup suppers, now that's something you don't want to get involved with more times than you have to, not if you value variety in your diet. Or meat. I've not yet seen that man eat a piece of meat. So I waited until he bundled you off out here to bed and let myself in and had a little talk with him. Uncle Lex, he can't keep much from me I tell you that right up front. To most folks he's a zipper-mouth but I can wheedle about anything out of him. I call him Uncle Lex but he's my great-uncle which I'm not about to call him because it would swell his head and seeing how he's already tilted off some little bit it would do neither one of us any good. He's a regular squirrel I tell you, the same as me. The only difference is he's a man and a old one too so people let him be instead of fussing after him like they do me, behind my back and to my face too, how I should be carted off I guess for a rest cure somewhere. Up to the mountains, to Asheville where there's sanitariums thick as ticks although I don't even like the sound of that word. Sanitarium. It sounds like I'm not clean enough. Or what they really want is to marry me off so I can get stuck out on some dirt farm somewhere and be as loopy as I want and only have a husband to inflict myself on but I don't want any of that either. The only husbands I've seen so far I'd probably have to do in with a axe, that's how tedious they seem to me, and the only other ones would probably take the same axe to me, which doesn't strike me as much fun either. There's boys that can be fun but they all turn into husbands sooner or later too. Not that I rule anything out. I can tell you this though, I'm not one of those brainless little girls who wants to run off to California and be in the pictures. There is some kind of evil in that notion, some pure evil is what I think. So what do you want to do?"

"Me? You're the one woke me up."

They were standing in the alley beside the Chrysler. As soon as he'd gotten dressed she'd taken him by the hand and led him silent out through the yard, her hand hot wrapped around his, he following her, still bare-footed, following the white of her sleeveless dress through the dark, her bare arms darker than the cloth, long slender sweeps of arm down from her shoulderblades, the collar of the dress low enough behind to show her nape below the bob of thick soft blond hair white in the moonlight. As soon as they went through the gate into the alley she dropped his hand as if all she wanted was to get him away from the house, beyond earshot of sleepless old men. Foster looked back. The upstairs light was out. His hand she'd held was moist and cooling in the night.

"You want to waste a perfectly good night, is that what you're telling me?"

"I'd thought I'd get some sleep is all. I been on the road some days."

"God, I could just stand here and listen to you. That funny accent."

"It's you that talks funny." Gawky and awkward immediately. She was not short but he felt himself a loose-limbed clamor just standing beside her. Facing her, her face tilted up, lips parted. She was older. Nineteen.

She tilted her head a little. "Don't sleep. Let's go ride around. The nighttime, the nighttime is the only time I can really stand being alive. Everything goes away and the world's made just the way you want it to be. There's this piece of time where even the hours are gone. You know what I mean?"

And he recalled those nights riding with his father and knew well what she meant and had even seen enough dawns murder those nights to know how they all ended. And he would not admit it but she was standing two feet away from him, crushing him.

"You should let me drive."

"Why should I do that?"

"Because you're barefoot and I know my way around and you don't."

"Well let's take your car then. You didn't walk here, did you?"

"I don't want to take my car. It's just a ruint wore-out old flivver that Daddy wouldn't even let me drive except I told him if I couldn't use the car I'd just walk out the road and thumb down a ride with the first criminal that came along. But I knew he wasn't worried at all about criminals but that some neighbor would happen along and see that crazy Pettigrew girl out thumbing like some plain country hussy. I want to drive this car. This car looks like fun."

He stood silent, rubbing one bare foot against the hard clay of the alley. Wondering if he should go back and get his boots. Wondering if the dogs would howl if he left them. Wondering how far this girl would run circles around him and if she even knew.

"Well, Foster Pelham," she said, "don't you trust me?"

"No."

She laughed then and he liked her laugh. Heard the sadness in it and liked that too. She said, "It's not many boys are honest." Her voice dropped down. "You just keep it like that."

She drove through the downtown with a smoothness and precision that calmed him. The town was silent in the warm night but for the cicadas ringing off in the trees. Past the spare downtown blocks she turned off and they were in the night then, leaving the pale tangerine streetlamps behind. They crossed the river over a low bridge of heavy uneven planks with railroad tie railings, the whole bridge heaving piece by piece under the motion of the automobile. Then twisted up through tight uncobbled pitted streets past shack houses set tight one against the other, random with the uneven fall of land. Daphne twisting the wheel with an expert slide of open lank wrist. Some of the houses dark and others showing the glimmer of lantern light behind pulled shades. But people on the street. Children and adults, men and women both, all throwing tilted glances at the slow-moving churn of the automobile. All colored. The children in rag shirts and pull-over dresses. Long naked legs moving like shadows against shadows in the dark. The eclipse of headlight-caught eyes turning away. The men some in suits and some in overalls, some of each bareheaded and some in porkpies or even hats of a finer block. The women also some fine and some in everyday wear. But all tilted back along the side of the street as the car passed. Watching it pass by averting their heads. Looking away, off to the other side. But he could feel them. Not their eyes so much as their minds, tightly focused on the Chrysler as it came abreast of them and moved on.

"Fishtown," she announced. "What we're after is a man what will sell me some bottles of beer. A little liquor. It's corn liquor clean as a whistle, I swear. Can you take a drink of liquor, Foster?"

"I can." Thinking he could twist around in his seat and reach back under the backseat and lift out a bottle of bonded scotch probably better than anything she'd ever tasted and was proud of himself that he did not. The best he could hope for at this time, right now, was to let this blond self-declared crazy girl lead him through the night. The air washed over him warm as a bath and the people around him scared him and he did not want to be anyplace but right where he was.

She left the engine running and told him to stay and went in to buy the liquor. Parked alongside a house no different from the others around it, the same dim shades. But a handful of men squatting on their heels on the porch, all watching the car. This time no eyes turned away. Hats tilted back on their heads. In the headlamp light their eyes did not show white but red. Staring hard at him. He could not look back at them. He opened the glovebox and took out the box with the single last of his father's cigarettes and smoked. The smoke dangling in soft ropes out the open window. He looked at his knee propped up on the dash and watched also for the flash of light that would be Daphne coming out of the house. He felt the men on the porch could ignore him or kill him and either way would take the same pleasure in it. But they did not move. He understood that they were in some ways more afraid of him than he was of them. Which, he guessed, would not stop them from killing him if he stepped from the car.

She had two quart bottles of beer in a paper sack already sweated through and a fruit jar with a screw-on lid of clear corn liquor. They'd gone on through the hill broken apart by the lanes and homes of Fishtown and then were up away from the river bottom and out onto the great rolling pine flats and swaled fields of the Piedmont countryside, Daphne driving faster now with the road ahead open and clear under the moon, a smooth pale swath in the dark land, the even darker hemmed woods.

"You got a opener in here?"

"A what?"

"A opener. For the beers. Someway to prize them open."

"I can do them against the door handle."

"Just open one. We'll pass it back and forth. What you do is sip some of the liquor and swallow some beer to smooth it down. By the time the beers are gone they'll be warm anyhow but we won't care then and be happy with the liquor straight."

Foster said nothing but opened one of the quarts and handed it over to her and unscrewed the fruit jar lid and took a swallow, holding it in his mouth a moment for it to bite against his teeth. It was good, smooth, lacking what his father would have described as "fumey" from being hurried. He took a little more and then passed it over to her and took the bottle she held out. He didn't like beer and this beer was pretty bad, flat and oily, bitter, but he thought he'd do things her way, this time anyhow. She wanted the beer right back after the liquor and he was happy to let it go. She pressed her dress down between her thighs and nested the bottle in there. He thought it was pretty bad beer to be treated so well. He was glad to have the liquor back.

"Uncle Lex tells me we're cousins, you and me, in a mighty slender nigger-in-the-woodpile kind of way," she said, one hand lying flat on top of the wheel as she drove fast, not looking at him. "Don't worry, he also told me to keep that quiet and you might not think so to listen to me but that is one thing I am real good at doing. And, it doesn't make any difference to me." She modulated her tone then, said, "It don't make me no nevermind," as if mocking something—herself, some unknown listener—and went on. "The truth is—you want the truth Foster? The truth is there's most likely plenty 'cousins' out there that we don't look at or think about or pay any attention to at all. Some of us even with brothers and sisters too. But they're not. They're *colored*. They're *Negroes*. That's what we say—what we say if we're nice people like my Mama is, likes to think she is—but the truth is that we all, each and every one of us, we say those words and all the time what we hear in our heads is Nigger, Nigger. And those are the ones we like. The good ones. The others, we don't talk about. But the men, the men can talk about them. Those others. Those bad niggers. And the women they hear that talk and their mouths get all tight like they're biting down hard onto a sour apple and you know what, Foster? Part of it is because each and every one of those women knows or suspects— and you tell me which is worse, to know a thing or just suspect it— each of them knows there's little *Negro* children running around that's half brothers and sisters to their own precious little children. And more than that. Each one of us knows that anywhere within a two–three-mile circle of any one of our homes there is more than that; there's aunts and uncles and some split-off piece and parcel of every type of relative you can think of. Pettigrews. But they's *colored* Pettigrews. So what do you do, Foster? Why, you clamp those sweet little dried-up old lips together and you don't think about it. So there. Just in case you were feeling unique. Just in case you thought you were some walking one-and-only. But people found out about you, that's what they'd think you were. And you'd flat disappear. Standing right before them you would change and go away. Unless of course you were pushy about it. Then you'd become one of those bad ones. They'd all look twice at this big car then I can tell you. What happened to me was I was at the University and had a breakdown was what they liked to call it and so they brought me home. Mama took me down to Dorothea Dix hospital? In Raleigh? Where some doctors talked to me for days on end and then finally one of them told my mama I was suffering from neuroses. He had to tell her something. He had to give her some word to cling on to. What could he do? Tell her I was the sane one in a crazy world? That wouldn't pay the bills, I don't imagine. So. What happened to you?"

"Seems to me," Foster said, wondering what Mebane had told her, wondering what he himself might choose to tell her, and not sure of either one, "you already know about me what you need to know."

"You can do that, baby," she said, "if that's what you want. But it's not why I'm sitting here."

"You're the one driving the car."

"But it's your car, isn't it?" She looked over at him. He did not know what that look was intended to convey. She said, "Give over that fruit jar." She took it and drank and shuddered and handed it back and lifted up the beer from the incubator of her thighs and drank some of that and offered it and when he declined she made no argument but settled it back down. They were driving with the windows open and the night warm and comfortable flowing over them, the land all but lost in the headlights and the speed, just here and there openings, sometimes the white shabby dribble of cotton and othertimes the dense rank of woods and here and there would be a farmhouse or shed or shack and he could not always tell which was habitation and which was not. Once there was a vast looming shape twisting in the air above the road before them and she braked the car hard and they sat silent while a froth-mouthed, red-eye mule turned to face the headlights, blowing from its nostrils before it smelled them or smelled the car or just came to some decision from mule-sense and bolted from the road. And she drove on then, hard, going up through the gears and when they were back up to speed she said, "All Uncle Lex told me about you was the parts important to him. You can figure out what those were. And I'm not saying that's not of interest to me, it is. But it's not why we're out riding around. Now is it?"

He was quiet then. He drank a little from the fruit jar. He wished he hadn't squandered that last cigarette. Then had one of those rare wondrous moments of illumination where the past was not passed but breathing, working alongside him. And he leaned over her and with his right arm bracing himself against the dash to not touch her said, "Excuse me," and leaned over her lap with the scent of her like a dozen campfires each burning a different fuel rising into him. He used his free hand to fumble down in the side pocket of the driver door and came up with a box of cigarettes. Because too many times to forget he'd seen his father set some partial almost-gone pack down into there when he wanted a fresh unopened one to take with him out of the car. And this was perfect knowledge to Foster. He dug in the glovebox and found a box of matches and struck up the smoke and worked with the fruit jar a little more. The girl Daphne just driving, the speed the same. Although he'd felt the hover of her breasts and the catch of her breath when he leaned over her. In that moment he understood that her talk was not all talk—she was fragile as he was and something in her searching was honest.

He said, "My father died nearly two months ago. My mother and baby sister ten years ago with the influenza. I didn't know a thing about North Carolina or what went on here until after Father died. He was his own man was all he was, I never knew a thing about his family. Then I went looking. It's all strange to me. I'm just trying to sort it out. That business you talk about—who's white and who's colored and why—it doesn't make any sense to me. Except it's starting to. Because my father never talked about his family. But what I don't know is what does it have to do with me? I guess something because I'm here. All I'm trying to do is figure out what happened to somebody a long time ago. It's not something that has much to do with who I am. Except maybe to you people. What I think, you people pay too much attention to what doesn't matter all that much. I've got a simple question and your uncle is determined to not give a simple answer. Maybe that's because he doesn't have one. Or maybe it's because he doesn't want to."

He had been watching the road. It was like driving with his father, the road tearing out from under them. Daphne had not looked at him as he spoke. When he was done, sometime after that, she lifted and drained the beer and then backhanded the bottle out the window into the night. Still she did not look at him. She was flexed away from the back of the seat, driving fast and peering ahead at once. Then she braked hard and dropped the gears and the car fishtailed and she let it do that, her one hand sliding and then gripping the wheel. As she made the turn off the road onto a shallow dirt track between files of tall pines she said, still not looking at him, "Don't confuse me with him."

"You're the one brought it up."

"If I hadn't," she said, "you'd of had to."

"You think?"

"I do." She was quiet then, driving slow down through a stand of woods. She killed the headlights and they were just in moonlight and the columns and shadows of the woods. The pines thinning to hard-woods, big canopied trees still holding their leaves. Then those thinned and he could smell the river before he saw it. An opening that spread out under the reach of the trees and then there was the broad slow drift of the water and the Chrysler came to a stop in the dark. She turned the engine off and twisted sideways on the seat to look at him, one knee poking free of her dress. Pale round bone under the moon. She said, "It's a strange thing all right. You're a perfect stranger but you're not. There's all that mess back there and if you don't know it or like it I can't help that but it's there."

"Seems to me it doesn't have to matter much. To you and me."

"Is that what you think?" She did not wait for answer or argument from him but threw open the door and stepped out and walked around in front of the car and down toward the river, a floating solid form of white dress and blond hair in the sparse moonlight. He sat in the car and watched her hunker before the broad silent river, her arms around her drawn-up knees, the dress pulled tight over her curled body. He felt very still, warm and comfortable with the liquor and also as if he were in another world altogether from any he'd ever known. And thought that what he would do was tiptoe his way as quiet as he could through this whole place to learn what he might and then load his dogs and head right back to New Hampshire and live quiet. Be a dog-man. Maybe see those two old women time to time. Maybe not. Maybe go to school. Maybe not. All he wanted right now was some slice of old solid earth to put his feet down on. And recalled the afternoon just passed when the quail rose up in the evening out of the creek bottom in their breathless wonder. And felt that moment was the end of something. Just what it was he could not say and he wasn't sure if the sadness was real or just the liquor. As if the fruit jar could hold sadness that the world did not contain.

He got out of the car and walked down and knelt beside Daphne, not too close. He wanted to say something to her but would not wait to rehearse it and so was still not sure of the words as he knelt but she turned to him quick and reached out and put her hand on his knee and asked him, "Tell me Foster. Do you think I'm crazy?"

And he rocked a little under her touch and said, "Well. It's hard to say. I've only known you a couple hours. But you don't seem dangerous."

And she laughed then, the laugh a splendid thing as if she opened her mouth and moonlight billowed soft out of it into the air to drift over him and beyond, on over the water where it fell apart under the cicada drone. And he wondered then if she was a little bit crazy.

She said, "You know what I thought? When Uncle Lex told me about you and why I came to wake you up? You want to know what I was thinking?" Her hand still on his knee, as if she were balancing herself. Or just wanted to touch him.

"What's that?"

"I thought, Here's this person come who doesn't know me at all. Who's never laid eyes on me, never heard the first thing about me. But who's some part of me. Not the distant cousin part so much as maybe the one who would recognize me, who would know me. I don't know what made me think it would be you but I did. Maybe some way Uncle Lex talked about you. Maybe just something I thought I heard. You know what I mean, Foster? You know?"

He looked at her then, seeing not just her but himself as well, the two of them in the dark on the bank of the river. And knew just what she was saying and at that moment did recognize her, as if each part and line and tissue of her was known to him. And was frightened now truly for the first time. He thought if he didn't get his hands into her hair, along her arms, hovering over her face, he would lose the ability to draw breath. So he looked from her to the river and was quiet.

She took her hand from his knee then. He did not know what this meant. She took the fruit jar from him and drank a little bit from it and rocked on her haunches and he wanted to reach and steady her, just his hand along her shoulder, her upper arm, but he did not. And she said, "You can't ever tell, can you?"

Then she rose without warning and he rose up with her and both unsteady, turning and reaching out for each other, hands on forearms, elbows, holding each other upright, steadying, not touching otherwise. Her breath against his face, warm and sweet with corn and the faint edge of charcoal. Then she said, "Oh," and let him go and turned to walk up to the car and he followed her, lifting up the fruit jar forgotten on the riverbank. She went around the side of the car and got in the passenger seat. He stopped in front. The moon breaking apart fleet clouds driven by some high wind, the air down below still. He looked at her through the windshield. He took the lid from the jar and drank a little bit. Then went around and got behind the wheel.

She was low in the seat with her knees up against the dash, her dress pushed between her legs. She was smoking one of his cigarettes, lazy smoke dribbling from her mouth as she turned to him and said, "Tell me something, Foster?"

"What's that?" His voice rough, torn with itself.

"What's the craziest thing you ever did?"

He did not have to think about that. "This right now. I mean coming south chasing after something happened a long time ago to somebody I never knew. Some part of me feels like it's all for someone else, I mean for my grandmother. I guess I'm trying to figure out what it all means to me."

"Don't you know already?"

"Thought I did."

"What happened?"

He looked at her. "How much did that Alexander Mebane tell you?"

"That your grandmother was a colored woman his family owned and that she ran away right before the end of the war. And came back years later looking to find her own mother and then went away again."

"That's all?"

"And that she—your grandmother—was his half sister. That his father was father to both him and her. He told me that part."

Foster drank from the fruit jar and looked straight ahead and said, "Whatever happened when she came back looking for her mother, I don't think she found her. But when she went home, back to Vermont, she went crazy. Not crazy like you but crazy crazy. Talking to herself. Not talking to anybody else. Before she killed herself."

The blond girl looked at him, her bottom lip out and down a little. "She killed herself?"

"That's right."

"How?"

"She hanged herself. My grandfather found her. Up in the woods."

"He didn't tell me that."

"Well he knows all right. Because I told him. And he knows something of why. But he hasn't told me. Not yet at least. I can't figure him out. So far, in one afternoon and evening he's baited me, teased me, threatened me and been nice to me. Sometimes it seems all at the same time."

"That's because he likes you. Or is intrigued by you. Or both. Most people can't get past his door. And he hasn't told you what you want to know I guess because once he does then you'll be done with him."

"A lonely old man, is that what you're telling me?"

She ran a hand over her face and looked away from him a moment out into the dark and said, "I think it's more than that. I think whatever it is you're after, is something after him too."

Both quiet then. Foster drank a little more of the fruit jar and silent handed it over and she took it and drank also and then set it up on the dash like she wanted it out of the way. Then she said, "You're sixteen is what he told me."

"That's right."

"I turned nineteen the end of May."

"Well, I can't help that."

"Orphan boy. Are you ever going to say my name?"

"What?"

"You haven't once called me by name. Since I introduced myself."

"Well. I will I guess."

She laughed again, a low thing out of her throat. Then said, "And you're not going to touch me unless I touch you first. Are you?"

"I don't know. I guess not."

"Foster? Let's get in the back. I want to get in the backseat now."

There was a moment, not during the first fumbling awkward fast time but during the second when she was over him, there was a moment then that was not thought or feeling or even the illumination of earlier by the riverbank but an understanding that flowed throughout him, a moment when it seemed for the first time of his life everything he understood to be himself was all of one piece, as if his body and mind and that other, that unknowable soul, had fused to unity: her over him, her breath shredded, broken by small cries that no longer alarmed him but seemed instead to enter directly into his blood, those cries small paper boats that would float forever through his veins toward his heart; her ragged breath against his face, her hands on his shoulders as she leaned her tipped breasts toward him; the moment then when her wet wrapped around him and the drops of sweat that beaded and flung from both of them straining toward the other and the air through the open car window and the silent tug of the passing river and the smell of her and the smell of the wet riverbank and her cries and the cicada echo and his hands wondrous sliding over the globe of her sliding against him and the hot writhe of her mouth against his and the sudden swift wet probe of her tongue and the tobacco liquor smell of the car and the pale thread-smell of dying leaves—when all these things were one thing and all things made sense; when the world became known to him and it was not bad or good but bitter and unbearably sweet. And he would live forever. If he died tomorrow. And he wrapped his arms around her tight and drew her close and hard against him, arresting her so she could not move before he spoke her name against her ear. Over and over.

He woke sheathed in sweat, the sleeping bag thrown open beneath him also wet, the air in the cabin dense and sullen, unmoving, swelled-up to some liquid state around him. Hot. Bright angled heat breaking in bars through the window and open door. He did not know where he was. He sat up naked on the sleeping bag laid over the old feather tick. His dogs were missing. His penis was staring up at him from between his legs. She had brought him back in the long flown-together hours before dawn and jerked him to her and kissed his mouth as if she would take it with her and then let go of him and walked down the alley, looking back once to say, "Bye, Foster." He'd stood there swaying until he heard the rupture of the old Ford firing before the house and traced its passage through the town and away until it was gone from sound. And there was nothing then. Some nightbirds pealing in the bushes. And he'd come in through the yard and piled himself into the bed with his sleeping dogs and had not thought he would sleep at all but replay her forever. But now was up sweating and blinded and without dogs. He stood off the bed, losing balance before stepping into his trousers, hopping one leg around after the other. Then out into the day. Through the open door. Which he was sure he had not left open. So he was elated and rebuked and terrified all at once. As if he had made a fatal error he could not yet name.

The midday cascaded upon him. His eyes were broken to pieces. There was a pump between the cabin and the house and he went there stumbling with his head down and worked the handle until the water was surging and bent down to hold his head under the gush, tipping to one side to drink, the water over him cold and riveting, bringing him back. And he recalled the vast liquid of the night before and could not understand how both the pump and that night could fit into the same world. He raised his wet head and shook it. His dogs were lying up in the shade of the house at the edge of the ruined garden. Tilted back in a broken-legged kitchen chair out in the middle of the yard, in full sun, was Alexander Mebane. His cane hooked over the chairback. One leg crossed over the other.

"It's a beautiful day, isn't it?" Mebane observed. "Your dogs was fussing so I let them out. You were dead to it all."

Foster raked his hair back with his fingers, wiping at his brow, trying to do it in such a way as to blinder the sunlight. "Good morning." He needed half an hour, some time to gather himself.

Mebane said, "Afternoon. It was high noon the last I looked at a clock. That girl'll lead you to damnation."

"I was willing enough."

Mebane nodded. "Of course you were. Wouldn't be natural, you wasn't. What you want is a cup of coffee."

"That'd be all right."

Mebane grinned at him, tight lips drawn back over yellow teeth. "There isn't any. I don't keep it in the house. Life itself works me up all I need to be worked up."

"I imagine I'll live."

Mebane jerked his head toward the house. "You go dig around in the icebox you'll find you a bottle of Coca-Cola in the back of it. That'll do you better than the coffee anyhow. Settle your stomach."

"My stomach's all right."

"Go on. Get something in you. I don't want to sit here and watch you get sick. You look like fishguts right now."

"It's hot out here."

"I sit out for an hour or so every day. The sun is healthful. And the inside of the house feels so cool afterward."

"I'll go get that soda pop maybe."

"You do that."

Foster turned to the house. Lovey and Glow in the shade, watching him, their tongues heavy. Behind him Mebane called out, "Get your drink, come back out here."

Foster stumbled in the kitchen dim after the outside, found the icebox and squatted before it and reached around in the back of it and found the bottle and lifted it out. Shaped like a woman. Everything in the world was changed. He wondered where she was, doing what. When he'd see her again. He rolled the bottle in his hands. Everything could go away. He already knew that. He went to the screen door and called out, "Is there an opener?"

"Drawer under the toaster. In there somewheres."

He popped the cap from the bottle and took a couple of swallows. It was good. She had such great power, he thought. And wondered if it was her age or if that only added to it. He would not hunt her down. He drank off half the bottle and went back outside, already feeling better, his feet more steady.

"I thought you two might get along," Mebane said. "Of course there was no way to know if you could keep up with her or not. But that would not be any disaster—there's not many that can, I understand. It's possible she makes a career of that sort of thing is what some think. Myself, I just think she's looking for someone what can hold pace with her. From the looks of you, I couldn't say. What do you think?"

"I'm all right."

"Is it your nature or the situation that keeps you so tight-lipped?"

Foster grinned. "Both I guess."

"Well you two managed to stir up the neighbors. Old Winifred Coxe was over here this morning bright as a birdbath telling me all sorts of things I had no interest in knowing or hearing and all the time her head swiveling around so she could listen to the upstairs trying to figure out where you were. I wasn't about to tell her you were camped out in the nigger cabin. These old birds they don't miss a thing. If I was to move a flowerpot from over here to over there, if I had flowerpots to move, they'd not only note it but attach a meaning to it that would be lost on me. But it would be some reading of my character, of who I am, of who they think I am. It's their job, the only job they have I guess. Or at least the one they're best disposed for. Just so you know all I told her was you were the grandson of a friend of mine from Chapel Hill who moved north after the war. It was close enough to the truth so I felt fine about it and just far enough from the truth so's to shut them up. My business is not theirs and never has been, never will be. As far as Daphne is concerned, I can't help her in the eyes of these old ladies. It's not as if she wants my help anyhow."

"I like her."

"Of course you do. I like her myself. I'll tell you a secret."

"What's that?"

"The way you feel? Right now? About her? That's the way you're always going to feel about women. Now, it'll get wrapped up and tamped down and turned around and pushed back into some little corner mostly by the actions of women theirselves as time goes on and time to time you'll forget it and othertimes you'll feel that way and think you shouldn't for all sorts of reasons but there will always be that part of you. And you pay attention to it. There's worse things a man can do."

"I don't understand you."

"I wasn't asking you to understand. I was asking you to remember is all."

"All right."

"You do that."

"Yes sir."

"That drink helping?"

"It is. Thank you."

"Don't you thank me. It's the last one though. I'll have to send around an order for more, you keep on nightcrawling."

"You don't need to do that."

"You say that now. See how you feel about it tomorrow."

Again Foster grinned. "Nothing says I'll be out raising hell again."

"Oh she'll be back. Don't you worry about that."

"She talked about something that happened to her at college. What was that all about?"

"What'd she tell you?"

"Said she had a breakdown."

Mebane wiped his hands along the tops of his thighs, scrubbing his trousers. He said, "That's her mama talking. There is not one thing wrong with Daphne except she's restless in a place that makes no room for restlessness. And she hasn't figured out what to do about that yet. If she should cave or run."

"So what happened?"

"She didn't tell you?"

"No sir."

"Well that's a sign of some sort. She doesn't mind telling the tale has been my experience. They threw her out is what happened. October of her first year. That would be a year ago. Pissheads. If it'd been a boy they would've told him not to do that sort of stunt again and all the time all of them, him too, laughing about it, knowing it would become a little legend that would follow him around the rest of his life and that not a bad thing but something good, some signal of the sort of man he would be. But she is no boy and they did not know how to fit it in with their ideas of how things should be. So they heaved her out. And every one of those little chit-mouthed girls over there glad to see her gone only because it meant they didn't have to provide for themselves the same way; all they had to do was sit around and talk about it, how horrible it was, how deformed she was. It is a gift of women, in case you don't know it yet, to turn on one of their own once she steps away from what they all think is the way they should be. Women are the keepers of the pack, I tell you that. We could not do without them but they are not kind, in the end. Most likely for good reason, I give them that. What she did was like any other good boy or girl just off at school: She drank too much one night. But was not content with doing that or just screwing some fraternity boy what had been panting after her all night long like her good sisters did; no, what she had to do was hike down Franklin Street all the way into Carrboro which is its own town piled right up against Chapel Hill, where she went into a colored man's backyard at dawn to steal his mule from the shed and then she rode that mule back up right through the middle of town wearing only a sheet she'd stole off somebody's laundry line and singing "In My Merry Oldsmobile". She always had a good voice in Sunday school and I'd guess she looked pretty good up on that old mule's back but still it was not what anybody wanted to face first thing in the morning with each and every one of those people doing their best to forget what their own nights were like, what lizards lay down in their nightsouls, and the last thing they could abide was a vision of that come to life right before them. Which is what she was.

Because she is a girl. I can tell you that right now. If it had been a boy, like I said, it would be laughed off and forgot for the most part except where it would be helpful to him. But they would not laugh at her and they would not forgive her. So they turned her away, back to us."

"What happened to her clothes?"

"What?"

"When she stole the sheet off the line? What happened to her clothes?"

Mebane looked at him, his mouth clamped down tight. Then he reached over his shoulder for the cane and brought it before him and stood up out of the chair. Rocking a little before Foster. "Let's go in the house. I've had enough sun. Come on. I don't know what happened to her clothes. She's got you good, doesn't she?"

In a small iron skillet varnished with ancient grease Mebane fried an egg on the electric coil and charred two thick slices of bread in the toaster and spread butter over the toast and slid the egg out onto a plate from the drainboard and set it on the counter for Foster to eat standing up. While Foster ate Mebane said, "What I hate about getting old is it gets harder and harder to get a good night's sleep because you don't do enough during the day to tire you out but then you can't sleep so you feel like you don't have the energy to get anything done. It's a little circle that goes round and round. All it does is leave you wide awake come the middle of the night with nothing but a weary old brain and the tinkerings you make from that. I was up much of the night considering your arrival. It's a little like the man waiting so long for some event that when it arrives he doesn't know what to do with it. Because through-out the long waiting he's turned into that—the man who waits. It be-comes a condition of the soul. Were you raised in the church, Foster Pelham?"

"No sir."

"You've not been baptized, christened, saved, or otherwise amended?"

"No."

"Well you're a free man then. You can come to learn God as you go along. As a student of your own life and as an experiment of whatever it is that sets us up walking and talking and breathing and thinking, whatever that mystery is, you can do your best to cipher it out on your own. Faith and grace are not empty words but you'll have to fill them out your own self and not just accept some translation."

"I haven't thought about it too much. Sometimes. Thinking about my parents, my little sister."

"Of course you haven't. Unless there is something wrong with you it's not a young man's sport. What I was thinking was, we'd take a little road trip in your automobile. Nothing far but just a bit of history that isn't quite dead yet. And perhaps you'll begin to learn what you're after."

They drove the main highway back north and west out of town, the road Foster had come in on. It was hot and the dogs sat up on the backseat, a pair of wind-twisted gargoyles splayed out the open windows, their tongues spread wide with the wind of the moving car. Mebane had pumped them a bucket of water and Foster knew they were hungry but they would have to wait. It felt like they were all on slender rations. For himself, he thought that was good; he felt alert and liked it. The dogs would just have to partner along with him.

Mebane talked as they drove. "Used to be I'd come up here a couple times a month, at least once a month with the winter weather. But that was when G T Kress was alive. He did the driving. I'm talking a pair of horses here and a ragged old ruint covered buggy. After he died there was no one to do it with regular and I hate to ask someone to do what they're not at least a little interested in. Still I used to get up here a couple times a year. But with G T it was regular. Every second Tuesday evening unless the weather was bad and then we'd just wait until the next. That little buggy of his was in bad shape but his horses was always fine. I never kept horses. A one-armed man would be a idiot to mess with horses."

"How'd you get around otherwise?"

"Briefly I owned a bicycle. But my balance is not good and I lacked the courage to make a spectacle of myself for however long it would've taken to get the hang of it. Before that, in my short undistinguished career at the bar the boy who kept the yard also tended a driving team and would take me where I needed to go. This was not the one I was speaking of yesterday—Fred—but one before him."

Foster thought of the story told him by his aunts of the colored man Peter who was burned and hanged for helping his grandmother. And wondered if Mebane guessed that Foster knew that story and wondered if he was being baited here or not. He said nothing. They were up on a rolling plain of land, big pastures of cattle broken by woodlots and fields, mostly of tobacco. It was a fine bright hot day with much wagon traffic and the air sweet from the tobacco flues.

Mebane went on. "Now G T was a younger man although he's dead now. Killed by one of these automobiles after he sold off his horses, which is a cautionary tale itself right there but not the one we're after today. See, he wasn't even alive when the war ended. Born most near ten years after that, I'd make it. One of his uncles was killed at Fort Fisher and another shot up bad in The Wilderness but his own daddy did not fight a lick although I don't know how not. Kresses was not the sort of folk to've found an easy out. Country people, poor farmers, I don't think at the time they owned but two three coloreds anyhow. And that was before his time. G T's I mean. Now hold on, slow down here. Pull in up there. No, there."

They went onto a narrow dirt half circle of drive with patchy grass growing up through it before a long three-story stone building with a sagging porch the length of the front and many of the windows missing glass, the rows of windows so many blank eyes onto the day. Very large old red oaks grew to shade the building and the drive was covered over with green acorns that broke with a harsh wet sound under the tires as Foster came to a stop in the shade. The blocks of stone rough-faced and dark gray, as if they still held some moisture from the earth they'd been quarried from, as if the endless heat and even neglect could not dry them.

"It was a little military academy for boys run by a veteran of the war with Mexico right up until 'sixty-one when it emptied out so all those boys could go off and get shot up. The colonel too, which I guess if they'd known it not many of them boys would've grieved over. It sat empty not very long and then was turned into a hospital." Mebane turned in his seat, hitching his upper body around to glare at Foster. "Not the one I ended up in. That was nothing but a pitched row of rotten tents up in southern Virginia." He looked back at the building and went on. "After the war it was a home for survivors. Men worse off than me. Men with-

out legs or both arms gone or men torn up in the body or mind so awful
they could not tend to themselves. There was a subscription taken up
to keep it going and I guess some money came down from the government too. It was closed up six–eight years ago when it came down to
just a handful of old men what they moved down to Raleigh to another
home. Before that G T and I used to come up here and visit with those
old men. G T liked to get them talking, hear their stories. There was
some anxious to tell it all over again. Me, I'd rather sit and read or write
letters for them unable to do it for themselves. In a way it all came down
to the same thing—he heard the same stories over and over and I wrote
the same letters. But it was what we could do. What someway suited
each of us. G T was after something he'd just missed, what he felt someway cheated out of. The way a man will when he makes most of something out of his head rather than having lived it. Me, I'd like to say all I
was up to was trying to help those poor old creatures what way I could
but, truth is, more like I was chasing after something too, something
closer to home. Maybe my dead brother, maybe my own dead boyhood,
maybe something part of each. That's not why we're here. Not really.
That's just the cartoon and newsreel, we still got the feature picture
ahead of us. Do you go to the pictures?"

"No sir. Not much."

"Well I enjoy them. Perhaps only because I can walk downtown easy
on my own of an evening. Perhaps because I can leave myself alone for
the time I sit there in the dark. Well, get out of the car. Let's walk
around. Your dogs'll like this."

They walked out, not up to the building, which had a pair of planks
nailed crosswise to bar the door and trash, bottles and such on the wide
rotting steps of the porch, but out through the tall brittle-stemmed grass
beyond the oaks, the dogs crashing ahead, grasshoppers flinging themselves off in reckless short bursts with each step. Out of the shade it was
bright and the sun was not a point in the sky but a spread of white haze
that blended without clear ending into the pale blue. There was a cemetery beyond the building, a long rectangle enclosed by a spiked-tipped
iron fence with an iron gate turned back, and they went in. It was not
like any cemetery Foster had seen. There was a single peastone path
straight down the middle and out at the far end a single shadetree oak
with an iron bench under it and otherwise just the flanks of graves, each

stone alike, a squat thick white marble slab laid into the ground equidistant from the next, uniform in size and height. The names and dates chiseled almost invisible in the white marble. Before each stone a small iron circular marker held a small rebel flag. Silent and solemn, without the distractions of monuments and stone angels, without variety of any sort. What death, Foster realized, might be like: small white spaces in endless files and ranks, all manner of identity pared and paled to be unseen.

The cemetery grass was well-mown. "The Daughters pay a man to keep it up," Mebane said. "I find it peaceful out here. It's a colored man that does the work, I've seen him at it. He does a good job. I wonder though what he thinks. Getting paid to tend after these old Confederate boys."

"Well, they're dead," Foster said. "Probably he's just glad to have the job, make the money."

"Could be, could be. Could be he feels he can't get free of those sonsabitches no matter what. I wouldn't know. Tell you what we're going to do: we're going to sit on that bench there and talk about the nature of evil. Except I doubt a young man like you is much interested in that, has much faith in that sort of talk. So what I'll do is tell you a story, a true story." Mebane reached the bench, his cane striking hard to not slide among the peastone, and anchored the cane and pivoted around and settled himself. The shade seemed dusty, the leaves of the oak also dusty as if they were tired of living. Foster did not want to sit beside him and so squatted in the gravel before the bench, a little to one side of Mebane. His dogs off nosing among the stones. He kept his head tilted to keep them in his sight—all they'd need would be a breath of scent and they'd slip through the iron fencing and be off.

"What it is," Mebane said, "is some family history for you."

"I already told you. I'm not after anything like that." Foster went on, not knowing he would say this until he did. "I've got all the family I want. There's Pelhams been on the same Vermont farm since just before the Revolution and my mother's family is up in French Canada, probably been there a hundred years longer than those Pelhams in Vermont."

"It's blood we're talking about here," Mebane said. "It's not some single isolated event you're looking to learn about. There's swampwater and rice in your veins too and it don't matter if you like it or not, it's a fact."

Foster rocked back on his heels, craned around to seek his dogs, spotted them and followed them a time with his eyes. Then looked back at Mebane and waited.

"My father was Caswell Mebane and he had one brother older by eight years named Buchanan. My grandfather, Coleman Mebane, was the youngest of three brothers and so what came down to him was whittled away at pretty good—it was right much by any terms I could imagine but for him in that time and place he was bound to feel thwarted by fate as his two older brothers got the pie and he got the crust or so he always felt. But this isn't so much about him. Although he did what you would expect in a man feeling that his place in line had determined his lot in life; he favored his older son and not the younger. You might squat there and think it would be the other way around but that's not human nature. And to forgive him what I can, perhaps he felt it just was the way things were done. Perhaps he believed he had no choice. Perhaps his nature was such that he saw no choice. Every man is a curious thing—each one of us thinks we are nothing so much as our ownselves even as we fume about what has been done to us by others but we almost never see how we pass those wrongs along; we have our reasons for doing what we do and believe them not only to be right but the way things are, the way they have to be. If each man could see truly how they are and the way they fit some pattern laid down and could see it fair and true then likely they would all quit, the way I have, and we wouldn't get anywhere. We'd die out. Which might not be such a bad thing. But is not likely to happen.

"What happened was there was these two brothers far apart in age who hated each other. The way I think only brothers can. Because one brother knows someway the secret workings of the other and each knows the other knows it. And they either make peace with that and are friends rare and precious or they don't and so are bitter with hatred. Because they know there is that one man who can undo them in any number of ways at any time he chooses. It doesn't even have to happen in public; it could just be between the two of them and one of them would be destroyed. Maybe able to carry on outside but flanked and pinned and bereft inside, always after. And that is what happened.

"My father and his father were alike in their temperament. They were both men who, in the end, could not comprehend how to respond to the world. Both men who flailed as they grasped and so almost always came up holding the wrong stick. And they were both men of appetite, always hungry for something and unable to determine what that was so they chased after whatever might be right before them. And in between them was my uncle, Buchanan, who was steady as a pivot that could look both before and after and see what was coming and where it came from, see that and know also where it was headed, which neither of those other two could do. And so my grandfather could not stand my father who was the image of himself and loved his other son and my father could not stand his own father and loved his brother but hated him also with every pulse of his blood. And what's important is to know that my uncle, Buchanan, knew how both the others felt about him and did not care. He did not have to care and not because he had the land and not because he had the money but because he had the other two, the elder and the younger, in thrall to him. He didn't care if they would admit it or not. He knew. Now you see, we're getting close on to what is evil. Not that he was evil itself. Evil is not a thing that just sums up in a man. No. It is a thread that begins to run in a small way and then falls down through the years and generations to gain weight as it goes.

"Now my father Caswell when he went off to the university he knew he was leaving the Cape Fear for good. He didn't have to. He could've gone up and taken his degree and gone back to Wilmington and read law there and life would've been good for him where his name and people was known. Where there were plenty of other less fortunate sons in professions and trade that he would've done business with. But it was not his way. I can't tell you the entire why of his wanting a fresh start in a new place but it's something plenty of men do, have done and always will. At least some it's safe to say was to put distance between himself and his brother and father. And so he looked around and found this place which needed a lawyer but was big enough so there was some town to it, and close enough to Raleigh so he could reach beyond Sweetboro without too great an effort. And he met my mother and took her down there to the big rice farm on the Cape Fear enough times so she thought she knew what she was getting and married him before she'd even heard of Sweetboro. And if it was not what she was expecting it was still not so shabby; it's not always a bad thing to be exotic without having to make much effort at it. And she was not unaware that he had political intentions. Raleigh might've been upstart compared to Wilmington but she was a young woman and young women can point their noses into the wind better than most.

"So he built that house there in town which you would not know to look at but was a pretty nice place at the time. And they—Grandfather and Uncle Buchanan—sent up as a wedding present a pair of Negroes, an old woman to keep the house and an old man to tend the yard and horses. And my mother went right ahead and had my brother Spence and then a pair of girls, Audrey and Deborah. And somewhere along the time those girl babies were arriving my father decided more help was needed around the house, to keep up with all those babies, to help my mother. Now, he could've looked around the area and found some girl to suit. But he didn't do that. Some men are unable to keep themselves out of where they shouldn't be. What he did was, he sent down eight hundred dollars to his brother and asked for a girl to be sent up. Maybe he thought he would get a better deal that way. Eight hundred was not a lot for a strong healthy girl. And so there was Buchanan Mebane with a bank check for eight hundred dollars in his hand from his only brother.

"There's been three hundred years of colored people owned by white people. There's very few white boys that did not start out their manhood with a black girl. And there was some that would continue right on all their lives, without regard of their own wives and children. Some of those did it because they could. Because it was there and could not say no. Some kept on because it was a reach into some other life, something wild and unfettered missing in their own lives, regardless of how fettered it might be on the other end. And there was some, some few, who did it because they could not stop themselves, because their hearts bolted away from them. And the ones who did not, who left the colored women be after that first initiation or maybe even did not partake of that, they came down into two groups also. There was the ones who understood pure and simple that it was wrong. And there was the others who did not understand that but knew it was true. Do you understand the difference? To not do something because it's wrong and not do the same thing because everyone else thinks it's wrong?

"I do." Foster, back on his heels, his legs asleep from his knees down, unable to move, his eyes on the face of the man seated above him.

Mebane said, "Coleman Mebane was one of those ones with the bolted heart. And his son, his heir, Buchanan, knew that about his father and hated him for it. I don't have to tell you he was one who held himself above it all. Or if he had to rut on some girl you could bet it was a girl off in some corner hid well from everybody else. But there he stood. With that eight hundred dollars in his hand. And knowing his father and his brother were men from the same piece of work. With that softness of heart he so despised. You see, it was not like some men that would spread it around. Grandfather Coleman had just the one woman in her own little cabin down the end of the row of cabins and each one of those babies the same dun color as the next, not a one with a father different from the next.

"It was a good-sized place, sixteen hundred acres. And it was Buchanan's. But that didn't mean his father just sat off to the side of things. What that meant, for our story here, is that those dun-colored children were not just left down there at the end of the row. The boys were taught trades, smithing or wheel-wrighting, coopers, masons. The girls were all brought to the house. They did not work in the fields, those children. Well there was Uncle Buchanan, with that eight hundred dollars to commission household help for his brother. So with his genius for stabbing both ends from the middle, he picked out the middle girl, a pretty girl just fourteen years old called Helen and sent her upcountry to his brother. Half sister to the both of them and he sent her along, knowing somehow that his brother, my daddy, would not be able to refuse her and would not be able to refuse his own heart either, anymore than their own father had been able to do. Buchanan knew my father would hate that girl and love her too and hate himself for both and so poison himself. Would love her because he could not help it and hate himself for allowing what he could not help. It was poison perfect, innocent if untouched. So he sent her off. Everything his brother had asked for. And I do not fail to blame my father. As I said, some part of him must've known it would be that way. You do not ask the man who chopped off your foot if your hand is sound as well."

Foster was flat down on the peastone gravel now, cross-legged, his hands loose in his lap, open. He had not seen his dogs in some time and it seemed terribly important that he locate them but he would not look away from the old man. Who sat with his palm capped over his cane-crook, looking down at him. He wrapped his tongue around the inside of his cheeks for moisture and wetted his lips and said, "So my grandmother then: she was not only half sister to you. But her own mother was half sister to her father. Is that right?"

Mebane looked away from him then. Peering off into the sky above the empty shell of hospital. Without looking back he said, "It is blood-soaked. All of it is. Already now and more in years to come what we will recall is the big event of it. What people did to other people. But it will all be turned into something abstract, removed from each of us. Both colored and white I expect. I seen it happening already with G T Kress. And what will be forgot is the small everyday things that made it real. Because each man has to contribute someway to keep such a flimsy tent aloft. But once it is down we all can step away from it and say it was the other fellow—the other fellow that pitched it in the first place and the other fellow as well that helped hold it up. And so we walk away from it, from the ruins of it. And it will never be made right. It will never be repaired. Because some things are beyond repair. Those things that need it most, it's beyond the scope of man to do the job. Because all we're up to, most of the time, is trying to get a little bit back of what we think we lost. It's human nature. We could flourish I guess. But it will not happen. Perhaps because in our hearts we don't deserve it. Perhaps because it's easier to lie between the legs of that dark sister than to call her by name."

"Is that what you told her," Foster asked, his voice rasped thick, "when she came back down looking for her mother. Is that what you told my grandmother?"

Mebane looked back at him. Foster had to look around the hand on the cane tip to see his face. As he watched. the hand clenched hard and the old man stood. Way up over him, looking down. Dry-skinned in the heat of the day, his face blotched with color, blanched and ripe at once. Then he turned away and went down the gravel path between the graves, a tall lean figure bent to one side, the sunlight soft as bathwater over him, the cane stabbing out hard and angry ahead. As he went he called back without turning his head. "No. I did not tell her that. I did not. I was a coward, what I was. I did no better than my father or any of them before him."

He did not look back again but kept on going and Foster watched him until he reached the car and once there Mebane stood, his one hand holding on to the side of the car, his back still to Foster. Foster could see him breathing, the small hump of his shoulders rising and falling within his back. He looked away from the old man, down at the ground beneath him. He raked his fingers through the gravel, the stones smooth against his fingers. Then he stood. Once up, he rocked from side to side and stamped his feet against the earth. Ran a hand through his hair, down over his face. The muscles of his cheeks and jaw tight as drawn bolts. He looked out away from the files of headstones toward the pine-stand beyond the fence. The light there in sharp angles between the trees. He whistled for his dogs.

They rode back silent to town: the old man slumped down against the seat and doorframe, his face turned to catch the wind through the window, his pale stringy hair blown up away from the stretched-paper skin of his skull in some awful halo; Foster driving one-handed, his right arm draped across the seat down into the back where his hand rested on one of his dogs, driving through the deadstill middle of the afternoon where even the muledrawn wagons they passed seemed to swim in the dust, the mules trudging each step with a sideways yaw as if belabored more by the strike of the heat than the load behind. Foster no longer raising a hand in greeting to the black men driving the loads, no longer able to see them as other working men but recognizing that they inhabited landscape unknowable to him, one that he could not penetrate regardless of what blood he shared with any of them or not; it was not blood anymore than it was the common shares of dreams and hopes and fears that bonded them but rather the dark bay of the soul that the one race had opened unhindered upon the other. Slavery he knew then was not the whips and chains of the school history books, not the breaking apart of families or the unending driving labor but some stain far greater and deeper, something that had been unleashed and then bloomed up, between and within at once, both races, white and black, forever without surcease, tenacious, untouchable and unchangeable. And wondered how a man might know this and go on. And for the first time since driving up to the farmhouse in Vermont and seeing the face of his aunt come out the open door he thought he understood something of his father. And he thought then, That is how it's done, how we go on; we make it personal because we can bear that. And recalled Mebane saying something like that and looked over at the old man as if to see something of himself there. But this man was a stranger to him, in a way that other old man, that faded yellow ferocious old man on the parlor wall a thousand miles away would never be. And Foster then also thought Don't be so sure.

He parked in the alley and opened the gate in the back fence for Alex Mebane and left the old man to make his way unaided to the house while Foster opened the trunk of the Chrysler and fed the dogs tinned meat out of there, sitting on the seat with the door open and his feet out in the sand of the alley under the speckled shade of the live oaks as the dogs wolfed the gray meat from a shared tin plate. Then he let them into the yard and worked the pump to fill their bucket with fresh water. He brought in the tin water can from the car and filled that also at the pump, wanting things as much in order as he could make them. He refilled the bucket for the dogs and watched as they switched ends of the yard from earlier to lie up in the shade now against the side of the unused barn. Then he went quiet into the house.

Alex Mebane was asleep in the padded rocking chair in the dining room, his head tilted back, mouth open. Foster stepped back into the kitchen and let the quiet door swing shut. He took a tin basin down from a nail in the kitchen wall and carried that and a bar of handsoap from the sink out to the pump where he filled the basin and then on to the cabin. Where he closed the door against the bright light and stood in the dim dull heat and washed himself and then stepped back into his trousers but left his feet and chest bare and lay down on his back on the sleeping bag, sweating again where he'd just washed but thinking he might not smell as strong.

Then he stood again and went to call the dogs in and close the door. He wanted them with him. They came fast as if they'd been waiting for him. Glow circled around up on the tick and lay where his head had

been. Lovey, older, wiser, went straight to the hearth and stretched out
there, disregarding the snakeskin for the cool old bricks. Foster lay back
down, pushing the young dog away, not wanting the heat of her against
him. Both dogs speckled with the green triangular pods of beggar-lice.
There was a steel-toothed comb in the Chrysler that he needed to run
through them. He closed his eyes, a great stripped-down fatigue over
him. He felt he should leave the place he was in. He could not get away
from the sense of some unknown looming event, some disaster before
him. But knew also he was not done here. He did not trust any of this
but could not step away from it. It could be the heat. It could even, he
thought, be everything all at once come down on him. He was lonely,
with a pain that spread out from his chest throughout his body. He laid
his hands open on his belly and breathed the closed dread air of the little
shut-up miserable cabin, his eyes closed; the room around him burned
into him as if he had spent winter nights by lantern light memorizing
each split and splinter in the squared-log walls, each pouch and pout of
the clay-mud daub between the logs, each smokestain on the stone chimney, each grease stain on the hearth. The air itself he sucked into his
lungs, air that had been expelled by those before him: dense, wet, close,
only just enough to live on.

When he woke the light through the now open door was pale, quivering with dusk, and he came up startled with her sitting there beside him
on the bed watching him and as he cried out in fear he knew who she
was. She did not move when he called out, did not shrink from his
abrupt fear. Sitting sideways at his waist, wearing a pale green skirt with
a white blouse open at her neck where a fine gold chain fell holding a
slender gold cross. Glow lying alongside her thigh, the dog's head up
on top of the skirt. Two sets of eyes watching him. His first clear thought
how close her sex was to his and how little there was in between and his
penis moved inside his trousers and he stayed sitting up, putting his
hands down in his lap. His face a foot from hers.

"You haven't been lying here all day sleeping waiting for me." It was
not a question.

"Daphne," he said.

"That's better," she said. "Just the sight of me should not make you scream."

"I was startled was all."

"That's all right. I don't mind that."

"Oh shoot. Boy I was asleep." He wanted to kiss her. He said, "That's what I hear."

"What do you hear?"

"That you don't mind startling people."

"That's true enough. Up to a point. But you're aiming at some detail. You want to fill me in?"

"I spent the day with Alex Mebane. He took me for a little trip. And talked the whole time through it."

"I see," she said. "So, you're learning what you came after. That's good, isn't it? But you're not being straight with me, Foster. Foster? I thought maybe we understood each other."

"Maybe we do," he said. "But I'm not sure that's a good thing."

She spouted her lips and blew air at him. "What else is there? But you hold on and back up. I want to know what you heard. About me."

"Isn't that the way it is? We always need to know about ourselves first."

"Well shoot boy. What's the alternative?" And she grinned at him.

"I don't know."

And she heard the despair in his voice and she was quiet a long moment. She did not move away or toward him but she looked at him close. Then she said, "I don't guess there is one."

He said, "I heard about you over at the college. Riding that mule."

She sighed. "I always felt bad about that mule. He didn't want to go. I had to get off him and break a branch off a bush to whip him on with. I never thought it was because he knew it was wrong. I just figured he knew it was the wrong time of day to have to work at all. It was so early in the morning. A mule knows what time is his and what time is not." And she grinned at him.

"Seems to me, you wearing only some kind of toga made out of a sheet, even a mule would be happy to rouse himself to carry you."

"Is that what he told you? Well, I had a slip on. My underwear. I was not jaybird naked."

He reached for her face. She stood up. "Are these your dogs?"

"This here is Glow and that one is Lovey. They're English setters."

"I know what they are. They're pretty."

"They are pretty." He sat without moving, watching her. She stood beside the bed not looking down at him but off. She was very still but he felt that she was in some motion within herself. Some perturbation, some conflict rising up. It's me, he thought and reached for her hand. Even as he reached thinking it was the wrong thing to do.

She stepped away from the bed and went before the small single-pane window of old bubbled glass. He could just see the side of her face. She reached up and ran a finger slow in the dust on the glass. Without turning her head she said, "I don't know what's wrong with me. People just make me so damn sad. I can't stand it. You know, when I was a little baby my daddy used to carry me around with him all the time. I remember it, hugged up against his side. Took me with him everywhere. I went out in the fields, went to town, to the gin, the tobacco warehouse. The livestock sales. And he'd introduce me to everybody—I remember that, shaking big old grown men's hands. I can't tell you what that was like, the world of men. All in their overhauls and suitcoats and their big boots and the heavy stained cattle prods they carried, the smell of their sweat and tobacco and the earth on them. Bending down to shake my hand solemn as if I was one of them. Doing that even as they smiled at me in the way they would not smile at one another and those smiles telling me I was someway special. But still let in! Still in with them. Even after I started school I'd come home afternoons and run out to find Daddy and like as not he'd be watching for me, see me coming. Stop what he was doing to hoist me up or squat down talking to me, asking me about my day and then telling me about his, what he was doing. What we were doing. That's what it felt like. That it was all something we were doing, the two of us. Like my absence was just something temporary. As if he was holding some place for me. I'm the youngest you know. Two brothers and a sister all older and those brothers worked along-side Daddy ever since I can remember but it never seemed the same with them as it was with me. He drove them hard. Still does. They hate him and he hates them but they all love each other and they don't ever say a word about it. What they talk about is what work they need to be doing. But now he can barely bring himself to look at me, much less speak to me." She turned from the window and looked at Foster. "But nothing changed with me. I'm no different than I ever was. So, what happened? I tell you what. I don't know. What's wrong with me? I don't know." She walked halfway back to where he sat on the bed and stopped again, her hands out before her as if grabbing something from the air, her face turned full upon him, working upon itself and before he could speak she said, "Do you think I'm a slut, Foster? Was last night just some slut to you? You tell me the truth, Foster. I'm counting on you for the truth."

He spoke slow. "I guess I know what it was to me. I'm not sure I can tell you what that is though. What words."

She nodded.

He went on. "The question it seems, is what it was to you. That's how it seems."

"How can I know what it was?"

He shrugged. "I don't know. I guess you either do or you don't. And I guess if you don't then it isn't."

She cocked her head at him. "It was your first time wasn't it."

He looked at her awhile. Then said, "Why are you so worried about what I might think about whatever you might have done before with anybody else?"

"Do you think that's what it is?"

"Well. It doesn't seem like you trust me."

"I don't trust much of anything."

"What I've found, there's not much to trust. Not much that stays."

"So why do you trust me?"

He grinned at her. "Didn't say I did."

"What about those words you can't say?"

"I don't know. I'm not even sure what they are."

"Yes you are. You know exactly what they are. You just don't want to say them for fear you'd be wrong."

"I'm not sure it's worry about being wrong so much as wanting to get things right."

She smiled at him then. "That's a pretty thing to say."

He looked at her again for some time. Then said, "You're the last thing I expected when I came down here. The last thing on my mind. The last thing I thought to find."

"It can be funny how that works."

"I guess so. Some ways it makes sense."

"It's funny. The first thing I thought when I heard about you was that this was someone I had to find out. Someone who was here for me."

He was very serious then. "It's complicated. There's business between your uncle—your great-uncle—and myself that's just starting to get worked out. And I don't know where it will lead but already I can tell you some of it's not so nice. There's no reason to think it will get better as it goes. If it goes any further. He could clam up on me anytime I think. Although I don't guess he will. He's going slow with it, bits and dabs, but what I think is that's more to let each piece sink in all the way with me before we go on. Anyway, I don't know what's going to happen with it all. And I don't know how much he'd want you involved in it."

"You're afraid I might mess it up for you and him, my being around?"

"No. I don't see it as a problem. If anything, it seemed to me he took some delight over me this morning, teasing me about you. But serious too. It seems to me he cares for you."

"He's got a soft spot for me, somehow."

"Thing is, what he's telling me, it's not exactly making us close, him and me."

She was quiet then, studying him, understanding what he was saying. Then she said, "I'm not stupid, Foster. I know plenty about him, those others too."

"Well I figure you do. Still, you know what they say. About blood."

She came then to the bed and sat beside him and reached her hands up to his shoulders, just resting her hands there, the droop of her arms between them. He did not move. Her eyes broken shards of winter sky. She said, "It's all blood, baby."

The blankets, their skin, the very air of the room a swamp, everything rich, glutinous, gelid and pure as he imagined some ocean, some forgotten lost sea might be. The dogs, both of them now, off on the hearth, watching them, their heads up, their eyes alert, curious and somewhat alarmed.

"I'm not a bad girl. Not really. I just want. I want."

"I don't think you're bad. I think you're some kind of wonder is what you are."

"No, no, no. Foster. Anybody, any girl, could do this for you."

"I'm not talking about this. I don't know what it is. It's not what you think it is, what you seem afraid I'll think it is. I'm just all scrambled up inside is all."

"You boy. You sweet boy."

"What is it?" he asked. "What is it you want?"

"Oh Lord," she said. "Everything."

Late dunrose dusk, pale light dimmed free of shadow. The blanket off them. Still hot. Still-hot. Something passed, not sleep, not waking but some nether nuzzle between the two of them, drifting up and down.

The door opened. The dogs shot out. Alexander Mebane standing in the door, his cane leaned in like something extended out before him. His head tipped sideways to look at them. Daphne scrabbling the blanket over them, her movements clumsy against Foster as the rough army blanket tented them.

"Children," Mebane said. And shut the door.

"Oh Jesus wept." She was up in the half-light, tipped awkward on one foot then the other as she stepped into her underwear. For the brief moment before she pulled the rest of her clothes on as glowing white as a peeled onion. It was the first time he'd seen her this way, naked and struggling with her body, and he sat welled with tenderness, thinking that the very way she lived within space was different from him, that the world someway was not made right for either one of them alone but together they might find balance one against the other. She said, "I'm dead. I am dead. Oh shit I'm shot and skinned and hung out to dry."

He got up from the bed, languid, pulled only by her urgency. He pulled on his trousers and said, "He didn't seem that worked up about it."

Her blouse over her head, she was running her hands through her hair. He could not see that this changed the way it fell. She said, "You don't know anything about it. What it is, is I carried Mama in to Wednesday night church and brought a sack of food for you two which is all I was supposed to do was come over and get you all fed and then be back there to pick her up. Do you know what time it is? I am god damn dead. She's setting over there, waiting and pretending not to wait and there's two or three other ladies setting with her pretending to chat about any god damn thing they can pretend to be interested in but all any of them is doing is waiting to see when I show up, if I show up, and they'll all each and every one of them be sniffing the air, each one trying to figure out if I've been drinking or screwing or both or whatever else they can dream up."

Foster buttoned his shirt, then reached out and straightened the little gold cross where it was caught bottom end up in the chain around her throat. "Well," he said, "at least you haven't been drinking."

She batted his hand away. "Don't you make fun. It wasn't you that rolled in at a quarter to four this morning with Daddy already out in the sheds and Mama setting at the table with coffee already made, me stinking of corn liquor and everything else and cross-eyed and her reminding me that however old I might be or think I was as long as I was living under their roof there was things I could and could not do and I was just about done calming her down when Daddy came in and started up all over again. So I got through that and slept and got up and worked my tail off to make this mess of food for everyone just so they'd let me plead to bring you two stranded odd boys something to eat other than soup out of a can while my mama was at church and me making promises left and right and then here I am and I screw it up, screw it right up. Don't you make fun with me."

"Was that what it was," he asked. "Quarter of four?"

"No it was not." She was sitting on the bed, lacing her shoes. "I must of left you off here about two or so. I don't know. What I did was swipe the rest of that liquor jar from your car and rode out in the country and set there stopped, just drinking and thinking. Until some old colored man came along on a bicycle and I knew it was later than I wanted it to be and so got along home."

He wanted to ask what it was she had been sitting thinking about. But she was up, brushing her clothes with her hands. She said, "Don't you have any idea what time it is?"

"It must be eight o'clock or so. Maybe later."

"You think that's all?"

"It's starts getting dark early this time of year."

"That's right. Still, I'm awful late."

"I could come along. Explain things."

She looked at him, half-grinned. "Explain just what?"

"Well. Maybe distract her."

"You'd do that all right. No. What you do. Damn it. I was going to build a fire in that stove and warm things over. Listen. There's a sack of food in there. You two can warm it or eat it cold, I don't care. But I got to go."

"What about you?"

"I'll be fine. Mama and me, we'll have the ride home to get things worked out. I just want you to go in and eat that food. I can't stand to cook. And there I was all afternoon in the kitchen, any minute feeling like I might could be sick, just to fix food for you. So you go in there and set down with that old man and eat you that food what was good once, before it got cold. And do your business with him. You've got business to do with him, isn't that right?"

He stepped back, again feeling the faint threat of distance. He could not help himself and said, "When can I see you?"

She stepped up close and kissed him fast. "I don't know."

"It's early," he said. "I've been sleeping all day. He's an old man. Even if he gets worked up I don't bet he's good for more than three–four hours."

She looked at him. He could tell she wanted to go but still she stayed. Then she said, "You remember how to get out to the crossroads? Pettigrew?"

He nodded, pretty sure he did.

She said, "Between one and two, I'll do my best to be down along the road. Not right by the house but somewhere along there. If you get out there and don't see me just drive on to the crossroads and set a bit and then turn around and come back slow. I'll slip up out of the ditch. If I can get out there. Don't do it more than twice. Don't drive by more than twice. Two times, I'm not there, I won't be. You hear me?"

"I'll be there."

"If you're not," she said, "I'll know it's because you couldn't help it."

*   *   *

It was an odd meal. Mebane had it out of the sack, arrayed on the counter-top. Wide-mouth jars of vegetables, snap beans and cutup yellow squash and a smaller jar of tomatoes stewed with peppers and okra. A cloth napkin tied around a heap of crumbling cookie-cutter biscuits. And a square tin box that had once held lard or lye or some such now filled with flattened pieces of beefsteak in a thick gravy the color of oatmeal. Chicken-fried steak.

They ate it room temperature off old wide featherweight china plates that Mebane removed wordless from a china safe and wiped clean with a rag, taking each plate down one at a time and setting it on the counter and then lifting the rag to wipe it off, slow and cautious. As if, Foster thought, making clear that all his life had been conducted one patient slow step after another, every action thought out beforehand in a world where there was no free hand to arrest a fall, to catch a mistake.

Mebane disregarded the meat, dabbing spoonfuls of vegetable distinct on the plate, taking up a single biscuit. Foster loaded his own plate, digging deep into the tin of meat with a wide spoon to bring up the warmest slabs out of the thickened gravy. Then followed Mebane into the shabby dining-room where again they ate side by side at the single spare bare area of the table. He felt soft and easy, wide awake and, because of this, wary. He felt this was when he might miss something. He could not help but think of Daphne cooking this food for him. Regardless of anything else, this meant something. Thinking that it is the small things that stitch us one to another. And wanting to be stitched. As simple as a longing toward home. A home that might grow from a plate of food. Seeing her naked and stumbling into her clothes. Thinking he could not find the way to tell her that her being in the world set him to tremble, throughout his soul.

"Okra," Mebane said, "is not edible." He was lifting the chunks of green wheel free of the stewed tomatoes and stacking them at the side of his plate. "It was brought from Africa by the coloreds. Or to feed them with. Somehow we all got stuck with it. You can stew it like this or you can batter and fry it but all you're doing is eating what it is cooked with. Still, everyone grows it and swears how much they love it. I'd rather eat treebark." He glared sideways at Foster.

Foster put his fork into the stewed vegetables, lifting up a piece of skinned tomato and one of okra together, and ate them. The tomatoes were sweet with the peppers and seasoning and the okra was a sidelong crunch, something to chew and seep out the other flavors. He said, "I like it."

"Of course you do," Mebane said. "From her sweet hands. Eat it up. Eat it up, all of it. Eat that meat too. Used to be when I was a young man I could not eat enough meat. For a time I thought it was on account of not getting much through the war. But it occurred to me that it was something else I was after. Some big bite-hold that would never be mine. I've been happier since I gave it up. Better for my bowels, too."

"I'm hungry is all."

"I bet you are. Well, eat on it. Whatever you don't will go bad and get fed to your dogs."

"They'll have to stand in line."

"Boy, they already are. Your attention grows more divided by the minute."

"I haven't forgot why I'm here."

"That's right." Mebane speared a chunk of squash, lifted it to examine and set it back down. Took up his biscuit and broke off a crumb-edge with his bright corn-kernel teeth. "You're the one after the truth."

The meat did not need a knife but came apart under the fork tines. It was not anything that he thought of as beef but he figured he could get close to the bottom of the tinful anyway. He said, "What happened, that you never got married?"

"Who says I never did?" Mebane now peering down his flung-up nose at Foster.

Foster looked around at the discord of the room. "Nobody. I just assumed—"

"Which you shouldn't do. Young sir after the truth. No I never got married. What woman would want a one-armed man?" Stabbing green beans one at a time and lifting them to his mouth, eating the food as if angry with it.

"I don't know," Foster said. "I'd imagine there might be some. Depending on the woman." Then he added, "Depending on the man, too."

"Well, there," Mebane said. "In one step you arrived at the conclusion of every busybody I ever met in my life. Which is to put the blame for it on me. As if it's a lack just because everybody else does it. Or most everybody. There's one–two old maids whose theories are the most severe concerning me. But mostly it's a simple thing. Regardless of how two people start out, from what I can see, and the view is pretty far from these years, for most it comes down to the little things and the little things for me are ten steps for everybody else's two or three. And I think anybody patient enough to put up with me that way for years and years would have to be stupid enough that I would hate her. Maybe that's just an excuse. Maybe I never found the right person. Maybe it just was not meant for me. Maybe I'm not the marrying sort of person. It looks that way, don't it?"

"I guess so," Foster said. He laid his knife and fork on the side of his plate and let his hands rest loose on the table edge. Upright in his chair, looking at Mebane next to him. "Are you a queer?"

Mebane chewed on biscuit. His eyes on Foster. Some of the anger paled, some of the wry twist lifted in his eyes. He swallowed and said, "You're a regular man of the world ain't you?"

Foster shrugged. "It's not anything to me. I told you my father worked those White Mountain resorts. Saw every kind and stripe. Warned me of it too."

"There is plenty think I'm queer. But not the way you mean. A bale shy of a load is what they mean. But no, to answer your question. My own needs are unfulfilled and will always be that way. They are beyond the reach of life is what they are."

His arm was what Foster thought he was speaking of. Foster pushed back his chair and stood, taking up his empty plate. He said, "I'm going to get a little more of this food. Can I bring you something?"

"Eat it all. I believe I've had enough of it." He pushed his plate, still with dots of food, away from him. "What you can do is carry this into the kitchen for me. So I don't have to sit looking at it."

"I can do that." Foster lifted up the other plate.

"What else you can do you're out there in the kitchen? I could use a little drink. If I recall, down in the cabinet under the sink, back behind the bottles of soap and disinfectant and all that mess I don't bother with anymore, back of all that I think you'll find a fruit jar with a little corn liquor in it. You could bring that in to me along with a glass. Two, if you want some. I know you're no stranger to it."

Foster carried the plates through that silent door that each time he passed through left him feeling he'd moved some great distance he could only guess at. He set both plates down in the sink and then stood over the sink and with his hands ate three more pieces of the beef, the gravy thick on his hands, all of it ripe with seasoning. Then ate a biscuit and rinsed his hands. Looked out the window set in over the sink into the reflection of himself in the dark glass. Wondered how many times his grandmother had done the same thing. And her mother. And what they had seen looking back at them. He dried his hands on the old piece of sacking Mebane had used to wipe the plates. Took up the tin of left-over meat and gravy and stepped with it outside and stood silent a moment before his dogs came up out of the dusk. Then set the tin on the ground, pausing bent as they began to eat to run his hands over their backs. Unmindful of him, the dogs gulping at the food, swallowing pieces of beef whole without chewing, each wanting to get someway ahead of the other. Dogs knowing no one would wait for them to catch up, mother–daughter or not.

He went out across the yard and through the gate into the alley where the Chrysler was parked. He lifted out the backseat and opened the crate of liquor and brought out a bottle of his father's hoarded scotch. Set that in the sand at his feet. Then opened the wood case holding the L. C. Smith and took it out and used the oiled rag laid flat in the bottom of the case to run over the gun. Then broke it open and reached again down into the backseat and rummaged for his vest and pulled free a pair of shells. No. 6 birdloads. It was what he had. He slid them into the gun and snapped it shut. With the shotgun in one hand he bent and carried the bottle of scotch with him back into the yard. At the slave cabin he went in and laid the shotgun upright in the corner by the head of the bed. Once the gun was laid up he slid his hand down to make sure the safety was off. His hands running over the gun in the dark an old familiar thing. Something known top to bottom. He could not say for sure why he wanted it there but knew he did. Something simple. The way you checked to make sure your shirt was tucked in before going in someplace. Then he took the bottle of whiskey and went back to the house. Passing Glow down on her stomach, her front paws pinning down the empty tin, her head up inside it. Her teeth scraping against the folds of soldered tin. Eating nothing but flavor. The scent of something.

There were jelly glasses on the drainboard but he left them there and went to the china safe and opened the wide double doors and peered in at the neat dust-ribboned stacks. Found a set of short squat tumblers and lifted down two in one hand. Light as holding a pair of postcards. He took them to the sink and rinsed and dried them, running the sacking rag over them until they shone bright in the light. And carried it all into the dining room. Again through that silent door.

He set the glasses on the table and made no show with the bottle but twisted off the seal and poured both glasses half full and set the bottle on the table and sat down. His chair now pushed a little back and to one side from Mebane. Without waiting he said, "My dad had a couple crates of this buried out back of the house. When he was killed I dug one up and brought it with me."

Mebane leaned to peer at the bottle, took up the glass and sniffed at it, then sipped. "That's the real thing, ain't it."

Foster drank off some of his own and immediately wished he'd brought cigarettes in with him. But went forward, where he was determined to go. He said, "I been thinking about all you had to say this afternoon. Up there in the cemetery. It was a pretty good job, seems like. I felt like I was being led around. But what I came after is why my grandmother came back down here after her mother and couldn't find her and so went home where she was loved and needed and chose instead to walk up in the woods and kill herself. You haven't told me one thing that gets close to explaining that. Why she did it. And what I think is if anybody knows it's you. Maybe I'm wrong, but it seems to me that her daddy being her mother's half brother or whatever the point of your story this afternoon was, it doesn't make anything clearer to me."

Mebane lifted his glass and sighted along the rim at eye level and then drank some. Put the glass down and looked at it. "In its way," he said, "it was part of it."

"Her part or your part?"

"Could be they're much the same thing."

Foster drained down his own glass and set it on the table and poured for himself from the bottle and turned to look at Mebane. "The way I heard it, when she got back home she kept talking to herself about some old man set up on a block with a rope around his neck and doused down with kerosene and set afire so he burned up until he jumped off the block to kill himself. You know what I'm talking about? Mister Mebane? Sir?"

Mebane sat silent gazing off across the table, into the piles of books and newspapers and old ledgers there as if it was a place he longed to go. He ran his one index finger around the rim of his glass without looking down at it. "I do." His voice loose upon itself, a soft strangle. He added, "Mister Pelham. Sir."

Foster said, "I didn't intend to be rude."

"A man can't handle his whiskey hadn't ought to drink."

"I can handle it just fine. What's giving me a problem is feeling like I'm in the middle of some old duck-and-dodge. I think I'm patient, otherwise."

"But you have an end to that patience, is that what you're telling me?"

"Everybody does, I guess."

"Are you threatening me?"

"No sir." Then added, "Not yet."

"Good," said Mebane. He took up his whiskey and sipped. "Good for you Foster Pelham. You see, we're beginning to understand each other."

"I don't see that."

"Oh yes you do. It just hasn't occurred to you that way yet."

"Sir?"

"What there is between us is something not either one of us wants. But it's here. It's what we have."

Foster was quiet.

Mebane filled up his glass and let it set on the old stained green blotter. As if he just wanted the glass full. He still had not looked at Foster. In the same quiet voice he said, "The man you're talking about was called Peter. He was yardboy to my parents. And he took care of the driving horses and mostly except when my father got a burr under his butt did the driving for them. Now Peter was a horseman. This is something you need to know; most white people that owned Negroes would brag about them. If they wasn't complaining. But it was all how good a cook this one was or how good with the children that one was or what a hand with the flowers or the horses." Mebane looked then at Foster and held up his hand palm out flat. "Thing is, most of the time what we're talking about is one people that elevated simple everyday skills to something special and appointed some of those other people to hold them. Not because the first people couldn't have had those same skills, mostwise. But because it held the whole delicate balance a little more firmly. As if there were some things one set could do better than the other. What they disregarded was that it was a simple matter of what you have to do. If being treated well depends on how well you cook or fertilize a rose garden, then you're going to do it well. And if you don't have to do that, you can attribute some special level of skill to those who can. Most especially if you don't have to know anything about it. If you can just set down and eat the food or walk through the garden and see how pretty it all is. You understand?"

Foster said nothing.

Mebane went on. "With that said, Peter was a horseman. Now, you have that automobile. Do you know anything of horses?"

"Not much."

"You see? It's a new world. All the time there are old worlds slipping away from us that we don't even see going. What you're here after is one old world, one thing, but there's countless of them. Horses is one. Your children, their children certainly, will think there was never anything but motorcars. Yet they're brand new. And behind them is ten thousand years of men and horses working together. Think about that. All going away. The horse will be a plaything in the world to come. And fewer and fewer will be the men who understand them, who know them down in their blood and sinew and sweat. I guess there will be men what know automobiles that way. I wouldn't care to meet one. But forever, there have been horsemen. It's not just grease and bearings and pistons and such. It's the souls of two creatures that somehow line up. Link up. So one knows the other. The best of them, those horsemen, did not do well with people. But they could walk up to a strange horse and twist up its lower lip in one hand and lift the head to look up straight into that creature's eye and talk to it and they would understand one another."

"There's men like that with dogs."

"Ah yes, you're the boy with the dogs. And some way you're right. But allow this: Horses and dogs are different animals. It is the nature of a dog to bend to a man. It is not that way with a horse. A horse is a fragment more wild than a dog. There is always something in a horse's eye we cannot see. Some place they look beyond us."

"Dogs can be the same way. Good ones."

"It's the rare dog can kill you if you misstep."

"All right."

Mebane took up his whiskey and without pause drank it down. He said, "What happened to Peter was nothing of my doing. I didn't even know about it until afterward. I was in bed at the time, insensible. I don't remember any of it. All I know is what I learned later. But I will not lie to you. When I was awake enough to hear of it I was not unhappy. Not then. At that time it felt right to me. But I was not there. It was not me who called out for it, not me who stood by and watched. If I'd been able, would I have watched? Yes, I believe I would have. But it was not Peter I would have been watching. It was everything else. Things I would not have even known I was seeing then, the same as the men who did it. Most of them I guess. But I was not there. I was laid up in the bed."

"Because she brained you with a flatiron is what I heard."

Mebane lifted up the bottle and drank straight from it. He did not look at Foster. He tipped his head, the bad flowered ear toward Foster. His eyes still out in the dim reach of the room. The place, Foster guessed, where his eyes rested most of the time. "I was a boy. Younger than you. With my arm gone just three-four months. She stove in my head. And me already wounded. There was no one to look after me. No one that would tend to me. I was left to myself. I was alone. I still have dreams that soak the sheets and I wake from in a panic, right back there."

"So who was it killed that old man Peter. And why him?"

"It was some few around. I was not among them."

Foster nodded. "All right. But why?"

"Because it was him that helped her get away after she attacked me."

Foster drank a little of his whiskey. Feeling now that he was firm-footed, following a way laid before him. He said, "How did they know that? That he helped her?"

Mebane looked down at the blotter before him. "When word got out what happened to me the men come up here and talked to Peter. I was not there. It was a wild hard time. These men come to talk to Peter, thinking he must know something of where she went, how she got away. A sixteen-year-old girl never been five miles from home before does not just pick up and disappear, not in the middle of everything coming apart. She had to have help, they knew that. But what happened, what I heard, was, instead of being a dumb nigger or a scared one or any kind they expected, not even a wild angry one, instead of any of that what I heard was old Peter stood out there in the yard, at the door of his little quarters up against the barn and in a voice so soft each and every one of those white men had to lean close to hear it, in that voice he told them they were evil, that the retribution of the Lord was loose upon the land and it would all end in blood and fire and sorrow for them and each one of them would walk the stones of eternity with the cup of their sorrows empty in their parched hands, their souls bound in the chains of their sins, the sins of their commission and the sins of their omission. It was quite a little speech and I guess those boys did not take well to it."

"For somebody not there you seem to know it pretty good."

"It got repeated to me. There was more I guess but that's what I recall. And likely I've not even got that right. But the heart of it—that's stayed with me."

Foster did not ask who repeated Peter's words. Instead he said, "If all she wanted was to run away why did she try to brain you with that flatiron?"

Mebane looked at him, looked away. Looked off. Then back at Foster, his face grim and tight, some old anger betraying the set of his face. Like his mouth was putrid he said, "You know why she did that."

Foster sat silent. Like a trigger-line between his crotch and brain flared a sudden burst of images: Daphne first and rolled right over her was the idea of some other, some girl always there who could not say no. Whose no did not matter. As if some boil in him was lanced and spread through him. And understood the taint upon him and recalled also his father speaking to him once of women, bidding him to recall always that he once had a sister. And so because it was all he could say, all the authority he could claim, very softly said, "She was your sister."

Mebane turned then, his mouth a pale working wretched line, his eyes a scrim of inflamed veins as he hitched his body sideways to face Foster. He said, "You're not listening. Everything I've been trying to tell you is how we can find it in ourselves to let things exist or not. Of course she was my sister. And I knew that but did not admit it. The same way my father did not admit it, either about the girl that was his daughter or the girl's mother that was his own sister. Anymore than my own mother would admit what she walked around in between each and every day. And all of that, all that just the small version under our own roof, but a piece of what all things were made up of. Can't you understand that?"

Foster said, "Even if she hadn't of been your sister—" And stopped.

"Don't you rebuke me. You, out rolling around with that girl. Your own cousin. However distant you want to make it that fact remains. You see, you think it's so far it can't be traced, that it can't touch you. It's what we all do—we find a way to allow what we want but should not. It's not so different, is it?"

Foster lifted up his glass and let whiskey onto his tongue and set it down and said, "I never asked her to do anything she didn't want to do."

Mebane was quiet then a time. Looked away from Foster, not off into the shadows of the room but down at the blotter before him. He closed his eyes and sat motionless. After a while Foster began to think he'd gone to sleep. He had the urge to rise and walk through the rest of the house. Through all the rooms, opening all the doors, cupboards and closets, all of it. Feeling someway he had that right. Even feeling Mebane would maybe expect it of him. But did not move. He did not want to see the preserved unused rooms he knew lay down the hall and up the stairs. Did not want to see the rank or spare room where Mebane slept. Or the furniture, the ornaments, the pictures, the spent detritus of the lives before of this house. He wanted none of it. He felt up on tiptoes, poised, on view only to himself; he felt he was stronger for disregarding everything else and staying right where he was. He felt he could tear the house down with his bare hands and knew he would only walk away from it and leave it behind him. As a man walks, he thought.

Without stirring, somnolent, Mebane spoke. "I was a boy. Your age, a year younger I guess. But I did not know what you do. I was still wrapped up in childhood. I don't know what it was. Perhaps it was the war. Perhaps it was just the way I was made. But for me that winter was all about what I had not done. And that had-not-done was all laid up alongside what I thought I ought to've done. And you see, that was all Spencer. Spencer in my mind. Dead Spencer. I could spend the night talking about the ways I tried to track after him. Because they was countless; they informed and re-formed each breath and thought and step I took. Now, is that just the younger brother or is it something else? How can you know? There is the example of my father and Uncle Buchanan. Who came to my father's funeral and stood solemn and silent watching the earth get thrown in under a winter rain, not saying a word to me or anybody else that I could see. Him in his brushed wool overcoat with the rest of us arrayed in clothes three years outgrown. But him watching that box go down. Like maybe it was something he'd been waiting for.

"I was fifteen. My brother dead more than a year. Me alone in the house with an arm gone. And there was that girl there. Your grandmother. I can't see her as a grandmother. All my life what I see is her long lean body and that bright sudden smile and the way she walked as if every ounce of her body walked all over an earth that was held away from me, was something I could not touch. You see? I'm not talking about a sister here. And there was this: She and Spencer adored each other. As a boy that was all I could see. It seemed he had something I did not. And, to be fair, he would not admit to me what it was between them. That took me most the rest of my life to learn. Because at the time he was a boy too. So what he told me was not the truth. It was what he wanted me to believe. No. It wasn't even that. It was what he thought I should believe. But beyond all that there is a more simple truth. Spencer did not bother to see her but as his sister. Spencer was able to step away from all the rest of it. That's what he would not tell me. Or anybody else. Except of course her and I guess he did not have to tell her. They both knew it. But he would talk otherwise to me. I guess he thought he was protecting her someway doing that. Keeping their tenderness hidden. He would see that as more dangerous than any empty brag he could come up with. Because when all around you is built up of lies then where do you allow the truth in? You cloak it is what you do. You hide it anyway you can. You do not think about how one lie may twist around and allow another. You have no choice. So I was an empty boy. I did not have what my brother had."

Foster drank a little whiskey. The electric bulb suspended overhead was arcing, dancing shadowy light. He waited a pause and then said, "Who was it?"

"Who was who?"

"When my grandmother did her best to strike you dead and ran off out of here and left you? You talk about being alone then. But you were just a boy. Bad hurt. So who was it that took care of you? Who was that person?"

Mebane nodded. Took up his whiskey. Did not drink but set it down and looked at Foster. He said, "Did you hear me?"

"I did."

"All right." Mebane nodded again. Then took up his cane and rose up, using the table edge to push his body against to stand. Clamped hard on the cane looking down at Foster. He said, "It was her mother. It was the only one here. It was Helen took care of me."

Foster studied him. Then said, "She must've known what you'd done. To get your head laid open."

"Well, I sure didn't tell her."

"But she knew."

"I don't know what she knew. What I can say for sure is I was hurt and her daughter was run off and one man was dead on account of her running off. So who can say why she did what she did? What she knew? What her reasons was? Maybe it was just to save herself. Maybe it was nothing more than that."

"Now wait. You're telling me there was just the two of you here alone and her nursing you and you two did not talk at all? Not one bit beyond what you needed or wanted? With everything else gone away you did not talk to her?"

Mebane weaved against the cane. As if the cane was the one reliable piece in the upright grouping of himself. A single slender raised vein pumped on his forehead. He said, "I tell you what. Some of this work you have to do yourself. I can't lead you through like a child at a medicine show. What I'm doing. Is to go pee. I'm an old man. My bladder can't hold that whiskey like it used to. Then I'm going to bed." He scowled at Foster. "Other than that, I'm not going anywhere."

"Well I guess I'm not either anytime soon."

"There you go."

"One thing."

"What's that?"

"I understand why you're telling me all this. But sometime you've got to tell me the rest. The part I came after. Just so you know."

Mebane looked at him a long time. The old man's eyes watery with fatigue. Foster began to think Mebane would say nothing, was waiting for Foster to say something more.

Finally Mebane said, "You watch yourself with that girl. She is the only creature on this earth I love even a little bit. Do you follow me?"

"I guess so."

"You'll get what you want, in my way and my time. When I'm satisfied that I've got it right."

Foster sat silent.

"Well," Mebane said. "Goodnight then. Turn those lights off when you're done setting there. I don't trust that electric."

He sat at the table for the time it took the sounds of the other life in the house to cease, the faint scrapings of movement from the second floor, the pad of uneven feet. Then a time more while the house settled to rest around him. He corked the bottle of whiskey still half full but drank off what was left of his own glass, left it there on the blotter as some rough evidence of the night for the morning and carried the bottle out with him, leaving the room dark behind him; also the kitchen where he paused before the dark to study the remains of the uneaten dinner— the jars of vegetables and the biscuits. It was not just food. He was pretty sure of that.

Outside the evening haze had thickened. There were no stars. It was still warm, the air heavy, a thing immediate to walk through, to breathe in. The rub of cicadas pierced the air as if the insects inhabited all living space. As if they would bore into his ears.

He let the dogs out of the slave cabin and kept the door open to sit and watch them, white ghosts scouting the fenced yard. Then left them be and lighted the lantern inside, leaving it on the floor as there was no place but the bed to set it otherwise. Went and knelt by the hearth and took up the snakeskin there and broke the segments apart in his hands. Dry hard shackles of some body passed by. Then reached into the hearth and rubbed one hand there. Squatting on his haunches. Just old stones, long cold.

The dogs came in and lay up on the bed and watched him. As if they wanted to see what he would do next. He turned and sat crosslegged on the floor with the lantern turned to a low wicker and looked back at them. He drank a little from the bottle of his father's scotch.

Twice he went out across the yard through the gate to the Chrysler in the alley. He sat there and smoked cigarettes. He could take off the brake and hold down the clutch and coast silent down the alley to where it dropped to the street and there pop the clutch and drive off as quiet as driving could be. Out to the crossroads. Pettigrew. Where she said she would wait for him. He turned sideways on the seat and propped his feet up on the far side of the dash and with the bottle between his legs sat smoking. He had no idea why he did not go to her. Each time he went to the car he intended to leave and find her and each time he did not. Each time he left the car to return to the cabin where the lantern, the wick turned low, was blackening the chimney so the cabin grew more and more dim. Just shadows. Shadows of walls and floor and hearth and rising rough chimney stones and the jut of bed into the dim space and the two forms on the bed with their eyes yellow and pale as from another world watching him.

The rain began sometime while he slept, not waking him but entering into him someway as it struck soft against the old rotting split-cedar shakes overhead so his dreams were of rivers, of swimming underwater through windowglass water, some brown-skinned girl swimming alongside him, streams of bubbles sweeping from her mouth back into her short twisted glistening hair, her body naked but never quite seen altogether. Together they skimmed over the smooth riverbed stones.

He woke to a rain-dimmed early dawn, fresh and sharp-edged, bouncy. He stood up in his trousers and opened the door and watched the water run slantwise into the overgrown dried-up backyard. The dogs went past him, quick-footed with the sudden cool, after rabbits in the tall broken grass. The rain came through the open door and streaked an oval on the old floorboards around his bare feet. He ran out to the back fence and through the gate to the Chrysler where he rolled up the left-down windows, thinking, Stupid. He should've guessed it would rain. Feeling again that he was in a place where he could not recognize simple signs. He dug in the backseat and got his canvas coat.

Everything—the yard, the old carriage shed, the still-dark house, the trees beyond—was distinct yet close. As if color had been drained from the world and with it simple perspective. Back in the cabin he took off the coat and got a shirt on and his socks and boots. Roughed his wet hair with his fingers and then put the coat back on. The dogs splattering damp marks, traces of themselves, in the dirt layer of the floorboards. Wet and happy, both of them, smelling like dogs, eyes pitched up on him.

He stepped again into the wet day and shut the door behind him, closing them in. He stood a moment studying the dark house. It was early. He crossed over the yard to the carriage barn and went in a small man-sized door set into the two larger doors that would open out. To one side a row of vehicles: a covered buggy, an open carriage, a two-wheeled fancy gig. All dull with grime and dust, spiderwebbing like the hands of ghosts over them. The cloth sunscreen of the carriage rotted off its slender frameworks. The other side a row of straight stalls, empty, cleared of all manure or bedding, of anything at all. Except— when he went up into one and ran his hand along the planks of the stallside where the wood had been smoothed by years of rubbing—some few long dark horsehairs still caught in splinters of the wood. And the wood of the feed manger worn down where hungry necks had pushed down into it, time after time, day after day. Old tie-chains welded with rust lay in the bottom of the mangers.

At the end of the stalls a row of feed bins and beyond that a door let into the wall and he went through there and was in a small slope-roofed shed built onto the side of the barn. The shed empty. Nothing there at all. At one end a small hearth and rough chimney. Against the inner barn wall, high up, was a set of eight spaced wooden pegs the thickness of his wrist, a foot long and curved up. Harness pegs. That was all. Even the hearth had been swept clean. The room was dark, just a single paned window set high on the shed wall, dark with grime, not cleaned by the rain. Foster squatted and looked around him, studying the walls, the floor. And finally could see where there had once stood a bedstead built into the wall like the one in the cabin he was staying in. Along the wall at the end of where the bed had been, found some nails where clothing had once hung. Thought he could see patches on the floor where perhaps a chair had been scraped back and forth from a table over the years.

That was all. At the end of the shed was a door that opened into the yard and he went out through there. Against the side of the carriage barn, right up close under the eaves, was a stack of stovewood. The stack had at some point come right up to cover over this outer entrance to the small shed. Where Peter had lived.

A pall of dense sour woodsmoke hugged close down over the yard. He looked at the house and from one of the two chimneys a thick oily spume rose up, the color of wet black wool. He crossed over to the house and went in through the kitchen. In the dining room he found Mebane down on his knees before the grate. Stacked up smoldering against the andirons was the stack of ledgers from the table. Beside Mebane was a pile of yellow newspaper, from which he was removing sections and crumpling them against his chest and then feeding them under the ledgers, prodding with a poker lying before him on the hearth. His cane was upright, within reach, against the hearthside. He looked around when Foster came in and then back at his work, reaching for another sheaf of newspaper.

"What're you doing?"

Without looking back at him Mebane spoke. Into the fire. "Nothing. Burning trash."

"What was in those books?"

Mebane took up the poker and stabbed hard at the mess before him and the ledgers gave way, sliding one off the other. Fresh fire licked up. "Nothing." He stabbed again. Still not looking back.

Foster left the old man to his burning and went through into the kitchen where he stood at the sink washing up from the night before. Wiping down the counters. He fried eggs on the electric coil and toasted bread and laid the food out on plates. The work made him melancholy, the rain against the windows. The meals he'd cooked alone or for his father, the water dripping off the tamaracks and hemlocks. He was a long way from home. Even if the house was still there, even if it was his, it seemed long gone. He was terribly sad. It seemed the farther he went the less he had.

He carried the plates into the dining room and silent put them down. Took up the glasses from the night before and carried them to the kitchen. The fire was burning well now, Mebane standing to the side of the fireplace, a couple of sticks of wood atop the stacked ledgers. The room was warm, drying the moisture from the air. Foster came back in and together they sat and ate.

Mebane mopped eggyolk with breadcrust. "I thought you'd be out running all night."

"No sir. I stayed in."

Mebane nodded as if they'd agreed upon something. "I was awake myself much of the night. Pitch and thrash. Then just about daybreak the time I got to sleep that girl called me up to make sure I hadn't killed you or run you off."

"Daphne called here?"

"Wasn't you supposed to meet her?"

"It wasn't anything firm."

"Un-huh," Mebane said. "Are you going to run off on her? Treat her bad? Time comes you're done with me?"

"I don't know what I'm doing."

Mebane looked at him. "Life is a misery, isn't it?"

"Seems like."

"You're lucky, you know."

"How's that?"

"Most people, it takes up half their life or more to figure that out."

"I don't know. There's ones that seem to do all right. That it seems things work out all right for."

"All that is, is them not paying attention."

"Could be luck."

"Is that what you're thinking? Luck? Let me tell you. Unless you get hit in the head, every one of us sooner or later comes down to lying there reworking each and every inch of our lives. Gasping for breath. Imagine how that is—to not be able to draw breath. And you lie there wondering what mercy the Lord can provide. Because it's clear the tired old earth is out of mercy if it ever had any to start with. And the Lord, the Lord He is silent. He don't go peep. Now tell me, what kind of luck is that?"

Foster grinned at him. "Not much I guess."

"It's not funny. Not much is right. Look over there in the fireplace. You know what that is burning up?"

"No sir."

"That's right you don't. What that is, is years of trying to write out what happened in my life, long afternoons, midnights, long hours, chewing on a pen-tip, trying to get things right. Because it seemed like it was all I had. Some way to get it out of me and before me in a way I could see it. That would make sense to me. Something I could touch, could review."

"Why'd you burn it up?"

"Why boy, because I got you. Because you're the one I can give it to. Because you're the single one needs it as bad as I do."

"I don't want all this. Some single answer is enough."

"You're close," Mebane said. "You're closer than you think. You been adding two and two and you just about got it. Except you got that extra one thrown in and you're still trying to make her fall in and add up to four. But she's a sum all of her own. Part of this but her own also. The same way you are."

"You lost me there."

Mebane scowled at him. "There is always some other one that keeps us hopeful. That makes us believe things can change. Or at least keep us smoking onward, intent on reaching the next bend. The place where it all comes together. Where it all makes sense."

Foster leaned back in his chair and looked at the old man beside him. Mebane creased and white, his eyes up to a high glitter, a chatter of iris and pupil. Foster said, "You're talking about love, aren't you?"

Mebane said, "Sometimes it can be love I suppose. Or at least start out that way. Othertimes—"

"Othertimes what?"

"Othertimes, I don't know what to call it. Something that eats at you, that burns at you, that consumes you. That you can't touch. That you can't even see. But that is with you every livelong day. It's a fair thing to call it a passion. But you got to recall, passion is one of those things that is individual, complicated, as many-faced and -sided as a person. As the person that bears that passion. Do you understand?"

"I guess so."

"Listen. Your grandmother. Leah. I'm going to call her Leah. That's how I knew her, how I thought of her. You never met her. Is that all right with you? If I call her Leah?"

Foster was silent.

"There you see. It's coming now. And you know it don't you? What you came after. What you thought you wanted to know."

Foster was very still. He said, "Tell me."

"I killed her, boy. It was me. Yes." He held up his hand palm out. "As sure as if I'd followed her back up there to those Vermont woods and tied the rope myself. I did."

"Now what you have to do is forget everything I've told you. Because this is the part that is not about any of that. I don't mean for you to discard it, just let it slide off to a corner of your mind and hold it there for later. For you. Right now feature only this—a man who twenty-five years past harmed a woman and the woman did her best to harm him even worse but failed. See that man, not young anymore but still one with a hint, a faint stir of hope that the mess of his life could change someway. See him there, right out the front of this house sitting up on the front porch in a hot September afternoon, not so different from the one you walked in on. Except he's out there like he does most every afternoon. Waiting. Because there has not been a day go by but what he thinks of her. Not a single solitary one. She, who could be dead for all he knows. Except she is not. He knows this. And it is not just daytimes. At least once a week he wakes from dreams of her, dreams where her skin and voice, where the touch of her is so vivid that waking he wants to hurt himself to get back there. To that dreamland. And he wonders how many of those dreams occur that he sleeps right through. On the one hand he likes to think it's not many of them and on the other he likes to think that she flows through him all the time without stopping. Because he knows it is not his brain that labors over her, not his mind but his soul. His heart. Where each and every day he is disturbed by her. Where he has long since worn out all the could-have-beens. All the ways he could have been different. Acted otherwise. Where he has made some peace with himself and does not quite think she will have done the same but still knows it will be different if he should see her again. And you see, he expects this to happen. Except he has been expecting this for so long it is expectation he has become. The actual woman, she is a fragment. She is only a portion of all that waiting. She could be anywhere on the earth, doing anything. And so he sits right where he is, because it is the only way he can think that she might ever find him. Because, you see, he cannot find her. And that is not a question of knowing where she is or not.

"All he wants is to explain he was a boy. That he did not know what he was doing. That he was a stupid boy. And that he is sorry. So sorry. It's all he wants, all he thinks he wants through those long years. Because he knows when she does come, which he no longer quite believes will happen, it will be enough. Because he thinks that would be what she is looking for. And more—he thinks it's all he's looking for. The chance to say how sorry he is. But what he does not know, what he cannot know until he looks up and there she is, is neither of them are the same people. She is not that young girl. As important, he is not that young boy. He would be if he could. He thinks he will be. But he is not. He is a man grown into himself.

"So then there is that afternoon. Weather aside, one like any other. Except he looks up and there she is. Standing down at the end of the walk. Looking at him up on the porch. Her face revealing in one look that everything he'd thought this would be will be something else. Because what he sees there is only just a little fear of him but the rest a mask of pure loathing, a disgust of him so true as if she sees down into that empty soul of his and knows it better than he even can. And he feels shabby, feels caught out, found out. And he sits thinking perhaps she will just look at him and walk on, that her purpose will be satisfied. But she pauses only long enough for him to hope she'll go on and then comes up the walk. Lifting the front edge of her dress each time she steps up the bricks. It was all still tended then. Until she is at the bottom of the porch steps, in the shade of the house where she can look him right in the eye.

"She tells him she'd thought he was dead. Nothing in her voice to show she wished it was otherwise.

"He told her she'd tried but not hard enough.

"And she just stood looking up at him. As if measuring him. She already knew him. So it was something else she was studying and he looked away from her gaze, knowing it was pity of him she felt. And he was still looking away when she asked him what had become of her mother.

"And there you see. He had her then. All the pretense of those years fell away just like that. He was revealed to himself as purely and cleanly as a tooth. So when he looked back at her he smiled. And he raised up his hand, his one hand, and ran it over this scar right here upside his temple, still smiling at her. And she looked serious at that smile and watched him stroke himself like that and he saw her fall away just a little bit. Not too much. Just what he was hoping for.

"It was a moment of miracles. She there before him: no longer some remembered teenage girl so much older than him but a full-blown woman still young and lovely, arched upright down there before him. In her best clothes better than any he owned by appearance but still he could look at her and see she was a countrywoman, a country colored woman who'd done well for herself and had dressed as such to make her journey back. And he could sit there, feeling ruined and proud and stronger than he had in years, maybe all his life, and look down at her and know that the both of them, each helpless before it, were right back in that rain-pouring-down kitchen all those years before. And he did not know any reason not to trail her over with his eyes, sitting silent that long time with her quest still out unanswered in the air between them, but sweep her with his eyes and let her watch him doing that. Because that was what lay between them. Then, and before, and always. And each knew it.

"Now it seems to me that you have begun to learn about sorrow. And that's good. Good for you. But what you still don't understand is desire. As a poet, Foster Pelham, you have to understand desire. We have, I believe, covered a portion of it. When we talked about the nature of man, of evil. That was yesterday. Or was it the day before? It don't matter. Because man is at least an octagon. And desire is the one point that will lead. Where you have no choice. So, the poet is after desire."

("No," he said. "I'm not a poet.")

"A truth-seeker. And you should not disclaim that. I don't need long stories to explain desire. Desire is not what the preachers talk about. What they talk about is what they fear most simply in themselves: chasing after whatever they can get. That is not desire. That's not passion. That's simply old root-hog-or-die. It's why I can't abide religion. They will not get down in the dirt and talk about how things really are. The best they can do is prate about the little common things that afflict each

and every one of us. But they shy from the big ones. Because the big ones
are so vast, reaching out to all of life, that there is no way to make a neat
parable of them. There is no simple right or wrong. Desire then, desire
is when you are helpless. It's not a lapse, you see. It's the truth of yourself. It's all you have. All you can ever hope for. Right here on the sweet
old earth. It is everything. It is, when you have it, something you know
the Lord would bow His head before. Because, if He knows nothing
more, the Lord understands desire. And when you have that, when it
owns you, directs you, you have no choice but to surrender to it.

"So that man up on the porch revealed to himself. It was very simple
what he did. He held his smile while he told her: what she should do.
Told her to go over to Fishtown, to Niggertown, and went on then,
enjoying the loss of twenty-five years to describe to her where he was
talking about. Because when she'd left Sweetboro there was of course
no such place. So he journeyed back and laid out the geography to her.
Told her to go over there and ask around. Because he knew she would
find no answer there. Because he knew there was none to tell her. But
wanted her to do that first, because he knew there was only him. Wanted
her to know for her ownself he was the only one she could come to.
Reminded her she was a fugitive woman. And then told her what it
would cost her to learn what she wanted. He sat up straight in that
rocker, leaving that goddamn cane flat on the porch floor and forced
himself erect to look down at her. Still smiling at her. And told her what
she would have to trade for what she wanted. And did not wait to watch
her face but bent and scrabbled for his cane and stood sideways a moment on the porch, looking off away from her, letting her see that some
part of him still worked exactly right.

"It did not matter what she told him then. He looked down at her
face all blotched with anger, still so pretty and fine. Fine like an animal, the sort of creature a man would make if he could make anything
he wanted, to his own specifications—wasn't that after all what those
old Greeks were up to with their nymphs and naiads, the woman as a
creature of the world, out of stone, rock, wood or some such thing, some
material that we strive to join with? Some other beyond just the simple
frail humanity of a woman?

"So he waved her off, just waved a hand at her response. Told her
again to go over to Niggertown and see for herself, then come back. Not

sure she would go anywhere. Just wanting her to have to wait. And he turned then and went on in the house, shutting the door behind him, sliding home the bolt he almost never used. So she could hear him do that. He wanted her to hear the sound of the lock sliding home. Wanted her to know she'd have to come up on the porch when she returned and knock at that door. That he would not be out waiting on her. Wanted that locked door to make clear there was no negotiation.

"Because the thing about desire and regret, when you've harmed someone and then have years to shred it and play it over time and again—the thing is you fail to comprehend the origin of that initial episode. You attach layers of meaning to it and feel it was an aberration, some moment of yourself out of yourself. That is what regret does. It allows you to live with yourself. You know what they say—all men in prison are innocent? It's not that they are and it's not even that they truly believe they are; it's that they grow to understand themselves in such a way as to see that moment, the trigger that set them off in the first place, that got them to where they are, they see that as something separate from themselves. They come to believe, to know, that ever again their choice would be a different one. Not only in the past but in the future. Because they cannot allow the truth.

"The truth, Foster Pelham, is very simple. The nature of man is divided. And because we cannot live in the light we refuse to see the dark surrounding us. Until it owns us.

"So he sat up in that locked house the remainder of the afternoon. Because it was as if time had gone away. It was just hours of the day. Twenty-five years. More than that. He had no regret you see, no sorrow or remorse. All that was a confection he'd built around himself over the years. So he could live to that day. Because it was not love you see. What he thought it had been. There was terrible anger in it. Elemental is the word comes to mind. Possession is another one. To possess her in a way she would never be able to deny. That she could walk away from but would follow her, always. Yes, always.

"Now you can sit there looking at me like I'm some sort of monster. I don't mind it one bit. You don't know any better. But it is something that every man feels, at least once in his life. If he is lucky. That's right. Lucky. That sort of passion. Beyond caring about anything. Any goddamn thing at all.

"So he did not move but sat in this chair right here. Waiting. For the first time in twenty-five years just waiting. Not thinking at all. Only a man, every bit and morsel of him. Roused, unstoppable. Needing nothing. Not food, not a drink of water, nothing at all. Not even that fucking cane. Which he laid up flat on the table and left there. So when late afternoon that knock at the door he knew was coming came he left that cane, and walked straight and steady and thoughtless as if he was fourteen years old again, down to the door. Where he could see her through the glass, her face turned down, her shoulder pressed close to the door. Waiting for him. He stopped some feet away. He knew she'd heard him coming but he did not care. He wanted to see her there. Waiting.

"When he opened the door she started to speak. But he reached out and laid his fingers flat over her mouth and held them there. Until she lifted her head to look at him. Her eyes wide and flat all at the same time upon him. And every bit of her piled up in those eyes. He leaned forward and kissed her forehead. It did not matter that she flinched from him. He expected she would flinch more than once in the time ahead of them. In truth, he liked that, he wanted it. He wanted to hear her moan, not only with pleasure but agony. Because it was the only way she could apprehend him, could understand all of him. Which he knew she could do.

"When she was quiet, he took her by the hand and led her into the house. Down the hall and up the stairs. And got her all the way to the landing, at the door to his bedroom where she stopped him. She reached her free hand and took his shoulder, his short one, and turned him to face her. She stood like that a long moment. Looking at him. And he saw not just the rage and anger that he expected but also some fracture in her soul, some infirmity, an ancient chasm. And he wondered then if she might kill him, might finish the job she failed at so many years ago. Thinking that the same way she had returned him to his essential self, perhaps he'd done the same for her. This did not frighten him. It was excitement, was what it was.

"When she spoke he saw the hatred of him there in her eyes, as if her voice was something apart from her. And it was that hatred he wanted. He wanted to own it. Not tame or change or make it go away. But to own. He held his eyes on hers then and saw the shrink of retreat. Ferocious, he gazed upon her. For as long as it took for her to look away.

Because there was no negotiation. Then, her head turned, toward the door she was already entering even though she had not yet moved; then, she told him she'd heard what happened to Peter. He was confused a moment. He had to think who Peter was. He had been sure no one would talk to her. Because they would not know her, and they would know *him*. But Peter did not matter to him, then or ever. What mattered was she was now moving ahead and he was following, toward the bed."

Still raining, hard. The fire burned down, the room hot and close. The long windows steamed inside and oily from driven rain, the room at midmorning dark as dawn. Foster stiff, holding himself from motion, wet under his arms, his skin rippling in the moisture and heat with recoil. Looking down at the stained green blotter. He could not recall when he'd taken his eyes from the old man seated up close beside him. The smell in the room strong of the old body, astringent, sour, blooded, as if some must, some musk, came off the old man as he talked, rising up in pitch as he went on, the smell one of decay and excitement all at once. All Foster wanted was away. He dreaded the old man reaching out that one claw hand to touch him someway, to draw his attention, his eyes back to that bitter bright maniac old face. He did not move.

Quiet but for the lash and splatter of rain. Time to time the low fire settled and would pop, some small chuckle of fire. After a long silent while, Mebane rose up groaning from his chair, leaning on the cane. He hitched his way around the table to the grate, where he took up the poker and stirred the sifting coals. The movement a terrible labor. As if sitting so long had crippled him more. And Foster thought maybe this was the old man's natural gait, that his liveliness, his seeming ability of the past days, had been an effort. Some illusion for Foster. Or even for both of them. To get through it. To get here.

Finally Foster spoke. "So what was it? What did you tell her?"

Mebane's one hand was up on the slender dark wood mantelpiece over the fireplace. Slowly he turned and leaned forward, his body a crane up over the tripod of the cane and his two feet. He smiled at Foster.

"Why, boy, I had to give her something. Her coming that long way and all. I had to give her something for the effort. And she knew about that old nigger Peter, what happened to him. So it was an easy place to start. What I told Leah, what I told your grandmother, was that after those boys done that way with Peter her mama and I had a little talk. It was Helen anyway tended me with my bashed-in head and mashed ear. It was a bad time. Everything was gone to hell. She was too scared to run. She'd seen Peter after they were done with him. She was still a young woman, even to a boy like me. That high fine round ass. Oh my. It was a beautiful story. It had Leah stunned right back down sitting on the bed still just wrapped in a sheet. And me standing there with my trousers back up, still feeling her against me as I told her how I'd made her mother my woman for fifteen years. Told her my father, our father, was dead. So Helen was my woman then. My housekeeper yes but my woman as well. Whenever I wanted her, however way. It was some moment, I can tell you. Grace is what comes to mind. All of it, as I told her, I could see it. Some rarefied moment of the mind. It makes you wonder what makes truth, where truth begins or ends. Because what I was telling her became my memory as I told her and I stood with the words coming and saw it becoming her memory too. It was lovely. I could not stop.

"So I went on. I made a child come, a girl child but an idiot. An imbecile. Soft-brained. Her name was Nell. Now that was pure genius. Just like that, rolling off my tongue. Her own mother's name turned around. I described how Helen tried to keep her hid, hid away from everybody as much she could but that little girl could not be stopped. And I suggested to Leah that her mother was not without complicity, to go from the father to the son like that, the blood all mixed around. As if it was the one thing she knew. As if she could not stop herself from being what she was. And watched your grandmother's face then, knowing that what she'd just done with me was no different, that it fell the same way.

"But I did not stop there. It had to come all the way from the night she brained me and run off in the rain to that afternoon twenty-five years later when she hunched naked sweating in my bed. So what I told her I had done with her mother, and what her mother had done with me, was someway a version of what she and me had just done. Some better version. One in which both parties knew exactly what they were doing and why. Where there was no hazard like there had just been that one time I'd waited twenty-five years for but something else altogether. Where it was not love pictured but need. Dreadful terrible need that would not go away. Could not be slaked. For either one. Because it was what I wanted, you see. It was what I wanted it to have been with Leah.

"So the story goes on. There was that Nell. She made it come all the way around. An inspiration, she was. I made her an idiot but that could not stop her body. All she was was body. I drew her tangled whole out of the air. What a daughter! Sister to your grandmother and cousin all at once. Who was fourteen years old when her throat was cut open in the middle of the night by someone unknown over in Niggertown where she'd been sneaking off for two-three years. Some jealous wife I suggested. Maybe even just some man sick of her. A simple creature-child who just wanted to lay back and splay her legs. The way any of us do. Leah fallen silent then, the sheet dropped off her shoulders. Flies landing on her and her not even aware. The smell of her still strong in the room. Her face like something broken by stone.

"Give me credit here—I made it short. Of course I was ready to wash myself. Get something to eat. It's true, I wanted her gone. I had my reasons. But I did not torture her further. There was nothing left to tell anyway. It was just a detail to finish it off. How her mother then went out that night and walked the tracks to where the span is high over the river and dropped herself down into that water. That was all. I told her there was no grave. No marking. The niggers is afraid of suicides. But then, we all are, aren't we? Then I left her. Alone in my room. So she could pull herself together and leave. I thought that was a nice touch, giving her that privacy. Even as I wanted her again and likely could have had her. But I was weary with it all. Some ways it had been so much for so long for so little. In the end, so little. Still, it was a good job. Wasn't it?"

Foster could taste his eggs, the whiskey from the night before. His stomach was tight. Mebane was no longer smiling but his face was bright, pitched up. Foster ran his tongue over the roof of his mouth and swallowed. He said, "It was all a trick. Is that right? It wasn't true?"

Mebane made a sound, a sigh, a hiccup of sadness, despair. It could have been a chopped-off laugh. He said, "I never knew where Helen went to. What happened to her. I was bad sick with fevers and somebody—it could have been her—got word to my mother in Raleigh who

came after me. It was a terrible time to travel. The railroads was all torn
up and shut down, the roads filled with Yankee patrols and every other
sort of criminal you could think of. I don't know how she did it. She
got a man and a team and made that trip for me. Thirty miles. But by
the time my mother got to me I was alone. Helen was gone, the other
old nigger woman too. I didn't know where, didn't care. I recall lying
on a tick in the back of that wagon sweating under a stretched canvas,
crying with every step and jounce of the way."

Foster stood. "It was all a lie then. What you told her was lies."

"I was not interested in anything," Mebane said, "except watching
her break. All I wanted then was her gone. She needed something and
I gave it to her. What did it matter? She needed that bad news the same
way she needed to make the deal with me to get it. She did you know!
She needed that deal. Maybe more than me. She had tried to trade her
way into a new life. Fancy-go-to-town nigger woman! I wanted her to
know what it cost. Cost me. I wanted her to have that weight over her
every walking moment of her life."

"Jesus," Foster said. "Why? I don't understand why."

And for a brief moment Mebane's eyes were focused on Foster, and
when he spoke his voice was triumphant, soft.

"What I'm trying to tell you," Mebane said. "She had that debility,
stronger even than doubt. So there was that. But mostly," he added,
"because I could."

"Because you could," Foster repeated. He had grasped the top of the
chair before him, the chair tipping on its casters, his arms shaking.

Mebane did not move. His face was pink, filmed with sweat. His shirt
beneath his arms drooped dark along his sides. Foster could smell him.
He let go of the chair and swung his arms loose along his sides. Mebane
smiled once more, gray lips a rictus against the blot of his face. He said,
"It wasn't even that good a piece of tail. She was on top of me of course,
her eyes closed. Just slapping up and down against me. I've paid for
better. It was not the pussy I expected it to be."

Foster started around the table. Mebane stepped back, away from the
flue and leaned against the wall. He raised up the cane and cut several
passes with it. "That's it. Come on, boy," he cried out. "I've been waiting for you."

Foster stopped. He turned from the old man. The rain mapped dissolving continents down the window glass. He thought then of his father, of what he would've done. After a moment, he looked back at Mebane, the cane pointed at the ceiling, ready to descend. He said, "No."

"No? What do you mean, No? It's what you came after. It's why you're here."

Foster put his hands in his pockets. He stood very still. Again, he said, "No."

"No? A hunting man like yourself? You got those dogs. I seen you out in the woods with them. What's the matter with you? Can't you do the right thing?"

Foster stood silent. Mebane took a step forward, waved the cane in the air. Foster did not move. Mebane looked at him. There was a long silence.

Mebane was wheezing. He placed the cane-tip before him and leaned upon it. His breath broke. "I know you got a gun. I seen you carrying it in to the nigger cabin."

Foster walked up to stand before him. He was as close as he had been to the man. He reached over with his left boot and tapped the cane-tip. "The worst thing I can think of. Is to leave you just the way you are."

"Don't do it."

"Tell you what," Foster said. "I'll see you later." And stepped around the man, aiming for the swinging kitchen door.

Mebane wracked, "Come on back here."

Foster, already in the kitchen, straight for the back door, heard some crashing in the room behind him. Some flailing, some thing breaking. Breaking apart as it fell.

He went across the yard with his head bent down, the rain striking hard his humped back. He opened the door of the cabin but the dogs failed to pour out as he expected. He stepped up inside, shaking the water off his head. The dogs were up on the bed, one either side of Daphne. Who sat crosslegged, her hair in wet matted ropes, peeled away from her face, the L. C. Smith held over her lap.

"Jesus Christ," he said and stepped forward to take the shotgun up from her, her hands coming off it and held up a moment in the air after it. He broke it open and drew out the two shells and put them in his trouser pocket and snapped the gun to and leaned it against the wall. Her eyes wide upon him, her face damp with rain from her hair. He said, "What're you doing?"

"I got scared," she said. "I thought something happened to you."

"I'm all fucked up," he said.

She stood off the bed. In heavy dark denim jeans too big for her belted high on her waist with four-inch cuffs over rough old boots also too big, a flannel shirt buttoned tight to her throat. The clothes splotched with rain, the boots rimed with red gumbo mud. She stood before him, not too close. When she stood the young dog Glow also rose up, sitting on the bed, watching. Daphne said, "When you didn't show up last night I woke up this morning feeling something was wrong. I called Uncle Lex on the telephone and he didn't sound right to me, sounded giddy and worked up, kept telling me everything was fine. The way a person does when it's not. There wasn't any way to get into town so I set off walking. I got a ride pretty quick."

"What were you up to with my shotgun?" Feeling offkey. He wanted to be alone. Yet there she was. Her lips parted, her breath coming onto him a little sour. Her fear, he thought.

"I came right in the front door, down the hall and stood looking in the dining room at the two of you. He was off, wild, talking about somebody, I don't know who. And you, braced back in your chair like you'd been hit. And not either one of you aware I was there. So I went out and came around here. And seen that gun leaned up against the wall and knew you had a reason for it being there. I didn't know what to do. All I could do was sit here and wait, thinking if you came through the door in a hurry I could maybe stop whatever was coming after you."

He looked at her then, the wet girl. "Is that what you thought?"

"Don't make fun of me."

He shook his head. "Whatever is after me, that shotgun wouldn't be much good. I'm not making fun."

Both quiet then. She was so lovely. He thought This is how it is, with all of them. Someway. His father and mother. His grandfather and grandmother. Even all skewed and twisted the old man in the house thirty feet away through the rain and that same grandmother. He was unbearably sad. He wanted to touch her and would not. He felt more than saw her waver toward him and it made him want to cry out. He was very still. Felt his own waver. Saw her lips open again and close. He wanted to dry her hair, to build a fire in the ancient hearth, to sit before it cradling her in his arms to warm her. He did not move. No. No was what he thought.

She said, "You're already gone. Isn't that right?"

His voice low and broken. "I got to go." Stricken.

"Did he tell you to go?"

"No. No. He wants—I won't tell you what he wants."

"It's some kind of big trouble, isn't it?"

Foster shook his head. "It's not something I can do anything about. It's not anything I want to be around any longer though."

"Are you going to tell me?"

"I don't think so. It's not anything about me—"

"I know that."

"—but it's not just about him either. It's something I feel I got to keep inside me."

"Everybody's got things like that. There's things about me, things I've done, things been done to me too, that I could know a person all my life and never tell about."

He looked at her. He thought he knew what her meaning was. Trying to explain, he said, "Only part of what he had to tell me was about him. There's things about him would make you sick. I don't care about that. But there was other people involved, people who are gone and can't do a thing about what he did or what he said he did or even what he said about them. It's for those people I need to hold it inside me. Because it's like a trust. It's all I can do for them. Is to carry it with me."

"Oh baby." And stepped forward that one step and held him against her, her arms around him, her head turned down, held him until he held her back. And without any idea he was about to he began to cry. She held him through it, not moving, silent, uttering no words to soothe or distract him from his grief. Just stood for him to stand against as he wept for everything, for all the people before him, for himself. And as he wept he took in the smell of the girl up against him, her wet hair, the pale clean scent of her skin, her wet clothes. Her head laid sideways against his chest, her face turned down so he saw the crown of her head, the split-through to her scalp where her hair fell apart, the delicate rib of the back of her ear, the smooth swelling column of her neck going into the collar of the shirt. And when he stopped crying he still stood holding her, held her until they were both silent and still and he could feel her life against him, the beating of her heart. And stepped away when he felt himself begin to rise against her.

"Oh boy," he said, turning from her, "am I ever fucked up." And he took the box of his father's stale cigarettes from the pocket of his jacket and lighted one and squatted in the rain at the open door of the cabin. And then, as if released, the two dogs came off the bed and went out the door into the rain, tracking again through the yard. He squatted there smoking, watching the dogs. The smoke came off in slow wrought spirals that held out in the rain before breaking apart. Behind him he heard her sit once again on the bed, the faint clicking sound as the tick settled.

"Where are you going to go?"

"I don't know." He did not look back at her.

"Back north?"

"I don't know," he said again. "I don't think so. Not right off." Thinking of the house in Bethlehem, the two old women on the Vermont farm. Them he would need to send some kind of word to. Some letter. Without any idea what he would say. Get away from here first, he thought. Then write something simple, painless, fill it up with his love of them, whatever it was he would finally be doing.

Behind him she said, "Take me with you."

Where the rain ran off the shake roof there was a line of beading streams that were trenching pods into the earth, into the mire of mud, forming a shallow little trench. He said, "Before my dad died he talked of going out west. New Mexico. Arizona. We joked about it. I wonder how serious he was about it now. Maybe I'll drive out there. Drive right on through the fall. Quail-hunt these dogs all the way, wherever I can find a place to do it. Right on through the fall and winter. See what it's like. See what all that country is about. I don't know."

She was silent behind him.

After a bit he flicked the cigarette out into the mud and watched as it drenched through with rain and fell apart. When he couldn't see any of it anymore, when the paper and tobacco were all mixed with the mud and gone, he said, "The thing is, I took you along, what I'm afraid of is everytime I looked at you I'd think about this place. And what I got to do. What I've got to do is put all this behind me." He still did not look at her.

Her voice was very low. "You're wrong. If you were to carry me along I'd just become a part of everywhere we went. You've got it backward. You leave me here, everytime you think of me you'll think of everything else happened here. And I'll get all mixed up with that. I'll never be just me, to you, again. I've got forty-two dollars."

He did not smile at this. But felt what he thought was a smile turn over within him. He stood, one last long look at the rain and turned to look at her. He did not say anything, just looked at her. As if reading every line of her, every part he could know or hope to know. To hold it with him. To take away with him. She saw him doing this.

"Then go," she said.

"Daphne."

"No. Just go. Go on."

"Listen to me."

"No. Go on, Foster Pelham. Look! What've you got here? That old ruint suitcase? Your gun? Those dogs'll carry themselves out to your car. There's this old sleeping bag. Here." And without getting off the bed she rolled sideways and pulled it from under her and still sitting on the bed folded it and placed it on the end of the tick. "There. You're all set."

"Daphne—"

"You be quiet! Whatever it is you want to say, I don't want to hear it! Maybe you found what it was you couldn't say the other night. Well, that's an old song and dance. I don't want any part of it. Keep it, Foster. Keep it for yourself. Tell yourself those things. I don't want to hear it. Just go. Just get out of here. Get away from me."

He stood silent before her. Feeling crude, shambling, struck by her fury. After a time, knowing it was the wrong thing but not clear what else he might do, he said, "At least let me give you a lift out to your house."

Her head jerked up to look at him, her eyes wild with anger. "I'm not going anywhere. I'm going to set right here. I don't want any rides from you. Just get the fuck out of here."

*   *   *

He carried his things out to the lane where the Chrysler was parked and sat in the car and used the oiled rag to wipe down the L. C. Smith and then shut it in its case and set the case down in the compartment with the whiskey and money under the rear seat and replaced the heavy seat cushion. Then back to the yard gate where Glow and Lovey waited him and he let them out and into the backseat of the car. They lay curled as if knowing it would be a long ride this time. He sat in the car, the rain streaming down outside, the day all brown and gray, even the leaves on the live oaks just a deep gray, a neutral tone against the downpour. Soon he could not see outside at all as the windows fogged from the wet dogs and everybody breathing. He opened the window and let the rain fall in to wet his left side and he smoked another of the cigarettes. And knew he would not leave her, would not abandon her to this place, certain that she trusted him because she was right to trust him. That he could be trusted. And then knew he could not leave her, and this had nothing to do with trust and all to do with her. That he could not leave her anymore than he could leave himself. He threw the cigarette out and sat a moment longer. Aware that for once his life was about to change because he wanted it to. Not as a result of what some other person had done or said. Thinking that right then, that moment was the true beginning of his life. He got out of the car and went back through the yard to the cabin door where he stood outside a minute looking in. She was seated still crosslegged on the bed, her elbows on her knees as her hands held her face, her shoulders rocking back and forth. She could have been laughing but no sound came from her but a desperate ceaseless suck for air. He watched her a moment and then stepped in and said, "I got no idea how far we can get today with all this rain. What I'd like is to get this place a ways behind us. Then, somewhere, we'll hunt down some maps."

She lifted her head, her face moist and blotched. She dropped her hands into her lap and studied him. Her chin was tilted off toward her shoulder, her lips as if she were silently whistling.

Then, somehow satisfied, she said, "You think we need maps?"

Acknowledgments

I'd like to thank Ginger West &
Allan Wolf for their reading of the work in progress; Dan Morgan for
generous and thorough research assistance; Kim Witherspoon for her
outstanding advocacy; Elisabeth Schmitz, Morgan Entrekin and the entire crew at Grove/Atlantic for the dedication and focus brought to this
project; extended family members who, regardless of their private
doubts, never offered anything but encouragement over the years; and
finally, my mother, who, among other passions, instilled in me the love
of reading and books beginning all those years ago on the lawn of the
North Pomfret farmhouse.